A TEXT BOOK OF

QUANTITY SURVEYING, CONTRACTS AND TENDERS

FOR
SEMESTER – II
FINAL YEAR (B.E.) DEGREE COURSE IN CIVIL ENGINEERING

As Per the New Revised Syllabus of Savitribai Phule Pune University (2012 Pattern)

G. B. DESHPANDE
B. E. (Civil), M. Sc. (Engg.)
Formerly Govt. College of Engineering,
Shivajinagar.
Pune – 411005.

J. P. NAYAK
M.Tech (Environment)
Associated Professor and Head
Civil Engineering Department,
Sandip Foundations,
Sandip Institute of Technology and Research Center
Nasik 422213.

NIRALI PRAKASHAN
ADVANCEMENT OF KNOWLEDGE

N 3717

QSCT (BE CIVIL SEM. II)   **ISBN 978-93-5164-876-5**

First Edition	:	**January 2016**
New Edition	:	**January 2017**
©	:	**Authors**

Published By :
NIRALI PRAKASHAN
Abhyudaya Pragati, 1312, Shivaji Nagar,
Off J.M. Road, PUNE – 411005
Tel - (020) 25512336/37/39, Fax - (020) 25511379
Email : niralipune@pragationline.com

☞ **DISTRIBUTION BRANCHES**

PUNE
Nirali Prakashan : 119, Budhwar Peth, Jogeshwari Mandir Lane, Pune 411002, Maharashtra
Tel : (020) 2445 2044, 66022708, Fax : (020) 2445 1538
Email : bookorder@pragationline.com, niralilocal@pragationline.com
Nirali Prakashan : S. No. 28/27, Dhyari, Near Pari Company, Pune 411041
Tel : (020) 24690204 Fax : (020) 24690316
Email : dhyari@pragationline.com, bookorder@pragationline.com
MUMBAI
Nirali Prakashan : 385, S.V.P. Road, Rasdhara Co-op. Hsg. Society Ltd.,
Girgaum, Mumbai 400004, Maharashtra
Tel : (022) 2385 6339 / 2386 9976, Fax : (022) 2386 9976
Email : niralimumbai@pragationline.com

☞ **DISTRIBUTION BRANCHES**

JALGAON
Nirali Prakashan : 34, V. V. Golani Market, Navi Peth, Jalgaon 425001,
Maharashtra, Tel : (0257) 222 0395, Mob : 94234 91860
KOLHAPUR
Nirali Prakashan : New Mahadvar Road, Kedar Plaza, 1st Floor Opp. IDBI Bank
Kolhapur 416 012, Maharashtra. Mob : 9850046155
NAGPUR
Pratibha Book Distributors : Above Maratha Mandir, Shop No. 3, First Floor,
Rani Jhanshi Square, Sitabuldi, Nagpur 440012, Maharashtra
Tel : (0712) 254 7129
DELHI
Nirali Prakashan : 4593/21, Basement, Aggarwal Lane 15, Ansari Road, Daryaganj
Near Times of India Building, New Delhi 110002
Mob : 08505972553
BENGALURU
Pragati Book House : House No. 1, Sanjeevappa Lane, Avenue Road Cross,
Opp. Rice Church, Bengaluru – 560002.
Tel : (080) 64513344, 64513355,Mob : 9880582331, 9845021552
Email:bharatsavla@yahoo.com
CHENNAI
Pragati Books : 9/1, Montieth Road, Behind Taas Mahal, Egmore,
Chennai 600008 Tamil Nadu, Tel : (044) 6518 3535,
Mob : 94440 01782 / 98450 21552 / 98805 82331,
Email : bharatsavla@yahoo.com

niralipune@pragationline.com | www.pragationline.com
Also find us on f www.facebook.com/niralibooks

PREFACE TO THE NEW EDITION

We are glad and excited to announce that the First Edition of this book received an overwhelming response from the engineering student community, compelling us to release its New Edition within a very short period of time.

This New Edition has been updated with including all University Question Papers from December 2011 to May 2015 and we also given University Question Papers (2012 Pattern) In Sem. February 2016, End Sem. May 2016 and November 2016.

Special care has been taken to maintain high degree of accuracy in the theory and numericals throughout the book.

We take this opportunity to express our sincere thanks to Dineshbhai Furia of Nirali Prakashan, a reputed pioneer in the publication field. Our special thanks to Jignesh Furia for their effective cooperation and great care in bringing out this revised edition. We also appreciate the efforts of M. P. Munde and the entire staff of Engineering Books Deptt. of Nirali Prakashan namely Mrs. Deepali Lachake (Co-ordinator) for bringing this book to the students in a timely manner.

We sincerely hope that this "New Edition" will also be warmly received by all concerned as in the past.

Valuable suggestions from our esteemed readers to improve the book are most welcome and highly appreciated.

Pune   **Authors**

PREFACE TO THE FIRST EDITION

We are very glad to present a textbook on **"Quantity Surveying, Contracts and Tenders"**. This book is strictly written as per the New Revised Syllabus of Savitribai Phule Pune University, Pune (2012 Pattern) for the students of final year degree course in Civil Engineering.

This book is as per new revised examination scheme which has been implemented from this academic year. According to this, In-semester examination carries 30 Marks over first three units and End-semester examination carries 70 marks for entire syllabus of which the first three units will carry 20 marks and unit 4, 5, and 6 will carry 50 marks.

We have given University Question Papers at the end of the book. Also we have given Sample Question Papers of In-Semester University Examination (30 Marks) and End-Semester University Examination (70 Marks) in this book for the practice.

We have tried to provide the best possible material in simple and lucid language to the students preparing for degree course. The subject is divided in to 6 units and each unit is explained thoroughly with diagrams and examples. So, we are sure that this book will fulfill all needs of the subject. Sufficient numbers of questions are also included at the end of each chapter for the revision of the subject.

We would like to express our gratitude to the many people who saw us through this book; to all those who provided support for this book.

We are very thankful to the management of our respective institutes for their continuous support and encouragement.

Above all, we want to thank our family members and friends, who supported and encouraged us in spite of all the time it took us away from them. It was a long and difficult journey for them.

We gratefully acknowledge co-operation from **Shri. Dineshbhai Furia, Shri. Jignesh Furia, Mrs. Nirali Verma, Shri. M.P. Munde** and **Mrs. Deepali Lachake** (Co-ordinator) of **Nirali Prakashan.**

Though every effort has been made to eliminate all types of errors, yet some error might have been left unnoticed. However, further improvement if you find any, you can mail on **jyotiprakash.nayak@sitcc.org.**

Pune   **Authors**

SYLLABUS

Unit I : Introduction and Approximate Estimates   [6 Lectures]

(a) Introduction to Estimates and Related Terms: Definitions of estimation and valuation. Significance (application) of the Course. Purpose of estimation. Type of estimates, data required for estimation as a pre requisite. Meaning of an item of work, and enlisting the items of work for different Civil Engineering projects. Units of measurement. Mode of measurement of building items/ works. Introduction to components of estimates: face sheet, abstract sheet (BOQ), measurement sheet, Rate Analysis, lead statement. Provisional sum and prime cost items, contingencies, work charge establishment, centage charges. Introduction to D. S. R

(b) Approximate Estimates: Meaning, purpose, methods of approximate estimation of building and other civil engineering projects like roads, irrigation/ water supply, sanitary engineering, electrical works.

Unit II : Taking out quantities and Detailed estimate up to plinth   [6 Lectures]

(a) Methods of Estimating : P.W.D. and center-line methods of working out quantities. Calculation of quantities for Load bearing and R.C.C framed structures up to plinth,

(b) Detailed Estimates, Factors to be considered while Preparing Detailed Estimate, Detailed estimates of Load bearing and R.C.C framed structures up to plinth only.

Unit III : Detailed Estimation for Super Structure and Valuation   [6 Lectures]

(a) Calculation of quantities and detailed estimate for Load bearing and framed structures above plinth (super structure).Deduction rules for different items of work as per IS: 1200.

(b) Valuation: Purpose of valuation. Meaning of price, cost and value. Factors affecting 'value'. Types of value: only Fair Market Value, Book Value, Salvage/ Scrap Value, Distressed Value and Sentimental Value. Concept of free hold and lease hold property. Estimation versus valuation. Meanings of depreciation and obsolescence.

Unit IV : Specifications and Rate Analysis   [6 Lectures]

(a) Specifications: Meaning and purpose, types. Drafting detailed specifications for materials, quality, workmanship, method of execution, mode of measurement and payment for major items like, excavation, stone/ brick masonry, plastering, ceramic tile flooring, R.C.C. work.

(b) Rate Analysis: Meaning and factors affecting rate of an item of work, materials, sundries, labour, tools and plant, overheads and profit. Working out Rate Analysis for the items mentioned in specifications above. Task work or out turn, factors effecting task work.

Unit V : Tendering and Execution of Works [6 Lectures]

(a) Tenders: Definition. Methods of inviting tenders, tender notice, tendering procedure, Pre and post qualification of contractors, tender documents. 3 bid/ 2 bid or single bid system. Qualitative and quantitative evaluation of tenders. Comparative statement, Pre-bid conference, acceptance/ rejection of tenders. Various forms of BOT and Global Tendering, E-tendering.

(b) Methods of Executing Works: PWD procedure of work execution, administrative approval, budget provision, technical sanction. Methods of execution of minor works in PWD: Piecework, Rate List, Daily Labour. Introduction to registration as a contractor in PWD.

Unit V : Contracts and Arbitration [6 Lectures]

(a) Contracts: Definition, objectives and essentials of a valid contract as per Indian Contract Act(1872), termination of contract. Types of contracts: only lump sum, item rate, cost plus. Conditions of contract: General and Specific conditions. Conditions regarding EM, SD, and time as an essence of contract, conditions for addition, alteration, extra items, testing of materials, defective work, subletting, etc. Defect liability period, liquidated damages, retention money, interim payment or running account bills, advance payment, secured advance, final bill.

(b) Arbitration: Introduction to Arbitrations as per Indian Arbitration and Conciliation Act (1996) Meaning and need of arbitration, qualities and powers of an Arbitrator.

(c) Brief introduction to laws related to professional liabilities

CONTENTS

Unit I

Unit II & III (a)

Unit III (b)

Chapter 4 : Valuation of Properties **4.1-4.54**

Unit IV

Unit V

◈ ◈ ◈

Chapter 1

INTRODUCTION TO ESTIMATES AND RELATED TERMS

1.1 INTRODUCTION

Before any engineering project is to be constructed, it is necessary to know its estimated cost to ascertain whether the required funds can be made available for its completion or not. If the funds available are more than the estimated cost of the work, the execution of the work can be started. If, however, the available funds are less than the estimated cost, then either the work may be executed in parts or its specification can be altered to bring down its cost within the available funds. The actual cost of construction (which will be known after its completion) should not exceed the estimated cost of the work.

Definition : To know the cost of the proposed work, it is required to prepare a detailed estimate of the proposed work. An estimate is a probable cost of the work, arrived by mathematical calculations based on the measurement of quantities of various items of work involved in the work. The quantities of the various items of work are then multiplied by the present market rates for those items to arrive at the cost of all such items. Summation of costs of all such items gives the total estimated cost of the work.

1.2 DATA REQUIRED FOR PREPARATION OF AN ESTIMATE

In order to prepare a detailed estimate of the proposed work, the following information is required :

(i) **Complete Set of Detailed Drawings :** In order to work out the quantities of various items of work, a complete set of detailed drawings consisting of plan, elevation, sections and foundation details etc. is required. The relevant dimensions i.e. length, breadth, depth or height of the items, whose quantities are to be worked out, can be measured from such drawings.

(ii) **Specifications of Items of Works :** The rate of an item depends upon the specifications of the work. Specifications provide information regarding type of construction, quality of materials, proportion of mixes, manner in which the work is to be executed, etc.

(iii) **Prevalent Rates of Items of Construction :** After the quantities of various items of work involved are calculated, they are to be multiplied by the current market rates of those items. The Government department such as Buildings and Communication, Irrigation and Power Department prepares schedule of rates for all items of work pertaining to the department for a district or area, on the basis of analysis of rates of items. A booklet called 'District Schedule of Rates' (D.S.R) is available for sale in such Government Organisations.

(iv) **Standard Mode of Measurement :** I.S. 1200 has specified the procedure of measurement of various items of work, standard deductions to made if any, the accuracy of measurement etc. and is to be followed while preparing estimates.

(v) Details of foundation strata likely to encounter.

(vi) The exact location of the work site.

(vii) The physical condition of the work site.

It is usual practice to enclose a brief report containing information about the proposed work i.e. project as regards the following :

- The history and necessity of the proposed work.
- The exact location and condition of the work site.
- Details of soil strata at the site.
- The total cost of the proposed work.
- Source of the finance required for the completion of the work.
- Probable period of completion of the work.

1.2.1 Purposes of detailed estimate   (W-2010)

- In Government Organisation, a detailed estimate is required for obtaining *technical sanction* from the competent authorities for the proposed work.
- A detailed estimate is also required for the preparation of contract (agreement) document.
- The detailed estimates serve as a guide during the execution of the work.
- It helps in computing the quantities of materials required and labour to be employed for the completion of various items of construction.
- It is very useful in the efficient planning and programming of all activities required for the speedy completion of the work.
- It enables to prepare bar-chart, material schedules etc. for the work.

1.2.2 THE USES OF ESTIMATION   (W-2010)

- To get appropriate idea of the proposed work before its execution.
- It helps in working out the quantities of various materials required and also in preparation of material schedules.
- The labour force required for various items of construction can be worked out considering the specified work time.

- The various types of tools, plants and machinery required for the work can be ascertained.

- It helps in the preparation of bar-charts and cash flow schedules etc. for the speedy completion of the work.

- The overall economy in the completion of the project can also be achieved by the judicious combination of the various activities.

1.3 TYPES OF ESTIMATES   (W-2010)

The estimates are broadly classified as

   (i) Approximate Estimates, and (ii) Detailed Estimates

Before a detailed estimate of the proposed work is to be taken up, it is necessary to prepare its approximate estimate. An approximate estimate gives the approximate cost of the work and is prepared on the basis of cost of the similar works carried out in the past. Such an estimate is required to obtain administrative approval in case of Government works. Once the work is administratively approved by the Government, a detailed estimate is worked out. A detailed estimate is prepared after its complete set of drawings are ready. The quantities of various items of work are worked out from such drawings and are multiplied by the present rates of items of works to arrive at the estimated cost of the work.

Thus the various types of estimates prepared according to their requirements may be classified as follows:

- Preliminary or Approximate or Rough Cost Estimate
- Plinth Area Estimate.
- Cubic Contents Method
- Approximate Quantity Method
- Detailed Estimate (or Item Rate Estimate)
- Revised Estimate
- Supplementary Estimate
- Supplementary and Revised Estimate
- Annual Repair (A.R) or Annual Maintenance (A.M.) Estimate

Of the above estimates, the first four belong to approximate estimates and the remaining five are detailed estimates.

(i) Preliminary or Approximate or Rough cost estimate :

This approximate estimate is prepared for preliminary studies of the various aspects of the work and also to decide the financial position and policy for administrative approval by competent sanctioning authority. In case of commercial projects such as residential buildings, irrigation and power projects that earn revenue, the probable income is also mentioned and the investment in the project is justified. If the project is non-commercial, having no direct return, its necessity, utility, prospects in future and availability of finance etc. are considered before final decision is taken. This estimate is prepared on the basis of practical experience of carrying out similar works in the past and their rates. In this estimate, the approximate cost of all important works such as cost of land, roads, buildings, water supply, sanitary works, electrification etc. are mentioned separately. A brief report of the project indicating its necessity, utility and method of arriving at the cost of each item and the site or layout plan is also enclosed with the estimate.

(ii) Plinth Area Estimate :

As the name implies, this estimate is prepared by multiplying the plinth area of the proposed building by the plinth area rate of similar building having same specifications and height that is constructed very recently in the same locality. The plinth area of the proposed building is calculated for the covered i.e. roofed portion by measuring the outer dimensions at the plinth level. The area of courtyards, and other open areas are not to be included while calculating the plinth area. The plinth-area method of preparing estimate gives the approximate cost of the building to be constructed.

Even if the plan of the proposed building is not ready, the floor areas of different units (i.e. rooms) are worked out from the users requirements and about 35% of it is added for thickness of walls, circulation and waste to obtain the approximate total plinth area. This plinth area is then multiplied by the current plinth area rate in the locality to obtain the approximate cost of the proposed building. The method is simple and is usually adopted in practice.

(iii) Cubic Content Method :

The cubic content method is an approximate method of preparing an estimate of a proposed building and differs from the method (ii) described above in that, in addition to the total plinth area of the proposed building, it also takes into consideration its height. The total cubic contents of the building are obtained by multiplying its total plinth area by the height. Knowing the cubic content rate of recently constructed building having similar specifications in the locality, the approximate cost of the proposed building is worked out by multiplying the total cubic contents by its cubic content rate. In order to calculate the cubic contents of the building, the length and breadth are measured as the external dimensions at the floor level and the height of the building is measured from the floor level to the top of the flat roof or upto half way of the sloped roof. For multistoreyed building, the height is measured between floor level of one storey to the top of next floor above it. As per I.S. 3861, the foundation and plinth and the parapet above the roof are not taken into consideration in calculating the cubic contents.

The cubic content method is more accurate as compared to plinth area method as it accounts for the height of the building. In practice, however, this method is not used.

(iv) Approximate Quantity Method :

In this method the structure is divided into :

 (a) Foundation Inclusive of Plinth and

 (b) The Super Structure.

The cost per running meter of foundation inclusive of plinth is worked out and is multiplied by the total length of foundation to determine the total cost of foundation inclusive of plinth. Similarly the cost per running meter of the superstructure is found out and is multiplied by the total length of all the walls of superstructure to get the total cost of superstructure. The total cost of the structure is then obtained by the addition of total cost of foundation inclusive of plinth to the total cost of the superstructure. A line plan of the proposed structure is required for the above computations.

(v) Detailed Estimate (Or Item Rate Estimate) :   (W-2010)

This is the accurate method of estimating in which the entire building work is subdivided into individual items of work and the quantities of each item of works are calculated from the complete set of drawings (i.e. plan, elevation, sections etc.) and the abstract of the estimated cost is prepared by multiplying the quantities of each of the above items by the rate of the completion of that item. The rates of various items of work can be obtained from the 'schedule of rate' prepared by the Government organisation or from analysed rates of item. In order to make provision for unforeseen expenditure for miscellaneous petty items (for which no provision is made in the estimate) and contingencies a 3 to 5% of the estimated cost is added to it. An additional 1 to 2 % is also provided for the work-charged establishment i.e. for the salaries to be paid to the chawkidars, technical assistants, supervisors etc. appointed by the Government (or owner) to look after the work. The grand total of all the above cost is known as the total estimated cost of the proposed work.

After the administrative approval for the work is obtained, its detailed estimate is prepared and sent for obtaining technical sanction from the appropriate competent Government authorities. The actual execution of the work commences only after obtaining technical sanction (from the Government) and necessary allocation of funds are made available in the budget grants for that year.

The detailed estimate is accompanied by the following documents :

- A comprehensive report of the proposed work.
- General specifications of the work.
- Detailed specifications of various items of work.
- Detailed working drawings consisting of plan, elevations, sections, details of foundations etc. with site or layout plan.
- Calculation and design of component parts of the work.
- Analysis of rates for the items of work not included in the schedule of rate.

Detailed estimate is generally prepared in the following two steps :

   (a)   Taking out dimensions and squaring them i.e. the dimensions of the various items of work are taken from the relevant drawings and are multiplied (i.e. squared) to obtain its quantities and are entered in the 'Measurement Sheet Form'.

   (b)   Abstracting i.e. the quantities of the various items of work calculated as above are multiplied by the rates of those items obtained either from the schedule of rate or worked out by rate analysis and are entered in the 'Abstract Sheet Form'. If 'rate' and 'amount' columns in the abstract sheet form are left blank (to be entered by the contractor) then it is termed as the 'Bill of Quantity'.

(vi) Revised Estimate :   (W-2010)

It is also a detailed estimate and is to be prepared when :

- The original sanctioned amount of estimate exceeds by more than 5%.

- Amount spent on the work exceeds administratively sanctioned amount more than 10 %.

- When there are drastic changes in original proposal i.e. the original load bearing structure is now proposed to be converted into a framed structure, even if the cost of the work does not exceed the sanctioned amount.

The revised estimate is accompanied by a comparative statement in the prescribed format indicating the changes in each item of works, its rate and amount as per original and revised with full justification for such variations and excess etc.

(vii) Supplementary Estimate :   (W-2010)

It is a fresh detailed estimate which is to be prepared when additional works are required to supplement the original proposed work or when further development or extension of the work is required to be carried during progress of the work. The abstract must indicate the original amount of the estimate and the total amount including supplementary amount for which fresh sanction is to be obtained.

(viii) Supplementary and Revised Estimate :   (W-2010)

This estimate is prepared when a particular work is abandoned and the cost of the work remaining is less than 95 % of the original sanctioned amount of the work or where there are material deviations from the original proposed work which may result in substantial saving in the estimate. In such cases a fresh supplementary and Revised Estimate is to be prepared and sent for revised technical sanction.

(ix) Annual Repairs (A.R.) or Annual Maintenance (A.M.) Estimate :

Annual Repair (A.R.) or Annual Maintenance (A.M.) is a detailed estimate prepared to keep or maintain the building or roads in proper working and safe condition. In case of buildings, this includes items such as white washing, painting of doors and windows, inside and outside plastering and minor repairs etc. The amount of such estimate should be within 1.5

to 2% of the original cost of the building. In case of roads, it includes items such as filling patches, minor repairs to bridges and culverts, repairs to berms etc.

In case of damages caused to the works during monsoon, which cannot be repaired within the annual repair grants a 'Special Repair Estimate' is to be prepared.

1.4 ITEMS OF WORK

While preparing detailed estimate of a building it is necessary to split the entire building into different items preferably in the order of its construction. e.g. The load bearing structure to be constructed may be split into following items of work in the order of its execution as :

- Site clearance.
- Excavation for foundations.
- P. C. C. in foundations.
- U. C. R. masonry in foundations.
- C. R. masonary in plinth.
- Damp proof course at plinth level.
- Plinth filling with hard murum.
- Brick Work (or stone masonary) in Superstructure.
- Providing and fixing door and window frames.
- Lintels over openings.
- Flat R.C.C. or sloping roof.
- External and internal plastering and pointing.
- Providing and laying flooring.
- Door and Window shutters.
- Water supply and sanitary arrangement.
- Electrification.

The quantities of the above items of work are calculated from the relevant drawings (i.e. plan, elevation, section and foundation details etc.), the process being termed as 'taking out' (i. e. measuring the required dimensions of the items such as length, width, depth or height (or thickness) and 'squaring' (i.e. multiplying length by breadth and depth or height if the item is to be measured in m^3 or multiplying length by its width or height if the item is to be measured in m^2 etc.) The above measurements are then to be entered in a systematic manner in a specified *measurement sheet form*'. The next step is known as 'Abstracting' i.e. preparing the bill of quantities by multiplying the quantities of the above items by the corresponding rates (to be taken from the 'schedule of rate' prepared by the P.W.D. organisation of the State or Central Government) and entering them in a specified manner in the 'Abstract Sheet Form.' The summation of the cost of all the items of the work is then known as the *Estimated Cost of the Work*'.

1.5 DESCRIPTION OF AN ITEM OF WORK

An exact concise and complete description of all the items of work is to be framed so as to convey the clear and unambiguous meaning of all the items of work to be executed by the contractor. The rates to be quoted by the contractor in the tender form depends entirely upon the complete description of the item. e.g. a complete, correct and concise description of the item of excavation for foundations shall be as follows :

Excavation for foundation in ordinary soil such as sand, gravel, soft murum etc. including lift upto 1.5 m and removal of the excavated material up to a distance of 50 m beyond the building area including stacking and or spreading as directed, dewatering (if necessary), preparation of the bed for foundation, shoring strutting, back filling, ramming and watering etc. complete.

Similar complete description is required to be written in correct sequence for all the items of the work to be executed.

1.6 MEASUREMENT OF WORKS

The measurement of quantities of various items of building work forms an important stage in the planning and its execution from the commencement of first estimate to its final completion and settlement of the payments of the works. The procedure followed for taking out quantities of various items of work differs from State to State and for different departments in the same State. The task of bringing uniformity in the measurements was entrusted to the Indian Standard Institute (I.S.I.) (now renamed as Bureau of Indian Standards) in the year 1958. The procedure of measurement of building works as standardized by the I.S.I. is laid down in I. S. 1200 (par I to XXV) and is explained below.

The whole building work is divided into different subheads to have control over the finance and the material consumed. The items of work of similar nature are grouped under the following subheads:

Main head : Building works

Subheads :

- (a)   Earth work
- (b)   Concrete work
- (c)   Brick work
- (d)   Stone work
- (e)   Steel work
- (f)   Wood work
- (g)   Roofing
- (h)   Plastering and Pointing
- (i)   Finishing items such as white washing, Colour Washing
- (j)   Painting
- (k)   Miscellaneous items etc.

1.7 GENERAL GUIDE LINES FOR MEASUREMENTS (I.S. 1200)

(i)   All measurements shall be item wise for completed items of works and the description of each item should be complete, self explanatory and unambiguous.

(ii)   Taking out dimensions from the drawings and entering them in the measurement sheet shall be in the order of length (L), breadth (B) and depth (if measured below the ground level) or height (H) (if measured above the ground level) or thickness.

(iii)   All measurements shall be carried as follows :

    (a)   All dimensions to be measured to the nearest 0.01 m.

    (b)   All areas to be measured out nearest to 0.01 m^2.

    (c)   All Cubic contents (i.e. volume) shall be worked out to the nearest 0.01 m^3.

(iv)   Similar type of work can be carried out under different conditions to be measured separately.

(v)   Different items having similar description can be clubbed together.

(vi)   Minimum area defined for deduction of an opening or void shall be applicable to the opening or void within the measured space only.

(vii)   In case of stone masonry, brick work or concrete, the work shall be measured separately as follows :

    (a)   From the foundation to the plinth.

    (b)   From the plinth up to the first floor level.

    (c)   From first floor level up to the second floor level and so on.

(viii) The parapet shall be included with the corresponding item of the storey just below it.

(ix)   The bill of quantities shall include the full description of the materials, proportion of mix, workmanship and accurately represent the work to be completed. Items for which accurate measurements are not possible shall be included under ' provisional items'.

1.8 I.S. MODE OR UNITS OF MEASUREMENTS   (W-2010)

The units of measurement of various items of work are based upon their size, shape and nature. The general principles to be followed for units of measurement are as follows:

(a)   Voluminous work, whose length, breadth and depth or height can be measured easily, is calculated in cubic metre (i.e. L × B × d or H) e.g. Excavation for foundations, filling foundation with P.C.C.

(b)   The shallow or thin work whose depth or thickness cannot be measured accurately, is calculated in sq. m (i.e. L × B or H) e.g. plastering and flooring.

(c) Work having long length and small thickness shall be measured in running meters (i.e. m) e.g. water supply or drainage line.

(d) Items which cannot be measured accurately (by the Quantity Surveyor) are included under job work.

(e) Certain items such as Wash-hand basin, W.C. pan etc., are measured in numbers (Specifying its size).

(f) Steel work is measured in terms of its weight (i.e. total volume of steel × its weight density).

1.9 PLINTH AREA, FLOOR AREA, CARPET AREA AND F.S.I.

(i) **Plinth Area :** It is the maximum built up covered area which is measured from outside at the floor level or the area of any storey or the basement whichever is more. The plinth area is inclusive of thickness of wall, covered porches but exclusive of open balconies, lofts, sun breakers etc. The term 'plinth area' is synonymous to 'built up area'.

(ii) **Floor Area :** It is defined as the usable covered area of the building at any floor level and is equal to the total plinth area minus the area covered by the walls. The area covered by the walls is usually taken as 'one sixth' of the plinth area.

(iii) **Carpet Area :** It is defined as the net unstable area at any floor level. This is obtained by deducting the area of passages, corridors, verandahs, bathroom, water closets, kitchen, stores and staircases from the floor area.

(iv) **Floor Space Index (F.S.I.) :** It is equal to the total built up area on all floors divided by the total area of the open plot. i.e. If the area of an open plot is say 400 sq. m and the total built up area of all the floors is say 500 sq. m, then F.S.I = 500/400 = 1.25

The term 'Floor Area Ratio' is synonyms with the 'Floor Space Index'. Generally for town planning schemes, the permitted F.S.I. is 1.00 whereas for Gaothan areas it may be up to 1.5 (or even up to 2.00)

1.10 PRIME COST (P.C.) AND PROVISIONAL SUM (P.S.)

(a) Prime Cost (P.C.) :

While preparing detailed estimate of a building, it is necessary to determine the quantities of various items of work involved in its completion. However, there are certain items which cannot be decided by the architect at the time of preparation of detailed estimate. e.g. water supply and sanitary fitting, fixtures to the doors and windows etc. Such items are to be decided by the architect in consultation with the owner when the execution of the work comes to that stage. Thus all details of above such items are not worked out at the time of preparation of its detailed estimate, but a certain lump-sum amount is provided in the bill of quantities and the contractor is asked to specify in his bill the Prime Cost (P.C.) or the price for such items, and are to be finally adjusted against the actual cost of the article or item purchased by him. The contractor is supposed to specify in his tender a fixed amount or percentage as profit, inclusive of packing, forwarding and delivery of the article at the work-site and other incidental expenses etc.

(b) Provisional Sum (P.S.) :

There are certain items of work for which the contractor has to engage the services of some specialist firms for its completion. e.g. Air conditioning, installation of lift etc. For the completion of such items, a certain amount is specified as provisional sum (P.S.) in the Bill of Quantities, after consulting the specialist firms.

Thus the 'Prime Cost' (P.C.) is for the articles supplied by the shopkeeper and fixed in position by the contractor, whereas 'Provisional Sum' (P.S.) refers to the sum provided in the bill of quantity to be paid as per actual expenditure to the specialist firms.

1.11 PROVISIONAL QUANTITIES

At the time of preparing detailed estimate, there are certain items of work, which are not detailed on the drawings and as such their quantities cannot be worked out accurately. The actual measurements of such items of work will have to be carried out at the work site only and hence the quantities of such items of work are estimated approximately and entered in the measurement sheet (or Bill of Quantities) as 'Provisional Quantities' e.g. in case of excavation for foundations of gravity dam, which should rest on solid rock, if the trial pit investigations are not realistic, the quantity of excavation for foundations (based on the trial pits) specified in the estimate may not be exact, but approximate and are entered in the estimate as 'Provisional Quantity'. The fact that the actual quantity of excavation may be more or less than that specified in the estimate and thus needs adjustment after the completion of the work must be brought to the notice of the contractor at the time of accepting his tender and his consent in writing taken accordingly.

1.12 SPOT ITEMS

A quantity surveyor (or estimator) can prepare a detailed estimate of the proposed building from its complete set of drawings. However, there are certain items of work whose detailed estimate can be prepared by the estimator after the actual visit to work site to record the relevant measurements of the proposed work. Such items, for which spot inspection is necessary, are called as 'spot items'. Some of the spot items are as mentioned below.

- A new opening to be provided in the existing wall
- Site clearance
- An old building to be connected to a new one
- An old roof to be connected to a new roof.

A complete description of such items shall be specified in the tender so that the tender can offer competitive rates for such items.

1.13 CONTINGENCIES

The term 'contingencies' indicates the incidental expenses of a miscellaneous character that cannot appropriately be classified under any specified sub-head or work, but pertain to the work as a whole.

i.e. At the time of preparing a detailed estimate of a proposed work, the estimator has to take care to see that all probable items of work are incorporated into it. However, it is quite likely that a few small items might have passed unnoticed by the estimator that may result in the increase in the estimated cost of the work. In order to make provisions for all such small items and also to provide for the increase in rates of certain items (during its execution) and also to make allowance for minor changes in the design etc., a certain additional amount @ 5 % of the estimated cost of the work is added towards 'contingencies'. It may be noted that contingencies do not provide for increase in the cost of the item due to inflation etc.

Thus if the 'Estimated Cost' of the work = Rs. a/-

$$\text{then the amount provided for contingencies } = a \times \frac{5}{100} = \text{Rs. b (say)}$$

Thus the 'Total Estimated Cost' of the work = Rs. (a + b).

1.14 WORK-CHARGED ESTABLISHMENT

The various establishments in Government Organizations have been classified as 'Permanent', 'Temporary' and 'Work-charged'. In case of an employee on permanent establishment, his services can be terminated by giving three months notice (on either side) and in case of temporary establishment, the services can be terminated by giving one months notice (on either side). In case of work-charged establishment, the salaries of the persons employed, are charged directly to the work (under construction) and as soon as the work is completed, their services are no more required and are automatically terminated and hence the name 'work-charged' establishment. A certain percentage of about 1 to 2 %, say 1.5 % of the total estimated cost of the work is added to provide for the salaries of engineers, supervisors, watchman etc. employed on the work-charged establishment.

i.e. the amount provided for work-charged establishment = $(a + b) \times \frac{1.5}{100}$ = Rs. c (say).

∴   Grand total estimated cost of the work = Rs. (a + b + c)

1.15 CENTAGE CHARGES

Sometimes an Engineering (Government) Department of one organization has to carry out certain work belonging to another department. In such cases, an additional amount of about 10 to 15 % of the estimated cost is included in the estimate to provide for the expenditure incurred by the organizations (which is going to execute the work) towards the salaries of engineers, supervisors, etc. employed for the planning, designing, and completion of such works and are known as 'Centage charges' or *Departmental charges*'. Centage charges are also included on the 'contributory' and 'deposit works' of local bodies or private organizations etc. carried out by the State Public Works Department. Sometimes Central Government may also allot their work in a particular region to the State Government of that region. In such cases, the concerned State Government may add 10 to 15 % centage charges over the estimated amount towards the supervisor charges etc. of the works during its execution.

THEORETICAL QUESTIONS

1. What is meant by Estimating and Estimated Cost ?
2. Explain the importance of preparing an estimate of a proposed Civil Engineering Work.
3. State the complete information (or data) required by the 'Quantity Surveyor' before preparing an estimate of a proposed building.
4. What is the purpose of preparing an estimate of a proposed building before its construction starts ?
5. State how the estimates are broadly classified and explain the purpose of each.
6. State and explain the various types of estimates prepared according to their requirements.
7. Write explanatory notes on the following:
    (i)   Rough cost estimate
    (ii) Plinth Area (P.A.) estimate
    (iii) Cubic contents estimate
    (iv) Approximate Quantity method estimate
    (v)   Item rate estimate
    (vi) Revised estimate
    (vii) Supplementary estimate
    (viii)Supplementary and Revised estimate
    (ix) Annual repairs (A.R.) estimate
    (x)   Annual maintenance (A.M.) estimate
8. Explain the meaning of measurement of works and state the different guide lines followed during such measurements.
9. What is meant by an item of work ? What exact information is required while describing a particular item of work ?
10. What is meant by 'unit of measurement' for an item of work ? State the important principles in deciding the unit of measurement.
11. State the various 'Modes of Measurement' of building works as specified in I.S. 1200.

12. Explain the meaning of the following terms :

(i) Plinth Area (ii) Floor Area (iii) Carpet Area (iv) F.S.I.

13. Distinguish clearly between 'Plinth Area' and 'Carpet Area'.

Ans. **Plinth Area :** It is defined as the covered built up area measured at the floor level of the basement or at any Storey. In calculating the plinth area, following areas shall be included :

Area of wall at floor level exclusive of plinth offset, internal shaft for sanitary installation and garbage chute upto 2 sq. m area, porch, stair cover, machine room etc.

The following items shall not be included while calculating plinth area: Loft Area, Balcony, Cantilever Porch, Vertical sun breakers, Sanitary shaft and garbage chutes having more than 2 sq. m. area, open platform, spiral stair case, tower projecting above terrace level etc.

Carpet Area : It is defined as the usable covered area of all rooms situated at any floor level. It shall be obtained by deducting the areas of the following units from the plinth area : Area of all walls, stilted floor, passages, corridors, verandah, porch, staircase and stair cover, lift shaft, W. C., bath rooms, store room, kitchen, shaft for sanitary pipes, garage, air conditioning ducts etc.

14. State the purpose of having standard method of measurement of building works. Quote the relevant I.S. No. Explain the difficulties, that may arise if no such standard method is adopted.   (P. U. Dec. 1993)

Chapter 2
APPROXIMATE ESTIMATES

2.1 INTRODUCTION AND DEFINITION

Introduction : Before a detailed estimate of a proposed work is prepared, it is necessary to prepare its 'approximate estimate' to know the approximate cost of construction. For government works 'approximate estimate' is to be prepared first and sent to the Government authorities for obtaining 'administrative approval'. Once the administrative approval is accorded on the basis of approximate estimate, its detailed estimate is prepared and sent to the 'appropriate authorities of the Government for its technical sanction. After the technical sanction for the work is obtained, its execution can be carried out as per its approved plan, elevation etc.

Definition : "An estimate that gives the approximate cost of the proposed work and which is based upon the experience of carrying out similar works (i.e. having same specifications, heights etc.) in the past, is called as an approximate estimate". It is to be prepared before its detailed estimate is worked out.

2.2 PURPOSE OR NECESSITY OF PREPARING AN APPROXIMATE ESTIMATE

The purpose of preparing an approximate estimate of the proposed work, before its detailed estimate is prepared, is as follows :

- **Feasibility Studies :** The probable net benefits after the execution of the commercial work can be worked out and can be compared with the approximate cost of the work using the approximate estimate and it can be decided whether the investment in the proposed work is feasible or not.

- **Availability of Funds :** The preparation of an approximate estimate enables to know the approximate cost of the proposed work, which can be compared with the availability of funds for the work and the decision regarding the execution of the work can be taken.

- **Decision Regarding Preparation of Detailed Estimate :** From the approximate estimate, the approximate cost of the work is known, and the decision regarding whether the work is to be executed or not is taken. If the work is to be executed, then only its detailed estimate is to be worked out. If the work is not to be executed, the preparation of its detailed estimate is not required. Thus approximate estimate helps in deciding whether it is necessary to prepare its detailed estimate or not.

- **For Insurance :** If the proposed work is to be insured against natural calamities such as cyclone, earthquake etc., then approximate estimate helps in ascertaining the value of proposed work required for insurance purpose.

2.3 GENERAL PRINCIPLE OF PREPARING APPROXIMATE ESTIMATES

Even though there are different methods of preparing, approximate estimates of buildings and other civil engineering works, their basic or general principle remains the same; i.e. knowing the cost per unit of similar construction executed in the recent past, the approximate cost of proposed work can be worked out by multiplying the number of units in the proposed work by the unit cost of the similar work (executed in the recent past), due allowance being made for the likely escalation of prices of various items of construction during the execution of the proposed new work depending upon the "building cost index' prevalent at the time of its execution.

2.4 METHODS OF PREPARING APPROXIMATE ESTIMATES

The various methods adopted for preparing approximate estimates of buildings and other civil engineering works are as follows:

(I) Buildings :

The methods commonly used for preparing approximate estimates for buildings are as explained below:

- Service unit method or unit basis method.
- Plinth Area (or square metre) method
- Volumetric or cubic content method.
- Bay method.
- Approximate quantity method or running meter method.
- Building cost index method.

(i) Service Unit Method or Unit Basis Method :   **(W-2010)**

The service unit means the important unit in a structure that is supposed to give certain service to its users. e.g. in an auditorium or cinema house, the service unit is a seat or chair; in case of school building, it is a class room or a student; in a hospital, it is a bed; in a lodge, it is a room; in a stable, it is a horse and in case of elevated water reservoirs, it is a litre. Thus knowing the cost of providing one such unit, the approximate cost of the work can be determined by,

Approximate cost of the work

$$= \begin{pmatrix} \text{Number of such service} \\ \text{units proposed} \end{pmatrix} \times \begin{pmatrix} \text{Cost of constructing one service} \\ \text{unit in the similar structure} \end{pmatrix}$$

The method is very simple and it requires less time. However, as the method is very approximate, it is not used in practice except for mere comparison during casual discussion. The service units in the proposed work should be identical with service unit taken from the similar structure for computations.

(ii) Plinth Area (P.A.) or Square Meter Method :

The method commonly adopted for buildings consists in determining the plinth area of the proposed building in square metres and multiplying it by the cost per square metre of the recently constructed similar building having same specifications and same height. The plinth area is taken as covered area of a building measured at floor level by taking external dimensions (i.e. out-to-out dimensions) excluding plinth offsets, if any.

The following points need careful consideration while adopting this method :

- **Escalation of Prices :** While adopting this method, necessary allowance is to be made for change in the price level that may occur during the construction of the proposed work; i.e. cost per square meter taken from the similar construction in the past will have to be modified to account for the increase (or decrease) in the price level.

- **Height of the Proposed Building :** The plinth area method does not account for the height of the building. If the height of the proposed building is not same as the height of the similar structure taken for the computation of the approximate cost, then the cost per square metre of the similar structure is to be modified suitably. i.e. if the height of the proposed building is more or less than the similar structure, the cost per square metre of the new building will have to be increased or decreased proportionately.

- **Specification of the Building :** The specifications (i.e. type and quality of work) of the proposed building should be same as the specifications of the similar comparable building already constructed, to bring the approximate cost of the new building very near to its ultimate cost.

- **Transportation Cost :** The proposed new building should be situated in the same locality of a comparable building.

- **Shape of Building :** The proposed building should have the same shape and same ratio of plinth area to its perimeter as those of the similar building whose rate per square metre is to be taken for computations. It may be noted that the rectangular buildings have more perimeter of walls as compared with the square building having same area. Thus the cost of the rectangular building works out to be more than the cost of the square building having same area.

(iii) Volumetric or Cubic Content Method :

In this method, the cost per cubic content of a recently constructed similar building is worked out by dividing the total cost by the total cubic contents of the building. Thus knowing the cost per cubic meter of this building, the approximate cost of the proposed new building is worked out by multiplying the total cubic contents of the proposed new building by the cost per cubic metre of similar building. In order to calculate the cubic contents of the proposed new building, its total plinth area is worked out as in the method (ii) above and is multiplied by the height of the proposed building.

The proposed new building should have similar specifications, same height and situated in the same locality of the building taken for comparison of the cost. The length and width are measured from out-to-out of the wall at the plinth level and the height is usually taken from the floor level to the top of the flat roof or upto half the height of the sloping roof. The foundation and plinth and the parapet wall (constructed above the flat roof) are not to be accounted for calculating the cubic contents of the building, as per Bureau of Indian Standard recommendations.

This method is found to be more accurate as compared to plinth area method as the height of the building is also considered. However, the method is very little used in practice.

(iv) Bay Method :

The method is usually adopted in case of constructions where there is repetitive type of work i.e. which has several similar types of bays. A bay is space occupied between centre to centre of two similar supports; e.g. Arches of same length supported on similar piers or columns spanning a bridge. In this case cost of construction of one such bay of the work recently constructed is worked out and the approximate cost of the proposed new work is calculated by multiplying the total number of such bays (in the proposed work) by the cost per bay of the similar constructed work in the past. The method is usually applicable to cycle stands, grain godowns, factory buildings etc. where there is repetition of the similar work.

(v) Approximate Quantity Method or Running Meter Method :

In this method, the whole building is divided into 'Substructure' (which includes foundations and plinth) and 'Super structure' and the cost per running meter of construction of substructure is worked out and is then multiplied by the total running meter length of substructure to obtain the approximate cost of construction of substructure. Similarly the cost per running meter of the super-structure is also worked out and is multiplied by the total length in running meter of the super structure to get the approximate cost of construction of the super-structure. Summation of total cost of substructure and superstructure will be the approximate cost of the proposed building.

The items included under 'substructure' are site clearance, excavation for foundations, P.C.C. in foundation, stone or brick masonry in foundation and upto plinth and damp-proof course at the plinth level. The 'Superstructure' includes the items such as brickwork in superstructure, doors and windows, roof, flooring, plastering, white washing, colour washing etc. A complete plan of the proposed building is required for this method.

(vi) Building Cost Index Method :   (W-2010)

The 'building cost index' is a measuring device that indicates the relative changes in the prices of certain specific items such as cement, steel, teakwood, bricks, sand, coarse aggregates and labour employed etc. in a certain year with respect to the respective prices of the same items in the past year (which is considered as the base year).

The procedure of determining the building cost index in general consists as follows :

After selecting a base period, the important items (such as cement, steel, teakwood, bricks, and labour employed etc.) whose prices are likely to be appreciably affected during this period are decided and certain weightages are assigned to such items and the building cost index is worked out by any one of the following formulae.

(a) Laspeyre's Formula :

$$L_{In} = \frac{\sum P_1 Q_0}{\sum P_0 Q_0} \times 100$$

where, P_0 = Base year price

Q_0 = Base year weights

P_1 = n^{th} year i.e. current year price.

(b) Passche's Formula :

$$P_{In} = \frac{\sum P_1 Q_1}{\sum P_0 Q_1} \times 100$$

where, P_0, P_1 and Q_0 have the same meanings, as stated in (a) above, and Q_1 = current year weights.

(c) Fisher's Formula :

$$P \cdot F_{In} = \sqrt{\frac{\sum Q_0}{\sum P_0 Q_0} \times \frac{\sum P_1 Q_1}{\sum P_0 Q}} \times 100 = \sqrt{L_{In} \times P_{In}}$$

where, P_0, P_1, Q_0 and Q_1 have the same meaning as stated in (a) above and L_{In} and P_{In} are the Laspeyre's and Paasche's index constants respectively.

If the 'Building Cost Index' determined by any one of the method suggested above works out to be 2.5 for the current year, it means that there is a general price rise of all the items by 50 % in the current year over the assumed base period. However, this may not be true in practice.

[II] Other Civil Engineering Works :

(i) Highways : The unit to be adopted for determining the approximate cost of a new proposed highway is per kilometer length basis.

The cost per kilometer of length constructed depends upon the cost of the private land to be acquired, topography of terrain through which the highway passes (i.e. depending upon the undulation of the ground, the cost of earthwork i.e. cost of excavation or embankment varies), cost of the finished road surface (i.e. whether asphalted or concerted surface) and cost of crossings to be constructed (i.e. bridges, culverts etc.).

Thus knowing the cost of construction per kilometer length of a similar constructed highway, the approximate cost of the proposed new highway can be worked out immediately.

(ii) Railways : The method of preparing approximate estimate of a new railway line is similar to the method explained in (i) above; i.e. knowing the cost per kilometer of the recently constructed similar railway line (having same gauge, sleepers, ballasts etc.), the approximate cost of construction of the proposed new railway route can be worked out.

The cost of acquiring private land and topography of the ground through which the track passes will also have to be given due consideration while preparing approximate estimate.

(iii) Storage (Reservoirs and) Dams : The unit adopted for calculating the approximate cost of the dam that stores water in the reservoir on its upstream side is the hectare-meter i.e. the quantity of water spread over one hectare of land to a depth of one metre. Thus knowing the cost per hectare-meter of water of a similar constructed dam in the recent past, the approximate cost of the proposed new dam can be calculated.

However, the characteristics of all the reservoir basins may not be same and hence due consideration must be given to this aspect while determining the approximate cost of the new dam.

(iv) Water Supply Works : The basis of preparing approximate estimate in case of water supply projects is the population to be served by such works. Thus knowing the cost per capita (i.e. per head) of the population served by an existing similar project, the approximate cost of the new project can be worked out knowing the total population for which the new project is designed.

(v) Sanitary Engineering Projects : The basis of preparing an approximate estimate of a new sanitary engineering project is same as explained in (iv) above; i.e. knowing the cost per capita of the population served by an already constructed similar project, the approximate cost of the proposed new sanitary project can be worked out if the total population for which it is designed is known.

(vi) Bridges : From the known cost of construction of a recently completed bridge and its linear water way (calculated approximately by the formula $4.75\sqrt{Q_{max}}$), the rate of construction of the bridge per meter of linear water way is worked out. The (approximate) cost of construction of a new proposed bridge is then worked out by multiplying its total linear water way (in metres) by the rate of construction per meter of linear water way of the recently constructed similar bridge as stated above, due consideration being given to the escalation of the prices and the changes in the specifications, if any, of the proposed new bridge to be constructed.

(vii) Culverts and (Hume) Pipe Drains : If the length of a culvert or Hume pipe drain to be constructed is same as the one already constructed in the recent past, the (approximate) cost of such works can then be expressed per number of such new drains to be constructed.

2.4.1 Approximate Estimates

This is the most quick method of preparing rough cost estimate of the (proposed) project.

The method is based on the practical knowledge and experience of carrying out similar works in the past. The approximate quantities of the various materials required for the project can be ascertained by making use of *material consumption constants per sq. metres of built up area* based on the earlier similar types of projects (completed) in the past.

i.e. The total quantity of material required for the (proposed) project will be approximately equal to the proposed built up area of the project multiplied by the material consumptive constant.

Calculation of 'Built Up Area' of the Work :

In order to prepare an approximate estimate of the proposed work, it is necessary to determine its probable built up area as stated below.

- The (proposed) area on ground floor and on all other floors (if any) is considered as 100%.
- Space occupied by staircases, balconies and lift (any) is also considered as 100%.
- Parking floor i.e. spaces, stilt areas etc. is assumed as 50 % (of the area occupied by them).
- The total base area occupied by the overhead water tanks is also considered as 50%.

Cost of the Project :

The (approximate) cost of the (proposed) project depends upon its direct and indirect costs as stated below :

1. **Direct Cost :** It consists of the actual (direct) expenditure involved in the completion of the project. It includes the initial cost of acquiring the open land (including legal and brokerage expenses etc.) and also the cost of material, labour, tools and plants etc. required for the work.

2. **Indirect Cost :** It consists of any expenses other than that included in the direct costs (i.e. cost of land, materials and labour) as stated above.

It includes the following :

- Expenditure incurred on the development charges of the area.
- Expenses for the non agricultural clearance from Government authority.
- Local body taxes.
- 7/12 extract charges.
- Site cleaning expenses.
- Site development (i.e. construction of compound walls, and or fencing, approach and internal roads in the area water supply and drainage line, street lights etc.
- Fees to be paid to architects, R. C. C. experts and for services of other specialist required if any.
- Administrative expenses for the establishments of office at the site, stationary, printing, telephone, salaries to office staff etc.
- Supervision charges for technical person.

- Expenses towards the security staff employed.
- Running expenses on site during construction.
- Any other sundries or miscellaneous expenses etc.

The approximate break up of direct and indirect costs of the building may be as indicated below :

Sr. No.	Description of item	Approximate Rate/m²	Percentage cost
1.	Material cost (Direct cost)	₹ 2000/-	45%
2.	Labour cost (Direct cost)	₹ 950/-	26.5%
3.	Indirect expenses	₹ 550/-	28.5%
4.	Land cost	As per actual	–

THEORETICAL QUESTIONS

1. What is meant by an approximate estimate ? Why such an estimate is prepared ?
2. Explain clearly the purpose or necessity of preparing an approximate estimate of a proposed work.
3. State the general principles to be followed while preparing an approximate estimate.
4. State and explain the various methods of preparing approximate estimates and specify where these methods shall be adopted.
5. What are the various methods adopted for preparing approximate estimates of buildings ?
6. Explain the following methods of preparing approximate estimates of buildings :
   - (i) Service unit method
   - (ii) Plinth area (or square meter) method
   - (iii) Cubic content (or volumetric) method
   - (iv) Bay method
   - (v) Approximate quantity method
   - (vi) Building cost index method.

Chapter 3

TAKING OUT (OR MEASUREMENT OF) QUANTITIES

3.1 INTRODUCTION, DEFINITION

As already stated in chapter one, it is necessary to prepare an estimate of a proposed civil engineering work to know its probable cost of construction. To start with, an 'approximate estimate' is prepared by any one of the methods as explained in chapter two and once the owner agrees to spend that much amount or in case of Government works, once an 'administrative approval' is obtained, the next step is to prepare its 'detailed estimate' with the help of detailed drawings of the proposed work. While preparing a detailed estimate, the whole work is split up into different items of works in the order of their execution, and quantities of various items of works are calculated either by the English (i.e. M.E.S.) method or Public Works Department (P.W.D.) method, the procedure being termed as 'Taking Out Quantities'.

The methods of taking out quantities, as followed by Central and various State Governments are not same throughout. As taking out quantities of works occupies a very important place in planning, designing and execution of Civil Engineering Works from its first estimate to its final completion, there should be some uniformity in the procedure to be followed during the preparation of detailed estimate. The I.S. 1200 of 1960 has more or less standardised the procedure of measurement of Civil Engineering Works (i.e. taking out quantities) and shall be followed throughout the discussion of this chapter hereinafter.

A quantity surveyor preparing detailed estimates of works shall be conversant with the general procedure of mensuration and taking out quantities and shall be well versed in the art of reading the detailed drawings, accurately. Moreover, he should have thorough knowledge of the various types of construction, their specifications, construction materials etc. The work of computations of quantities of various items of work shall be carried out by him very precisely as per the norms laid down in IS 1200 of 1960.

3.2 GENERAL PROCEDURE OF MEASUREMENT OF WORKS

The norms laid down in I.S. 1200 of 1960 for the accuracy of measurements of various items of works are as follows :

- While recording dimensions, the order should be : length, width (or breadth) and depth (or height or thickness).

- All linear dimensions shall be measured to the nearest 0.01 metre.
- Computations of areas shall be carried out to the nearest 0.01 square metre.
- All volumetric (i.e. cubic contents) computations shall be to the nearest 0.01 cubic metre.
- Clubbing of items is permitted, provided, the break up of the items clubbed is on the basis of its complete description as mentioned under the item.
- Every item shall be described neatly and completely to include loading, transport, handling, unloading, storing etc. complete.
- Reinforcement items requiring cutting of bars etc. shall include the consequent waste also.
- For allowing deductions in case of items, where minimum area is defined for such deductions of openings, such area shall refer only to such openings within the space being measured.
- The work shall be measured into two stages, the one below the average ground level and the other above it.

Sr. No.	Particulars of Items	Units of Measurement
1.	Earthwork in excavation in ordinary soil, in mixed soil with kankar, bajri, in hard soil.	m^3
2.	Earthwork in excavation in foundation.	m^3
3.	Sand filling/Earth filling.	m^3
4.	Damp proof course – cement concrete, rich cement mortar, asphalt etc. (thickness specified).	m^2
5.	Brickwork in foundation and plinth in superstructure.	m^3
6.	Thin partition wall.	m^2
7.	Reinforced brickwork.	m^3
8.	Strip course, drip course, weather course, coping (projection specified).	m
9.	Stone masonry, random rubble masonry, coursed rubble masonry.	m^3
10.	Stone work in wall facing or lining (thickness specified).	m^2
11.	Wood work, door and window frame, chowkhat, rafter beams, roof trusses.	m^3
12.	Door and window shutters, panelled, battened, glazed, part panelled and part glazed (thickness	m^2

	specified).	
13.	Door and window fittings as hinges, sliding bolts, handles etc.	No.
14.	Wood work in position, plywood etc.	m^2
15.	Rolled steel joints, channels, angles, flats, squares, rounds etc.	quintal
16.	Steel reinforcement bars, in R.C.C., R.B. work.	quintal
17.	Binding, bending of steel reinforcement	quintel
18.	Welding of sheets, plates	cm
19.	Rivets, bolts and nuts, anchor bolts.	quintal
20.	Barked wire fencing	m
21.	Iron gate	m^2
22.	Iron hold fast	quintal/No.
23.	Iron grill, collapsible gate	m^2/quintal
24.	Steel doors and windows	m^2
25.	All types of roofs (tile roof, asbestos cement roof)	m^2
26.	Expansion, contraction joint in roof	m
27.	Centering and shuttering, form work – surface area of R.C.C. or R.B. work supported.	m^2
28.	Plastering.	m^2
29.	Pointing	m^2
30.	Pointing, varnishing (No. of coats specified)	m^2
31.	Flooring (thickness specified)	m^2
32.	Ornamental cornice	m

3.3 METHODS OF TAKING OUT QUANTITIES

The methods of taking out quantities of the works are classified as

    (i)   Public Works Department (P.W.D.) method (long wall-short wall method).

    (ii)   Centre-line method.

(i) Public Works Department (P.W.D.) Method :

This method commonly adopted in our country essentially consists of the following three steps :

    (a)   Taking out (dimensions from the relevant drawings),

    (b)   Squaring the dimensions, and

    (c)   Abstracting.

The term 'taking out' implies measuring the dimensions i.e. length, width and height (or depth) of the various items of construction from the relevant drawings and recording them in the measurement sheet form. The meaning of 'squaring the dimensions' indicates the multiplication of the dimensions length, width and depth (or height) to determine its quantity if the item is to be measured in cubic metres or multiplication of length and depth (or height) if the item is to be measured in square metres etc. and recording the result as 'quantities' in the measurement sheet form. The various items of construction, whose quantities are to be calculated, are entered in the measurement sheet form in the order of their execution of the work, so that there is little chance of omitting, any item of measurement.

Measurement Sheet :

A typical 'Measurement sheet' form is as shown below :

Item No. or Sr. No. of item	Description of item	Number	Length	Breadth or Width	Depth or Height or Thickness	Quantity	Total Quantity	Remarks
1	2	3	4	5	6	7	8	9

Once the measurement sheet as indicated above is prepared, i.e. the quantities of various items of work are calculated and entered in the measurement sheet, the next (or last) step is to prepare an abstract of the estimated cost i.e. Bill of quantities and to enter it in the 'abstract sheet' form as indicated below

Abstract Sheet :

Item No. or Serial Number of item	Description of item	Quantity	Rate	Per	Amount
1	2	3	4	5	6

It may be noted that the first two columns of the both the measurement and abstract sheets are identical and the entries in the column (3) of the abstract sheet are same as those in the column (7) of the measurement sheet. The total number of items in the abstract sheet and sequence of items shall be same as those in the measurement sheet.

The relevant rates of the items of the work are either worked out or taken from the Schedule of Rate, also called as District Schedule of Rates (D.S.R.) prepared by the Central or State Government Public Worked Department (i.e. C.P.W.D. or State P.W.D.) and are entered in the abstract sheet form. Multiplication of the quantities of items of works with their corresponding rates gives the cost i.e. amount of the items of work. Summation of all such costs (i.e. amounts) gives the estimated cost of the work. To this estimated cost, contingencies at 5%, which allows for unforeseen expenses, petty expenditure, variations in the rates, minor changes in the designs etc. are added. In addition, 1 to 2% of the estimated cost is also added to meet the expenditure of work-charged establishment to arrive at the grand total estimated cost of the work.

It is the method, most commonly adopted in practice for calculating the quantities of various items in the substructure and superstructure walls. The method in short consists in determining the length of long walls, usually (not necessarily) running in the longitudinal direction from out to out and that of the 'short wall' running in transverse direction in between the long walls from in to in. Such measurements of dimensions i.e. out to out and in to in are to be carried out at each and every changes in the thickness of the wall. It is interesting to note that with the decrease in the width of the walls from the foundation to superstructure, the length of the 'long wall' goes on decreasing by the sum of the offsets on either side and that of the 'short wall' goes on increasing by the sum of the offsets on either side as computations proceed from the foundation to superstructure level. It is better to draw different plans at different elevations e.g. plan at foundation trench level, plan at different footing levels etc. to calculate the lengths of the long walls and short walls separately at each level of the work.

The simple procedure to determine the length of 'long-walls' and 'short-walls' at each level is to calculate the length of the centre line for long walls and short walls separately from the plan and add one width of the item of work at that level to obtain the length of the 'long wall' and subtract one width of the item of work at that level to get the length of the 'short-wall' i.e.

$$\begin{pmatrix} \text{Length of the long wall} \\ \text{measured from out to out} \end{pmatrix} = \begin{pmatrix} \text{Centre line length} \\ \text{of long wall} \end{pmatrix} + \begin{pmatrix} \text{One width} \\ \text{at that level} \end{pmatrix}$$

and

$$\begin{pmatrix} \text{Length of the short} \\ \text{wall measured between} \\ \text{the long wall from} \\ \text{in to in} \end{pmatrix} = \begin{pmatrix} \text{Centre line length} \\ \text{of short wall} \end{pmatrix} - \begin{pmatrix} \text{One width at} \\ \text{that level} \end{pmatrix}$$

It may be noted that the very first wall taken in any direction, for computation of its quantity is termed as 'long wall' (even though its length may be shorter). All other walls running parallel to it (i.e. first wall) are called as other long walls (L), and those running at right angles to the 'long walls' are then termed as 'short walls'.

It may be noted that the common portion of the item of the work at the junction of the walls is always to be included in the long walls and is to be excluded from the short walls.

Measurement of length of long walls and short walls from the plan :

The plan shown on the drawings is at the plinth level. A beginner is supposed to draw different plans at various levels of construction from the foundation upto the plinth level. For example : in case of a load bearing structure, the foundation and plinth usually consist of the following items of works.

- Excavation for foundations below ground level upto the depth of foundation (as shown in the foundation detail drawing).
- P.C.C. (1 : 4 : 8) in foundations.
- U.C.R. masonry in foundation in cement mortar (1 : 6).
- C.R. masonry in plinth in cement mortar (1: 6) and
- Damp proof course over the entire plinth level.

Thus to calculate the quantities of the above items of construction by long wall and short wall (i.e. P.W.D.) method it is advisable to draw the following three different plans.

- Plan at foundation level which will be helpful in computing the quantities of 'excavation for foundation' and P.C.C. (1 : 4 : 8) in foundations.
- Plan at U.C.R. masonry level in foundations that will enable to calculate the quantity of U.C.R. masonry in foundation.
- Plan at C.R. masonry level in plinth which will be used for calculating the quantities of C.R. masonry in plinth and D.P.C. over plinth level.

Once the above three plans at different levels are drawn, the various walls are classified into two groups as 'long walls' and 'short walls', the 'first wall' measured in any one direction with common portion of the item included into it is then called as 'long wall', and all walls measured parallel to it are designated as other long walls. All other walls from which the common portion of the item is excluded and are measured at right-angles to the long walls are termed as 'short walls' (or cross walls). This convention once adopted, for taking out quantities, is not to be changed during the entire computation work. Thus, the following rules may be used for determining the length of the long wall and short wall at the various levels of the item of work as shown in the foundation details.

(i)   Length of the long wall (measured from outside to outside of the item of work)

$$= \begin{pmatrix} \text{Centre to centre distance} \\ \text{of that wall} \end{pmatrix} + \begin{pmatrix} \text{One width of that item} \\ \text{of work at that level} \end{pmatrix}$$

(ii) Length of the short wall (measured from inside to inside of the item of work)

$$= \begin{pmatrix} \text{Centre to centre distance} \\ \text{of that wall} \end{pmatrix} - \begin{pmatrix} \text{One width of that item} \\ \text{of work at that level} \end{pmatrix}$$

It may be noted that the length of 'long wall' goes on decreasing by the sum of offsets measured on the either side of the centre line and that of the 'short wall' is seen to increase by the sum of offsets, as measured from the foundation level to plinth level in successive stages.

Illustrations of computations of lengths of long walls and short walls at various levels :

Figs. 3.1 (a) and (b) indicate the procedure of determining the length of long walls and short walls at various levels of work i.e. at foundation level, U.C.R. and C.R. masonry levels etc. The common portion of the item of work is to be included in the lengths of the long walls, whereas the same is to be excluded from the corresponding lengths of short walls.

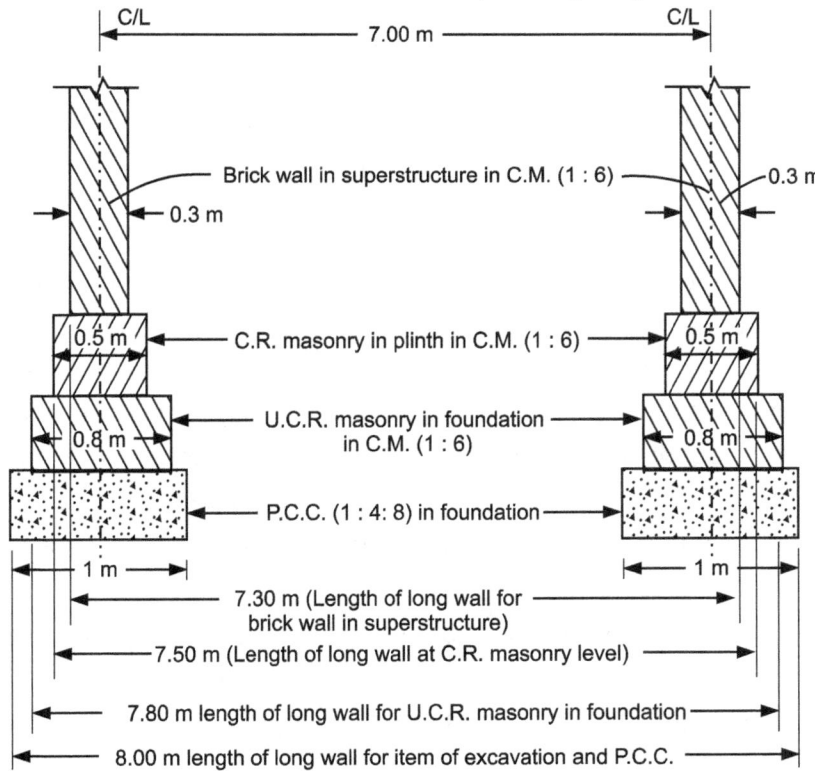

Fig. 3.1 (a) : Sectional elevation for long wall at various levels

(one room block) (Along length)

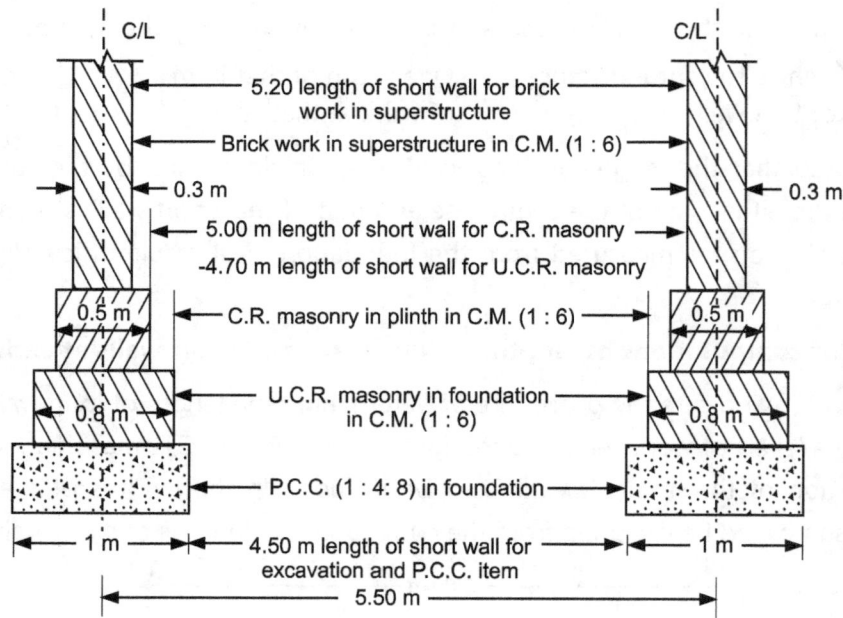

Fig. 3.1 (b) : Sectional elevation for short wall at various levels

(one room block) (Along width)

(ii) Centre-line Method :

As the name implies, the total centre line length of all the walls of same type having similar foundations is worked out from the plan of the proposed structure and is then multiplied by the respective breadth (or width) and depth (or height) to obtain the required quantities of the structure. The total length of the centre line remains same for the substructure (i.e. excavation for foundation, filling foundations with concrete, all footings etc.) and superstructure items except in cases where there are cross walls i.e. at the junctions of the walls. The method is simple and quick in computations for symmetrical structures having no cross walls.

However, if there are cross walls, then special care is to be taken in taking out dimensions at all such junction points. The simple rule is to deduct half the width (or breadth) of the respective item for each junction point from the total length of the centre line. e.g. in case of a plan of a building having one cross wall i.e. having two junctions, deduct one width (or breadth) of that item of work from the total length of the centre line and multiply it by the width and depth (or height) of that item to determine its quantity. In case of buildings having different types of walls, each set of wall is to be considered separately i.e. first determine the total length of the centre line of each type and make deductions for each junction as stated above and then multiply it by the respective width (or breadth) and depth (or height) of that item to calculate its quantity. The illustrative Example nos. 1 and 2 are solved by the centre-line method.

1. Referring to Fig. 3.2, which is a plan of a building having no re-entrant portion,

(i)   The total length of the centre line (of external walls)

= 2 (a + b) – 8 (half the thickness of the external walls)

= 2 (a + b) – 8 (t/2)

(ii)   Total outside length = 2 (a + b)

(iii)   Total inside length = 2 (a + b) – 8 (thickness of the external walls)

= 2 (a + b) – 8 (t)

2. Referring to Fig. 3.3, which is a plan of a building having one re-entrant portion,

(i)   The total length of the centre line (of external walls)

= [2 (a + b) – 8 (t/2) + 2c]

(ii)   Total outside length = 2 (a + b) + 2c

(iii)   Total inside length = [2 (a + b) – 8t + 2c]

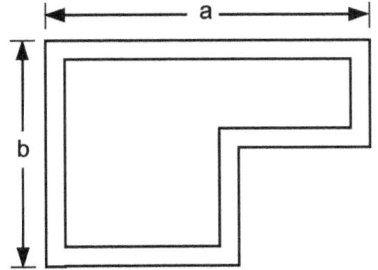

a = Outside length of the building
b = Outside width of the building

Fig. 3.2 : Plan of a building having no re-entrant portion

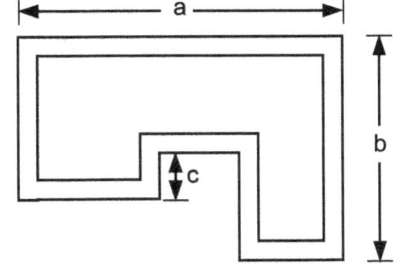

t = Thickness of the external walls
c = Re-entrant length

Fig. 3.3 : Plan of a building having re-entrant portion

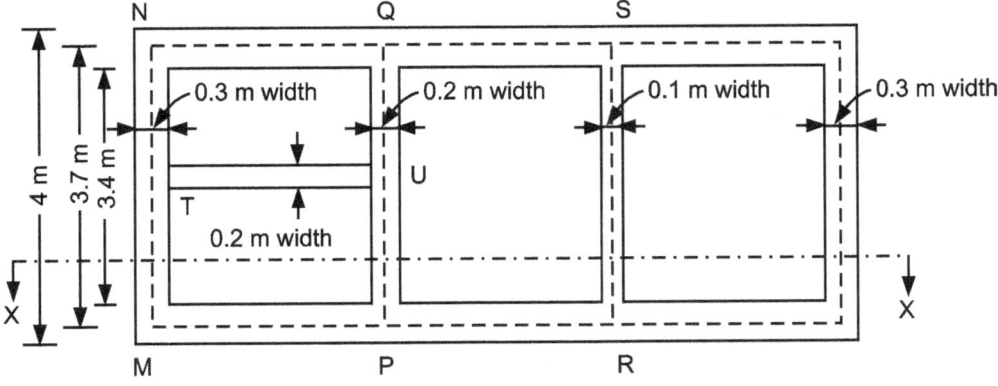

Fig. 3.4 (a) : Plan

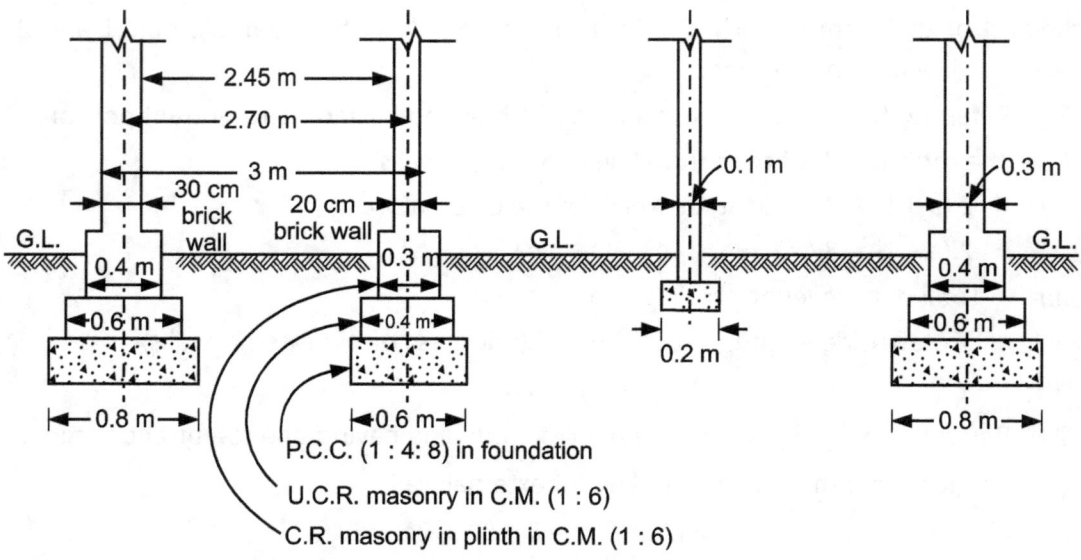

Fig. 3.4 (b) : Details of foundations of varying widths and varying depths
(Section along xy)

Computations of Quantites in Case of Buildings having Cross-walls :

In case of buildings having no cross wall, the quantities of the various items of substructure (i.e. excavation for foundations, P.C.C. in foundations, U.C.R. and C.R. masonry in foundations etc.) can be computed on the basis of the length of the centre line of the external walls without any difficulty. However, in case of building having cross walls, the effective length of the centre line will have to be worked out carefully (from the plan) by deducting the corresponding length of the work which is already measured and included in the external walls of the buildings. Referring to Fig. 3.4 (a) and (b),

(I)   In case of *cross-wall* PQ (that joints the external walls having same width) the c/c distance for cross wall PQ from the plan = 3.7 m.

(i) $\begin{pmatrix}\text{Effective length of the centre line}\\\text{for cross wall PQ for the items of}\\\text{excavation for foundations and}\\\text{P.C.C. in foundations}\end{pmatrix} = 3.70 - 2\left(\dfrac{0.80}{2}\right) = 2.9 \text{ m}$

(ii) $\begin{pmatrix}\text{Effective length of the centre line}\\\text{for cross wall PQ for the item of}\\\text{U.C.R. masonry in foundations}\end{pmatrix} = 3.70 - 2 \times \left(\dfrac{0.60}{2}\right) = 3.1 \text{ m}$

(iii) $\begin{pmatrix}\text{Effective length of the centre line}\\\text{for cross wall PQ for the items of}\\\text{C.R. masonry in plinth and}\\\text{D.P. cource}\end{pmatrix} = 3.70 - 2 \times \dfrac{0.40}{2} = 3.3 \text{ m}$

(iv) $\begin{pmatrix}\text{Effective length of the centre line}\\ \text{for cross wall PQ for the item of}\\ \text{brick work in superstructure}\end{pmatrix} = 3.70 - 0.2 \times \left(\dfrac{0.30}{2}\right) = 3.4 \text{ m}$

which is same as shown on the plan.

(II) In case of cross-wall TU (Fig. 3.4) (case of varying width of foundation), the c/c distance of the cross wall TU from the plan = 2.70 m. The widths of the two walls that join TU are not same, but are 0.3 m for external wall and 0.2 m for cross wall respectively and their foundation widths are also varying as shown in the section.

(i) $\begin{pmatrix}\text{Effective length of the centre line}\\ \text{for cross walls TU for the items of}\\ \text{excavation for foundation and}\\ \text{P.C.C. in foundation}\end{pmatrix} = 2.70 - \left\{\dfrac{0.8}{2} + \dfrac{0.6}{2}\right\} = 2 \text{ m}$

(ii) $\begin{pmatrix}\text{Effective length of the centre line}\\ \text{for cross wall TU for the item of}\\ \text{U.C.R. masonry in foundation}\end{pmatrix} = 2.70 - \left\{\dfrac{0.6}{2} + \dfrac{0.4}{2}\right\} = 2.2 \text{ m}$

(iii) $\begin{pmatrix}\text{Effective length of the centre line}\\ \text{for cross wall TU for the items of}\\ \text{C.R. masonry in plinth and D.P.C.}\end{pmatrix} = 2.70 - \left\{\dfrac{0.4}{2} + \dfrac{0.3}{2}\right\} = 2.35 \text{ m}$

and

(iv) $\begin{pmatrix}\text{Effective length of the centre line}\\ \text{for cross wall TU for the item of}\\ \text{the brickwork in superstructure}\end{pmatrix} = 2.70 - \left\{\dfrac{0.3}{2} + \dfrac{0.2}{2}\right\} = 2.45 \text{ m}$

which is same as shown on the plan.

(III) In case of the cross wall RS, it meets the external walls having same thickness of 0.3 m. However, the foundation depth of the cross wall (which is 0.1 m thick) is smaller than that of the external walls as shown in the section.

In this case, the effective depth of excavation for foundation and P.C.C. in foundation will not remain same, because the P.C.C. in foundation for this cross wall RS has to extend into the excavation for foundation for external walls upto the edge of 0.4 m width of the C.R. masonry offset of the external walls.

(i) $\begin{pmatrix}\text{Effective length of the centre line}\\ \text{for excavation for foundation}\\ \text{of cross walls}\end{pmatrix} = 3.70 - 0.8 = 2.9 \text{ m}$

(ii) $\begin{pmatrix}\text{Effective length of the centre line}\\ \text{for P.C.C. in foundation}\\ \text{of cross wall RS}\end{pmatrix} = 3.70 - 0.4 = 3.3 \text{ m}$

(iii) $\left.\begin{array}{l}\text{Effective length of the} \\ \text{centre line for brick work} \\ \text{for cross wall RS}\end{array}\right\}$ = 3.70 – 0.3 = 3.4 m

Concept of free joint and overlapping joint in centre-line method :

Fig. 3.5 (a) represents the foundation trench plan of a room.

If the total centre-line length is multiplied by the breadth and the depth, we get the quantity of earthwork in excavation. By doing so, we take certain portion twice and leave an equal portion, but this does not affect the quantity. The quantity is not affected, since at every corner of the building, the joint is free joint. [A free joint occurs at the corner of the room/building and does not affect the quantity of the item of work.]

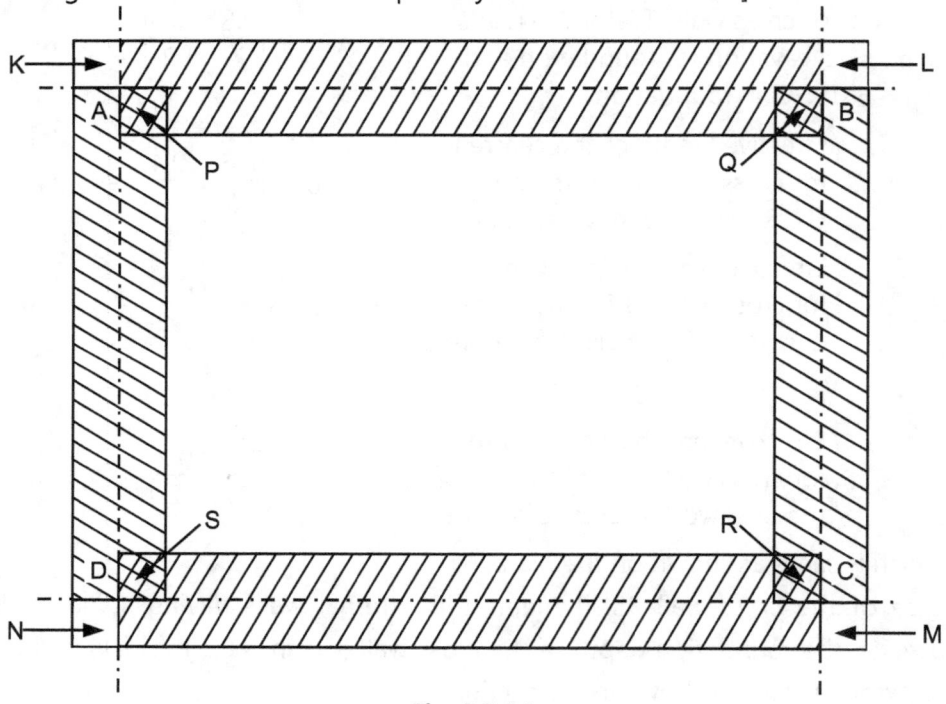

Fig. 3.5 (a)

The quantity of excavation = (AB × 90 cm × 90 cm) + (BC × 90 cm × 90 cm) + (CD × 90 cm × 90 cm) + (DA × 90 cm × 90 cm). It may be noticed that the portions P, Q, R and S marked with double hatch lines come twice, while the portions K, L, M, N left blank do not come at all, but these portions being equal in magnitude, we get the correct quantity.

An overlapping joint is formed when a cross wall meets with the main wall. The intersection of a cross wall with the main wall causes the formation of two number of overlapping joints. Whenever the overlapping joints are encountered, the centre-line length should be reduced, by considering the number of overlapping joints and the overlapping width. The order of deduction in the centre-line length will be equal to number of overlapping joints multiplied with half of the overlapping width.

This concept is explained as follows :

In this Example, there are two overlapping joints A and B of the cross wall with the main wall.

Total centre-line length of wall　=　(2 × centre to centre of long wall)

+ (3 × centre to centre of short wall)

= (2 × 10.60) + (3 × 6.30) = 40.10 m

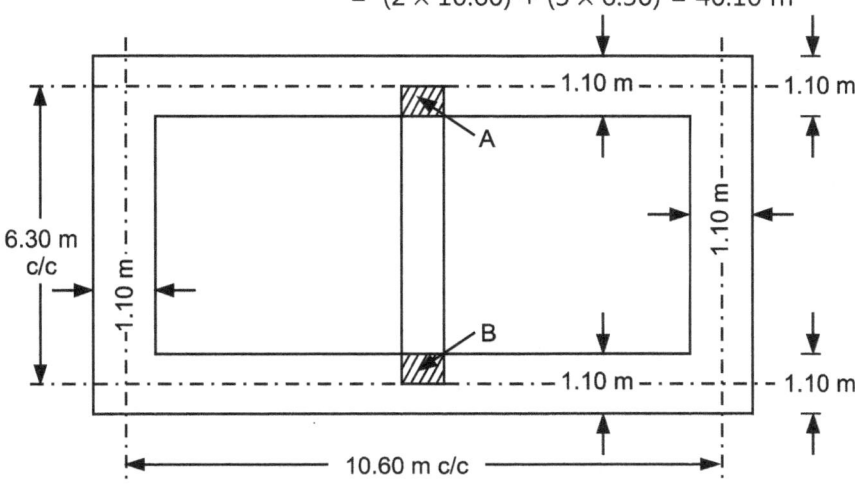

Fig. 3.5 (b)

If the total centre length is multiplied by the width and depth, at the junction the portions A and B shown by hatch lines in figure come twice and we get the quantity in excess by these portions. Therefore these excesses caused by overlapping joints shall have to be deducted.

So,　　　net centre-line length　=　Total centre-line length

$$- \left(\text{No. of overlapping joints} \times \frac{1}{2} \times \text{width} \right)$$

$$= 40.10 - \left[2 \times \frac{1}{2} \times 1.0 \right] = 39.0 \text{ m}$$

So, the quantity of earthwork in excavation = 39.0 × 1.10 × 1.0 = 42.90 m³.

[Depth of trench is taken as 1.00 m]

3.4 COMPARISON OF ENGLISH METHOD AND P.W.D. METHOD

Sr. No.	English method	P.W.D. method
1.	The quantities of items of work are worked out in the order of its execution.	The quantities of items of work are determined in the sequence of measurement.
2.	Grouping of items is not carried out.	Grouping of items is carried out.
3.	Chances of omitting any measurement of item of work are very less.	Possibility of missing some of the items of work.
4.	Method is tedious and time consuming.	Method is simple, easy and takes less time.
5.	The method is used by the Military Engineering Service (M.E.S.) of Government of India.	The method is followed by Central and State Government Public Works Department.
6.	The computations are carried out in duo-decimals.	The computations are in decimals.

3.5   VARIOUS ITEMS OF WORK (IN THE ORDER OF THEIR EXECUTION)

The various items of work to be considered in the order of their execution in case of detailed estimates shall be as stated below :

1.   Earth Work :

As per I.S. 1200 of 1974, the measurement of the item of earth work shall be carried out as follows : Earth work in excavation and earthwork in filling or embankment are to be considered separately under different items and shall be measured in cubic metres by multiplying the length of excavation (or filling) by its width (or breadth) and the depth (or height).

i.e. Quantity of earth work = L × B × D (or H) cubic metres subject to the dimensions of L, B and D (or H) as shown on the drawings.

It is necessary to record the measurement of excavation item separately for every additional 1.5 m lift and also for additional different leads (i.e. disposing off the excavated material beyond the boundary of the proposed work) as the rates of excavation will vary according to different lifts and leads.

As the same excavated material is usually used for 'back filling' (i.e. return fill and ramming the portion of the gap between the original portion of the excavated ground and the completed masonry in foundations) no separate provision is necessary for this work.

In case of sand filling in plinth, this item is to be taken separately and measured in cubic metres.

The *Excavation* in different soil strata is usually classified as follows :

    (i)   Ordinary loose soft soil
    (ii)   Hard soil
    (iii)   Soft murum
    (iv)   Hard murum
    (v)   Soft rock
    (vi)   Hard rock requiring blasting.
    (vii)   Hard rock requiring chiseling.

Usually shoring, strutting, preparing the foundation bed and dewatering, if necessary, is also included under this item.

2.   Concrete :

It may be plain cement or reinforced cement concrete :

(a) Plain Cement Concrete (P.C.C.) :

The item of foundation concrete is calculated in cubic metres, by multiplication of length, width and depth of concrete. The length and width of the foundation concrete shall be same as for excavation item, only the depth or thickness of concrete being different. The usual proportion of foundation plain cement concrete is 1 : 4 : 8 or 1 : 5 : 10 and its depth varies from 15 cm to 40 cm.

$$\text{As a check}\quad \begin{pmatrix} \text{Quantity of} \\ \text{foundation} \\ \text{concrete} \end{pmatrix} = \begin{pmatrix} \text{Quantity of} \\ \text{excavation} \\ \text{for foundation} \end{pmatrix} \times \frac{\begin{pmatrix} \text{Depth of} \\ \text{foundation} \\ \text{concrete} \end{pmatrix}}{(\text{Depth of excavation})}$$

Foundation concrete may also be of lime concrete (i.e. instead of cement, lime will be used while preparing concrete). Lime concrete in foundations is also to be measured in cubic metres.

(b) Reinforced Cement Concrete (R.C.C.) :

The reinforced cement concrete may be required for slabs, beams, columns, footings and lintels etc. and is measured in cubic metres.

R.C.C. slabs having depth less than 15 cm, R.C.C. partitions, pardi, jali etc. are measured in square metres specifying the thickness in the description column. The item of reinforced cement concrete is usually split up into three parts :

- Concrete to be measured in cubic metres.
- **Form work :** Unless otherwise specified, it is to be measured separately. The surface of the form work in contact with the concrete is usually measured in square metres.
- **Reinforcement :** Unless otherwise specified, the item of reinforcement is to be measured separately. If the details of reinforcement bars are not shown on the structural drawings, then the item is measured as percentage of concrete in which it is embedded. For slabs, it is usually assumed as 0.8 % approximately; for beams, it is usually taken as 1% approximately and for columns, it is taken as 1.5% approximately.

When the details of reinforcing bars are shown on the drawings, then knowing the total lengths of bars and their diameters, the total volume of steel required can be calculated. This volume, when multiplied by its weight density, gives the total weight of steel reinforcement required.

In case of precast cement concrete, the item shall include moulds for its casting, reinforcement steel required and finishing etc. according to the description specified for the item. Hoisting and erection of items in position shall usually be included in the item. Reinforcement, if specified, shall be measured as a separate item.

Precast cement concrete items having small thickness, such as slabs upto 12 cm thickness, jali work, partition walls etc., are measured in square metres. Precast concrete units of uniform cross-section having long length such as columns, fencing poles, posts, beams etc. are measured in number or running metres, specifying its sectional area in the description of the item. Solid block work in precast concrete may be measured in cubic metres. Stair-case in R.C.C. is usually measured in terms of number of steps specifying its dimensions in the description column.

Measurement of Concrete in Columns, Beams and Slabs :

(i) Columns :

The length or height of the column shall be measured from the top of the footing on which column rests to the underside of the first slab for the ground floor and from the top of the floor slab to the underside of the floor slab immediately above it. (See Fig. 3.6).

(ii) Beams :

The length of the beam shall be measured clearly between the two columns and shall be inclusive of haunches between columns and beams, if any. (See Fig. 3.7).

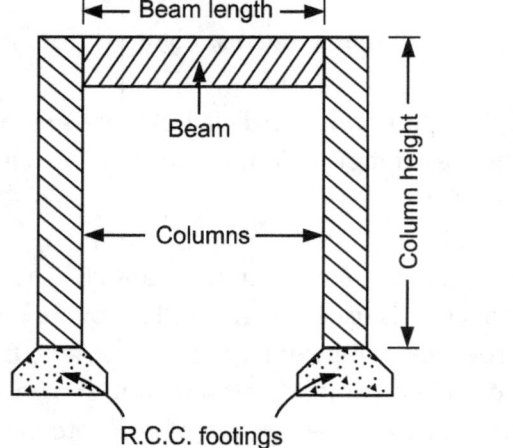

Fig. 3.6 : Column and beam   **Fig. 3.7 : Slab and rectangular beam**

The depth of the ordinary beam shall be measured from the bottom of the beam to the bottom of the slab above it. In case of inverted beams, however, it is measured from the top of the slab to the bottom of the beam.

(iii) Slab :

The depth of the slab shall be measured from the top of the slab to the top of the rectangular beam lying below it. (See Fig. 3.7). In case of slab and T or L-beam, the common portion shall be measured in the T-beam. (See Fig. 3.8).

In case of concrete chajjas combined with lintels or beam, the common portion shall be included into lintel only. (See Fig. 3.9).

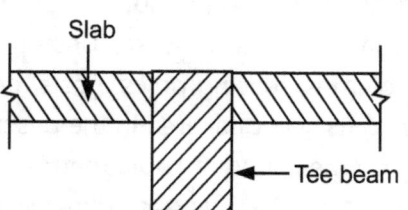

Fig. 3.8 : Slab and T or L-beam

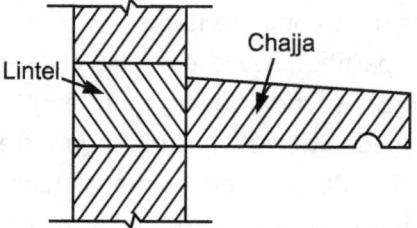

Fig. 3.9 : Lintel and Chajja

The common portion at the junction of two similar members is usually included with only one item e.g. in case of junction of column and beam, the common portion of the work is included in the column (See Fig. 3.6), and in case of slab and rectangular beam, the common portion is included in the slab (See Fig. 3.7), whereas in case of slab and T-beams (or L-beam), the common portion is to be included in the T (or L beam) (See Fig. 3.8) and in case of lintel and chajja the portion common to it is measured in the lintel. (See Fig. 3.9).

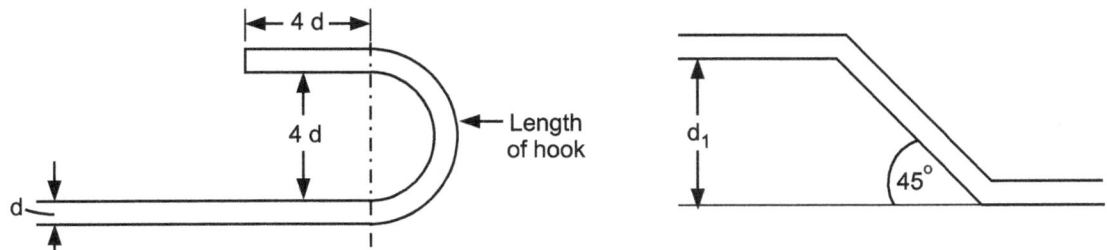

Fig. 3.10 : Bar with standard hook   **Fig. 3.11 : Bar with 45° bent**

The item of Reinforced Cement Concrete (R.C.C.) work is usually divided into two parts i.e. the concrete work required inclusive of centering, shuttering, form work etc. complete (excluding reinforcement) is measured as one item and the steel reinforcement required is considered as another separate item, no deductions being made for the space occupied by the steel from the volume of concrete. Binding wire required is to be included in this item and separate measurements are required for it.

The quantity of concrete work in R.C.C. is calculated in cubic metres knowing the length, width and depth of the concrete. The quantity of reinforcement steel to be laid in position is also worked out from the details shown on the drawings, making due allowance for overlaps, hooks and cranks etc. In the absence of such detailed reinforcement drawings, the quantity of reinforcement steel may be worked out approximately on the percentage of the volume of concrete as specified below.

   (i)   For foundation footings = About 0.5% of volume of concrete

   (ii)   For column = About 1.2 to 2.5% of volume of concrete

   (iii)   For beam = About 1 to 1.5% of volume of concrete

   (iv)   For slab and lintels = About 0.8 to 0.9% of volume of concrete

A thin rich cement plaster may be applied to the exposed R.C.C. surfaces to give uniform smooth finished surface, without making separate item. No deductions are to be made for the volume of the reinforcing bar from the volume of concrete.

End and Side Covers :

The end and side cover for the steel reinforcement usually provided is 40 to 50 mm, whereas the cover at the top and bottom may be 10 to 20 mm in case of R.C.C. slabs and 20 to 50 mm for R.C.C. beams.

The density of steel reinforcement is assumed as 78.5 quintals/m^3 or 7.85 grams/cm^3.

Determination of the Length of Reinforcement Bars :

Consider a bar with standard hook as shown in Fig. 3.10. The length of the hook = d + 4d + 4d = 9d, where d represents the diameter of the bar.

∴   Length of the straight bar of length L, with hook at both ends

$$= L + 9d + 9d = L + 18d$$

For a 45° bent up bar (Fig. 3.11),

Additional length required   =   Hypotenuse (i.e. slant length) – Horizontal length

$$= \left(\frac{d_1}{\sin 45°} - d_1\right) = \left(\frac{1}{0.707} - 1\right) d_1 = 0.42\, d_1 \approx 0.45\, d_1$$

For 30° bent,

$$\text{Additional length} = \left(\frac{d_1}{\sin 30°} - d_1\right) = 0.27\, d_1 \approx 0.30\, d_1$$

For 60° bent,

$$\text{Additional length} = \left(\frac{d_1}{\sin 60°} - d_1\right) = 0.58\, d_1 \approx 0.60\, d_1.$$

where, d_1 = Vertical distance between lower and upper portions of the bent up bar.

Schedule of (Reinforcement) Bars :

It is usual practice to prepare a schedule of reinforcement bars which will be useful for bar bender and supervisors etc. It consists of a list of reinforcement bars specified in a tabular form, indicating its diameter, shape of bending with neat sketches, length of each angle of bent, its total weight etc. Such a schedule of bars is prepared separately for each type of R.C.C. work such as slabs, beams, columns etc. From the schedule of bars, it is possible to determine the total requirement of reinforcement for that item of work with its length, diameter etc. and accordingly the job of bending of bars etc. as per the drawings can be carried out before it is placed in the position before casting of that member.

Some of the usual types of reinforcement bars with the length of hooks and the total length of the bar required are as mentioned below.

Table showing types of reinforcement bars commonly used in R.C.C. construction

Sr. No.	Particulars of bar	Hook length	Total length of bar required
1.	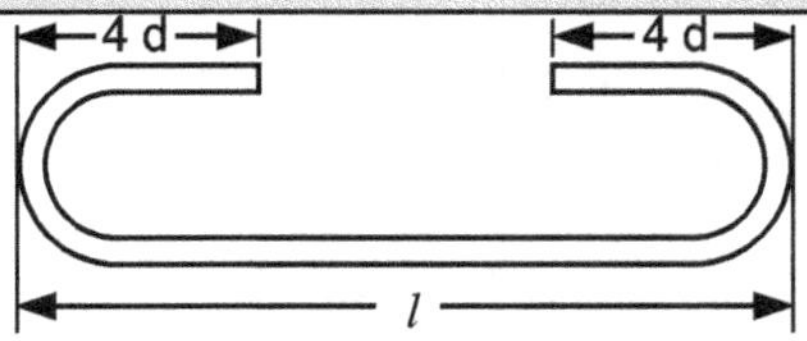 Fig. 3.12	$2 \times 9\,d = 18\,d$	$(l + 18\,d)$
2.	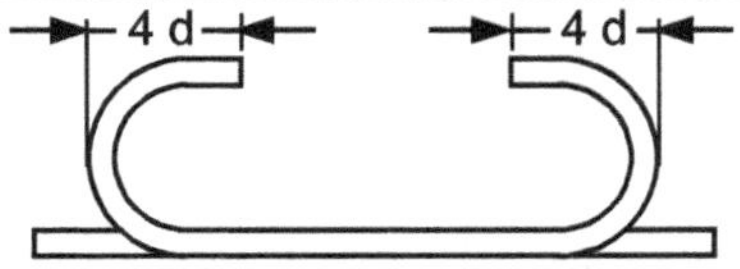 Fig. 3.13	$2 \times 9\,d = 18\,d$	$(40\,d + 18\,d)$ or $(45\,d + 18\,d)$
3.	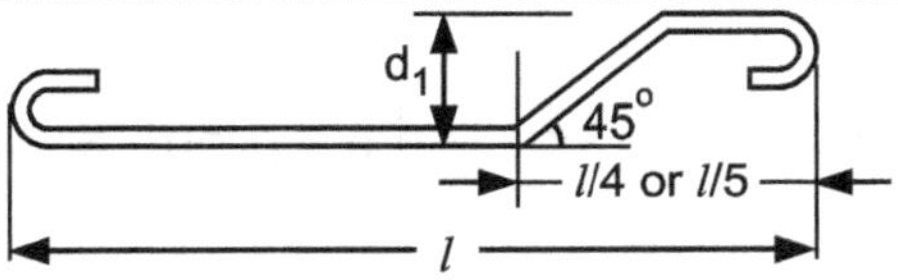 Fig. 3.14	$2 \times 9\,d_1 = 18\,d_1$	$l + 18\,d_1 + 0.45\,d_1$
4.	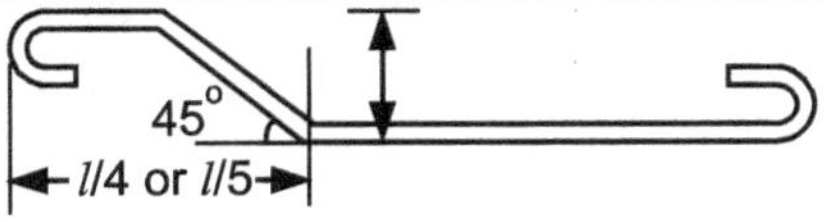 Fig. 3.15	$2 \times 9\,d_1 = 18\,d_1$	$l + 18\,d_1 + 0.45\,d_1$
5.	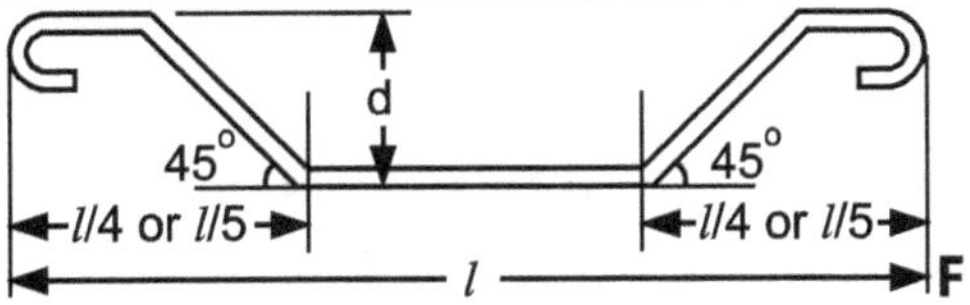 Fig. 3.16	$2 \times 9\,d_1 = 18\,d_1$	$l + 18\,d + 2 \times 0.45\,d_1$ $= l + 18\,d + 0.9\,d_1$
6.	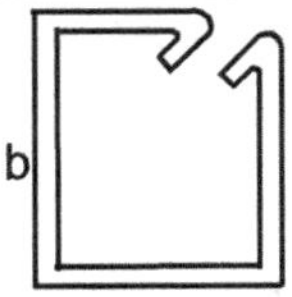 Fig. 3.17	$2 \times 12\,d = 24\,d$	$2a + 2b + 24d$ $= 2(a + b + 12d)$
7.	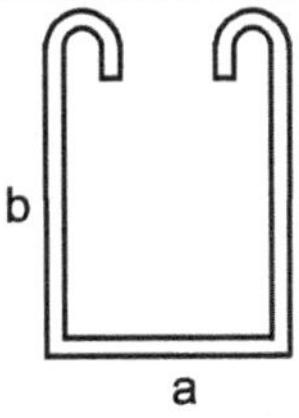 Fig. 3.18	$2 \times 14\,d = 28\,d$	$a + 2b + 28d$

where,   d = Diameter of the bar

d_1 = Vertical distance between lower and upper portions of bent up bar

3. Damp Proof Course (D.P.C.) :

Damp proof course about 25 mm thickness in cement concrete (1 : 1.5 : 3 or 1 : 2 : 4) combined with standard water proofing agent is applied evenly to the entire width of plinth level and is measured by multiplying the length of the D.P. course by its width in square metres. D.P.C. is not to be applied at the verandah openings, sills of the door etc. for which necessary deductions are to be made from the measured quantity.

The D.P.C. in horizontal and vertical directions are to be measured separately.

Guniting :

Full description of the item shall be specified mentioning the thickness. The item shall be measured in square metre.

4. Brick Work :

The size of the bricks, its type, thickness of the joints, bond etc. and the proportion of mortar shall be specified in the description of the item.

The main brick work is measured in cubic metres, and brick work in partition i.e. one brick thickness is measured in square metere specifying its thickness. Brick masonry in foundation and upto plinth is included under one item and the brickwork in superstructure is measured separately. In case of multistoreyed building, the brick work of each floor is to be measured separately as the rates of the item go on increasing from ground floor to subsequent higher floors.

The general procedure of calculating the quantities of brick work in superstructure is to assume all walls as solid and find out its cubic contents, and then allow for the deductions for the openings into it e.g. doors, windows, ventilators, lintels etc. Different types of brick work with different proportion of mortar etc. shall be measured separately.

Honey combed brick work is measured separately, specifying the thickness in square metres, no deductions being made for the holes into it.

Rules for Deductions to be Made for Openings in Brick Wall are as Follows :

- No deductions are to be made for openings upto 0.1 square metre areas, ends of beams, rafter, purlins etc. upto 0.05 square metre in areas and wall plate, bed plates etc. upto 100 mm depth.
- Full deductions are to be made for the rectangular openings by multiplying the length of the opening by its width and the thickness of the wall.

  The brick work in arches is to be measured separately.
- For lintels over openings, the length of the lintel is found out by adding twice the thickness for bearing to the clear span.

Thus, the quantity of deduction to be made shall be equal to :

$(l + 2t) \times$ (Thickness of lintel) $\times$ (Wall thickness)

where, t = Thickness of lintel and l = Length of the opening.

It may be noted that lintels also form separate item to be measured in cubic metres; the quantity being equal to :

$$= (l + 2t) \times t \times \text{Wall thickness}$$

Brick work in columns and pillars shall be described fully and shall be measured separately in cubic metres.

Circular brick work above 6 m radius shall be measured in the general item of brick work in cubic metres.

Brick work in staircases, arches etc. shall be measured separately in cubic metres.

5. Stone Masonry :

The stone masonry in uncoursed rubble or coursed rubble etc. shall be measured separately in cubic metres. Usually stone masonry in foundation and upto plinth (if of the same type) is included under one item and the masonry in superstructure is considered as separate item. For multi-storeyed buildings, the masonry at each floor is to be measured separately.

The procedure of calculating the net quantity of stone masonry is to assume all walls as solid and to calculate its cubic contents, and then deductions are to be made for the various openings such as doors, windows, ventilators etc.

The rules of deduction for the openings in stone masonry are same as for openings in the brick work already explained in item (4) above.

The stone work for sill and parapet copings are measured in running meters, specifying the item fully in the description column.

The face stone work for weather sheds, shelves, slabs etc. are measured in square metre.

6. Lintels :

Lintels provided over openings such as doors, windows etc. are to be measured separately in cubic metres. The length of the lintels shall be taken as length of the clear span (l) between openings and twice the thickness of lintel (t).

The quantity of lintel = $(l + 2t) \times$ (Thickness of lintel) $\times$ (Wall thickness).

7. Form Work :

The form work required for the various items of construction such as slab, beam, columns etc. shall be taken as the actual surface of the form work in contact with the concrete and is measured in square metres as per I.S. 1200 part IV.

8. Sloping Roofs (i.e. Roof Coverings) :

The roof covering over the building structure consists of two parts :

(a) Supporting structure and

(b) Roof proper (i.e. roof cover)

The supporting structure consisting of rafter, purlins etc. is measured separately in cubic metres. The cubic contents of the wood work are calculated by multiplying the length of the members (i.e. purlin, rafter, etc.) by its cross-sectional area.

The roof cover consisting of either Mangalore Tiles, (M.T.), Galvanised Iron (G.I.) sheets, or Asbestos Cement (A.C.) sheets is measured separately in square metres, specifying the thickness of the cover in the description column.

Ridges, valleys and hips are measured separately in running metres.

9. Flooring :

The flooring to be provided may be on the ground, first or second floor etc.

- **(a) Flooring on Ground Floor :** The item usually includes the base course of lime or cement concrete over which the floor finish of Shahabad stone or plain cement concrete or mosaic tiles etc. of specified thickness is to be laid as described in the description column of the item. The combined item is measured in square metres by the multiplication of length and the width to be covered measured from inside to inside of walls of the superstructure.

- **(b) First Floor etc. :** The supporting structure, over which the flooring rests i.e. R.C.C. slab etc., is measured separately in cubic metres, and floor finish laid over it is measured separately in square metres specifying its thickness in the description of the item.

Dado and Skirting : Dados (including raking dados) shall form a separate item to be measured in square metres. Skirting (including raking skirting) shall form a separate item and shall be measured in running metres, specifying the height to which it is to be carried out. Alternatively it may also be measured in square metres.

10. Doors and Windows :

The item of doors and windows shall be split into the following two sub-items :

- **(a) Wooden Frame or Chowkat :** This sub-item shall be measured separately in cubic metre. The cubic contents are calculated by adding the entire length of chowkat (i.e. two vertical members and two horizontal members or one horizontal member if the door sill is not provided) and multiplying it by its cross-sectional area. Additional length for the horns, if provided, shall also be considered.

- **(b) Shutters for Doors and Windows :** This sub-item is to be measured separately in square metres by multiplying the height of the shutters by its width. If the door is not provided with the sill, a clearance of about 6 mm is to be provided at the bottom portion of the door.

Different types of shutters e.g. glazed, panelled, panelled and glazed etc. shall be measured separately.

Various fittings to doors and windows may be considered under separate items on square metre basis or lump-sum amount is provided in the estimate.

11. Other Wood Works :

Other wood works such as wooden trusses, beam, poles, etc. shall be measured separately in cubic metres.

12. Iron Work :

All iron work required shall be measured separately on weight basis in quintal or kilogram. The total cubic contents of the iron work are calculated by multiplying the length of the members by its cross-sectional area. Total cubic contents when multiplied by the weight density of iron gives the total weight of the iron work. The mass density of Mild Steel (M.S.) is taken as 7850 kg/cubic metre.

13. Plastering and Pointing Works :

(a) Plastering :

Plastering in lime and cement mortar shall be measured separately, specifying the thickness of plaster in the description column and is to be measured in square metres. In the description column of this item, the proportion of the mix of lime or cement mortar, the number of coats to be applied etc. shall be specified clearly. If the external and internal plasters are different, then it shall be measured separately. Usually internal plastering is with neeru finish (of thickness 1.5 mm) and the external plastering is rough cast sand faced plaster.

Plastering to walls, ceilings and on roofs shall be taken separately and measured in square metres.

The usual procedure of determining the net quantity of plastering to wall surface is to assume them as solid and to calculate its contents in square metres and then allow for deductions of openings depending upon its size (i.e. area) as follows :

- There shall be no deductions, made for the ends of beams, rafter etc.
- For openings having areas upto 0.5 square metre, no deduction is made from either face and also no additions are to be made for jambs, soffits, sills etc. of such openings.
- For openings having areas greater than 0.5 square metre but less than 3 square metres, deduction is to be made from one face (preferably inferior face) only and the other face (superior face) allows for jambs, soffits, sills etc. without making any separate provision for them.
- For openings having areas greater than 3 square metres, deductions are to be carried out for both the faces of openings and jambs, soffits, sills etc. being considered separately and added to the area to be plastered. The outer jamb portion being smaller than the inner ones, the deduction is carried out from the outer face usually.

If the proportion of mix of the cement plaster is different, i.e. richer than from the wall plaster, it is measured as a separate item in square metres.

(b) Pointings :

The type of pointing, the proportion of the cement mortar mix etc. shall be described fully and the item is to be measured separately in square metres. As the rate of various types of pointings is not same, different types of pointings e.g. tuck pointing, groove pointing, V-pointing etc. shall be measured separately in square metres. Similarly, plastering to different types of wall surfaces, roofs etc. shall be measured separately in square metres. The item of pointing usually includes the raking of joints also.

Pointing of honey combed surfaces shall be measured separately in square metres without allowing any deductions for openings.

Rules of deductions to be made for openings in the surface to be pointed are same as described in the item of plastering above.

14. White Wash, Colour Wash and Distempering :

The finishing items such as white washing, colour washing, distempering etc. shall be measured separately in square metres. The above item usually includes cleaning the surface such as brooming, steel wire brushing, washing, cleaning, rubbing etc.

The white washing, colour washing, distempering etc. to wall surfaces, sloping roof portions and ceiling is to be measured separately in square meteres. Rules for deductions to be made for opening are same as described in the item of plastering explained above.

Work on corrugated surfaces shall usually be measured considering it as flat and not girthed. The measured quantities shall then be increased by the following multiplying factor to allow for corrugations etc.

Sr. No.	Type of surface	Multiplying factor
1.	Corrugated A.C. sheets	1.10
2.	Semi-corrugated A.C. sheets	1.10
3.	Corrugated steel sheets	1.14

15. Painting, Varnishing, Polishing, Tarring :

Painting and varnishing works on different surfaces shall be considered separately and measured in square metres, specifying the measurements as flat or girthed. Multiplying factors for converting the plain surface to the corrugated for different surfaces are as follows :

Sr. No.	Type of surface	Multiplying factor
1.	Corrugated A.C. sheets	1.20
2.	Semi-corrugated A.C. sheets	1.10
3.	Corrugated steel sheets	1.14

Paintings to be carried out on down take pipes, eves gutters etc. shall be measured separately in running metres specifying its size or girth etc.

Varnishing : The item of varnishing is to be measured separately in square metres on the same lines of item of painting as explained above.

Polishing, Tarring etc. : It shall be accounted for separately in the same way as for item of painting described above.

16. Equivalent Plain Areas of Uneven Surfaces in a Tabular Form :

The I.S. 1200 part XV specifies the following multiplying factors for converting the plain or flat areas into the corresponding uneven or girthed surfaces.

Sr. No.	Description of item battened	Measured as	Corresponding multiplying factor
1.	Panelled or framed and braced or ledged joinery work	Measured flat inclusive of chawkat, chockes, edges, cleats etc.	1.30 for each side.
2.	Flush joinery (doors)	Same as above	1.20 for each side
3.	Fully glazed joinery	Same as above	0.80 for each side
4.	Partly panelled and partly glazed joinery	Same as above	1.00 for each side
5.	Louvered type joinery	Same as above	1.80 for each side
6.	Grills, grating, gates, etc.	Measured flat without deduction.	1.00 for painting all over
7.	Steel roller shutters	Measured flat exclusive of top cover.	1.10 for each side
8.	Fully glazed steel doors and windows	Measured flat inclusive of frame	50 for each side
9.	Partly glazed and partly steel sheet cladded steel doors	Same as above	0.80 for each side
10.	Collapsible gates or doors	Measured flat with size of opening.	1.50 for painting all over.

3.6 CHECKS OVER THE ACCURACY OF DETAILED ESTIMATES

In order to ensure that the quantities of the various items worked out in a detailed estimate are fairly correct it is necessary to apply cross-checks as specified below.

Sr. No.	Item of work whose quantity has been already worked out by detailed estimate	Cross-check over the quantity worked out by detailed estimate
1.	Excavation of foundations	The quantity of excavation shall be same as the quantity of excavated material disposed off.
2.	Earth work i.e. return fill (i.e. back filling) and earth or murum filling in plinth.	The quantity of excavation = $\left(\begin{array}{c}\text{Quantity of earth required}\\ \text{for back filling}\end{array}\right) + \left(\begin{array}{c}\text{Earth or murum}\\ \text{filling in plinth}\end{array}\right)$ $\pm \left(\begin{array}{c}\text{Surplus quantity of excavation}\\ \text{or quantity of earth or murum}\\ \text{borrowed from outside}\end{array}\right)$
3.	P.C.C. in foundations	$\left(\begin{array}{c}\text{The quantity}\\ \text{of P.C.C. in}\\ \text{foundation}\end{array}\right) = \left(\begin{array}{c}\text{The quantity}\\ \text{of excavation}\\ \text{for foundation}\end{array}\right) \times \left(\begin{array}{c}\dfrac{\text{Depth of}}{\text{P.C.C.}}\\ \overline{\text{Depth of}}\\ \text{excavation}\\ \text{for foundation}\end{array}\right)$
4.	Stone masonry for a 40 cm thick stone masonry throughout	Area of masonry = $\dfrac{1}{3.5}$ × Plinth area (approx.)
5.	Brick work for a brick wall 20 cm thick throughout	Area of brick walls = $\dfrac{1}{6}$ × Plinth area (approx.)
6.	Total area of flooring	Total area of flooring = Summation of areas of flooring at different storeys = N (Area of flooring at one storey) where, N = number of floors and if the area on each floor is same throughout.
7.	Internal plaster in to walls	Total area of internal plaster in = $(\sum L_E + 2\sum L_1) \times H$ where, $\sum L_E$ = Summation of lengths of external walls $\sum L_1$ = Summation of lengths of internal walls and H = Height of the room or floor. **Note :** The area of different openings such as doors, windows etc. is to be deducted as per the rules.

8.	White wash, colour wash distempering etc.	Total area of this item = total area to be plastered.
9.	R.C.C. work (i) For framed structure	$\dfrac{\text{Volume of reinforced}}{\text{concrete (in m}^3\text{)}}{\text{Weight of reinforcing bars}} \approx 1.25$ (approx.) (in quintals)
	(ii) For load bearing structure	$\dfrac{\text{Volume of reinforced concrete}}{\text{(in m}^3\text{)}}{\text{Weight of reinforcing bars}} \approx 1.00$ (approx.) (in quintals)

3.7 APPROXIMATE RELATION BETWEEN COST OF VARIOUS ITEMS OF WORK WITH RESPECT TO TOTAL COST OF BUILDING

1.	Earth work including excavation and filling	1% of total cost
2.	P.C.C. in foundations	5% of total cost
3.	Providing D.P. course at plinth level	1% of total cost
4.	Brick work in superstructure	35% of total cost
5.	Roof over the building	20% of total cost
6.	Doors and windows	15% of total cost
7.	Flooring	6% of total cost
8.	Plastering, pointing etc.	10% of total cost
9.	Finishing i.e. white wash, colour wash etc.	2% of total cost
10.	Miscellaneous items.	5% of total cost

In addition to above, the cost of water supply, sanitary arrangement and electric fitting will be taken approximately as follows :

1.   Water supply and sanitary arrangements

= 10 to 12% of total cost of building

2.   Electric fitting = 10 to 12% of total cost of building

Note : For preparing abstract sheet of any estimate, use latest rates of item as per dsr-pune 2011-2012 available at end of this chapter on page 3.164. (Under schedule of rates for various items of work.)

3.8 SOME TYPICAL ESTIMATES OF WORKS

3.8.1 Preparation of An Estimate of One Room Block As Shown Below In Fig. 3.19 (a) For The Following Items of Work

(i)   Excavation for foundations.

(ii)   P.C.C. (1 : 4 : 8) in foundations.

(iii)   U.C.R. masonry in foundations in C.M. (1 : 6).

(iv)   C.R. masonry plinth in C.M. (1 : 6).

(v)   D.P.C. at plinth level.

(vi)   Brick work in super structure in C.M. (1 : 6) and

(vii)   R.C.C. slab 15 cm thick by

    (a)   Centre-line method and

    (b)   Long wall-short wall method

(a) Preparation of an estimate of a one room block for the above items by centre line method :

Measurement Sheet

Item No.	Description	No.	Length L	Breadth B	Depth or Height	Quantity	Total
1.	Site clearance				Job	Item	
2.	Excavation for foundations in soft soil including removing the excavated material upto a distance of 50 m (and lift of 1.5 m) beyond the building area and spreading, stacking, and dewatering, preparing the bed for the foundation and back filling etc. complete.	1	25	1	0.90	22.5 m³	
3.	Providing and laying plain cement concrete (1 : 4 : 8) of trap or granite metal for foundation including bailing of water, form work, compaction and curing.	1	25	1	0.20	5.00 m³	

No.	Description					
4.	Providing and laying U.C.R. masonry of trap or granite stones in cement mortar (1 : 6) in foundations including bailing of water, striking of joints and watering etc. complete.	1	25	0.80	0.60	12.00 m^3	
5.	Providing and laying C.R. masonry, IInd sort in plinth of granite or trap stones in cement mortar (1 : 6) including bailing of water, striking of joints on inside and raking of joints on outside including watering complete.	1	25	0.50	0.50	6.25 m^3	
6.	Providing and applying damp proof course 5 cm thick in cement concrete layer (1 : 2 : 4) with bitumen or cement with water proofing material.	1	25	0.50	–	12.50 m^2	
7.	Providing second class burnt brick masonry with I.S. or conventional type bricks in cement mortar (1 : 6) in superstructure including raking out and striking joints including scaffolding, watering etc. complete.	1	25	0.30	2.00	15 m^3	(a)
	Deductions for						
	(i) Door D	1	1.20	0.30	2.00	0.72 m^3	
	(ii) Window W_1	2	1.00	0.30	1.5	0.90 m^3	
	(iii) Window W_2	1	1.00	0.30	1.00	0.30 m^3	
	(iv) Lintel over door D	1	1.50	0.30	0.15	0.068 m^3	
	(v) Lintel over window W_1	2	1.30	0.30	0.15	0.12 m^3	
	(vi) Lintel over window W_2	1	1.30	0.30	0.15	0.06 m^3	
				Total deductions		2.17 m^3	(b)
	∴ Net quantity of brick masonry	=	(a – b)		=	12.83 m^3	
8.	Providing and casting in situ cement concrete M – 15 (i.e. 1 : 2 : 4) of trap metal for R.C.C. slab 15 cm thick including centering, form work, compacting and curing etc. complete excluding reinforcement.	1	7.40	5.90	0.15	6.55 m^3	

Centre Line Method – One Room Block

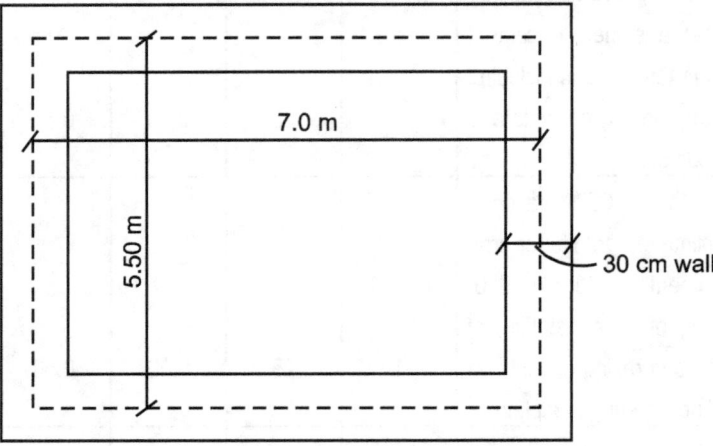

Fig. 3.19 (a) : Plan at a plinth level

Total length of centre line = 7.0 + 5.5 + 7.0 + 5.5 = 25 m

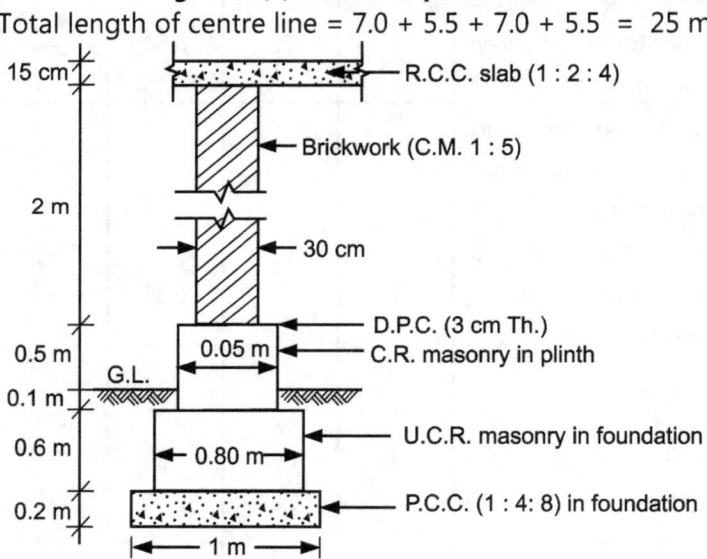

Fig. 3.19 (b) : Foundation details

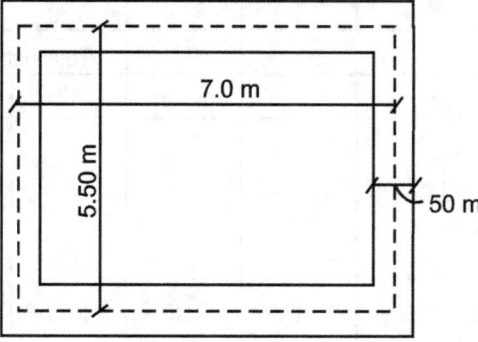

Plan at C.R. masonry level

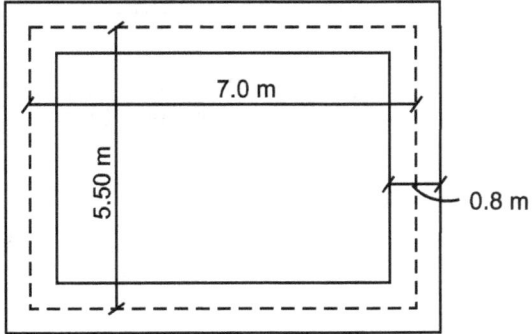

Plan at U.C.R. masonry level

Fig. 3.19 (c)

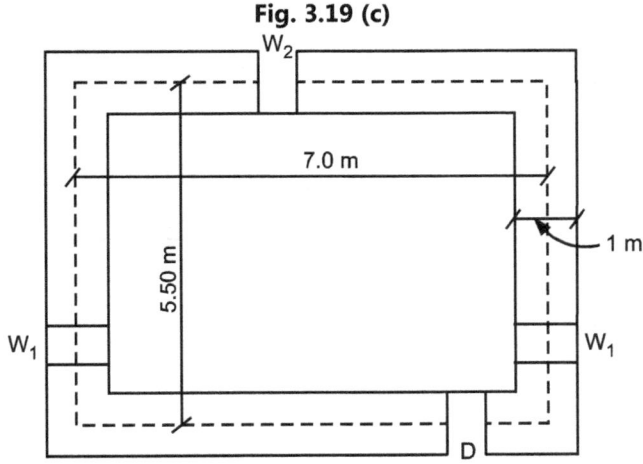

Fig. 3.19 (d) : Plan at a foundation level

Schedule of door and windows

Door   – 1.2 m × 2 m – 1 No.

Window 1   – 1.0 m × 1.5 m – 2 Nos.

Window 2   – 1.0 m × 1.0 m – 1 Nos.

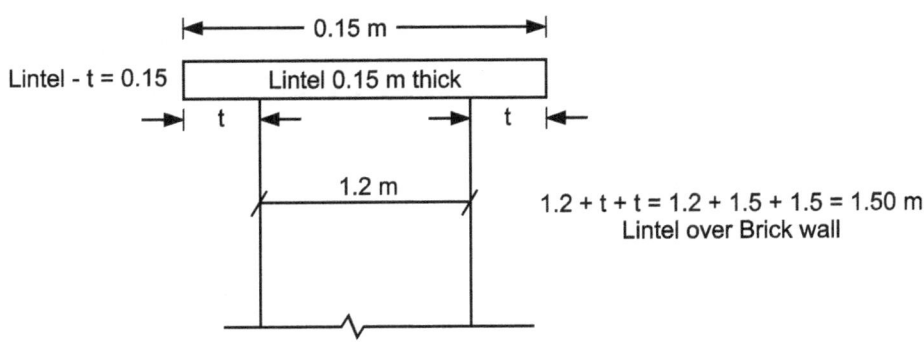

Fig. 3.19 (e)

(b) Preparation of an estimate of the same one room block by Long wall and Short wall method :

Measurement Sheet

Item No.	Description	No.	Length L	Breadth B	Depth or Height	Quantity	Total
1.	Site clearance		–	Job	Item	–	
2.	Excavation for foundations in earth, soil of all types, removal of the excavated material upto a distance of 50 m beyond the building area and stacking and spreading as directed and lift upto 1.5 m, preparing the bed for foundations with necessary back filling, ramming, watering including shoring and strutting etc. complete. (i) Long walls (ii) Short walls	2 2	8.00 4.5	1 1	0.90 0.90	14.40 m^3 8.10 m^3	22.50 m^3
3.	Providing and laying in situ, cement concrete (1 : 4 : 8) of trap metal for foundation and bedding including bailing out water, form work, compacting and curing etc. complete. (i) Long walls (ii) Short walls	2 2	8.00 4.50	1 1	0.20 0.20	3.2 m^2 1.8 m^3	5 m^3
4.	Providing uncoursed rubble masonry of trap stones in cement mortar (1 : 6) in foundations including bailing out of water, striking joints on unexposed faces and watering etc. complete (i) Long walls (ii) Short walls	2 2	7.80 4.70	0.80 0.80	0.60 0.60	7.48 m^3 4.52 m^3	12.00 m^3
5.	Providing coursed rubble masonry IInd sort of trap stores in cement mortar (1 : 6) in external walls of plinth including bailing out water, striking joints inside and racking out joints from outside and watering. (i) Long walls (ii) Short walls	2 2	7.50 5.00	0.50 0.50	0.50 0.50	3.75 m^3 2.50 m^3	6.25 m^3

6.	Providing and laying damp proof course 5 cm thick in cement concrete (1 : 2 : 4) layer and bitumen using cement with water proofing compound						
	(i) Long walls	2	7.50	0.50	–	7.5 m^2	12.5 m^2
	(ii) Short walls	2	5.00	0.50	–	5.00 m^2	
7.	Providing second class burnt brick masonry with I.S. type bricks or conventional type in cement mortar (1 : 6) in superstructure including raking out and striking joints including scaffolding, watering etc. complete						
	(i) Long walls	2	7.30	0.30	2	8.76 m^3	15 m^3
	(ii) Short walls	2	5.20	0.30	2	6.24 m^3	(a)
	Deductions for						
	(i) Door D	1	1.20	0.30	2.00	0.72 m^3	
	(ii) Window W_1	2	1.00	0.30	1.5	0.90 m^3	
	(iii) Window W_2	1	1.00	0.30	1.00	0. 30 m^3	
	(iv) Lintel over door D	1	1.50	0.30	0.15	0.068 m^3	
	(v) Lintel over window W_1	2	1.30	0.30	0.15	0.12 m^3	
	(vi) Lintel over window W_2	1	1.30	0.30	0.15	0.06 m^3	
				Total deductions =		2.17 m^3	(b)
	∴ Net quantity of brick masonry			= (a – b) =		12.83 m^3	
8.	Providing and casting in situ cement concrete M-15 (i.e. 1 : 2 : 4) of trap metal for R.C.C. slab 15 cm thick including centering formwork, compacting and curing etc. complete.	1	7.40	5.90	0.15	6.55 m^3	

One room block
P.w.d. Method (Long Wall-Short Wall Method)

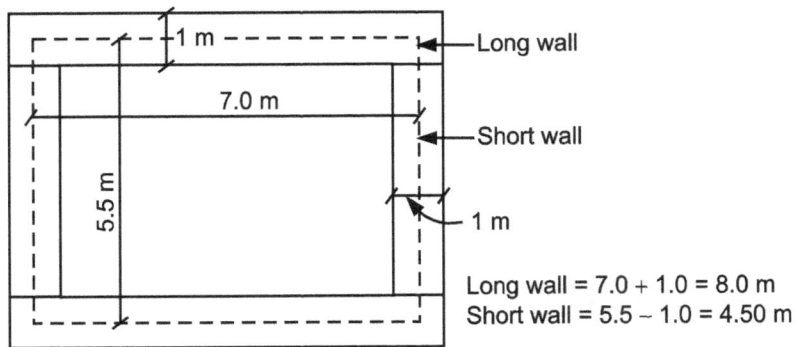

Long wall = 7.0 + 1.0 = 8.0 m
Short wall = 5.5 – 1.0 = 4.50 m

Fig. 3.20 (a) : Plan at a foundation level

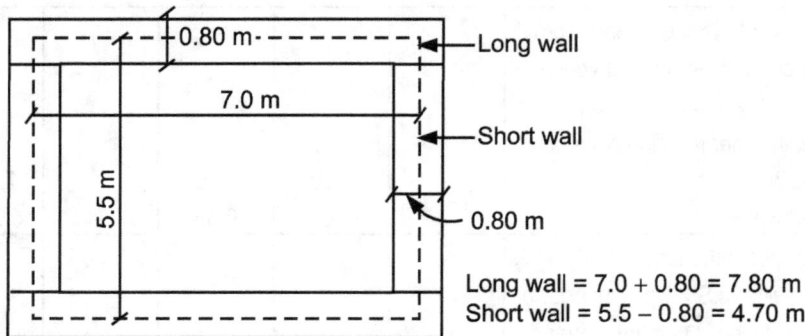

Long wall = 7.0 + 0.80 = 7.80 m
Short wall = 5.5 − 0.80 = 4.70 m

Fig. 3.20 (b) : Plan at a U.C.R. masonry level

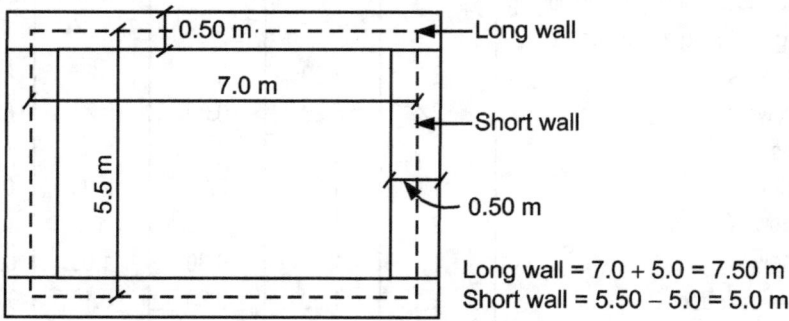

Long wall = 7.0 + 5.0 = 7.50 m
Short wall = 5.50 − 5.0 = 5.0 m

Fig. 3.20 (c) : Plan at a C.R. masonry level

3.8.2 Preparation of An Estimate of One Room Block

Abstract Sheet

Item No.	Description	Quantity	Rate		Per	Amount	
			₹	Ps.		₹	Ps.
1.	Site clearance	L.S.				100	00
2.	Excavation for foundations in soft soil including removing the excavated material upto a distance of 50 m and (lift upto 1.5 m) beyond the building area and spreading stackling, dewatering, preparing the bed for the foundation and back filling etc. complete.	22.5 m³	23	10	m³	519	75
3.	Providing and laying plain cement concrete (1 : 4 : 8) of trap or granite metal for foundation including bailing of water, form work, compaction and curing.	5 m³	600	00	m³	3000	00

4.	Providing and laying U.C.R. masonry of trap of granite stones in cement mortar (1 : 6) in foundations including bailing of water, striking of joints and watering etc. complete.	12 m³	423	00	m³	5076	00
5.	Providing and laying C.R. masonry IInd sort in plinth of granite or trap stone in cement mortar (1 : 6) including bailing of water striking of joints and raking of joint on outside including watering complete.	6.25 m³	570	00	m³	3562	50
6.	Providing and applying damp proof course 5 cm thick in cement concrete layer (1 : 2 : 4) with bitumen or cement with water proofing materials.	12.5 m²	66	00	m²	825	00
7.	Providing IInd class burnt brick masonry with I.S. or conventional type bricks in cement mortar (1 : 6) in superstructure including raking out and striking joints including scaffolding, watering etc. complete.	12.83 m³	728	00	m³	9340	24
8.	Providing a casting in situ cement concrete M-15 (i.e. 1 : 2 : 4) of trap metal for R.C.C. slab 15 cm thick including centering, form work, compacting and curing etc. complete.	6.55 m³	1380	00	m²	9039	00
					Total	**31462.49**	

Total = ₹ 31462.49

Add 5% for contingencies = ₹ 1573.12

= ₹ 33035.61

Add 1% for work charged establishment = ₹ 330.35

Grand total estimated cost = ₹ 33365.96

= ₹ 33366.00

3.8.3 Preparation of An Estimate of Two Room Block As Shown in Fig. 3.21 (A) for The Following Items of Work

(i)   Excavation for foundations.

(ii)   P.C.C. (1 : 4 : 8) in foundation.

(iii) U.C.R. masonry in foundations in C.M. (1 : 6).

(iv)   C.R. masonry in plinth in C.M. (1 : 6).

(v)   D.P.C. at plinth level by

    (a)   Centre-line method and

    (b)   Long wall-short wall method.

Measurement Sheet

Item No.	Description	No.	Length L	Breadth B	Depth or Height	Quantity	Total
1.	Site clearance		Job	Item			
2.	Excavation for foundations in soft soil including removing the excavated material upto a distance of 50 m beyond the building area and spreading, stacking, (lift upto 1.5 m) and dewatering, preparation of the bed for foundations and back filling etc. complete						
	(i) C.L. method	1	32.00	1.10	0.95	33.44 m^3	
	(ii) P.W.D. method						
	Long walls	2	9.70	1.10	0.95	20.27 m^3	33.44 m^3
	Short walls	3	4.20	1.10	0.95	13.17 m^3	
3.	Providing and laying plain cement concrete (1 : 4 : 8) of trap or granite metal for foundations including bailing of water, form work, compaction and curing etc. complete.						
	(i) C.L. method	1	32.00	1.10	0.15	5.28 m^3	
	(ii) P.W.D. method						
	Long walls	2	9.70	1.10	0.15	3.20 m^3	5.28 m^3
	Short walls	3	4.20	1.10	0.15	2.08 m^3	

4.	Providing and laying U.C.R. masonry of trap or granite stones in cement mortar (1 : 6) in foundations including bailing of water, striking of joints and watering etc. complete					
	(i) C.L. method	1	32.30	0.80	0.55	14.21 m³
	(ii) P.W.D. method					
	Long walls	2	9.40	0.80	0.55	8.27 m³ ⎫ 14.21 m³
	Short walls	3	4.50	0.80	0.55	5.94 m³ ⎭
5.	Providing and laying C.R. masonry, IIⁿᵈ sort in plinth of granite or trap stone in cement mortar (1 : 6) including bailing of water, striking of joints inside and raking of joints from outside including watering etc. complete.					
	(i) C.L. method	1	32.60	0.50	0.45	7.34 m³
	(ii) P.W.D. method					
	Long walls	2	9.10	0.50	0.45	4.10 m³ ⎫ 7.34 m²
	Short walls	3	4.80	0.50	0.45	3.24 m³ ⎭
6.	Providing and applying D.P. course 5 cm thick in cement with water					
	(i) C.L. method	1	32.60	0.50	–	16.30 m²
	(ii) P.W.D. method					
	Long walls	2	9.10	0.50	–	9.10 m² ⎫ 16.3 m²
	Short walls	3	4.80	0.50	–	7.20 m³ ⎭

Centre-Line Method : Two Rooms Block

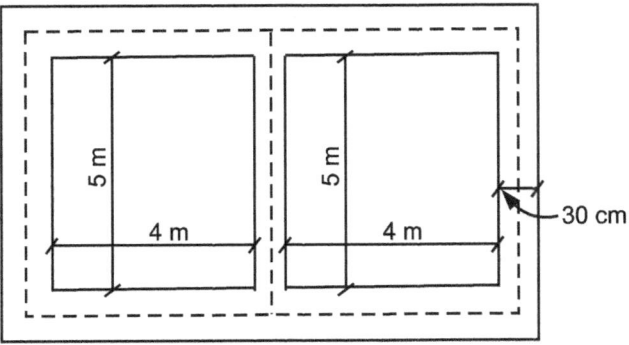

Fig. 3.21 (a) : Plan of a two rooms block

Plan of Two Rooms Block :

Total length of centre-line at foundation level

$$= 8.60 + 5.30 + 8.60 + 5.30 + (5.30 - 1.10)$$
$$= 27.80 \text{ m} + 4.20 \text{ m}$$
$$= 32.00 \text{ m}$$

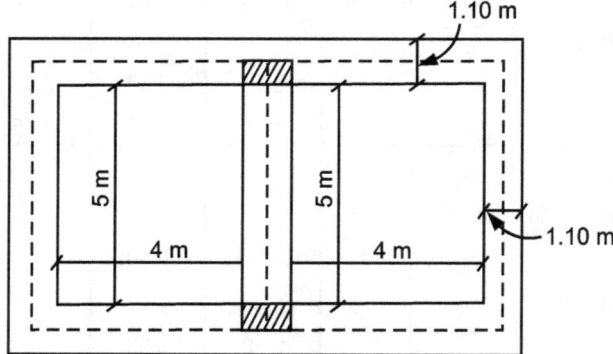

Fig. 3.21 (b) : Foundation details

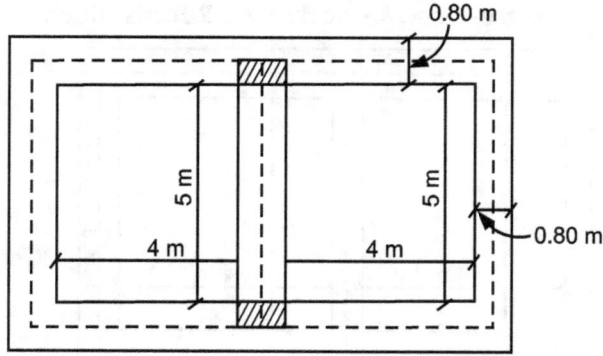

Fig. 3.21 (c) : Plan at a foundation level

Length of centre-line at U.C.R. level = 27.80 + (5.30 – 0.80) = 27.80 + 4.50 = 32.30 m

Fig. 3.21 (d) : Plan at a U.C.R. masonry level

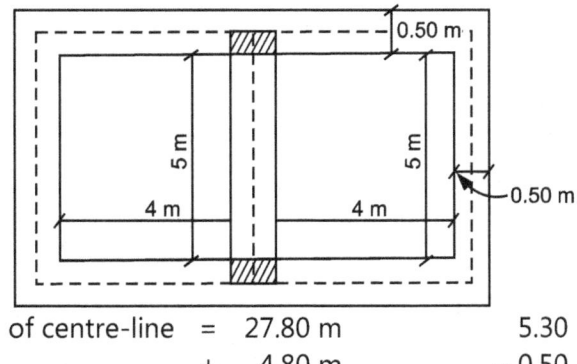

Length of centre-line	=	27.80 m	5.30
	+	4.80 m	− 0.50
Total length at C.R.M. level	=	32.60 m	4.80

Fig. 3.21 (e) : Plan at a C.R masonry level

P.W.D. Method : Two Rooms Block

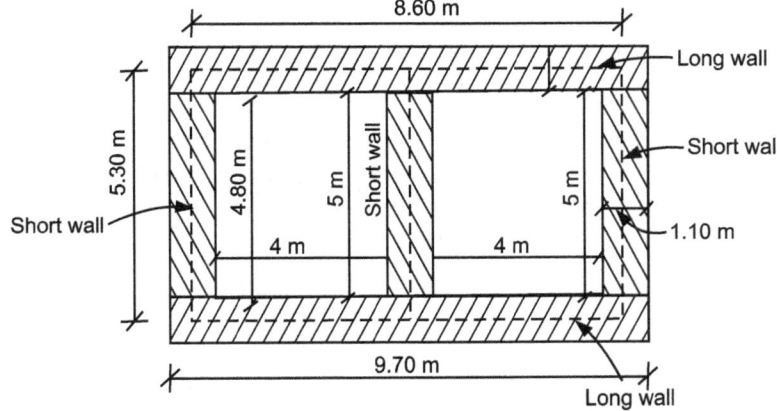

Length of long wall = 8.60 + 1.10 = 9.70 m
Length of short wall = 5.30 − 1.10 = 4.20 m

Fig. 3.22 (a) : Plan at a foundation level

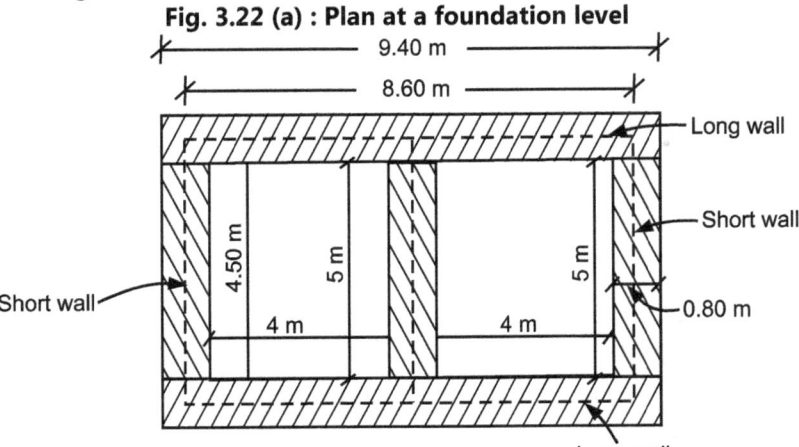

Length of long wall = 8.60 + 0.80 = 9.40 m
Length of short wall = 5.30 − 0.80 = 4.50 m

Fig. 3.22 (b) : Plan at a U.C.R. masonry level

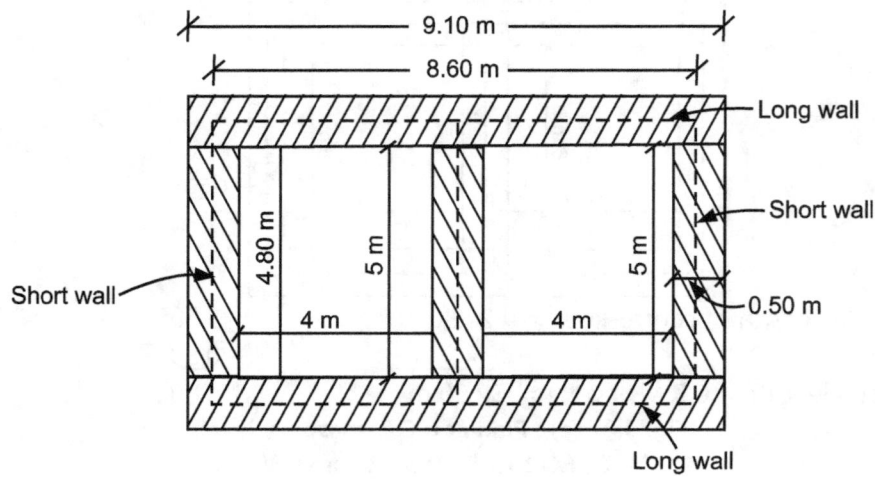

Length of long wall　=　8.60 + 0.50　=　9.10 m
Length of short wall　=　5.30 − 0.50　=　4.80 m

Fig. 3.22 (c) : Plan at a C.R. masonry level

3.8.4 Preparation of An Estimate of Two Rooms Block

Abstract Sheet

Item No.	Description	Quantity	Rate		Per	Amount	
			₹	Ps.		₹	Ps.
1.	Site clearance	L.S. Amount				200	00
2.	Excavation for foundations in soft soil including removing the excavated material upto a distance of 50 m beyond the building area and spreading, stacking, lift upto 1.5 m and dewatering, preparation of the bed for the foundation and back filling etc. complete.	33.44 m³	23	10	m³	771	54
3.	Providing and laying plain cement concrete (1 : 4 : 8) of trap or granite metal for foundations including bailing of water, form work, compaction and curing etc. complete.	5.28 m³	600	00	m³	3168	00

4.	Providing and laying U.C.R. masonry of trap of granite stones in cement mortar (1 : 6) in foundations including bailing of water, striking of joints and watering etc. complete.	14.21 m^3	423	00	m^3	6010	83
5.	Providing and laying C.R. masonry IInd short in plinth of granite or trap stone in cement mortar (1 : 6) including bailing of water, striking of joints and raking of joints from outside including watering etc. complete.	7.34 m^3	570	00	m^3	4183	80
6.	Providing and applying damp proof course 5 cm thick in cement concrete layer (1 : 2 : 4) with bitumen or cement with water proofing material.	16.30 m^2	66	00	m^2	1075	80
				Total		₹ 15209.97	

Adding 5% of contingencies = 760.49

= **15970.46**

Adding 1% for work charged

Establishment ₹ 159.70

Grand total ₹ 16130.16

≈ ₹ **16131.00**

3.8.5 Prepare an Estimate of A Four Rooms Block as Shown Below for The Following Items of Work

(i)   Excavation for foundations.

(ii) P.C.C. (1 : 4 : 8) in foundations.

(iii) U.C.R. masonry in foundations in C.M. (1 : 6).

(iv) C.R. masonry in plinth in C.M. (1 : 6).

(v)   D.P.C. 5 cm thick of plinth level.

(vi) B.B. masonry in superstructure IInd sort in C.M. (1 : 6).

Enter your results in a measurement and abstract sheet forms :

Preparation of an estimate of four rooms block for the above items by

(1)   Centre-line method.

(2)   Long wall and short wall method.

MEASUREMENT SHEET

Item No.	Description	No.	Length L	Breadth B	Depth or Height H	Quantity	Total
1.	Site clearance		Job	item			
2.	Excavation for foundations in earth, soil of all types, sand, gravel, and soft murum including removing of the excavated material to a distance of 50 m beyond the building area (and lift upto 1.5 m) and staking and spreading as directed, dewatering, preparing the bed for foundation and back filling, ramming, watering, shoring, strutting, etc. complete.						
(A)	Centre-line method	1	45.6	1.00	1.00	45.6 m^3	45.6 m^3
(B)	Long and short wall method						
	(i) Long walls L$_1$	3	9.60	1.00	1.00	28.8 m^3	
	(ii) Short walls S$_1$	3	2.30	1.00	1.00	6.90 m^3	45.6 m^3
	(iii) Short walls S$_2$	3	3.30	1.00	1.00	9.90 m^3	
3.	Providing and laying in situ cement concrete (1 : 4 : 8) of trap material in foundations and bedding including bailing out water, form work, compacting and curing complete.						
(A)	Centre-line method	1	45.6	1.00	0.20	9.12 m^3	9.12 m^3
(B)	Long wall and short wall method						
	(i) Long walls L$_1$	3	9.60	1.00	0.20	5.76 m^3	
	(ii) Short walls S$_1$	3	2.30	1.00	0.20	1.38 m^3	9.12 m^2
	(iii) Short walls S$_2$	3	3.30	1.00	0.20	1.98 m^3	
4.	Providing uncoursed rubble masonry of trap stones in cement mortar (1 : 6) in foundations including bailing out of water, striking joints on unexposed faces and watering etc. complete.						
(A)	Centre-line method	1	46.5	0.70	0.40	13.02 m^3	13.02 m^3
(B)	Long wall and short wall method						
	(i) Long walls L$_1$	3	9.30	0.70	0.40	7.812 m^3	
	(ii) Short walls S$_1$	3	2.60	0.70	0.40	2.184 m^3	13.02 m^3
	(iii) Short walls S$_2$	3	3.60	0.70	0.40	3.024 m^3	

5.	Providing coursed rubble masonry IInd sort of trap stones in cement mortar (1 : 6) in plinth including raking of joints where plastering is to be done and striking joints when no plastering is to be done, watering, scaffolding etc. complete.						
(A)	Centre-line method	1	47.4	0.40	0.60	$11.376 m^3$	$11.376 m^3$
(B)	Long wall and short wall method						
	(i)　Long walls L_1	3	9.00	0.40	0.60	$6.48 m^3$	
	(ii)　Short walls S_1	3	2.90	0.40	0.60	$2.088 m^3$	$11.376 m^3$
	(iii)　Short walls S_2	3	3.90	0.40	0.60	$2.808 m^3$	
6.	Providing and laying damp proof course 5 cm thick in cement concrete (1 : 2 : 4) layer and bitumen/using cement with waterproofing compound etc. complete.						
(A)	Centre-line method	1	47.4	0.40	–	$18.96 m^2$	$18.96 m^2$
(B)	Long wall and short wall method						
	(i)　Long walls L_1	3	9.00	0.40	–	$10.80 m^2$	
	(ii)　Short walls S_1	3	2.90	0.40	–	$3.48 m^2$	$18.96 m^2$
	(iii)　Short walls S_2	3	3.90	0.40	–	$4.68 m^2$	
7.	Providing IInd class burnt brick masonry with I.S./conventional type bricks in cement mortar (1 : 6) in superstructure including raking out and striking of joints where plastering is to be done including watering, scaffolding etc. complete						
(A)	Centre-line method	1	47.70	0.30	3.00	$42.93 m^3$	... (a)
(B)	Long wall and short wall method						
	(i)　Long walls L_1	3	8.90	0.30	3.00	$24.03 m^3$	
	(ii)　Short walls S_1	3	3.00	0.30	3.00	$8.10 m^3$	$42.93 m^3$
	(iii)　Short walls S_2	3	4.00	0.30	3.00	$10.80 m^3$	... (a)
	Deductions for openings						
	(i)　Door D_1	4	1.2	0.30	1.50	$2.16 m^3$	
	(ii)　Door D_2	2	1.00	0.30	1.50	$0.90 m^3$	
	(iii)　Window W_1	2	1.00	0.30	1.2	$0.72 m^3$	
	(iv)　Window W_2	2	0.80	0.30	1.2	$0.576 m^3$	
	(v)　Lintels over door D_1	4	1.50	0.30	0.15	$0.27 m^3$	
	(vi)　Lintels over door D_2	2	1.30	0.30	0.15	$0.117 m^3$	
	(vii)　Lintels over window W_1	2	1.30	0.30	0.15	$0.117 m^3$	
	(viii)　Lintels over window W_2	2	1.10	0.30	0.15	$0.099 m^3$	
					Total	4.959	... (b)
	∴ Net quantity of brick masonry in superstructure.	= (a–b)				$37.971 m^3$	

Explanation for (i) Centre-Line Method :

1. $\left[\begin{array}{l}\text{Total length of the centre-line}\\ \text{at the foundation level}\end{array}\right]$ = 2 (8.60) + 2 (7.60)

   $\quad$ + (8.60 − 1.00) + (7.60 − 1.00 − 1.0)
   $= 17.2 + 15.2 + 7.60 + 5.60 = 45.6$ m

2. $\left[\begin{array}{l}\text{Total length of the centre-line}\\ \text{at P.C.C. level}\end{array}\right]$ = 45.6 m (same as (1) above)

3. $\left[\begin{array}{l}\text{Total length of centre-line}\\ \text{at the U.C.R. masonry level}\end{array}\right]$ = 2 (8.6) + 2 (7.60)

   $\quad$ + (8.60 − 0.70) + (7.60 − 0.70 − 0.70)
   $= 17.2 + 15.2 + 7.90 + 6.20 = 46.5$ m

4. $\left[\begin{array}{l}\text{Total length of the centre-line}\\ \text{at the C.R. masonry level}\end{array}\right]$ = 2 (8.60) + 2 (7.60)

   $\quad$ + (8.60 − 0.40) + (7.60 − 0.40 − 0.40)
   $= 17.2 + 15.2 + 8.20 + 6.80 = 47.40$ m

5. $\left[\begin{array}{l}\text{Total length of centre-line}\\ \text{at plinth level}\end{array}\right]$ = 47.40 m (same as (4) above)

6. $\left[\begin{array}{l}\text{Total length of centre-line}\\ \text{at B.B. masonry level}\end{array}\right]$ = 2 (8.60) + 2 (7.60)

   $\quad$ + (8.60 − 0.30) + (7.60 − 0.30 − 0.30)
   $= 17.2 + 15.2 + 8.30 + 7.00$
   $= 47.7$ m

Explanation for (ii) Long wall and short wall method :

1. At foundation level
   - (a) Length of long walls L (3 in Nos.) $\quad$ = (8.60 + 0.50 + 0.50) = 9.60 m
   - (b) Length of short walls (S_1) (3 in Nos.) $\quad$ = (3.30 − 0.50 − 0.50) = 2.30 m
   - (c) Length of short walls (S_2) (3 in Nos.) $\quad$ = (4.30 − 0.50 − 0.50) = 3.30 m

2. At P.C.C. level
   - (a) The length of long walls (L) (3 in Nos.) $\quad$ = 9.60 m same as in (1) above
   - (b) Length of short walls (S_1) (3 in Nos.) $\quad$ = 2.30 m same as in (1) above
   - (c) Length of short walls (S_2) (3 in Nos.) $\quad$ = 3.30 m same as in (1) above

3. At U.C.R. level
   - (a) Length of long walls (L) (3 in Nos.) $\quad$ = 8.60 + 0.35 + 0.35 = 9.30 m
   - (b) Length of short walls (S_1) (3 in Nos.) $\quad$ = (3.30 − 0.35 − 0.35) = 2.60 m
   - (c) Length of short walls (S_2) (3 in Nos.) $\quad$ = 4.30 − 0.35 − 0.35 = 3.60 m

4. At C.R. level and plinth level
   - (a) Length of long walls (L) (3 in Nos.) $\quad$ = 8.60 + 0.20 + 0.20 = 9.00 m
   - (b) Length of short walls (S_1) (3 in Nos.) $\quad$ = 3.30 − 0.20 − 0.20 = 2.90 m
   - (c) Length of short walls (S_2) (3 in Nos.) $\quad$ = 4.30 − 0.20 − 0.20 = 3.90 m

5. At B.B. masonry level

(a) Length of long walls (L) (3 in Nos.)   = 8.60 + 0.15 + 0.15 = 8.90 m

(b) Length of short walls (S_1) (3 in Nos.) = 3.30 − 0.15 − 0.15 = 3.00 m

(c) Length of short walls (S_2) (3 in Nos.) = 4.30 − 0.15 − 0.15 = 4.00 m

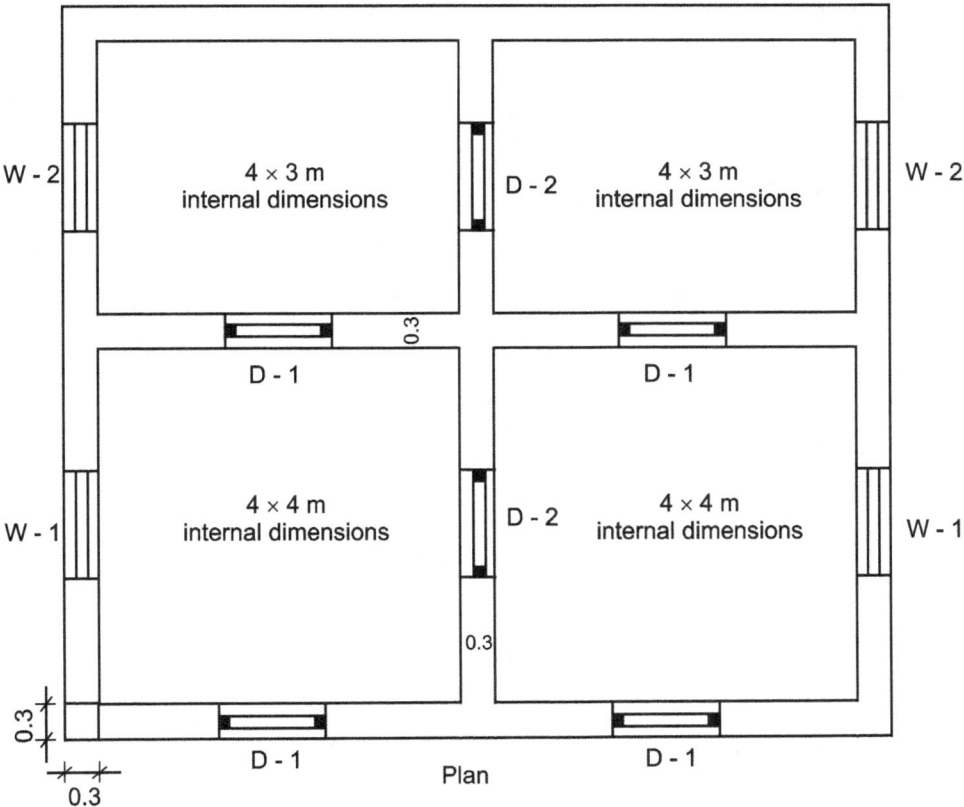

Fig. 3.23 (a) : Four rooms block

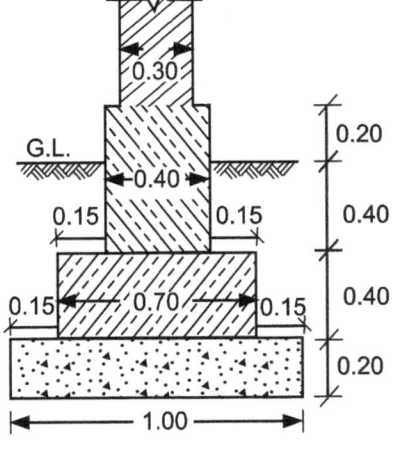

Fig. 3.23 (b)

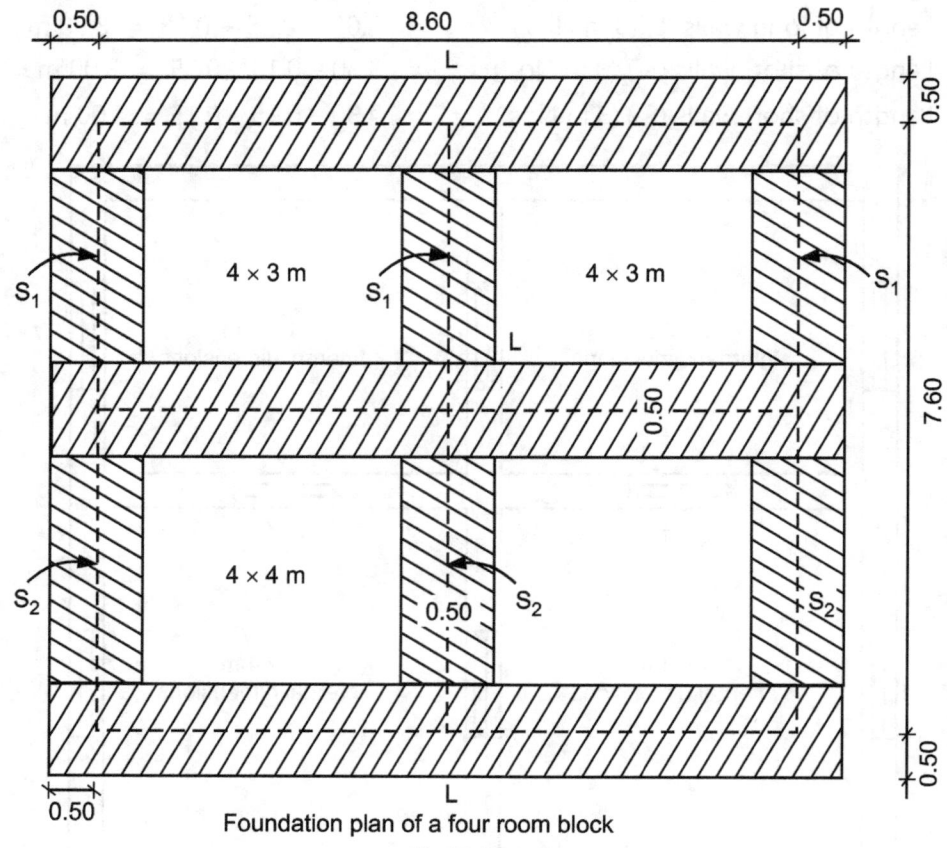

Foundation plan of a four room block

Fig. 3.23 (c)

3.8.6 Preparation of an Estimate of A Four Rooms Block

ABSTRACT SHEET

Item No.	Description	Quantity	Rate		Per	Amount	
			₹	Ps.		₹	Ps
1.	Site clearance	L.S.				300	–
2.	Excavation for foundations in earth, soil of all types, sand, gravel and soft murum including removing of the excavated material to a distance of 50 m beyond the building area (and lift upto 1.5 m) and stacking and spreading as directed, dewatering, preparing the bed for foundations and back filling, raming, watering, shoring, strutting, etc. complete.	45.6 m^3	23	10	m^3	1053	36

3.	Providing and laying in situ cement concrete (1 : 4 : 8) of trap metal in foundation and bedding including bailing out water, form work, compacting, curing complete.	9.12 m³	600	00	m³	5472	00
4.	Providing uncoursed rubble masonry of trap stones in cement mortar (1 : 6) in foundations including bailing out of waters, striking joints on unexposed faces and watering etc. complete.	13.02 m³	423	00	m³	5507	46
5.	Providing coursed rubble masonry of trap stones in cement mortar (1 : 6) in plinth including raking of joints where plastering is to be done and striking joints when no plastering is to be done, watering, scaffolding etc. complete.	11.376m³	570	00	m³	6484	32
6.	Providing and laying damp proof course 5 cm thick in cement concrete (1 : 2 : 4) layer and bitumen using cement with waterproofing compound etc. complete.	18.96 m²	66	00	m²	1251	36
7.	Providing IInd class burnt bricks masonry with I.S./conventional type bricks in cement mortar (1 : 6) in superstructure including raking out and striking of joints where plastering is to be done including watering, scaffolding, etc. complete.	37.971m³	728	00	m³	27642	89

$$= ₹ \quad 47411.39$$

Adding 5% towards contingencies $= ₹ \quad \underline{2370.57}$

Total $= ₹ \quad 49781.96$

Adding 1% for work charge establishment $= ₹ \quad \underline{497.81}$

Grand total estimated cost $= ₹ \quad 50279.77$

$$\approx ₹ \quad \mathbf{50280.00}$$

3.8.7 Construction Steps To The Building [Refer Fig. 3.24 (a), (b) & (c)]

MEASUREMENT SHEET

Item No.	Description	No.	Length L	Breadth B	Depth or Height H	Quantity	Total
1.	Site clearance		Job item				
2.	Excavation for foundations of steps in earth, soil of all types including removing the excavated material upto 50 m beyond the building area (and upto a lift of 1.5 m), stacking, spreading, dewatering, preparing the bed for foundations, back filling ramming, watering, shoring, strutting complete.	1	2	1.05	0.15	0.315 m^3	... (a)
	Less quantity of the excavation already carried, out for plinth walls.	1	2	$\dfrac{0.70 - 0.30}{2}$ $= 0.20$	0.15	0.06 m^3	... (b)
	∴ Net quantity of excavation	=	a – b			0.255 m^3	0.255 m^3
3.	Providing and laying in situ cement concrete (1 : 4 : 8) of trap metal for foundations and bedding, bailing out water, formwork, compaction, curing etc.	1	2	1.05	0.15	0.315 m^3	... (a)
4.	Providing first class brunt brick masonry with I.S. or conventional type bricks in cement mortar (1 : 6) for steps including striking of joints, raking of joints and pointing with cement mortar (1 : 3) on exposed faces, watering complete.						
	(i) For the first step	1	0.80	0.90	0.15	0.243 m^3	
	(ii) For the second step	1	1.30	0.60	0.15	0.117 m^3	0.3825 m^3
	(iii) For the third step	1	0.50	0.30	0.15	0.0225 m^3	

Explanation :

(1)   The total length of excavation from the plan = 2 m and the total width of excavation from the section = 0.15 + 0.30 + 0.30 + 0.30 = 1.05 m and the depth of excavation from the section is 0.15 m.

(2)   Rise and tread for the steps are 0.15 and 0.30 m respectively.

(3)   The length and width of the first step are 1.80 m (from the plan) and

(1.05 – 0.15) = 0.90 m (from the section) respectively.

(4) Similarly, the length and width of the second step are 1.30 m and
     (1.05 – 0.15 – 0.30) = 0.60 m respectively.

(5) And the length and width of the third step are 0.50 and
     (1.05 – 0.15 – 0.30 – 0.30) = 0.30 m respectively.

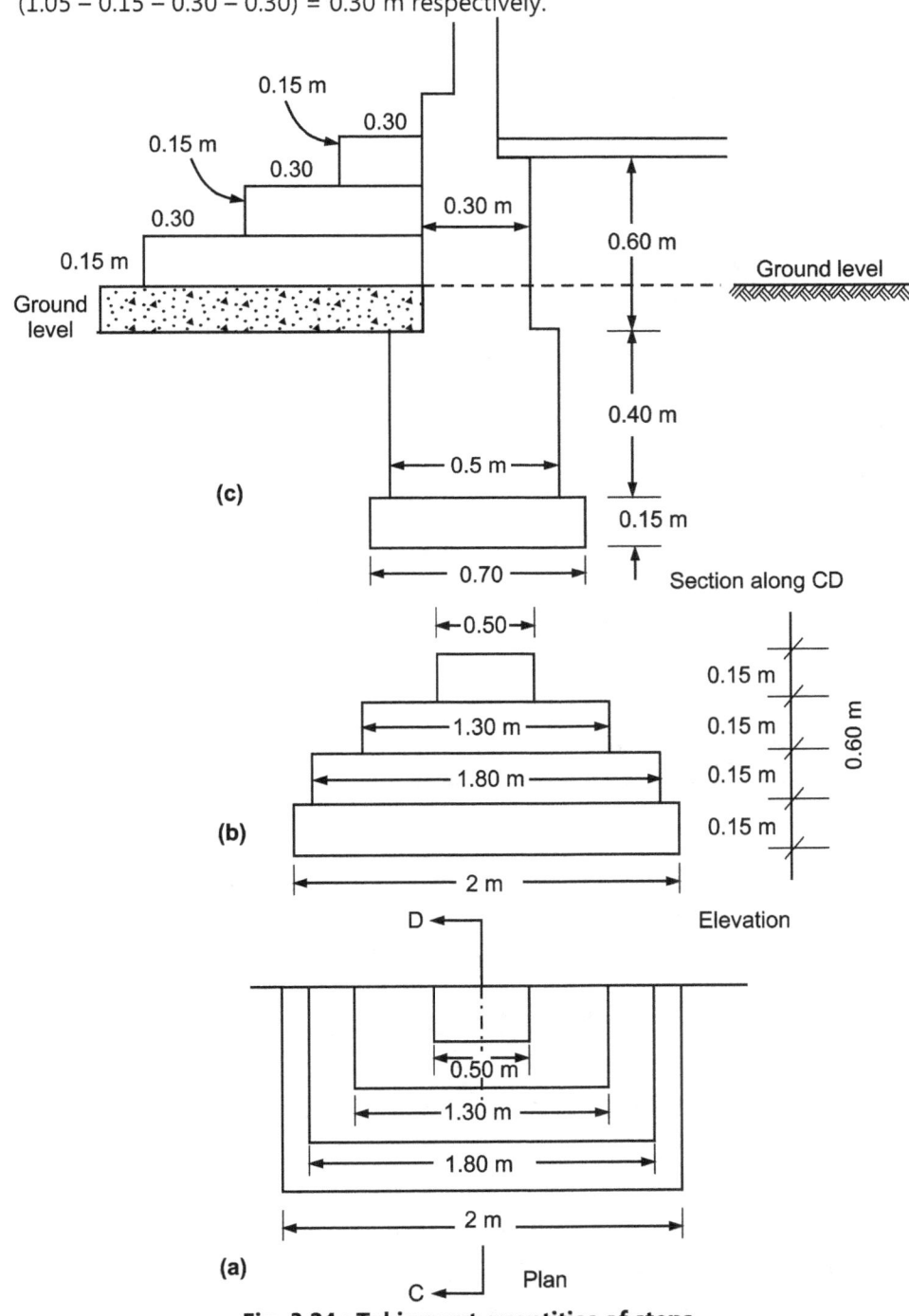

Fig. 3.24 : Taking out quantities of steps

3.8.8 Construction of Steps to The Building

Abstract Sheet

Item No.	Description	Quantity	Rate		Per	Amount	
			₹	Ps.		₹	Ps.
1.	Site clearance	L.S.				100	–
2.	Excavation for foundations of steps in earth, soil of all types including the removing of excavated material upto 50 m beyond the building area (and upto lift of 1.5 m), stacking, spreading, dewatering, preparing the bed for foundations, back filling, ramming, watering, shoring, strutting complete. Less quantity of the excavation already carried out for plinth walls.	0.255 m³	23	10	m³	5	89
3.	Providing and laying in situ cement concrete (1 : 4 : 8) of trap metal for foundations and bedding, bailing out water, form work, compaction, curing etc.	0.315 m³	600	00	m³	189	00
4.	Providing first class burnt brick masonry with I.S. or conventional type bricks in cement mortar (1 : 6) for steps including striking of joints, raking of joints and pointing with cement mortar (1 : 3) on exposed faces, watering complete.	0.3825 m³	760	00	m³	290	70

Estimated cost   =   ₹ 485.59
Add 5% towards contingencies   =   ₹ 24.28
Total cost   =   ₹ 509.87
Add 1% towards work charged establishment   =   ₹ 5.099
Ground total estimate cost   =   ₹ 514.969
Say   ≈   **₹ 515.00**

SOLVED EXAMPLES

Example 3.1 :

Estimate the quantity of following items of work, for the 3-BHK (symmetrical) building shown in Fig. 3.25.

1. Earth work in excavation in foundation.

2. Plain cement concrete 1 : 3 : 6 in foundation.

3. 1st class brick work in foundation and plinth.

4. D.P.C. 2.5 cm thick provided at plinth level.

5. 1st class brick work in superstructure.
6. 2.5 cm cement concrete (1 : 2 : 4) flooring.
7. 12 mm plastering in walls.
8. R.C.C. work excluding steel reinforcement.
9. Steel reinforcement including bending.

Note : Use both long wall-short wall method and centre-line method separately for the estimation of the items of work.

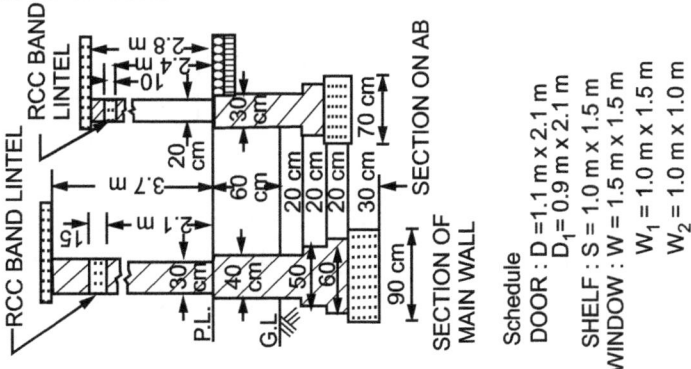

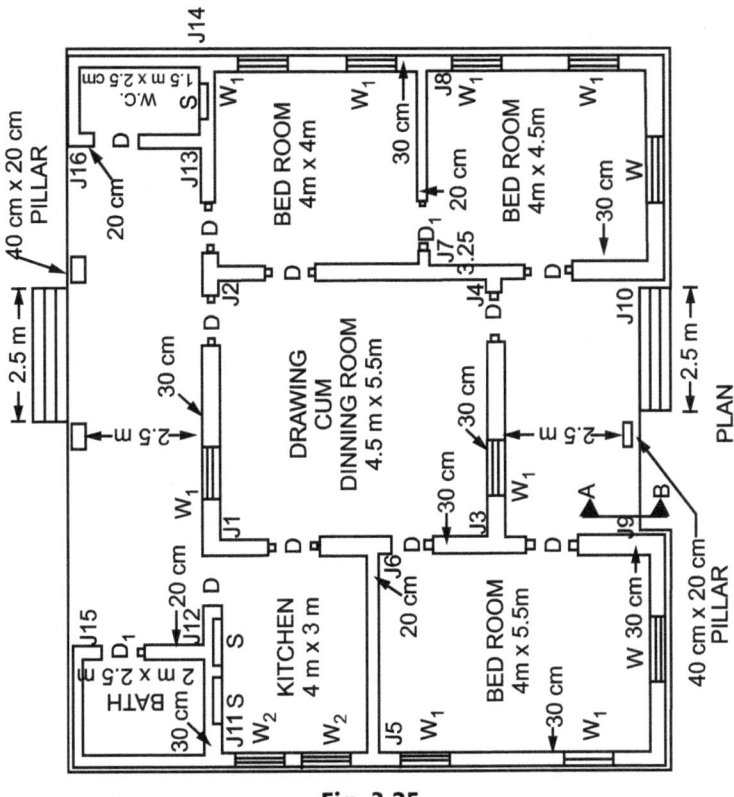

Fig. 3.25

LONG WALL-SHORT WALL METHOD FOR 3-BHK (SYMMETRICAL) BUILDING

Sr. No.	Name of item	No.	L (m)	B (m)	H (m)	Quantity	Remark
1.	Earth work in excavation in foundation :						
	Kitchen and Bed (combined)						
	Long walls	2	9.90	0.90	0.90	16.04	L = 9.0 + 0.9 = 9.9 m
	Short walls	2	3.40	0.90	0.90	5.51	L = 4.3 – 0.9 = 3.4 m
	Right side bedrooms (Combined)						
	Long walls	2	9.9	0.90	0.90	16.04	L = 9.0 + 0.9 = 9.9 m
	Short walls	2	3.40	0.90	0.90	5.51	L = 4.3 – 0.9 = 3.4 m
	Partition short walls	2	3.40	0.70	0.6	2.86	L = 4.3 – 0.9 = 3.4 m
	[Available between right side bedrooms and left side kitchen and bedroom]						
	Drawing cum dining room, back and front side						
	Short walls	2	3.90	0.90	0.90	6.32	L = 4.8 – 0.9 = 3.9
	Front verandah, front						
	Short wall	1	3.90	0.70	0.60	1.64	L = 4.8 – 0.9 = 3.9
	Back verandah, back						
	Long wall	1	14.2	0.70	0.60	5.96	L = [0.2 + 4.0 + 0.3 + 4.5 + 0.3 + 4.0 + 0.2] + 0.7 = 13.5 + 0.7 = 14.2 m
	Sides and front of bath, W.C. as short walls	4	1.95	0.70	0.60	3.28	$L = 2.75 - \dfrac{0.7}{2} - \dfrac{0.9}{2}$ = 1.95 m
					Total =	63.16m³	
2.	Plain cement concrete 1 : 3 : 6 in foundation :						
	Kitchen and bed (combined)						
	Long walls	2	9.90	0.90	0.30	5.35	L = 9.0 + 0.9 = 9.9 m
	Short walls	2	3.40	0.90	0.30	1.84	L = 4.3 – 0.9 = 3.4 m

	Right side bedrooms					
	Long walls	2	9.90	0.9	0.30	5.35	$L = 9.0 + 0.9 = 9.9$ m
	Short walls	2	3.40	0.90	0.30	1.84	$L = 4.3 - 0.9 = 3.4$ m
	Partition short walls	2	3.70	0.70	0.20	1.04	$L = 4.30 - 0.6 = 3.70$ m
							[Since 0.6 m is width of main wall footing at the level of P.C.C. in partition wall.]
	Drawing cum dining room, back and front						
	Short walls	2	3.90	0.90	0.30	2.11	
	Front verandah, front						
	Short wall	1	4.20	0.70	0.20	0.59	$L = 4.8 - 0.6 = 4.2$ m
							[At the level of P.C.C. of partition wall 0.6 m wide footing of main wall is available.]
	Back verandah, back						
	Long walls	1	14.20	0.70	0.20	1.99	
	Short walls	4	2.10	0.70	0.20	1.18	
					Total =	21.29m^3	
3.	1st class brick work in foundation and plinth **Kitchen and bed (combined)** Long walls						
	Ist footing	2	9.60	0.60	0.20	2.30	$L = 9.0 + 0.6 = 9.6$ m
	IInd footing	2	9.50	0.50	0.20	1.90	$L = 9.0 + 0.5 = 9.5$ m
	Plinth wall	2	9.40	0.40	0.80	6.02	$L = 9.0 + 0.4 = 9.4$ m
	Short walls						
	Ist footing	2	3.70	0.60	0.20	0.89	$L = 4.3 - 0.6 = 3.70$ m
	IInd footing	2	3.80	0.50	0.20	0.76	$L = 4.3 - 0.5 = 3.80$ m
	Plinth wall	2	3.90	0.40	0.80	2.50	$L = 4.3 - 0.4 = 3.90$ m
	Right hand side bedrooms						
	Long walls						
	Ist footing	2	9.60	0.60	0.20	2.30	
	IInd footing	2	9.50	0.50	0.20	1.90	
	Plinth wall	2	9.40	0.40	0.80	6.02	

Short walls						
Ist footing	2	3.70	0.60	0.20	0.89	
IInd footing	2	3.80	0.50	0.20	0.76	
Plinth wall	2	3.90	0.40	0.80	2.50	
Partition walls as short wall						
Ist footing	2	3.80	0.40	0.2	0.61	L = 4.3 – 0.5 = 3.8 m
Plinth wall	2	3.90	0.30	0.8	1.87	[At the level of 0.4 m wide footing of 20 cm wall, 0.5 m wide footing of main wall is available.]
Drawing cum dining room						
Short walls						
Ist footing	2	4.20	0.60	0.20	1.01	L = 4.8 – 0.6 = 4.2 m
IInd footing	2	4.30	0.50	0.20	0.86	
Plinth wall	2	4.40	0.40	0.80	2.82	
Front verandah, front as short wall						
Ist footing	1	4.30	0.40	0.20	0.34	L = 4.8 – 0.5 = 4.3 m
Plinth wall	1	4.40	0.30	0.80	1.06	L = 4.8 – 0.4 = 4.4 m
Back verandah, back as long wall						
Ist footing	1	13.9	0.40	0.20	1.11	L = 13.5 + 0.4 = 13.9 m
Plinth wall	1	13.8	0.30	0.80	3.31	L = 13.5 + 0.3 = 13.8 m
Sides and front of bath and W.C.						
As short walls						
Ist footing	4	2.30	0.40	0.20	0.74	$L = 2.75 - \dfrac{0.4}{2} - \dfrac{0.5}{2} = 2.30$ m
Plinth wall	4	2.40	0.30	0.80	2.30	$L = 2.75 - \dfrac{0.3}{2} - \dfrac{0.4}{2} = 2.40$ m
4.	D.P.C. 2.5 m thick provided at plinth level					
Kitchen and bedroom (combined)						
Long walls	2	9.40	0.40	–	7.52	L = 9.0 + 0.4 = 9.4 m
Short wall s	2	3.90	0.40	–	3.12	L = 4.3 – 0.4 = 3.9 m

Right side bedrooms						
Long walls	2	9.40	0.40	–	7.52	L = 9.0 + 0.4 = 9.4 m
Short walls	2	3.90	0.40	–	3.12	L = 4.3 – 0.4 = 3.9 m
Partition walls						
As short walls	2	3.90	0.30	–	2.34	L = 4.3 – 0.4 = 3.9 m
Drawing cum dining room side walls as						
Short walls	2	4.40	0.40	–	3.52	L = 4.8 – 0.4 = 4.4 m
Backside of bathroom as						
Long wall	1	2.50	0.30	–	0.75	L = 2.2 + .0.3 = 2.5 m
Backside of W.C. as						
Long wall	1	2.00	0.30	–	0.60	L = 1.7 + 0.3 = 2.0 m
Side walls of W.C. & bath as						
Short walls	4	2.40	0.30	–	2.88	$L = 2.75 - \dfrac{0.4}{2} - \dfrac{0.3}{2} = 2.40$ m
					Total = 31.37 m^2	
Deductions						
Door sills – D type	9	1.10	0.40	–	3.96	
Door sills – D$_1$ type	3	0.90	0.30	–	0.81	
					Total = 4.77 m^2	

Net Total = 31.37 – 4.77 = 26.60 m^2.

Note : D.P.C. will not be provided at top of plinth wall in front and back verandah, since they are open to atmosphere.

5.	Ist **class brick work in superstructure**						
	Kitchen and bed (combined)						
	Long walls	2	9.30	0.30	3.70	20.65	L = 9.0 + 0.3 = 9.3 m
	Short walls	2	4.00	0.30	3.70	8.88	L = 4.3 – 0.3 = 4.0 m
	Right side bedrooms						
	Long walls	2	9.30	0.30	3.70	20.65	L = 9.0 + 0.3 = 9.3 m
	Short walls	2	4.00	0.30	3.70	8.88	L = 4.3 – 0.3 = 4.0 m
	Partition walls						
	As short walls	2	4.00	0.20	3.70	5.92	L = 4.3 – 0.3 = 4.0 m

Drawing cum dining room						
Short walls	2	4.50	0.30	3.70	9.99	L = 4.8 – 0.3 = 4.5 m
Front verandah, Front						
As short wall	1	4.50	0.20	0.30	0.27	H = 2.8 – 2.5 = 0.3 m
						[In front and back verandah, brick wall of 0.3 m height is available, above lintel]
Back verandah, back						
As short wall	1	9.40	0.20	0.30	0.56	L = 13.3 – 2.2 – 1.7 = 9.4 m
Back wall of bathroom						
As long wall	1	2.40	0.20	2.8	1.34	L = 2.0 + 0.4 = 2.4 m
Back wall of W.C.						
As long wall	1	1.90	0.20	2.80	1.06	L = 1.5 + 0.4 = 1.9 m
Side walls of bath and W.C.						
As short walls	4	2.50	0.20	2.80	5.60	L = 2.75 – 0.1 – 0.15 = 2.50 m
Pillars	3	0.40	0.20	2.40	0.58	
				Total = 84.38 m^3		
Deductions						
Door openings	9	1.10	0.30	2.10	6.24	Provided in 20 cm wall
	3	0.90	0.20	2.10	1.13	
Window openings	2	1.50	0.30	1.50	1.35	
	8	1.00	0.30	1.50	3.60	
	2	1.00	0.30	1.00	0.60	
Shelves	3	1.00	0.20	1.50	0.90	
Lintel over door D	9	1.40	0.30	0.15	0.57	15 cm bearing
Lintel over door	3	1.10	0.20	0.10	0.07	10 cm bearing
Lintel over window W	2	1.80	0.30	0.15	0.16	15 cm bearing
	8	1.30	0.30	0.15	0.47	
	2	1.30	0.30	0.15	0.12	
Lintel over shelves	3	1.30	0.30	0.15	0.18	
			Deductions (Total) =		15.39m^3	

Net Total = 84.38 – 15.39 = 68.99 m^3

Note : It is assumed that lintels have been provided only over doors, windows and shelves. Lintels not provided over entire length of walls.

Ch. 3 | 3.56

6.	2.5 cm cement concrete (1 : 2 : 4) flooring :					
	Kitchen	1	4.00	3.00	–	12.00	
	Left side bedroom	1	4.00	5.50	–	22.00	
	Right side bedroom 1	1	4.00	4.00	–	16.00	
	Right side bedroom 2	1	4.00	4.50	–	18.00	
	Drawing cum dining room	1	4.50	5.50	–	24.75	
	Front verandah	1	4.50	2.75	–	12.38	$B = 2.50 + 0.2 + 0.05 = 2.75$ m
	Back varandah	1	9.40	2.75	–	25.85	[After pillar considering 5 cm
	Bathroom	1	2.00	2.50	–	5.00	projection on front side]
	W.C.	1	1.50	2.50	–	3.75	
					Total =	139.73 m^3	
	Deductions						
	Pillars	3	0.40	0.20		(–)0.24	
	Additions						
	Door sills D	9	1.10	0.30	–	2.97	
	D$_1$	3	0.90	0.20	–	0.54	
					Total =	(+) 3.51 m^2	
	Net Total = 139.73 − 0.24 + 3.51 = 143.0 m^2						
7.	12 mm plastering in walls						
	Inside plastering						
	Kitchen						
	Long walls	2	4.00	–	3.70	29.6	
	Short walls	2	3.00	–	3.70	22.2	
	Left side bedroom						
	Long walls	2	5.50	–	3.70	40.7	
	Short walls	2	4.00	–	3.70	29.6	
	Right side bedroom 1						
	Long walls	2	4.00	–	3.70	29.6	
	Short walls	2	4.00	–	3.70	29.6	
	Right side bedroom 2						
	Long walls	2	4.50	–	3.70	33.3	
	Short walls	2	4.00	–	3.70	29.6	

Drawing cum dining room						
Long walls	2	5.50	–	3.70	40.7	
Short walls	2	4.50	–	3.70	33.3	
Bathroom						
Long walls	2	2.50	–	2.80	14.00	
Short walls	2	2.00	–	2.80	11.20	
W.C.						
Long walls	2	2.50	–	2.80	14.0	
Short walls	2	1.50	–	2.80	8.40	
Jambs, sills & soffits of shelves	3	5.00	0.20	–	3.00	$L = 2(1.5) + 2(1.0) = 5.0$ m
Deductions						
Door openings D	9	1.10	–	2.10	20.79	Deduction on only one face, since area of openings are $0.5 - 3.0$ m^2
D_1	3	0.90	–	2.10	5.67	
Window opening W_1	1	1.00	–	1.50	1.50	Deductions for remaining openings done in outside plastering
					Total = 27.96 m^2	

Net (Total) Plastering = 368.8 – 27.96 = 340.84 m

Net (Total) Plastering = 368.8 – 27.96 = 340.84 m^2

Outside Plastering						
For outer wall of 3.7 m height	1	48.10	–	3.70	177.97	Total over length of 3.7 m height wall = 9.3 + 4.6 + 3.2 + 4.5 + 3.2 + 4.6 + 9.3 + 9.4 (back verandah) = 48.1 m.
For outer wall of 2.8 m height	1	15.10	–	2.80	42.28	Total over length of 2.8 m height wall = $(2.7 \times 4) + 2.4 + 1.9$ = 15.1 m
Backwall of bathroom and W.C. above the slab.	1	4.30	–	0.75	3.22	H = 3.7 – 2.8 – 0.15 (slab thickness) = 0.75 m (Above the slab) L = 2.4 + 1.9 = 4.3 m
Pillars	3	1.20	–	2.40	8.64	
Total length of plinth wall of 30 cm – main wall = 9.3 + 0.1 + 4.6 + 0.1 + 0.45 + 2.25 + 0.45 + 0.1 + 4.6 + 0.1 + 9.3 = 31.35 m						

	Total length of plinth wall of 20 cm secondary wall $= 13.8 + (2.75 \times 2) = 19.3$ m Total length of plinth wall $= 31.35 + 19.3 = 50.65$ m						H = 0.60 + 0.5 (side) + 0.05 (inside ground) = 0.70 m
	So quantity for plinth wall	1	50.65	–	0.70	35.46	
	Masonry wall above lintel in front verandah	1	4.50	–	1.00	4.50	H = 0.4 + 0.2 + 0.4 = 1.0 m
	Masonry wall above lintel in back verandah	1	9.40	–	1.00	9.40	
	**Total outside plastering = 281.47 m²**	

	Deductions						
	Window openings W	2	1.50	–	1.50	4.50	Deduction of only one face.
	W_1	7	1.00	–	1.50	10.50	
	W_2	2	1.00	–	1.00	2.00	
	Slab of front verandah entering into 3.7 m high wall	1	10.10	–	0.15	1.52	L = (2.8 × 2) + 4.5 = 10.1 m H = 0.15 m (slab thickness)
	Slab of back verandah entering into 3.7 m high wall	1	9.40	–	0.15	1.41	

Total   =   **19.93 m²**

Net outside plastering   =   281.47 – 19.93 = 261.54 m²

Total plastering   =   Inside plastering + Outside plastering

=   340.84 + 261.54 = 602.38 m²

8.	R.C.C. work excluding steel and its bending but including centering and shuttering and binding steel **Roof slab of** Kitchen and bedroom (combined)	1	9.50	4.80	0.15	6.84	L = 9.3 + 2 (0.1) = 9.5 m [10 cm projection outside wall]
	Right side bedrooms	1	9.50	4.80	0.15	6.84	
	Drawing cum dining room	1	6.30	4.30	0.15	4.06	L = 5.5 + 0.6 + 2(0.1) = 6.3 m
	Front verandah	1	4.70	2.90	0.15	2.04	L = 4.5 + 2(0.1) = 4.7 m [10 cm projection of slab taken inside wall] B = 2.5 + 0.2 + 2(0.1) = 2.9 m

Bathroom, W.C. and back verandah as a whole	1	13.90	2.90	0.15	6.04	L = 13.7 + 2(0.1) = 13.9 m B = 2.50 + 0.2 + 2(0.1) = 2.90 m
Lintels over doors, windows and shelves					1.57 m³	Quantity taken from Ist class brick work item
				Total = 27.39 m³	

9.	Mild steel including bending in reinforcement	

$$@ \ 1 \text{ \% of R.C.C.} \ = \ 27.39 \times \frac{1}{100} \ = \ 0.2739 \text{ m}^3$$

$$\text{So, mass of steel} \ = \ 0.2739 \times 7850 \text{ kg/m}^3 \ = \ 2150.12 \text{ kg}$$

Mild steel in windows
Assuming 1.0 cm ϕ bars
At 10 cm c/c spacing
provided only horizontally

$$W_2 : \ 2 \times 9 \times \frac{\pi}{4} \times (0.01)^2 \times 1.0 \ = \ 1.41 \times 10^{-3} \text{ m}^3$$

$$W_1 : \ 8 \times 14 \times \frac{\pi}{4} \times (0.01)^2 \times 1.0 \ = \ 8.79 \times 10^{-3} \text{ m}^3$$

$$W : \ 2 \times 14 \times \frac{\pi}{4} \times (0.01)^2 \times 1.5 \ = \ 3.30 \times 10^{-3} \text{ m}^3$$

So,　Total volume of steel bars = $[1.41 + 8.79 + 3.30] \times 10^{-3}$

　　　　　　　　　　　　　= $13.5 \times 10^{-3} \text{ m}^3$

So,　　Mass of steel bars　= $7850 \text{ kg/m}^3 \times 13.5 \times 10^{-3} \text{ m}^3 = 105.97 \text{ kg}$

So,　　Total mass of steel　= $2150.12 + 105.97 = 2256.10 \text{ kg}$

　　　　　　　　　= 22.56 quintal

Centre-Line Method For 3-Bhk [Symmetrical] Building

1.　Total length of centre-line for main wall of 30 cm :

Kitchen and bedroom (combined)　= 2 [0.15 + 5.5 + 0.2 + 3.0 + 0.15] + 2 [0.15 + 4.0 + 0.15]

　　　　　　　　　　　　= 18.0 + 8.6 = **26.60 m**

Right side bedrooms (combined)　= 2 [0.15 + 4.5 + 0.2 + 4.0 + 0.15]

　　　　　　　　　　　+ 2 [0.15 + 4.0 + 0.15]

　　　　　　　　　　　= 18.0 + 8.6 = **26.60 m**

Drawing cum dining room (back and front side only) = 2 [4.8] = **9.60 m**.

So, **Total centre-line length for 30 cm wall** = 26.60 + 26.60 + 9.60 = **62.80 m**

No. of overlapping joints of 30 cm wall with 30 cm wall = 4.0 No.

[J1, J2, J3 and J4 – As shown in the drawing]

2. **Total centre-line length for 20 cm wall of verandah and partition wall**

$$= 2 (4.0 + 0.3) = \textbf{8.6 m}$$

[4.0 No., overlapping joints with 30 cm

main wall, shown as J5, J6, J7, J8]

Front verandah, front side = 4.5 + 0.3 = **4.8 m**.

[2.0 No. of overlapping joints with 30 cm main wall, shown as J9 and J10]

Backside of entire back verandah = 0.2 + 4.0 + 0.3 + 4.5 + 0.3 + 4.0 + 0.2 = **13.5 m**

Sides of bath 2 W.C. $= 4 \left(2.5 + \dfrac{0.20}{2} + \dfrac{0.30}{2} \right) = \textbf{11.0 m}$

[4.0 No. of overlapping joints with 30 cm wall, shown as J11, J12, J13, J14 and

2.0 No of overlapping joints with 20 cm wall, shown as J15, J16].

So, **Total centre-line length for 20 cm wall** = 8.6 + 4.8 + 13.5 + 11.0 = **37.90 m**

Total overlapping joints – 10 No. with 30 cm and 2.0 No. with 20 cm wall.

(2a) Total centre-line length for 20 cm thick, 3.7 m height wall = **8.6 m**

[4.0 No. overlapping joints with 30 cm wall]

(2b) Total centre-line length for 20 cm thick, 2.8 m height wall = **29.3 m.**

[6 No. overlapping joints with 30 cm wall and 2.0 No. with 20 cm wall]

Centre-Line Method For 3 Bhk (Symmetrical) Building

Sr. No	Name of item	No.	L (m)	B (m)	H (m)	Quantity	Remark
1.	Earth work in excavation in foundation for						
	30 cm thick main wall	1	61.0	0.90	0.90	49.41	$L = 62.80 - 4 \times \dfrac{0.9}{2} = 61.0$
	20 cm thick secondary wall	1	32.70	0.70	0.60	13.73	$L = 37.90 - 10 \times \dfrac{0.9}{2}$ $- 2 \times \dfrac{0.7}{2} = 32.70$ m
					Total = 63.14 m³		
2.	P.C.C. 1:3:6 in foundation						
	30 cm thick main wall	1	61.0	0.90	0.30	16.47	$L = 37.9 - 10 \times \dfrac{0.6}{2} - 2 \times \dfrac{0.7}{2}$ $= 34.20$ m [At the level of P.C.C. of 20 cm wall, 0.6 m wide footing of 30 cm wall is available.]
	20 cm thick secondary wall	1	34.20	0.70	0.20	4.79	
					Total = 21.26 m³		

3.	First class brick work in foundation and plinth **30 cm thick main walls**					
	I^{st} footing	1	61.60	0.60	0.20	7.39	$L = 62.8 - 4 \times \dfrac{0.6}{2} = 61.60$ m
	IInd footing	1	61.80	0.50	0.20	6.18	$L = 6.28 - 4 \times \dfrac{0.5}{2} = 61.80$ m
	Plinth wall	1	62.00	0.40	0.80	19.84	$L = 62.8 - 4 \times \dfrac{0.4}{2} = 62.0$ m
	20 cm thick secondary walls I^{st} footing	1	35.00	0.40	0.20	2.80	$L = 37.9 - 10 \times \dfrac{0.5}{2}$ $- 2 \times \dfrac{0.4}{2} = 35.0$ m
	Plinth wall	1	35.60	0.30	0.80	8.54	$L = 37.9 - 10 \times \dfrac{0.4}{2}$ $- 2 \times \dfrac{0.3}{2} = 35.60$ m
					Total = 44.75 m³	

4.	D.P.C. 2.5 cm thick provided at plinth wall					
	30 cm thick main wall	1	62.0	0.40	–	24.80	
	20 cm thick secondary wall	1	35.60	0.30	–	10.68	
					Total = 35.48 m³	
	Deductions					
	For front and back verandah	1	13.90	0.30	–	4.17	$L = 9.4 + 4.5 = 13.9$ m
	For door sills, D	9	1.10	0.40	–	3.96	
		3	0.90	0.30	–	0.81	
					Total = 8.94 m²	

Net Total = 35.48 – 8.94 = 26.54 m²

5.	First class brick work in superstructure					
	30 cm thick main walls	1	62.20	0.30	3.70	69.04	$L = 62.80 - 4 \times \dfrac{0.3}{2} = 62.20$ m
	20 cm thick partition walls of 3.7 m height	1	8.0	0.20	3.70	5.92	$L = 8.6 - 4 \times \dfrac{0.3}{2} = 8.0$ m
	20 cm thick walls in bathroom, W.C. & verandah [as solid] of 2.80 m height	1	28.20	0.20	2.80	15.79	$L = 29.30 - 6 \times \dfrac{0.3}{2}$ $- 2 \times \dfrac{0.2}{2} = 28.20$ m
					Total = 90.75 m³	

Deductions					
For DWRs, windows, shelves opening				13.82	Taken from long wall - short wall method directly.
For lintel over door, window and shelves				1.57	Taken from long wall - short wall method directly.
For lintel and opening in front verandah	1	4.50	0.20	2.50	2.25	H = 2.4 + 0.1 = 2.5 m
For lintel and opening in back verandah	1	9.40	0.20	2.50	4.70	
				Total = 22.34 m³	
Addition for pillars	3	0.40	0.20	2.40 = 0.58 m³	
Net Total = 90.75 – 22.34 + 0.58 = 68.99 m³					

Note : The method of estimation for the remaining items, will remain the same, as used in long wall – short wall method. Therefore, estimation of the remaining items have not been done in centre-line method.

Example 3.2 :

Estimate the quantity of following items of work, for the unsymmetrical building shown in Fig. 3.26.

1. Earth work in excavation in foundation.
2. P.C.C. 1 : 3 : 6 in foundation.
3. 1st class brick work in foundation and plinth.
4. 1st class brick work in superstructure.
5. 12 mm plastering in walls.

The height of all rooms (including bathroom, W.C., verandah, kitchen) is 3.5 m above floor level.

Note : Use both long wall-short wall method and centre-line method separately for the estimation of the items of work.   **(May 1999 – 20 Marks)**

Doors	**Windows**
$D_1 - 0.9 \times 2.1$	$W_1 - 1.5 \times 1.1$
$D_2 - 0.8 \times 2.1$	$W_2 - 0.8 \times 1.1$
$D_3 - 0.6 \times 2.0$	$W_3 - 0.5 \times 0.8$

Notes :

1. Unless stated, all dimensions are in metres.
2. Assume suitable data (if required) and mention it, at appropriate place.
3. Lintels 10 cm thick/height have been provided over doors and windows and has 10 cm bearing on both sides.

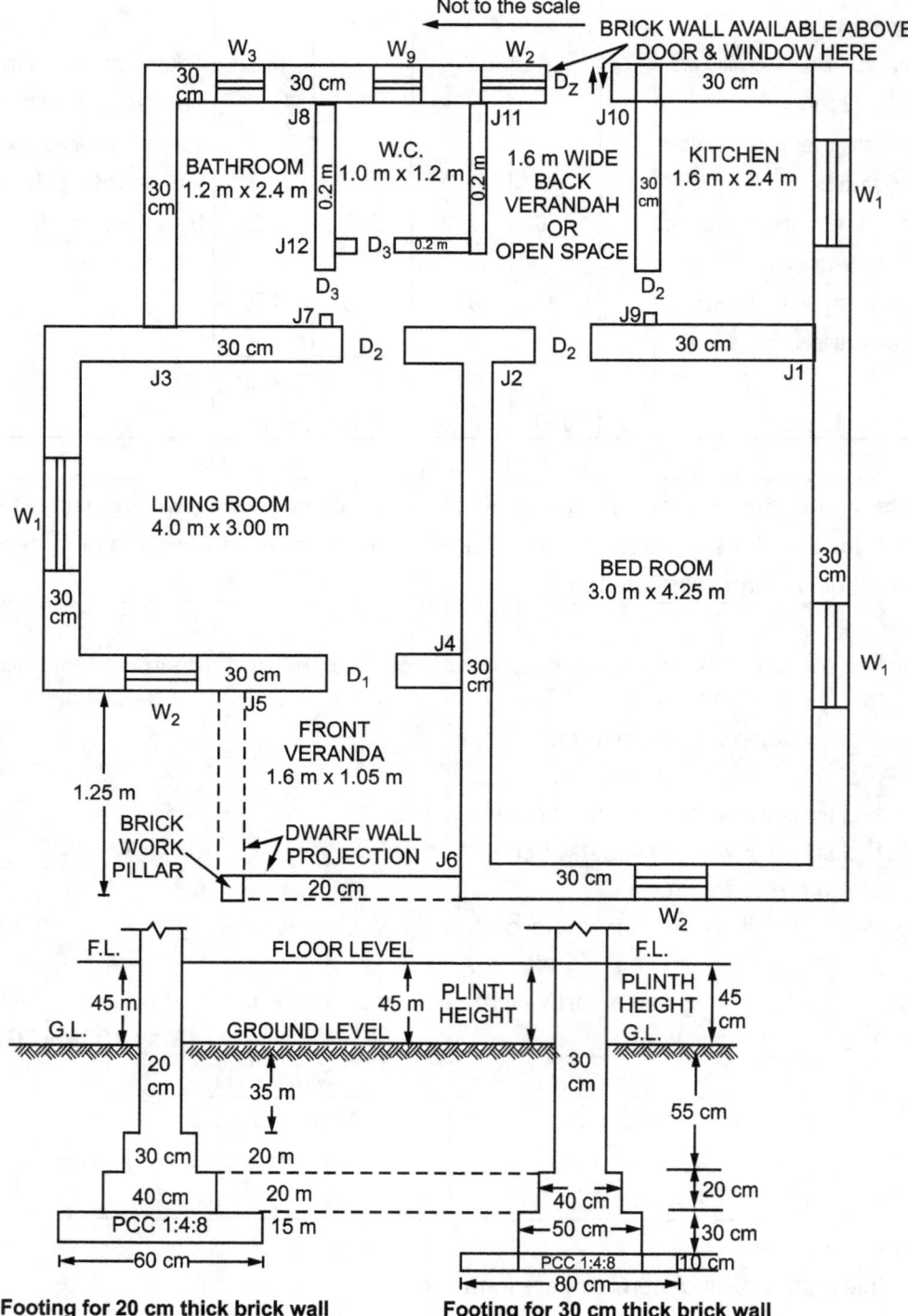

Fig. 3.26

Note : In front verandah at 2.8 m height, 20 cm thick/height R.C.C.
lintel have been provided, over which 0.5 m height of brick wall available below R.C.C. roof

Sr. No.	Name of item	No.	L (m)	B (m)	H (m)	Quantity	Remark
1.	Earthwork in excavation in foundation						
	Bedroom						
	Long walls	2	5.35	0.80	1.15	9.84	L = 4.55 + 0.8 = 5.35 m
	Short walls	2	2.50	0.80	1.15	4.60	L = 3.3 − 0.8 = 2.5 m
	Living room						
	Long wall	1	4.10	0.80	1.15	3.77	L = 3.3 + 0.8 = 4.1 m
	Short walls	2	3.50	0.80	1.15	6.44	L = 4.3 − 0.8 = 3.5 m
	Front verandah						
	Long wall	1	1.75	0.60	0.90	0.95	$L = 1.85 + \dfrac{0.6}{2} - \dfrac{0.8}{2} = 1.75$ m
	Short wall	1	0.60	0.60	0.90	0.32	$L = 1.3 - \dfrac{0.6}{2} - \dfrac{0.8}{2} = 0.60$ m
	Backside wall of bath, W.C., back verandah and kitchen						
	Long wall	1	7.10	0.80	1.15	6.53	L = [0.15 + 1.2 + 0.2 + 1.0 + 0.2 + 1.6 + 0.2 + 1.6 + 0.15] + 0.8 = 6.3 + 0.8 = 7.1 m
	Over short walls [30 cm thick]	2	1.90	0.80	1.15	3.50	L = 2.7 − 0.8 = 1.9 m
	Inner short walls [20 cm thick]	2	1.90	0.60	0.90	2.05	L = 2.7 − 0.8 = 1.9 m
	W.C.　　Long wall	1	1.35	0.60	0.90	0.73	L = 1.45 + 0.3 − 0.4 = 1.35 m
	Short wall	1	0.60	0.60	0.90	0.32	L = 1.2 − 0.6 = 0.6 m
					Total =	39.05m³	
2.	Plain cement concrete 1 : 3 : 6 in foundation						
	Bedroom						
	Long walls	2	5.35	0.80	0.10	0.86	L = 4.55 + 0.8 = 5.35 m
	Short walls	2	2.50	0.80	0.10	0.40	L = 3.3 − 0.8 = 2.50 m
	Living room						
	Long wall	1	4.10	0.80	0.10	0.33	L = 3.3 + 0.8 = 4.10 m
	Short walls	2	3.50	0.80	0.10	0.56	L = 4.3 − 0.8 = 3.50 m
	Front verandah						
	Long wall	1	1.90	0.60	0.15	0.17	$L = 1.85 + \dfrac{0.6}{2} - \dfrac{0.5}{2} = 1.9$ m

	Short wall	1	0.75	0.60	0.15	0.07	$L = 1.3 - \dfrac{0.6}{2} - \dfrac{0.5}{2} = 0.75$ m

	Backside wall of bathroom, W.C., back verandah and kitchen					
	Long wall	1	7.10	0.80	0.10	0.57	$L = 6.3 + 0.8 = 7.1$ m
	Outer short walls	2	1.90	0.80	0.10	0.30	$L = 2.7 - 0.8 = 1.9$ m
	Inner short walls	2	2.20	0.60	0.15	0.40	$L = 2.7 - 0.50 = 2.2$ m
	W.C.					
	Long wall	1	1.50	0.60	0.15	0.13	$L = 1.45 + \dfrac{0.6}{2} - \dfrac{0.5}{2} = 1.50$ m
	Short wall	1	0.60	0.60	0.15	0.05	$L = 1.2 - 0.6 = 0.6$ m

						Total =	3.84 m³	

3.	**First class brick work in foundation and plinth**					
	Bedroom					
	Long walls					
	Ist footing	2	5.05	0.50	0.30	1.52	$L = 4.55 + 0.50 = 5.05$ m
	IInd footing	2	4.95	0.40	0.20	0.79	$L = 4.55 + 0.40 = 4.95$ m
	Plinth wall	2	4.85	0.30	1.00	2.91	$L = 4.55 + 0.3 = 4.85$ m
	Short walls					
	Ist footing	2	2.80	0.50	0.30	0.84	$L = 3.30 - 0.50 = 2.80$ m
	IInd footing	2	2.90	0.40	0.20	0.46	$L = 3.30 - 0.40 = 2.90$ m
	Plinth wall	2	3.00	0.30	1.00	1.80	$L = 3.30 - 0.30 = 3.0$ m
	Living room					
	Long walls					
	Ist footing	1	3.80	0.50	0.30	0.57	$L = 3.30 + 0.5 = 3.8$ m
	IInd footing	1	3.70	0.40	0.20	0.30	$L = 3.30 + 0.40 = 3.7$ m
	Plinth wall	1	3.60	0.30	1.00	1.08	$L = 3.30 + 0.30 = 3.6$ m
	Short walls					
	Ist footing	2	3.80	0.50	0.30	1.14	$L = 4.3 - 0.5 = 3.8$ m
	IInd footing	2	3.90	0.40	0.20	0.62	$L = 4.3 - 0.4 = 3.9$ m
	Plinth wall	2	4.00	0.30	1.00	2.40	$L = 4.3 - 0.3 = 4.0$ m
	Front verandah					
	Long walls					
	Ist footing	1	1.85	0.40	0.20	0.15	$L = 1.85 + \dfrac{0.4}{2} - \dfrac{0.4}{2} = 1.85$

IInd footing	1	1.85	0.30	0.20	0.11	$L = 1.85 + \dfrac{0.3}{2} - \dfrac{0.3}{2} = 1.85$
Plinth wall	1	1.80	0.20	0.80	0.29	$L = 1.85 + \dfrac{0.2}{2} - \dfrac{0.3}{2} = 1.80$
Short walls						
Ist footing	1	0.90	0.40	0.20	0.07	$L = 1.30 - \dfrac{0.4}{2} - \dfrac{0.4}{2} = 0.90$ m
IInd footing	1	1.00	0.30	0.20	0.06	$L = 1.3 - \dfrac{0.3}{2} - \dfrac{0.3}{2} = 1.0$ m
Plinth wall	1	1.05	0.20	0.80	0.17	$L = 1.3 - \dfrac{0.2}{2} - \dfrac{0.3}{2} = 1.05$ m
Backside of bathroom, W.C., back verandah and kitchen						
As long wall						
Ist footing	1	6.80	0.50	0.30	1.02	$L = 6.3 + 0.5 = 6.80$ m
IInd footing	1	6.70	0.40	0.20	0.54	$L = 6.3 + 0.4 = 6.70$ m
Plinth wall	1	6.60	0.30	1.00	1.98	$L = 6.3 + 0.3 = 6.60$ m
Over short walls						
Ist footing	2	2.20	0.50	0.30	0.66	$L = 2.7 - 0.5 = 2.20$ m
IInd footing	2	2.30	0.40	0.20	0.37	$L = 2.7 - 0.4 = 2.30$ m
Plinth wall	2	2.40	0.30	1.00	1.44	$L = 2.7 - 0.3 = 2.40$ m
Inner short walls						
Ist footing	2	2.30	0.40	0.20	0.37	$L = 2.7 - 0.4 = 2.30$ m
IInd footing	2	2.40	0.30	0.20	0.29	$L = 2.7 - 0.3 = 2.40$ m
Plinth wall	2	2.40	0.20	0.80	0.77	$L = 2.7 - 0.3 = 2.40$ m
W.C.						
Long walls						
Ist footing	1	1.45	0.40	0.20	0.12	$L = 1.45 + \dfrac{0.4}{2} - \dfrac{0.4}{2} = 1.45$ m
IInd footing	1	1.45	0.30	0.20	0.09	$L = 1.45 + \dfrac{0.3}{2} - \dfrac{0.3}{2} = 1.45$ m
Plinth wall	1	1.40	0.20	0.80	0.22	$L = 1.45 + \dfrac{0.2}{3} - \dfrac{0.3}{2} = 1.40$ m
Short walls						
Ist footing	1	0.80	0.40	0.20	0.06	$L = 1.20 - 0.4 = 0.80$ m
IInd footing	1	0.90	0.30	0.20	0.05	$L = 1.20 - 0.3 = 0.90$ m
Plinth wall	1	1.00	0.20	0.80	0.16	$L = 1.20 - 0.2 = 1.0$ m
				Total	**= 23.42 m^3**	

4.	1st class brick work in superstructure					
	Bedroom					
	Long walls	2	4.85	0.3	3.5	10.18	L = 4.55 + 0.3 = 4.85 m
	Short walls	2	3.0	0.3	3.5	6.30	L = 3.3 – 0.3 = 3.0 m
	Living room					
	Long wall	1	3.6	0.3	3.5	3.78	L = 3.3 + 0.3 = 3.6 m
	Short walls	2	4.0	0.3	3.5	8.40	L = 4.3 – 0.3 = 4.0 m
	Front verandah					
	Long wall	1	1.8	0.20	0.50	0.18	L = 1.85 + 0.1 – 0.15 = 1.8 m
	Short wall	1	1.05	0.20	0.50	0.10	L = 1.3 – 0.15 – 0.1 = 1.05 m
	Backside of bathroom, W.C., back verandah and kitchen					
	As long wall	1	6.60	0.30	3.50	6.93	L = 6.3 + 0.3 = 6.6 m
	Outer short wall	2	2.40	0.30	3.50	5.04	L = 2.7 – 0.3 = 2.4 m
	Inner short wall	2	2.40	0.20	3.50	3.36	L = 2.7 – 0.3 = 2.4 m
	W.C.					
	Long wall	1	1.40	0.20	3.50	0.98	L = 1.45 + 0.1 – 0.15 = 1.4 m
	Short wall	1	1.00	0.20	3.50	0.70	L = 1.2 – 0.2 = 1.0 m
					Total	**= 45.95 m³**	
	Addition for pillar	1	0.20	0.20	2.80	0.11	
	Deductions						
	DWR openings	1	0.90	0.30	2.10	0.57	
		3	0.80	0.30	2.10	1.51	Provided in 30 cm wall.
		1	0.80	0.20	2.10	0.34	Provided in 20 cm wall.
		2	0.60	0.20	2.00	0.48	
	Window openings	3	1.50	0.30	1.10	1.49	
		3	0.80	0.30	1.10	0.79	
		2	0.50	0.30	0.80	0.24	
	Lintel over door openings						
		1	1.10	0.30	0.10	0.03	L = 0.90 + 2(0.10) = 1.10 m [Bearing is 10 cm]
		3	1.00	0.30	0.10	0.09	
		1	1.00	0.20	0.10	0.02	L = 0.80 + 2(0.10) = 1.00 m
		2	0.80	0.20	0.10	0.03	
	Lintel over windows						

		3	1.70	0.30	0.10	0.15	L = 1.5 + 2(0.1) = 1.7 m [10 cm bearing]
		3	1.00	0.30	0.10	0.09	
		2	0.70	0.30	0.10	0.04	
							Total = 5.87
		Net Total = 45.95 + 0.11 − 5.87 = 40.19 m³					
5.	**12 mm plastering in walls** **Internal Plastering** **Bedroom**						
	Long walls	2	4.25	–	3.50	29.75	
	Short walls	2	3.00	–	3.50	21.00	
	Living room						
	Long walls	2	4.00	–	3.50	28.00	
	Short walls	2	3.00	–	3.50	21.00	
	Front verandah						
	Long wall	1	1.60	–	0.70	1.12	H = 0.2 [lintel] + 0.5 [brick wall] = 0.7 m
	Short wall	1	1.05	–	0.70	0.73	
	Bathroom						
	Short walls	2	1.20	–	3.50	8.40	
	Long walls	2	2.40	–	3.50	16.80	
	Backside-long wall	1	1.00	–	3.50	3.50	
	W.C.						
	Long wall	2	1.20	–	3.50	8.40	
	Short wall	2	1.00	–	3.50	7.00	
	Backside-short wall	1	1.20	–	3.50	4.20	
	Backside-long wall	1	1.40	–	3.50	4.90	
	Passage						
	Long walls	1	2.40	–	3.50	8.40	
	Short walls	1	1.60	–	3.50	5.60	
	Backside of living and bedroom in passage	1	2.80	–	3.50	9.80	L = 1.2 + 1.60 = 2.80 m
	Kitchen						
	Long walls	2	2.40	–	3.50	16.80	
	Short walls	2	1.60	–	3.50	11.20	
	Front verandah						
	Long wall	1	1.60	–	3.50	5.60	
	Short wall	1	1.05	–	3.50	3.68	
					Total =	215.88 m²	

Deductions						
Door openings	1	0.90	–	2.10	1.89	
	4	0.80	–	2.10	6.72	
	2	0.60	–	2.00	2.40	
Total = 11.01 m²						
Net inside plastering = 215.88 – 11.01 = 204.87 m²						
Outside plastering So, quantity of outside plastering in 3.5 m high wall	1	27.85	–	4.00	111.40	Total over length of wall of 3.5 m high wall = 4.85 + 2.7 + 6.6 + 2.7 + 1.3 + 3.6 + 2.5 + 3.6 = **27.85 m** H = 3.5 + 0.45 (plinth) + 0.05 (inside ground) = 4.0 m
Front verandah						
Walls above lintel	1	2.65	–	0.90	2.39	L = 1.6 + 1.05 = 2.65 m H = 0.7 + 0.2 = 0.90 m
Plinth wall	1	3.05	–	0.50	1.53	L = 1.8 + 1.25 = 3.05 m
Total = 115.32						
Addition for pillar	2	0.2	–	3.50	1.40	
Deductions						
Window openings	3	1.50	–	1.10	4.95	
	3	0.80	–	1.10	2.64	
	2	0.50	–	0.80	0.80	
Total = 8.39						
Net outside plastering = 115.32 + 1.40 – 8.39 = 108.33 m²						
Total plastering = Net inside + Net outside plastering						
= 204.87 + 108.33 = **313.20 m²**						

Centre-Line Method For Unsymmetrical Building

Determination of total centre-line length for 30 cm walls :

Bedroom = $(4.55 \times 2) + (3.30 \times 2) = 9.1 + 6.6 = 15.70$ m

Living room = $3.30 + 2(4.30) = 3.30 + 8.60 = 11.90$ m

Backside of bathroom, W.C., back verandah and kitchen = 6.30 m

Side walls of bathroom and kitchen = $2 \times 2.70 = 5.40$.

Total centre-line length of 30 cm – main wall = 39.30 m

No. of overlapping joints of 30 cm wall with 30 cm wall = 4.0 No.

[Shown as J1, J2, J3 and J4 in the drawing.]

Determination of total centre-line length for 20 cm walls :

Front verandah = $1.85 + 1.30 = 3.15$ m

Side walls of bathroom and kitchen = $2 \times 2.7 = 5.40$ m

Wall of W.C. = $1.45 + 1.20 = 2.65$ m

Total centre-line length of 20 cm walls = 11.20 m

No. of overlapping joints of 20 cm wall with 30 cm wall = 7.0 No.

[Shown as J5, J6, J7, J8, J9, J10, J11 in the drawing]

No. of overlapping joints of 20 cm wall with 20 cm wall = **1.0 No. [J12]**

Sr. No.	Name of item	No.	L (m)	B (m)	H (m)	Quantity	Remark
1.	Earthwork in excavation in foundation						
	30 cm wall	1	37.70	0.80	1.15	34.68	$L = 39.3 - 4 \times \dfrac{0.8}{2} = 37.70$ m
	20 cm wall	1	8.10	0.60	0.90	4.37	$L = 11.2 - 7 \times \dfrac{0.8}{2} - 1 \times \dfrac{0.6}{2}$ $= 8.10$ m
					Total = 39.05 m³		
2.	P.C.C. 1:3:6 in foundation						
	30 cm wall	1	37.70	0.80	0.10	3.02	$L = 39.3 - 4 \times \dfrac{0.8}{2} = 37.70$ m
	20 cm wall	1	9.15	0.60	0.15	0.82	$L = 11.2 - 7 \times \dfrac{0.5}{2} - 1 \times \dfrac{0.6}{2}$ $= 9.15$ m
					Total = 3.84 m³		[At the level of P.C.C. of 20 cm wall, 50 cm wide footing of 30 cm wall is available]
3.	Iˢᵗ class brick work in foundation and plinth						
	30 cm wall Iˢᵗ footing	1	38.30	0.50	0.30	5.75	$L = 39.3 - 4 \times \dfrac{0.5}{2} = 38.30$ m
	IInd footing	1	38.50	0.40	0.20	3.08	$L = 39.3 - 4 \times \dfrac{0.4}{2} = 38.50$ m
	Plinth wall	1	38.70	0.30	1.00	11.61	$L = 39.3 - 4 \times \dfrac{0.3}{2} = 38.70$ m
	20 cm wall Iˢᵗ footing	1	9.60	0.40	0.20	0.77	$L = 11.2 - 7 \times \dfrac{0.4}{2} - 1 \times \dfrac{0.4}{2}$ $= 9.6$ m
	IInd footing	1	10.00	0.30	0.20	0.60	$L = 11.2 - 7 \times \dfrac{0.3}{2} - 1 \times \dfrac{0.3}{2}$ $= 10.0$ m

	Plinth wall	1	10.05	0.20	0.80	1.61	$L = 11.2 - 7 \times \dfrac{0.3}{2} - 1 \times \dfrac{0.2}{2}$ $= 10.05$ m
					Total = 23.42 m³	
4.	Ist class brick work in superstructure						
	30 cm wall	1	38.7	0.30	3.50	40.63	$L = 39.3 - 4 \times \dfrac{0.3}{2} = 38.70$ m
	20 cm wall	1	10.05	0.20	3.50	7.03	$L = 11.2 - 7 \times \dfrac{0.3}{2} - 1 \times \dfrac{0.2}{2}$
					Total	47.66m³	$= 10.05$ m
	[As solid wall including front verandah]						
	Deductions						
	For DWR, window and lintel over doors and windows					5.87	Taken directly from long wall-short wall method
	For front verandah opening including lintel	1	2.65	0.2	3.0	1.59	$L = 1.6 + 1.05 = 2.65$ m $H = 2.8 + 0.2$ (lintel) $= 3.0$ m
					Total = 7.46	
					Net Total = 47.66 – 7.46 = 40.20 m³	

Note : Estimation of quantity of plastering in walls in centre-line method is to be done, in the same manner, as it was done in long wall-short wall method. Therefore, plastering in walls not estimated separately in centre-line method.

Comparison of results of both the methods

Sr. No.	Name of item	Long wall-short wall method	Centre-line method
1.	Earthwork in excavation in foundation	39.05 m³	39.05 m³
2.	P.C.C. 1 : 3 : 6 in foundation	3.84 m³	3.84 m³
3.	Ist class brickwork in foundation and plinth	23.42 m³	23.42 m³
4.	Ist class brickwork in superstructure	40.19 m³	40.20 m³

Note : Quantity of different items of work obtained using both the methods are exactly same.

Example 3.3 : Fig. 3.27 shows the plan the section of an office building. Determine the quantities of following items and prepare the measurement sheet with appropriate description of each item.

(i)   Earth work in excavation in hard murrum for foundation.

(ii) UCR masonry in C.M. (1 : 6) in plinth and foundation.

(iii) Brick masonry in C.M. (1 : 6) in superstructure.

(iv) RCC M20 in slab and lintels assuming 15cm projection on either side of openings.

(Nov. 2012)

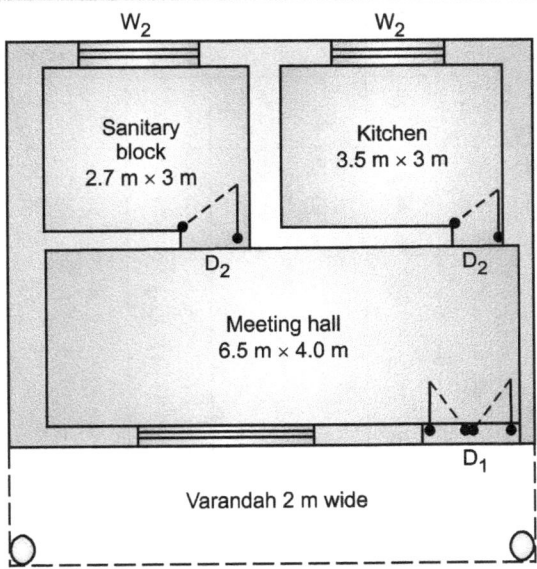

Fig. 3.27 : Plan

Solution :

No.	Name of item	No.	L	B	H	Quant.	Remark
1.	Earth work in excavation in hard murrum for foundation.						
	Side Walls as Long Wall	2	10.5	1.00	0.80	16.80	L = [0.15 – 3.0 + 0.3 + 4.0 + 0.3 + 2.0 – 0.25] + 1.0
							L = 9.5 + 1.0 = 10.5
	Front Walls as Short Wall	4	5.80	1.00	0.80	18.56	L = 6.8 + 1.0 = 5.80
	Wall Between Sanitary Block and Kitchen as Short Wall	1	2.30	1.00	0.80	1.84	L = 3.3 – 1.0 = 2.30
					Total	= 37.20 m³	
2.	U.C.R. masonary in e.m. (1 : 6) in plinth and foundation						

No.	Description		No.	Length	Breadth	Depth	Quantity	Remarks
	Side Walls as Long Wall							
	Footing		2	10.20	0.70	0.60	8.57	L = 9.5 + 0.7 = 10.20
	Plinth Wall		2	10.00	0.50	0.60	6.00	L = 9.5 + 0.5 = 10.00
	Front Wall as Short Wall							
	Footing		4	6.10	0.70	0.60	10.25	L = 6.8 – 0.7 = 6.10
	Plinth Wall		4	6.30	0.50	0.60	7.56	L = 6.8 – 0.5 = 6.30
	Wall Between Sanitary Block and Kitchen as Short Wall							
	Footing		1	2.60	0.70	0.60	1.09	L = 3.3 – 0.7 = 2.60
	Plinth Wall		1	2.80	0.50	0.60	0.84	L = 3.3 – 0.5 = 2.80
						Total	= 34.31 m³	
3.	**Brick Masonary in C.M. (1 : 6) in Superstructure**							
	Side Walls as Long Wall		2	9.80	0.30	3.50	20.58	L = 9.5 + 0.3 = 9.80
	Front Wall as Short Wall		4	6.50	0.30	3.50	27.30	L = 6.8 – 0.3 = 6.50
	Wall Between Sanitary Block and Kitchen as Short Wall		1	3.00	0.30	3.50	3.15	L = 3.3 – 0.3 = 3.00
						Total	= 51.03 m³	
	Deduction for							
	Door Opening	D_1	1	1.50	0.30	2.10	0.95	
		D_2	2	1.00	0.30	2.10	1.26	
	Window Opening	W_1	1	1.50	0.30	1.20	0.54	
		W_1	2	1.20	0.30	1.20	0.86	
	Deductions for Lintels							
	Door Openings	D_1	1	1.80	0.30	0.20	0.11	L = l + 2t
		D_2	2	1.30	0.30	0.20	0.16	15 cm Projection on both Sides
	Window Openings	W_1	1	1.80	0.30	0.20	0.11	
		W_2	2	1.50	0.30	0.20	0.18	
						Total	0.56 m³	
	Net Total = 51.03 – 3.61 – 0.56 = 46.86 m³							
4.	**RCC M20 in Slab and Lintels Assuming 15 cm Projection on either Side of Openings**							
	RCC Slab		1	9.90	7.10	0.15	10.54	L = 0.3 + 3.0 + 0.3 + 4.0 + 0.3 + 2.0 = 9.9 m B = 0.3 + 6.5 + 0.3 = 7.1 m
	RCC in Lintel						0.56	Refer Item 3 for Deductions for Lintels
						Total	11.10 m³	

Example 3.4 : A person wish to construct a building as per the following plan Fig. 3.28 Explain the utility of plan, sectional elevation in working out the detailed estimate.

(May 2015)

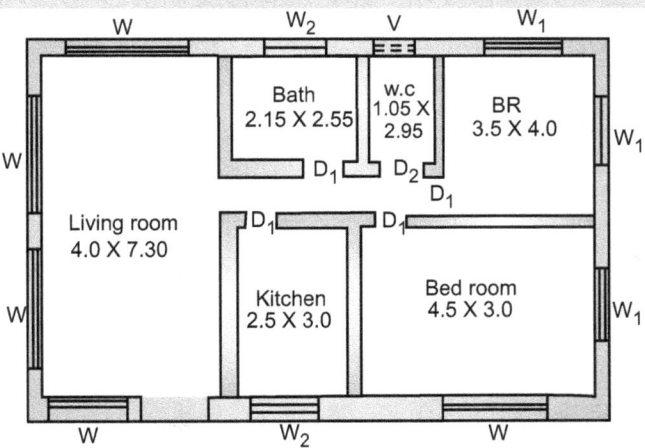

Fig. 3.28 : Plan

Solution :

No.	Name of item	No.	L	B	H	Quant.	Remark
			(m)	(m)	(m)		
1.	P.C.C. in Foundation Outside Front and Back Walls						
	As Long Wall	2	12.8	0.90	0.20	27.65	L = [0.15 + 4.0 + 0.3 + 2.5 + 0.3 + 4.5 + 0.15] + 0.9 = 12.8 m
	Side Walls As Short Wall	2	6.7	0.90	0.20	2.41	L = 7.6 – 0.9 = 6.7 m
	Kitchen and Bedroom [Combined]						
	Back Wall as Long Wall	1	7.60	0.90	0.20	1.37	L = [0.15 + 2.5 + 0.3 + 4.5 + 0.15] + $\frac{0.9}{2} - \frac{0.9}{2}$ = 7.6 m
	Side Walls as Short Wall	2	2.40	0.90	0.20	0.86	L = 3.3 – 0.9 = 2.4 m
	Bath and W.C. [Combined]						
	Front Wall as Long Wall	1	4.70	0.90	0.20	0.85	L = [0.15 + 2.15 + 0.3 + 1.05 + 0.15] + 0.9 = 4.7 m
	Side Walls as Short Wall	3	2.35	0.90	0.20	1.27	L = 3.25 – 0.9 = 2.35
					Total	34.41 m³	

2.	**Damp Proof Course (D.P.C) Outside Front and Back Walls as Long Wall**					
	As Long Wall	2	12.30	0.40	-	9.84	L = 11.90 + 0.4 = 12.30 m
	Side Walls as Short Wall	2	7.20	0.40	-	5.76	L = 7.60 – 0.4 = 7.20 m
	Kitchen and Bedroom [Combined]					
	Back Wall as Long Wall	1	7.60	0.40	-	3.04	$L = 7.60 + \frac{0.4}{2} - \frac{0.4}{2}$ = 7.60 m
	Side Walls as Short Wall	2	2.90	0.0	-	2.32	L = 3.30 – 0.40 = 2.9 m
	Bath and W.C. [Combined]					
	Front Wall as Long Wall	1	4.20	0.40	-	1.68	L = 3.80 + 0.4 = 4.2 m
	Side Walls as Short Wall	3	2.85	0.40	-	3.42	L = 3.25 – 0.4 = 2.85 m
					Total	26.06 m²	
3.	**R.C.C. Lintel and Beam Assuming Steel at 1% of RCC**					
	Lintel over Door D	1	1.20	0.30	0.15	0.054	L = 0.9 + (2 × 0.15) = 1.2 m [15 cm Bearing]
	Lintel over Door D_1	4	1.05	0.30	0.15	0.189	15 cm Bearing
	Lintel over Door D_2	1	0.90	0.30	0.15	0.041	15 cm Bearing
	Lintel over Window W	5	1.80	0.30	0.15	0.41	15 cm Bearing
	Lintel over Window W_1	3	1.50	0.30	0.15	0.20	
	Lintel over Window W_2	2	1.20	0.30	0.15	0.11	
	Lintel over Ventilator	1	0.75	0.30	0.15	0.03	
					Total	1.038 m³	

Note: It is assumed that lintels have been provided only over doors windows and ventilators. Lintels not provided over entire length of walls.

	MILD Steel in Lintel [Beam] @ 1% of RCC = $1.038 \times \frac{1}{100}$ = 0.0104 m3 So, Mass of Steel in Lintel = 0.0104 × 7850 kg/m³ = 81.48 kg					

4.	**Brick Masonary 1:6 for Superstructure [Assuming Floor to Roof Height as 3.0 m]**					
	Outside Front and Back Walls					
	As Long Wall	2	12.20	0.30	3.00	21.96	$L = 11.9 + 0.3 = 12.2$ m
	Side Walls as Short Wall	2	7.30	0.30	3.00	13.14	$L = 7.6 - 0.3 = 7.30$ m
	Kitchen and Bedroom [Combined]					
	Backwall as Long Wall	1	7.60	0.30	3.00	6.84	$L = 7.6 + \dfrac{0.3}{2} - \dfrac{0.3}{2}$ $= 7.6$ m
	Side Walls as Short Wall	2	3.00	0.30	3.00	5.40	$L = 3.3 - 0.3 = 3.0$ m
	Bath and W.C. [Combined]					
	Front Wall as Long Wall	1	4.10	0.30	3.00	3.69	$L = 3.8 + 0.3 = 4.1$ m
	Side Walls as Short Wall	3	2.95	0.30	3.00	7.97	$L = 3.25 - 0.3 = 2.95$ m
					Total	59.00 m³	
5.	**Deductions**					
	Door Openings D	1	0.90	0.30	2.10	0.57	
	D1	4	0.75	0.30	2.10	1.89	
	D2	1	0.60	0.30	1.80	0.32	
	Window Openings W	5	1.50	0.30	1.20	2.70	
	W1	3	1.20	0.30	0.90	0.97	
	W2	2	0.90	0.30	1.05	0.57	
	Ventilator V	1	0.45	0.30	0.60	0.08	
	Lintel					1.04	Refer Item No. 3
					Total	7.10 m³	
	Net Total = 59.00 – 7.10 = 51.9 m³						

Example 3.5 : Fig. 3.29 shows the plan for an ottah provided infront of a building. Determine the quantities of following items.

(i) Earthwork in excavation.

(ii) Brick masonry in C.M. (1 : 6)

(iii) Tile flooring

(iv) Plastering to the surfaces   **(Nov. 2014)**

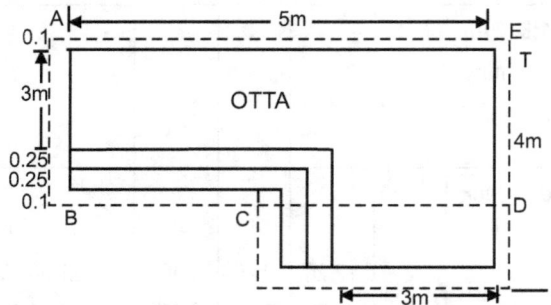

Fig. 3.29 : Plan at foundation trench level

Solution :

No.	Name of item	No.	L (m)	B (m)	H (m)	Quant.	Remark
1.	**Earthwork in Excavation**						
	For Part ABCDEA [Longer Part]	1	5.20	3.70	0.20	3.85	B = 0.1 + 3.0 + 0.25 + 0.25 + 0.1 = 3.7 m
	For Part BFGCB [Shorter Part]	1	3.70	0.50	0.20	0.37	L = 0.1 + 5.0 + 0.1 = 5.2 m
							L = 0.1 + 0.25 + 0.25 + 3.0 + 0.1 = 3.7 m
					Total	4.22 m³	
2.	**Brickwork in Masonary in C.M. (1:6)**						
	At the Level of 1ˢᵗ Step						
	For Longer Part	1	5.00	3.50	0.175	3.06	B = 3.0 + 0.25 + 0.25 = 3.5 m
	For Shorter Part	1	3.50	0.50	0.175	0.31	L = 0.25 + 0.25 + 3.0 = 3.5 m
	At the Level of 2ⁿᵈ Step						
	For Longer Part	1	5.00	3.25	0.175	2.85	
	For Shorter Part	1	3.25	0.75	0.175	0.43	
	At the Level of OTTAH						
	For Longer Part	1	5.00	3.00	0.175	2.63	
	For Shorter Part	1	3.00	1.00	0.175	0.53	
					Total	9.81 m³	
3.	**Title Flooring**						
	At the Top of OTTAH						

	For Longer Part	1	5.00	3.00	-	15.00	
	For Shorter Part	1	3.00	1.00	-	3.00	

Note: It is assumed that in steps [Both Rise and Tread] Tiles are Provided						
	For 1st Step						
	For Tread	1	2.25	0.25	-	0.56	L = 1.75 + 0.5 = 2.25 m
	For Rise	1	2.00	0.175	-	0.35	L = 1.50 + 0.5 = 2.0 m
	For 2nd Step						
	For Tread	1	2.75	0.25	-	0.69	L = 2.0 + 0.75 = 2.75 m
	For Rise	1	2.50	0.175	-	0.44	L = 1.75 + 0.75 = 2.50 m
	Above 2nd Step [on OTTAH Side]						
	Only Rise	1	3.00	0.175	-	0.53	L = 2.0 + 1.0 = 3.0 m
					Total	20.57 m^2	
4.	**Plastering to the Surfaces**						
	It is assumed that rooms of building are available on both 5 m and 4 m side, so plastering not required on these sides.						
	Front Side of OTTAH	1	3.00	-	0.525	1.575	H = 3 × 0.175 = 0.525 m
	Left Side of OTTAH	1	3.00	-	0.525	1.575	
	Side of 1st Step	2	0.25	-	0.175	0.09	H = 0.175 m
	Side of 2nd Step	1	0.25	-	0.35	0.18	H = 2 × 0.175 = 0.35 m
					Total	3.42	

Example 3.6 : Fig. 3.30 shows plant of a residential building. Determine quantities of the following items :

    (i) Excavation of foundation for tooting.

    (ii) R.C.C. in footing.

    (iii) R.C.C. in columns.

    (iv) R.C.C. in slab.

    (v) R.C.C. in beam.

    (vi) Steel reinforcement, if percentage of steel for various element is

        Column : 2%, Beam and lintel : 1.2%, Slab : 1%, Footing : 0.8%.   **(May 2013)**

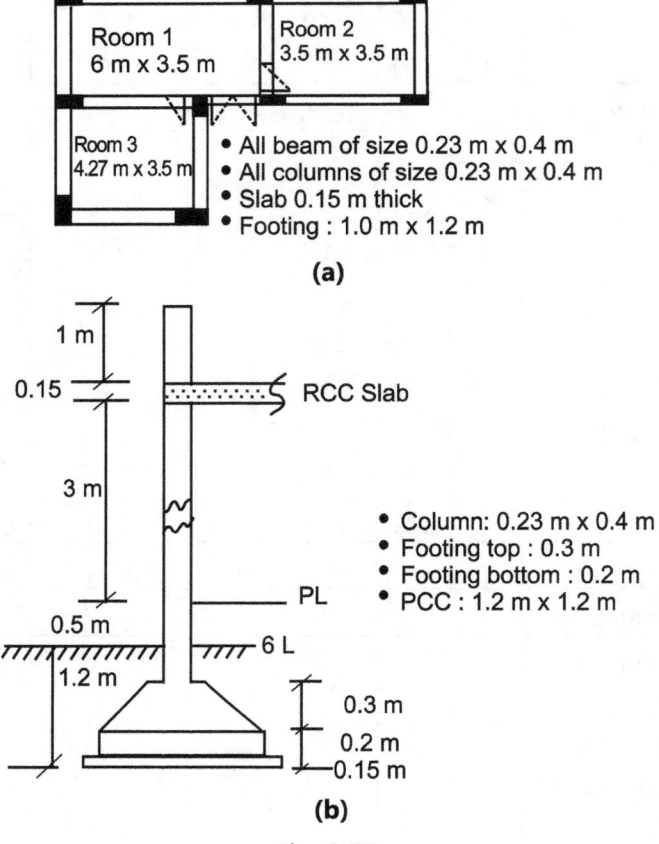

Fig. 3.30

Solution :

No.	Name of item	No.	L (m)	B (m)	H (m)	Quant. m³	Remark
1.	**Excavation for Foundation for Footing**						
	Column Footings	9	1.20	1.40	1.20	18.14	Column Fooring = 1.20 m × 1.40 m
Assuming plinth beam of 0.4 m depth is available at ground level. Plinth beam has 0.2 m depth below ground level and 0.2 m above G.L.							
	For Plinth Beam						
	For Wall of Room 3	1	3.20	0.23	0.20	0.15	L = 4.27 + 0.23 – 0.6 – 0.7 = 3.20 m
	Side Walls of Room 3	2	2.43	0.23	0.20	0.22	L = 3.50 + 0.23 – 0.6 – 0.7 = 2.43 m
	Intermediate Long Wall	1	5.96	0.23	0.20	0.27	L = 6 + 2 (0.23) + 3.5 – 2 (1.4) – 1.2 = 5.96 m

	Backside Long Wall	1	7.16	0.23	0.20	0.33	L = 6 + 2 (0.23) + 3.5 – 2 (1.4) = 7.16 m
	Side Walls of Room 1 and Room 2	3	2.53	0.23	0.20	0.35	L = 3.5 + 0.23 – 1.2 = 2.53 m
					Total	19.46 m³	
2.	**R.C.C. in Footing**						
	Square Bottom of Column Tradezoidal Portion	9	1.00	1.20	0.20	2.16	
	$= \dfrac{h}{6}[A_1 + A_2 + 4A_m]$	9	$\dfrac{0.30}{6}[(1.0 \times 1.2) + (0.3 \times 0.5) + 4\left(\dfrac{1.2 + 0.15}{2}\right)] = 1.82$				
					Total	3.98 m³	
3.	**R.C.C. in Column**	9	0.23	0.40	4.90	4.06 m³	H = (1.2 – 0.65) + 0.5 + 3.0 – 0.15 + 1.0 = 4.90 m At beam and column junction, RCC is considered in column, not in beam. So, deduction not made for beam depth.
4.	**RCC in SLAB**						
	Slab over Room 1 and 2	1	10.19	3.96	0.15	6.05	L = 6+ 3.5 + 3(0.23) = 10.
	Slab over Room 3	1	4.73	3.73	0.15	2.65	B = 3.5 + 2(0.23) = 3.9 L = 4.27 + 2(0.23) = 4 m³
					Total	8.70 m³	
5.	**RCC in BEAM** **RCC in Plinth Beam**						
	Front Wall of Room 3	1	4.10	0.23	0.40	0.38	L = 4.27 + 2(0.23) – 0.23 – 0.4 = 4.10 m
	Side Walls of Room 3	2	3.33	0.23	0.40	0.61	L = 3.5 + 0.23 – 0.4 = 3.33 m
	Backside Wall as Long Wall	1	8.99	0.23	0.40	0.83	L = 6 + 3(0.23) + 3.5 – 3(0.4) = 8.99 m
	Intermediate Long Wall	1	8.76	0.23	0.40	0.81	L = 8.99 – 0.23 = 8.76 m
	Side Walls of Room 1 and Room 2	3	3.50	0.23	0.40	0.97	

					Total	= 3.60	
	Same Quantity will Exist for Beam below Slab (Like Plinth Beam)					= 3.60	
					Total	= 7.20 m³	
6.	**Steel Reinforcement**						
	For Column @ 2%	$4.06 \times \dfrac{2}{100} \times 78.59$				= 6.379 = 6.789	
	For Beam @ 1.2%	$7.2 \times \dfrac{1.2}{100} \times 78.59$				= 6.829 = 2.509	
	For Slab @ 1.0%	$8.70 \times \dfrac{1.0}{100} \times 78.59$					
	For Footing @ 0.8%	$3.98 \times \dfrac{0.8}{100} \times 78.5$					
					Total	= 22.47 quintal	

3.8.9 Estimate Of an R.C.C. Framed Structure [Refer Fig. 3.27 (a), (b), (c)]

Measurement Sheet

Item No.	Description	No.	Length L	Breadth B	Depth or Height H	Quantity	Total
1.	Site clearance						
2.	Excavation for foundations of footings of columns in earth, soil of all types, sand, gravel and soft murum, including removing the excavated material upto a distance of 50 m beyond the building area (and lift upto 1.5 m) and stacking and spreading, dewatering, preparing the bed for the foundation, backfilling ramming, watering, shoring and strutting etc. complete.	4	1	1	1.8	7.2 m³	
3.	Providing and laying in situ, cement concrete M-15 of trap metal for foundation block and bedding including bailing out of water, form work compacting and curing, finishing etc. complete.	4	1	1	0.20	0.8 m³	

4.	Providing and laying in situ, cement concrete (1 : 2 : 4) of trap metal for R.C.C. work in footings of R.C.C. columns including bailing out of water, form work compaction, curing and roughening the surface (excluding reinforcement)	4	Mean area = $\frac{(1 \times 1) + (0.30 \times 0.30)}{2}$		0.30	0.654 m^3	
5.	Providing and casting in situ, cement concrete M-15 (1 : 2 : 4) of trap metal for R.C.C. columns as per drawings, centering, form work, compaction and roughening, curing complete (Excluding reinforcement)	4	4.5	0.30	0.30	1.62 m^3	1.62 m^3
6.	Providing and casting in situ, M-15 cement concrete of trap metal for R.C.C. beams as per drawings, centering, form work, compaction and roughening, curing complete (Excluding reinforcement) : (i) B$_1$ (ii) B$_2$	 3 2	 4.80 6.40	 0.20 0.20	 0.35 0.45	 1.008 1.152	2.16 m^3
7.	Providing and casting in situ, cement concrete M-15 (i.e. 1 : 2 : 4) of trap metal for R.C.C. slabs as shown on the drawing, centering, form work, compaction, roughening and curing complete (excluding reinforcement)	1	7	5.40	0.15	5.67 m^3	5.7 m^3

Notes :

- The length of the column is to be measured from the top of the footing to the bottom of the R.C.C. slab.
- The length of the beam is to be measured in between the two columns.
- The common portion between the slab and beam (rectangular) is to be measured in the slab portion.

- The volume of the trapezoidal portion of the footing is calculated by the average area method i.e. Volume = V.

$$\frac{(\text{Area of footing at bottom} + \text{Area of footing at top})}{2} \times \text{Height of footing}$$

- The exact volume of footing can be determined by the formula :

Volume of footing $V = \dfrac{h}{3} [A_1 + A_2 + \sqrt{A_1 \times A_2}]$

where h = height or depth of footing and A_1 and A_2 are the areas of cross-section of the footing at bottom and top respectively.

Framed Structure :

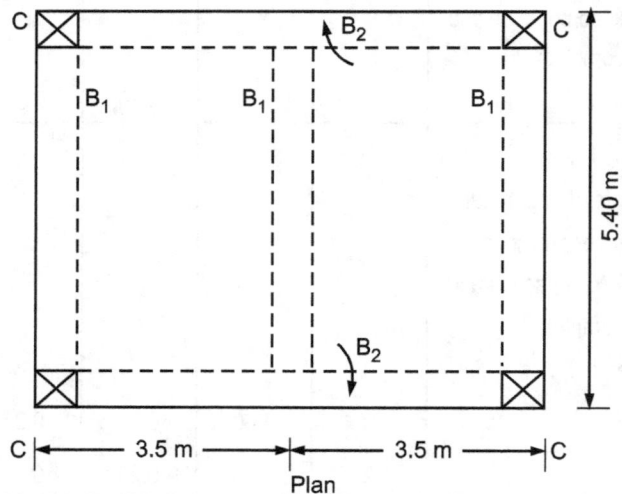

Fig. 3.31 (a)

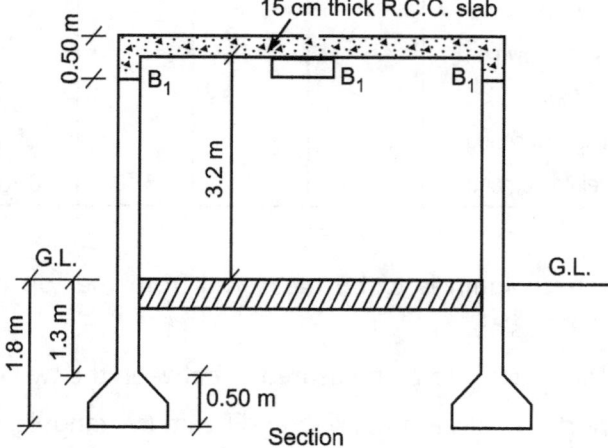

Fig. 3.31 (b)

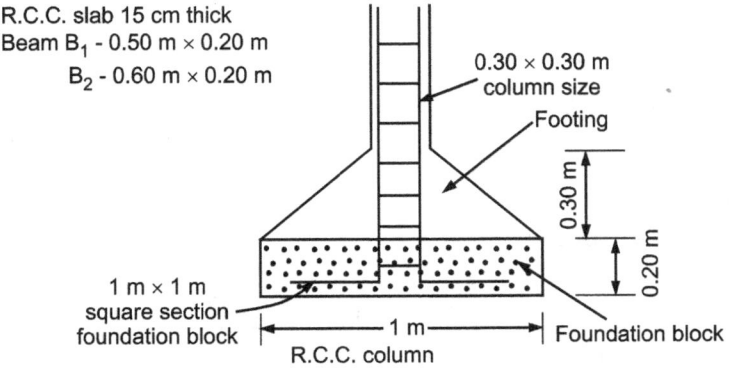

Fig. 3.31 (c)

3.8.10 R.C.C. Framed Structure

ABSTRACT SHEET

Item No.	Description	Quantity	Rate		Per	Amount	
			₹	Ps.		₹	Ps.
1.	Site clearance		L.S. Amount			200	00
2.	Excavation for foundations of columns in earth, soil of all types, sand, gravel and soft murum, including removing the excavated material upto a distance of 50 m beyond the building area (Lift upto 1.5 m) and stacking and spreading, dewatering, preparing the bed for the foundations, back filling, ramming, watering, shoring and strutting etc. complete.	7.2 m³	23	10	m³	166	32
3.	Providing and laying in situ, cement concrete M-15 of trap metal for foundation block and bedding including bailing out of water, form work, compacting, curing, finishing etc. complete.	0.8 m³	900	00	m³	720	00

4.	Providing and laying in situ, cement concrete (1 : 2 : 4) of trap metal for R.C.C. work in footings of R.C.C. columns including bailing out of water, form work, compaction, curing and roughening the surface (excluding reinforcement)	0.654 m³	980	00	m³	640	92
5.	Providing and casting in situ, cement concrete M-15 of trap metal for R.C.C. columns as per drawings, centering, formwork, compaction & roughening, curing complete (Excluding the reinforcement)	1.62 m³	1420	00	m³	2300	40
6.	Providing and casting in situ, M-15 cement concrete of trap metal for R.C.C. beams as per drawings, centering, form work, compaction and roughening, curing etc. complete (excluding reinforcement)	2.16 m³	1300	00	m³	2808	00
7.	Providing and casting in situ, cement concrete M-15 of trap metal for R.C.C. slab as shown on the drawing, centering, form work compaction, roughening and curing complete (excluding reinforcement)	5.67 m³	1380	00	m³	7824	60

Estimated cost = ₹ 14460.24

Add 5% towards contingencies = ₹ 732.01

Total cost = ₹ 15192.25

Add 1% towards work charged establishment = ₹ 151.92

Ground total establishment cost = ₹ 15344.17

Say ≈ ₹ **15345.00**

3.8.11 Estimate of an R.C.C. Column (Fig. 3.28)

Measurement Sheet

Item No.	Description	No.	Length (L)	Breadth (B)	Depth or Height (H)	Quantity	Total
1.	Excavations for foundations in soil upto a depth of 1.5 m including removing the excavated material upto a distance of 50 m beyond the building area and all lift, stacking, spreading as directed, dewatering, shoring and strutting, preparing the bed for foundation and necessary backfilling.	1	1.8	1.8	1.1	3.564m³	
2.	Providing and casting in situ P.C.C. (1 : 4 : 8) of trap metal for foundation and bedding including dewatering, form work, compacting and curing etc. complete.	1	1.8	1.8	0.1	0.324m³	
3.	Providing and casting in situ C.C. (1 : 2 : 4) of trap metal for R.C.C. foundations as per detailed designed drawing or as directed including dewatering, centering, form work, compaction, finishing the formed surface with cm (1 : 3) of sufficient minimum thickness to give a smooth and even surface or roughening them if special finish is to be provided and curing etc. (excluding MS reinforcement)						
	Rectangular	1	1.6	1.6	0.2	0.512m³	
	Trapezoidal	1	$\frac{1}{2}$ {1.6² + 0.6²}		0.3	0.438m³	
							0.950 m³
4.	Providing and casting in situ. C.C. (1 : 2 : 4) of trap metal for R.C.C. columns as per detailed designed and drawing or as directed including dewatering, centering, form work, compaction, finishing the formed surfaces with cm (1 : 3) of sufficient minimum thickness to give a smooth finish or roughening them if special finish is to be provided and curing (excluding MS reinforcement)						
	Sect. 0.50 × 0.50	1	0.5	0.5	1.2	0.3 m³	
	Sect. 0.4 × 0.41	1	0.4	0.4	3.1	0.496m³	
						0.796m³	

5.	Providing and fixing in position MS bars as reinforcement of various diameter for RCC column and footing as per detailed design and drawing and schedules including cutting, bending, hooking the bars, binding with wires or tack welding and supported as required etc. complete.					
	(A) Footing					
	18 mm diameter	22	1.824m	$\pi/4 \times (0.018)^2$		$0.0102113\, m^3$
	150 mm bothways					
	$L = (1.60 - 2\text{ cover} + 2\text{ hooks})$					
	$= (1.60 - 0.1 + 9 \times 2 \times 0.018)$					
	$= 150 + 0.324$					
	$= 1.824$ m					
	No. of bars $= \left(\dfrac{160 - 10}{15} + 1\right)$					
	$=$ 11 numbers one way					
	$\therefore$ 22 Nos. bothways					
	(B) Main steel in column	4	5.58	$(\pi/4 \times 0.02^2)$		$0.00701\, m^3$
	4 Nos. – 20 mm diameter					
	$L = 1 + 0.7 + 3.10 + 0.52 - 0.10$					
	(cover) + two bends					
	$= 5.22 +$ two bends					
	$= 5.58$ m					
	(C) Ties	33	1.344	$(\pi/4)$ $\times (0.006)^2$	$0.001254\, m^3$	
	6 mm dia. @ 150 mm c/c					
	Nos. $= \dfrac{4.70}{0.15} + 1$ say 33 Nos.					
	$L = 4 \times (0.40 - 0.10) + 24 \times 0.006$			Total =	$0.018475\, m^3$	
	$= 1.20 + 1.44 = 1.344$ m					
	5% of wastages					$0.00092375\, m^3$
						$0.01940\, m^3$
	Weight of reinforcement @ 7850 kg/m³					152.30 kg

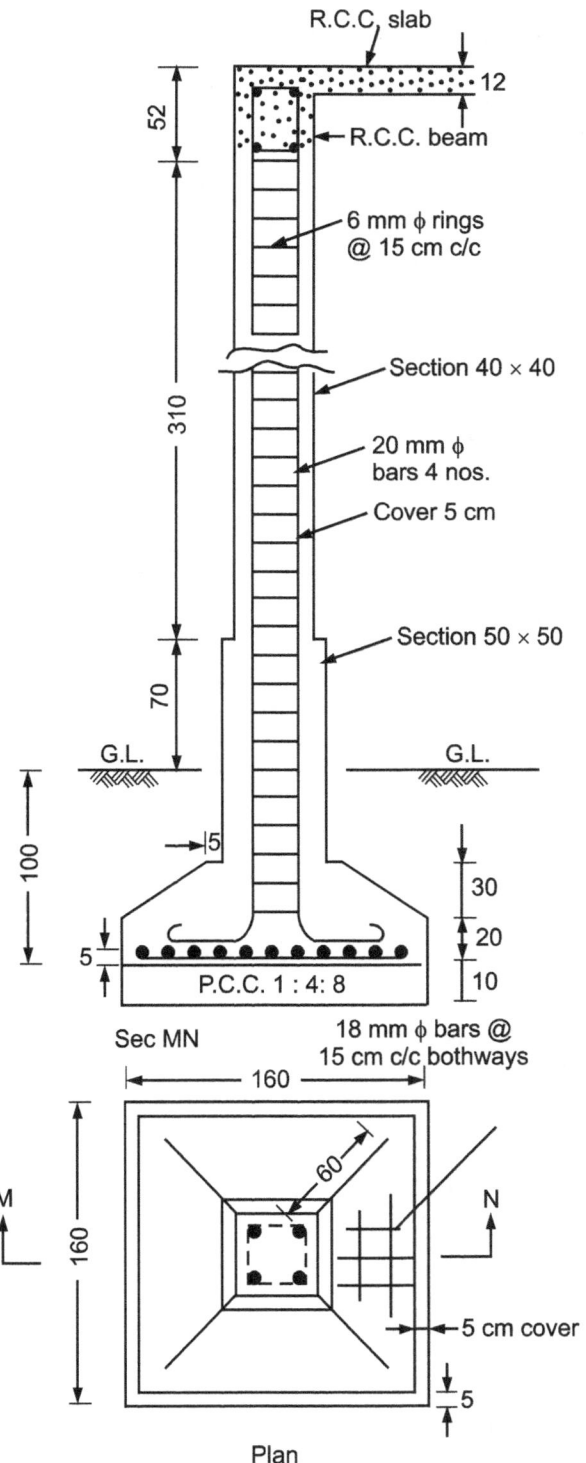

Fig. 3.32 : Estimate of an R.C.C. column

3.8.12 Estimate of an R.C.C. Column

Abstract Sheet

Item No.	Description	Quantity	Rate		Per	Amount	
			₹	Ps.		₹	Ps
1.	Excavation for foundations in soil upto a depth of 1.5 m including removing the excavated material upto a distance of 50 m beyond the building, area and all lift, stacking and spreading as directed dewatering, shoring, strutting, preparing the bed for foundation and necessary back filling	3.564 m³	23	10	m³	82	33
2.	Providing a casting in situ. C.C. (1 : 4 : 8) of trap metal for foundation and bedding including dewatering, form work, compacting and curing etc. complete.	0.324 m³	600	00	m³	194	40
3.	Providing and casting in situ. C.C. (1 : 2 : 4) of trap metal for RCC foundations as per detailed design and drawings or as directed including dewatering, centering, form work, compaction, finishing the formed surface with cm (1 : 3) of minimum thickness to give a smooth and even surface or roughening them if special finish is to be provided and curing etc. (Excluding M.S. reinforcement)	0.95 m³	900	00	m³	855	00
4.	Providing and casting in situ. C.C. (1 : 2 : 4) of trap metal for RCC columns as per detailed design and drawing or as directed including dewatering, centering, form work, compaction, finishing the formed surface with cm 1 : 3 of sufficient minimum thickness to give a smooth and even surface or roughening them for special finish and curing etc. (excluding MS reinforcement)	0.796 m³	1420	00	m³	1130	32

5.	Providing and fixing in position mild steel bars reinforcement of various diameters for RCC column footing as per detailed drawings and design and schedules including cutting, bending, hooking the bars and binding with wires or tack welding and supporting as required etc. complete.	0.1523 tonne	13000	00	tonne	1979	90
	Add 5% for contingencies					Total	4241.94
							221.10
							4454.04
	Add 1% for W.C. establishment						44.54
							4498.58
						Say ₹	**4499.00**

Example 3.7 :

A beam of width 380 mm × 660 mm total depth has a total length of 6.0 metres. The reinforcement details are as follows :

(1)   Top steel : 2 Nos. – 12 mm dia., mild.

(2)   Bottom steel : 4 Nos. – 22 mm dia., mild (2.0 No. bent up).

(3)   Stirrups : 6 mm dia., mild steel from each end @ 150 mm c/c upto 1.2 m length from each end and remaining 6 mm dia., @ 300 mm in the central portion.

The width of the two supporting columns is 300 mm. Draw a suitable sketch of the beam with reinforcement. Determine the following :

(i)   Quantity of

    (a)   6 mm dia. steel in kg.

    (b)   12 mm dia. steel in quintal and

    (c)   22 mm dia. steel in tonne.

(ii)   Percentage of total steel with respect to concrete.

Assume clear cover of 3.0 cm to bar from all sides and other allowances can be assumed. The beam is taken 150 mm inside the column support.

Solution :

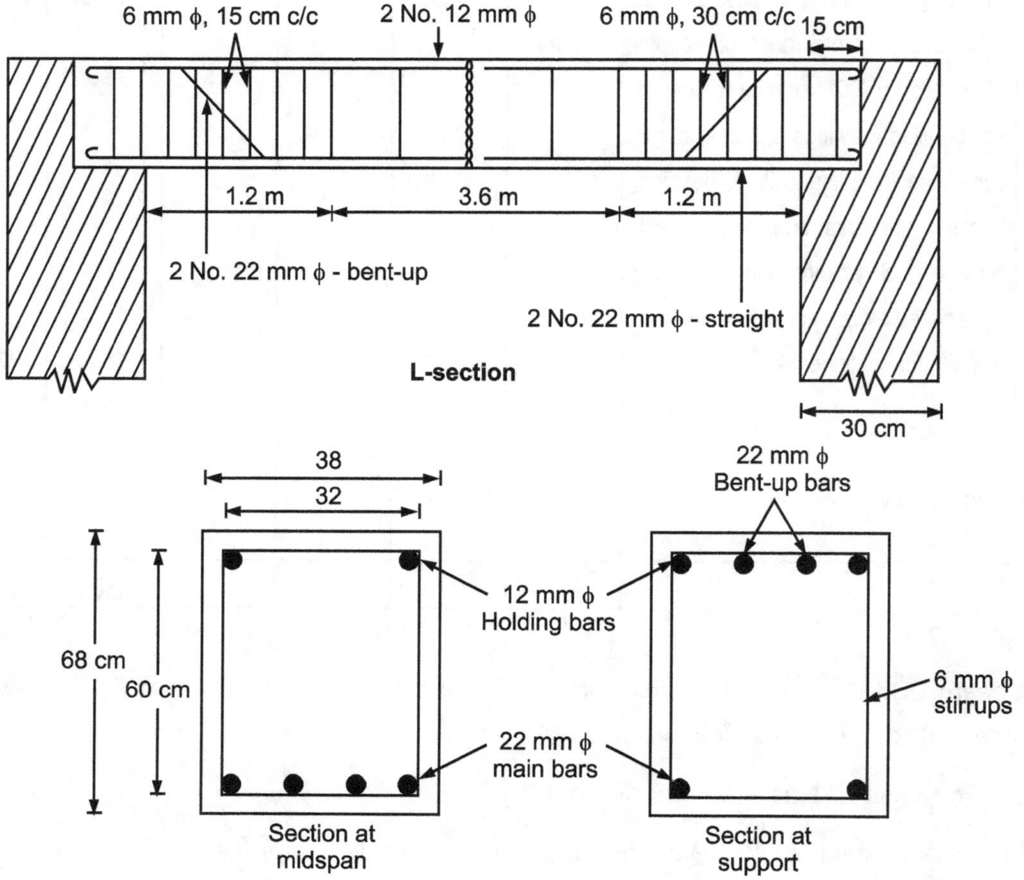

6 mm φ, 15 cm c/c   2 No. 12 mm φ   6 mm φ, 30 cm c/c 15 cm

1.2 m   3.6 m   1.2 m

2 No. 22 mm φ - bent-up

2 No. 22 mm φ - straight

L-section

30 cm

38

32

68 cm

60 cm

22 mm φ
Bent-up bars

12 mm φ
Holding bars

6 mm φ
stirrups

22 mm φ
main bars

Section at
midspan

Section at
support

Fig. 3.33

Estimation of R.C.C. Beam :

Sr. No.	Name of item	No.	L (m)	B (m)	H (m)	Quantity	Remark
1.	R.C.C. work [1 : 2 : 4] excluding steel and its bending but including centering and shuttering and binding of steel.	1	6.30	0.38	0.66	1.58 m³	No deduction for volume of steel bars.
2.	Steel bars including bending in R.C.C. work						
	Main bars 22 mm φ straight bars @ 2.98 kg/m	2	6.64	= 13.28 × 2.98 = 39.57		39.57 kg	L = 6.30 – 2 end covers + 2 hooks = 6.30 – (2 × 0.3) + (2 × 9 × 0.022) = 6.64 m

22 mm φ bent up bars @ 2.98 kg/m	2	7.12	= 14.24 × 2.98 = 42.43	42.43 kg	L = 6.30 – 2 end covers + 2 hooks + [0.84 × effective depth] = 6.30 – (2 × 0.03) + (2 × 9 × 0.022) + (0.84 × 0.57) = 7.12 m
12 mm φ holding bars @ 0.89 kg/m	2	6.46	= 12.92 × 0.89 = 11.50	11.50 kg	L = 6.30 – 2 × 0.03 + 2 × 9 × 0.012 = 6.46 m
6 mm φ stirrups @ 0.22 kg/m at 150 mm c/c spacing	8 × 2 = 16	2.25			L = (60 × 2) + (32 × 2) + 2 hooks + Extra 30 cm = 184 + (2 × 9 × 6) + 30 = 224.8 cm = 2.25 m
6 mm φ stirrups @ 0.22 kg/m at 300 c/c spacing $\text{No. of bars} = \frac{3.6}{0.3} + 1 = 13.0$	13	2.25			
Total no. of 6 mm φ stirrups	29	2.25	= 65.25 × 0.22 = 14.36	14.36 kg	
				Total mass of steel = 107.86 kg	

$$\text{Volume occupied by steel in concrete} = \frac{107.86 \text{ kg}}{7850.00 \text{ kg/m}^3} = 0.0137 \text{ m}^3$$

(ii) Percentage of volume of steel in concrete $= \dfrac{0.0137}{1.58} \times 100 = \textbf{0.87\%}$

Example 3.8 :

The plan and past cross-section of a watchman's cabin are given in Fig. 3.30. The watchman's cabin is a **regular hexagon** of internal side 3.0 m. Work out quantities of following items and enter the same in a measurement sheet :

1. Excavation in ordinary soil for foundation.
2. P.C.C. (1 : 3 : 6) in foundation bed.
3. First class brickwork in foundation and plinth.
4. Damp proof course.
5. First class brick work in superstructure.
6. R.C.C. work in roof including chajja and lintels.
7. 8.0 cm lime concrete in roof terracing.
8. 2.5 cm cement concrete over 7.5 cm L.C. floor.
9. 12 mm cement plastering 1 : 6 inside and outside walls.   **(June 2003 – 20 Marks)**

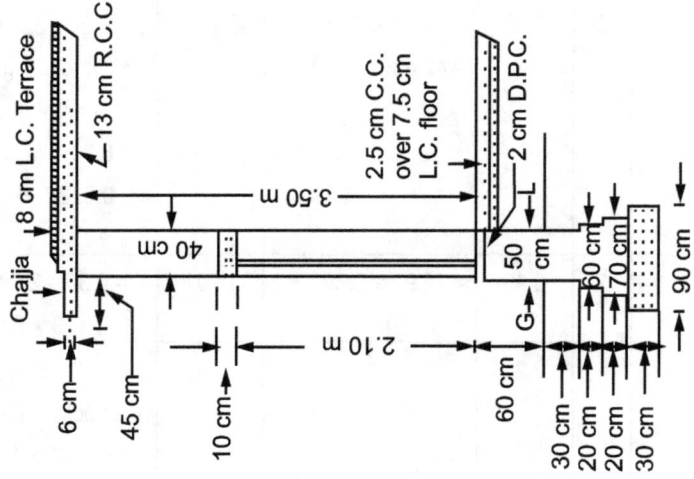

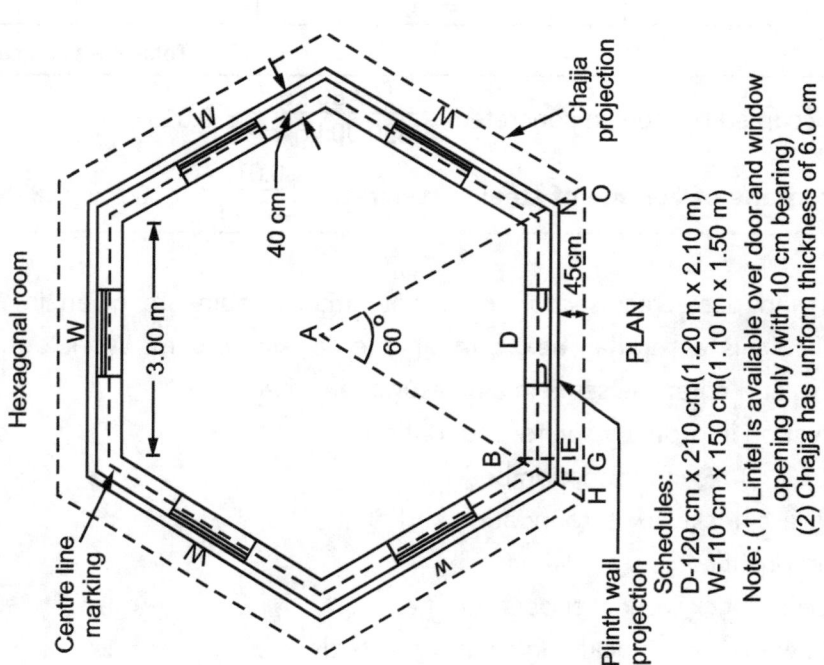

Fig. 3.34

Solution : The length of the centreline and the area of the hexagon may be calculated as follows :

Fig. 3.35 represents $(1/6)^{th}$ of the hexagon. The sides of a hexagon form equilateral triangles at the centre.

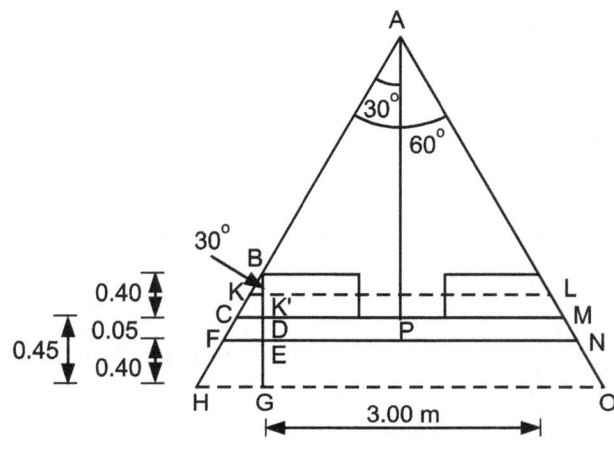

Fig. 3.35

In the figure, for triangle BKK′, $\tan 30° = \dfrac{KK'}{BK'}$.

So,　　　　　　　　$KK' = BK' \tan 30° = 0.2 \tan 30° = 0.115$

So, centre-line length KL = $3.0 \text{ m} + 2\,KK' = 3.0 + 2\,(0.115) =$ **3.23 m.**

Therefore, total length of centreline for hexagon $= 6 \times 3.23 =$ **19.38 m**

Calculation for $(1/6)^{th}$ portion of hexagon [shown in Fig. 3.31]

Outer length of superstructure wall $= CM = 3.0 + 2\,CD = 3.0 + (2 \times 0.23) = 3.46$ m

Outer length of plinth wall $= FN = 3.0 + 2FE = 3.52$ m

Outer length of chajja $= HO = 3.0 + 2\,HG = 3.0 + [2 \times 0.85 \tan 30°] = 3.98$ m

$$\text{Total floor area} = 12 \times \text{Area of } \triangle\ APC$$

$$= 12 \times \frac{1}{2} \times AP \times PC = 12 \times \frac{1}{2} \times 1.5 \times \frac{1.5}{\tan 30°}$$

$$= 23.38 \text{ m}^2$$

$$\text{Total roof area} = 6 \times \text{Area of } \triangle\ AHO = 6 \times \left[\frac{1}{2} \times 3.98 \times \frac{3.98}{2 \tan 30°}\right]$$

$$= 31.10 \text{ m}^2$$

Measurement sheet for hexagonal room : Centre-line method :

Sr. No.	Name of item	No.	L	B	H	Quantity	Remark
1.	Earthwork in excavation in foundation	1	19.38	0.90	1.00	17.44m^3	No overlapping joint, so net centre line length = 19.38 m
2.	P.C.C. [1 : 3 : 6] in foundation bed	1	19.38	0.90	0.30	5.23 m^3	
3.	First class brickwork in foundation and plinth						
	Ist footing	1	19.38	0.70	0.20	2.71	
	IInd footing	1	19.38	0.60	0.02	2.33	
	Plinth wall	1	19.38	0.50	0.90	8.72	
					Total = 13.76 m^3		
4.	Damp proof course	1	19.38	0.50	–	9.69	
	Deduction – Door sill	1	1.20	0.50	–	0.60	
					Total = 9.09 m^2		
5.	First class brick work in superstructure	1	19.38	0.40	3.50	27.13	
	Deductions						
	Door openings	1	1.20	0.40	2.10	1.01	
	Window openings	5	1.10	0.40	1.50	3.30	
	Lintel over door	1	1.40	0.40	0.10	0.06	
	Lintel over windows	5	1.30	0.40	0.10	0.26	
					Total = 4.63 m^3		
			Net Total = 27.13		– 4.63 = 22.50 m^3		
6.	R.C.C. work in roof including chajja and lintels Roof slab					4.043	Qty = $6 \times \dfrac{1}{2} \times 3.46 \times$ $\dfrac{3.46}{2 \tan 30°} \times 0.13 = 4.043$ m^3
	Chajja	6	3.72	0.45	0.06	0.603	Qty = 6 × Mean length × Breadth × Thickness where mean length
	Lintels					0.32	$= \dfrac{3.46 + 3.98}{2} = 3.72$ m
	[Same as in item No. 5]					Total = 4.996 m^3	

7.	8.0 cm lime concrete in roof terracing				31.10m²	Qty = $6 \times \frac{1}{2} \times 3.46 \times \frac{3.46}{2 \tan 30°}$ = 31.10 m²
8.	2.5 cm cement concrete over 7.5 cm L.C. floor				23.38m²	Total floor area = 23.38 m²
	Addition for door sill	1	1.20	0.40	–	0.48	
				Net Total = **23.86 m²**		
9.	**12 cm cement plastering 1 : 6 in walls**						
	Inside	6	3.00	–	3.50	63.00	
	Outside above plinth	6	3.46	–	3.50	72.66	
	Outside plinth wall	6	3.52	–	0.70	14.78	H = 0.6 + 0.05 [plinth projection] + 0.05 [inside ground] = 0.70 m
					Total = **150.44 m²**		
	Deductions						
	Door opening	1	1.20	–	2.10	2.52	
	Window opening	5	1.10	–	1.50	8.25	
					Total = **10.77 m²**		
			Net Total = 150.44 – 10.77 = **139.67 m²**				

3.8.13 Estimate of a Two Storeyed Building (Fig. 3.31)

Measurement Sheet

Sr. No.	Name of item	No.	Length L (m)	Breadth B (m)	Depth or Height H (m)	Quantity	Total
1.	Cleaning the side before and after the work including removing all debris, shrubs etc.			Job item			
2.	Excavation of foundation in (soil or H.M.) upto a depth of 1.5 m including removing the excavated materials upto a distance of 50 m beyond the building area and all lift stacking and spreading as directed, dewatering, shoring and strutting, preparing the bed for foundation and necessary back filling complete.						

Sr. No.	Name of item	No.	Length L (m)	Breadth B (m)	Depth or Height H (m)	Quantity	Total
(A)	Excavation for footing for column numbers.		(Depth of excavation for all column footings is 1.2 m)				
	(i) C_{18}, C_{19}	2	1.05	1.05	1.2	2.646	
	(ii) C_{10}, C_{12}, C_{16}	3	1.50	1.45	1.2	7.830	
	(iii) C_2, C_3, C_6, C_7, C_8, C_9, C_{11}, C_{13}, C_{14}, C_{17}	10	1.275	1.20	1.2	18.36	
	(iv) C_1, C_4, C_5, C_{15}	4	1.2	0.9225	1.2	5.3136	34.15 m³
(B)	For footing of external wall (excluding the excavation for col. footings)						
	Long wall (Left)	1	8.475	0.60	1.2	6.102	
	Long wall (Right)	1	8.32	0.60	1.2	5.99	
	Short wall (Back)	1	4.86	0.60	1.2	3.50	
	Short wall (Front)	1	5.76	0.60	1.2	4.15	19.74 m³
							53.90 m³
3.	Providing and laying in situ cement concrete of trap metal for foundation and including dewatering, formwork, compacting and curing etc.						
(A)	P.C.C. for column foundations						
	(i) C_{18}, C_{19}	2	1.05	1.05	0.15	0.33	
	(ii) C_{10}, C_{12}, C_{16}	3	1.5	1.45	0.15	0.97	
	(iii) C_2, C_3, C_6, C_7, C_8, C_9, C_{11}, C_{13}, C_{14}, C_{17}	10	1.275	1.20	0.15	2.295	
	(iv) C_1, C_4, C_5, C_{15}	4	1.2	0.9225	0.15	0.67	4.127 m³
(B)	P.C.C. for wall footings (External)						
	Long wall (Left)	1	8.475	0.60	0.15	0.762	
	Long wall (Right)	1	8.325	0.60	0.15	0.749	
	Short wall (Back)	1	4.86	0.60	0.15	0.437	
	Short wall (Front)	1	5.76	0.6	0.15	0.518	2.446 m³
					Total P.C.C. for foundation		6.593 m³

Remarks :

$L = 14.625 - 3(1.2) - 2(0.275)$

$\quad = 8.475\ m$

$L = 14.625 - 4(1.275) - 1.2$

$\quad = 8.325\ m$

$L = 8.55 - 2\left(\dfrac{0.52}{2}\right) - 2\left(\dfrac{0.225}{2}\right)$

$\quad\quad - 2(1.275)$

$\quad = 4.86\ m$

$L = 8.55 - 2\left[\dfrac{0.225}{2}\right] - \dfrac{0.92}{2} - \dfrac{1.2}{2} - 1.5$

$\quad = 5.76\ m$

Sr. No.	Name of item	No.	Length L (m)	Breadth B (m)	Depth or Height H (m)	Quantity	Total
4.	Providing and casting in situ. cement concrete (1 : 2 : 4) of trap metal for R.C.C. footings as per detailed designs and drawings or as directed, including dewatering, centering, formwork, compaction, finishing and curing etc. complete (excluding reinforcement)						
	(i) For C_{18}, C_{19} (square footing)	2	0.75	0.76	0.3	0.34	
	(ii) For C_{10}, C_{12}, C_{16}		$\dfrac{(0.525 \times 0.375) + (1.2 \times 1.15)}{2} \times 0.2$				
	(a) Trapezoidal part	3	$= \dfrac{0.197 + 1.38}{2} \times 0.2 = 0.158$			0.474	
	(b) Rectangular part	3	1.2	1.05	0.2	0.891	
	(iii) C_2, C_3, C_6, C_7, C_8, C_9, C_{11}, C_{13}, C_{14}, C_{17}		$\dfrac{0.45 \times 0.375 + 0.975 \times 0.9}{2} \times 0.2$				
	(a) Trapezoidal part	10	$= \dfrac{0.169 \times 0.878}{2} \times 0.175 = 0.917$			0.917	
	(b) Rectangular part	10	0.975	0.9	0.2	1.75	
	(iv) C_1, C_4, C_5, C_{15} (square footing)	4	0.90	0.825	0.3	0.756	
							5.131 m³
5.	Providing and casting in situ cement concrete 1 : 2 : 4 of trap metal for R.C.C. columns as per detailed drawings and design or as directed including centering, formwork, compaction, finishing and curing etc. complete (excluding reinforcement) for column from footing to plinth level.						
	(i) C_{18}, C_{19}	2	0.225	0.225	1.125	0.114	

1.425

0.3

Sr. No.	Name of item	No.	Length L (m)	Breadth B (m)	Depth or Height H (m)	Quantity	Total
	(ii) C_{10}, C_{12}, C_{16}	3	0.375	0.225	1.025	0.26	
	H = 1.425 − 0.4 = 1.025 m						
	(iii) C_2, C_3, C_6, C_7, C_8, C_9, C_{11}, C_{13}, C_{14}, C_{17}	10	0.30	0.225	1.05	0.708	
	H = 1.425 − 0.375 = 1.05 m						
	(iv) C_1, C_4, C_5, C_{15}	4	0.3	0.225	1.025	0.30	
	H = 1.425 − 0.3 = 1.125 m						
							1.38 m^3
6.	Providing Random (U.C.R.). Rubble Masonry of trap stones in C.M. (1 : 6) in foundation and plinth of walls including striking joints on exposed faces. Masonry for external walls.						
	Long wall (Left)	1	13.125	0.375	1.425	7.01 m^3	
	L = 14.625 − 1.5 = 13.125 m						
	Long wall (Right)	1	13.05	0.375	1.425	6.97 m^3	
	L = 14.625 − 4 (0.3)						
	− 0.375 = 13.05						
	Short wall (Back)	1	1.50	0.375	1.425	4.00 m^3	
	L = 8.55 − 2 (0.225) − 2 (0.3)						
	= 7.50 m						
	Short wall (Front)	1	7.725	0.375	1.425	4.13 m^3	
	L = 8.55 − 2 (0.225) − 0.375						
	= 7.725 m						
							22.11 m^3
7.	Providing and casting in situ cement concrete (1 : 2 : 4) of trap metal for R.C.C. plinth beams as per detailed designs and drawings or as directed, including dewatering, centering, formwork, compaction, finishing the formed surface with cm (1 : 3) of sufficient minimum thickness to give smooth and even surface of roughing, if special finish is to be provided and curing etc. complete (excluding reinforcement).						

Sr. No.	Name of item	No.	Length L (m)	Breadth B (m)	Depth or Height H (m)	Quantity	Total
	(i)　　External plinth beams						
	Long walls	2	14.25	0.375	0.15	1.603m^3	
	Short walls	2	8.1	0.375	0.15	0.92m^3	
	$8.55 - 2\left(\dfrac{0.42}{2}\right) = 8.1\ m$						
	(ii)　　Internal plinth beams						
	(a)　　PB$_{18}$, PB$_{22}$	2	3.6	0.225	0.225	0.36 m^3	
	(b)　　[PB$_4$ + PB$_5$ + PB$_6$] and [PB$_7$ + PB$_8$]	2	8.1	0.225	0.225	0.82 m^3	
	(c)　　PB$_{19}$	1	2.1	0.225	0.225	0.107m^3	
	(d)　　PB$_9$ + PB$_9$	1	5.1	0.225	0.225	0.259 m^3	
	(e)　　PB$_{10}$	1	3.75	0.225	0.225	0.189m^3	
	(f)　　PB$_{17}$	1	2.1	0.225	0.225	0.107m^3	
	(g)　　PB$_{21}$	1	4.2	0.225	0.225	0.212m^3	**4.58 m^3**
8.	Filling in between plinth and floor ...						
	(i)　　Providing dry trap rubble soling (15-23 cm thick) including hard packing etc. complete						
	L　=　14.25 – 2 (0.375) = 13.5 m	1	13.5	7. 8 m	0.225	23.7 m^3	
	B　=　8.55 – 2 (0.375) = 7.8 m						23.7 m^3
	(ii)　　Filling in between plinth and floor with murum in (15-30 cm layers) including watering and compaction complete.	1	13.5	7.8	0.30	31.59m^3	31.59 m^3
9.	Providing and laying in situ cement concrete of trap metal for bedding including dewatering, formwork, compacting and curing etc. complete.						
	(i)　　Store room	1	3.6	2.4	0.075	0.648	
	(ii)　　W.R./Bath/Passage	1	3.6	2.25	0.075	0.60	
	(iii)　　Bed	1	3.6	3.0	0.075	0.81	
	(iv)　　Dining-drawing	1	8.1	4.05	0.075	2.46	
	(v)　　Kitchen	1	3.75	3.6	0.075	1.01	
	(vi)　　Stair room	1	5.1	2.1	0.075	0.80	
	(vii)　　Master bed	1	4.2	3.6	0.075	1.13	
	(viii)　Toilet	1	2.1	2.1	0.075	0.33	
	(ix)　　Pooja room	1	2.1	1.5	0.075	0.23	

Sr. No.	Name of item	No.	Length L (m)	Breadth B (m)	Depth or Height H (m)	Quantity	Total
							8.10 m³
10.	Providing and casting in situ cement concrete (1 : 2 : 4) of trap metal for R.C.C. columns, as from plinth level to first floor level as per detailed drawings and design or as directed including centering, finishing and curing etc. complete and finishing the formed surface with C.M. (1 : 3) of sufficient minimum thickness to give smooth and even surface or roughening, if special finish is to be provided and curing (excluding reinforcement)						
	(i) $C_1, C_3, C_4, C_5, C_6, C_7, C_8$	7	0.3	0.225	2.75	1.26	
	$H = 3 - 0.25 = 2.75$ m						
	(ii) C_2	7	0.3	0.225	2.825	0.19	
	$H = 3 - 0.179 = 2.825$ m						
	(iii) $C_9, C_{11}, C_{14}, C_{15}$	4	0.3	0.225	2.6	0.704	
	$H = 3 - 0.4 = 2.6$ m						
	(iv) $C_{10}, C_{12}, C_{16}, C_{17}$	4	0.375	0.225	2.6	0.876	
	$H = 3 - 0.4 = 2.6$ m						
	(v) C_{13}	1	0.3	0.225	2.55	0.172	
	(vi) C_{18}, C_{19}	2	0.225	0.225	2.975	0.301	
	$H = 3 + 0.225 - 0.25 = 2.975$ m						3.493 m³
11.	Providing and casting in situ cement concrete (1 : 2 : 4) of trap metal for R.C.C. beams as per detailed designs and drawings or as directed including dewatering, centering, formwork, compaction, finishing the formed surface with cement mortar (1 : 3) of sufficient minimum thickness to give smooth and even surface or roughening if special finish is to be provided and curing (excluding steel reinforcement)						
	(i) FB_1	1	2.58	0.225	0.3	0.175	
	$L = 2.4 + 0.3375 - 0.15$						
	(ii) FB_2	1	2.5125	0.225	0.30	0.17	
	$L = 2.2 + 2 (0.15)$						
	(iii) FB_3	1	3.18	0.225	0.375	0.269	
	$L = 3 + 0.33 - 0.15$						

Sr. No.	Name of item	No.	Length L (m)	Breadth B (m)	Depth or Height H (m)	Quantity	Total
(iv)	FB$_4$	1	2.59	0.225	0.375	0.218	
	L = 2.4 + 0.33 − 0.15						
(v)	FB$_5$	1	2.51	0.225	0.375	0.22	
(vi)	FB$_6$	1	3.19	0.225	0.375	0.269	
	FB$_7$	1	4.125	0.225	0.525	0.488	
	L = 4.2 + 0.225 − 0.3						
	FB$_8$	1	4.425	0.225	0.525	0.53	
	FB$_9$	1	4.425	0.225	0.45	0.448	
	FB$_{9A}$	1	0.75	0.225	0.45	0.076	
	FB$_{10}$	1	2.325	0.225	0.525	0.275	
	L = 2.1 + 0.225 = 2.325 m^3						
	FB$_{11}$	1	4.125	0.225	0.525	0.488	
	FB$_{12}$	1	4.425	0.225	0.525	0.523	
	FB$_{13}$	1	2.10	0.225	0.3	0.14	
	FB$_{14}$	1	3.9	0.225	0.375	0.329	
	L = 3.6 + (0.15) × 2	1	4.35	0.225	0.375	0.367	
	FB$_{15}$						
	L = 4.05 + 2 (0.15)						
	FB$_{16}$	1	3.9	0.225	0.375	0.329	
	FB$_{17}$	1	2.1	0.225	0.30	0.142	
	FB$_{18}$	1	3.9	0.225	0.45	0.395	
	FB$_{19}$	1	2.325	0.225	0.3	0.175	
	FB$_{20}$	2	3.225	0.225	0.375	0.272	
	FB$_{21}$	1	3.6	0.225	0.525	0.426	
	FB$_{22}$	1	3.9	0.225	0.45	0.385	
	FB$_{23}$	1	3.6	0.225	0.375	0.304	
	FB$_{24}$	1	2.325	0.225	0.375	0.196	
	FB$_{25}$	1	4.350	0.225	0.375	0.369	
	FB$_{27}$	1	2.4	0.225	0.375	0.2025	
	L = 2.85 − 2 (0.225)	1	3.9	0.225	0.375	0.329	8.5 m^3
	FB$_{26}$						

Sr. No.	Name of item	No.	Length L (m)	Breadth B (m)	Depth or Height H (m)	Quantity	Total
12.	Providing and casting in situ. C.C. (1 : 2 : 4) of trap metal for R.C.C. (1st floor) slabs upto 12.5 cm thick to 15 cm thick as per detailed design and drawings including formwork, compacting, finsihing the formed surface with C.M. (1 : 3) of sufficient minimum thickness to give a smooth and even surface or roughening them, if special finish to be provided and curing (excluding steel reinforcement)						
	Store room – S_1	1	3.60	2.4	0.125	1.08	
	Bed – S_2	1	3.6	3.0	0.125	1.35	
	Kitchen – S_3						
	(A)	1	3.6	2.85	0.125	0.938	
	(B)	1	1.35	0.75	0.125	0.127	
	W/C and Bath – S_3 and Passage	1	3.6	2.1	0.125	0.945	
	Toilet – S_3	1	2.1	2.1	0.125	0.551	
	Canopy Slab – S_1	1	2.85	2.25	0.125	0.80	
	Pooja Room – S_5	1	2.1	1.5	0.125	0.394	
	Canopy – S_6	1	2.85	0.75	0.125	0.267	
	Master Bed – S_1	1	4.2	3.6	0.125	1.89	**8.34 m³**
	Dining and Drawing – S_4	1	8.1	4.05	0.15	4.92	**4.92 m³**
13.	Providing class II B.B. masonry with conventional sized bricks in C.M. (1 : 6) in superstructure including striking joints, facing out joints, watering and scaffolding complete						
	(A)　External walls						
	Store　–　Long wall	1	3.6	0.225	2.75	2.23	
	–　Short wall	1	2.4	0.225	2.825	1.53	
	W.C. and Bath – Short wall	1	2.22	0.225	2.825	1.41	
	Bed Rood – Long wall	1	3.6	0.225	2.75	2.23	
	–　Short wall	1	3.0	0.225	2.75	1.86	

Sr. No.	Name of item	No.	Length L (m)	Breadth B (m)	Depth or Height H (m)	Quantity	Total
	Dining and Drawing – Short wall	2	4.05	0.225	2.775	5.06	
	H = 3.15 – 0.375 = 2.775						
	Kitchen – Short wall	1	3.6	0.225	2.75	2.227	
	Pooja – Long wall	1	2.1	0.225	2.825	1.335	
	– Short wall	1	1.5	0.225	2.60	0.88	
	Toilet – Long wall	1	2.22	0.225	2.6	1.29	
	L = 2.1 + 0.12						
	Master Bed – Long wall	1	4.2	0.225	2.6	2.457	
	– Short wall	1	3.6	0.225	2.75	2.227	
	Staircase room – Long wall	2	2.1	2.225	2.75	2.58	
	– Short wall	2	0.6	2.225	2.75	0.75	**28.07 m³**
	Deduct – Door openings :						
	(i) DSF	1	2.4	0.225	2.025	1.09	
	(ii) D	1	1.05	0.225	2.025	0.478	
	(iii) D_2	1	0.75	0.225	2.025	0.342	
	Window openings :						
	(i) W	1	2.4	0.225	1.575	0.85	
	(ii) W_1	1	1.80	0.225	1.275	0.516	
	(iii) W_2	1	1.80	0.225	0.975	0.395	
	(iv) W_3	3	1.2	0.225	1.275	0.688	
	(v) W_4	3	0.6	0.225	1.275	0.516	
	(vi) W_5	1	0.9	0.225	0.9	0.183	
	(vii) W_6	2	0.6	0.225	0.9	0.243	
	(viii) W_7	2	0.45	0.225	1.9	0.385	
	Lintels						
	Above DSF	1	2.7	0.225	0.225	0.136	
	Above D	1	1.35	0.225	0.225	0.068	
	Above D_2	1	1.05	0.225	0.225	0.053	

Sr. No.	Name of item	No.	Length L (m)	Breadth B (m)	Depth or Height H (m)	Quantity	Total
	Above W	1	2.7	0.225	0.225	0.136	
	Above W_1	1	2.1	0.225	0.225	0.106	
	Above W_2	1	2.1	0.225	0.225	0.106	
	Above W_3	3	1.5	0.225	0.225	0.228	
	Above W_4	3	0.9	0.225	0.225	0.136	
	Above W_5	1	1.2	0.225	0.225	0.061	
	Above W_6	2	0.9	0.225	0.225	0.091	
	Above W_7	2	0.75	0.225	0.225	0.076	
	Note : Bearing of 15 cm on both sides.						
					Total deductions =	7.227 m^3	
					Net Total		20.84 m^3
13. (A)	Providing and casting in situ. C.C. (1 : 2 : 4) of trap metal for R.C.C. lintels as per detailed design and drawings for ground floor including centering, formwork, compaction, finishing the formed suface with C.M. (1 : 3) of sufficient minimum thick to give a smooth and even surface or roughening if special finish is to be proved curing etc. (excluding reinforcement)						
	Lintels						
	DSF	1	2.7	0.225	0.225	0.136	
	D	1	1.35	0.225	0.225	0.068	
	D_2	1	1.05	0.225	0.225	0.053	
	W	1	2.70	0.225	0.225	0.136	
	W_1	1	2.10	0.225	0.225	0.106	
	W_2	1	2.10	0.225	0.225	0.106	
	W_3	3	1.50	0.225	0.225	0.228	
	W_4	3	0.9	0.225	0.225	0.136	
	W_5	1	1.2	0.225	0.225	0.061	

Sr. No.	Name of item	No.	Length L (m)	Breadth B (m)	Depth or Height H (m)	Quantity	Total
	W_6	2	0.9	0.225	0.225	0.091	
	W_7	2	0.75	0.225	0.225	0.076	1.197 m³
	Note : 15 cm bearing on either side						
13. (B)	Providing and laying polished shahabad store flooring, 25 mm thick and 25 cm wide in plain pattern on a bed of C.M. (1 : 4) including cement float, fittings, joints with neat cement slurry, curing, polishing and cleaning complete.						
	W.C.	1	0.9	1.2	–	1.08	
	Bath	1	2.1	1.2	–	2.52	
	Toilet	1	2.1	2.1	–	4.41	8.01 m²
13. (C)	Providing and fixing white glazed tiles 148.5 × 148.5 mm @ 6.6 mm thick for dado in required positions on plaster of c.m. (1 : 4) including all sphericals required like round corner files, angles, cups etc. filling joints with white cement slurry, curing and cleaning complete.						
	Bath 1 – Long wall	2	2.1	–	1.2	5.04	
	– Short wall	2	1.2	–	1.2	2.88	
	W.C. – Long wall	2	1.2	–	1.2	2.88	
	– Short wall	2	0.9	–	1.2	2.16	
	Toilet Long wall/Short wall	4	2.1	–	1.2	10.08	23.04 m²
14.	Providing class II B.B. masonry with conventional type bricks in C.M. (1 : 4) in half brick thick wall including M.S. longitudinal reinforcement of 2 bars of 6 mm dia. placed at every third course, properly bent and bounded at ends, scaffolding, raking out joints and watering complete.						
	Store – Long wall	1	3.6	–	2.675	9.63	
	H = 3.125 – 0.45						
	W.C. – Short wall	1	0.9	–	2.10	1.89	

Sr. No.	Name of item	No.	Length L (m)	Breadth B (m)	Depth or Height H (m)	Quantity	Total
	Bath — Long wall	1	2.1	–	2.10	4.41	
	— Short wall	1	1.2	–	2.10	2.52	
	Bed — Long wall	1	3.6	–	2.675	9.63	
	Dining and Drawing						
	Long wall - (Back)	1	7.5	–	2.625	19.68	
	L = 8.1 – 2 (0.3) = 7.5 m						
	H = 3 – 0.375 = 2.625						
	Long wall (Front)	1	7.65	–	2.475	18.93	
	L = 8.1 – 0.45 = 7.65 m						
	H = 3 – 0.525 = 2.475 m						
	Kitchen — Long wall	1	3.75	–	2.475	9.28	
	Master bed — Long wall	1	4.2	–	2.47	10.37	
	— Short wall	1	3.6	–	2.55	9.18	
	Toilet — Long wall	1	2.1	–	2.7	5.67	$101.19 m^3$
	Deduct						
	Door openings						
	D_1	4	0.9	–	2.025	7.29	
	D_2	5	0.75	–	2.025	7.59	
	D_3	1	0.9	–	2.025	1.83	
	Total of deductions						$16.71 m^2$
	Net Total					$16.7 m^2$	$84.48 m^2$
15.	Providing and casting in situ C.C. (1 : 2 : 4) for R.C.C. loft of trap metal – 10 cm thick (max.) as per detailed design and drawing including formwork, compacting, finishing the formed surface with cm (1 : 3) of sufficient min. thickness to give a smooth and even surface or roughening them, if special finish to be providing and curing (excluding steel reinforcement)						

Sr. No.	Name of item	No.	Length L (m)	Breadth B (m)	Depth or Height H (m)	Quantity	Total
	Above DSF	1	2.7	0.75	0.081	0.164	
	D	1	1.35	0.75	0.081	0.082	
	D_2	1	1.05	0.75	0.081	0.064	
	W	1	2.7	0.75	0.081	0.064	
	W_1	1	2.1	0.75	0.081	0.128	
	W_2	1	2.1	0.75	0.081	0.128	
	W_3	2	1.5	0.75	0.081	0.182	
	W_4	3	0.9	0.75	0.081	0.164	
	W_7	2	0.75	0.75	0.081	0.091	**1.167 m³**
16.	Providing and casting in situ C.C. (1 : 2 : 4) for R.C.C. loft of trap metal – 10 cm thick as per detailed design and drawing including formwork, compacting, finishing the formed surface with C.M. (1 : 3) of sufficient min. thickness to give a smooth and even surface or roughening them, if special finish is to be provided and curing (excluding steel reinforcement)						
	Over W.C.	1	1.2	0.9	0.075	0.081	
	Over Bath	1	2.1	1.2	0.075	0.189	**0.270 m³**
17.	Providing sand faced plaster in C.M. (1 : 4), 25 mm thick using Kasaba or similar type of sand in all positions including base coat, scaffolding, keeping the base coat rough to receive the sand faced treatment, finishing the surface by taking outgrains and curing etc. complete						
	External – Long wall	2	14.25	–	3.0	85.5 m²	136.8 m²
	– Short wall	2	8.55	–	3.0	51.3 m²	
	Deduct – Door openings						

Sr. No.	Name of item	No.	Length L (m)	Breadth B (m)	Depth or Height H (m)	Quantity	Total
	DSF	1	2.4	–	2.025	4.86 m^2	
	D	1	1.05	–	2.025	2.12	
	D$_2$	1	0.75	–	2.025	1.52	
	W	1	2.4	–	1.575	3.78	
	W$_1$	1	1.8	–	1.275	2.295	
	W$_2$	1	1.8	–	0.975	1.76	
	W$_3$	3	1.2	–	1.275	4.59	
	W$_4$	3	0.6	–	1.275	2.295	
	W$_5$	1	0.9	–	0.9	0.81	
	W$_6$	2	0.6	–	0.9	1.08 m^2	
	W$_7$	2	0.45	–	1.9	1.71 m^2	**–25.45m^2**
	Add for jambs and sills						
	DSF	1	4.425	0.08	–	0.354	
	L = (2.025 + 2.4) = 4.425 m						
	W						
	L = 2 × 2.4 + 2 × 1.575 = 7.95 m	1	7.95	0.12	–	0.954	+ 13.08
							112.66m^2
18.	Providing cement plaster 12 mm thick in two coats in c.m. (1 : 5) without neeru furnish to concrete or brick surface in all positions including scaffolding and curing complete						
	Store – Long wall	2	3.6	–	3.0	21.6	
	– Short wall	2	2.4	–	3.0	23.04	
	– Ceiling	1	3.6	2.4	–	8.64	
	W.C. – Long wall	2	1.2	–	3.0	7.2	
	– Short wall	2	0.9	–	3.0	5.4	
	– Ceiling	1	1.2	0.9	–	1.08	
	Bath – Long wall	2	2.1	–	3.0	12.6	
	– Short wall	2	1.20	–	3.0	7.2	
	– Ceiling	1	2.1	1.2	–	2.52	
	Passage : L = 2.1 + 3 (1.2) + 0.9 + 2.4 = 9.0	1	9.0	–	3.0	27.0	
	(Perimeter of base)						

Sr. No.	Name of item		No.	Length L (m)	Breadth B (m)	Depth or Height H (m)	Quantity	Total
Ceiling	(i)		1	2.4	0.9	–	2.16	
	(ii)		1	1.2	0.9	–	1.8	
Bed	–	Long wall	2	3.6	–	3.0	21.6 m^2	
	–	Short wall	2	3.0	–	3.0	18.0 m^2	
	–	Ceiling	1	3.6	3.0	–	10.8 m^2	
Dining and Drawing	–	Long wall	2	8.1	–	3.0	48.6	
	–	Short wall	2	4.05	–	3.0	24.3	
	–	Ceiling	1	8.1	4.05	–	32.81	
Kitchen	–	Long wall	2	3.75	–	3.0	22.5	
	–	Short wall	2	3.6	–	3.0	21.6	
	–	Ceiling	1	3.75	3.6	–	13.5	
Pooja room	–	Long wall	2	2.1	-	3.0	12.6	
	_	Short wall	2	1.5	-	3.0	9.0	
	_	Ceiling	1	2.1	1.5	-	3.15	
Toilet	_	L.W./S.W.	2	2.1	-	3.0	25.2	
	_	Ceiling	1	2.1	2.1	-	4.41	
Master Bed Room								
	_	Long wall	2	4.2	-	3.0	25.2	
	_	Short wall	2	3.6	-	3.0	21.6	450.23m^3
	_	Ceiling	1	4.2	3.6	-	15.12	
Add - For Jambs and Sills								
		DSF	1	4.425	0.08	-	0.354	
L = 2 × 2.025 + 2.4 = 4.425 mW			1	7.95	0.12	9.45		+1.308m^2
L = 2 × 2.4 + 2 × 1.575 = 7.95								
Deduct								
		DSF	1	2.4	-	2.025	4.86 m^2	
One face only		D$_1$	5	0.9	-	2.025	9.15 m^2	

Sr. No.	Name of item	No.	Length L (m)	Breadth B (m)	Depth or Height H (m)	Quantity	Total
	One face only　　　D$_2$	6	0.75	-	2.025	9.12 m²	
		1	2.4	-	1.575	3.78 m²	−26.01 m²
						Net =	424.63 m²
						Say	425 m²
19.	Providing neeru finish to plastered surface in all positions including scaffolding and curing complete.						
	Same as that for internal plaster i.e. item 18						425 m²
20.	Providing and laying marble mosaic tiles of approved colour and pattern with white and coloured marble chips upto a maximum size of 6 mm for flooring required positions, set on a bed of 1 : 6 cm including neat cement float, filling the joints with coloured cement slurry, curing, polishing and rubbing complete without border and pattern of tiles of different colours and designs as directed. (Use grey cement).						
	Store Room	1	2.4	3.6	-	8.64 m²	
	Passage　　(i)	1	0.9	2.25	-	2.025	
	(ii)	1	1.2	1.35	-	1.62	
	Bed Room	1	3.0	3.6	-	10.8	
	Dinning and Drawing	1	8.1	4.05	-	32.81	
	Kitchen	1	3.75	3.6	-	13.5	
	Master Bed	1	4.20	3.6	-	15.12	
	Pooja Room	1	1.5	2.1	-	3.15	87.66 m²
21.	Providing and applying white wash in 3 coats on plastered surface or masonry including scaffolding and preparing the surface by brushing and brooming down complete.						
	Same as that for plaster i.e. Item No. 18						425 m²

Sr. No.	Name of item	No.	Length L (m)	Breadth B (m)	Depth or Height H (m)	Quantity	Total
22.	Providing and fixing C.C.T.W. door frames w/o ventilator of size 60 mm × 100 mm for doors including chamfering, rebating, hold fast of size 300 × 40 × 3 mm finishing with 3 coats of oil painting complete						
	DSF	1	6.45	0.06	0.1	0.039m³	
	D	1	5.1	0.06	0.1	0.03 m³	
	D$_1$	5	4.95	0.06	0.1	0.149m³	
	D$_2$	6	4.8	0.06	0.1	0.173m³	**0.39 m³**
22.	Providing and fixing door shutters - solid core flushed with all fixtures and fastenings of aluminium and finishing the wood work with oil painting 3 coats complete.						
(A)	DSF	1	2.40	-	2.025	4.86 m²	
	D	1	1.05	-	2.025	2.12 m²	
	D$_1$	5	0.90	-	2.025	9.15 m²	
	D$_2$	6	0.75	-	2.025	9.12 m²	**25.25 m²**
23.	Providing and fixing steel windows of various sizes as per detailed drawings without hot dip-zinc coating, w/o ventilators including fabricating, glazing with plain obsecured and of approved type of quantity and fixtures and fastenings and finishing with oil painting 2 coats complete.						
	W	1	2.4	-	1.575	3.78 m²	
	W$_1$	1	1.80	-	0.516	0.93	
	W$_2$	1	1.80	-	0.975	1.76	
	W$_3$	3	1.20	-	1.275	4.59	
	W$_4$	3	0.6	-	1.275	2.295	
	W$_5$	1	0.9	-	0.90	0.810	
	W$_6$	2	0.6	-	0.90	1.08	

Sr. No.	Name of item	No.	Length L (m)	Breadth B (m)	Depth or Height H (m)	Quantity	Total
	W_7	2	0.45	-	1.90	1.71	**16.95 m²**
24.	Providing and appling washable distemper of approved colour and shade to new surfaces in three coats including scaffolding, preparing the surfaces to receive the priming coat and finishing coat complete.		Same as that of white wash excluding total ceiling area				**425.00m²**
	Deduct ceilings First Floor					Net	**425.00m²** **32931 m³**
25.	Providing and casting in situ. C.C. of trap metal (1 : 2 : 4) for (F.F. to Roof) R.C.C columns as per detailed design and drawings or as directed including centering, form work, compaction, finishing the formed surface with c.m. (1 : 3) of sufficient min. thickness to give smooth and even surface or roughening if special surface is to be provided and curing etc. (excluding M.S. Reinforcement). Column Nos.						
	(i)　　$C_1, C_3, C_4, C_5, C_6,$	5	0.225	0.225	3.75	0.95	
	(ii)　　C_2	1	0.225	0.225	3.825	0.19	
	(iii)　$C_8, C_7,$	2	0.225	0.225	2.75	0.28	
	(iv)　C_9, C_{14}, C_{15}	3	0.225	0.225	3.6	0.55	
	(v)　　C_{10}, C_{12}	2	0.30	0.225	4.85	0.65	
	(vi)　$C_{11}, C_{13},$	2	0.225	0.225	4.85	0.49	
	(vii)　C_{16}	1	0.3	0.225	3.475	0.23	
	(viii)　C_{17}	1	0.225	0.225	3.475	0.17	**3.51 m³**
26.	Providing and casting in situ. C.C. (1 : 2 : 4) for R.C.C. Roof beams of trap metal as per detailed design and drawings or as directed including centering, formwork, compaction, finishing the formed surface with C. M. (1 : 3) with sufficient min. thick to give a smooth and even surface or roughening if special finish is to be provided and curing etc. (excluding M.S. Reinforcement) RB_1						

Sr. No.	Name of item	No.	Length L (m)	Breadth B (m)	Depth or Height H (m)	Quantity	Total
RB_1		1	2.625	0.30	0.225	0.177	
L = 2.58 + 0.0375							
	RB_2	1	2.587	0.30	0.225	0.175	
	RB_3	1	3.225	0.375	0.225	0.272	
	RB_4	1	2.625	0.225	0.375	0.221	
	RB_5	1	2.587	0.225	0.375	0.22	
	RB_6	1	3.225	0.225	0.375	0.272	
L = 3.187 + 0.037							
	RB_7	1	4.613	0.225	0.525	0.491	
	RB_8	1	4.463	0.225	0.520	0.530	
	RB_9	1	4.46	0.225	0.450	0.452	
L = 4.425 + 0.0375							
	RB_{9A}	1		0.225	0.450	0.079	
	RB_{10}	1		0.225	0.525	0.275	
	RB_{11}	1		0.225	0.525	0.492	
	RB_{12}	1		0.225	0.525	0.527	
	RB_{13}	1		0.225	0.300	0.149	
L = 2.1 + 0.75							
	RB_{14}	1		0.225	0.375	0.335	
	RB_{15}	1		0.225	0.375	0.373	
	RB_{16}	1		0.225	0.375	0.335	
	RB_{17}	1		0.225	0.300	0.142	
	RB_{18}	1		0.225	0.450	0.395	
	RB_{19}	1		0.225	0.30	0.157	
	RB_{20}	1		0.225	0.375	0.272	
	RB_{21}	1		0.225	0.525	0.426	
	RB_{22}	1		0.225	0.450	0.395	

Sr. No.	Name of item	No.	Length L (m)	Breadth B (m)	Depth or Height H (m)	Quantity	Total
	L = 3.6 + 0.0375						
	RB$_{23}$	1		0.625	0.375	0.310	
	RB$_{24}$	1		0.225	0.375	0.202	
	RB$_{25}$	1	4.425	0.255	0.375	0.313	
	RB$_{26}$	1	3.70	0.255	0.375	0.332	823 m^3
27.	Providing and casting in situ. C.C. (1 : 2 : 4) of trap metal for roof slabs of thickness 12.5 cm/ 15 cm as per detailed design and drawing, including formwork, compacting, finishing the formed surface with C.M. 1 : 3 of suff. min. thickness to give a smooth and even surface or roughhening if special finish is to be provided and curing (excluding M.S. reinforcement)						
	(A) 12.5 cm thick						
	Store - S$_1$	1	3.6	2.4	0.125	1.08	
	Bed - S$_2$	1	3.6	3.0	0.125	1.35	
	Kitchen - S$_3$						
	(i)	1	3.6	2.85	0.125	0.938	
	(ii)	1	1.35	0.75	0.125	0.127	
	W.C./Bath S$_3$	1	3.6	2.1	0.125	0.945	
	Toilet S$_3$	1	2.1	2.1	0.125	0.551	
	Pooja Room - S$_5$	1	2.1	1.5	0.125	0.395	
	Master Bed S$_1$	1	4.2	3.6	0.125	1.89	7.275 m^3
	(B) 15 cm thick Dining and Drawing	1	8.1	4.05	0.15	4.92	4.920 m^3
28.	Providing Class II B.B. masonry with conventional bricks in cm (1 : 6) in superstructure incl. striking joints, facing out joints, watering and scaffolding complete.						
	External walls						
	Store - Long wall	1	3.712	0.225	2.750	2.30	

Sr. No.	Name of item		No.	Length L (m)	Breadth B (m)	Depth or Height H (m)	Quantity	Total
		- Short wall	1	2.44	0.225	2.825	1.55	
	W.C./Bath	- Short wall	1	2.29	0.225	2.825	1.45	
	Bed	- Long wall	1	3.713	0.225	2.750	2.30	
		- Short wall	1	3.04	0.225	2.750	1.88	
	Dining and Drawing							
		- Short wall	2	4.125	0.225	2.775	5.15	
	Kitchen	- Short wall	1	3.675	0.225	2.75	2.27	
	Pooja	- Long wall	1	2.213	0.225	2.825	1.40	
		- Short wall	1	1.50	0.225	2.60	0.878	
	Toilet	- Short wall	1	1.533	0.225	2.60	0.897	
	Master bed	- L.W.	1	4.237	0.225	2.60	2.48	
		- S.W.	1	3.72	0.225	2.75	2.297	
	Stair Room	- L.W.	2	2.175	0.225	2.75	2.70	
		- S.W.	2	0.6	0.225	2.75	0.75	
	Parapet wall	- 1 m high	1	38.625	0.225	1.00	8.69	
								36.96 m³
	Deduct							
	Door openings							
		D_2	1	0.75	0.225	2.025	0.34	
	Window openings							
		W	2	2.40	0.225	1.575	1.700	
		W_1	1	1.80	0.225	1.275	0.520	
		W_2	1	1.80	0.225	0.975	0.395	
		W_3	3	1.20	0.225	1.275	1.033	
		W_4	3	0.60	0.225	1.275	0.520	
		W_5	1	0.90	0.225	0.90	0.180	
		W_6	2	0.60	0.225	0.90	0.243	

Sr. No.	Name of item	No.	Length L (m)	Breadth B (m)	Depth or Height H (m)	Quantity	Total
						$-4.93m^3$	
					Net	$32.05m^3$	
	Deduct						
	Lintels						
	Above D_2	1	1.05	0.225	0.225	0.053	
	W	2	2.70	0.225	0.225	0.270	
	W_1	1	2.10	0.225	0.225	0.110	
	W_2	1	2.10	0.225	0.225	0.106	
	W_3	3	1.50	0.225	0.225	0.228	
	W_4	3	0.9	0.225	0.225	0.136	
	W_5	1	1.20	0.225	0.225	0.06	
	W_6	2	0.90	0.225	0.225	0.091	
						-1.068	
	Note : Bearing of 15 cm on either side				Net	**30.99m³**	
29.	Providing Class II BB Masonry with Conv. Brick in C.M. (1 : 4) in 1/2 Brick thick wall incl. mild steel long reinfocement of 2 bars of 6 mm dia. placed at every third course properly bent and bounded at ends scaffolding, raking of joints and watering etc. complete.						
	Same as that for ground floor i.e.				Net	**84.48m²**	
30.	Providing and casting in situ. C.C. (1 : 2 : 4) of trap metal for R.C.C. chajjas for 1st floor 10 cm thick as per detailed design and drawing incl. formwork, compaction and finishing the formed surface with C.M. (1 : 3) of suff. min. thickness to give and even surface or roughening if special finish to be provided and curing etc. complete. (excl. M.S. Reinforcement)						
	Same as that for ground floor i.e.				Net	**1.167m²**	

Sr. No.	Name of item	No.	Length L (m)	Breadth B (m)	Depth or Height H (m)	Quantity	Total
31.	Providing and casting insitu C.C. (1 : 2: 4) or trap metal for R.C.C. Lofts for 1st floor 10 cm thick as per detailed design and drawing incl. formwork, compaction and finishing the formed surface with C.M. (1 : 3) of sufficient min. thickness or to give a smooth surface or roughening for special finish and curing etc. (excl. M.S. Reinforcement)						
	Same as that for ground floor i.e.					Net	0.270 m^2
32.	Providing sand faced plaster in C.M. (1 : 4) 25 mm thick using kasaba or simllar type of sand in all positions incl. base coat, scaffolding, keeping the surface of base coat rough to receive the sand faced treatment. Finishing the surface by taking out grains and curing complete. Same as that for ground floor except the deduction for D.S.F.						
	Deduct						
	W instead of						
	DSF and add sill					117.46m^2	
	W	1	2.4	-	1.575	−3.76m^3	
	Add for parapet wall						
	L = 2 (14.25) + 2 (8.55)	2	45.6	-	1.00	+91.2m^2	
	∴ Total Plaster						204.88m^2
33.	Providing cement plaster 12 mm thick in double coat in C.M. (1 : 5) w/o neeru finish to conc. or brick surface in all positions including scaffolding and curing complete.						
	Same as that for ground floor.					Net	4.25 m^2
34.	Providing neeru finish to plastered surface in all positions including scaffolding and curing complete.						
	Same as that for internal plaster					Net	4.25 m^2

Sr. No.	Name of item	No.	Length L (m)	Breadth B (m)	Depth or Height H (m)	Quantity	Total
35.	Providing and laying marble mosaic tiles of approved colour and pattern with white and coloured marble chips upto max. size of 6 mm for flooring, required positions set on a bed of 1 : 6 cm including neat cement float filling the joints with coloured cement slurry curing, polishing and rubbing complete w/o border and pattern of tiles of different colour and design as directed in gray cement.						
	Same as that for ground floor					Net	87.66 m²
36.	Providing and applying white washing, three coats on plastered surface or masonry surface inlcuding scaffolding and preparing the surface by brushing and brooming down complete.						
	Same as that for Plaster						425 m²
37.	Providing and fixing C.C.T.W. door frames without ventilator of size 60 mm × 100 mm for doors including chamfering, rebating, hold fast of size 300 × 40 × 3 mm finishing with 3 coats of oil painting complete.						
	D_1	6	4.95	0.06	0.1	0.1782	
	D_2	4	4.80	0.06	0.1	0.1152	0.2934m³
38.	Providing and fixing steel windows of various sizes as per detailed design and drawings w/o hot dip-zinc coating, w/o ventilators including fabricating, glazing with plain obscured glass and of approved type and quantity and fixtures and fastenings and finishing with oil paint in two coats.						
	W	2	2.4	-	1.575	7.56 m²	
	W_1	1	1.85	-	0.516	0.93	
	W_3	4	1.2	-	1.275	6.12	
	W_4	2	0.6	-	1.275	1.53	

Sr. No.	Name of item	No.	Length L (m)	Breadth B (m)	Depth or Height H (m)	Quantity	Total
	W$_5$	1	0.9	-	0.9	0.81	
	W$_6$	2	0.6	-	0.9	1.08	**16.59 m²**
39.	Providing and applying washable distemper of approved colour and shade to new surfaces in 3 coats including scaffolding, preparing the surfaces to receive the priming coat and finishing coat complete. Same as internal white-wash quantity except ceilings.						**329.31m²**
40.	Providing and casting in situ cement concrete (1 : 4 : 8) of trap metal for R.C.C. lintels as per detailed designs and drawings including centering, formwork, finishing the formed surface with cm (1 : 3) of suff. min. thick to give a smooth and even surface or roughening if special finish is to be provided and curing etc. (excluding M.S. reinforcement). Same as that for ground floor						**1.197 m³**
40. (A)	Providing and laying polished shahabad flooring 2.5 cm thick and 25/30 cm wide in plain/dia. pattern on a bed of C.M. 1 : 4 incl. cement float, filling joints with neat cement slurry, curing, polishing and cleaning complete. (for W.C., bath, toilet) Same as that for ground floor						**8.01 m³**
40. (B)	Providing and fixing white glazed tiles 148.5 × 148.5 in size and 6.6 mm thick for flooring (dado) in required positions laid on a bed of 1 : 4 cm incl. neat cement float, add special sperial required like round corner, angles, cups, fillings joints with neat cement slurry, curing and cleaning complete.						

Sr. No.	Name of item	No.	Length L (m)	Breadth B (m)	Depth or Height H (m)	Quantity	Total
	Same as that for ground floor						**25.04 m²**
41.	Providing and fixing 3 cm thick solid core flush doors with fixtures and fastenings including 3 coats of oil paint etc. complete with Aluminium fastenings						
	D_1	6	0.9	-	2.025	10.935	
	D_2	4	0.75	-	2.025	6.075	
							17.01 m²
42.	STAIRCASE						
	Providing and casting in situ. C.C. (1 : 2 : 4) of trap metal for R.C.C. stair (landing + steps) as per detailed design and drawing, including centering, formwork and finishing the surface with C.M. (1 : 3) of sufficient min. thickness to give a smooth and even surface or roughening if a special finish is to be provided and curing etc. (excl. M.S. Reinforcement)						
	(A)　Landing						
	(i)　(0.75 m wide)	2	2.1	0.75	0.15	0.470	
	(ii)　2nd Type　(a)	2	2.1	1.2	0.15	0.76	**1.83 m³**
	(b)	2	1.92	1.05	0.15	0.60	
	(B)　Steps (R = 0.16 m, T = 0.27)	36	0.975	A=0.0216		0.758	**0.758 m³**
	$A = \frac{1}{2} \times 0.27 \times 0.16 = 0.0216$						
	(C)　Waist Slab						
	(i)　$L = \sqrt{2.1^2 + 3.5^2} = 4.1$ m	2	4.1	0.975	0.15	1.2	
	(i)　$L = \sqrt{0.9^2 + 1.35^2}$	2	1.62	0.975	0.15	0.46	**1.66 m³**
							4.25 m³
	(D)　Pardi (R.C.C.)	1	14.08	0.075	1.0	1.05 m³	
	L = 2 (3.50) + 2 (1.72) + 2 (1.62) = 14.08						

Sr. No.	Name of item	No.	Length L (m)	Breadth B (m)	Depth or Height H (m)	Quantity	Total
					Total R.C.C. for Stair =		5.3 m³
43.	Providing cement plaster 12 mm thick in 2 coats in C.M. without neeru finish, to concrete or brick surface in all positions incl. scaffolding and curing complete.						
(A)	Stair Room - Long wall	2	4.2	-	8.25	69.3 m²	
	- Short wall	2	2.1	-	8.25	34.65m²	112.77m²
	- Ceiling	1	4.2	2.1	-	8.82 m²	
	Deduct						
	Door Openings						
	D	1	1.05	-	2.025	2.13	
	D₁	5	0.9	-	2.025	9.11	
	D₂	1	0.75	-	2.025	1.52	
						−12.76m²	
					Net	100.01m²	
(B)	R.C.C. Pardi (2 faces)	2	14.08	-	1.0	28.16m²	28.16 m²
(C)	Stair Slab	1	14.08	1.05		14.78m²	
(D)	Landings - from below						
	Type 1	2	2.1	1.2		5.04 m²	
	Type 2	2	0.75	2.1		3.15 m²	8.19 m²
						Total	151.13m²
44.	Providing neeru finish to plastered surface in all positions incl. scaffolding and curing complete Same as that for plaster					=	151.13m²
45.	Providing and applying white washing in three coats on plastered surface incl. scaffolding and preparing the surface by brushing and brooming down complete. Same as that for plaster					=	151.13m²
46.	Providing and applying washable distemper of approved colour shade to new surface in 3 coats including scaffolding, preparing the surface to receive the priming coat and finishing coat complete.						
	(A) Stair Room						
	Long Wall	2	4.2	-	8.25	69.3 m²	
	Short Wall	2	2.1	-	8.25	34.65m²	103.95m²
	Deduct -						

Sr. No.	Name of item	No.	Length L (m)	Breadth B (m)	Depth or Height H (m)	Quantity	Total
	D	1	1.05	-	2.025	2.13	−12.76m²
	D$_1$	5	0.9	-	2.025	9.11	
	D$_2$	1	0.75	-	2.025	1.52	
	(B) Pardi (R.C.C.)	2	14.08	-	1.0	28.16m²	
					Total Distemper		119.35m²
47.	Providing and laying polished shahabad stone flooring 25 mm to 30 cm thick and 30 mm wide in plain pattern on a bed of 1.6 C.M. including cement float, filling joints with neat cement slurry, curing, polishing and cleaning complete.						
	(A) Steps	36	0.975	0.27	-	9.47 m²	
	(B) Landings (i)	2	2.1	0.75	-	2.48	
	(ii)	2	2.1	1.2	-	5.04	
	(iii)	2	1.92	0.975	-	3.75	20.75 m²
48.	STEEL Providing and fixing in position mild steel bar reinforcement of various diameters for R.C.C. footings, foundations, slabs, beams, columns, canopies, staircases, chajja, lintels, pardis, couplings, fins, arches, etc. as per detailed design, drawings and schedules, incl. cutting, bending, hooking the bars, binding with wires or tack wedding and supporting as required complete.						

(A)   Upto Plinth

Total Qty. of concrete

$=$ 5.191 m³   (footings)

$+$ 1.38 m³   (columns)

$+$ 4.58 m³   (plinth beams)

11.15 m³

$\therefore$ Volume of steel $(0.115 \times 7850) \times 10^{-3}$ $=$ 0.875 tonnes

$=$ 1 % of 11.15

$=$ 0.115 m³

(B)   Upto First Floor

Total quantity of concrete

$=$ 3.493 m³   (column)

$+$ 8.5 m³   (beam)

$+$ 13.26 m³   (slab)

$+$ 0.270 m³   (loft)

$+$ 1.197 m³   (lintels)

Sr. No.	Name of item	No.	Length L (m)	Breadth B (m)	Depth or Height H (m)	Quantity	Total
	+ <u>1.167 m³</u> (chajjas) 27.887 m³ ∴ Vol. of steel 1 % of 27.887 = 0.27887 m³		$(0.27887 \times 7850)/1000$			2.189 tonnes	
	(C) Upto roof level Total concrete = 3.51 m³ (columns) + 8.23 m³ (beams) + 12.195 m³ (slabs) + 0.270 m³ (lofts) + 1.197 m³ (lintels) + <u>1.167 m³</u> (chajjas) 26.569 m³ ∴ Vol. of steel 1 % of 26.569 = 0.26569 m³		$(0.26569 \times 7850)/1000$			2.085 tonnes	
	(D) Stair (R.C.C.) + R.C.C. pardi Volume of concrete = 5.3 m³ ∴ Vol. of steel 1 % of 5.3 = 0.053 m³		$(0.053 \times 7850)/1000$			0.416 tonnes	
					Total	**5866 tonnes**	
49.	Providing and laying water proofing treatement with average thickness of 10 cm injecting the water proofing compound, containing the treatment to inner side of parapet or adjoining wall (A) (B) Parapet wall L = 2(13.8 + 8.1) Deduct : - Stair Room	1 1 1	13.8 43.8 4.2	8.1 - 2.1	- 1.0 -	111.78m² 43.8 m² 155.58m² −8.82m²	
					Net	**146.76m²**	

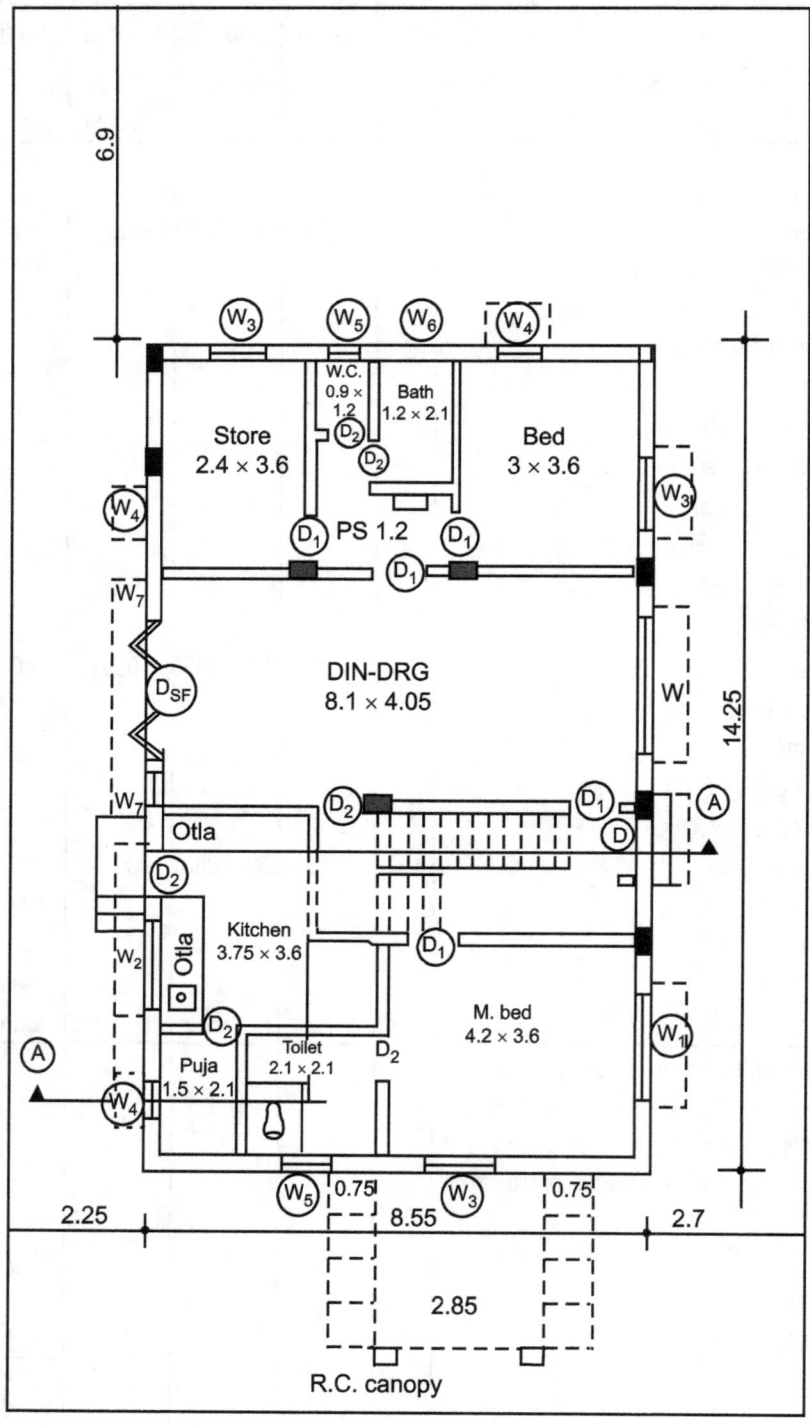

Fig. 3.36 : Ground Floor Plan

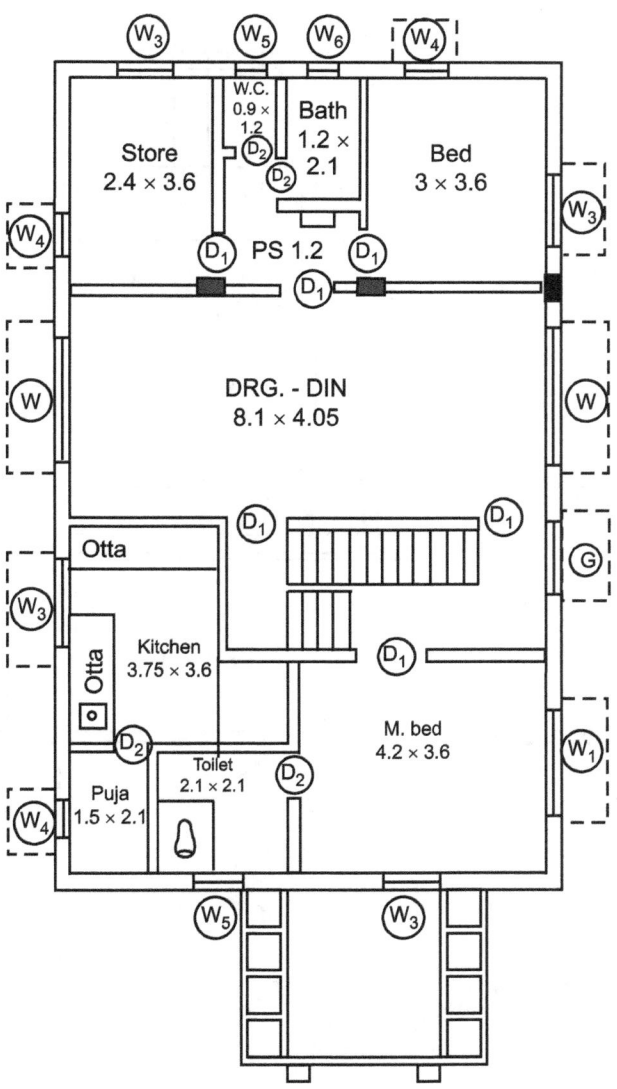

Fig. 3.37 : First Floor Plan

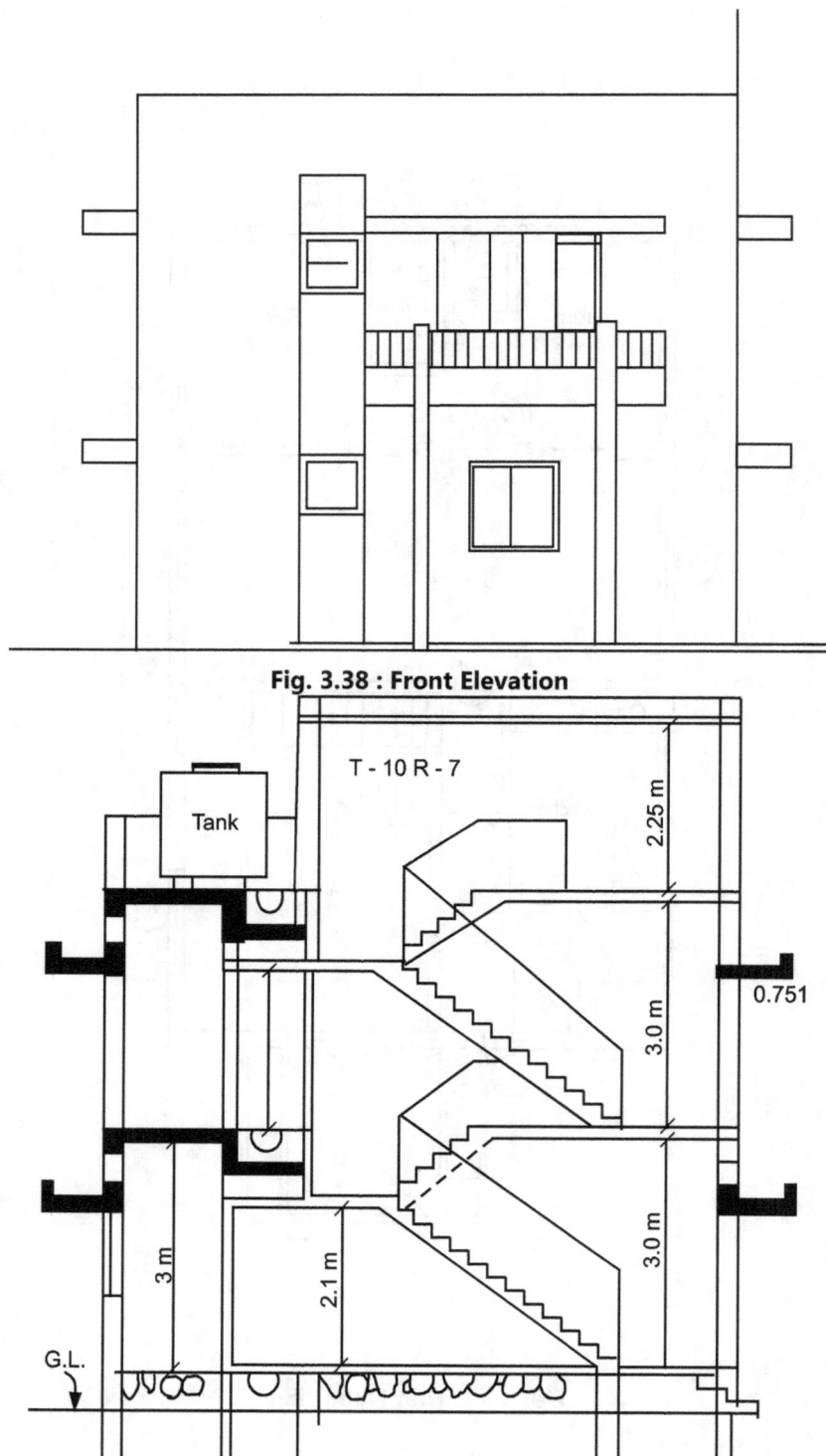

Fig. 3.38 : Front Elevation

Fig. 3.39 : Section A-A

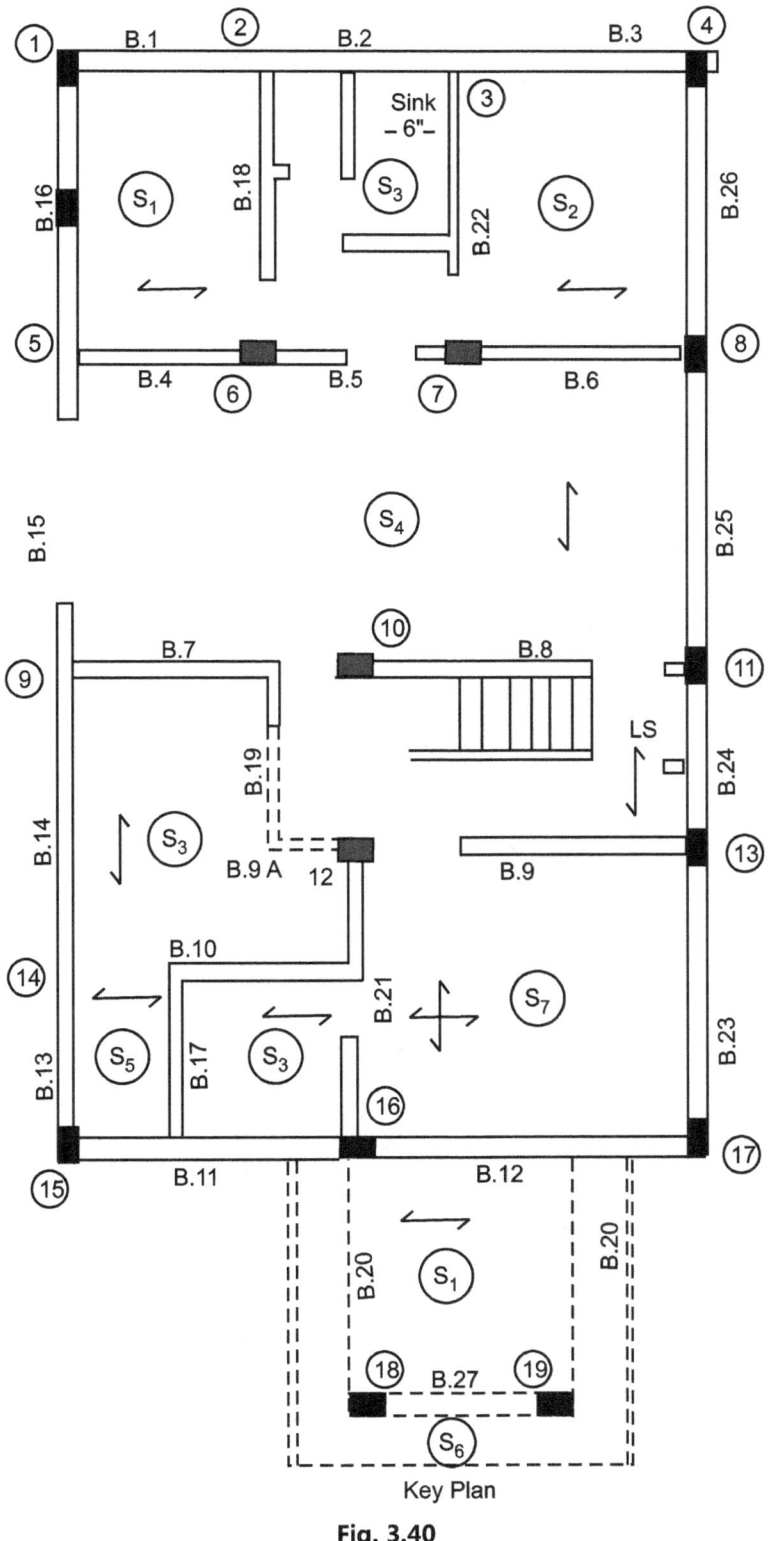

Fig. 3.40

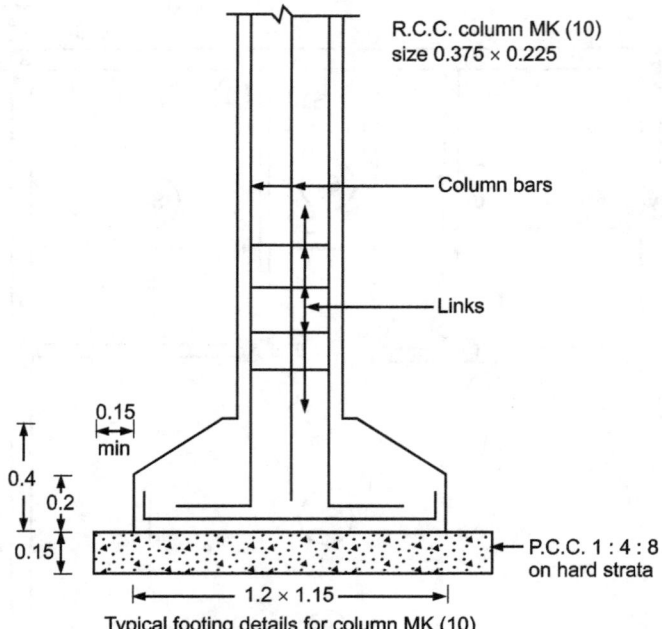

R.C.C. column MK (10)
size 0.375 × 0.225

Column bars

Links

0.15 min

0.4
0.2
0.15

P.C.C. 1 : 4 : 8
on hard strata

1.2 × 1.15

Typical footing details for column MK (10)

Fig. 3.41 (a)

0.375

0.15

External on masonry

0.225

0.225

Internal on soling

Fig. 3.41 (b)

DOORS AND WINDOWS			
		W	2.4 × 1.575
D_5	2.4 × 2.025	W_1	1.8 × 1.275
D	1.05 × 2.025	W_2	1.8 × 0.975
D_1	0.9 × 2.025	W_3	1.2 × 1.275
D_2	0.75 × 2.025	W_4	0.6 × 1.275
		W_5	0.9 × 0.9
		W_6	0.6 × 0.9
		W_7	0.45 × 1.899

Fig. 3.41 (c)

BEAM - SIZES			
Beam		Beam	
MK	Size	MK	Size
FB - 1	0.3×0.225	FB - 15	0.375×0.225
FB - 2	0.3×0.225	FB - 16	0.375×0.225
FB - 3	0.375×0.225	FB - 16 A	0.375×0.225
FB - 4	0.375×0.225	FB - 17	0.3×0.225
FB - 5	0.375×0.225	FB - 18	0.45×0.225
FB - 6	0.375×0.225	FB - 18 A	0.375×0.225
FB - 7	0.575×0.225	FB - 19	0.30×0.225
FB - 8	0.575×0.225	FB - 20	0.375×0.225
FB - 9A	0.45×0.225	FB - 21	0.525×0.225
FB - 9	0.45×0.225	FB - 22	0.45×0.225
FB - 10	0.525×0.225	FB - 23	0.375×0.225
FB - 11	0.525×0.225	FB - 24	0.375×0.225
FB - 12	0.525×0.225	FB - 25	0.375×0.225
FB - 13	0.3×0.225	FB - 26	0.375×0.225
FB - 14	0.375×0.225	FB - 27	0.375×0.225

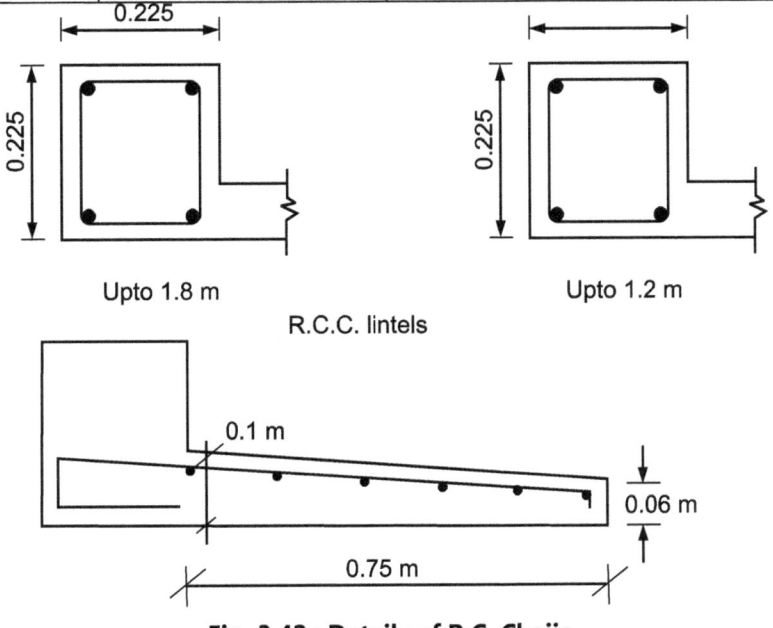

Upto 1.8 m   Upto 1.2 m

R.C.C. lintels

Fig. 3.42 : Details of R.C. Chajja

Table 3.1

Schedule of R.C. Columns and Footings (Ground + 1 Upper)

18, 19	10, 12, 16	2, 3, 6, 7, 8, 9, 11, 13, 14, 17	1, 4, 5, 15	Column Mark
0.225×0.225	0.375×0.225	0.3×0.225	0.3×0.225	Size upto 1st slab
4 - 12 HT	6 - 12 HT	6 - 12 HT	4 - 12 HT	Reinforcement Links
6 φ @ 6" c/c	6 φ @ 6" c/c In Pairs	6 φ @ 6" c/c In Pairs	6 φ @ 6" c/c	
$0.75 \times 0.75 \times 0.3$	$1.2 \times 1.05 \times 0.4 - 0.2$	$0.975 \times 0.9 \times 0.4 \times 0.2$	$0.9 \times 0.625 \times 0.3$	Footing
8 HT @ 6" c/c each way	8 HT @ $4\frac{1}{2}$" c/c each way	8 HT @ $4\frac{1}{2}$" c/c each way	8 HT @ 5" c/c each way	Footing Reinforcement
	0.3×0.225	0.225×0.225	0.225×0.225	Size upto Roof
	4 - 12 HT 6 φ @ 6" c/c	4 - 12 HT 6 φ @ 6" c/c	4 - 12 HT 6 φ @ 6" c/c	Reinforcement Links

Table 3.2

Schedule for R.C. Slabs

| Type | Thickness | Main Steel | | Distribution | Remark |
		Short Steel	Long Steel		
S - 1	0.125 m	8 HT @ 6" c/c A.B. BENT		6 φ @ 6" c/c	One Way
S - 2	0.125 m	8 HT @ 5" c/c A.B. BENT		6 φ @ 6" c/c	One Way
S - 3	0.125 m	8 HT @ 4" c/c A.B. BENT		6 φ @ 6" c/c	One Way
S - 4	0.15 m	10 HT @ 5" c/c A.B. BENT		$6\phi @ 4\frac{1}{2}"$ c/c	One Way
S - 5	0.125 m	8 HT @ 8" c/c A.B. BENT		6 φ @ 6" c/c	One Way
S - 6	0.125 m	8 HT @ 5" c/c Top Face Only		6 φ @ 6" c/c	0.75 m Cant
S - 7	0.125 m	8 HT @ 6" c/c A.B. BENT	8 HT @ 7 c/c A.B. BENT	6 φ @ 6" c/c	Two Way
S - 8	0.125 m	8 HT @ 4" c/c Top Face Only		6 φ @ 6" c/c	1.2 m Cant Bal
LS	0.15 m	8 HT @ 4" c/c A.B. BENT		$6\phi @ 4\frac{1}{2}"$ c/c	Landing Slab One Way

3.8.14 Estimate of a Two Storeyed Building

Abstract Sheet

Item No.	Description	Quan.	Rate ₹	Rate Ps.	Per	Amount ₹	Amount Ps.
1.	Cleaning the site, before and after the work, including removal of debris and shrubs etc.			- Lump sum -		300	00
2.	Excavation for foundation in soil upto a depth of 1.5 m including removing the excavated material, upto a distance of 50 m, beyond the building area and all lift, stacking and spreading as directed dewatering, shoring, strutting, preparing the bed for foundation and necessary backfilling complete.	53.90 m³	23	10	m³	1245	09
3.	Providing and laying in situ cement concrete of trap metal for foundation and including dewatering, formwork, compacting and curing etc. C.M. (1 : 3 : 6)	6.593 m³	720	00	m³	4746	96
4.	Providing and casting cement concrete (1 : 2 : 4) of trap metal of R.C.C. footings as per detailed design and drawings or as directed including, dewatering, centering, formwork, compaction, finishing with C.M. (1 :3) and curing complete	5.191 m³	980	00	m³	5087	18
5.	Providing and casting in situ cement (1 : 2 : 4) of trap metal for R.C.C. columns as per detailed design and drawings or as directed including, centering, formwork, compaction, finishing with C.M. (1 : 3) and curing etc. complete (excluding reinforcement).	1.38 m³	1420	00	m³	1959	60
6.	Providing U.C.R. masonry of trap stones in cm (1 : 6) in foundation and plinth of walls including striking joints on exposed faces.	22.11 m³	423	00	m³	9352	89
7.	Providing and casting a situ C.C. (1 : 2 : 4) of trap metal for R.C.C. plinth beams as per detailed design and drawings or as directed including dewatering, centering, formwork, compaction and finishing with C.M. (1 : 3) and curing etc. complete.	4.58 m³	1300	00	m³	5954	00
8.	Filling in between plinth and floor in layers of :						

Item No.	Description	Quan.	Rate		Per	Amount	
			₹	Ps.		₹	Ps.
	(A) Rubble soling (15 - 23 cm) thick including hand packing.	23.7 m³	90	00	m³	2133	00
	(B) Murum (15 - 30 cm thick) including watering and compaction, etc. complete.	31.59 m³	35	00	m³	1105	65
9.	Providing and laying in situ. C.C. of trap metal for bedding, including, dewatering, formwork, compaction and curing etc. complete (1 : 3 : 6).	8.10 m³	720	00	m³	5832	00
10.	Providing and casting in situ cement concrete (1 : 2 : 4) of trap metal for R.C.C. columns, from plinth level to first floor level, as per detailed designs and drawings or as directed including, centering formwork, compaction and finishing with C.M. (1 : 3) and curing etc. complete.	3.493 m³	1420	00	m³	4960	06
11.	Providing and casting in situ C.C. (1 : 2 : 4) of trap metal for R.C.C. beams as per design and drawings or as directed including centering, formwork, compaction and finishing with C.M. (1 : 3) and curing etc. complete.	8.5 m³	1300	00	m³	11050	00
12.	Providing and casting in situ (C.C.) (1 : 2 : 4) of trap metal for R.C.C. slab (first floor) as per detailed design and drawings including centering, formwork, compaction and finishing with C.M. (1 : 3) and curing etc. complete.						
	(A) 12.5 cm thick	8.34 m³	1380	00	m³	11509	20
	(B) 15 cm thick	4.92 m³	1380	00	m³	6789	60
13.	Providing B.B. Masonry with (Class II) with conventional bricks in C.M. (1 : 6) in super-structure, including striking joints, raking out joints, watering and scaffolding complete.	20.84 m³	728	00	m³	15171	52
13 (A)	Providing and casting in situ C.C. (1 : 2 : 4) of trap metal for R.C.C. lintels as per detailed designs and drawings or as directed for ground floor including centering, form work, compaction and finishing with C.M. (1 : 3) and curing etc. complete	1.197 m³	1300	00	m³	1566	10

Item No.	Description	Quan.	Rate		Per	Amount	
			₹	Ps.		₹	Ps.
13 (B)	Providing and laying polished shahabad stone flooring, 25 mm thick and 25-30 cm wide in plain pattern on a bed of 1 : 6 cm, including cement float, filling joints with heat cement slurry, curing, polishing and cleaning complete.	8.01 m²	160	00	m²	1521	90
13 (C)	Providing and fixing white glazed tiles 148.5 × 148.5 mm size and 5 to 6 mm thick for dado in required positions on plaster 1 : 4 cm including round corner files, angles, cups etc., filling joints with white cement slurry, curing and cleaning etc. complete	23.04 m²	354	00	m²	8156	16
14.	Providing B.B. Masonry, Class II (internal walls) with conventional type bricks in C.M. (1 : 4) in $\frac{1}{2}$ brick thick wall including m.s. longitudinal reinforcement of 2 nos. 6 mm φ, placed at every third course, properly bent and bounded at end, scaffolding, raking out joints and watering complete.	84.48	128	00	m²	10813	44
15.	Providing and casting in situ. C.C. (1 : 2 : 4) of trap metal for R.C.C. chajjas 10 cm thick. (max.) as per detailed designs and drawings or as directed including centering, formwork, compaction and finishing with C.M. (1 : 3) and curing etc. complete.	1.167 m³	1300	00	m³	1517	10
16.	Providing and casting in situ C.C. (1 : 2: 4) for R.C.C. lofts as per detailed design and drawings or as directed including centering, formwork, compaction and finishing with C.M. (1 : 3) and curing etc. complete	0.270 m³	1300	00	m³	351	00
17.	Providing sand faced plaster in C.M. (1 : 4) 25 mm thick using kasaba sand or similar type in all positions including base coat, scaffolding, keeping the surface of base coat rough to receive the sand faced treatment, finishing the surface by taking out grains and curing etc. complete.	112.66 m²	78	30	m²	8821	28

Item No.	Description	Quan.	Rate		Per	Amount	
			₹	Ps.		₹	Ps.
18.	Providing cement plaster 12 mm thick in two coats in C.M. (1 : 5) w/o neeru finish to concrete or brick surface in all positions including scaffolding and curing complete.	425 m²	24	00	m²	10200	00
19.	Providing neeru finish to plastered surface in all positions including scaffolding and curing complete.	425 m²	7	90	m²	3357	75
20.	Providing and laying marble, mosaic tiles of approved colour and pattern with white and coloured marble chips upto a max. size of 6 mm for flooring required positions, set on a bed of 1 : 6 (cm) including neat cement float, filling the joints with coloured (gray) cement, slurry, curing, polishing and rubbing complete, w/o border and/or of tiles of different colours and design as directed.	87.66 m²	220	00	m²	1928	52
21.	Providing and applying white wash in 3 coats on plastered surface or masonry surface including scaffolding and preparing the surface by brushing and brooming down complete.	425 m²	2	60	m²	1105	00
22.	Providing and fixing C.C. T.W. door frames w/o ventilator of size 60 × 100 mm, for door including chamfering, rebating, hold fast of size 300 × 40 × 3 mm finishing with 3 coats of oil painting complete.	0.39 m³	18000	00	m³	7020	00
22 (A)	Providing and fixing solid core flushed door shutters with all fixtures and fastenings of aluminium and finishing the wood work with 3 coats of oil paint complete.	25.25 m²	1100	00	m²	27775	00
23.	Providing and fixing steel windows of various sizes as per detailed drawings w/o hot dip-zinc coating, w/o ventilators, including fabricating, glazing with plain obscured glass and of approved type and quantity and fixtures and fastenings and finishing with oil paint 2 coats complete.	16.95 m²	1000	00	m²	16960	00

Item No.	Description	Quan.	Rate		Per	Amount	
			₹	Ps.		₹	Ps.
24.	Providing and applying washable distemper of approved colour and shade to new surfaces in 3 coats, including scaffolding, preparing the surface to receive the priming coat and finishing coat comp.	329.31 m²	6	00	m²	1975	86
	FIRST FLOOR						
25.	Providing and casting in situ. C.C. (1 : 2 : 4) of trap metal for R.C.C. columns as per detailed designs and drawings or as directed including centering, formwork, compaction and finishing with C.M. (1 : 3) and curing etc. complete	3.51 m³	1435	00	m³	5036	85
26.	Providing and casting in situ. C.C. (1 : 2 : 4) of trap metal for R.C.C. Roof Beams as per detailed designs and drawings or as directed, incl. centering, formwork, compaction and finishing with C.M. (1 : 4) and curing etc. complete.	8.23 m³	1315	00	m³	10822	45
27.	Providing and casting in situ C.C. (1 : 2 : 4) of trap metal for R.C.C. slab (roof) as per detailed design and drawing or as directed including centering, formwork, compaction and finishing with C.M. (1 :3) and curing etc. complete.						
	(A) 12.5 cm thick	7.275 m³	1395	00	m³	10148	62
	(B) 15 cm thick	4.920 m³	1395	00	m³	6853	40
28.	Providing B.B. Masonry (II class) in C.M. (1 : 6) with conventional bricks in superstructure including strutting joints, facing out joints, watering and scaffolding complete.	30.99 m³	743	00	m³	23025	57
29.	Providing B.B. Masonry (IInd class) with conventional bricks in C.M. (1 : 4) in 1/2 brick thick wall including M.S. longitudinal reinforcement of 2 Nos. 6 mm ϕ placed at every third course properly bent and bonded at ends, scaffolding, raking of joints and watering etc. complete.	84.48 m²	132	00	m²	11151	36

Item No.	Description	Quan.	Rate ₹	Rate Ps.	Per	Amount ₹	Amount Ps.
30.	Providing and casting in situ C.C. (1 : 2 : 4) of trap metal for R.C.C. chajjas for 1st floor as per detailed design and drawings or as directed including centering, fromwork, compaction, finishing the surface with C.M. (1 : 3) and curing etc. complete.	1.167 m³	1315	00	m³	1534	60
31.	Providing and casting in situ. C.C. (1 : 2 : 4) of trap metal for R.C.C. lofts as per detailed design and drawings or as directed including centering, formwork, compaction and finishing the surface with C.M. (1 : 3) and curing etc. complete.	0.27 m³	1315	00	m³	355	05
32.	Providing sand faced plaster in C.M. (1 : 4) 25 mm thick using Kasaba or simillar type of sand in all positions including base coat, scaffolding, keeping the surface of base coat rough to receive the sand faced treatment, and finishing the surface by taking out grains and curing complete.	204.88 m²	83	50	m²	17107	48
33.	Providing cement plaster 12 mm thick in double coat in cm (1 : 5) w/o neeru finish to concrete or brick surfaces in all positions including scaffoldings and curing complete.	425 m²	27	00	m²	11475	00
34.	Providing neeru finish to plastered surface in all positions including scaffolding and curing complete.	425 m²	11	00	m²	4675	00
35.	Providing and laying marble mosaic tiles of approved colour and pattern with white and coloured marble chips upto a max. of comm. size for flooring, required positions set on a bed of cm (1 : 6) including neat cement float, filling the joints with coloured cement slurry, curing, polishing and rubbing complete w/o border and pattern of tiles of different colur and design as directed in grey cement.	87.66 m²	225	00	m²	19723	50
36.	Providing and applying white washing, three coats in plastered surface or masonry surface incl. scaffolding and preparing the surface by brushing and brooming down complete.	425 m²	3	50	m²	1487	50

Item No.	Description	Quan.	Rate ₹	Rate Ps.	Per	Amount ₹	Amount Ps.
37.	Providing and fixing C.C.T.W. door frame w/o ventilator of size 60 × 100 mm for doors including chamfering, rebating hold fast of size 300 × 40 × 3 mm finishing with 3 coats of oil painting complete.	0.2934 m²	18000	00	m³	5281	20
38.	Providing and fixing steel windows of various sizes as per detailed drawings w/o hot dip-zinc coating, w/o ventilators, including fabricating, glazing with plain observed glass and of approved type and quantity and fixtures and fastenings and finishing with oil paint of 2 coats complete.	16.59 m²	1100	00	m²	18249	00
39.	Providing and applying washabale distemper of approved colour and shade to new surfaces in 3 coats including scaffolding, preparing the surface to receive the primary coat and finishing the coat complete.	329.31 m²	8	00	m²	2634	48
40.	Providing and casting in situ. C.C. concrete (1 : 2 : 4) for R.C.C. lintels as per detailed design and drawings or as directed including centering, formwork, compaction and finishing the surface with C.M. (1 : 3) and curing etc. complete.	1.197 m³	1315	00	m³	1574	05
40 (A)	Providing and laying polished shahabad flooring 2.5 cm thick and 25 - 30 cm wide in plain pattern on a bed of C.M. 1 : 6 including cement float, feeling joints with neat cement slurry, curing, polishing and cleaning complete (for W.C.), bath and toilet.	8.01 m²	195	00	m²	1561	95
40 (B)	Providing and fixing white glazed tiles 148.5 × 148.5 and 6.6 mm thick for flooring is dado in required positions laid on a bed of C.M. (1 : 4) incl. neat cement float all special spherical required like round corner, angles, cups etc. filling joints with clean cement slurry, curing and cleaning complete.	23.04 m²	600	00	m²	13824	00

Item No.	Description	Quan.	Rate		Per	Amount	
			₹	Ps.		₹	Ps.
41.	Providing and fixing solid core flushed door shutters with all fixtures and fastenings of aluminium and finishing the woodwork with 3 coats of oil paint complete.	17.01 m²	1000	00	m²	17010	00
	STAIRCASE						
42.	Providing and casting in situ. C.C. (1 : 2 : 4) of trap metal for R.C.C. stair (landings and steps pardi) as per detailed designs and drawings or as directed including centering, formwork, compaction and finishing the surface with C.M. (1 : 3) and curing complete.	5.3 m³	1390	00	m³	7367	00
43.	Providing cement plaster 12 mm thick in 2 coats in C.M. (1 : 4) w/o neeru finish to concrete or brick surface in all positions including scaffolding and curing complete.	151.13 m²	27	00	m²	4080	51
44.	Providing neeru finish to plastered surface in all positions incl. scaffolding and curing complete.	151.13 m²	11	00	m²	1662	43
45.	Providing and applying white washing in 3 coats on plastered surface including scaffolding and preparing the surface by brushing and brooming down complete.	151.13 m²	3	50	m²	528	96
46.	Providing and applying washable distemper of approved colour and shade to new surface in 3 coats incl. scaffolding, preparing the surface to receive the priming coat and finishing coat complete.	119.35 m²	4	25	m²	507	24

Item No.	Description	Quan.	Rate ₹	Rate Ps.	Per	Amount ₹	Amount Ps.
47.	Providing and laying polished shahabad stone flooring 25 - 30 mm thick and 30 cm wide in plain pattern on a bed cm (1 : 6) including cement float, filling joints with neat cement slurry, curing, polishing and cleaning complete.	20.75 m^2	190	00	m^2	3942	50
48.	Providing and fixing in positing MS bar reinforcement of various dia. for R.C.C. footings, foundations, slabs, beams, columns, canopies, stair, chajja, lintels, pardis, couplings, fins, arches, etc. as per detailed design and drawings and schedules including cutting, bending, hooking the bars, binding with wires or tack welding and supporting as required complete.						
	(A)　　Upto Plinth	0.875 t	13000	00	t	11375	00
	(B)　　Upto First Floor	2.189 t	13000	00	t	28457	00
	(C)　　Upto Roof	2.085 t	13000	00	t	27105	00
	(D)　　Staircase	0.416 t	13000	00	t	5400	00
49.	Providing and laying water proofing treatment with average thickness of 10 cm injecting the water proofing material containing the treatment to inner side of parapet wall or adjacent wall.	146.76 m^2	115	00	m^2	16877	40

		498153.78
Add 10 % for electrification	+	49815.38
Add 10 % for water supply and sanitation	+	49815.38
		597784.54
Add 5 % for contingencies	+	29889.22
	=	627673.76
Add 1 % for work charge establishments	+	6276.73
		633950.51
	Say	**633951.00**

3.8.15 Estimation Of An Excavation And Construction Of An Open Well (Fig. 3.39)

Measurement Sheet

Item No.	Description	No.	Length L	Breadth B	Depth or Height H	Qty.	Total
1.	Excavation for well in ordinary soil including the removing of excavated material upto a distance of 30 m stacking and spreading as directed, dewatering, shoring, strutting and necessary backfilling etc. complete. (from G.L. to 1.2 m depth)		Area	$= \dfrac{\pi \times 5.3^2}{4}$ $= 22.06 \text{ m}^2$	1.2 m	26.50 m³	26.50 m³
2.	Excavation for well in hard murum including removing of excavated material upto a distance of 30 m. stacking and spreading as directed, dewatering, shoring, strutting and necessary backfilling etc. complete. (from 1.2 m to 3 m depth)		Area	$= \dfrac{\pi \times 5.3^2}{4}$ $= 22.06 \text{ m}^2$	0.3 m	6.62 m³	6.62 m³
3.	Excavation for well in hard murum including removing of excavated material upto a distance of 30 m. stacking and spreading as directed, dewatering, shoring, strutting and necessary backfilling etc. complete. (from 1.5 m to 3 m depth)		Area	$= \dfrac{\pi \times 5.3^2}{4}$ $= 22.06 \text{ m}^2$	1.5 m	33.10 m³	33.10 m³
4.	Excavation for well in hard rock by blasting including trimming where necessary and removing the excavated material within a distance of 30 m. stacking, dewatering and necessary backfilling etc. complete (3 to 4.5 m)		Area	$= \dfrac{\pi \times 3.7^2}{4}$ $= 10.75 \text{ m}^2$	1.5 m	16.13 m³	16.13 m³
5.	Excavation for well in hard rock by blasting including trimming where necessary and removing the excavated material within a distance of 30 m. Stacking, dewatering and backfilling (from 4.5 m to 6 m depth)		Area	$= \dfrac{\pi \times 3.7^2}{4}$ $= 10.75 \text{ m}^2$	1.5 m	16.13 m³	16.13 m³
6.	Providing and laying the in situ cement concrete (1 : 2 : 4) of trap metal for R.C.C. ring below brick masonry steining wall including dewatering, formwork, compaction, finishing, curing, M.S. reinforcement etc. complete		Area	$= \dfrac{\pi}{4}(5.3^2 - 3.7^2)$	0.3 m	3.40 m³	3.40 m³

Item No.	Description	No.	Length L	Breadth B	Depth or Height H	Qty.	Total
7.	Providing second class B.B. masonry in cement mortar (1 : 6) for steining wall including dewatering, racking of joints on exposed faces, scaffolding and watering etc. complete						
	(a) Bottom layer		Area	$= \dfrac{\pi}{4}(5^2 - 4^2)$ $= 7.068 \text{ m}^2$	1.5 m	10.60 m³	18.90 m³
	(b) Top layer		Area	$= \dfrac{\pi}{4}(4.8^2 - 4^2)$ $= 5.53 \text{ m}^2$	1.5 m	8.30 m³	
8.	Providing second class B.B. masonry in C.M. (1 : 6) for steining wall including dewatering, racking of joints on exposed faces, scaffolding and watering etc. complete (from 3 m to 6 m height)		Area	$= \dfrac{\pi}{4}(4.8^2 - 4^2)$ $= 5.53 \text{ m}^2$	0.3 m	1.66 m³	1.66 m³
9.	Providing and laying in situ cement concrete (1 : 2 : 4) of trap metal for coping on parapet including formwork, compacting, finishing, curing etc. complete		Area	$= \dfrac{\pi}{4}(4.8^2 - 4^2)$ $= 5.53 \text{ m}^2$	0.2 m	1.11 m³	1.11 m³
10.	Providing cement pointing (1 :3) to brick masonry work including scaffolding, watering etc. complete (from top of R.C.C. ring to 3 m height)		Area	$= \pi \times 4.0$ $= 12.56 \text{ m}$	3 m	37.7 m²	37.7 m²
11.	Providing cement pointing (1 : 3) to brick-masonry work including scaffolding, watering etc. complete						
	(a) Inside surfaces		Area	$= \pi \times 4.0$ $= 12.56 \text{ m}$	0.3 m	3.77 m²	12.82 m²
	(b) Outside surface of parapet wall		Area	$= \pi \times 4.8$ $= 15.08 \text{ m}$	0.6 m	9.05 m²	

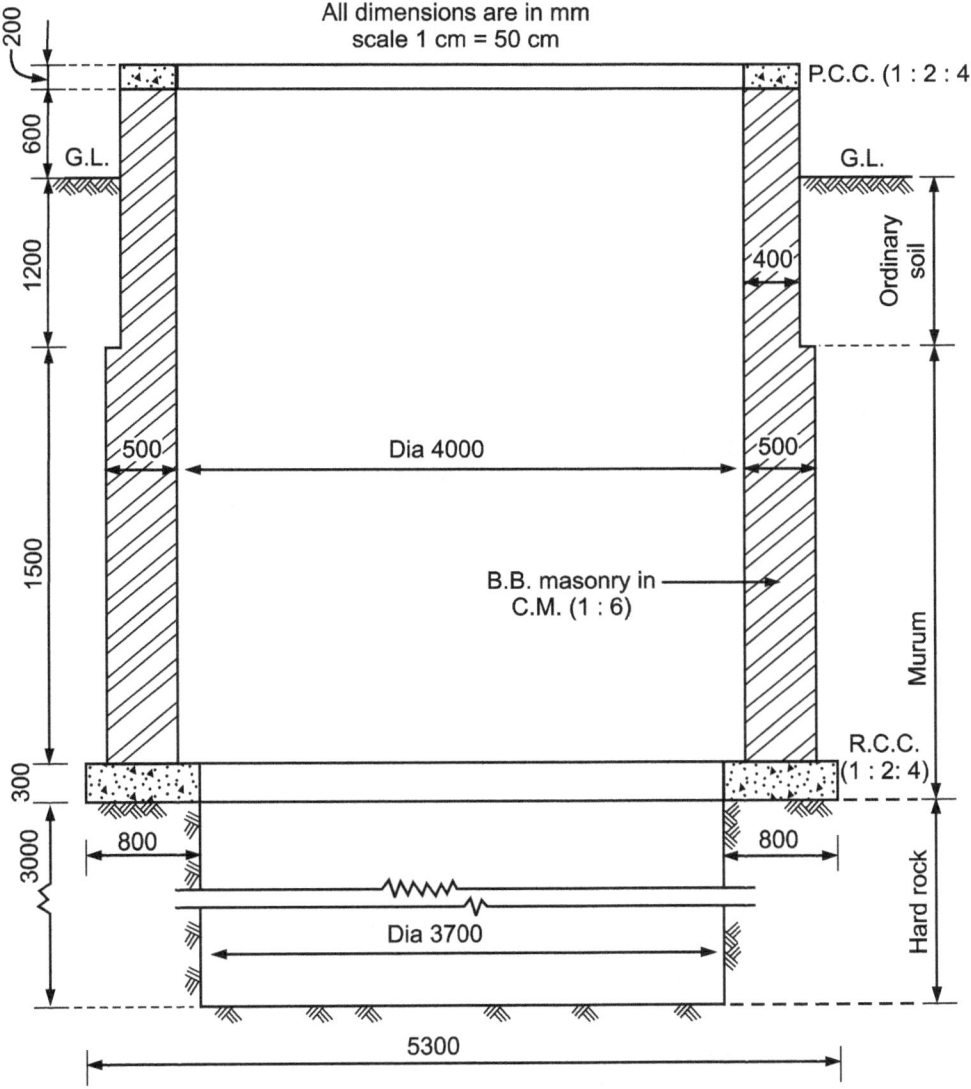

Fig. 3.43 : Vertical section of a circular well

3.8.16 Estimate Of An Excavation And Construction Of An Open Well

Abstract Sheet

Item No.	Description	Quantity	Rate		Per	Amount	
			₹	Ps.		₹	Ps.
1.	Excavation for well in soil including removing the excavated material upto a distance of 30 m, stacking and spreading as directed, dewatering, shoring, strutting and necessary backfilling etc. complete (from G.L. to 1.2 m depth)	26.5	23	10	m³	612	15

Item No.	Description	Quantity	Rate		Per	Amount	
			₹	Ps.		₹	Ps.
2.	Excavation for well in hard murum including removing excavated material upto a distance of 30 m, stacking and spreading as directed, dewatering, shoring, strutting and necessary backfilling etc. complete. (from 1.2 m to 1.5 m depth)	6.62	29	00	m³	191	98
3.	Excavation for well in hard murum including removing the excavated material upto a distance of 30 m stacking and spreading as directed. Dewatering, shoring, strutting and necessary backfilling etc. complete from 1.5 m to 3 m depth.	33.10	30	50	m³	1009	55
4.	Excavation of well in hard rock by blasting including trimming where necessary and removing the excavated material and stacking within a distance of 30 m. Dewatering and backfilling etc. complete (from 3 m below G.L. to a depth of 4.5 m)	16.13	88	00	m³	1419	44
5.	Excavation for well in hard rock by blasting including trimming where necessary and removing the excavated material and stacking within a distance of 30 m, dewatering and backfilling etc. complete (from 4.5 m below G.L. to a depth of 6 m)	16.13	95	00	m³	1532	35
6.	Providing and laying the in situ cement concrete (1 : 2 : 4) of trap metal for R.C.C. ring below brick masonry. Steining wall including dewatering formwork, compaction, finishing, curing, M.S. reinforcement etc. complete.	3.40	1600	00	m³	5440	00
7.	Providing second class B.B. masonry in cement mortar (1 : 6) for steining wall including dewatering, raking of joints on exposed faces scaffolding and watering etc. complete (from top of R.C.C. ring to 3 m height)	18.90	745	00	m³	14080	50
8.	Providing second class B.B. masonry in C.M. (1 : 6) for steining wall including dewatering, raking of joints on exposed faces, scaffolding and watering etc. complete (from 3 m to 6 m height)	1.66	765	00	m³	1269	90

Item No.	Description	Quantity	Rate		Per	Amount	
			₹	Ps.		₹	Ps.
9.	Providing and laying in situ cement concrete (1 : 2 : 4) of trap metal for coping on parapet including formwork, compacting, finishing, curing etc. complete.	11.1	1120	00	m²	1243	20
10.	Providing flush grooved cement-pointing (1 : 3) to brick masonry work including scaffolding, watering etc. complete (from top of R.C.C. ring to 3 m height)	37.7	19	20	m²	723	84
11.	Providing cement-pointing (1 : 3) to brick-masonry work including scaffolding, watering etc. complete (from 3 m to 6 m height)	12.82	22	00	m²	282	04

Total estimated cost	₹		27804.95
Add 5 % for contingencies	₹		1390.25
Total cost	₹		29195.20
Adding 1 % for W.C. establishment	₹		291.95
Grand Total	₹		29487.15
	Say ₹ =		**29488.00**

Earthwork Calculations In Road Project:

If road has to be constructed above natural ground level then longitudinal section and cross-section at any point between points (1) and (2) will be as shown in Fig. 3.44 and 3.45 respectively.

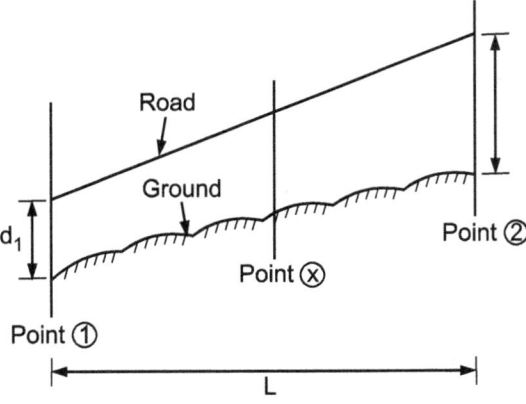

Fig. 3.44 : Longitudinal section

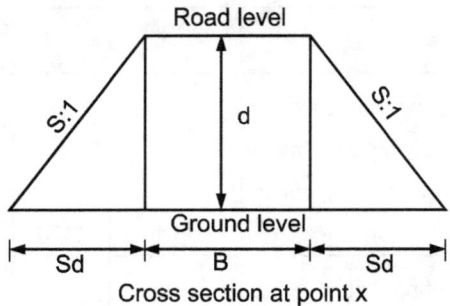

Fig. 3.45

In above case of road i.e. above ground level for entire length of road L, the filling of earth will have to be done, so all cross-sections between points (1) and (2) will be in filling or banking as shown in Fig. 3.45.

But if road is to be constructed below ground level, then excess earth available above the decided road level has to be cut or removed. Then in this case at every point in considered length, the section will be under cutting as shown in Fig. 3.46.

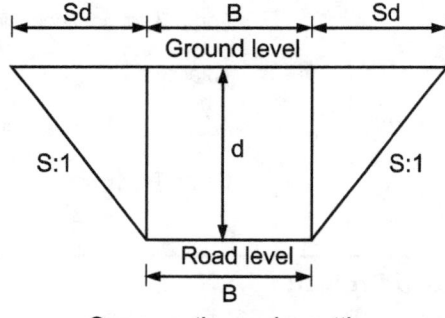

Fig. 3.46

For calculation of volume of earthwork in cutting or filling, undermentioned 3 methods are used :

1. Mid sectional area method :

$$\text{Volume of earthwork } = V = A_{MID} \times L = [Bd + Sd^2] \times L$$

where, $d = \text{Mid point} = d_{MID} = \dfrac{d_2 + d_2}{2}$

2. Mean sectional area method :

If $A_1 = B_1 d_1 + S_1 d_1^2$ and $A_2 = B_2 d_2 + S_2 d_2^2$

then   Mean sectional area $= \dfrac{A_1 + A_2}{2} = A_{MEAN}$

and   Volume of earthwork $= A_{MEAN} \times L$

3. Prismoidal formula method :

$$\text{Volume of earthwork} = \frac{L}{6} [A_1 + A_2 + 4A_{MID}]$$

where A_{MID} is as shown in method (1) and A_1 and A_2 are as shown in method (2).

Example 3.9 : Calculate the quantity of earthwork for 200 m length for a portion of a road in an uniform ground, the height of banks at the two ends being 1.0 m and 1.60 m. The formation width is 10.0 m and side slopes 2 : 1 [H : V]. Assume that there is no transverse slope. Use 3 different methods, you can use in this case.   **(Dec. 2008, 6 M)**

Solution : 1. Mid sectional area method :

$$d = d_{MID} = \frac{1.0 + 1.6}{2} = 1.3 \text{ m}$$

$$A_{MID} = Bd + Sd^2 = 16.38 \text{ m}^2$$

$$\text{Volume of earthwork, V} = (Bd + Sd^2) \times L$$

$$V = [(1.0 \times 1.3) + (2 \times 1.3^2)] \times 200 = 16.38 \times 200 = 3276 \text{ m}^3$$

2. Mean sectional area method :

$$A_1 = B_1d_1 + S_1d_1^2 = (10 \times 1.0) + (2 \times 1^2) = 12 \text{ m}^2$$

$$A_2 = B_2d_2 + S_2d_2^2 = (10 \times 1.6) + (2 \times 1.6^2) = 21.12 \text{ m}^2$$

$$\text{Mean sectional area} = A_{MEAN} = \frac{A_1 + A_2}{2} = \frac{12 + 21.12}{2} = 16.56 \text{ m}^2$$

$$V = A_{MEAN} \times L = 16.56 \times 200 = 3312 \text{ m}^2$$

3. Prismoidal formula method :

$$V = \frac{L}{6} [A_1 + A_2 + 4A_{MID}]$$

where,

$$A_{MID} = \text{Mid sectional area} = 16.38 \text{ m}^2$$

$$V = \frac{200}{6} [12 + 21.12 + 4 \times 16.38] = 3288 \text{ m}^2$$

Example 3.10 : Workout the quantities of earthwork for the following portion of the road by mid-sectional area method :

Chainage	300	350	400	450	500	550	600	650	700	750	800
R.L. of ground	184.50	184.75	184.90	185.20	186.20	184.70	182.80	183.30	185.0	185.50	186.40

(1) Width of earthwork at formation level in embankment is 7.0 m.

(2) Width of earthwork at formation level in cutting is 7.9 m.

(3) Earth formation level at chainage 300 is 186.0.

(4) Side slopes are 2.5 to 1.0 and 1.75 to 1.0 in banking and cutting respectively.

(5) Falling gradient of 1 in 100 is to be provided upto chainage 600 and thereafter rising gradient of 1 in 75.   **(Dec. 2008, 10 M)**

Solution : Determination of point of intersection of ground and formation lines :

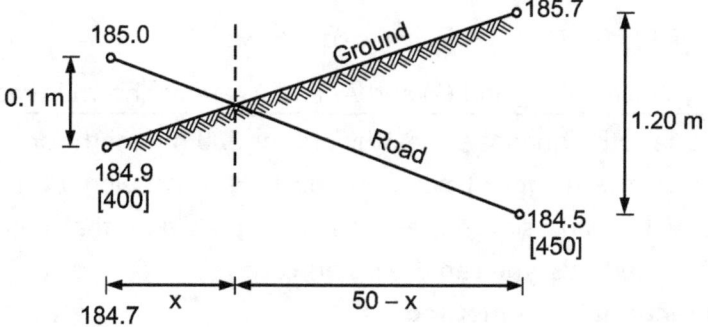

Fig. 3.47

$$\frac{x}{0.1} = \frac{50 - x}{1.2}$$

So $12x = 50 - x$

$\therefore$ $13x = 50 \Rightarrow x = \dfrac{50}{13} = 3.84 \ (4.0 \text{ m})$

So, point of intersection will occur at chainage = 400 + x = 404.0 m.

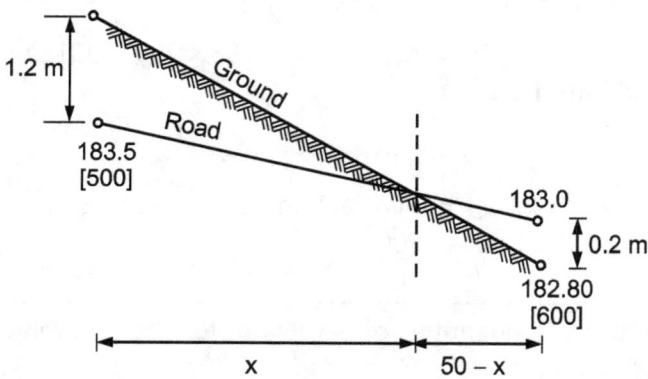

Fig. 3.48

$$\frac{x}{1.2} = \frac{50 - x}{0.2}$$

$\therefore$ $2x = 600 - 12x$

$\therefore$ $14x = 600$

$\therefore$ $x = \dfrac{600}{14} = 42.86 \ (43.0 \text{ m})$

Filling : B = 7.0 m, S = 2.5   Cutting : B = 7.9 m, S = 1.75

Chainage	R.L. of Formation	R.L. of Ground	Depth = R.L. of F.L. – R.L. of G.L.	Mean Depth (d)	Central Area [Bd]	Side Area [Sd²]	Total Sectional Area = Bd + Sd²	Distance Between Stations (L)	Quantity of Earthwork = L × [Bd + Sd²]	
									$(10) = (8) \times (9)$	
(1)	(2)	(3)	(4) = (2) – (3)	(5)	(6)	(7)	(8) = (6) +(7)	(9)	Banking	Cutting
300	186.00	184.50	(+) 1.50	(+) 1.12	7.84	3.14	10.98	50	549.00.00	
350	185.50	184.75	(+) 0.75	(+) 0.42	2.94	0.44	3.38	50	169.00	
400	185.00	184.90	(+) 0.10	(+) 0.05	0.35	0.006	0.35	04	1.40	
404	–	–	0	(–) 0.60	4.74	0.63	5.37	46		247.02
450	184.50	185.70	(–) 1.20	(–) 1.70	13.43	5.06	18.49	50		924.50
500	184.00	186.20	(–) 2.20	(–) 1.70	13.43	5.06	18.49	50		924.50
550	183.50	184.70	(–) 1.20	(–) 0.60	4.74	0.63	5.37	43		230.91
593	–	–	0	(+) 0.10	0.70	0.02	0.72	07	5.04	
600	183.00	182.80	(+) 0.20	(+) 0.28	1.96	0.20	2.16	50	108.00	
650	183.67	183.30	(+) 0.37	(+) 0.18	1.26	0.08	1.34	18	24.12	
668	–	–	0	(–) 0.33	2.61	0.19	2.80	32		89.60
700	184.34	185.00	(–) 0.66	(–) 0.58	4.58	0.59	5.17	50		258.50
750	185.01	185.50	(–) 0.49	(–) 0.60	4.74	0.63	5.37	50		268.50
800	185.68	186.40	(–) 0.72							
								Total	856.56 m³	2943.53m³

Example 3.11 : Estimate the quantity of earthwork between chainage 0 to 100. The formation level at chainage 0 is 400 and rises @ 2% for certain distance and thereafter decreases @ 4%. The formation level at chainage 100 is found to be 398.4. The ground level at various chainages are given below :

Chainage (m)	0	10	20	30	40	50	60	70	80	90	100
Ground level (m)	400.0	399.6	400.2	400.9	401.0	401.6	401.0	399.0	398.7	398.6	398.0
Formation level (m)	400.0	Rising @ 2% →								← Rising @ 4%	398.4

Assume width of formation in cutting and in embankment as 12 m and 10 m respectively and side slopes in cutting and embankment as (1 : 1) and (2 : 1) respectively. Tabulate the results.   **(May 2009, 13 M)**

Solution : In the given question, the chainage upto which the formation level rises is not given. So with the given information, we will determine it by determining the number of intervals of rise and fall.

Let,   A = Number of intervals for rise and

[In 100 m, rise is 2 m (2%). So in 10 m, rise will be 0.2 m]

                                        B = Number of intervals for fall

So,   A + B = 10   ... (1)

            0.2 A – 0.4 B = 398.4 – 400.0 = – 1.6   ... (2)

[Taking rise as positive and fall as negative]

On solving equations (1) and (2), we get A = 4, B = 6.

So, formation level will rise upto 4 intervals (i.e. upto chainage 401.0) and after that fall will occur @ 4%.

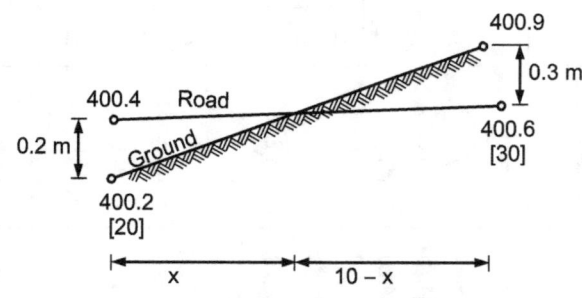

Fig. 3.49

$$\frac{x}{0.2} = \frac{10 - x}{0.3}$$

∴ $\frac{x}{2} = \frac{10 - x}{3}$

∴ $3x = 20 - 2x$

∴ $5x = 20$ ∴ $x = 4.0$ m

So point of intersection is chainage.

            $20 + x = 20 + 4.0 = 24.0$ m

Banking : B = 10.0 m, S = 2.0 Cutting : B = 12.0 m, S = 1.0

Chainage	R.L. of Formation	R.L. of Ground	Depth = R.L. of F.L. − R.L. of G.L.	Mean Depth (d)	Central Area [Bd]	Side Area [Sd²]	Total Sectional Area = Bd + Sd²	Distance Between Stations (L)	Quantity of Earthwork = L × [Bd + Sd²] (10) = (8) × (9)	
									Banking	Cutting
(1)	(2)	(3)	(4) = (2) − (3)	(5)	(6)	(7)	(8) = (6) + (7)	(9)		
0	400.0	400.0	0	(+) 0.3	3.0	0.18	3.18	10	31.80	
10	400.02	399.6	(+) 0.6	(+) 0.4	4.0	0.32	4.32	10	43.20	
20	400.4	400.2	(+) 0.2	(+) 0.1	1.0	0.02	1.02	4	4.08	
24	–	–	0	(−) 0.15	1.8	0.02	1.82	6		10.92
30	400.6	400.9	(−) 0.3	(−) 0.25	3.0	0.06	3.06	10		30.60
40	400.8	401.0	(−) 0.2	(−) 0.70	8.4	0.49	8.89	10		88.90
50	400.4	401.6	(−) 1.2	(−) 1.10	13.2	1.21	14.41	10		144.10
60	400.0	401.0	(−) 1.0	(−) 0.50	6.0	0.25	6.25	6		37.50
66	–	–	0	(+) 0.30	3.0	0.18	3.18	4	12.72	
70	399.6	399.0	(+) 0.6	(+) 0.55	5.5	0.61	6.11	10	61.10	
80	399.2	398.7	(+) 0.5	(+) 0.35	3.5	0.25	3.75	10	37.50	
90	398.8	398.6	(+) 0.2	(+) 0.30	3.0	0.18	3.18	10	31.80	
100	398.4	398.0	(+) 0.4							
								Total	222.20 m³	312.02 m³

3.8 (XVII) ESTIMATE OF A ROAD FOR EARTH WORK (Fig. 3.46 & 3.47)

Measurement Sheet

	Chainage	G.L.	F.L.	Depth of		c/s Area		Mean Area	Dist.	Volume	
				Cutting	Embankment	Cutting	Embankment			Cutting	Embankment
1	0	106.40	105.00	1.4	-	22.159		11.08	40	443.184	
2	40	105.20	105.20	-	-			2.488	10		24.88
3	50	104.90	105.25	-	0.35		4.977	3.525	50		176.25
4	100	105.35	105.50	-	0.15		2.073	1.036	12.5		12.95
5	112.50	105.58	105.58	-	-			3.447	37.5	129.26	
6	150	106.20	105.75	0.45	-	6.894		14.612	50	730.6	
7	200	107.40	106.0	1.40	-	22.33		13.785	50	689.25	
8	250	106.60	106.25	0.35	-	5.339		2.669	10.66	28.45	
9	260.6	106.30	106.30	-	-			17.52	39.33		689.06
10	300	104.50	106.50	-	2.00		35.04	17.52	35.09		614.77
11	335.09	106.68	106.68	-	-			6.624	14.91	94.789	
12	350	107.60	106.75	0.85	-	13.249		10.072	50	503.6	
13	400	107.40	107.00	0.4	-	6.115		6.505	50	325.25	
14	450	107.70	107.25	0.45	-	6.894		17.735	50	886.75	
15	500	108.20	107.50	0.70	-	10.041				Σ 3831.133 m³	Σ 1517.91 m³

Volume of cutting $= 2 \left[\frac{1}{2}(0.3 + 0.75) \times 0.15\right] [40 + 37.5 + 50 + 50 + 10.6 + 14.91 + 150] = 55.599$

∴ Total cutting $= 3831.133 + 55.599 = 3886.733$ m³

∴ Cutting $>$ Filling ∴ Spill

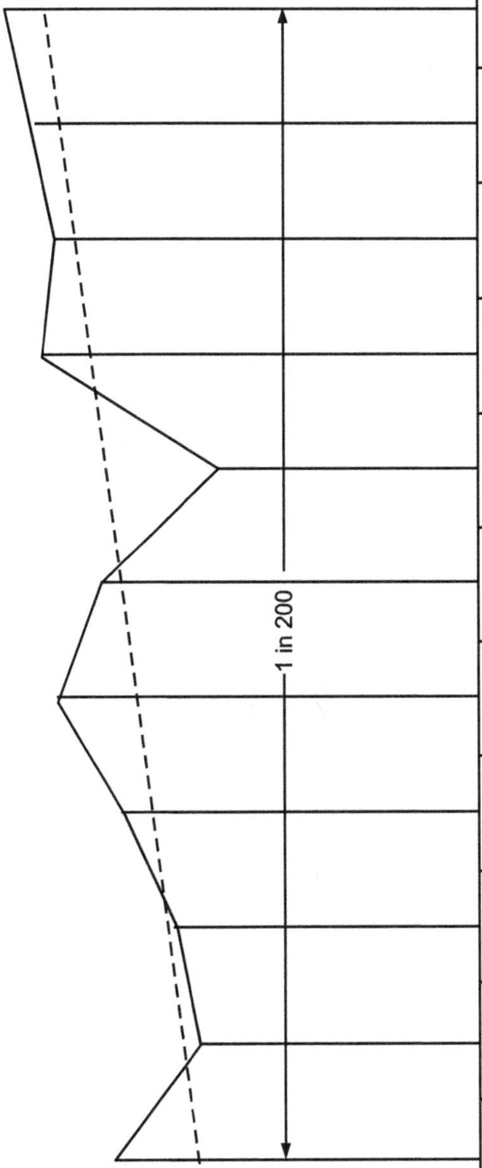

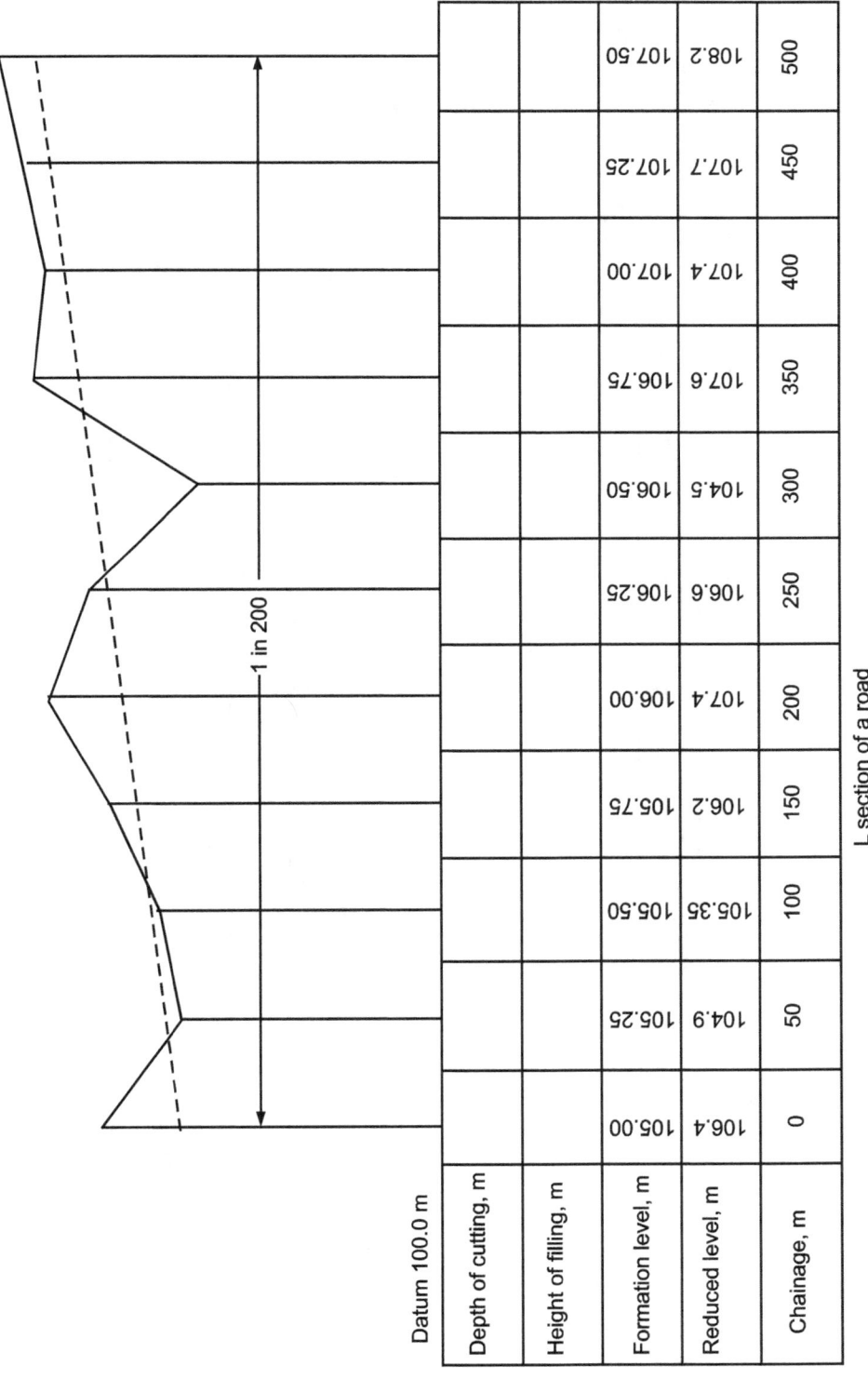

Datum 100.0 m

Chainage, m	Reduced level, m	Formation level, m	Height of filling, m	Depth of cutting, m
0	106.4	105.00		
50	104.9	105.25		
100	105.35	105.50		
150	106.2	105.75		
200	107.4	106.00		
250	106.6	106.25		
300	104.5	106.50		
350	107.6	106.75		
400	107.4	107.00		
450	107.7	107.25		
500	108.2	107.50		

L section of a road

Fig. 3.50

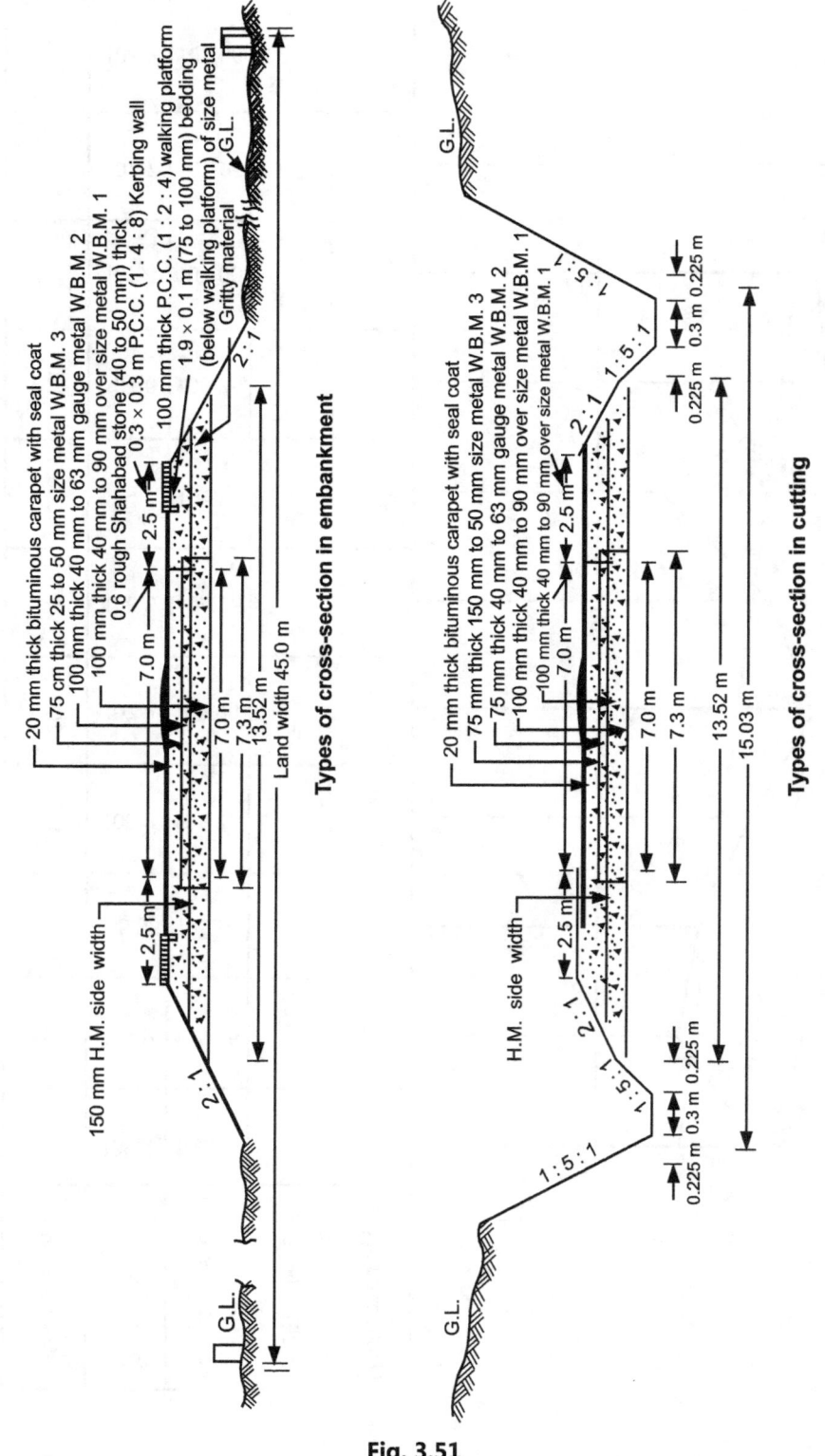

Types of cross-section in embankment

Types of cross-section in cutting

Fig. 3.51

Ch. 3 | 3.156

3.8.18 Estimate of A Road For Earth Work (Fig. 3.50 & Fig. 3.51)

Abstract Sheet

Item No.	Description	Quantity	Rate ₹	Rate Ps.	Per	Amount ₹	Amount Ps.
1.	Clearing the site before and after the work including removing all the debris, shrubs etc.	Lumpsum				500	00
2.	Excavation of hard murum upto a depth of 1.4 m including removing the excavated material upto a distance of 50 m beyond the highway area and all lift and stacking and spreading as directed dewatering, shoring and strutting preparing the bed and necessary back filling complete.	3886.73 m³	29	70	m³	115435	88
3.	Providing hard murum filling incl. laying in layers of 15 - 20 cm watering compaction complete.	1517.91 m³	35	00	m³	53126	85

Total	**168562.73**
Add 5 % contingencies	= 8428.14
Total	176990.87
Add 1 % work charged establishment	**1769.90**
Total cost	₹ 178760.77
	≈ **178761.00**

3.8.19 Estimate Of A Pipe Culvert (Fig. 3.52)

Measurement Sheet

Item No.	Description	No.	Length L	Breadth B	Depth or Height H	Qty.	Total
1.	Clearing the site before and after the work including removal of debris, shrubs, etc.			Job item			
2.	Excavation for foundations in soil upto a depth of 1.5 m including removal of the excavated materials upto a distance of 50 m beyond the building area and all lift, stacking, spreading as directed, dewatering, preparing the bed to foundation and necessary backfilling, etc.						
	(A) Trenches	2	4.0	0.95	0.75	5.70 m³	**8.025 m³**

Item No.	Description	No.	Length L	Breadth B	Depth or Height H	Qty.	Total
	(B) Below the base of pipe for laying P.C.C.	1	25	62	0.15	2.325 m³	
3.	Providing and casting in situ C.C. (1 : 4 : 8) of trap metal for foundation and bedding, including dewatering, formwork, compacting and curing etc. complete.						
	(A) Trenches	2	4.0	0.95	0.25	1.90 m³	
	(B) Surrounding the pipe						
	(i) Rectangular	1	2.5	6.5	0.15	2.4375m³	
	(ii) Trapezoidal	1	2.5	6.55	0.35	5.73125m³	
	Deduct	2	6.55		0.1924	− 2.52	
	For pipes					7.5483	
	Diameter of pipe = 70 cm Outer			$(\frac{\pi}{4} \times (0.70)^2 \times \frac{1}{2})$ $= 0.1924 \ m^3$				
4.	Providing U.C.R. masonry in trap stones in C.M. (1 : 6) in foundation and plinth of walls including dewatering, striking joints on exposed faces						
	Below G.L.	2	3.7	0.65	0.5	2.405 m³	
	Above G.L.	4	3.5	$\frac{0.4 + 0.65}{2}$	1.5	5.5125m³	**7.0068 m³**
	Deductions for pipes	4		0.3848	0.592	−0.91069	
5.	Providing and laying cast iron pipes of class B 60 cm ϕ, 5 m thick with socket and spigot joints (end, flanges and cast centrifugals verticals, including special excavation, laying pipes and backfilling the trench etc. complete.	2	7.8	-	-	15.6 m	
6.	Filling the plinth and floors with murum 15 - 20 cm layers, including watering, compaction complete (lead 50 m considered)	1	3.5	6.4	3.625	22.5268	m³
		2	6.558	0.5	0.35	2.2953	m³
	Deductions for pipes	2	6.675		0.1924	− 2.5685	m³

Item No.	Description	No.	Length L	Breadth B	Depth or Height H	Qty.	Total
						22.2536m³	
7.	Providing class I B.B. masonry with conventional bricks in C.M. (1 : 6) in parapet and external walls including dewatering, striking joints on unexposed faces and raking on exposed faces and watering etc. complete.						
	II I	I. 2	3.5	0.4	0.15	0.42 m³	1.05 m³
		II. 2	.35	0.3	0.3	0.63 m³	
8.	Providing a casting in situ cement concrete (1 : 2 : 4) of trap metal to R.C.C. coping to plinth or parapet and sills of doors, windows, moulded as per designs and drawings approved by the Engineer including centering, formwork, compaction, finishing the exposed faces and C.M. (1 : 3) of sufficient minimum thickness to give a smooth and even surface or roughening them if special finish is to be provided and curing (excluding M.S. reinforcement)	2	3.6	0.35	0.1	0.252 m³	
9.	Providing dry trap rubble soling as metalling 20 cm thick including hand packing etc. complete	1	3.5	7.033	0.2	4.9233m³	
10.	Providing pointing with C.M. (1 : 3) for masonry including scaffolding and curing complete						
	External surface	2	3.5	-	1.95	13.65 m²	
	Deduction for pipes	2	0.38	48		0.76969m²	
	Parapet wall	2	3.5		0.45	3.15 m²	

Item No.	Description	No.	Length L	Breadth B	Depth or Height H	Qty.	Total
		2	3.5	0.1		0.7 m²	
						16.73031m²	
		2	3.5	0.1		0.7 m²	
						16.73031m²	

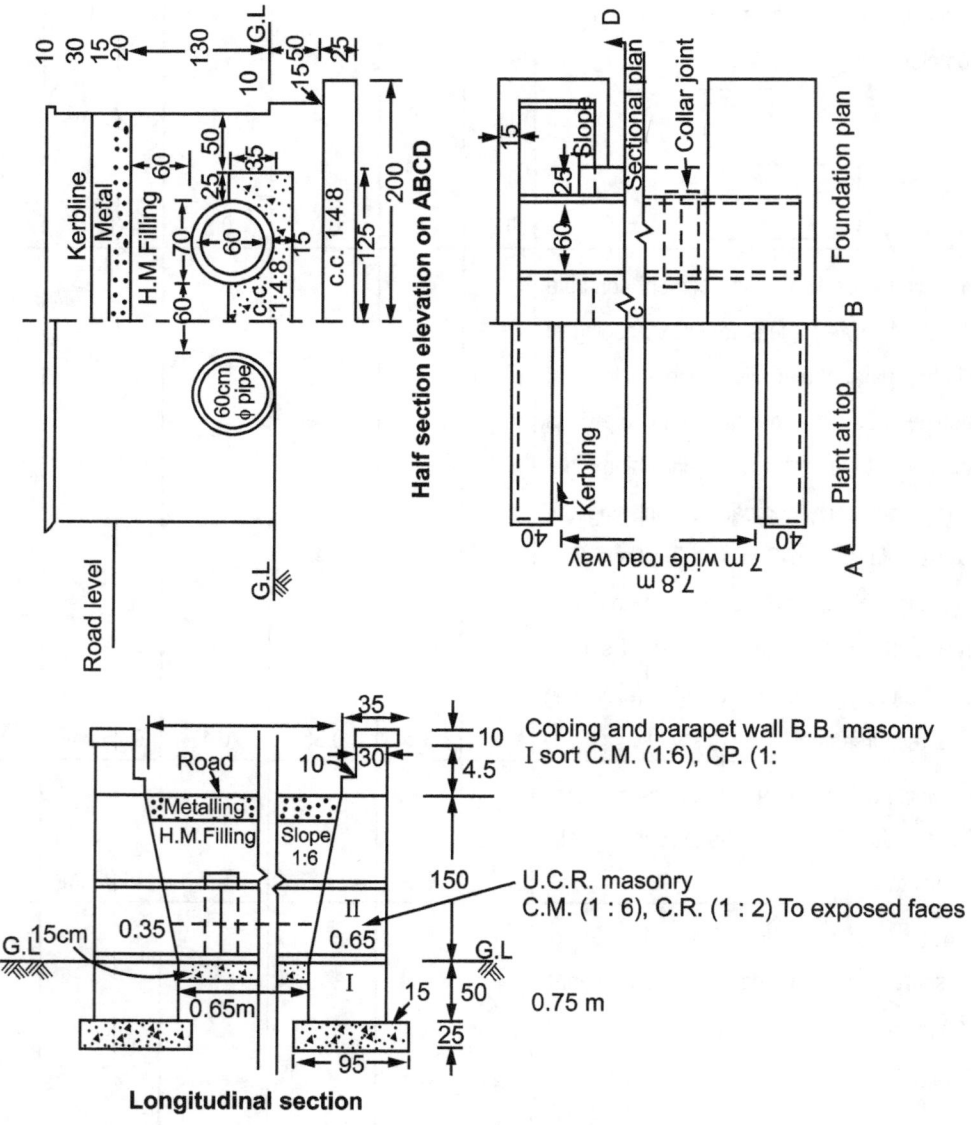

Fig. 3.52 : Pipe culvert

3.8.20 Estimate of A PIPE CULVERT

Abstract Sheet

Item No.	Description	Quantity	Rate		Per	Amount	
			₹	Ps.		₹	Ps.
1.	Clearing the site before and after the work including removing all the debris, shrubs etc.	Lumpsum				200	00
2.	Excavation for foundation in soil upto depth 1.5 m including removing of the excluding material upto a distance 50 m beyond the building area and all lift, staking and spreading as directed, dewatering, shorting and strutting, preparing the bed for boundation and necessary back filling.	8.025 m³	23	00	m³	184	58
3.	Providing a casting in situ C-C (1 : 4 : 8) of trap metal for foundation and bedding including dewatering, formwork, compacting and curing etc. complete.	7.5483 m³	600	00	m³	4528	78
4.	Providing UCR masonry of trap stones in C.M. 1 : 6 in foundation and plinth walls including dewatering, striking joints on exposed faces.	7.0068 m³	423	00	m³	2963	88
5.	Providing a laying CI pipes of class B of 60 cm φ 5 cm thickness with socket and spigot end flanges a cast centrifugals, verticals, including special excavation, laying pipes and back filling the trench etc. complete.	15.6 m	150	00	R.M.	2340	00
6.	Filling the plinth and floors with murum in 15-20 cm layers including watering, compaction complete (considering 50 m lead).	22.2536 m³	35	00	m³	778	88
7.	Providing class II BB masonry with conventional bricks in C.M. (1 : 6) in parapets and external walls including striking of joints on unexposed faces, raking out joints on exposed faces and watering etc. complete.	1.05	723	00	m³	759	15
8.	Providing and casting in situ cement concrete (1 : 2 : 4) of trap metal for R.C.C. coping to plinth/parapet/walls/as per detail designs and drawings and approved by the Engineer including centering, formwork, compacting, finishing the exposed surfaces with C.M. (1:3) of sufficient minimum thickness to give a smooth and even surface or roughening them if special finish is to be provided and curing (excl. M.S. Reinforcement).	0.252 m³	1420	00	m³	357	84

Item No.	Description	Quantity	Rate		Per	Amount	
			₹	Ps.		₹	Ps.
9.	Providing dry trap rubble soling as metalling 20 cm thick including hand packing etc. complete.	4.9233 m³	90	00	m³	443	10
10.	Providing flush groove pointing with CM 1 : 3 for masonry including scaffolding and curing complete.	16.7303 m²	19	20	m²	321	22

Total cost	₹	12677.83
Adding 5 % for contingencies		633.89
		13311.72
Adding 1 % for work charged establishment		133.11
Grand Total Cost	₹	13444.83
Say	≈ ₹	**13445.00**

3.9 SCHEDULE OF RATES FOR VARIOUS ITEMS OF WORK

The rates mentioned below for various items of work for the year 2011-2012 are to be taken for guidance and are not to be quoted as authority. The actual rates may be (slightly) more or less than those specified below :

Sr. No.	Full Description of item	Rate for completed item
(I)	**Excavation**	
1.	Excavation for boundations in earth and ordinary soil, sand, gravel, soft murum upto a lift (or depth) of 1.5 m and removing the excavated material to a distance of 50 m and stacking and spreading as instructed including dewatering, shoring and strutting, preparing the bed for foundation and including back filling, ramming, watering etc. complete.	₹ 111.00/m³
2.	Excavation for foundations in earth and ordinary soil, sand, gravel, soft murum for a lift (or depth) from 1.5 to 3 m and removing the excavated material to a distance of 50 m and stacking and spreading as instructed including dewatering, shoring and strutting, preparing the bed for foundation and including back filling, ramming, watering etc. complete.	₹ 119.00/m³
3.	Excavation for foundations in hard murum to a lift (or depth) of 1.5 m including removal of excavated material to a distance of 50 m and stacking and spreading as instructed, dewatering, preparation of bed for foundations and back filling, ramming, watering including shoring, strutting, etc. complete.	₹ 119.00/m³

Sr. No.	Full Description of item	Rate for completed item
4.	Excavation for foundations in hard murum to a lift (or depth) from 1.5 to 3 m including removal of excavated material to a distance of 50 m and stacking, spreading as instructed, dewatering, preparation of bed for foundations and back filling, ramming, watering including shoring, strutting, etc. complete.	₹ 136.00/m³
(II)	**Structural Steel Work**	
5.	Providing and fabricating structural steel work in rolled sections such as joists, channels, angles, tees, etc. as per drawing including fixing in position without connecting plates, braces etc. with two coats of oil painting over one coat of anti-corrosive paint.	₹ 57,424/M.T.
6.	Providing structural steel work in trusses with all bracing, gusset plates, etc. as per drawing including cutting, fabricating, hoisting, erecting and fixing in position with 2 coats of oil paint over one coat of anticorrosive paint.	₹ 64,802/M.T.
7.	Providing and fixing in position 50 mm dia. G.I. pipe gate with all fixtures and fastenings in two leaves with hold fast firmly embeded in cement concrete (1 : 2 : 4) block at bottom and top including cutting, bending with one primer coat.	₹ 3,216/m²
(III)	**Plain Cement Concrete (P.C.C.)**	
8.	Providing and laying in position plain cement concrete M-15 (i.e. 1 : 2 : 4) of trap or granite broken stone for foundations and bedding, inclusive and bailing out of water form work and compacting, curing etc. complete. (cement 5.90 bags/cub.m.)	₹ 3762/m³
9.	Providing and laying in position plain cement concrete M-10 (i.e. 1 : 4 : 8) of trap or granite broken stone for foundations and bedding including removal of water from work and compacting, curing etc. complete.	₹ 3001/m³
10.	Poviding and cast in situ cement concrete M-15 (i.e. 1 : 2 : 4) of trap or granite metal for steps inclusive of centering, form work, compacting, curing, finishing, etc. complete (cement 5.90 bags/cub.m.)	₹ 3850/m³
11.	Providing and cast in situ M-20 cement concrete (i.e. 1 : 1.5 : 3) of trap or granite metal for steps inclusive of centering, form work, compacting, curing and finishing etc. complete.	₹ 4173/m³
(IV)	**Reinforced Cement Concrete (R.C.C.)**	
12.	Providing and laying in position cement concrete M-20 (i.e. 1 : 1.5 : 3) of trap or granite metal for R.C.C. work in foundations and footings of R.C.C. columns inclusive of removing water, formwork, compaction and curing complete. (excluding reinforcement)	₹ 3939/m³

Sr. No.	Full Description of item	Rate for completed item
13.	Providing and casting in situ cement concrete M-20 (i.e. 1 : 1.5 : 3) of trap or granite metal for R.C.C. columns including centering, formwork, compacting and curing complete (exclusive of reinforcement (cement 5.9 bags/cub.m.).	₹ 5316/m³
14.	Providing and casting in situ cement concrete M-20 (i.e. 1 : 1.5 : 3) of trap or granite metal for R.C.C. Lintels and R.C.C. beam inclusive of centering, tormwork, compacting and curing complete. (excluding reinforcement) (cement 5.9 bags/cub.m.)	₹ 5470/m³
15.	Providing and casting in situ cement concrete M-20 (i.e. 1 : 1.5 : 3) of trap or granite metal for R.C.C. slab and landings and chajja inclusive of centering, formwork, compaction and curing complete. (excluding reinforcement).	₹ 5946/m³
16.	Providing and casting in situ cement concrete M-20 (i.e. 1 : 1.5 : 3) of trap or granite metal for coping of R.C.C. to parapet plinth and sills of doors and windows inclusive of centering, formwork, compaction, curing complete. (excluding reinforcement)	₹ 4446/m³
17.	Providing and casting in situ cement concrete M-20 (i.e. 1 : 1.5 : 3) of trap or granite metal for waist slab and steps of R.C.C. including centering, formwork, compaction and curing complete. (excluding reinforcement)	₹ 5280/m³
18.	Providing and casting in situ cement concrete M-20 (i.e. 1 : 1.5 : 3) of trap or granite metal for R.C.C. newel posts of stair case, including centering, formwork, compaction and curing complete. (excluding reinforcement)	₹ 4730/m³
(V)	**Brick Work (or Masonry)**	
19.	Providing IInd class burnt brick masonry (I.S. size or conventional size bricks) in cement mortar (1 : 6) in foundations and plinth inclusive of bailing out water striking joints of unexposed faces and raking joints of exposed faces, watering etc. complete.	₹ 3612/m³
20.	Providing IInd class burnt brick masonry (with conventional or I.S. type bricks) in cement mortar (1; 6) in superstructure inclusive of striking of joints, and raking of joints including scaffolding, watering complete.	₹ 3662/m³
21.	Providing IInd class burnt brick masonry (with I.S.) or conventional size bricks in cement mortar (1 :4) in half brick thick wall including M.S. reinforcement (longitudinal at every) third course including scaffolding, raking of joints, watering complete.	₹ 523/m²
22.	Providing IInd class burnt brick masonry with I.S. or conventional bricks in cement mortar (1 : 4) for rectangular pillars including scaffolding, raking of joints and watering complete.	₹ 3744/m³

Sr. No.	Full Description of item	Rate for completed item
(VI)	**Stone Masonry**	
23.	Providing U.C.R. masonry of trap or granite stones in cement mortar (1 : 6) in foundations and plinth inclusive of bailing out of water, striking of joints of unexposed faces, watering etc. complete.	₹ 2307/m³
24.	Providing U.C.R. masonry of trap or granite stones in cement mortar (1 : 6) inclusive of bailing out water, striking of joints of unexposed faces, watering for superstructure including raking or striking of joints, scaffolding and watering etc. complete	₹ 2338/m³
25.	Providing R.R. masonry IInd sort of trap or granite stones in cement mortar (1 : 6) in plinth including removal of water, striking joints on unexposed faces, watering complete.	₹ 2262/m³
26.	Providing R. R. masonry IInd sort of trap or granite stones in cement mortar (1 : 6) in superstructure including removal of water, striking joints on unexposed faces, watering, superstructure including watering, scaffolding complete.	₹ 2340/m³
27.	Providing coursed rubble masonry IInd sort of trap or granite stone in cement mortar (1 : 6) in plinth including removal of water, striking for raking joints and watering.	₹ 4905/m³
28.	Providing coursed rubble masonry IInd sort of trap or granite stone in cement mortar (1 : 6) in superstructure including removal of water, striking for raking joints and watering for superstructure including scaffolding complete.	₹ 5114/m³
(VII)	**Cement Conrete Hollow Block Masonry**	
29.	Providing and laying Indian standard hollow block in cement concrete, of size 100 × 200 × 400 mm in cement mortar 1 : 6 portion, finished with neeru etc. complete.	₹ 339/m²
30.	Providing and laying Indian hollow block in cement concrete of size 200 × 200 × 400 mm in cement mortar 1 : 6 for superstructure including scaffolding, cement pointing from outside, watering etc. complete.	₹ 520/m²
(VIII)	**Water Proofing Course**	
31.	Providing and laying damp proof course 5 cm thick in cement concrete (1 : 2 : 4) and bitumen/using cement with water proofing compound.	₹ 224/m²
32.	Providing and laying bitumen layer @ 2 kg per m² over the terrace structural slab.	₹ 108/m²

Sr. No.	Full Description of item	Rate for completed item
(IX)	**Plastering, Pointing**	
(i)	**Plastering**	
33.	Providing and applying 6 mm thick internal cement mortar (1 : 4) without neeru finish to concrete surfaces including scaffolding, curing complete.	₹ 80/m²
34.	Providing and applying internal cement plaster 12 mm thick in cement mortar without neeru finish to concrete or brick surfaces including scaffolding, curing.	
	(i) 1 : 5 cement mortar	₹ 109/m²
	(ii) 1 : 4 cement mortar	₹ 117/m²
	(iii) 1 : 3 cement mortar	₹ 124/m²
35.	Providing and applying neeru finish to the plastered surfaces including scaffolding, curing (excluding for ceiling)	₹ 21/m²
36.	Providing neeru finish to the plastered surface for ceiling.	₹21/m²
(ii)	**Pointing**	
37.	Providing and applying pointing (grooved) with cement mortar 1 : 3 for brick work inclusive of scaffolding, curing.	₹ 69/m²
38.	Providing and applying pointing with cement mortar (1 : 3) for stone masonry inclusive of scaffolding, curing.	
	(i) Tuck pointing	₹ 74/m²
	(ii) Weathered pointing	₹ 72/m²
	(iii) Vee-pointing	₹ 67/m²
	(iv) Flush-pointing	₹ 65/m²
(X)	**Flooring**	
39.	Providing and laying Shahabad stone flooring 25 to 30 mm thick and a bed of cement mortar (1 : 6) including cement float, striking joints, pointing in cement mortar (1 : 3) including, curing, cleaning.	
	(i) Rough Shahabad	₹ 384/m²
	(ii) Polished Shahabad	₹ 460/m²
40.	Providing and fixing skirting or dado of polished Shahabad stone slabs 25 to 30 mm thick and 300 cm wide on 1 : 4 cement plaster or 1 : 2 lime plaster inclusive of cement float, filling joints, cement slurry, curing, polishing, cleaning etc. complete.	₹ 460/m²

Sr. No.	Full Description of item	Rate for completed item
41.	Providing and laying cement concrete flooring 40 mm thick with 1 : 2 : 3 cement concrete, compaction, filling joints marking lines diagonally or square size 30 cm × 30 cm including curing etc. complete.	₹ 241/m²
	Flooring	
42.	Providing and laying **polished Kotah stone flooring 25 mm to 30 mm thick** in required width in plain/diamond pattern on a bed of 1:6 cement mortar including cement float, filling joints with neat cement slurry, curing, polishing and cleaning complete.	₹ 732/m²
43.	Providing and fixing **black Kadappa stone shelves**, 25 mm thick machine polished, extending the polish upto 20 cm width on lower side rounding corners, laying in position jointly with cement mortar bedding cement mortar 1:4 proportion curing etc. complete.	₹ 650/m²
44.	Providing and laying **ceramic tiles** of approved quality 30 cm × 30 cm × 8 mm for flooring in required position laid on a bed of 1:4 cement mortar including cement float, filling joint with white/colour cement slurry cleaning curing complete.	₹ 650/m²
45.	Providing and laying **vitrified matt finish decorative type tiles** of size 590 mm to 605 mm × 590 mm to 605 mm of 8 to 10 mm thickness and confirming I.S. 15622-2006 [Group B/a] of approved make, shade and pattern for flooring in required position laid on a bed of 1:4 cement mortar including neat cement float, filling joints, curing and cleaning etc. complete.	
	(a) Flooring	₹ 1150/m²
	(b) Skirting	₹ 1412/m²
(XI)	**Colour or White Washing and Distempering**	
46.	Providing and applying white or colour wash in one coat or two coats on old/new plastered or masonry faces inclusive of scaffolding and preparing the surface by brushing and brooming etc. complete.	
	(i) White wash one coat	₹ 2.80/m²
	(ii) White wash two coats	₹ 4.60/m²
	(iii) Colour wash one coat	₹ 3.55/m²
	(iv) Colour wash two coats	₹ 7.00/m²
	(v) Colour wash three coats	₹ 9.00/m²
47.	Providing and applying powder distemper (washable) of desired colour to old and new faces in one or two coats inclusive of scaffolding, preparing the surface (exclusive of prime coat)	
	(i) One coat	₹ 8.00/m²
	(ii) Two coats	₹ 12.00/m²

Sr. No.	Full Description of item	Rate for completed item
48.	Providing and applying oil bound distemper (washable) of desired colour to old and new surfaces, in one or two coats inclusive of scaffolding, and preparing the surface (exclusive of prime coat)	
	(i) One coat	₹ 17.00/m^2
	(ii) Two coats	₹ 25.00/m^2
	(iii) Three coats	₹ 29.00/m^2
(XII)	**Roofing**	
49.	Providing and fixing in position Mangalore tiled (AA - class type) roofing including fastening the last course of tiles near the eaves with steel flat (40 mm × 3 mm × 1.25 mm) wire fixing teak wood battens (25 mm × 12 mm) sloping and horizontal battens (50 mm × 25 mm) over sloping battens, nailing, tarring, etc. complete (exclusive of trip and ridge tiles).	₹ 540/m^2
50.	Providing and fixing Mangalore hip or ridge tiles (AA class type) inclusive of scaffolding, pointing, curing etc. complete.	₹ 120/m^2
51.	Providing and fixing galvanised iron sheets (corrugated) of 0.8 mm thickness i.e. (22 BWG) for roofing including fastering, bolting etc. complete.	₹ 560/m^2
52.	Providing and fixing zinc sheeting of 0.8 mm thickness for ridge and hip valley for G.C.I. sheet roofing including fastering, bolting etc. complete.	₹ 650/m^2
53.	Providing and fixing 6 mm thick asbestos semicorrugated sheet roofing including G.I. J. or 1 Books, washers, clamps, nuts and bolts and scaffolding complete.	
	(i) Big size sheets	₹ 300/m^2
	(ii) Trafford sheets	₹ 285/m^2
54.	Providing and fixing 6 mm thick A.C. ridge capping to roofing inclusive of hooks, washers, clamps, nuts and bolts inclusive of scaffolding.	₹ 225/RM
(XIII)	**Doors, Windows**	
55.	Providing and fixing door frame having ventilator frame 60 mm × 100 mm including chamfering, rounding, rebating, hold fast of size 30 mm × 40 mm size painted with oil. (Door sizes are inclusive of frame).	
	(i) 1.2 m × 2.6 m - Double leaf shutters with C.C.T.W.	₹ 2139/m^2
	(ii) 1 m × 2.6 m for double and or single leaf shutters of C.C.T.W.	₹ 3530/m^2
56.	Providing and fixing door frame without ventilator frame 60 mm × 100 mm including chamfering, rounding, rebating, hold fast of size 30 mm × 40 mm size painted with oil.	
	(i) 1.2 m × 2.1 m for double leaf shutters with C.C.T.W.	₹ 2700/m^2
	(ii) 0.9 m × 2.1 m for single leaf shutter with C.C.T.W.	₹ 3432/m^2

Sr. No.	Full Description of item	Rate for completed item
57.	Providing and fixing window frames with ventilators frame inclusive of chamfering, rounding, rebating, hold fast 0.3 m × 0.04 m × 0.005 m, with oil paint three coats.	
	(i) 1.2 m × 1.7 m for double leaf shutter C.C.T.W.	₹ 1992/m²
	(ii) 1 m × 1.7 m for double leaf shutter with C.C.T.W.	₹ 1725/m²
58.	Providing and fixing window frames without ventilators frame inclusive of chamfering, rounding, rebating, hold fast 0.3 m × 0.04 m × 0.005 m, with oil paint three coats.	
	(i) 1.2 m × 2.1 m for double leaf shutter with C.C.T.W.	₹ 2388/m²
	(ii) 1 m × 1.2 m for double leaf shutter with C.C.T.W.	₹ 2718/m²
(XIV)	**Iron Work**	
59	Providing and fixing M.S. Grill for windows and ventilator at 20 kg/m² with fixtures, welding and one coat of painting (anti corrosive) and two oil paint coats.	
	(i) 20 kg/sq.m	₹ 979/m²
	(ii) 25 kg/sq.m	₹ 1230/m²
	(iii) 15 kg/sq.m	₹ 762/m²
	Note : For the items other than those mentioned above, please refer schedule of rates published by P.W.D., Maharashtra Government.	

3.10 DETAILED ESTIMATE OF R.C.C. RETAINING WALL

Item No.	Particulars	Quantity Unit	Rate ₹	Rate Ps.	Per Unit	Amount ₹	Amount Ps.
1.	Cleating site before and after the work including removing all the debris, shrubs etc.		Lumpsum			500	00
2.	Excavation for foundation in earth, soils of all types, sand, gravel and soft murum, including removing the excavated material upto a distance of 50 m and stacking and spreading as director dewatering, preparing the bed for the foundation and necessary backfilling, ramming, watering including shoring and strutting etc. complete.						
	(i) Lift from 0 to 1.50 m	4.125 m³	35	00	m³	144	35
	(ii) Lift from 1.50 to 3.00 m	0.275 m³	37	00	m³	10	15

Item No.	Particulars	Quantity Unit	Rate ₹	Rate Ps.	Per Unit	Amount ₹	Amount Ps.
3.	Providing and laying in position plain cement concrete M 15 (1 : 2 : 4) of trap or granite broken stone for foundations and bedding, inclusive of bailing out of water, formwork and compacting, curing etc. complete	0.4125 m³	1307	00	m³	539	15
4.	Providing and laying in situ (1 : 2 : 4) cement concrete of trap/granite/quartzite/gneiss metal for RCC work including ramming, vibrating, finishing and curing complete in main/cross girders, diaphragms etc. (including formwork, centering, finishing in cement plaster and excluding reinforcement)						
	(i) Upto 3 m height	2.065 m³	2357	00	m³	4867	20
	(ii) Above 3 m height (Add 5% extra)	0.215 m³	2475	00	m³	532	10
5.	Providing cutting, bending, hooking, laying in position and tieing HYSD bars for reinforcement as per detailed drawings for all R.C.C.	0.2656 t	19000	00	M.T.	5127	15
6.	Providing selected hard murum filling including laying in layers of 15 cm to 20 cm, watering and compacting complete.	7.45 m³	67	20	m³	501	00

Total		12220.65
Add 5 % contigencies	-	611.05
Total		**12831.90**
Add 1 % work charged established	-	128.30
Total cost	-	₹ **12960.20**

∴ The estimated total cost per metre length of the retaining wall ≈ ₹ 12961 - 00/-

Estimate of R.C.C. Retaining wall

Item No.	Description	No.	Length	Breadth	Depth	Quantity	Total Quantity
1.	Clearing site			Job item			
2.	Excavation for foundation in earth, soils of all types, sand, gravel and soft murum, including removing the excavated material upto a distance of 50 m and stacking and spreading as directed, dewatering, preparing the bed for the foundation and necessary back filling, ramming, water including shoring and strutting etc. complete.						
(i)	Lift from 0 to 1.5 m	1	1.00	2.75	1.50	4.125	m^3
(ii)	Lift from 1.50 to 3.00 m	1	1	2.75	0.10	0.275	m^3
3.	Providing and laying in position plain cement concrete M-15 (i.e. 1 : 2 : 4) of trap or granite broken stone for foundations and bedding, inclusive of bailing out of water, formwork and compacting, curing etc. complete.	1	1.000	2.75	0.15	0.4125	$0.4125\ m^3$
4.	Providing and laying in situ (1 : 2 : 4) cement concrete of trap/granite/quartzite/gneiss metal for RCC work including ramming, vibrating, finishing and curing complete in main/cross grinders, diaphragms etc. (including formwork, centering, finishing in cement plaster and excluding reinforcement).						
	(i)　Height upto 3 m						
	(a)　Base slab	1	1.000	2.60	0.450	1.17	
	(b)　Stem	1	1.000	A = 0.895 m²		0.895	$2.065\ m^3$
	Area $= \left(\dfrac{0.2025 + 0.5}{2}\right) \times 2.55 = 0.895\ m^2$						
	(ii)　Above 3 m						
	(a)　Trapezoidal portion	1	1.000	A = 0.08 m²		0.08	
	$A = \left(\dfrac{0.15 + 0.025}{2}\right) \times 0.45 = 0.08\ m^2$						
	(b)　Rectangular portion	1	1.000	A = 0.135 m²		0.135	$0.215\ m^3$
	$A = 0.15 \times 0.90 = 0.135\ m^2$						
	(Add 5% for height from 3 m to 6 m)						

Item No.	Description	No.	Length	Breadth	Depth	Quantity	Total Quantity
5.	Steel work						
	Providing cutting, bending, hooking, laying in position and tieing HYSD steel bars for reinforcement as per detailed drawings for all RCC members						
	(A) Stem : Right side						
	(i) 16 mm R (a) 200 mm c/c (full height)	6	8.014 Total length $\Big\}$ 48.084m				
	Length = 0.038 + 0.828 + 0.302 + 0.45 + 2.478 + 2 × 0.35 + 0.5 = 8.014 m						
	No. of bars $= \dfrac{1.00 - \text{covers}}{0.20} + 1$						
	$= \dfrac{1.00 - 0.05}{0.20} + 1$						
	$= 5.75 \approx 6$ Nos.						
	(iii) 16 mm diamater upto 3.6 @ 100 mm c/c length = 8.014 − (0.038 + 0.828) = 7.148 m	7	7.148	Total	length	= 50.036	m
	No. of bars $= \dfrac{0.95 - 0.05 \times 2}{0.20} + 1$						
	$= 6.25 = 7$ Nos.						
	Area of 16 mm bars						
	$= \dfrac{\pi(0.016)^2}{4} = 1.131 \times 10^{-4}\,m^2$						
	Vol. of steel = (48.084 + 50.036) ×						
	$2.0106 \times 10^{-4} = 0.01972\,m^3$						
	Wt. of steel = 0.01972 × 7850 = 155 kg					0.155 t	
	(B) Stem : Left side						
	12 mm diameter @ 150 c/c	87	108	Total	length =	56.864 m	
	Length = 0.05 + 4.25 + 2.484 + 0.324 = 7.108 m						
	No. of bars $= \dfrac{1.00 - 0.05}{0.15} + 1 = 7.3$						
	≈ 8 Nos.						

Item No.	Description	No.	Length	Breadth	Depth	Quantity	Total Quantity
	Area $= \dfrac{\pi(0.012)^2}{4} = 1.131 \times 10^{-4}$ m^2						
	Vol. of steel						
	$= 56.864 \times 1.131 \times 10^4 = 6.431 \times 10^{-3}$ m^3						
	Wt. of steel =						
	$6.431 \times 10^{-3} \times 7850 = 50.4846$ kg					0.0505 t	
	(C)　Distribution Reinforcement						
	10 mm diameter @ 130 c/c						
	(i)　Right side of stem :						
	Nos. $= \dfrac{3848}{130} + 1 = 30.6 \approx 31$	31	1.06	Total	length	= 32.86 m	
	length = 1.00 - 20 covers + 2 hooks						
	$= 1.00 - 2 \times 0.05 + 2 \times 0.08 \approx 1.06$ m						
	(ii)　Left side of stem						
	Nos. $= \dfrac{0.05 + 3.90}{0.13} + 1$	32	1.06	Total	length	= 33.92	
	$= 31.38 \approx 32$						
	(iii)　Base slab :						
	Nos. $= \dfrac{(2.6 - 0.05)}{0.150} + 1 \approx 29$	29	1.06	Total	length	= 30.74	
	Area $= \dfrac{\pi(0.01)^2}{4} - 7.85 \times 10^{-4}$ m^2						
	Vol. of steel $= 7.85 \times 10^{-4} \times$	95.52 m $= 7.66 \times 10^{-3}$ m^3					
	Wt. of steel $= 7.66 \times 10^{-3} \times$	7850					
	$= 60.125$ kg					0.0601 t	
	Total wt. of HYSD steel						0.2656 t
6.	Providing selected hard murum filling laying in layers of 15 cm to 20 cm, watering and compacting complete.						
	(i)　Trapezoidal portion						
	Area $= \left(\dfrac{2.516 + 2.60}{2}\right) \times 2.0 = 5.116$ m^2	1	1.000	A = 5.116		5.116 m^3	
	(ii)　Rectangular portion	1	1.000	0.90		2.340 m^3	7.45 m^3

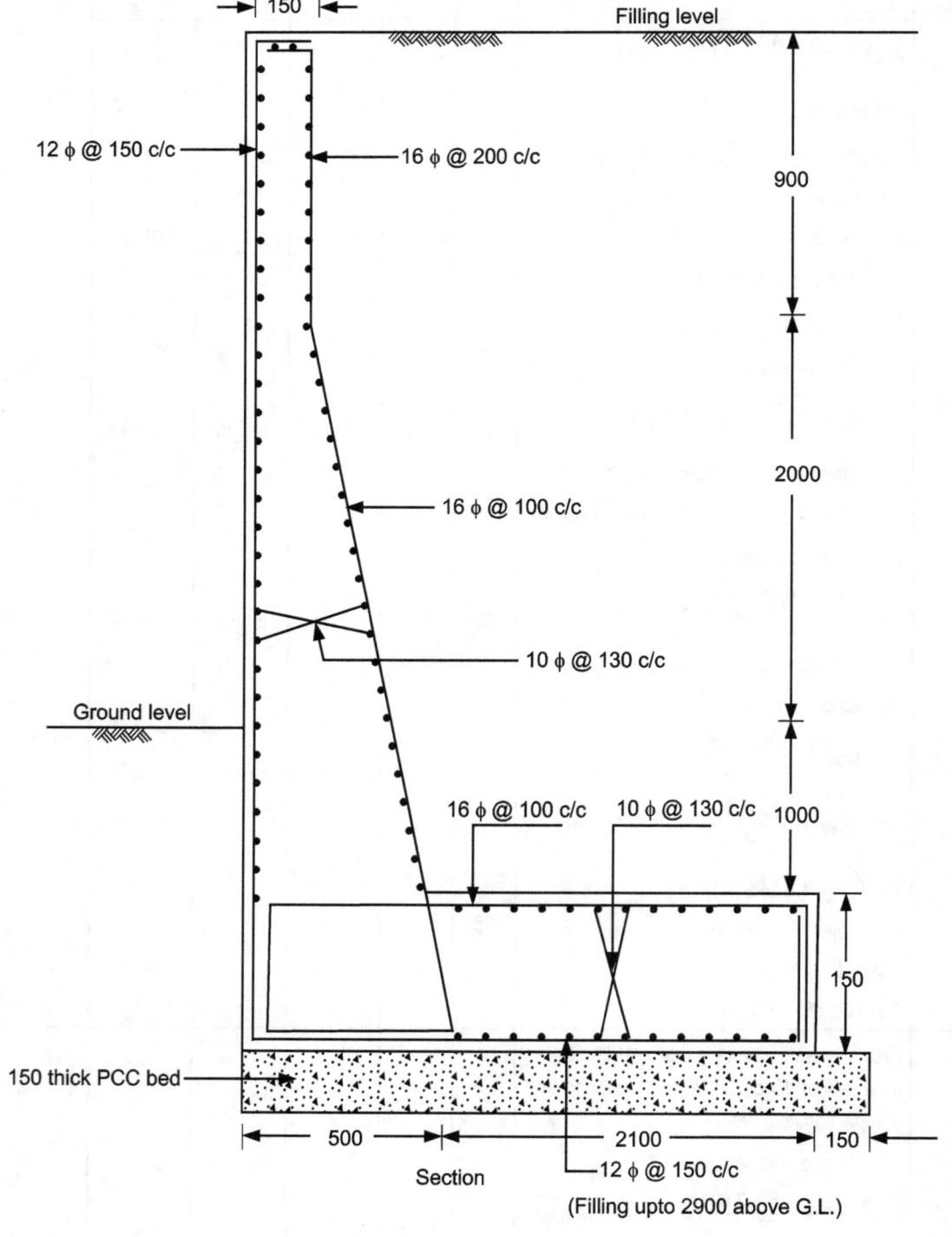

150

Filling level

12 φ @ 150 c/c

16 φ @ 200 c/c

900

16 φ @ 100 c/c

2000

10 φ @ 130 c/c

Ground level

16 φ @ 100 c/c   10 φ @ 130 c/c   1000

150

150 thick PCC bed

500   2100   150

Section

12 φ @ 150 c/c

(Filling upto 2900 above G.L.)

Fig. 3.53 : Retaining wall

THEORETICAL QUESTIONS

1. Explain the meaning of taking out quantities.
2. State the general procedure of measurement of works of various items of works.
3. Explain the various methods of taking out quantities.
4. Compare English and P.W.D. methods of estimating.
5. Enumerate the various common items of construction involved in the construction of a load bearing structure with : (i) Flat roof of R.C.C. and (ii) Sloping roof of Mangalore tiles.
6. Distinguish between Prime cost and Provisional sum.
7. Write short notes on : (i) Provisional quantities, (ii) Spot items.
8. What is meant by contingencies ? Why is it provided in detailed estimates ? State two items that can be included under contingencies.
9. What is meant by work-charged establishment ? Why this establishment is called as work-charged establishment ?
10. Explain the term 'centage charges'.
11. Explain the terms Lead and Lift used in the description of excavation item.
12. State the rules for deductions for openings to be made from brick masonry work in superstructure.
13. Explain the terms work charged establishment and contingencies.
14. Distinguish between revised estimate and supplimentary estimate.
15. Write the standards laid down for deduction for openings in brick masonry wall.
16. Write short notes on : (i) District schedule of rates, (ii) Prime cost, (iii) Provisional sums.
17. State the rules for deduction to be made for openings for plaster work.
18. What are provisional quantities and sums ? When are these provided in an estimate ?
19. Explain in detail the mode of measurement of the following items of work as per I.S.
    (i)   R. C. C. work
           (a)   Columns
           (b)   Beams
           (c)   Slab
           (d)   Staircase step
    (ii)   Painting work
           (a)   Oil painting to wood work,
           (b)   Structural steel work,
           (c)   Doors and windows.
    (iii) B. B. masonry work for different thickness of walls.

20. What are different modes of measurement of brick work ? State the rules for deductions for openings to be made from brick work.

21. State the particular accuracy for measuring thickness or cross-sectional dimensions, required to be adopted in case of any two of the following works as per I.S. 1200.
(i) Concrete work, (ii) Brick work, (iii) Timber work.

22. Write short notes on : (1) Data required for preparing estimate, (2) Centre-line method of estimating, (3) Centage charges, (4) Multiplying factor for equivalent plane area in case of painting.

23. State the standards laid down for the following : (1) Measurement of painting for fully glazed window, (2) Deductions for opening in brick masonry wall, (3) Measurement of T beams.

24. State the units of measurement for the following : (1) Door frame, (2) Stair railing, (3) Stone ware pipe, (4) M.S. reinforcement.

25. State the units of measurement for the following : (1) Excavation for pot holes for erecting ballies of pendal, (2) C.C. (1 : 2 : 4) DPC course in plinth, (3) Urinal partitions of polished kadappa, (4) Pointing in C.M. (1 : 3) to exposed stone work, (6) M.S. Grill work.

26. Differentiate between Revised estimate and Supplimentary estimate.

27. What is bill of quantity ? State its importance.

28. Write a note on D.S.R.

29. Why are contingencies and work charged establishments added to estimated cost ?

30. Write short notes on : (i) Schedule of Rate, (ii) Provisional sums.

31. Define contingencies and prepare a list of items which will be covered under the head 'Contingencies'.

32. Define and explain in detail how you will calculate : (i) Carpet area of a tenament, (ii) Cubic contents of a building.

33. (a) Explain the principles underlying selection of a unit for measurement of an item of work.

    (b) State any three items of brick work along with their units of measurement.

34. State the standard mode of measurement for the following items :

(i)	Mangalore Tile Roofing	(ii)	G.I. pipe
(iii)	Inspection chamber	(iv)	Excavation
(v)	R.C.C. beam	(vi)	Dado
(vii)	Ridge tiles	(viii)	Flush pointing
(ix)	Wash hand basin	(x)	Flooring
(xi)	M. S. bar reinforcement	(xii)	20 cm thick brick masonry
(xiii)	U.C.R. masonry	(xiv)	Plastering

35. State the mode of measurement (I.S.) for the following items : (1) M.S. Reinforcement for R.C.C. work, (2) Teak wood for door frame, (3) G.I. Pipe line for carrying water, (4) Mangalore Tile Ridge, (5) Damp proof course, (6) Cement pointing in C.M., (1 : 3) for brick work, (7) A.C. Sheet roof covering, (8) M.S. Grill for windows.

36. Write correct and complete description for the item of providing mosaic tile flooring on lime mortar.

37. What is the necessity of preparing detailed estimate for any construction project ?

38. (a)   State different types of estimates and explain their appropriate use under different conditions.

    (b)   What data is required to be collected before preparing an any estimate ?

39. State the multiplying factor required to be adopted for converting the following curved areas into equivalent plane areas : (i) Fully panelled door, (ii) Fully glazed window,   (iii) M. S. Grill in opening, (iv) A. C. sheet roofing.

40. What are establishment charges ? At what stage are they included in the estimate ? What is the quantum of establishment charges?

41. Write short notes on :

    (1)   Prime cost items

    (2)   Revised estimate

    (3)   Contingencies

    (4)   Abstract of an estimate

    (5)   Works included in the item of excavation

42. Explain the term 'Prime cost item' in a building contract and state how the payment due to the contractor under the prime cost item is arrived at.

43. What is meant by 'extra item' in bill of quantities ?

44. State the mode of measurement for the following items of work :

1.	Site clearance	2.	Steps of stair case
3.	Concrete Jallis	4.	R.C.C. sun breakers
5.	String course and cornices	6.	R.C.C. pile
7.	Honey combed brick work	8.	Brick coping
9.	Half brick work in partition	10.	Stone masonry
11.	Plain or corrugated sheets	12.	Evaes gutter
13.	M.S. rolling shutters	14.	Steel windows
15.	Spiral stair case	16.	Iron work
17.	C.I. brackets	18.	Window frame
19.	Door shutter	20.	Balustrades
21.	Pot holes		

Ans. 1. Job item – L.S. provision   2. Number
      3. Square metres   4. Square metres
      5. Running metres   6. Cubic metres or running metres
      7. Square metres   8. Square metres
      9. Square metres   10. Cubic metres
     11. Square metres   12. Running metres
     13. Square metres   14. Square metres
     15. Per number of steps   16. Quintal or kg
     17. Per number   18. Cubic metres
     19. Square metres   20. Square metres
     21. Per number

45. State the mode of measurements for the following items of walls :

      1. Mangalore tiled roof cover   2. Plastering 12 mm thick
      3. Pointing   4. Oil painting
      5. Floor pavement   6. White washing
      7. Glazing work   8. Brick bat coba
      9. Drainage line   10. Water supply pipe
     11. Vent pipe   12. Water storage tank
     13. Taps and cocks   14. Lead pipes
     15. Nahni trap   16. W.C. Pan
     17. Urinals   18. Wash hand basin
     19. Man hole   20. Inspection chambers
     21. Gullies   22. Intercepting trap
     23. Excavation for cables   24. Excavation for gulley trap chamber
          and pipes

Ans. 1. Square metres   2. Square metres
      3. Square metres   4. Square metres
      5. Square metres   6. Square metres
      7. Square metres   8. Square metres
      9. Running metres   10. Running metres
     11. Running metres   12. Per litre capacity
     13. Per number   14. Running metre
     15. Per number   16. Per number
     17. Per number   18. Per number
     19. Per number   20. Per number
     21. Per number   22. Per number
     23. Running metres   24. Per number

46. State the standard mode of measurements for the following items (any five) :

    (i)   Mangalore tile roofing   (ii) G.I. pipe

    (iii) Inspection chamber   (iv) Excavation

    (v)   R.C.C. beam   (vi) Dado

47. State the current market rates for (any five) :

    (i)   Glazed tile   (ii) Mangalore tiles

    (iii) Cement bag   (iv) M.S. bars

    (v)   Teak wood   (vi) Bricks

48. A compound wall in stone masonry is to be constructed for a newly built residential bungalow. Write down all possible items of work involved in this giving full description of each item as you would write in a measurement sheet form.

49. A compound wall in U.C.R. masonry in cement mortar (1 : 6) 10 m long, 20 cm thick and 1.10 m height including semi-circular coping of P.C.C. (1 : 3 : 6) of 10 cm radius over the top of the entire wall is to be constructed with the following details.

    (i)   Depth of excavation in ordinary soil = 30 cm below ground level.

    (ii)   Depth and width of P.C.C. (1 : 4 : 8) block below the entire compound wall to be 15 cm and 30 cm respectively.

    (iii) Semi-circular coping is of P.C.C (1 : 3 : 6) of 10 cm radius over the top of the entire wall.

    (iv) The compound wall above the ground level is to be pointed in cement mortar (1 : 6) from both the faces.

        (a)   Draw a neat dimensioned section of the compound wall showing all the details.

        (b)   List out all the items of works and calculate their quantities and enter them in a measurement sheet form.

        (c)   Assuming prevalent market rates for the above items, work out the cost of the above work and enter the results in an abstract sheet form.

    Assume suitable data whenever necessary.

50. Work out the quantity of earth work for 90 m road length. Formation width = 7 m. Side slope in embankment is 2 : 1 and in cutting, it is $1\frac{1}{2}$: 1.

Chainage (m)	Ground level (m)	Formation level (m)
0	125.00	123.60
30	124.60	124.00
60	122.90	123.60
90	121.60	123.20

51. A two room block with a common wall consists of :

   (i)   Living room 4 m × 4 m (internal dimensions)

   (ii)   Kitchen room 4 m × 3 m (internal dimensions)

   (iii) All the brick work in superstructure including the partition wall is load bearing and 30 cm thick.

   (iv)   Width of foundation at the bottom of excavation is 90 cm.

   (v)   U.C.R. masonry in foundation is 70 cm in width and 30 cm in depth.

   (vi)   Depth of P.C.C. (1 : 4 : 8) in foundation is 15 cm throughout.

   (vii) C.R. masonry in plinth is 50 cm in width and 75 cm in height.

   (viii) Height of brick wall in superstructure is 3.00 m.

   (ix)   Schedule of doors and windows.

Door	D	2 Nos.	1 m × 2.6 m
Window	W	2 Nos.	1 m × 1.4 m

   (a) Draw a centre line and foundation plan for the above building.

   (b) Work out the quantities of the following items of work, giving their full description. Enter your results in measurement sheet form.

   (i)   P.C.C. (1 : 4 : 8) in foundation

   (ii)   B. B. masonry IInd sort in cement mortar (1 : 6) in superstructure.

   (iii) 12 mm thick internal plastering in cement mortar (1 : 3) with neeru finish to brick walls.

52. The plan and section of a building are given in the accompanying sketch. Assuming any other data if required, find out the quantities for the following items of work using a standard measurement sheet. Write full description of each and every item :

   (a) Excavation for foundation

   (b) C.C. Bed for foundation

   (c) B.B. Masonry for superstructure

   (d) Doors and windows

   (e) Lintels over doors and windows.

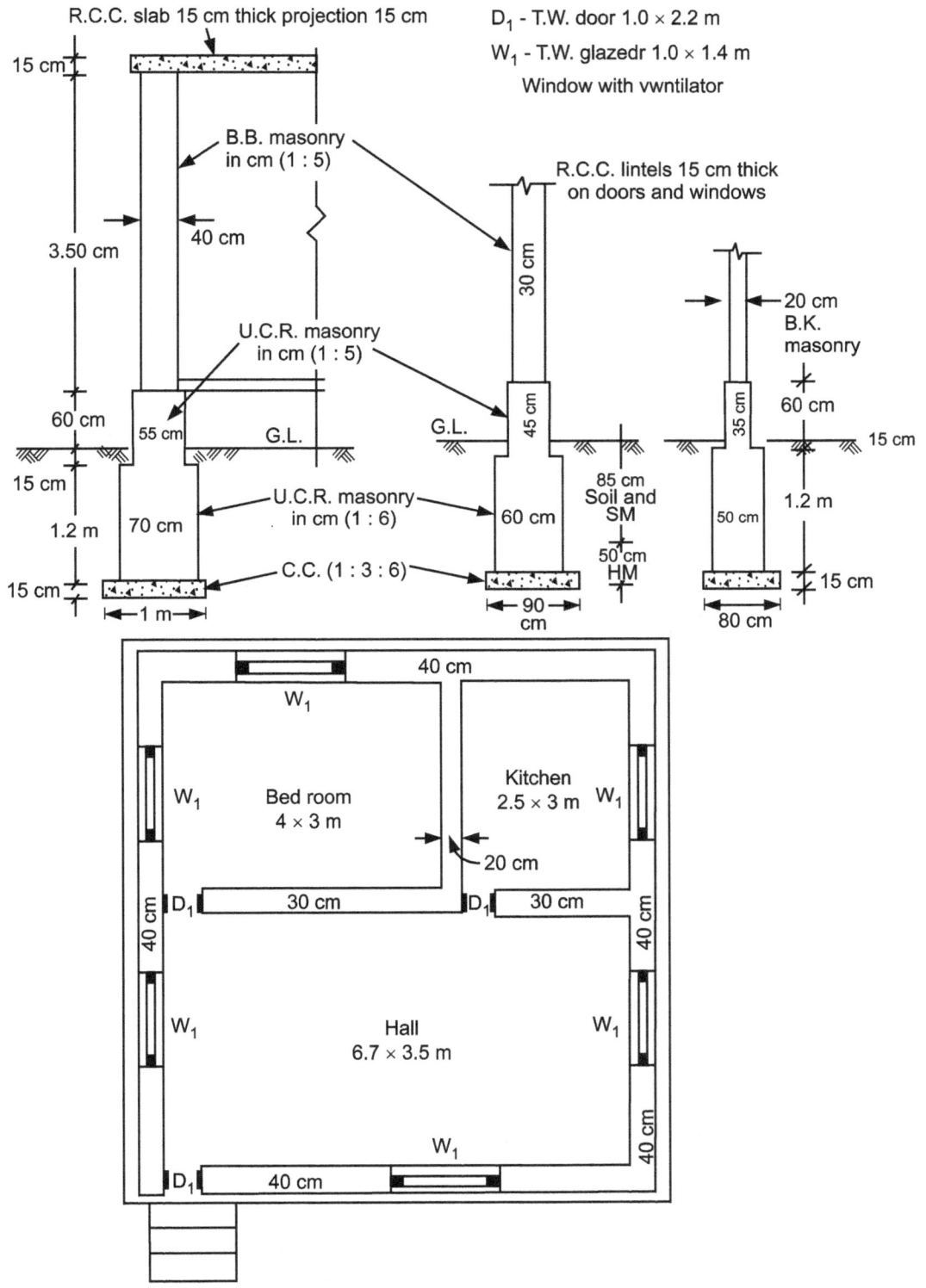

Fig. 3.54 : Plan and section of a building

53. Fig. 3.51 shows a plan and a section of a small bungalow. Following are the concerned construction details :

   (i)   Depth of foundation upto hard stratum – 1.2 m.

   (ii)   30 cm thick IInd class B.B. work in C.M. (1 : 6) in superstructure except kitchen and bedroom of internal walls of 20 cm thickness and sanitary block internal walls of 10 cm thickness.

   (iii) Mangalore tiled roof on T.W. supports.

   (iv)   13 mm thick neeru finished cement plaster in C.M. (1 : 4) on internal faces of all walls.

   (v)   20 mm thick sand faced cement plaster in C.M. (1 : 4) on external faces of all walls.

   (vi)   M. M. tile flooring in all rooms except sanitary block.

   (vii) Polished Shahabad stone flooring in sanitary block except W.C.

   (viii) White glazed tile flooring in W.C.

   (ix)   White glazed tile dado 45 cm. in W.C. and 1.2 m in bath.

Find out the quantities of any five of the following :

   (i)   Excavation in average soil.

   (ii)   U.C.R. masonry in C.M. (1 : 6) in foundation and plinth.

   (iii) IInd class B.B. work in C.M. (1 : 6) in superstructure.

   (iv)   T.W. work supporting roof. (Trusses to be measured on no basis)

   (v)   13 mm thick neeru finished cement plaster in C.M. (1 : 4) on internal faces of all walls.

   (vi)   (a) M.M. tile flooring

          (b) Polished Shahabad stone flooring.

          (c) White glazed tile dado.

Prepare an abstract for the four items you have chosen above. Write proper description of the items, adopt correct prevailing rates, and complete the estimate for those five items by adding usual contingencies and establishment charges.

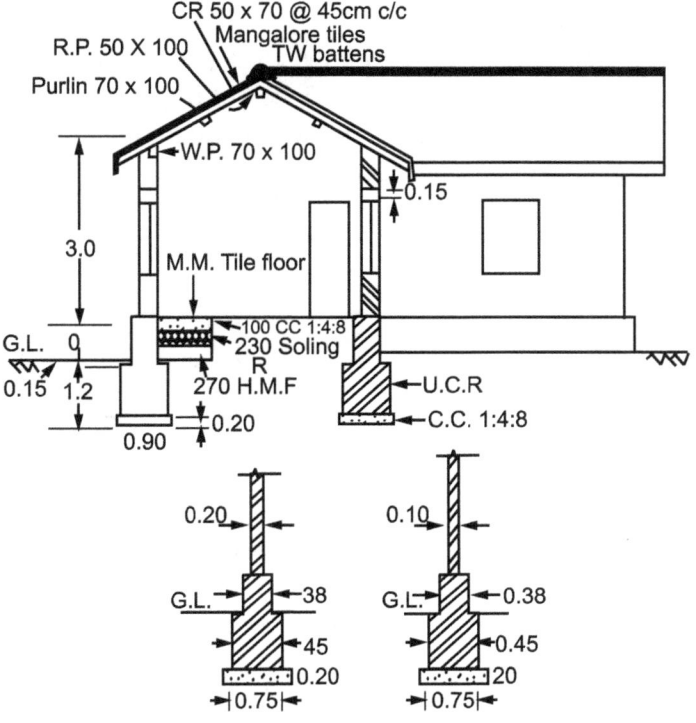

(a) Plan and section of small bungalow

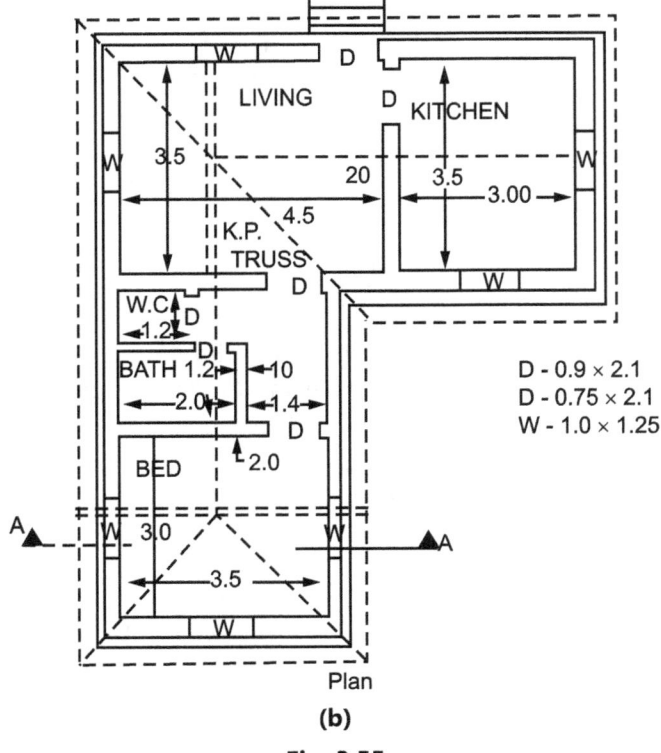

D - 0.9 × 2.1
D - 0.75 × 2.1
W - 1.0 × 1.25

Plan

(b)

Fig. 3.55

54. Solve any two of the following :

A bridge pier consists of the following dimensions. (Fig. 3.56).

Top width = 1.0 m, side face batters = 1 in 6, height of pier = 9 m and length of pier = 7 m. Assume end faces to be vertical. Find out the quantities of (i) C.R. masonry in pier, (ii) Cement pointing to the battered faces.

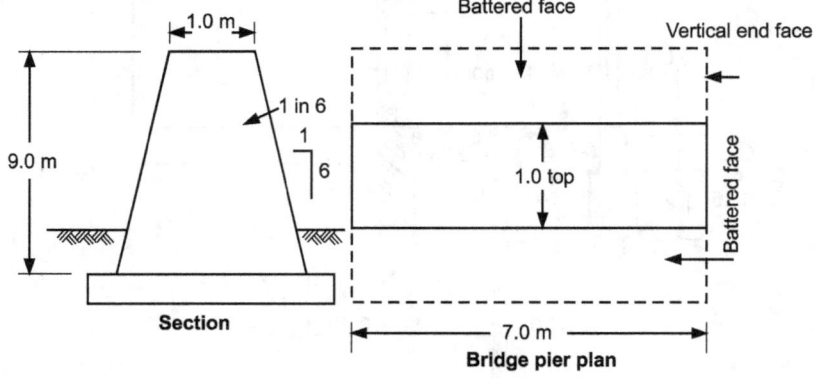

Fig. 3.56

55. Find out the quantity of cement concrete (1 : 2 : 4) required for the R.C.C. footing. (Fig. 3.57).

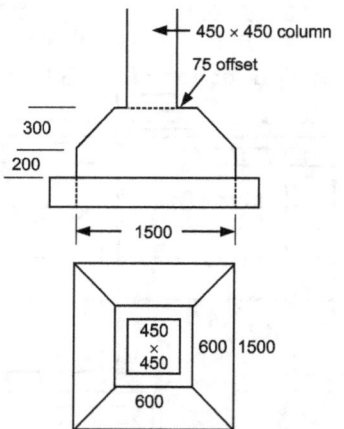

Fig. 3.57 : R.C.C. footing

56. A canal in embankment consists of side banks of following dimensions :

(Fig. 3.58). Length = 1 km, Top width = 1.5 m, Side slopes = 2 horizontal, 1 vertical, Height of bank = 1.5 m throughout the length. Assume that there is no cross slope. Work out the quantity of embankment required on both the banks of the canal.

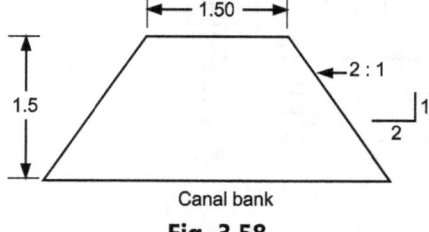

Canal bank

Fig. 3.58

57. Fig. 3.59 indicates L-section of a road. G.L.'s and Earth Formation Level (EFL) at starting point (Ch. O) are shown. Gradients are also mentioned.

(i)   Work out the EFL's for all other points.

(ii)   Find out chainages of points of intersection of GL and EFL, between chainages 0 to 30 and 180 to 210.

(iii)   Find out the total quantity of earth work in embankment and cutting, given that the formation width = 7.0 m, side slopes $2\frac{1}{2}$: 1 for embankment and $1\frac{1}{2}$: 1 for cutting and no cross slope.

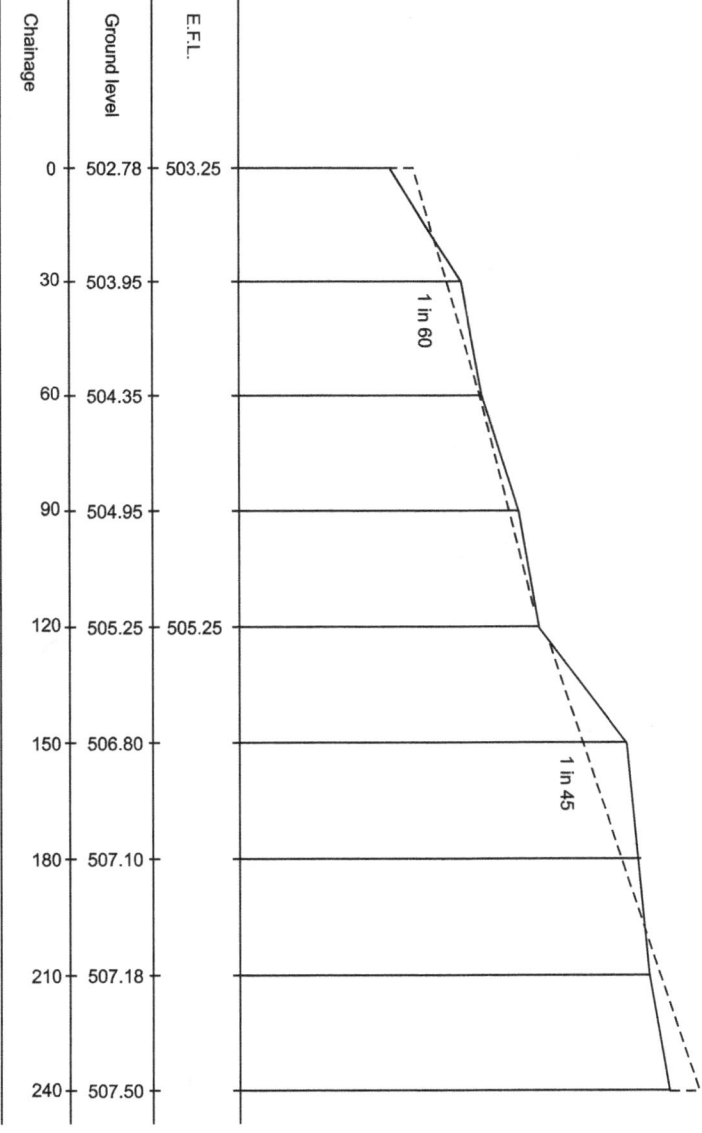

Fig. 3.59

58. Fig. 3.60 shows plan of a small bungalow. Depth of foundation be assumed as 1.5 m, plinth height to be 60 cm and floor to floor height 3.20 m.

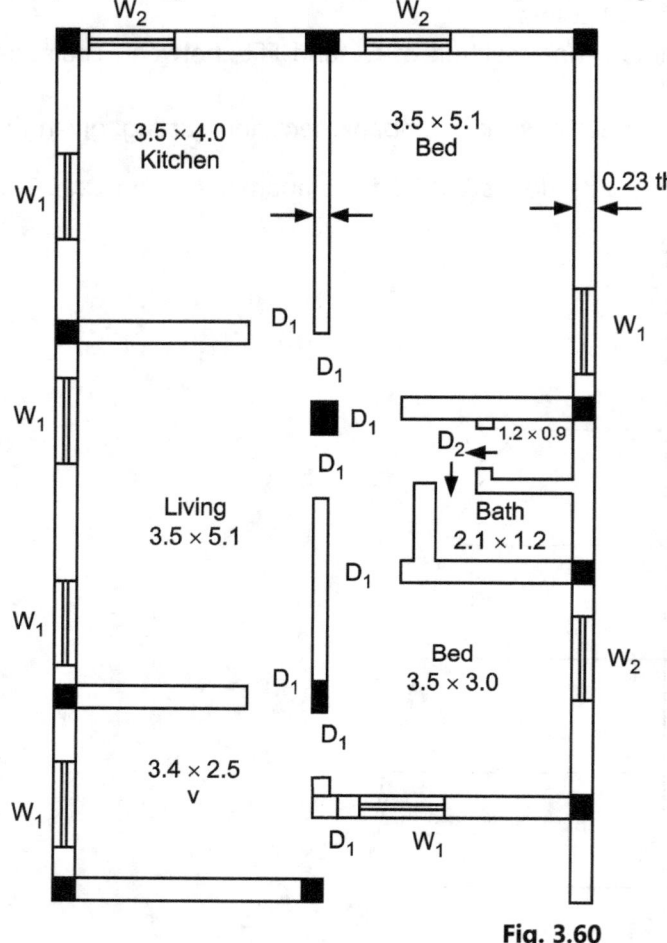

All columns 0.23 x 0.30 m

Footings: 1.0 x 1.2 m,

d = 45 m

All plinth beams - 0.23 x 0.45 m

and floor beams

Bottom of plinth beams

15 cm below G.L.

Slab = 12 cm thick.

D_1 = 0.9 x 2.1 m t.w. panelled

D_2 = 0.75 x 1.2 m t.w. panelled

W_1 = 1.5 x 1.2m

W_2 = 1.2 x 1.2m

Fig. 3.60

Find out the quantities of item no. (v) below and any two of the remaining items.

(i)   Excavation for footings and plinth beams.

(ii)   C.C. (1 : 2 : 4) in footing.

(iii) C.C. (1 : 2 : 4) in columns.

(iv)   C.C. (1 : 2 : 4) in slabs.

(v)   20 mm thick plaster in c.m. (1 : 4) with neeru finish internally.

59. Fig. 3.61 shows the L/S of a road. Top width of earth work is 7.0 m; side slopes in embankment are 2.5 : 1 and in cutting are 1.5 : 1. Assuming that there is no cross-slope, find out the quantities of earth work.

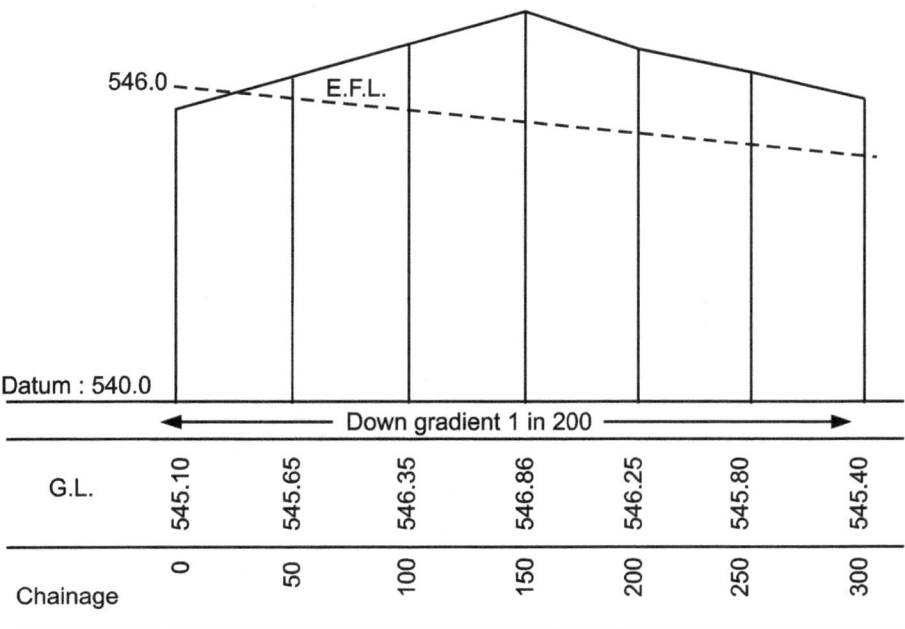

Fig. 3.61

60. An R.C.C. beam 23 × 45 cm size, is continuous over two spans, one 5.0 m c/c and the other 4.0 m. c/c. It is supported by columns 23 cm wide. It consists of 4 bottom bars, 20 mm diameter of Tor steel - two straight and two bent. It has two top bars 10 mm diameter Tor. It also possesses 8 mm diameter (Tor) rings. In 5.0 m span, five rings are placed @ 10 cm c/c from either end and in 4.0 m span, four rings are placed at 10 cm c/c from either end. In the remaining portions of both the spans, the rings are placed at 30 cm. c/c.

Find out the quantity of Tor steel reinforcement.

61. Fig. 3.62 shows details of a Bus-stand building. Work out the quantities for the following items of work on a measurement sheet.

(i)　　Excavation for foundation.

(ii)　　Brick work in cement mortar 1 : 6 in superstructure.

(iii)　　Plaster in cement mortar (1 : 3) with neeru finish for inside of walls of tea stall and office.

(iv)　　Sand faced plaster for all other surfaces of brick masonry.

(v)　　Providing and fixing A.C. sheet roof.

(vi)　　Painting wood work in doors, windows and counters.

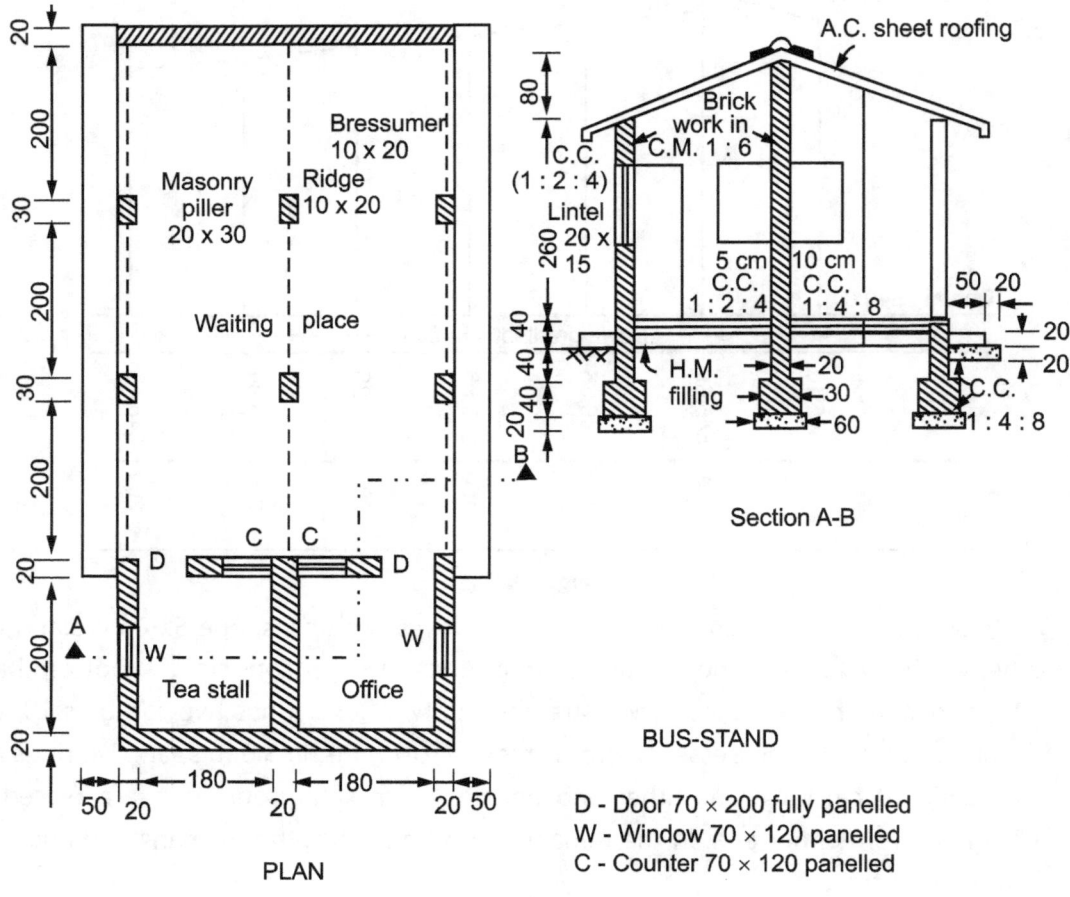

Fig. 3.62

62. For the plan and section of residential building shown in Fig. 3.63, work out the quantities of the following items describing them fully and recording the measurements in proper form.

   (a) U.C.R. masonry in C.M. (1 : 6) in plinth and foundation.

   (b) Rubble filling 200 mm thick in plinth.

   (c) Marble mosaic flooring in rooms and passages.

   (d) 15 cm thick sand faced cement plaster (1 : 4) to all external surfaces of brick masonry.

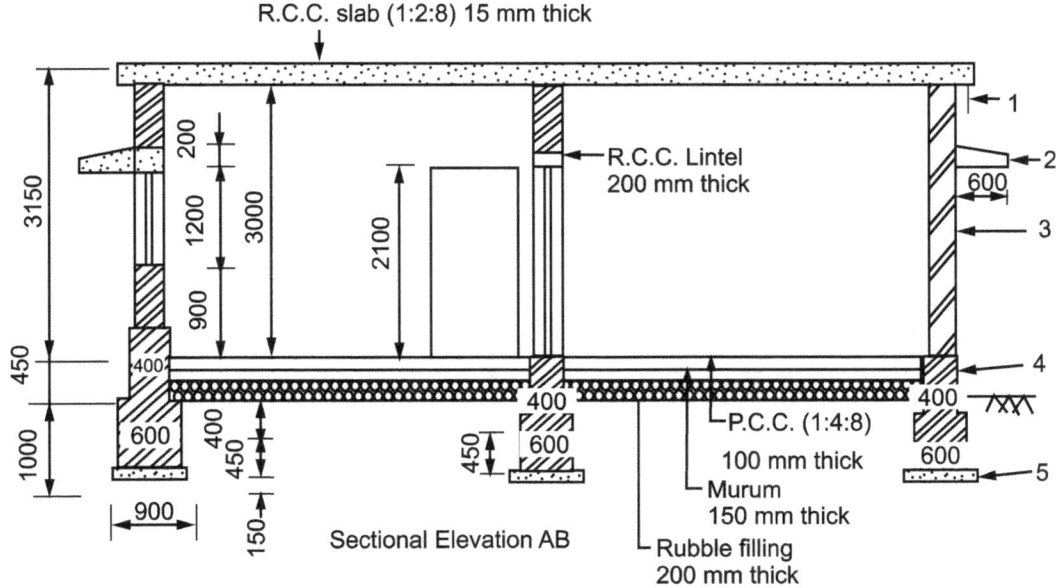

Sectional Elevation AB

R.C.C. slab (1:2:8) 15 mm thick

R.C.C. Lintel 200 mm thick

P.C.C. (1:4:8) 100 mm thick

Murum 150 mm thick

Rubble filling 200 mm thick

(1) 150 SLAB projection.

(2) Chajja 100 mm thick (average).

(3) B.B. masonry wall in C.M. (1 : 6) 300 mm thicknes in superstructure.

(4) U.C.R. masonry in C.M. (1 : 6) in plinth and foundation.

(5) P.C.C. (1 : 4 : 8) 150 mm thick.

Schedule of openings

Sy.	Size	Description
W_1	1000×1200	Steel window
W_2	1500×1200	Steel window
W_3	2000×1200	Steel window
V	600×600	Louvered
D_1	1000×2100	CCTW fully
D_2	800×2100	Panelled
op	1000×2100	Opening

Fig. 3.63 (a)

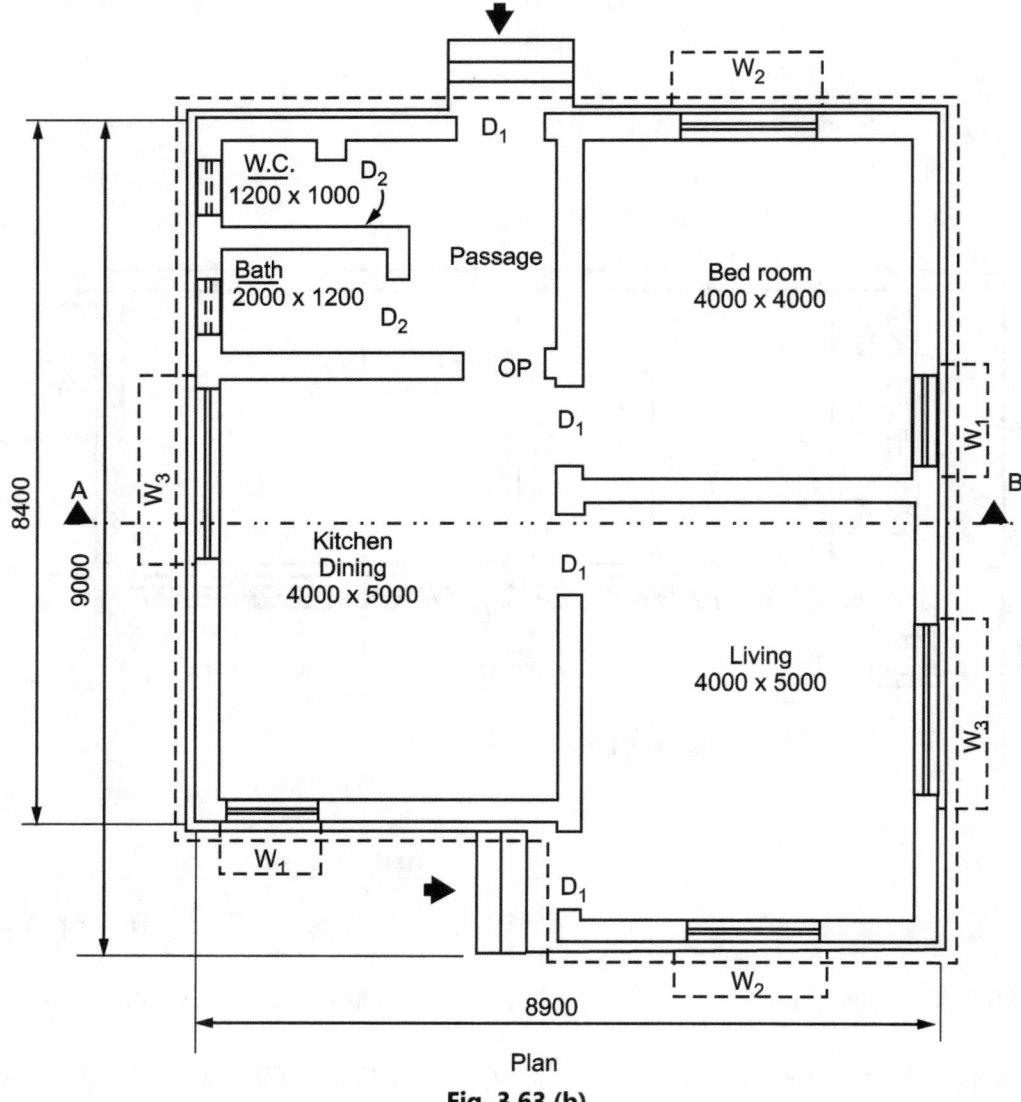

Plan

Fig. 3.63 (b)

Notes :

1. Hard murum is available at 0.8 m depth from G.L.
2. Marble mosaic flooring in all rooms and passage.
3. White glazed tiles for flooring and dado in W.C. and bath.
4. B.B. masonry for steps :
    Tread = 300 mm
    Rise = 150 mm
5. 15 mm thick sand faced cement plaster in C.M. (1 : 4) provided to all external surfaces of brick masonry.

6. 100 mm thick R.C.C. slab (1 : 2 : 4) is provided over W.C. bath at 2.1 m height from floor level.

    Scale : 1 cm = 1.0 m (All dimensions in mm)

63. Accompanying Fig. 3.64 shows the plan and section of residential building. Work out the quantities of the following items :

    (a)   P.C.C. (1 : 4 : 8) in foundation.

    (b)   IInd class B. B. masonry in C.M. (1 : 8) in superstructure.

    (c)   15 mm thick sand faced cement plaster (1 : 4) to external surfaces of B.B. masonry walls.

    (d)   Marble mosaic flooring in all rooms and passages except W.C. and bath.

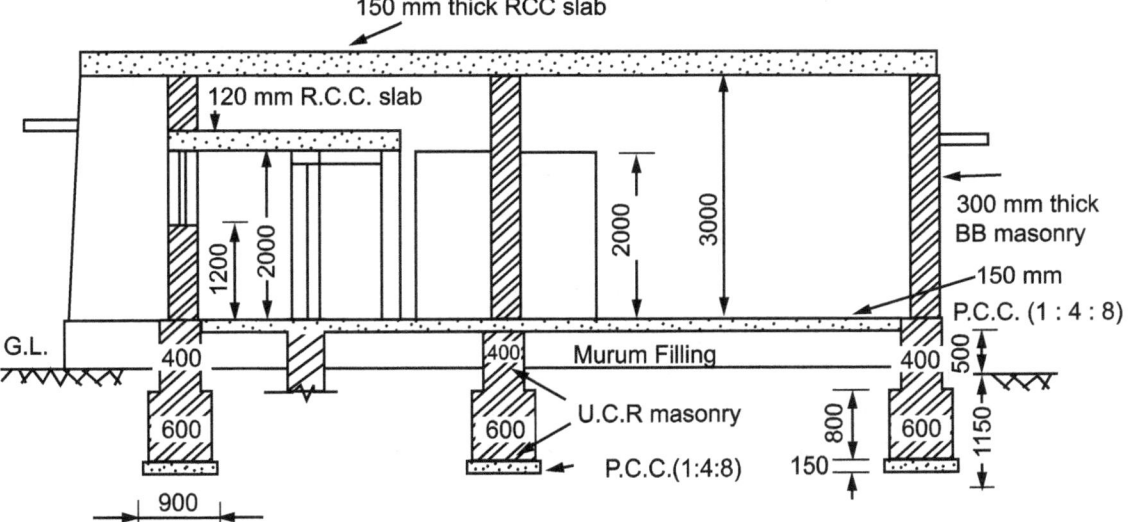

Section on AA

Shedule of openings

	No.	Type	Size	Description
Assume lintel thickness and	1	D$_1$	900 × 2000	Full paneled
mention it clearly	2	D$_2$	800 × 1900	Full paneled
Size of bath 2200 × 1200	3	W$_1$	900 × 1200	Full paneled
Size of W.C. 1200 × 1000	4	W$_2$	600 × 800	Fully glazed
	5	op	900 × 2000	Opening in masonry

(All dimensions are in mm)

Fig. 3.64 (a)

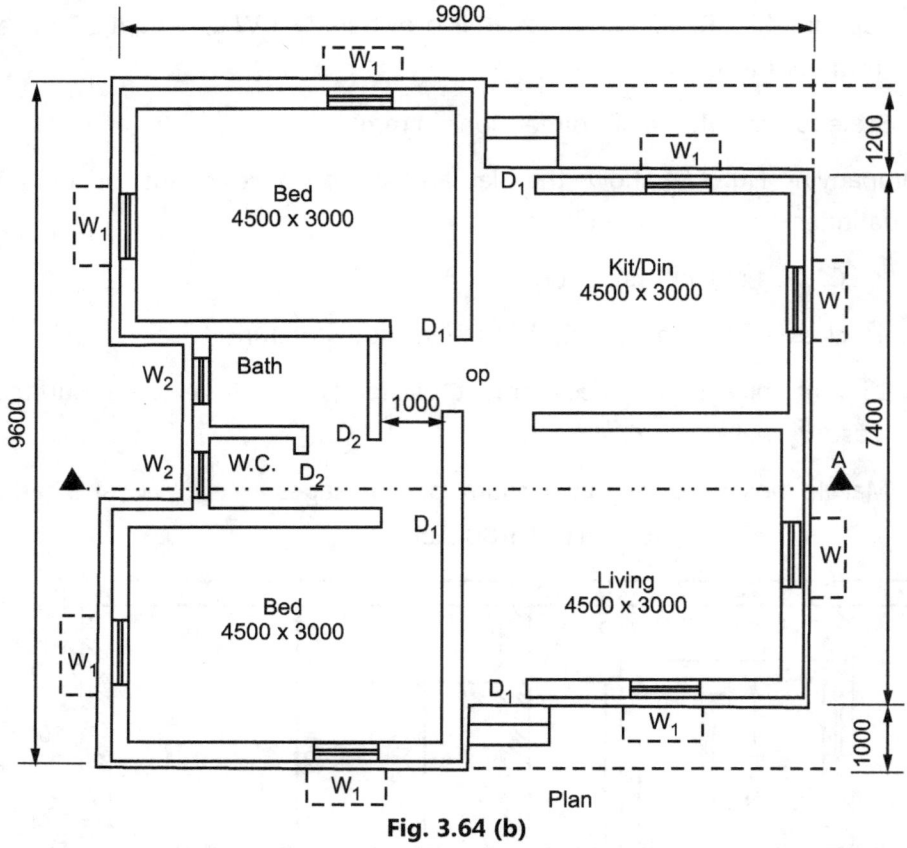

Fig. 3.64 (b)

Notes :

1. Hard murum is available at 1.15 m.
2. P.C.C. (1 : 4 : 8) 150 mm thick in foundation.

   All foundation and plinth masonry is U.C.R. in C.M. (1 : 6).

   All walls are provided with same size of foundation.
3. All walls are provided with B.B. masonry 300 mm thick except bath and W.C. partition walls which are 200 mm thick.
4. All rooms are provided with marble mosaic flooring except bath and W.C.
5. 15 mm thick sand faced cement plaster (1 : 4) externally and 12 mm thick cement plaster (1 : 4) with Neeru finish internally.

64. Fig. 3.65 shows the details of underground water tank. Work out the quantities of the following items of works :

   (a) Excavation for foundation in ordinary soil and murum separately considering the usual lift.

   (b) P.C.C. (1 : 3 : 6) in foundation.

   (c) Brick masonry in C.M. (1 : 6).

   (d) R.C.C. (1 : 2 : 4) for beams and slab.

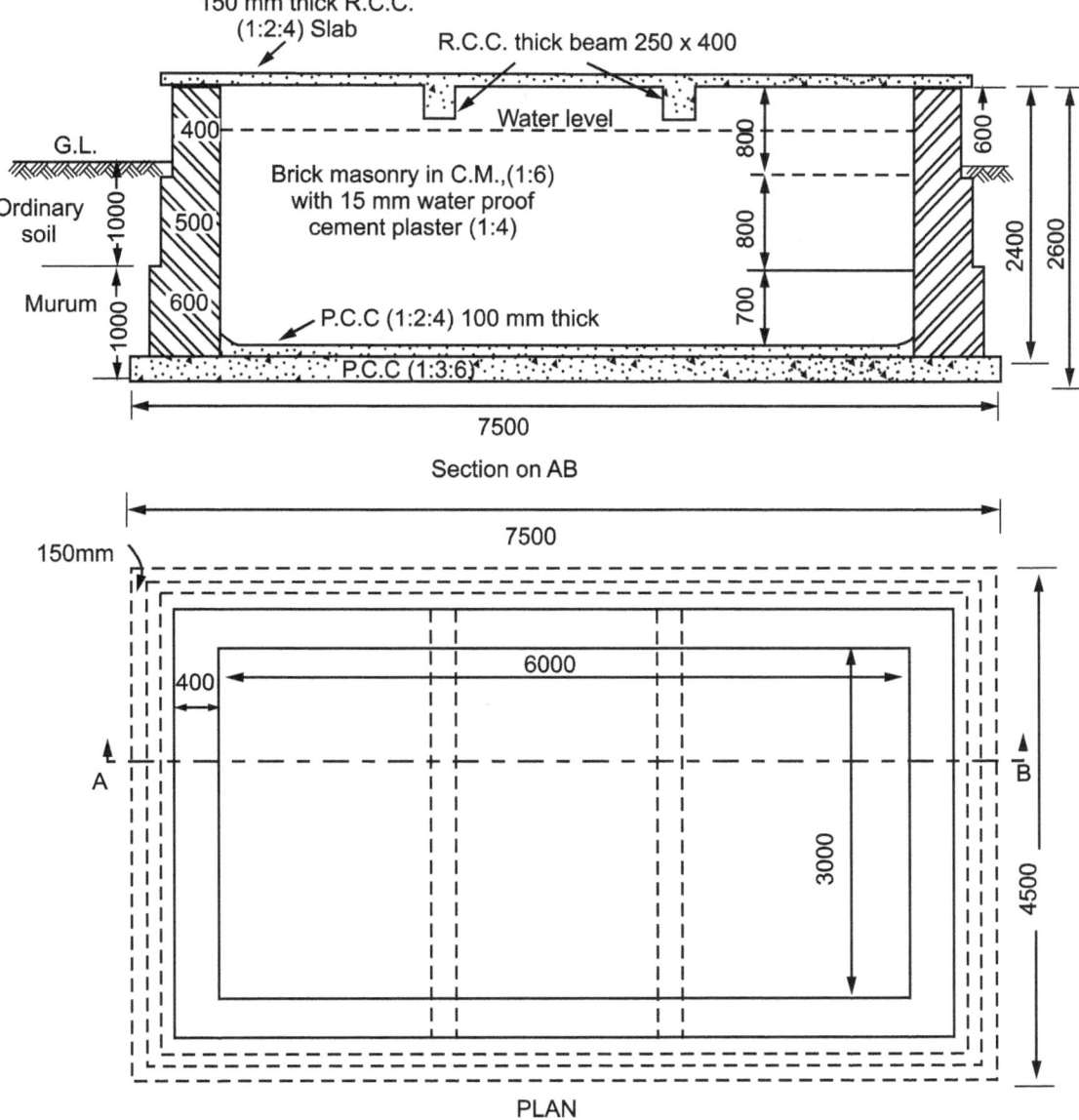

Fig. 3.65 : Details of underground tank

65. Fig. 3.66 shows the plan and section of a residential building. Work out the quantities of following items, describing the item fully and recording the measurements in proper form.

(a)   P.C.C. (1 : 4 : 8) in foundation;

(b)   B.B. masonry in C.M. (1 : 6) in superstructures;

(c)   Floor bed of P.C.C. (1 : 4 : 8) 100 mm thick.

(d)   12 mm thick cement plaster (1 : 4) with neeru finish to all internal surfaces of brick masonry.

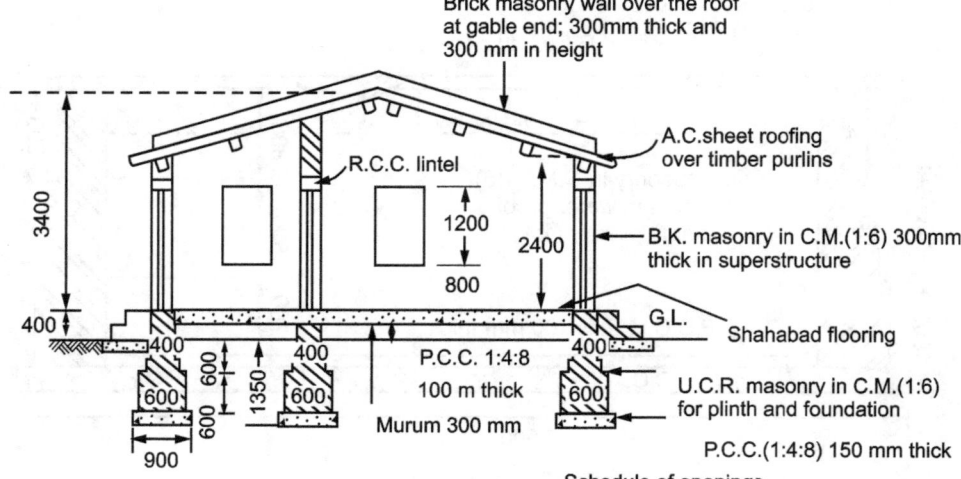

Brick masonry wall over the roof at gable end; 300mm thick and 300 mm in height

R.C.C. lintel

A.C.sheet roofing over timber purlins

B.K. masonry in C.M.(1:6) 300mm thick in superstructure

G.L.

Shahabad flooring

P.C.C. 1:4:8 100 m thick

Murum 300 mm

U.C.R. masonry in C.M.(1:6) for plinth and foundation

P.C.C.(1:4:8) 150 mm thick

3400

1200

800

2400

400

400

400

400

600

600

1350

600

600

900

600

Schedule of openings

Sym	Size	Description
W	800x1200	CCTW fully glazed
D	800x1200	CCTW fully panelled

(a)

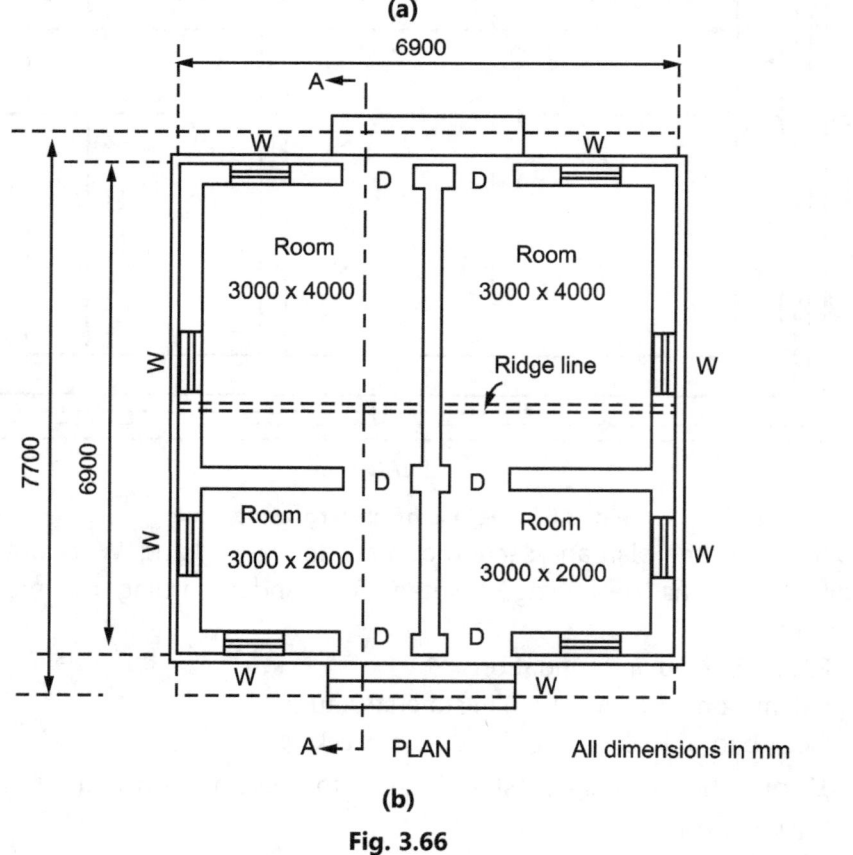

6900

7700

6900

A

W   W

D   D

Room
3000 x 4000

Room
3000 x 4000

Ridge line

W   W

D   D

Room
3000 x 2000

Room
3000 x 2000

W   W

D   D

W   W

A   PLAN   All dimensions in mm

(b)

Fig. 3.66

Notes :

1. Hard murum is available at 1.0 m depth from G.L. upto 1.0 m ordinary soil.

2. Polished shahabad flooring 25 mm thick provided in all rooms.

3. 12 mm thick cement plaster (1 : 4) with Neeru finish is provided to all internal surfaces of brick masonry. (All dimensions are in mm)

66. Fig. 3.68 shows details of pipe culvert. Work out the quantities involved in the construction of the culvert. (Exclude road items).

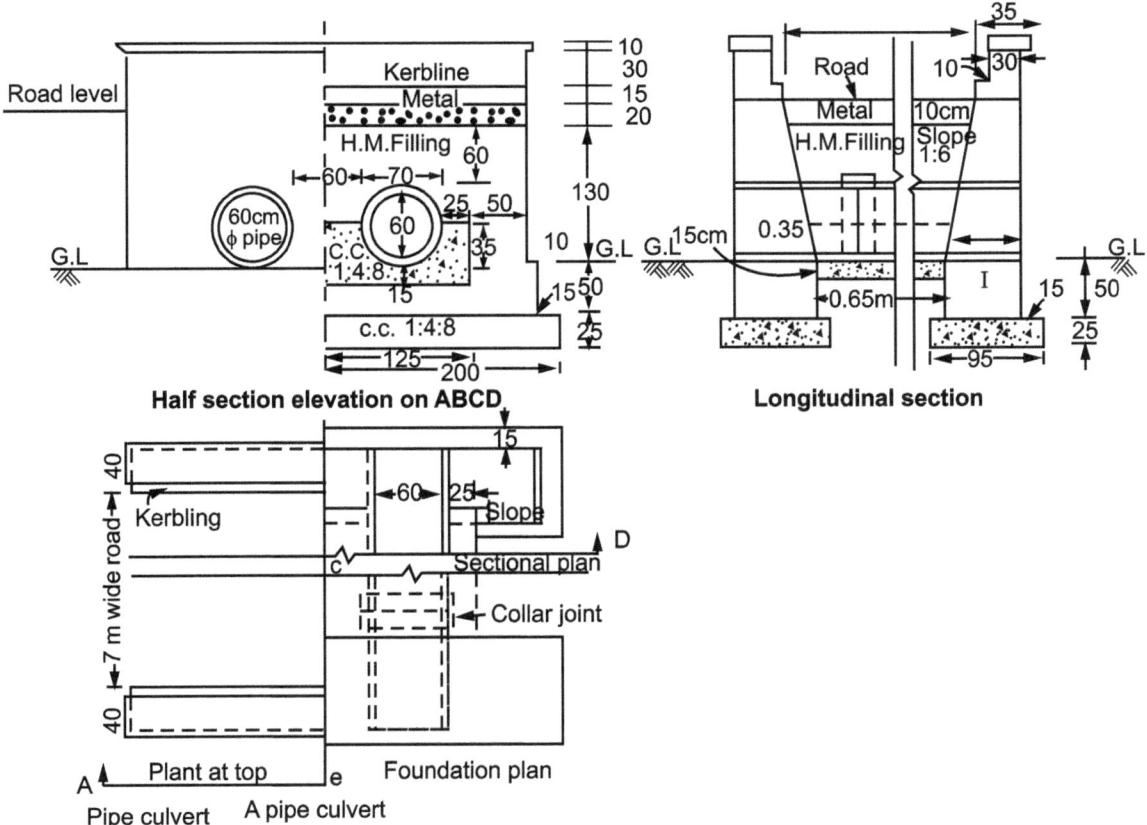

Fig. 3.68 : Details of culvert

1. Walls in R.R. masonry in C.M. (1 : 5), C.P. (1 : 3) to exposed faces.

2. Parapet and kerbing in C.R. masonry first sort in C.M. (1 : 5), C.P. (1 : 3) to exposed faces.

3. Coping P.C.C. (M 200).

4. All dimensions in cm.

Chapter 4
VALUATION OF PROPERTIES

4.1 INTRODUCTION

Valuation is the procedure of determining the present value of an existing property such as building, land, factory etc. Depending upon its selling price in the market or the income it fetches in the form of rent, its present value is decided. Other factors affecting the value of a property are its present condition, remaining future life, location and demand and supply position in the market.

4.2 COST, PRICE AND VALUE

In our day to day talk, we frequently use these three terms to specify the cost, price and 'value' of a commodity.

- **Cost :** The term 'Cost is used to indicate the initial investment incurred in manufacturing a particular commodity. Such a commodity having utility, and demand possesses certain value if it is exchangeable. It is used to determine the loss of value of the commodity due to wear and tear etc. i.e. depreciation.

- **Price :** As the manufacturer of the commodity would like to sell his product by adding reasonable profit for his labour and capital to its cost, it becomes the price of the commodity. i.e.

    (Price of an item) = (Cost of the item) + (Profit as a reward for his initial investment and labour)

- **Value :** The term 'value' indicates the present price of the commodity and mainly depends upon its utility and demand and supply position in the market. The value may be more or less than the actual cost of construction of that commodity.

For a commodity to possess value, it should have the following four quantities :

- It must be scarce.
- It should have demand.
- It must possess utility.
- It should be transferable.

The value of a commodity varies from place to place and also at the same place from time to time depending upon its qualities as specified above e.g. Air, even though it has greatest utility, has no value as it is freely available any where.

4.3 PURPOSE (OR OBJECT) OF VALUATION

The purpose or object of valuation of the property may be as follows :

- When a person wants to sell or buy a property.
- For the determination of municipal tax, property tax etc.
- For advancing loans against security of property, its valuation is required.
- In order to pay compensation for the property acquired by the government, its valuation is to be carried out.
- For the fixation of rent of a property, its valuation is required.
- Valuation of the property is necessary for the insurance purposes.
- In case of disputed property, its valuation is required to determine the court fees etc.
- In order to determine the capital gains, valuation of property is required to be carried out.
- For calculation of 'gift tax', valuation is to be carried out.
- Valuation of property is required for wealth tax purposes.

Thus the valuation of the property depends upon its purpose. The amount of valuation will differ with different purposes and hence it is quite essential to know the purpose of valuation to determine its fair market value.

4.4 FACTORS AFFECTING VALUATION OF A PROPERTY

The various factors affecting the value of a property are as follows :

- **Demand and Supply :** The value of the property depends upon the demand and supply position in the market. If the demand exceeds the supply (i.e. availability), the value of the property will increase and vice-versa.

- **Replacement Cost :** This is another important factor that affects the valuation of the built up property, for sale having vacant possession. The owner is interested in knowing the present cost of construction of similar building in the locality i.e. valuation of the building at present less the depreciation for the life of the building already over.

- **Annual Rent :** The valuation of a property depends upon the net annual rent the prospective purchaser is likely to get after the purchase of the property. The net rent is worked out after deducting all the annual outgoings from the gross rent obtainable from the property.

- **Returns from the Investment and its Security :** The prospective purchaser will work out the interest he is likely to get after investing the amount required for purchasing the property, from general trend of investment in other markets and its security. Usually, when the capital investment is secured and can be converted into liquid asset any time, the rate of interest may be lower as in case of land and buildings.

- **Future Development of the Area :** If the property is situated in an area which is likely to be provided with all amenities such as water supply, drainage, electricity, roads etc. the value of the property is likely to increase considerably.
- **Unforeseen Circumstances :** In case of communal riots, civil wars, earthquakes etc., the value of the property in such areas is likely to fall down abruptly.
- **Obsolescence :** If the design or construction of an existing building becomes old and outdated e.g. a recently constructed building with detached toilet units looses its value as compared with the modern design of self contained buildings (i.e. with attached toilet units), and this phenomenon is known as **'obsolescence'**.

4.5 DIFFERENT NOMENCLATURE OF VALUE

The different nomenclature commonly used in connection with the value of a property are as follows :

- **Book Value :** It is the amount shown in the account book after allowing for necessary depreciation. Thus the book value of the property at a particular year is equal to its original cost minus the total amount of depreciation upto the previous year. Thus the book value of the property goes on decreasing every year and becomes equal to the scrap value at the end of its useful life.
- **Scrap Value :** It is the value of the property that becomes useless at the end of its life. It is the value of the property in the dismantled condition after its life is over. It is usually taken as 10% of the total cost of construction. The cost of demolition is to be deducted from the value of the dismantled material to arrive at the scrape value.
- **Salvage Value :** It is the value of the property, at end of its useful life, without being dismantled and which has not yet become useless.
- **Market Value :** It is the value of the property one can get at particular time in open market after it is has been kept for sale. It depends upon its locality, future life, type of construction, demand and supply etc. It changes from place to place and at the same place from time to time.
- **Accommodation Value :** During rapid expansion of towns and cities, the surrounding agricultural land is to be converted into the accommodation land by taking permission from the competent Government authority. Thus the value of such accommodated land increases and usually lies between the value of adjacent building land and the (surrounding) agricultural land.
- **Distress Value :** When a property is sold at a price lower than the market value, it is said to have 'distress value'. This may happen due to the following reasons :

(a)   Fear of communal riots, war, earthquake etc.

(b)   Financial difficulties of the owner

(c)   To favour the person purchasing the property.

- **Monopoly Value :** It is sometimes happens that a particular property possesses certain advantages as regards its location, frontage, shape etc. In such cases the owner demands the value which is much higher than its market value and is known as **'Monopoly Value'**.

- **Replacement Value :** It is the value of the replacement of the property, either in full or part, at the prevailing market rates.

- **Sentimental Value :** Sometimes the sentiments of the owner are attached to the property and thus he demands exorbitant price for his property, having no relevance to its market value. Such a value of the property is then said to be **'Sentimental value'**.

- **Rateable Value :** It is the net annual letting value from the property and is obtained by deducting annual repair charges from the 'gross rent'. Municipal taxes etc. are assumed as certain percentage of the rateable value.

- **Speculative Value :** Some real estate dealers are interested in purchasing certain property and then selling them with profit after certain time. Such dealers only speculate on the property with a view to earn profit from such dealings and are not interested in developing the property. The price paid by the dealers in purchasing the property only with the intention of selling it at latter date with profit is known as **'Speculative Value'**. Speculative price is found to be always lower than its market value.

- **Assessed Value :** The value of the property entered in the register of local authorities, for ascertaining the property taxes etc., to be recovered from the owner is known as **'Assessed value'**.

- **Capital Cost :** The total cost of constructing the property inclusive of cost of land, boundary walls etc., is known as capital cost i.e. It is the original cost of the entire property which do not change. The present cost of this property is known as its value.

- **Capitalised Value :** The capitalised value of the property is defined as that amount of money whose annual interest at the highest prevailing rate of interest will be equal to net income from the property. Thus to calculate the capitalised value of any property it is necessary to known the 'net income' (which is equal to gross income minus all the outgoings) from the property and the prevailing highest rate of interest (on investment in such type of properties).

4.6 YEARS PURCHASE (Y.P.)

It is a numerical figure which when multiplied by the net income from the property determines its capitalised value.

The Y.P. is found by the equation :

$$\text{Y.P.} = \frac{100}{\text{Rate of interest}} = \left(\frac{100}{i}\right)$$

or $\qquad = \dfrac{1}{i}$ where i is expressed in decimals

However, to obtain interest from the capital and also to provide for annual sinking fund (i.e. for redemption of capital) the above expression is to be altered as follows :

i.e. $\qquad \text{Y.P.} = \dfrac{1}{i + I}$

where $\qquad$ i = Percentage rate of interest (i.e. in decimals)

and $\qquad$ I = Sinking fund required to replace ₹ 1/- at the end of given years = Sinking fund coefficient

Now if $\qquad$ i' = Rate of interest on sinking fund

and $\qquad$ n = Number of given years,

then $\qquad$ $I = \left[\dfrac{i'}{(1 + i)^n - 1}\right]$

where $\qquad$ i = Rate of interest (expressed in decimal) on capital

and $\qquad$ i' = Rate of interest for redemption of capital i.e. for sinking fund

Note :
- If i and i' are equal, then, Y.P. is supposed to be calculated on *'single rate basis'*.
- Usually, the rate of interest i' on sinking fund is very small as compared to the rate of interest on the capital, and hence the Y.P. is to be calculated considering the above two different rates of interest and is known as *dual rate basis.*

4.7 SINKING FUND AND SINKING FUND INSTALLMENT

(i) Sinking Fund :

The capital invested in a property consists of two parts viz. the one invested in the building and the other in the land. As the building is subjected to normal wear and tear, its value goes on decreasing with its age. Thus the owner shall be losing certain part of his capital each year till it becomes equal to the 'scrap value' at the end of the useful life of the building. Thus the owner is left with the land only and the part capital in the form of land cost shall be retained by him. Instead of investing his money, in the above property, if he had invested in the form of deposits in the nationalised bank or Government securities he would have received regular income in the form of interest from it, keeping the entire capital in tact. Thus before the life of the building expires the owner has to make certain provision by depositing certain amount every year to recover his part capital invested in the building at the end of useful life of the building else the capital invested in the building will be completely lost at the end of its life. Such a provision is made by depositing every year certain small portion of the gross rent in a nationalised banks or Government securities and is known as **'Sinking fund installment'**. Thus at the end of the useful life of the building the owner is in a position to receive the entire value of his building either from the nationalised bank or Government securities. As the investment in the sinking fund is required to recover capital invested in the building, it is considered as one of the outgoing.

The sinking fund to be calculated depends upon the following factors :

- Life of the building.

- Rate of interest on bank deposits or Government securities and

- The scrap value of the building, which is assumed as 0.1 times the cost of construction, at the end of its useful life.

Thus sinking fund may be defined as the amount deposited every year from the gross rent of the building at compound interest in a bank or securities, so that owner recovers the pre-determined value to meet the cost of replacement of the building. Thus there will be regular annual deposit in the form of sinking fund for depreciation and there shall be accumulation of interest on such deposits.

Computation of Annual Sinking Fund :

The annual sinking fund to be deposited to recover ₹ 1 (Rupee one) in 'n' number of years

$$= \left[\frac{i'}{(1-i)^n - 1} \right]$$

where i' = Rate of interest on sinking fund amount invested

$$= \left[\frac{1}{\text{Amount of Rupee 1 at the end of 'n' number of years}} \right]$$

The amount of Rupee 1 in 'n' number of years at the rate of interest 'i'

$$= \left[\frac{(1+i)^n - 1}{i'} \right]$$

(ii) Sinking Fund Installment (S_i) :

The amount of sinking fund installment to be deposited every year can be worked out as follows :

Let $\qquad S_i$ = Sinking fund installment

$\qquad\qquad n$ = Life of building in years

$\qquad\qquad i'$ = Rate of interest on sinking fund

$\qquad\qquad$ S.F. = Total sinking fund to be accumulated in the period of n years

$\therefore\quad$ Sinking fund accumulated at the end of 1st year = S_1 = S_i

and sinking fund accumulated at the end of 2nd year = S_2 = $S_i + S_i\,(1 + i')$

and sinking fund accumulated at the end of 3rd year = $S_i + S_i\left[(1 + i') + S_i\,(1 + i')^2\right]$

Therefore sinking fund accumulated at the end of the nth years,

$$\text{S.F.} = S_1 + S_i\,(1 + i') + S_i\,(1 + i')^2 + S_i\,(1 + i')^3 + \ldots + S_i\,(1 + i')^{n-1} \qquad \ldots \text{(a)}$$

Multiplying both the sides of equation (a) by $(1 + i')$, we get,

$$\text{S.F.}\,(1 + i') = S_i\,(1 + i') + S_i\,(1 + i')^2 + S_i\,(1 + i')^3 + \ldots + S_i\,(1 + i')^n \qquad \ldots \text{(b)}$$

$\therefore\quad$ Subtracting equation (b) from equation (a), we have,

$$\text{S.F.} - \text{S.F.}\,(1 + i') = S_i - S_i\,(1 + i')^n$$

or $\qquad\quad \text{S.F.}\,[1 - 1 - i'] = S_i\,(1 + i')^n - S_i$

$$\text{S.F.}\,(i') = S_i\left[(1 + i')^n - 1\right]$$

i.e. $\qquad\qquad\quad \text{S.F.} = \text{Total sinking fund} = S_i\left[\dfrac{(1 + i')^n - 1}{i'}\right]$

or Sinking fund installments,

$$S_i = \text{S.F.}\left[\dfrac{i'}{(1 + i')^n - 1}\right]$$

4.8 VALUATION TABLES

For the different methods of valuation explained above lot of laborious calculations are to be carried out to determine the value of the property. To reduce the calculation work, ready-made valuation tables are prepared and are used during computation to save the valuable time and also to eliminate the mistakes in mathematical computation etc.

Some of the ready made valuation tables commonly used during computation are briefly explained below :

(i)$\quad$ Amount of Rupee one 1/- invested at compound rate of interest will accumulate to rupees $(1 + i)^n$,

$\qquad$ where $\qquad\qquad\qquad i$ = Rate of interest

$\qquad$ and $\qquad\qquad\qquad\quad n$ = Number of years of investment

(ii)   Present value of ₹ 1/- i.e. the amount to be invested today to accumulate Re. 1/- at the end of 'n' number of years

∴   Present value of ₹ 1/- to be accumulated over n years

$$= \frac{1}{(1 + i)^n}$$

(iii) Amount of ₹ 1/- deposited at the end of each year will accumulate in a period of n years at the compound rate of interest

$$\text{Amount accumulated} = \left[\frac{(1 + i)^n - 1}{i}\right]$$

(iv) Sinking fund installment (S_i) i.e. the sinking fund installment to be deposited every year at compound rate of interest so as to collect ₹ 1/- in given number of n years

$$S_i = \left[\frac{i}{(1 + i)^n - 1}\right]$$

(v)   Present value of ₹ 1/- deposited every year,
    (a)   Single rate Y.P.

$$\text{Present value (P.V.)} = \left[\frac{\left\{1 - \frac{1}{(1 + i)^n}\right\}}{i}\right]$$

    (b)   Dual rate Y.P.

$$\text{Present value (P.V.)} = \left[\frac{1}{\left\{1 + \frac{i'}{(1 + i')^n - 1}\right\}}\right]$$

4.9 ANNUITY

It is the annual periodic payment made towards repayment of the capital amount invested. It is usually paid at the end (or sometimes in the beginning) of the year. If the annuity is paid for a specified number of years, it is called as **Annuity certain** and if paid at the beginning of each year, for a specified number of years, it is termed an *Annuity due*. If annuity payment continues for indefinite period, it is called as *'perpetual Annuity'*. Sometimes the annuity payment becomes due after certain number of years and is known as **'Deferred Annuity'**.

4.10 OWNERSHIP OF THE PROPERTY

The ownership of the property (also called as tenure) is divided into: (i) Free-hold and (ii) Lease-hold.

   (i)   Free-hold Property : A property is said to be free hold when it is in absolute possession of the owner for indefinite period and he can deal with such property according to his will. i.e. he can develop, gift, or sell or lease to any body for a certain period. After the expiry of lease period, the owner repossesses the property again.

(ii) **Lease-hold Property :** As already state above the owner of the free-hold property may permit some other person to use his property for specified number of years and then the property is said to be leased for which the 'lessee' (i.e. the person who accepts the property on lease) has to make some annual payment to the 'lessor' (i.e. the original owner). After the expiry of the lease period, the property again belongs to its original owner (i.e. lessor). Usually, the lease period is sufficiently long (e.g. 99 years etc.) so as to enable the 'lessee' to recover his investment on the development of the property.

The various types of lease in common practice are as follows :

(a) Building lease and (b) Occupation lease.

(a) Building Lease :

The Government or owner leases out an open land for the construction of residential buildings or factories etc. to the lessee for a long period of about 99 or 999 years. The lessee has to pay annual lease rent (also called as ground rent) to the lessor.

The lesse then constructs the structure on such land at his own cost and maintains it in good working condition. After the expiry of the period of lease, the entire property including the land and the building constructed by the lessee, belongs to the lessor.

(b) Occupation Lease :

In this type of lease the owner constructs the building on his land and the land with the building is given on lease for annual payment known as 'rack rent' i.e. the rent of the property is equal to the existing market rent for similar buildings. However, if this rent is less than the existing market rent, it is called as 'head rent'. The difference between these two rents represents the lease holder's interest. Usually, the period of occupation lease is of short duration varying from 5 to 30 years. Sometimes the property is leased out on 'rising rent' basis i.e. the lease rent goes on increasing with the increase in the lease years.

Sometimes, the lessee may sublease the portion of the building, depending upon the terms and conditions of the original lease document, to another person. Thus the original lease holder (i.e. lessee) becomes the lessor for the sub-lessee. The sub-lease period should obviously be less than the original lease period.

4.11 RETURNS FROM THE PROPERTY

(i) **Gross Income :** It is the total income or receipts from various sources from the property without any deductions for operational and collection charges.

(ii) **Net Income :** It is the income from the property obtained after deducting all operational and collection charges from the gross income. Such operational and collection charges are termed as 'outgoings'. Thus

Net income or return   = Gross income – Outgoings.

(iii) Outgoings : These are the expenses which are to be incurred by the owner for maintaining the revenue (i.e. income) from the building. The various 'outgoings' are classified as follows :

(a) Taxes : The owner of the building has to pay certain taxes such as municipal tax, property tax, wealth tax etc. based on the annual rental value of the property after deducting the amount spent on annual repairs of the building.

(b) Maintenance and Repair Charges : In order to maintain the property in safe and good condition, the owner has to spend certain amount on its maintenance and repairs. This amount generally depends upon its age, type and construction of the building. This amount is usually assumed as 10 to 15% of the 'gross income' or 1 to 1.5 times the monthly rent from the property. For annual maintenance and repairs an amount of 1 to 1.5 % of the total cost of building is usually assumed.

(c) Management and Collection Charges : These are the expenses to be incurred for collection of rent from the large properties and other expenses such as salaries for the services of the watchman, sweeper, liftman, pump attendants etc. It is usually assumed as 5 to 10% of the gross income from the property. In case of small building, the collection and management charges are not at all required.

(d) Loss of Rent : The portion of the building which is not occupied will not fetch any rent, and thus suitable amount from the gross income is to be deducted under outgoings.

(e) Sinking Fund Provision : A certain fixed amount from the gross rent is to be deducted annually as 'sinking fund' to accumulate the total cost of construction of building when the entire life of the building will be over.

(f) Miscellaneous Expenses : These expenses include the expenditure incurred by the owner towards electric charges for running pumps, lifts, lightings of common places, etc.

(g) Insurance Charge : Sometimes the property is insured to cover the risk against fire, accidents etc. by paying certain amount (known as premium) to the insurance companies. Such expenses are also included under 'outgoings'.

4.12 DEPRECIATION AND METHODS OF COMPUTATIONS OF DEPRECIATION (W – 2010)

(i) Definition : Depreciation is defined as the loss in the value of the property due to its wear and tear, structural deterioration, obsolescence etc. The usefulness of the property gradually decreases due to its age thus reducing its value. It is usual practice to allow certain percentage of the total cost of the building as 'depreciation' to calculate its present value. 'Annual depreciation' is the term used to denote the gradual annual decrease in the value of the property. The percentage of depreciation of the property in the beginning is usually less and it gradually increases with its age.

Thus the depreciation cost being known, the value of the property can be determined by deducting the depreciation from its original cost.

(ii) Methods of Computing Depreciation : The various method of determining the depreciation of the structure are as follows :

(a) Straight Line Method (Fig. 4.1) : This is the simplest method of determining the depreciated cost of the structure. The method assumes that the loss in the value of the property is same every year and at the end of its useful life it is equal to its scrap value i.e.

$$\text{Yearly or Annual depreciation} = \frac{\text{Original cost of structure} - \text{Scrap value}}{\text{Life of the structure in years}}$$

or $$D = \frac{C - S}{n}$$

where
- D = Yearly or annual depreciation
- n = Life of the structure in years
- C = Original cost of the structure
- S = Scrap value which is usually assumed as 10% of the original cost of the structure

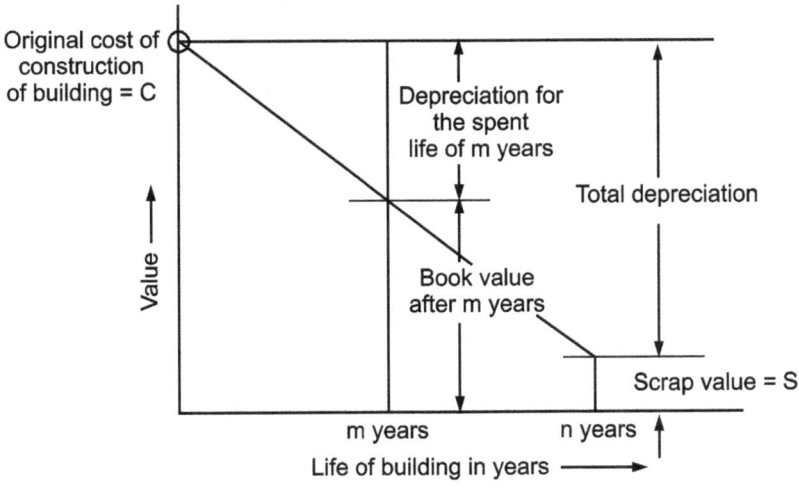

Fig. 4.1 : Straight line method of depreciation

The life of the structure constructed with first class specifications is assumed as 100 years and for the structure constructed with second class specifications is taken as 75 to 80 years.

(b) Constant percentage method : This method assumes that the property loses its value by a constant percentage of its value at the beginning of each year.

i.e.
$$D = 1 - \left(\frac{S}{C}\right)^{1/n}$$

where

D = Yearly or annual depreciation

S = Scrap value of the property

C = Original cost of the property

n = Life of the property in years

Thus the value of the property at the end of m years

$$= C\left(\frac{S}{C}\right)^{m/n}$$

Notes :

(a) If $S = 0$, the above formula does not hold good.

(b) For very small values of S/C the depreciation during the first year will be considerable.

(c) Sinking fund method : The method assumes that the depreciation is equal to the annual sinking fund plus the interest on the fund for that year which is supposed to be invested in the interest bearing securities.

For example, if A_s = Annual sinking fund installment

b, c, d, etc. = Interest on the sinking fund for the subsequent years

and C = Original cost of the structure

then, the table of depreciation and book value will be as shown below :

At the end of year	Depreciation for the year	Total depreciation	Book value
1st	A_s	A_s	$C - A_s$
2nd	$A_s + b$	$A_s + A_s + b$	$C - (2A_s + b)$
3rd	$A_s + c$	$A_s + A_s + b + A_s + c$	$C - (3A_s + b + c)$
4th	$A_s + d$	$4A_s + b + c + d$	$C - (4A_s + b + c + d)$
–	–	–	–

(d) Quantity survey method : In this method, the property is inspected in detail and the loss in the value due to wear and tear, deterioration, age etc., is actually worked out. Each and every step is based on sound reasoning without assuming any fixed percentage to the original cost of the property. The method is based on logic and is therefore most realistic. Valuer with sufficient experience can determine the amount of depreciation and work out the value of the property by this method.

4.13 MORTGAGE

(i) Definition : When any person wants to borrow money against the security of his property, then it is known as *'Mortgage loan'*. The person who accepts loan against his property is called as "*Mortgager*" and the person who grants loan is known as "*Mortgagee*". The loan is to be returned by the 'mortgager' to the 'mortgagee' within the stipulated time. Usually, the amount of loan granted is 50 to 70% of the present value of the property. The repayment of the loan is generally done in installments along with interest as per the terms and conditions agreed upon. The loan transaction when completed is known as *'mortgage deed'*. In case the mortgager is unable to refund the loan with interest for number of years, the mortgagee has a right to sell the entire property and recover his full amount of loan with interest. The surplus money if any is to be refunded by the mortgagee to the mortgager.

After the repayment of the full amount of loan with interest, the mortgager can repossess his property from the mortgagee and is known as *'Equity of redemption'*.

(ii) Equitable mortgage : If the mortgager has to deposit the title of the property with the mortgagee at the time of accepting the loan, it is termed as 'equitable mortgage'. In case the mortgager fails to repay the loan as per the terms and conditions, the mortgagee has to file a suit in the court of law for recovery of the loan.

(iii) Legal mortgage : At the time of deposition of the title if the loan transaction is entered on the stamp paper then it is called as 'legal mortgage'. In such cases, the mortgagee can sell the loaned property if the mortgager fails to repay the loan with interest in the specified period of time. The mortgager, may, however, request the court authorities for extension of time for repayment of loan.

4.14 EASEMENT

Easements are the rights which one owner of property possesses over the property of another. The person over whose property the rights are enjoyed is known as *'servient owner'* and the person who possesses and enjoys the rights (i.e. easement) is called the *'Domiant owner'*.

According to Indian Easement Act, 1882 an easement is a right which the owner (or occupier) of certain land, possesses, as such for the beneficial enjoyment of that land, to do and continue to do something or to prevent and to continue to prevent something that is being done, in or upon or in respect of, certain other land which is not his own.

Some of the important easement rights are as follows :

- Right to use air and (natural) light from over the adjoining owner's property.
- Right of access from the adjoining property.

- Right to allow rain water to flow over adjoining property.
- Right to lay and maintain water supply and drainage pipes through the adjoining property.
- Right to support one's building from the adjoining neighbours land.

It may be noted that the easements are attached to the properties and are possessed in any one of the following ways :

- Easement by necessity which may be qualified or otherwise.
- When a right is enjoyed continuously without any interruption for a period of 20 years.
- By custom or
- By legislative action etc.

4.15 METHODS OF VALUATION OF PROPERTY

(1) Factors to be considered :   **(W-2010)**

The various factors to be considered in valuation of building are as follows :

- Type of building
- Durability
- Materials of construction used
- Size, shape and frontage of building
- Height of buildings, type of roof, etc.
- Height of plinth and type of foundations, wall thickness etc.
- Location of the building

The buildings located in the commercial zone will fetch more value as compared to a similar one in residential areas. Similarly, building constructed on freehold plots will be valued more than similar building on lease hold plot. Building in developed zones will have more value than buildings in underdeveloped areas. Demand and supply also play major role in valuation of the building. If the demand is more and supply is less the value will increase and vice-a-versa.

(2) Methods of valuation :   **(W-2010)**

The various methods commonly adopted for valuation of the building are as follows :

- (i)   Land and Building method
  - (a) Book value method
  - (b) Present land value method
  - (c) Replacement value method
- (ii)   Rental method
- (iii) Direct comparison with the capital value
- (iv) Valuation on profit basing
- (v)   Development methods
- (vi) Depreciation method of valuation

(i) Land and Building methods :

(a) Book value method (based on original cost of the land) :

It is the simplest method of valuation usually adopted for properties which do not fetch any rent such as property occupied by the owner, school or college buildings etc. The method is particularly suitable for recording valuation of the assets in the balance sheet of companies or government office records etc.

Knowing the original cost of construction, the depreciation cost for the past (or spent) life is calculated by the straight line method. The book value of the property is then determined by subtracting the depreciated cost from the original cost of construction plus the original cost of the land i.e.

$$\text{Book value} = \begin{bmatrix} \text{Original cost of} \\ \text{construction} \end{bmatrix} - \begin{bmatrix} \text{Depreciation by} \\ \text{straight line method} \end{bmatrix} + \begin{bmatrix} \text{Original} \\ \text{cost of land} \end{bmatrix}$$

The drawback of this method is that the value obtained is far less than its real value; and as such is not used in practice.

(b) Present land value method :

In the book value method explained above, the original cost of the land was taken for determining the valuation of the property. Even though the value of the building depreciates, the value of the land on which the building is constructed, appreciates. Thus in calculating the valuation of the property, instead of original cost of land, the present market value of the land is taken by comparing the land under consideration (i.e. whose market value is to be found out) with the recent sale transactions of similar land in its neighbourhood.

Thus valuation of property

$$\begin{bmatrix} \text{Original cost of} \\ \text{construction} \end{bmatrix} - \begin{bmatrix} \text{Depreciation for} \\ \text{the past life} \end{bmatrix} + \begin{bmatrix} \text{Present market} \\ \text{value of the land} \end{bmatrix}$$

(c) Reproduction and replacement value method :

In this method of valuation, the fair market value of the property is determined on the land and building basis considering the current rates of constructions of structure and the present rate of land on which the structure is constructed.

Procedure :

- Determine the present cost of similar new structure in the area.
- Calculate the depreciated cost for the past or spent life of the building by sinking fund method.
- Work out the cost of the land on which the building is constructed, by comparing it with the recent sale transactions of similar land in the neighbourhood, and

- Determine the replacement value (also known as actual fair market value) of the property by the following mathematical expression.

$$\begin{bmatrix} \text{Replacement or} \\ \text{fair market value} \\ \text{of property} \end{bmatrix} = \begin{bmatrix} \text{Present cost of} \\ \text{construction of} \\ \text{similar building} \end{bmatrix} - \begin{bmatrix} \text{Depreciated cost} \\ \text{by sinking} \\ \text{fund method} \end{bmatrix} + \begin{bmatrix} \text{Present value of} \\ \text{the land at current} \\ \text{market rate} \end{bmatrix}$$

The above method is more realistic and is usually followed for the valuation of properties for sale and purchase transactions.

(ii) Rental method of valuation :   (W-2010)

The method is usually adopted if the building is used on rental basis or when the probable rent from the building can be ascertained by local enquires. The procedure in short consists as follows:

- Determine the 'gross rent' from the property from actual rent collected or by making local enquires in the area.
- Calculate all the outgoings to which the property is subjected.
- Work out the 'net rent' from the property by subtracting the total outgoings from the gross rent.
- Assume suitable rate of interest by comparison with the rate of interest offered by the Nationalised Banks and Government securities and calculate the years purchase (Y.P.) $\left(\text{i.e. Y.P. } = \dfrac{100}{\text{Assumed rate of interest}} \right)$
- Determine the capitalised value of the property by multiplying the net income by the year's purchase (Y.P.)

(iii) Direct comparison of the capital value :

The method is usually adopted when the rental value of the property is not available but recent sale prices of similar properties are obtainable. The method consists in determining the capitalised value of the property under consideration by direct comparison with the sale records of capitalised value of similar property situated in the same area.

(iv) Valuation on profit basis :

The method is usually adopted for the valuation of properties such as hotels, cinema houses, etc. for which the capitalised value depends solely on its profit from the business. The procedure in short consists in estimating the *gross profit* from the business and from this 'gross profit' the usual outgoings, working expenses (of running the business) and the interest on the capital (invested in the business) are all deducted to arrive at the 'net profit' (which is similar to net income in rental method of valuation). This net profit is then multiplied by the years purchase (Y.P.) to calculate the capitalised value of the property. The following points need consideration :

- The net profit to be used for the valuation is to be taken as the average profit of the last three years.
- The profit depends partly on the turn over and good will.

The valuation obtained by this method is too high and should therefore be verified by some other suitable method of valuation.

(v) Development method :

The method is suitable for the properties which are either in under developed or developing stages: When a large area of the land is to be sub-divided into smaller plots after providing for roads, open spaces, parks etc., the development method of valuation is usually adopted. The probable selling price of the divided plots, open spaces, parks etc. are determined. The valuation of the property is then carried out after assuming certain net future returns after its development. This net future return (which is similar to net rent) when multiplied by the suitable value of year's purchase (Y.P.) determines the capitalised value of the property.

(vi) Depreciation method of valuation :

According to this method of valuation, the building should be divided into four parts viz. (i) Walls, (ii) Roofs, (iii) Floor and (iv) Doors and Windows. The cost of each part should first be worked out on the present day rates by detailed measurements. The life of each of the four parts should then be ascertained with the help of table given in next page [Form 1, Annexure (B) to Chapter XIII of the Financial Hand Book Volume V, (Part 2)] and the depreciated value of each part is ascertained by the formula

$$D = P \left[\frac{100 - rd}{100} \right]^n$$

where D is the depreciated value, P is the cost at present market rate and rd is the fixed percentage of depreciation (rate of depreciation, r stands for rate and d for depreciation) and n the number of years, the building had been constructed. The value of rd may be taken as below :

Structures with 100 years life – rd = 1.0, Structures with 75 years life – rd = 1.3, Structures with 5 years life – rd = 2.0, Structures with 25 years life – rd = 4.0, Structures with 20 years life – rd = 5.0.

The values arrived at will be exclusive of cost of land water supply, electric and sanitary fittings etc. and will apply to those buildings only which have been properly maintained. If the repairs had been neglected in the past and the present condition is bad or dilapidated, suitable deduction should be made from the values as deducted above, for neglected repairs.

The present value of land and water supply, electric and sanitary fittings etc. should be added to the valuation of the building to arrive at total valuation of the property.

Life of various items of works in building :

Details of items and works	Life of the works
Masonry :	
1. Brickwork in lime or cement, Boulder masonry in lime or cement, Cut stone work in lime or cement	100 years and above
2. Brickwork in clay, Coursed rubble in mud	100 years
3. Brick arches in lime or cement mortar, Rubble stone arches in lime or cement mortar	100 years
4. Sundried brickwork in clay	75 years
Flooring :	
5. Brick-on-edge or flat flooring over 7.5 cm L.C.	40 years
6. Cement concrete floor, Granolithic floor, stone flooring	50 years
7. Terraced floor or lime concrete	20 years
Roofing :	
8. R.C.C., R.B., Terraced roofing over stone flags, Jack rack Roofing with L.C. terracing	75 years
9. Iron work in roofing	80 years
10. Sal wood work in roof	60 years
11. Country wood in work	15 years
12. Allahabad lock tiling	25 years
13. G.I. Sheet roofing of 22 B.W.G. sheet	50 years
14. Sal ballies in roof	20 years
15. Pine wood ceiling	30 years
Doors and windows :	
16. Teak wood doors and windows, Sal wood doors and windows	40 years
17. Country wood doors and windows	30 years
Iron work :	
18. Rolled steel joint	75 years
19. Wrought iron work	80 years

4.16 FIXATION OF RENT OF A PROPERTY

In order to determine the rent of a property, it is necessary to calculate the capitalised value of the property by valuation method. The capitalised value is then divided by the Year's Purchase (Y.P.) to get the net income from the property. To this net income from the property all possible outgoings are added to determine the gross annual rent (or income) from the property. The gross rent or income is then divided by 12, to calculate the rent per months from the property and is known as **'Standard rent'** from the property. However, the actual rent from the property may be higher or lower than the standard rent depending upon the locality in which the property is situated, type and materials of construction, and demand and supply of the property. It may be noted that while fixing the reasonable rent of the property it should be seen that the owner gets reasonable return of at least 10 to 15, on the capital he has invested in purchasing the property (i.e. the cost of the land and the cost of construction of building).

4.17 REVERSIONARY VALUE OF LAND (OR LAND VALUE IN REVERSION)

The two important aspects of method of valuation based on the rental or yield basis are as follows :

- Capitalised value of the structure that enables to receive income in future till the end of its life and

- Present value of the open land that can be obtained at the end of life of the building.

It may be noted that the owner shall be receiving income from the property in the form of rent till the end of the life of the building. At the end of the life of the building, the building being in the dismantled stage, no further income is possible from it and the owner is left only with the open land and is known as *'reversion to land'*.

The present worth of the full amount of the open land that will be obtained by the owner after the life of structure or (building) is over is termed as 'land value on reversion' or 'reversionary' or 'deferred value of the land'.

$$\begin{bmatrix} \text{Reversionary value of the land} \\ \text{or land value of reversion} \\ \text{or deferred value of land} \end{bmatrix} = \begin{bmatrix} \dfrac{\text{Present cost of the land}}{(1 + i_L)^n} \end{bmatrix}$$

where i_L = Rate of interest on land investment which is usually assumed as 6 to 7%

   n = Expected future life of the building

SOLVED PROBLEMS

Problem 4.1 :

   A concrete mixer was purchased for ₹ 50,000/-. Assume salvage value of ₹ 5000/- after five years and calculate the book value each year by calculating depreciation by

(1)   Straight line method,

(2)   Constant percentage method,

(3)   Sinking fund method.

Solution :

(1) By Straight Line Method :

$$\text{Annual depreciation} = \frac{\text{Original cost} - \text{Salvage value}}{\text{Life of the mixer}}$$

$$= \frac{50000 - 5000}{5} = ₹\, 9000/\text{- per year}$$

$\therefore$　　Book value per year $=$ Original cost $-$ Depreciation per year

$\therefore$　At the end of 1st year $= 50000 - 9000 = ₹\, 41000/\text{-}$

At the end of 2nd year $= 41000 - 9000 = ₹\, 32000/\text{-}$

At the end of 3rd year $= 32000 - 9000 = ₹\, 23000/\text{-}$

At the end of 4th year $= 23000 - 9000 = ₹\, 14000/\text{-}$

At the end of 5th year $= 14000 - 9000 = ₹\, 5000/\text{-}$　　　　$\therefore$ O.K.

(2) By Constant Percentage Method : The method presumes that the property loses its value by a constant percentage of its value at the beginning of each year.

i.e.　　　　　$D = 1 - \left(\dfrac{S}{C}\right)^{1/n}$

where　　　　$S =$ Salvage value $= ₹\, 5000/\text{-}$

　　　　　　$C =$ Original cost $= ₹\, 50000/\text{-}$

$\therefore$　　　　　$D = 1 - \left(\dfrac{5000}{50000}\right)^{1/5} = 1 - \left(\dfrac{1}{10}\right)^{1/5}$

　　　　　　　$= 0.3690$

Life in years	Book value at the end of year	Depreciation	Total depreciation
0	₹ 50000	Nil	Nil
1	₹ 31550	18450	18450
2	₹ 19908	11643	30093
3	₹ 12561	7347	37440
4	₹ 7925	4635	42075
5	₹ 5000	2925	45000

(3) By Sinking Fund Method : Annual sinking fund to replace ₹ (50000 − 5000) = ₹ 45000/- in 5 years @ say 6% interest

$$= 45000 \times \left[\frac{0.06}{(1 + 0.06)^5 - 1}\right] = ₹\, 7982.838$$

Problem 4.2 :

A property holder has purchased a centrifugal pump for ₹ 10,000/-. Calculate the amount that should be set aside by him every year as sinking fund to accumulate ₹ 10,000/- at 6% compound interests, after 10 years.

Solution :

Annual sinking fund to provide rupee one at the end of 10 years

$$= \left[\frac{i}{(1 + i)^n - 1} \right]$$

where　　　　　　　　i = Rate of interest = 6% (Given)

　　　　　　　　　　n = 10 years

∴　Annual sinking fund for rupee one

$$= \left[\frac{0.06}{(1 + 0.06)^{10} - 1} \right] = 0.075867$$

∴　To accumulate ₹ 10,000

　　　　　　　　$= 0.075867 \times 10{,}000 = 758.67$

Problem 4.3 :

An electric motor was purchased for ₹ 12,000/-. Assuming life of the motor as 16 years and scrap value as 10% of the original cost, calculate its book value after 10 years.

Solution :

Original cost of the electric motor　=　₹ 12,000/-

　　Scrap value after 16 years　=　₹ 1200/-

　　Total depreciation at the end of 16 years　=　12000 – 1200　=　10800

　　Yearly depreciation (by straight line method) $= \dfrac{10800}{16} = $ ₹ 675 per year

∴　Depreciation in 10 years　=　675 × 10　=　₹ 6750/-

　　Its book value after 10 years　=　12000 – 6750　=　₹ 5250/-

Problem 4.4 :

Calculate the present book value of the property from the following data :

(1)　Built-up area of building　= 200 sq. m.

(2)　Area of the plot　= 600 sq. m.

(3)　Year of construction of building　= 1953

(4)　Cost of construction is 1953　= ₹ 400 sq. m.

(5)　Cost of land purchased　= ₹ 10 sq. m.

(6)　Assume scrap value　= 10% of original cost

(7)　The building was constructed with first class specifications

Solution : Using the expression for Book Value (Fig. 4.2)

$$\text{Book value} = \begin{bmatrix}\text{Original cost} \\ \text{of building}\end{bmatrix} - \begin{bmatrix}\text{Depreciation by} \\ \text{straight line method}\end{bmatrix} + \begin{bmatrix}\text{Original cost} \\ \text{of land}\end{bmatrix}$$

$$= (200 \times 400) - (\text{Depreciation for spent life}) + (600 \times 10)$$

$$= 80000 + 6000 - (\text{Depreciation for the period from 1953 to 1993}$$
$$\text{i.e. 40 years})$$

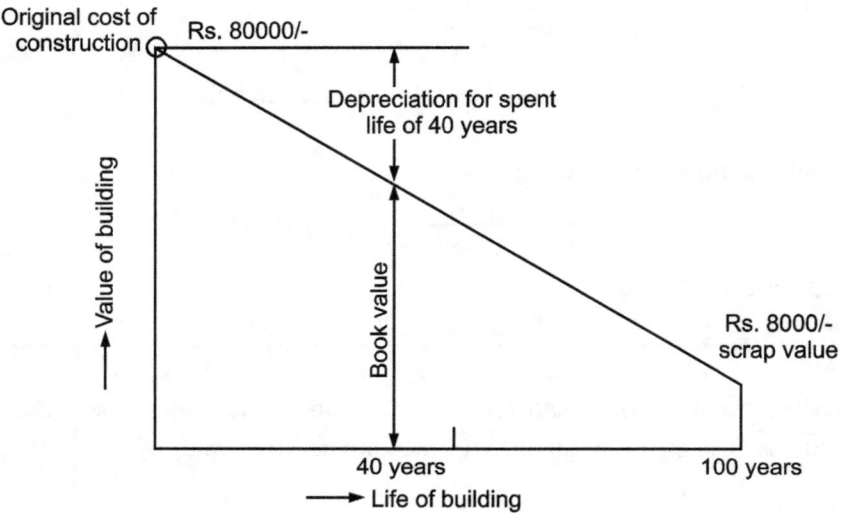

Fig. 4.2

To calculate the depreciation of the building :

As the building is constructed with first class specifications, its life is to be taken as 100 years.

∴   (Scrap value of building at the end of 100 years)

$$= \frac{1}{10}(80000) = 8000$$

$$\text{Annual depreciation} = \frac{\text{Original cost} - \text{Scrap value}}{\text{Life of the building}} = \frac{80000 - 8000}{1000} = \frac{72000}{100}$$

$$= ₹ 720/\text{- per year}$$

Depreciation for the period from 1953 to 1993 i.e. 40 years by straight line method

$$= 40 \times 720$$

$$= 28800$$

∴   Book value $= 80000 + 6000 - 28800$

$$= 86000 - 28800$$

$$= ₹ 57,200/\text{-}$$

∴   Book value of the property in 1993 $= ₹\ \mathbf{57200/\text{-}}$

Problem 4.5 :

Determine the 'Fair Market Value' of the property from the following data :

(1)   Built-up area of building = 200 sq. m.

(2)   Area of the plot = 600 sq. m.

(3)   Year of construction of building = 1973

(4)   Present rate of construction (in 1993) of similar structure = ₹ 2000/- sq. m.

(5)   Present cost of the land (in 1993) = ₹ 50 per sq.m.

(6)   Rate of interest on Govt. Securities = 6%

(7)   The building was constructed with first class specifications

(8)   Scrap value = 10%

Solution : The value of the property is to be determined by considering present rate of construction and the present cost of the land i.e. by replacement value method.

$$\therefore \begin{bmatrix} \text{Replacement value} \\ \text{of the property} \end{bmatrix} = \begin{bmatrix} \text{Present cost of} \\ \text{similar structure} \end{bmatrix} - \begin{bmatrix} \text{Depreciation by} \\ \text{sinking fund method} \end{bmatrix} + \begin{bmatrix} \text{Present cost} \\ \text{of the land} \end{bmatrix}$$

$$= (200 \times 2000) - \begin{bmatrix} \text{Depreciation by} \\ \text{sinking fund method} \end{bmatrix} + 600 \times 500$$

$$= 400000 + 300000 - \text{Depreciation by sinking fund method}$$

Now, $$\begin{bmatrix} \text{Total depreciation} \\ \text{for building} \end{bmatrix} = \begin{bmatrix} \text{Present cost of} \\ \text{similar structure} \end{bmatrix} - \text{Scrap value}$$

$$= 400000 - \frac{10}{100} (400000)$$

$$= ₹ 360000/-$$

This amount of total depreciation must be made available at the end of the building.

i.e.   The total sinking fund to be collected at the end of life of building = ₹ 360000/-

$$\therefore \quad \text{(Annual installment of sinking fund) } S_i = \frac{\text{S.F.} \times i'}{(1 + i')^n - 1}$$

where S_i = Annual instalment of sinking fund

               S.F. = Total sinking fund to be collected at the end of life of building

               i' = Rate of interest on securities

               n = Life of the building

In this problem,

               S.F. = 360000/-

               i' = Rate of interest on securities = 6% (Given)

               n = Life of building which is 100 years for a building having first class specification

$\therefore$ S_i = Annual sinking fund installment to be determined

$$\therefore \quad S_i = \frac{\left[360000 \times \dfrac{6}{100}\right]}{\left[\left(1 + \dfrac{6}{100}\right)^n - 1\right]} = \left[\frac{360000 \times 0.06}{(1 + 0.06)^{100} - 1}\right]$$

$$\therefore \quad S_i = \left[\frac{21600}{(1.06)^{100} - 1}\right] = 63.84$$

$\therefore$ Sinking fund collected so far for the spend life of property i.e. 20 years @ the above rate of sinking fund S_i

$$= S_i\left[\frac{(1 + i')^{n'} - 1}{i'}\right] = S_i\left[\frac{(1.06)^{20} - 1}{0.06}\right] = 2348.39$$

$$= \text{Depreciation by sinking fund law for the spend life of 20 years}$$

$\therefore$ Replacement value $= 400000 + 30000 - 2348.39 = 427651.61$

Problem 4.6 :

Determine the present fair market value (i.e. capitalised value) of the property from the following data :

(1) Gross income from the property = ₹ 30000/-

(2) Year of construction = 1963

(3) The expectancy of the property = 50 years

(4) Owner desires to have net return of 8% from the investment

(5) The rate of interest on Govt. securities = 5%

(6) Municipal taxes = 24% of gross income

(7) Annual repair charges = 3% of gross income

(8) Maintenance, insurance and other charges = 3% of gross income

Solution :

(1) Fair market value i.e. capitalised value of the property = (Net income from the property) × (Year's purchase)

(2) Net income = Gross income − Outgoings

$$= 30000 - \left(\frac{24}{100} + \frac{3}{100} + \frac{3}{100}\right) \times (30000)$$

$$= 30000 - 9000 = ₹ 21000/- \qquad \text{... (i)}$$

(3) Year's purchase = Y.P. (Here it is dual rate Y.P.)

$$\text{Y.P.} = \frac{1}{i + I}$$

where i = Rate of interest from capital investment

= 0.08 (given)

and I = Sinking fund coefficient

$$= \left[\frac{i'}{(1 + i')^n - 1} \right]$$

where i' = Rate of interest on Govt. securities

= 0.05 (given)

n = Expectancy of the building

= 50 years

$\therefore$ Y.P. $= \left[\dfrac{1}{0.08 + \dfrac{0.05}{(1.05)^{50} - 1}} \right] = \left[\dfrac{1}{0.08 + \dfrac{0.05}{10.46}} \right] = 11.79$ ... (ii)

$\therefore$ Capitalized or fair market value of the property

= (i) × (ii) = 21000 × 11.79

= ₹ 247590

Problem 4.7 :

Determine the monthly rent for the property from the following data :

(1)   Cost of the recently constructed building = ₹ 400000/-

(2)   Area of the plot = 1000 sq.m.

(3)   Cost of purchase of plot = ₹ 60 per sq.m.

(4)   Rate of return from capital invested on the building = 8%

(5)   Rate of return on land investment = 6%

(6)   Rate of interest on Govt. securities = 5%

(7)   Scrap value of property = 10%

(8)   Municipal taxes = 25% of rateable value

(9)   Rateable value = 85% of annual rent

(10) Annual repair charges = 2% of construction cost of building

(11) Management and other charges = 5% of annual rent

(12) Future life of building = 60 years

Solution :

Let the gross income i.e. annual rent from the property to be ₹ x.

Then, Gross income (i.e. Annual rent) = Net income + Outgoings

Now,   Net income = Income from investment in the building + Income from investment on land

$= \left(400000 \times \dfrac{8}{100} \right) + (1000 \times 60) \times \dfrac{6}{100}$

= 32000 + 3600 = 35600

and $\quad$ Outgoings $= (x)\left(\dfrac{25}{100} \times 0.85\right) + \dfrac{2}{100}(400000) + \dfrac{5}{100}(x)$

$$+ \text{ Sinking fund installment } (S_i)$$

where $\qquad S_i = (S.F.)\left[\dfrac{i'}{(1 + i')^n - 1}\right]$

$\qquad$ S.F. $=$ Total sinking fund to be collected at the end of life of building

$\qquad\quad = $ Total depreciation

$\qquad\quad = $ (Cost of building – Scrap value)

$\qquad\quad = 400000 - \dfrac{1}{10}(400000) = 360000/\text{-}$

and $\qquad\quad i' = $ Rate of interest on Govt. securities $= 5\%$

$\qquad\quad n = $ Future life of the building

$\qquad\quad = 60 \text{ years (given)}$

$\therefore \qquad S_i = 360000\left[\dfrac{0.05}{(1 + 0.05)^{60} - 1}\right] = 360000\left[\dfrac{0.05}{18.68 - 1}\right] = 1018.10$

$\therefore \quad$ Gross income or Annual rent $= x$

$\qquad\qquad = 32000 + 3600 + \text{Outgoings}$

$\qquad\qquad = 32000 + 3600 + 0.2125\,x + 8000 + 0.05\,x + 1018.10$

$\therefore \qquad x - 0.2125\,x - (0.05\,x) = 35600 + 1018.10 + 8000$

$\therefore \qquad\qquad 0.7375\,x = 44618.10$

$\therefore \qquad\qquad\qquad x = \dfrac{44618.10}{0.7375} = 60499.12$

$\therefore \qquad$ Monthly rent $= \dfrac{60499.12}{12} = ₹\,5041.60 = ₹\,5042.00$

Problem 4.8 :

Determine the present fair market value of the property from the following data :

(1) Built-up area of building $= 200$ sq.m.

(2) Area of plot $= 600$ sq.m.

(3) Year of construction $= 1973$

(4) Present cost of construction for similar structure $= ₹\,1500$ sq.m.

(5) Present value of land in the locality $= ₹\,400$ sq.m.

(6) Annual gross rent from the property $= ₹\,8000/\text{-}$

(7) Return on capital investment $= 5\%$

(8) Redemption of capital $= 5\%$

(9) Future life of the building $= 40$ years

(10) Total outgoings $= 30\%$ of annual gross rent

(11) Reversionary value of land at 6% rate of interest

Solution :

Gross income $= ₹ 8000/-$ (given)

∴ Net income $= 8000 - $ Outgoings

$$= 8000 - \frac{30}{100} \times 8000$$

$$= 8000 - 2400$$

$$= ₹ 5600/-$$

Now, Y.P. (dual rate) $= \dfrac{1}{i + I}$ $\qquad$ $i = 0.08$

$$= \frac{1}{0.08 + 8.278 \times 10^{-3}}$$ $\qquad$ $I = $ Sinking fund coefficient

$$= \frac{1}{0.08827}$$ $\qquad\qquad = \left[\frac{i'}{(1 + i')^n - 1} \right]$

$$= 11.32$$ $\qquad\qquad\qquad = \left[\frac{0.05}{(1.05)^{40} - 1} \right]$

$$\qquad\qquad\qquad\qquad\qquad = \frac{0.05}{7.04 - 1} = \frac{0.05}{6.04}$$

$$\qquad\qquad\qquad\qquad\qquad = 8.278 \times 10^{-3}$$

∴ Capitalized value $=$ N.I. $\times$ Y.P $+$ Reversionary value of land

$$= 5600 \times 11.32 + \left[\frac{\text{Current market value of land}}{(1 + 0.06)^{40}} \right]$$

$$= 63392.00 + \frac{600 \times 400}{(1.06)^{40}} = 63392 + \frac{240000}{10.285}$$

$$= 63392 + 23334.95$$

$$= ₹ 86726.95$$

Problem 4.9 :

Calculate the present value of the property from the following :

(1) Area of plot $= 800 \text{ m}^2$

(2) Plinth area of construction $= 200 \text{ m}^2$

(3) Expected future life of property $= 50$ years

(4) Gross rent received $= ₹ 4000/-$ P.M.

(5) Present sale rate of land $= ₹ 300/- \text{ m}^2$

(6) Rate of interest for building investment $= 12\%$ per year

(7) Rate of interest on land investment $= 5\%$ per year

(8) Rate of interest for sinking fund $= 4\%$ per year

Assume suitable outgoings and state them clearly.

Solution :

$$\text{Gross rent} = 12 \times 4000 = ₹\ 48000/\text{-}$$

$$\text{Cost of land} = 800 \times 300$$

$$= ₹\ 24000/\text{-}$$

Assumed outgoings :

$$\text{Municipal taxes} = 20\% \text{ of gross rent}$$

$$\text{Maintenance and repair charges} = 2\% \text{ of gross rent}$$

$$\text{Other outgoings} = 10\% \text{ of gross rent}$$

$$\therefore \quad \text{Total outgoings} = \frac{(20 + 2 + 10)}{100} \times 48000$$

$$= ₹\ 15360/\text{-}$$

$$\therefore \quad \text{Net income} = 48000 - 15360 = ₹\ 32640/\text{-}$$

$$\text{Dual rate Y.P.} = \frac{1}{i + I}$$

where

$$I = \frac{i'}{(1 + i')^n - 1} = \frac{0.04}{(1.04)^{50} - 1}$$

$$= 6.55 \times 10^{-3} = \text{Sinking fund coefficient}$$

$$\therefore \quad \text{Y.P.} = \frac{1}{0.12 + 6.55 \times 10^{-3}} = 7.90$$

$$\therefore \quad \text{Capitalised value} = (\text{Net income}) \times (\text{Y.P.})$$

$$= 32640 \times 7.90 \qquad \qquad \dots \text{(i)}$$

$$= ₹\ 257856/\text{-}$$

$$\text{Reversionary value of the land} = (\text{Present cost of land}) \times \frac{1}{(1 + i_L)^n}$$

$$= 240000 \times \frac{1}{(1 + 0.05)^{50}}$$

$$= 20928.89 \qquad \qquad \dots \text{(ii)}$$

$$\therefore \quad \text{Present value of the property}$$

$$= \text{(i)} + \text{(ii)} = 257856 + 20928.89 = ₹\ 278784.89$$

Problem 4.10 :

Find out the present market value of the property including reversionary value of land. It consists of a plot having 700 m² area on which stands a building fetching a gross monthly rent of ₹ 2800/-. The estimated future life of the building is 45 years. Assume usual outgoings. The owner desires to have 8% net return. Present cost of land in near vicinity is ₹ 300/m². Assume rate of interest on sinking fund @ 5% and that on land investment @ 6%.

Solution :

Gross income $= 2800 \times 12 = 22600/-$

$\therefore \quad \begin{bmatrix} \text{Capitalised value} \\ \text{of property} \end{bmatrix} = \begin{bmatrix} \text{Net} \\ \text{income} \end{bmatrix} \times (\text{Y.P.}) + \begin{bmatrix} \text{Reversionary} \\ \text{value of land} \end{bmatrix}$

Now,   Net income $=$ Gross income $-$ Outgoings

Assuming outgoings as :

(1)   Municipal taxes $= 30\%$ of $33600 = 10080/-$

(2)   Other repair and maintenance charges $= \dfrac{5}{100} \times 33600 = 1680/-$

$\therefore$ Total outgoings $= 10080 + 1680 = 11760/-$

$\therefore$ Net income $= 33600 - 11760 = 21840/-$

Now,   Dual rate Y.P. $= \dfrac{1}{i + I}$

where, $I = \dfrac{i'}{(1 + i')^n - 1}$ since n $= 45$

$= \dfrac{0.05}{(1.05)^{45} - 1} = 0.00626$

$=$ Sinking fund coefficient

$\therefore$ Y.P. $= \dfrac{1}{0.08 + 0.00626} = 11.60$

$\therefore \quad \begin{bmatrix} \text{Capitalised value} \\ \text{of property} \end{bmatrix} = [(\text{N.I.}) \times \text{Y.P.}] + \text{Reversionary value of fund}$

$= (21840 \times 11.60) + \dfrac{\text{Present cost of land}}{(1 + i_L)^n}$

$= (21840 \times 11.60) + \dfrac{700 \times 300}{(1 + 0.06)^{45}}$

$= 21840 \times 11.60 + 15256.50 = 268600.50$

Problem 4.11 :

A concrete mixer is purchased at ₹ 60000/-. Assuming salvage value equal to ₹ 10000/- at the end of five years, work out the book value of the mixer at the end of each years by calculating depreciation by constant percentage method.

Solution :

Depreciation (by constant percentage method)

$= 1 - \left(\dfrac{S}{C}\right)^{1/n}$

where   S $=$ Salvage value

and   C $=$ Original cost

$$\therefore \qquad \text{Depreciation} = 1 - \left(\frac{10000}{60000}\right)^{1/5}$$

$$\therefore \qquad D = 0.301$$

$$\therefore \qquad \begin{array}{c}\text{Value of the mixer} \\ \text{after n years}\end{array} = C(1-D)^n$$

(1) After first year, its book value

$$= 60000\,(1 - 0.031)^1$$
$$= ₹\,41940/\text{-}$$

(2) After second year, its book value

$$= 60000\,(1 - 0.031)^2$$
$$= ₹\,29316/\text{-}$$

(3) After third year, its book value

$$= 60000\,(1 - 0.031)^3$$
$$= ₹\,20492/\text{-}$$

(4) After fourth year, its book value

$$= 60000\,(1 - 0.031)^4$$
$$= ₹\,14324/\text{-}$$

(5) After fifth year, its book value

$$= 60000\,(1 - 0.031)^5$$
$$= ₹\,10000/\text{-}$$

The above results entered in a tabular form will be as follows :

Sr. No. of year	Description in ₹	Book value in ₹
0	Nil	60000
1	18060	41940
2	30684	29316
3	39508	20492
4	45676	14324
5	50000	10000

Problem 4.12 :

Calculate the capitalised value of the property (providing for a net yield @ 6%) from the following data :

(1) First class building.

(2) Estimated life of building = 75 years

(3) Annual rent of the plot on which the building is constructed = ₹ 500/-

(4) The gross rent from the building = ₹ 500/- per month

(5) Taxes and insurance charges = 20% of gross rent

(6) Repair charges = 10% of gross rent

(7) Management charges = 4% gross rent

(8) Miscellaneous expenses = 2% of gross rent

(9) Total replacement cost of the property = ₹ 90000/-

(10) Scrap value = 10%

(11) Rate of interest on sinking fund = 5%

(12) Return from the investment on building = 6%

Solution :

Gross rent from the property per annum

$$= 500 \times 12 = ₹ 6000/- \qquad \dots \text{(i)}$$

Outgoings

(1)   Annual plot rent = ₹ 500/-

(2)   Taxes and insurance $= \dfrac{20}{100} \times 6000 = ₹ 1200/-$

(3) Repairs management and miscellaneous charges

$$= \dfrac{16}{100} \times 6000 = ₹ 960/-$$

$\therefore$ Sinking fund coefficient $= \dfrac{i'}{[(1 + i')^n - 1]} = \dfrac{0.05}{[(1.05)^{75} - 1]}$

$$= 0.00132$$

and total sinking fund to be collected at the end of life of building

$$= 90000 - 9000 = ₹ 81000/-$$

(4)   Sinking fund installment $= 81000 \times 0.00132$

$$= 106.92 \approx ₹ 107/-$$

$\therefore$ Total outgoings $= 500 + 1200 + 960 + 107$

$$= 2767/- \qquad \dots \text{(ii)}$$

$\therefore$ Net income from the property $= \text{(i)} - \text{(ii)}$

$$= ₹ (6000 - 2767) = ₹ 3233/-$$

$\therefore$ Capitalised value of the property $= \text{Net income} \times \text{Y.P.} \qquad \dots \text{(iii)}$

$$= 3233 \times \dfrac{100}{6} = ₹ 53883/-$$

Problem 4.13 :

A building has been newly constructed at a cost of ₹ 240000/- including sanitary, water supply and electric fittings. The plot area is 300 m² and its cost is ₹ 150000/-. The building consists of four flats for four tenants. The owner expects 8% return on cost of construction and 5% return on land investment. Calculate the standard rent for each flat with the following assumptions :

(1)　Life of building, 60 years and sinking fund will be created on 5% interest basis.

(2)　Annual repairs = 1% cost of construction

(3)　Other outgoings including taxes at 30% of net return on building.

Solution :

(1)　Expected return on the cost of building = 8%

$$= \frac{8}{100} \times 240000 = ₹ 19200/-$$

(2)　Expected return on land investment = 5%

$$= \frac{5}{100} \times 150000 = ₹ 7500/-$$

∴　Total return from cost of building and land investment

$$= ₹ (19200 + 7500)$$
$$= ₹ 26700/-$$

(3)　Outgoings :

(a)　Annual repairs $= \frac{1}{100} \times 240000 = ₹ 2400/-$

(b)　Other outgoings $= \frac{30}{100} \times 19200 = ₹ 5760/-$

(c)　Sinking fund installment $= S_i = S.F. \left[\frac{i'}{(1 - i')^n - 1} \right]$

Total sinking fund to be collected at the end of the life of the building assuming 10% as scrap value

$$= \frac{90}{100} \times 240000$$

∴　　　　　　S.F. = ₹ 216000/-

and　i = Rate of interest = 5% (Given)

∴　Sinking fund installment

$$S_i = S.F. \left[\frac{i'}{(1 - i')^n - 1} \right]$$

$$= 21600 \left[\frac{0.05}{(1 + 0.05)^{60} - 1} \right]$$

where   n = Life of building = 60 years (Given)

∴ S_i = ₹ 610/-

∴   Total outgoings = ₹ (2400 + 5760 + 610)

                                = ₹ 8770/-

∴   Gross rent = Net rent + Total outgoings

∴   Gross rent = ₹ (26700 + 8770)

                                = ₹ 35470/- per year

∴   Rent per month = $₹\left(\dfrac{35470}{12}\right)$

                                = ₹ 2955/-

For the entire building, having four flats

∴ $\begin{matrix} \text{Standard rent} \\ \text{for each flat} \end{matrix}$ = $₹\dfrac{2955}{4}$ = ₹ 738.75 per month

Problem 4.14 :

A building has been rented on an annual rent of ₹ 12,000/-. The future life of the building in the present condition is expected to be 15 years. If the major repairs to the building are done, its life shall be increased by another 20 years. The major repairs will cost ₹ 30000/-. Determine whether it will be economical to do major repairs or not.

Assume rate of interest at 7%.

Solution :

Data : Rented building

                Annual rent = ₹ 12000/-

    Future life of building = 15 years

         Rate of interest = 7%

Assuming 30% total outgoings,

            Net income = Gross income – Outgoings

                        = $12000 - \dfrac{30}{100} \times 12000$

                        = ₹ 8400/-

∴   Value of the property (i.e. building)

                        = (Net income) × Y.P.

                        = 8400 × Y.P.

To determine the Y.P. :

$$\text{Y.P.} = \frac{1}{i + I}$$

where $\qquad i' = \%$ Rate of interest (i.e. in decimals)

and $\qquad I = $ Sinking fund required to replace ₹ 1/- at the end of given years

Now, if $\qquad i' = \begin{bmatrix} \text{Rate of interest} \\ \text{on sinking fund} \\ \text{in decimal} \end{bmatrix} = 7\%$ (assumed)

and $\qquad n = $ Number of given years

then $\qquad I = \left[\dfrac{i'}{(1 + i')^n - 1}\right] = \left[\dfrac{0.07}{(1 + 0.07)^{15} - 1}\right]$

$$= 0.0398 = \text{Sinking fund coefficient}$$

$\therefore \qquad \text{Y.P.} = \left(\dfrac{1}{i + I}\right) = \left(\dfrac{1}{0.07 + 0.0398}\right)$

$$= 9.11$$

$\therefore \qquad$ Value of the building $= $ Net rent $\times$ Y.P.

$$= 8400 \times 9.11 = ₹ \, 76524/- \qquad\qquad\qquad \text{... (i)}$$

Now, in the second case, if major repairs are carried out, the life of the building increases by 20 years and the cost of major repairs = 30,000.

i.e. Total future life after repairs = 15 + 20 = 35 years

$\therefore \quad$ Y.P. in the second case $= \dfrac{1}{i + I}$

where $\qquad I = \left[\dfrac{i'}{(1 + i')^n - 1}\right]$

where $\qquad i' = 0.07$ (assumed)

$$= \left[\dfrac{0.07}{(1 + 0.07)^{0.35} - 1}\right]$$

$$= \left[\dfrac{0.07}{(1.07)^{15} - 1}\right]$$

$$= 0.0072$$

$\therefore \quad$ Y.P. (in the second case)

$$= \frac{1}{0.07 + 0.0072}$$

$$= 12.95$$

∴   Value of the building (in the second case)

$$= \text{(net rent)} \times \text{(Y.P.)} = 8400 \times 12.95$$

$$= ₹ 108780/- \qquad\qquad\qquad ... \text{(ii)}$$

∴   Increase in the value of the property (i.e. building) of repairs

$$= \text{(ii)} - \text{(i)}$$

$$= 108780 - 76524 = ₹ 32256/-$$

Thus there is an increase in the value of the building by ₹ 32256/- after carrying out major repairs (by spending ₹ 30000).

Moreover the life of the building is also increased by another 20 years.

Therefore it is obviously economical to carry out the major repairs.

Problem 4.15 :

A building is constructed on a plot of land measuring 560 m². Size of building is 20 m × 10 m. Construction is first class with all ancillaries. The building is 25 years old and assume life of building as 80 years. Work out valuation of property. Assume suitable necessary data.   **(Nov. 2004, 4 M)**

Solution :

Built-up area $= 20 \times 10 = 200$ m²

Assuming present built-up area rate as 500 ₹/ft² $= 5500$ ₹/m²

[Including water supply, sanitary and electrification]

So present cost of construction $= 5500 \times 200 = ₹ 1100000/- = ₹ 11.00$ lakh

With the data available in the problem, valuation of property can be best done by depreciation method of valuation. For depreciation method, we know that :

Depreciated value of building $= D = P\left[\dfrac{100 - rd}{100}\right]^n$

Since life of building is 80 years, so $rd = \dfrac{100}{80} = 1.25$

n = Age of the building = No. of years before which building was constructed,

So, n = 25 years

P = Present value of building $= ₹ 11.00$ lakh

So $D = 1100000 \times \left[\dfrac{100 - 1.25}{100}\right]^{25} = 1100000 \times 0.73 = ₹ 803000/-$

Assuming present cost of land as 150 ₹/ft² $= 1650$ ₹/m²

So   present value of land $= 1650 \times 560 = ₹ 924000/-$

$$\therefore \quad \begin{array}{l} \text{Present value} \\ \text{of the property} \end{array} = \text{Value of building} + \text{Value of land}$$

$$= 803000 + 924000 = ₹ 1727000/-$$

$$= 17.27 \text{ lakhs}$$

Problem 4.16 :

A person desires to sell a well built property having a net rent of ₹ 18000/- per year in perpetuity. One of the conditions of the sale is that the purchases has to pay a sum of ₹ 22000/- once in every ten years to the owner. What is the value of property, if interest rate is 7.5% ?

Solution :

With the data available in the question, valuation of the building can be best done by determining its capitalised value.

We know that

$$\text{Capitalised value} = \text{Net rent} \times \text{Year's purchase}$$

$$\therefore \quad \begin{array}{l} \text{Capitalised value} \\ \text{of property} \end{array} = 18000 \times \frac{100}{7.5} = ₹ 240000/-$$

Problem 4.17 :

Based on the data given below, determine economic rent of the property :

(1) Cost of building = ₹ 4 lakh

(2) Expected future life = 60 years

(3) Plot area and land rate = 500 m² and 160 ₹/m²

(4) Yield on investment and on land 12% and 8%

(5) Outgoings @ 35% of gross income.

(6) Redemption of capital @ 4% per year.

Solution : Expected return on cost of building $= 400000 \times \dfrac{12}{100} = 48000$

Expected return on land investment $= 500 \times 160 \times \dfrac{8}{100} = 6400$

Total expected return from building and land $= 48000 + 6400 = 54400$

We know that,

$$\text{Gross annual income} = \text{Net income} + \text{Total outgoings}$$

Assuming that gross income is X ₹,

So,   Total outgoings = Annual installment of S.F. + Other outgoings

But,   Annual installment of S.F. $= 360000 \times \left[\dfrac{0.04}{(1.04)^{60} - 1} \right]$

                                    $= ₹\,1512.66$

and   Other outgoings $= 0.35\,X$

So,   Gross income $= X = [0.35\,X + 1512.66] + 54400$

∴ $0.65\,X = 55912.66$

So, $X = ₹\,86019.48$

∴   Economic rent $= \dfrac{X}{12} = \dfrac{86019.48}{12} = ₹\,7168.29$

4.18 VALUATION OF A (BUILDING) PROPERTY

Problem :

'X' is a prospective buyer who is a rich merchant and desires to have some immovable property in Pune. 'Y' is the present owner of the property. He wishes to sell the property and settle at his native place. The property is situated on the west side of Pune-Bangalore road in plot no. 4 of survey no. 40/A Parvati "Vivekanand Housing Society". The building was constructed in 1983. The other details are given in the description of the property.

The transaction is of sell and purchase type. Find the value of the property and advise the prospective buyer 'X' regarding the value at which he should purchase the property.

DESCRIPTION OF THE PROPERTY AND DATA :

The property is located on the west side of Pune-Bangalore road. The location of the property is as below :

Survey no. 40/A Parvati.

(1) East side - Plot no. 3 of the society.

(2) West side - Plot no. 5 of the society.

(3) North side - Plot no. 7 of the society.

(4) South side - 3.0 m wide road connecting main road.

Land Details :

The total land is 336 m³. The plot is rectangular in shape having the frontage on 30 m wide internal road. The depth of plot is 24 m the front width is 14 m. The land was used for agricultural purpose previously and has a surface layer of black cotton soil. The site plan is as given below.

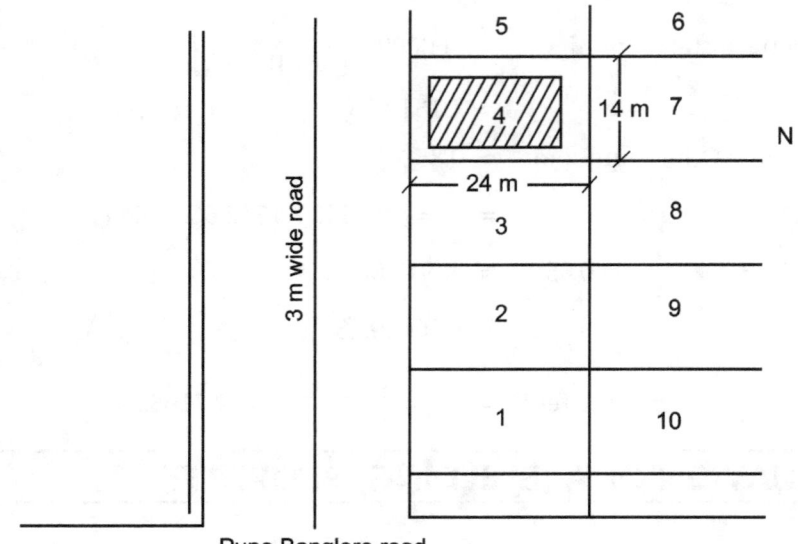

Fig. 4.3 : Site plan (not to scale)

(1)   Year of purchase of plot = 1961.

(2)   Rate of land in 1961 = ₹ 10 /m^2

(3)   Present rates of land in vicinity = ₹ 300 /m^2

(4)   Total area of plot = 24 × 14 = 336 m^2

Building Details :

The building is 2 storeyed with R.C.C. frame structure. It consists of 81.62 m^2 of plinth area of ground floor and the same built-up area on first floor.

Specifications :

1.   The external walls are of B.B. Masonry 20 cm thick in C.M. 1 : 6 with sand faced plaster in C.M. 1 : 4 for outer surface and 12 mm thick. Plaster in C.M. 1 : 4 with neeru finish for inside surfaces. Internal walls are 15 cm B.B. suitably finished.

2.   Marble Mosaic tiles paving for all rooms except kitchen, bath, W.C. and stair hall. Polished shahabad stone is provided in the kitchen, bath and stair hall. White glazed tiles are provided for W.C. floor and dados, bath dados and kitchen otta.

3.   The forms of doors and windows are C.C.T.W. 35 mm thick.

4.   Size of different rooms are as follows :

$$\begin{aligned}
\text{Drawing room} &= 4.2 \times 3.2 \text{ m} \\
\text{Two bed rooms} &= 3 \times 3.6 \text{ m and } 3 \times 4.2 \text{ m} \\
\text{Kitchen} &= 3 \times 4 \text{ m} \\
\text{Verandah} &= 4.2 \times 1.6 \text{ m} \\
\text{W.C.} &= 1.2 \times 1 \text{ m} \\
\text{Bath room} &= 1.9 \times 1.3 \text{ m}
\end{aligned}$$

Stair case :

The same area exists on 1st floor.

The plot has the following advantages :

- Nearness to Padmavati PMT bus stop.
- Nearness to National Highway.
- Swargate S.T. stand at the distance of 2 km.
- Nearness to market-yard area.
- Educational locality.

Plot has the following disadvantages :

- Major hospital is far away from the site.
- Railway station is far away from the site.
- Post office is 1 km away from the site.
- Entertainment facilities like theatre, parks, etc. are far away (@ 2.5 km).

Other Details :

- Year of construction (known from owner) = 1983
- Cost of construction (known from owner) = ₹ 90000/-
- Probable total life @ 80 years
- Plinth area = 81.62 m^2
- Cubic content of the building (G.F. + F.F.) = 604 m^3
- Present rate of construction (G.F. + F.F.) = ₹ 1500 /m^2
- Outgoings :
  - (a) Municipal taxes = 36% of gross income
  - (b) N.A. taxes = ₹ 0.80 /m^2/year
  - (c) Management and service charges = 2%
  - (d) Repairs = 16% of gross income
  - (e) Insurance charges 1/8 of 9/10 of original cost of building
- (8) For capitalisation adopt the following rates :
  - (a) Expected return = 8%
  - (b) Interest on S.F. = 45%
  - (c) Probable rate of rent/m^2 of carpet area/month = ₹ 16/-

Work out the property value and suggest the suitable value to the purchaser X.

Solution :

Method I : Valuation from present land value method :

$$\text{Cost of land} = (\text{Present rate of land in vicinity}) \times (\text{Total area of plot})$$
$$= ₹ 300 /m^2 \times 336$$
$$= ₹ 100800/-$$

Depreciation from S.F. (I) :

$$I = \frac{S \times i}{(i + 1)^n - 1} = \frac{90000 \times \frac{4.5}{100}}{(1 + 0.045)^{80} - 1}$$

$$= ₹ 123.36/-$$

∴ Depreciation for 10 years (i.e. from 1983 - 1993) is

$$= 123.36 \times \frac{(1 + 0.045)^{10} - 1}{0.045}$$

$$= ₹ 1515.90/-$$

∴   Book value = Original cost − Depreciation + Present land cost

$$= 90000 - 1515.90 + 100800$$

$$= ₹ 189284.1/-$$

Method II : Valuation from yield (rental method) :

Net area = Area (G.F. + F.F.) excluding area of W.C. and verandah

$$= 2 [(4.2 \times 3.2) + (3 \times 3.6) + (3 \times 4.2) + (3 \times 4)]$$

$$= 2 \times 48.84$$

$$= 97.68 \ m^2$$

Gross income = Net area × Rate of return

$$= 97.68 \ m^2 \times 16 \times 12$$

$$= ₹ 18754.56/-$$

S.F. coefficient = $S = \dfrac{i_n}{(1 + i_n)^n - 1}$

$$= \frac{0.045}{(1 + 0.045)^{80} - 1}$$

$$= 1.37069 \times 10^{-3}$$

Y.P. $= \dfrac{1}{i + s} = \dfrac{1}{0.08 + 1.37069 \times 10^{-3}}$

$$= 12.2894$$

Outgoings :

(a)   Municipal taxes = 36% of gross income

$$= \frac{36}{100} \times 18754.56$$

$$= 6751.64$$

(b)   N.A. taxes $= 0.80 \times 336 = 268.8$

(c)   Repairs = 16% of gross income

= 3000.73

(d)   Management and services charges

= 2% of G.I.

= 375.09

(e)   Insurance charges = $\frac{1}{8}$ % of $\left(\frac{9}{10}\right)^{th}$ of cost of building

= $\frac{1}{800} \times \frac{9}{10} \times 90000$

= ₹ 101.25/-

Total outgoings = 10228.71

∴   Net income = Gross income − Outgoings

= 18754.56 − 10228.71

= ₹ 8525.85

∴   Capitalised value = Net income + Y · P

= 8525.85 × 12.2894

= 10477.58

∴   Reversionary value of land

= $\frac{100800}{(1 + 0.045)^{80}}$ = 2979.60

∴   Total cost of property = Capitalised value + Reversionary value of land

= 10477.58 + 2979.60

= 107757.18

Method III : Valuation based on reproduction cost :

Present cost of land = 300 × 336

= ₹ 100800/-

Reproduction cost
of building = 1500 × 81.62

= ₹ 122430/-

Depreciation :

Total depreciation = Reproduction cost of building

= Total sinking fund

= ₹ 122430/-

Amount of annual installment = $\frac{S \times i}{(1 + i)^{n} - 1} = \frac{122430 \times 0.045}{(1 + 0.045)^{80} - 1}$

= ₹ 167.814/-

∴   Depreciation for 10 years (1983 to 1993)

$$= 167.814 \times \frac{(1 + 0.045)^{10} - 1}{0.045}$$

$$= 2062.1335$$

∴   Cost of building   = Reproduction cost – Depreciation

$$= 122430 - 2062.1335$$

$$= ₹ 120367.87$$

∴   Cost of property   = Cost of building + Valuation of land

$$= 120367.87 + 100800$$

$$= 221167.87$$

Comparison of three costs and cost to be compared to recommend purchaser 'X' :

Method of valuation	Cost of building	App. cost in lakhs
1. Valuation from life	₹ 189284.1	1.90 lakhs
2. Valuation from yield	₹ 107757.18	1.08 lakhs
3. Valuation from reproduction cost	₹ 221167.87	2.22 lakhs

The prospective buyer will be advised to purchase the property for a value lying between ₹ 1.90 lakhs to ₹ 2.22 lakhs, the justification being as follows :

1.   The area is quite a developing one and will be well developed in future.

2.   A good profitable business such as a hotel can be started as the property is situated on a highway.

3.   The area has many advantages as listed above.

4.   Life of the building is also satisfactory.

4.19 REPORT OF VALUATION OF IMMOVABLE PROPERTY

FORM - 0 - 1

PART I - QUESTIONNAIRE :

GENERAL :

1.   Purpose for which valuation is made.

Valuation is carried out because the prospective buyer 'X' desires to have an immovable property in 'Pune' and 'Y', the present owner of the property wishes to sell and desires to settle at his native place.

2.   Date on which valuation is made : 10 -1-1994.

3.   Name of the owner - 'Y'.

4.   If the property is under joint ownership / co-owner ship share of each owner ? Are the shares (individuals) undivided ?

     NO.

5.   Brief description of the property.

     The property is situated on west side of Pune-Bangalore Road in plot No. 4 of survey 40/A, Parvati, "Vivekananda Housing Society". The building was constructed in 1983. The total land is 336 m². The plot size is 24 m × 14 m. The building is 2 storeyed and R.C.C. framed structure. It consists of 81.62 m² of plinth area on ground floor and same built-up area on F.F. Other description is as given above.

6.   Location, street, ward number.

     The property is situated on the west side of Pune-Bangalore road in plot no. 4 of survey No. 40/A Parvati, "Vivekananda Housing Society".

7.   Survey plot No. of Land - as given above.

8.   Is the property situated in residential / commercial / mixed area / industrial area.

     Property is situated in residential area.

9.   Classification of locality - High Class / Middle class / Lower - poor class - Locality is of Middle Class.

10. Proximity to civic amenities like Schools, Hospitals, Offices, Market, Cinemas etc. Nearness to market area.

11. Means and proximity to surface communication by which the locality is served. Property is near to Padmavati PMT bus stop and the locality is served by bus service only.

     LAND

12. Area of Land supported by documentary proof, shape, dimensions, physical features.

     Area of land = 336 m²

     Plot is of rectangular shape of size (24 m × 14 m). The land was used for agricultural purpose previously and has a surface layer of B.C. soil.

13. Roads, streets or lanes on which the land is abutting: Land has a frontage of 30 m wide road meeting to Pune - Bangalore N.H.

14. Is it free hold / lease hold land.

     It is free hold land.

15. If lease hold, the name of the lessor/lessee, nature of lease, date of commencements, termination of lease and terms of renewal of lease.

    Not Applicable

    (i)   Initial premium

    (ii) Ground rent payable / year

    (iii) Unearned insurance payable to the lessor in the event of sale or transfer.

       NIL.

16. Is there any restrictive convenient in regard to use of land ?

    If so attach a copy of the convenient.

    NO.

17. Are there any requirements of easements ? If so attach copies.

    NO.

18. Does the land fall in an area included in any town planning plan of Government or any statutory body ? If so give particulars ?

    NO.

19. Has any contribution been made towards development or is any demand for each contribution still outstanding ?

    Full development has taken place.

20. Has the whole or part of the land been notified for acquisition by Government or any statutory body. Give dates of the notification.

    NO.

21. Attach a dimensioned site plan - As already given above.

Improvements :

22. Attach plans and elevation of all structures standing on land and a layout plan.
    NIL

23. Furnish technical details of the building on a separate sheet.

24. (i) Is the building owner-occupied / or tenanted / both owners occupied :
        Owner-occupied.
        If partly owner-occupied.

    (ii) Specify portion and extent of area under owner - occupation.
        NIL

25. What is the F.S.I. permissible and % actually utilized ?

    F.S.I. is 1.

Rents :

26. (i) Names of tenants / lessees / Licensees etc.

NIL

(ii) Portion in their occupation.

NIL

(iii) Monthly / annual rent / compensation licenses fee, etc. paid by each -

₹ 16 / m^2 of carpet area / month

.... = ₹ 1562.88 / month.

(iv) Gross amount received for the whole property. ₹ 18754.56 per year.

27. Are any of the occupants related to or close business associates of the owner.

NIL.

28. Is separate amount being recovered for the use of fixtures like fans, geysers, refrigerators etc. for service charges (Give details).

NIL.

29. Give details of water and electricity charges if any, to be borne by owner.

All changes are to be borne by owner as there are no tenants.

30. Has the tenant to bear whole of the cost of repairs and maintenance .

NO.

31. If a lift is installed who has to bear the cost of maintenance and operation.

No Lift.

32. If a pump is installed who has to bear the cost of maintenance and operation ? Tenant / Owner

Society Charges.

33. Who has to bear the cost of electricity charges for lighting of common space like entrance hall, stairs, passage, etc. Owner or tenant ?

All charges to be borne by owner.

34 What is the amount of property tax ? Who is to bear it ? Give details with documentary proof : Property tax will be as per prevailing rate and owner will bear it.

35. Is the building insured ? If so give policy no. amount for which insured and annual premium.

Yes, Insured for $\frac{1}{8}$ % of $\frac{9}{10}$ of original cost of building.

36. Is any dispute between land-lord and tenant regarding rent pending in court of law.

NO.

37. Has any standard rent been fixed for the premises under any law relating to the control of rent.

NO.

SALES :

38. Give instances of sales of immovable property in the locality on a separate sheet, indicating the name and address of the property, registration no., sale price and area of land sold : Not available.

39. Land Rate adopted in this valuation: - ₹ 200/m².

40. If sale instances are not available or not relied upon, the basis of arriving at the land rate.

    As already given above.

COST OF CONSTRUCTION :

41. Year of commencement of construction and completion.

    Year of completion = 1983.

42. What was the method of construction by contract / by employing labourers directly / both ?

    Employing labourers.

43. For items of work done on contract, produce copies of agreements.

    NIL.

44. For items of work done by engaging labour directly give basic rates of materials and labour supported by documentary proof.

    Information not available.

PART II - VALUATION :

Please refer attached calculations sheets discussing the detailed approach of valuation of the property and indicating how the valuation has been arrived at.

PART III - DECLARATION :

I hereby declare that :

1. I have personally inspected the property on 2nd January 1994.

2. I have no direct or indirect interest in the property.

3. I have not been convicted of any offence and sentenced to any imprisonment.

4. The information furnished in Part I is true and correct to the best of my knowledge and belief.

Sd/-

Signature of Registered Valuer

Registration Number

Date : 8-1-1994

Place : Pune

ANNEXURE TO FORM 0 - 1 :

Technical Details of (main building / Annexure / servants quarter) :

1. No. of floors and height; of each floor

No. of floors - G.F + F.F. = 2 floors

Height of each floor = 3 m

2. Plinth Area floor wise (As per I. S. 3861-1966)

G.F. = $10.6 \times 7.7 = 81.62$ m^2

F.F. = $10.6 \times 7.7 = 81.62$ m^2

3. Year of construction - (completion) - 1983

4. Estimated Future Life - 80 years.

5. Type of construction - load bearing walls / RCC frame / steel frame :
   - R.C.C. Framed Structure

6. Type of foundation - Open foundation

7. Walls -

   (a) Basement and plinth - 20 cm thick B.B. in cm (1.6)

   (b) Ground Floor - external wall - 20 cm B.B. masonry
        Internal walls - 15 cm B.B. masonry with suitable finish.

   (c) Superstructure above G.F.
        External wall - 20 cm thick B.B. masonry in C.M. 1.6 with sand faced plaster in C.M. 1 : 4 for outer surface and 12 mm thick cement plaster in C.M. (1 : 4) with neeru finish for inside surfaces.
        Internal wall - 15 cm B.B. masonry with suitable finish.

8. Partition - Internal partition walls are 15 cm thick B.B. masonry.

9. Doors and windows

   (a) G.F. - Both are C.C. T.W. and of size 70×100 mm

   (b) F.F. - The shutters are of size 35 mm thick and C.C. T.W.

10. Flooring (floor wise) : (a) Ground floor (b) 1st floor (c) 2nd floor.

    (a) G.F. - M.M. Tiles paving for all rooms except kitchen, bath and W.C. and stair hall. Polished Shahabad stone is provided in kitchen and bath and stair hall. White glazed tiles are provided for W.C. floor and dado.

11. Finishing - Floor-wise : (a) Ground floor (b) 1st floor (c) 2nd floor etc.

    (a) G.F. and FF - External walls have sand faced plaster and 12 mm thick cement plaster with neeru finish for internal walls (15 cm thick)

12. Roofing and Terracing

13. Special architectural feature / decorative feature, if any

14. (i)   Internal wiring - Surface or conduit surface

    (ii) Class of fitting - Superior/ ordinary/ poor-superior conduit wiring

15. Sanitary installations :

    (a) (i)   No. of water closets - One on each floor (1.2×1 m)

         (ii)   No. of lavatory basins - Two

         (iii) No. of urinals - One

     (iv)   No. of sinks - Two

     (v)   No. of bath tubs - One on each floor 1.9×1.3 m

     (vi)   No. of toilets - Two

     (vii)   No. of geysers - One

  (b) Class of fitting - superior coloured/superior white/ordinary-superior coloured

16. Compound wall
    (i) Height and length
    (ii) Type of construction.

17. No. of lifts and capacity - No lift

18. Underground sump capacity and type of construction

19. Overhead tank
    (i) Where located
    (ii) Capacity
    (iii) Type of construction.

20. No. of pumps and HP - NO pumps.

21. Roads and Pavings within the compound approximate area and type of paving.

22. Sewage disposal - weather connected to public sewer. If septic tanks are to be provided with - number and capacity
    - Connected to public sewer.

Sd/-
Signature of Registered Valuer

Registration No. -

THEORETICAL QUESTIONS

1. Define the following terms :
   (i) Cost
   (ii) Price
   (iii) Value
   (iv) Real estate

2. What is the purpose or object of valuation of a property ?

3. Explain the factors affecting the valuation of a property.

4. Explain the following terms :

(i) Book value	(ii) Scrap value	(iii) Salvage value
(iv) Market value	(v) Accommodation value	(vi) Distress value
(vii) Monopoly value	(viii) Replacement value	(ix) Sentimental value
(x) Rateable value	(xi) Speculative value	(xii) Assessed value
(xiii) Capital cost	(xiv) Capitalised value	

5. Explain the term Year's purchase (Y.P.) and distinguish between

   (i) Single rate Y.P. and (ii) Dual rate Y.P.

6. Define the term 'Annuity' and distinguish between :
   (i)   Annuity certain   (ii) Annuity due
   (iii) Perpetual Annuity   (iv) Deferred Annuity

7. What is a valuation table ? What is its utility ?

8. Distinguish between the following :
   (i)   Freehold property and Leasehold property.
   (ii)   Building Lease and Occupational Lease.

9. What do you mean by income from the property ? Distinguish between the 'Gross income' and 'Net income' from the property.

10. Define the term 'Sinking fund' and explain its necessity. Explain the method of calculating the 'Sinking fund installment'.

11. Define the term mortgage and explain the procedure of determining the mortgage loan from a property.

12. Distinguish between the following :
    Equitable mortgage and Legal mortgage.

13. What is an Easement ? State the important provisions of easement rights as per Indian Easement Act, 1882.

14. Distinguish between Depreciation and Depletion.

15. Explain the following methods of carrying out valuation of a property and state where you will adopt them.
    (i) Book value method
    (ii) Present land value method
    (iii) Replacement value (or cost) method
    (iv) Rental method of valuation
    (v) Direct comparison of capital value method
    (vi) Valuation on profit basis
    (vii) Development method of valuation

16. Explain clearly the procedure of determining the standard rent of a property.

17. Explain the term land value on reversion or reversionary value of the land.

18. Write short notes on :
    (i) Market value   (ii) Salvage value and scrap value
    (iii) Building lease   (iv) Book value
    (v) Capitalised value.

19. What are the different methods of calculating depreciation ? Explain the constant percentage method ? Where this method is generally used ?

20. Distinguish between the following :
    (i)   Building lease and occupation lease
    (ii) Sentimental value and speculative value
    (iii) Capital value and capitalised value
    (iv) Salvage value and scrap value.

21. Explain the situation where the following methods of valuation will be used :
    (i)   Rental method   (ii) Cost based method
    (iii) Profit based method   (iv) Development method.

22. What is depreciation ? Explain the different methods of depreciation.

23. Explain the following :
    (i)   Building lease   (ii) Occupational lease
    (iii) Sub-lease   (iv) Life lease
    (v)   Perpetual lease.

24. Define and explain 'Easement'.

25. What is the basis of valuation for the purpose of mortgage ? Explain.

26. What do you understand by obsolescence ?

27. Explain the terms 'cost' and 'price' of an item.

28. What is meant by value of a property ? What factors affect the value of property ?

29. Explain the following terms :
    (i)   Scrap value and salvage value
    (ii) Outgoings
    (iii) Year's purchase (Y.P.)
    (iv) Freehold and leasehold property.

30. How will you prepare a valuation report of a property consisting of a two storeyed residential building and a plot ?

31. What is depreciation ? State the types of depreciation.

32. Distinguish between 'depletion' and depreciation.

33. Explain the method of calculating book value of a property.

34. Explain any two methods of calculating depreciation.

35. Distinguish between sinking fund and depreciation.

36. Write short notes on :
    (i)   Easement rights   (ii) Mortgage
    (iii) Dual right Y.P.   (iv) Sinking fund.

37. Write in brief about valuation tables.

38. How will you prepare valuation of property ?

39. Explain the following :
    (i)   Annuity   (ii) Equitable mortgage.

40. State the meaning of the following :
    (i)   Present value   (ii) Book value
    (iii) Market value   (iv) Sentimental value
    (v)   Potential value   (vi) Monopoly value
    (vii) Reversionary value.

41. What is sinking fund ? How is the sinking fund installment calculated ?

42. Describe the following methods of valuation of property :
    (i)   Valuation from yield
    (ii) Valuation from depreciation

43. Explain the following terms :
    (i)   Nominal rent   (ii) Standard rent
    (iii) Rack rent   (iv) Ground rent.

44. Explain the following :
    (i)   Outgoings   (ii) Depreciation
    (iii) Sinking fund

45. Write various factors affecting the value of the property.

46. What is depreciation ? Distinguish between depreciation and depletion.

47. State and explain how depreciation is calculated by different methods. State where the above methods are used.

48. How will you prepare a valuation report of a property consisting of a two storeyed residential building and a plot ?

49. What is depreciation ? State types of depreciation. Distinguish between depletion and depreciation.

50. Explain the methods of calculating book value of the property.

51. What factors affect the value of property ?

52. State the different methods of valuation and explain any one of them.

53. Explain the situation where the following methods of valuation will be used.

    (i) Rental method   (ii) Cost based method

    (iii) Profit based method   (iv) Development method.

NUMERICAL PROBLEMS

1. A mixer brought at ₹ 16000/- has scrap value of ₹ 2000 after 5 years. Calculate constant percentage of depreciation.

2. A centrifugal pump was purchased in 1988 for ₹ 40000/-. The life of the pump as stated by the manufacturers is 10 years. Assuming any other suitable data, calculate the book value of the pump in 1993.

Given :

    (i)   ₹ 22000/- by straight line depreciation method.

    (ii)   ₹ 12649/- by constant percentage method.

            $P = 0.206$

    (iii)   ₹ 15815/- by sinking fund method.

3. A property consists of a plot 600 m² area and bungalow of 150 m² in area constructed in 1960. On inspecting the present condition of bungalow, future life of bungalow is predicted as 50 years. Find out the present value of property from the following data :

    (i) Present sale rate of land = ₹ 400/m²

    (ii) Present cost of construction of similar building = ₹ 2500 /m²

    (iii) Rate of interest for redemption of capital = 5% per year.

Assume any other data if necessary.

4. Determine the rent per month to be charged for the building having the following particulars :

    (i) Cost of land = ₹ 40000/-

    (ii) Cost of building = ₹ 250000/-

    (iii) Future life of building = 80 years

    (iv) Expected return on building = 8%

    (v) Expected return on land cost = 6%

    (vi) Annual repairs and maintenance = 1% of the building costs

    (vii) Other outgoings excluding sinking fund installments = 25% of gross rent of building.

    (viii) Rate of interest of sinking fund = 5%. Assume suitable data if necessary and mention it clearly.

5. Find out the present value of property from the data given below :

   (i)   Built-up area of the building = 300 m²

   (ii) Gross rent received per month = ₹ 3000/-

   (iii) Municipal taxes per year = 24% of gross rent per year

   (iv) Annual maintenance and other outgoings except sinking fund = 12 % of gross rent/ year

   (v)   Expected future life = 60 years.

   (vi) Area of plot = 800 m²

   (vii) Present sale rate of land = ₹ 400 /m²

   (viii) Net return expected from building investment = 10% per year.

   (ix) Net return expected from land investment = 6% per year.

   (x)   Rate of interest on redemption = 4% per year.

6. A property consists of a plot 1000 m² in area and a building with plinth area 300 m². The future life of building is estimated to be 40 years. The property is purchased for ₹ 200000/-. The cost of open plot in the nearly area is ₹ 500/m². The owner expects 10% return on cost of construction and 6 % on the cost of land. Calculate the standard rent of the property with the following assumptions.

   (i)   Rate of interest for sinking fund = 5%

   (ii) Annual repair cost = one months gross rent.

   (iii) All outgoings = 30% of annual gross rent. Assume any additional data if necessary and mention it clearly.

7. A property consists of a plot measuring 600 m² and a two storeyed building with total built-up area of 380 m². The building was constructed in 1950 and is expected to serve for future 40 years. The present rate of construction is ₹ 1600/m² of built-up area and that of the land in same locality is ₹ 600 /m².

   Find out the fair market value of the property considering :

   (i)   Redemption of capital at 5%.

   (ii) Reversionary value of land at 6%. Assume any additional data if necessary and state the same clearly.

8. The construction cost of a building is ₹ 280000/- the expected future life of building is 80 years. The plot area is 450 m² and the rate of land is ₹ 100/m² Expected yield is 12% on investment of building and 8% investment on land. Assuming the rate of redemption of capital at 4% per year and suitable percentage of outgoing of the gross rent, calculate the economic rent of the property.

9. A person has purchased a plot of land costing ₹ 100000/-. The building constructed cost is ₹ 250000/-. Allowing a net return @ 12% per year on cost of construction and @ 7% per year on cost of land, work out the standard rent of the property. Assume additional necessary data and clearly state the same.

10. Work out the valuation of Cinema theater and find the value per seat with the following details :

    (i)   Number of seats = 1700

    (ii) Gross annual income from = ₹ 540000 cinema shows

    (iii) Staff salary, electricity bill, stationery, taxes etc. = 40% of gross income

    (iv) Repairs and maintenance of machinery = 5% of capital cost

    (v)   Capital cost of machinery = ₹ 1000000/-

    (vi) Sinking fund on machinery = ₹ 20000/-

    (vii) Annual insurance premium = ₹ 10000/-

    (viii) Repairs to building 2% of gross income

    (ix) Assuming years purchase for 35 years at 8% of and redemption of capital at 5%. Differed value of land = ₹ 150000/-

    (x)   Income from slide advertisements = ₹ 30000/-

11. A building has been constructed on a plot costing ₹ 200000/-. The construction cost of building is ₹ 400000/- and the estimated life of the building is 80 years. The owner desires to have 9% return on construction cost and 6% return on land cost. The other details are as under:

    (i)   Annual cost of maintenance and repairs = 1% of construction cost of building.

    (ii) Annual taxes and other outgoings excluding sinking fund and = 30% of gross rent.

    (iii) Rate of interest for sinking fund = 4%.

    (iv) Scrap value of building at the expiry of its useful life = ₹ 40000/-

    (v)   Amount required for replacing the construction at the end of its useful life = ₹ 800000/-

    Calculate the standard monthly rent for the building.   **[Ans. :** ₹ 6300 /month]

12. A centrifugal pump set was purchased in 1990 for ₹ 45000/-. Assuming the life of pump as 12 years and scrap value as ₹ 2000/-, calculate the book value of the pump in 1994 using constant percentage method for depreciation.

    [Ans. : 12181.00]

Chapter 5
SPECIFICATIONS

5.1 INTRODUCTION

In order to prepare detailed estimate of the proposed building it is necessary to prepare a complete set of drawings i.e. plan, elevation, sections and details etc. These drawings, however indicate only the arrangement of various units, their shapes and sizes etc. included in the structure. Information as regards the quality of materials to be used and the workmanship expected during its construction is not mentioned on such drawings. The information regarding the quality of materials and expected workmanship is described separately in a contract document and is known as the "**Specifications of the work**". Thus, the detailed drawings along with the specifications will completely describe, physically and technically, the details of the structure. The specifications of the various items of work are written by the State Government organization e.g. P.W.D. for the works under their jurisdiction, and by the Central Public Works Department for the works undertaken by the Central Government. The Bureau of Indian Standards (earlier I.S.I.) has specified the specifications for the various items of construction and are available in the booklet form for sale in Government Book Depots.

5.2 DEFINITION OF SPECIFICATIONS

Specifications can be defined as furnishing detailed information about the qualities of materials, their property, the proportion in which they are to be mixed, mixing and laying in position etc. complete as regards the construction of the 'structure'. According to the quality of materials and workmanship the 'structure' is described as constructed with 'first', 'second' or 'third' class specifications. In short, specifications are the instructions in writing describing in detail the manner in which the work is to be executed. Due to the limitations of the space, the instructions regarding the quality of materials and the workmanship desired cannot be furnished on the drawings. Hence, specifications, which supply information as regards the quality of material to be used, the workmanship expected etc., are generally written separately to supplement the information given on the drawings. These specifications form part of the contract documents and are to be supplied to the intending contractors along with the tender papers.

5.3 PURPOSE OF SPECIFICATIONS

The purpose or object of writing specifications of the work are as follows :

- As the specifications furnish complete information as regards the quality of material and workmanship to be attained, the tenderer or contractor can quote correct rates for the various items of work.

- The detailed information furnished in the specifications of different items of work, serve as a guide to the contractor and supervisors (appointed by the owner or Government) during the actual construction of the work.

- As the cost of the work is directly related to its specifications, its estimated cost can be worked out precisely and compared with the availability of funds.

- Specifications clearly describe the responsibilities of both the owner and the contractor and thus help in avoiding conflict between them.

- Specifications serve the object of furnishing the detailed information which the engineer wants to convey so as to fulfill the requirement of his design.

- In case of conflict between the owner and the contractor, the specifications serve as an important legal document in the court of law.

Thus, it can be seen from the above, that specifications describe fully and specify the nature and quality of work and the method of construction. The information furnished on the drawings is very brief, and is supplemented by written instructions in the form of 'specifications' separately. In case if there is any discrepancy in the information between 'drawings' and 'specifications' that given on the drawings will always be taken as final.

5.4 TYPES OF SPECIFICATIONS

The specifications are broadly classified as follows :

- I.   Brief specifications and
- II. Detailed specifications

I. Brief Specifications :   (W-2010)

As the name suggests these are the specifications that describe briefly the items of construction and are useful to the quantity surveyor in preparing the estimate of the work. Such specifications do not form part of the contract document.

These specifications are in the form of brief description of various items of work indicating the various materials, their quantities, proportion and class of the work etc. and thus, furnish general idea about the work to be executed.

The brief or general specifications of the first class, second class, third class and fourth class of building works are given in a tabular form as shown below (page No. 4 and 5).

II. Detailed Specifications :   (W-2010)

The detailed specifications furnish the complete description of the various items of construction as regards the type and quality of materials and their workmanships, proportion of mix, mixing and laying etc. complete and the mode of measurement of items. These specifications form essential part of contract document. These specifications for various items of work are generally written in the order of execution of the works and are prepared by the State Government Agencies such as P.W.D. etc. and are published in the form of booklet named as **'Standard Specifications'**, (or Red Book). The publication of such a standard specification book by Government Agencies has helped in bringing uniformity in the wording of various items and their specifications in the tender papers, prepared by various departments and also in avoiding extra items of work during the execution of the work. All Government organizations are supposed to follow the instructions given in this book at the time of preparation of specifications for various items.

The detailed specifications are further sub-divided into three categories as follows :

(i)   General provisions

(ii)   Technical provisions

(iii)   Standard specifications

(i) General Provisions :

These general provisions which are known as conditions of contract are applicable to the work as a whole.

Table 5.1 : Brief or General Specifications of Various Class of Building Works

Sr. No.	Description of item of construction	First class	Second class	Third class	Fourth class
1.	Foundation and plinth work	Foundation shall be of lime or cement concrete (1 : 4 : 8). Plinth shall be of first class brickwork in lime or cement mortar (1 : 6).	Foundation of lime concrete. Plinth shall be of first class brickwork in lime mortar.	Foundation of lime concrete. Plinth shall be of second class brickwork in lime mortar.	Foundation and plinth of sun-dried second class bricks built in mud mortar.
2.	Damp proof course (D.P.C.)	It shall be in cement concrete 1 : 1.5 : 3, and 3 cm thick with bitumen layer of two coats.	2 cm thick cement concrete (1 : 2 : 4) mixed with impermo.	2 cm thick cement mortar (1 : 2) with water proofing material.	–

... Contd.

3.	Superstructure	It shall be in first class brickwork with cement mortar (1 : 6) with R.C.C. lintels over doors and windows.	Second class brickwork in lime mortar or cement mortar. R.B. work for lintels.	Second class brickwork in mud mortar. Brick arches of wooden planks for lintels.	Sun-dried brick work in mud mortar. Brick arches and wooden planks for lintels.
4.	Roofing	R.C.C. (1 : 2 : 4) slab with terrace of lime concrete.	R.B. slab with lime concrete terrace.	G.I. or A.C. sheet roof.	Made of tiles over wooden planks.
5.	Flooring	Shall be terrazo flooring for drawing, and dining, bath and W.C. For bed room, it should be coloured and polished in cement concrete.	3 cm thick cement concrete over lime concrete layer.	Brick floor placed over compacted murum.	Mud floor washed with cowdung.
6.	Finishing items	12 mm thick inside and outside plaster in cement mortar, distemper for bed room, drawing room and dining. From inside and outside shall be coloured snowcem.	12 mm thick cement mortar for inside and outside. Inside two colour wash coats over one white wash coat.	Inside and outside with lime mortar white washed.	Inside and outside plastered with mud.
7.	Doors and windows	of seaonal teakwood, panelled and glazed etc.	of seasonal wood, panelled and glazed etc.	of country cut wood.	of ordinary country wood.
8.	Miscellaneous	C.I. rain water pipes, painted. First class water supply and sanitary fittings.	C.I. rain water pipes painted.	–	–

(ii) Technical Provisions :

In the 'technical provisions' the details as regards desired quality of the finished products or items of construction are clearly specified. An arrangement for inspection and testing to be carried out during the construction stage to ensure the desired quality and workmanship is also included into such technical provisions. Moreover such technical provisions should be according to the provisions made in the working drawings.

The technical provisions, in short, include the following :

    (i)   Specifications regarding materials of construction and the workmanship.

    (ii)   Specifications for performance and

    (iii)   Specifications for proprietory commodities.

The part (i) deals with strict controls over the quality of materials of construction which consists of properties such as compressive and tensile strength, hardness and its chemical composition, precautions to be taken during its handling, transport and storage and the procedure of its inspection and tests to be carried out to ascertain its suitability, etc. Part (ii) includes the specifications regarding the performance of the finished items of equipment such as turbines, pumps, and their installation guarantee etc. and part (iii) deals with standardized or patented items or commodities from a particular manufacturer over which there is no direct control over its quality, workmanship and performance etc. The brand name of the product and the name of the manufacturing company is only mentioned.

(iii) Standard Specifications :

In order to avoid the lengthy procedure of writing the detailed specifications for the various items, of work, their specifications are standardized by the competent Government departments and are then serially numbered. At the time of writing specifications in contract documents for such items, only their serial numbers are written to save time and space in the contract documents. Such standard specifications are prepared by the concerned Central (i.e. C.P.W.D.) or State (i.e. P.W.D.) Govt. agencies. Such standard specifications are to be revised periodically to incorporate the latest techniques that may be developed in the construction industry.

5.5 CLASSIFICATION OF SPECIFICATIONS ACCORDING TO THE PURPOSE

Another classification of specifications based upon the purpose it serves, will be as follows :

- Standard specifications
- Guide specifications
- Particular specifications
- Manufacturer's specifications

- **Standard Specifications :**

These are the specifications prepared by the Bureau of Indian Standards, (former I.S.I.) New Delhi for the various common materials of construction. These specifications are the outcome of the critical study and experience of the experts in the concerned fields and are considered as authoritative in those fields. These standard specifications are to be referred to at the time of preparing specifications for a particular engineering project under consideration.

- **Guide Specifications :**

As the name implies, these are the typical specifications for various common items of construction prepared by the competent Government or private bodies and serve as a guide in preparing detailed specifications for any particular engineering project under construction.

- **Particular Specifications :**

These are the specifications written for a particular engineering project under construction to accompany the working drawings of the project. For each and every item of construction included in the schedule of quantities, detailed exhaustive specifications describing the type and quality of different materials required, their workmanship and the standard to be achieved etc. are specified in the same sequence in which they are written in the schedule of quantities. These specifications form important part of the contract document and are very useful to the contractor and supervisors at the time of actual construction of the work. In case of dispute between the contractor and the owner (or Government) their specifications serve as important documents in the Court of law.

- **Manufacturer's Specifications :**

These are the specifications published by the manufacturers for the items of (construction) materials or building products manufactured by them. Instructions regarding how to store, use and install them etc. during construction to achieve the desired standard are mentioned under such specifications. These specifications are to be followed by the contractor while utilizing such materials or building products prepared by the manufacturers.

5.6 REQUIREMENTS OF GOOD SPECIFICATIONS

When the specifications of the work are written by the engineer, he is not aware of the name of the contractor who is going to execute the work. In order that the specifications should be clearly understood by the contractor, supervisory staff, workmen etc. (who may have little or no technical knowledge), the following points should be carefully considered while drafting the specifications.

- **Wording :**

As the specifications form important part of contract document and are very useful during the execution of the works, they should be described in simple, concise, correctly worded and unambiguous manner without any repetitions.

- **Language :**

All the sentences describing the specifications should follow the rules of grammer. The style and tense should be maintained same throughout the description of specifications. The omission, addition and misplacement of a comma in the sentences should not alter its meaning.

- **Information :**

The description of specifications of different items should furnish the exact required information so that there is very little scope left for conflict between the owner and contractor.

- **Dual Meaning :**

The wording of the sentences describing the specifications should convey only one desired meaning and sentences conveying dual meanings should be avoided.

- **Fairness :**

The specifications should be balanced and fare to both owner and the contractor. No injustice should be made to the contractor by throwing all the risks on his shoulder.

- **Practical Consideration :**

The specifications should not be too theoretical but should be written by taking all practical difficulties of the contractor (during execution) into consideration.

- **Legal Complications :**

As the specifications form important legal documents it should be described in fewer words to avoid legal complications.

- **Use of Abbreviations :**

While writing specifications only the well established abbreviations should be used to avoid lengthy description and verbose.

- **'Shall' and 'Will':**

Since the specifications describe the quality of material to be used and the manner in which it is to be constructed by the contractor during its execution the word 'Shall' (and not will) must be used in the sentences.

5.7 DETAILED SPECIFICATIONS

As the name implies, these specifications describe the item of work in minute details and complete in all respects, to be completed as per the drawings of the proposed structure. The detailed specifications for each item of work should cover the following information :

- General scope of the item.
- Type of material, its quality and quantity.
- Instructions regarding transporting, handling and storing of material on site.
- Processing of the materials, proportion of the mix etc.
- Construction procedure such as mixing, conveying, laying, curing etc.
- Quality of work and workmanship desired.
- Standard test to be carried out to ensure the quality.
- Mode of measurement of completed item, deductions to be made if any, and payment to be made to the contractor.

5.8 STANDARD SPECIFICATIONS

After going through the tender papers prepared by the officers of various departments of the State and Central Government organization, it was noticed that there was no uniformity in the wording of items and specifications included in the tender documents. The use of incorrect and ambiguous wording in the items included in the tender papers and specifications and also due to not complying to the details shown on the drawings results in the creation of extra items of work during its execution.

In order to avoid the above difficulties and to bring uniformity in the wording of items and specifications in the tender document, the task of preparation of 'Specifications' of various items of construction was taken up by the Governments. Such specifications published by the (State or Central) Government are available in the booklet form called as 'Standard Specifications'. Such a standard specification booklet published by the P.W.D. of Government of Maharashtra is popularly known as 'Red (Hand) Book' due to its red cover.

5.9 DETAILED SPECIFICATIONS FOR COMMON ITEMS OF BUILDING WORK

The detailed specifications to be included in the tender documents for the various common items of work are as described below:

1. **Excavation for Foundations :**
   - **General :** The item of excavation will generally refer to excavation for foundations, wet or dry, carried out in soil, sand, gravel, soft or hard murum or rock etc.

- **Site Clearing :** The portion of the ground on which the structure is to be constructed should be cleared of all obstructions, loose materials, rubbish, small trees etc. to be arranged by the contractor.

- **Line Out :** After the site is cleared, the centre line of the proposed structure as shown on the drawings should be marked on the ground along with the reference marks (in horizontal plane) and bench marks (in vertical planes) by the contractor at his own cost.

- **Average Ground Level :** The contractor shall request the Engineer-in-charge to take levels of the ground before the excavation starts. The average ground level is then to be determined and used as a datum level for the measurement of depth of excavation.

- **Excavation :** The excavation work shall be carried out to the exact dimensions (i.e. length, width and depth) as indicated on the drawings and shall include the removal and disposal of the excavated material as directed by Engineer-in-charge. In case the contractor excavates to a depth more than as shown on the drawings the same shall be filled with the foundation concrete by the contractor at his own cost. If any unsound patch of the ground is encountered at the time of excavation, the same should be excavated to the depth as directed by the Engineer-in-charge and filled with concrete. The contractor shall, in such cases, claim extra payment for additional excavation and concrete.

- **Disposal of Excavated Materials :** The excavated material should not be placed nearer than 1.5 m from the outer edge of excavation.

  The unsuitable excavated material shall be disposed off beyond the construction site upto a lead of 50 m. The material useful for backfilling etc. shall be stacked as instructed by the Engineer incharge. The excavated material is the property of the Government or owner and the rate of excavation is inclusive of sorting out the materials and stacking them as directed. Backfilling material shall be placed in layers of 15 cm thickness, moistened and well compacted. All debris shall be removed from the site after the completion of the work.

- **Dewatering :** As the rate of excavation is inclusive of bailing out of water that may accumulate during excavation it shall be the responsibility of the contractor to arrange for dewatering by suitable pumps etc. Such pumping of water in no case should cause damage to the excavated foundation trenches.

- **Shoring :** All shoring etc. required to protect the sides of trenches shall be arranged by the contractor and the same shall be removed after the completion of the work.

- **Protection :** All the excavated portion of the ground shall be fenced properly and marked with red light during night time to avoid possibility of accidents.

- **Back Filling :** All material used for shoring shall be removed after their necessity is over and all space between foundation and sides of excavation shall be refilled to original ground level with approved materials in layers of 15 cm thickness, moistened and well rammed.

- **Mode of Measurement and Payment :** The payment to the contractor shall be made according to the type of strata met with (i.e. soft soil, hard soil, soft murum etc.) at the unit contract rate per cubic meter of excavation, limited to the dimensions given on the approved plan. No payment shall be made for the excess work carried out by the contractor. On the contrary, he shall have to fill up the excess depth with concrete without any additional payment.

Note : During the excavation process, all the materials encountered shall be classified as follows :

- Soil of all type, sand, gravel, soft murum etc.
- Hard murum
- Hard murum including boulders
- Soft rock
- Hard rock to be blasted
- Hard rock to be chiselled or drilled.

The Engineer in-charge will be the final authority in classifying the excavated material according to the group (i) to (vi) mentioned above, and payment will be mode to the contractor accordingly at the unit contract rate per cubic meter, limited to the dimensions shown on sanctioned drawings.

2. **Lime Concrete :**

   Materials required :

   (a) **Lime :** Lime for structural purposes shall be eminently hydraulic lime and for masonry work it shall be semi-hydraulic type. The physical and chemical properties of lime shall conform to the I.S. specifications. It should be stored in a water-proof and damp proof enclosed sheds. Only fresh lime i.e. within two weeks after it has been taken from the kiln should be used. It is to be measured in cubic meter.

   (b) **Sand (or Fine Aggregates) :** It shall satisfy all I.S. requirements and shall be clean, strong, hard, durable and free from dirt, dust and impurities etc. It shall be natural river sand or crusted aggregates. Particle size shall be 5 mm maximum. If it contains more than 4 % of dust, clay etc. it shall be washed thoroughly before use. Sea sand which contains salts shall not be used.

(c) Coarse Aggregate : It shall be broken stone of the required size (i.e. graded) and hard, strong, durable, clean. It shall not be elongated or flaky but only cubical shape be used. It should confirm to all I.S. tests. The minimum and maximum sizes vary from 20 mm to 80 mm.

Aggregates absorbing more than 5 % of water by weight after immersion for 24 hours, shall not be used. If necessary it should be washed before its use.

(d) Water : The water to be used shall be clean and free from salts, silts etc. Only potable water shall be used for mixing concrete.

- **Proportion :**

  The proportion of lime and sand shall be 1: 3 and mixed on volumetric basis.

- **Mixing of Lime Mortar :**

  The mixing of mortar shall be carried out by (bullock driven) **Ghani** or by using power driven mills.

  At first lime is ground with required quantity of water for 180 revolutions, moist sand is then added to it and further grinding is done for 180 revolutions, the mortar being stirred up well during the process of grinding. The mortar thus prepared is stored in moist conditions. It should be used, within one and half days of its preparation. Necessary I.S. test shall be carried out to ascertain the required strength of the mortar. The proportion of lime mortar to coarse aggregate shall be usually 1 : 2.

- **Mixing of Lime Concrete :**

  Mixing of lime concrete shall be carried out on impervious level platform. The lime mortar shall be spread uniformly on the coarse aggregate and then turned upside down, forward and backward atleast three times, till all the coarse aggregate is coated thoroughly with mortar. The mixing of lime mortar and coarse aggregates is to be done on volumetric basic.

Laying the Concrete :

The foundation to be concreted shall be thoroughly cleaned, wetted and compacted well. Form work if required shall be approved by the Engineer-in-charge. Fresh concrete should not be thrown but laid in foundation in layers of 15 cm thickness.

Compaction :

The concrete laid in foundation shall be well compacted by iron or wooden rammers for each layer till the slurry appears on the surface.

Curing :

The lime concrete layers should be kept wet at least for two weeks after it is laid in position. Only clean water be used for curing.

Mode of Measurement and Payment :

The lime concrete work shall be measured in cubic metre and paid for accordingly, limited to the dimensions shown on the approved drawing. No amount shall be paid for excess concrete work done by the contractor.

3. **Plain Cement Concrete (P.C.C.) :**
*   **Materials Required :**
    (a) Cement : It shall be Ordinary Portland Cement (O.P.C.) conforming to I.S. 269-1958. The cement shall be measured on weight basis and in whole bags, each bag weighing 50 kg which is equal to 35 litres in volume. All standard tests shall be carried out to ensure that the cement is of the required quality.

    (b) Storage : The cement brought on site shall be stored on wooden platform 15 cm above the floor and stacked 30 cm from the walls in a leak proof godown at the worksite. The stored cement shall be used in the chronological order i.e. first received first utilized. Spoilt or deteriorated cement shall never be used. Cement if stored for more than 60 days shall be tested before being used. It shall be measured by weight in tonnes.

    (c) Fine Aggregates (i.e. Sand) : As described under item (b) of specification No. 2 of lime concrete, the size of fine aggregates shall be from 0.15 mm to 5 mm (I.S. sieve No. 15 to 480).

    (d) Coarse Aggregates : As already described under item (c) of specification No. 2 of lime concrete the maximum size shall not be more than $1/4^{th}$ the thickness of concrete member subject to a maximum of 80 mm; the minimum size being 5 mm. The aggregate, shall be well graded to obtain a compact and dense volume of concrete consistent with workability. There shall be no segregation of aggregates during placing the concrete in position.

    (e) Water : Only potable water shall be used for mixing of concrete.

Mix of Concrete :

For usual mix of 1 : 2 : 4 cement concrete, the fine and coarse aggregates shall be measured dry on volumetric basis by suitable wooden boxes, due care being taken to allow for bulking of sand if it is in wet condition.

For a bag of cement weighing 50 kg, the quantities of sand, fine aggregates and water required for 1 : 2 : 4 concrete shall be 70 litres, 140 litres and 30 litres respectively, the water cement ratio being about 0.60.

*   **Mixing of Concrete :**

Mixing of concrete shall be done either manually or mechanically by mixers. When large quantity of concrete is required for important works, concrete mixers are invariably used. The mixer drum shall rotate for a minimum period of 1.5 minutes. For hand mixing it shall be carried out on a smooth specially prepared water tight platform. No foreign material shall be allowed to mix with the concrete. Cement, sand and coarse aggregates are first mixed dry and then just required quantity of water is added to it and tuned up and down, forward and backward till the whole mass appears to be homogeneous and of uniform colour. The concrete so formed shall be dense and workable.

Laying of Concrete :

The concrete prepared shall be laid in position before 30 minutes of adding water to the mix. Concrete shall not be dropped from a height more than 60 cm but laid gently in its position.

Compaction :

The concrete shall be well compacted by rods etc. after laying in its position to get dense concrete without any honey combing.

Curing :

Concrete after it has set shall be kept wet by ponding or by wet gunny bags for a period of 14 days.

Mode of Measurement and Payment :

The quantity of concrete is to be measured for length, width and height in cubic metres and paid accordingly subject to dimensions limited to given on drawings. No deduction shall be made for the reinforcement steel in the concrete.

4. Burnt Brick Masonry, First Sort (or Class) in Cement Mortar :

- **Materials Required :**
  - **(a) Bricks (First Class) :** The bricks shall be of uniform, regular shape, size and colour and very well burnt. The edges shall be sharp, straight and at right angles and free from defects with a frog of 10 mm depth on one of its flat surface. The bricks shall give ringing sound when struck against each other and shall not break when allowed to fall through a height of 60 cm.

    The size of the brick (I.S. type) shall be 19 cm x 9 cm x 9 cm or of conversional size 9 inch × 4.5 inch × 3 inch.

    The brick shall not absorb water more than 20% of its dry wet when submerged in a water.

    The brick shall be tested to give satisfactory results as per I.S. requirements.
  - **(b) Cement :** Fresh Ordinary Portland Cement (O.P.C.) satisfying all I.S. requirements shall be used. For more details see description (a) of item No. 3 of plain cement concrete of this chapter.
  - **(c) Fine Aggregates (i.e. sand) :** It shall be either natural river sand or broken stone satisfying all I.S. requirements. For further details refer description (b) of specification No. 2 of lime concrete of this chapter.
  - **(d) Water :** The water to be used for mixing shall be potable.

Preparation of Cement Mortar :

Cement and sand shall be intimately mixed first in dry condition in the predetermined proportion (e.g. 1 : 5 or 1 : 6 etc.) by volume and then just sufficient quantity of water shall be added to it and then turned up side down and forward and backward direction till a homogeneous mass of cement mortar is obtained.

For one cubic metre of brick masonry, usually the quantity of mortar to be used shall be about 0.26 cubic metre (i.e. about 260 litres). The mortar so prepared shall be used within 30 minutes of adding water to the dry mix.

Construction of Brickwork :

Bricks of only one size shall be used on the same work. Bricks shall be thoroughly soaked in water for about 2 hours before being used in masonry so that they will not absorb water contained in the mortar.

Only bricks of uniform colour and shape which are resistant to penetration of rain water and weathering shall be used for the face work if the brick work is not to be plastered.

No brickbats or cut portion of the bricks shall be used except in case of irregular openings.

Brick Laying :

The bricks shall be laid in mortar to lines and level as per the plan, slightly pressed and property bedded in mortar. All joints shall be filled carefully with mortar without leaving any cavities. The various courses shall be laid in horizontal position and the entire brickwall shall be vertical i.e. in a plumb.

The thickness of the joints shall not exceed 10 mm and raking of joints shall be to a depth of about 10 mm.

The brickwork shall be constructed either in English or any other bond as directed by the Engineer-in-charge.

The entire brickwork shall be raised uniformly, and the rate of raising shall not be more than 60 cm per day.

Suitable strong single or double scaffolding may be erected to have easy access to every part of the work. The contractor shall be responsible for any injury to the worker or damage to the work. All the faces of the brickwork shall either be plastered or pointed to give pleasing appearance to the structure.

All the put log openings shall be carefully filled with cement concrete (1 : 4 : 8). Any bad work detected during inspection shall be removed forthwith and replaced with good quality of work.

Watering :

The entire brick work shall be kept continuously wet by sprinkling water at least for 14 days, without allowing mortar to dry.

Mode of Measurement and Payment :

The brick work shall be measured in cubic metre correct to two decimal places for the completed work subject to the dimensions as shown on the drawings, without making any deduction for ends of dissimilar materials like lintels, beams, girder etc. upto an area of 500 cm^2 in section and for openings upto 0.1 cm^2 and shall be paid at the agreed rate specified in the contract document. The rate is for the completed item which includes providing (i.e. cost of material to be brought by the contractor), laying in position, necessary scaffolding, raking of joints, pointing, watering etc. complete.

5. **Random Rubble Masonry in Cement Mortar : (First Sort)**

*   **Material Required :**

    (a) **Stone for Masonry :** The stone shall be strong, hard, dense, durable obtained from the approved fresh quarries of trap or granite variety etc. It shall be impervious, weather resistant and free from defects. The water absorption capacity shall not exceed 5 % by weight.

    (b) **Cement :** Ordinary Portland cement (O.P.C.) satisfying all the I.S. requirements shall be used. For more details refer (a) of item No. 3.

    (c) **Fine Aggregates or Sand :** Natural river sand or broken stone satisfying all I.S. requirements shall be used. For further details refer (b) of item No. 2.

    (d) **Water :** The water to be used for preparing cement mortar shall be wholesome and potable.

*   **Proportion of Mix :**

    The cement and sand shall be mixed in the proportion as specified on the drawings on volumetric basis.

*   **Mixing :**

    Uniform mixing of cement and sand shall be carried out in dry condition and then just required quantity of water shall be added so as to obtain a homogeneous mass of cement mortar. It should be laid in position within 30 minutes of adding water to the dry mix, else it will start setting before it is used.

*   **Dressing of Stones :**

    All stones shall be rough tool dressed so as to remove weak projections, edges, corners etc. and shall be one line dressed.

*   **Laying of Stones :**

    The stone masonry shall be constructed in lines, levels etc. as shown on the drawings. Stones in the hearting shall be laid on their broader face so as to have an opportunity to fill the gap between the stones efficiently. Stratified stones are to be laid on their natural beds, all bed joints being perpendicular to the pressure coming on them. Stones shall be wetted before being placed in masonry else they will absorb moisture from the mortar. They shall be laid full in mortar and placed well in position with wooden mallet. Chips, spalls used to fill the space shall be wedged in the mortar joints and beds. The face work and hearting shall be completed evenly. The quantity of mortar required per cubic metre of masonry shall be about 0.30 cubic m and there shall be uniform raising of masonry limited to 0. 6 m.

- **Bonds :**

  To ensure proper bond, in lateral direction a stone laid is any course shall break the joint with the stone laid in the course above or below it.

  Through Stones : For every 0.5 square metre of facing one through stone shall be placed.

  Vertical Headers : For masonry having 1 m width, vertical headers of 0.45 m long shall be placed for every square metre area in plan.

  Hearting and Backing Stones : Such stones shall be atleast 0.15 m in any direction.

  Quions : They shall be of good quality stone having rough/fine tooled dressing and be of height of one course. The length of quions shall be more than twice its height.

- **Joints :**

  Face joints shall not be more than 6 mm thick and stones shall be laid to break the joints. If the masonry is to be pointed, all joints shall be raked to depth equal to its width (when the mortar is green). If it is not to be pointed, the mortar shall be pressed in the joints and is made smooth. The face joints shall be struck when the mortar is fresh.

- **Watering :**

  All masonry work shall be kept wet atleast for 14 days by sprinkling water over it, care being taken to see that mortar in the joints is not washed away in this process.

- **Scaffolding :**

  Single or double scaffolding required shall be provided by the contractor, sufficient care being taken to ensure its safety. The put log openings shall be filled by stones to match the face work, after removal of scaffold.

- **Mode of Measurement and Payment :**

  The mode of measurement for this item of construction is in cubic meters for the completed work subject to the limiting dimensions shown on the plan and the contractor shall be paid at the agreed rate per cubic meter of completed work.

6. Coursed Rubble Masonry in Cement Mortar (First Sort) :

*   **Materials Required :**

    (a) Stone : As explained under item 5 (a) of Random Rubble masonry in cement mortar (1st sort).

    (b) Cement : Refer item 5 (b) of specification for R.R. masonry in C.M. (1st sort).

    (c) Sand : Same as for item 5 (c) for item No. 5 of specifications for R.R. masonry in C.M. (1st sort).

*   **Dressing of Stones :**

    The Khandki stones shall be so dressed to have straight horizontal and vertical sides which will be perpendicular to adjacent sides. The face portion shall be in one plane. Such stones shall have its breadth larger than its height and shall project back into masonry, for 1.5 times its height and width 1/3rd such stones having their length twice its height, the height being not less than 15 cm.

*   **Hearting and Backing :**

    Such stones shall be as large as possible. One-third of such stones shall be 0.010 cubic metre in volume for 50 cm thick walls.

*   **Quions :**

    It shall be a good quality stone whose height shall be that of the course in which it is to be laid.

*   **Through Stones :**

    Through stones shall have their height equal to the height of the course and its width equal to its height. The dressing of such stones shall be similar to dressing of khandaki.

*   **Vertical Headers :**

    They are required for a masonry having one metre width and shall be 45 cm in length or depth of two courses whichever is higher.

*   **Laying of Stones :**

    They are to be laid in horizontal course of about 15 cm in height. All stones in one course shall have same height and all courses shall also be of same height.

    The through stones shall be laid 1.5 m apart and vertical headers shall be required for masonry of 1 m thickness. The quions shall be placed header and stretcher.

*   **Joints :**

    The thickness of joints shall not be more than 10 mm. In case the masonry is to be pointed, the raking of joints shall be carried out to a depth equal to the thickness of joint (i.e. 10 mm) when the mortar is still fresh and green.

    The mortar required shall be about 0.30 cubic meter per cubic meter of masonry.

*   **Raising of Masonry :**

    The whole masonry shall be raised uniformly limited to 60 cm height in one day.

- **Striking of Joints :**

  For the faces (unexposed) which are not to be plastered, shall be struck carefully when the mortar is fresh and green.

- **Scaffolding :**

  Single or double scaffolding as the case may be shall be arranged by the contractor. All put log opening shall be carefully filled with matching stones after the removal of scaffolding.

- **Mode of Measurement and Payment :**

  The completed masonry work shall be measured in cubic metres subject to limiting dimensions as shown on the plan. The contractor shall be paid at the agreed rate per cubic meter of completed masonry. The dimensions and quantities shall be calculated correct to two decimal places.

7. **Mild Steel Bar Reinforcement for Reinforced Cement Concrete Work :**

   The items of construction in general include the timely supply of mild steel bars, bending and cutting of bars and binding with wires as per the drawings etc. and placing it in position so as to serve as reinforcement in R.C.C. work.

Materials :

- **Mild Steel Bars :** Such bars to be used as reinforcement for R.C.C. work shall conform to the Bureau of Indian Standard specification (former I.S.I.) of 423 of 1960 and shall be tested and duly certified by the competent authorities of the test house. The cost of testing etc. shall be borne by the contractor. It shall also comply with I.S. 456 of 1957.

  The M.S. bars to be used as reinforcement shall be free from dirt, dust, rust, oil, paint, grease etc. Scrap steel shall never be used for this purpose.

  The M.S. bar reinforcement shall be stored on a platform above the ground surface and shall be protected from rust and corrosion etc. All bars of same type shall be stacked separately and marked accordingly.

- **Fabrication of Steel :** Before fabricating, all steel reinforcement shall be cleaned thoroughly of all dust, dirt, coating of any type etc. that would affect the bond.

  All reinforcing steel shall be bent cold to the dimensions as shown on plan. During bending the material shall not be injured. Bending of bar by heating may be carried out at 815°C for bars greater in diameter 25 mm. All dimensions of the reinforcing bars shall be got approved from the Engineer-in-charge.

- **Placing of Reinforcement :** All reinforcing bars shall be placed in correct position with exact spacing and cover as indicated on the drawings. Binding wires of 1.22 or 1.63 mm diameter shall be used for fastening at intersection points or it may be spot welded. Spacing of bars and the cover shall not be disturbed under any circumstances.

- **Inspection of Reinforcement :** No concreting shall be carried out till the entire reinforcement has been inspected and approved by the Engineer-in-charge, in writings. During placing of concrete, the spacing and cover provided shall not be disturbed.
- **Test Certificate :** If the reinforcing steel is brought by the contractor, he has to produce a certificate from the authorized test house regarding its suitability for the work.
- **Mode of Measurement and Payment :** All steel reinforcement shall be measured in quintal (i.e. weight basis) and shall be as shown on reinforcement details of the drawings. The length shall be measured correct to two decimal places in meters and weight measured correct to 0.1 kg and payment made at the agreed rate. No extra payment is to be made for wire used for tying of bars etc.

8. Plastering in Cement Mortar :

The exposed faces of concrete, brick or stone masonry are to be plastered in cement mortar of specified thickness etc.

- **Materials Required :**
  - **(a)** **Cement :** It shall be ordinary Portland cement satisfying all I.S. requirements etc. as described in item 3 (a) of specification of P.C.C.
  - **(b)** **Sand :** As described in item (b) of specifications of item No. 2 of lime concrete.
  - **(c)** **Water :** It shall be potable water free from all impurities
- **Cement Mortar Mix :** Cement and sand shall be mixed in the proportion as specified in the drawing e.g. 1 : 4 i.e. one part of cement to four parts of sand to be mixed thoroughly in dry condition and just sufficient water to be added in the desired proportion so as to give a homogeneous mass of cement mortar.
- **Scaffolding :** The necessary scaffolding shall be arranged by the contractor. It shall be single or double as the case may be.
- **Preparatory Work before Plastering :** All the joints on the surface to be plastered shall be raked to a depth equal to the width of the joints. Concrete surfaces etc. shall be roughened properly to serve as a bond for the plaster. All dust, dirt, oil, etc. that is likely to affect proper bond shall be removed. The surface to be plastered shall be wetted thoroughly for 6 hours before the plastering work starts.
- **Gauges :** Plaster patches about 15 cm × 15 cm shall be put approximately 3 m apart to serve as a gauge to obtain the plastered surface in one plane.
- **Applying Plaster :** During the process of plastering, all mortar shall be applied firmly and properly pressed into all joints and levelled by a flat wooden board to obtain uniform thickness throughout. All corners to be finished to their true angles (or rounded). The plastering can be carried out in squares or strips from top in downward direction.

- **Finishing Treatment :** After the surface is plastered, it may be given a finishing treatment of fine smooth cement slurry to increase its appearance.
- **Curing of Plastered Surface :** All plastered surface shall be kept continuously wet for a minimum period of 14 days at the contractor's cost.
- **Substandard Work :** Any substandard or bad plastered work shall be removed and replastered by the contractor as directed by the Engineer-in-charge.
- **Mode of Measurement and Payment :** All measurements of plastered work shall be carried out in square meter allowing for necessary deductions as per I.S. rule (I.S. 1200 of 1965) for openings for the specified thickness and payment made to the contractors for the completed work at the agreed rate on per square metre basis.

9. **Pointing in Cement (to Brick Work or Stone Masonry) :**
- **Materials Required :**
  - **(a) Cement :** As specified in item 3 (a) of specifications for P.C.C.
  - **(b) Sand :** As described in item 3 (b) of specification for P.C.C.
  - **(c) Water :** The water to be used shall be potable.
- **Scaffolding :** Necessary strong scaffolding, single or double to be arranged by the contractor.
- **Raking of Joints :** All joints shall be raked to a depth equal to the width of the joints or as instructed by the Engineer-in-charge. The joints shall then be brushed clean of all loose particles, dust etc.
- **Wetting :** The entire area to be pointed shall be washed and all joints wetted before the pointing work starts.
- **Pointing :** All the raked joints are filled with cement mortar of specified mix and pressed well and rubbed smooth. A clean string is then pressed with trowel into the centre line of pointing to form a semicircular depression of 3 mm diameter. Such depressions are then rubbed with nayla to make it 6 mm deep and 6 mm wide. The intersection of horizontal and vertical joints must be finished in such a way that they do not cross each other but just touch each other. Any superflous mortar seen outside the width of joints shall be removed immediately with trowel.
- **Curing of Pointings :** The pointed surface shall be kept wet continuously for 14 days.
- **Mode of Measurement and Payment :** All measurement shall be in square meters in accordance with I.S. 1200 of 1965. The contractor shall be paid for the completed work at the agreed rate per square meter of area plastered.

10. **Damp Proof Course (D.P.C.) :**

The item relates to the providing and laying of D.P.C. at the plinth level of 1 : 2 : 4 cement concrete and bitumen of specified thickness.

- **Materials Required :**
  - **(a) Cement :** It shall be as described in item 3 (a) of item plain cement concrete.
  - **(b) Sand :** As described in item 3 (b) of item P.C.C.
  - **(c) Coarse Aggregates :** As explained in 3 (c) of item (3) of P.C.C.
  - **(d) Water :** Only potable water shall be used for mixing.
  - **(e) Bitumen :** It shall be blown type satisfying all I.S. requirements 73 of 1961. The permissible penetration for bitumen tested as per I.S. 1203 of 1958 shall be 40.

- **Laying of D.P.C. :** A neat layer of cement concrete (1 : 2 : 4) of specifies thickness shall be applied to the entire width of the wall at the plinth level. The edges shall be even straight and vertical.

- **Curing :** The layer of concrete is to be cured for one week and then allowed to dry.

- **Application of Bitumen :** After the concrete layer has dried, the surface under the super structure shall be thoroughly cleaned by brushes and then with a cloth dipped in kerosene oil. The hot bitumen @ temp. 120°C is then applied uniformly over the entire surface coming below the superstructure and then allowed to set permanently.

- **Mode of Measurement and Payment :** The item of D.P.C. shall be measured in square meter and shall be equal to the entire length of the top surface of concrete multiplied by the width of the D.P.C. course. The contractor shall be paid for the completed work at the agreed rate on square meter basis.

11. **Shahabad Stone Flooring (of Specified Thickness) :**

- **Materials Required :**
  - **(a) Shahabad Stone :** The Shahabad stone shall be sound, hard, durable, tough and resistant to wear and tear with a minimum thickness of 25 mm with plain horizontal surface. It shall be either square or rectangular in shape.

  - **(b) Base of Cement Concrete :** A bedding of cement concrete of about 25 mm thickness shall be laid below the level of floor and compacted well to obtain a plain surface with required slope.

  - **(c) Cement Mortar Bedding :** Cement mortar required for bedding shall be mixed in required proportion with just sufficient quantity of water added to it to give a mortar of desired consistency. The thickness of mortar bedding shall be about 12 to 25 mm and placed uniformly over the properly wetted concrete bed.

- **Placing or Laying of Stone Slab :** The Shahabad stone shall be wetted well before its laying in position. The entire portion of mortar bed on which the slab is to be laid shall be covered with cement grout and Shahabad stone laid over it within 30 minutes. Each stone shall be tapped gently with a wooden mallet and firmly bedded without leaving any hollows into it.

- **Raking of Joints :** The joints shall then be filled properly to give uniform thickness of 6 to 10 mm in one straight line. The joints shall then be raked to a depth equal to its thickness when the mortar is still fresh and green.

- **Pointing :** All the joints shall be pointed with cement mortar mixed in the proportion as shown on the drawing. In case no pointing is to be carried out the joints shall be struck.

- **Watering and Curing :** The entire flooring is to be kept wet continuously for 14 days and left undisturbed at least for one week.

- **Cleaning :** The flooring is to be washed clean of all mortar stains etc. after the curing period is over.

- **Mode of Measurement and Payment :** The measurement for the completed work shall be as per IS 1200 of 1965 in square meters and paid to the contractor accordingly, for the completed work.

12. Doors, Windows and Ventilators :

The item of doors, windows and ventilators consists of wood work required for its 'frame' (i.e. chowkat) and for 'shutters', the former being measured in cubic meter, and the latter in square meter.

I. Wooden Frame (or Chowkat) :

- **Timber :** The timber (i.e. teak wood) to be used shall be cut from the full grown matured tree and shall be straight, free from sap, knots, flaws, bends etc. It shall be properly seasoned, uniform in colour and free from rot, defects etc.

- **Holdfasts :** The holdfasts made of iron shall be of size 30 cm x 4 cm x 5 mm. Each hold fast shall have two holes drilled into it for fixing screws. They shall be coated with tar and secured firmly into the wall.

- **Wood Work :** The entire woodwork shall have finished dimensions as shown on the detailed drawings.

  The length of the horn in heads and sills shall be 15 cm.

- **Finished Joints :** The joints shall be simple and shall fit correctly without filling or wedging.

- **Fixing the Frame :** The wooden frame with hold fasts shall be fixed in exact vertical position as specified in the drawing. The entire frame shall be painted with tar for the faces coming in contact with masonry and oil painted for the exposed faces of the frame.

- **Mode of Measurement and Payment :** The measurements for the completed item of the work shall be as laid down in I.S. 1200 of 1965, in cubic meter and payment to be made to the contractor subject to the limiting dimensions shown in the drawings at the agreed rate per cubic metre of completed wood work.

II. Shutters or Leafs (Door or Window) :

- **Timber :** As specified for timber (i.e. teak wood) required for the wooden frame of this item.

- **Fixtures and Fastenings :** The fixtures and fastenings to be provided to the shutters shall be as specified for that type of door and shall be strong and new and made of oxidized brass of good quality. The size, shape etc. shall be as specified on the drawings and approved by the Engineer-in-charge.

  Each shutter or leaf shall be hung with three butt hinges (of brass) with brass screws. Each door shall have aldrop, locking arrangement, handle, bolts etc.

- **Fixing in Position :** After the door frame is fixed in vertical position, the shutters or leafs shall be fastened to it as shown on the drawings.

  Each panel shall be made of single width piece and of size and pattern as indicated in drawings.

- **Glazing :** If the door or window is to be fully or partly glazed, the sizes of openings for glazing shall confirm to details as shown on the drawings. The standard quality of putty shall be used for fixing the glass panes into the frame.

- **Mode of Measurement and Payment :** The mode of measurement for the item shall be as specified in I.S. 1200 of 1965 in square meters and the contractor shall be paid for the completed work subject to the limiting dimensions for the item shown on the drawing at the agreed rate on square meter basis.

13. Iron Grill Works for Windows, Ventilators :

The item of construction pertains to providing and fixing in position iron or steel grill to the windows, ventilators etc.

- **Materials Required :**

  (a) **Mild Steel or Wrought Iron** as specified in the drawings shall confirm to I.S. 2090 of 1962 (for M.S.) or as per requirement specified for wrought iron. The section shall be round, flat etc. of the required dimensions as shown on drawings.

  (b) **Oil Paint :** The entire iron work shall be oil painted, the priming coat made up of red lead and the other remaining two coats of the shade and colour sanctioned by the Engineer-in-charge.

- **Fabrication and Fixing of the Grill :** The grill shall be fabricated as per the drawings and design approved by the Engineer. All joints shall be welded, riveted etc. as shown on the drawings. The fabricated grill shall be fixed into the window or ventilator frame before erecting them in position. The fixing of the grill to the frame shall be at the rate of one screw for 300 mm length of the outer strip. The screws are to be countersunk with their top flush with the face of the frame.

- **Mode of Measurement and Payment :** The mode of measurement shall be as laid in I.S. 1200 of 1965 in square meters, the length and width being measured from inside to inside of the frame (i.e. grill) and correct upto 5 mm length. The area of the grill shall be calculated to three decimal places of square metre and payment made to the contractor at the agreed rate on per square metre basis.

14. Colour Washing in two Coats to New Surface Over White Washing of Base Coat :

The item in general includes providing and applying colour wash can a base coat of while wash to unfinished surfaces.

Materials Required :

- **White Wash :** It shall be prepared from freshly burnt lime stone. The white wash shall be prepared by dissolving 1 kg of lime powder in about 4.5 litres of water and well stirred to obtain thin consistent cream. Good quantity of gum dissolved in warm water of required quantity then shall be added to the white wash.
- **Preparing Surface :** All surface to be white washed shall be thoroughly cleaned by removing foreign matter and mortar droppings with wire brush so as to make it even and clean.
- **White Washing (Base Coat) :** The white wash is then applied on the cleaned surface with a brush. The brushing is carried out from top downwards first and then from bottom upwards over the first and similarly one stroke from right to left and then from left to right before it dries, forming one coat of application. Each such coat shall be inspected and approved by the Engineer-in-charge. Splashing and dropping of white wash on doors, windows etc. shall be cleaned properly.
- **Scaffolding :** All the scaffolding, single or double type, required shall be arranged by the contractor and shall be removed after the completion of the work. The scaffolding shall be strong and no accident should take place during the process of while washing.
- **Colour Wash :** The next coat of colour wash is to be prepared by adding required colour to the (strained) white wash. The colour wash shall then be applied over the base coat, the method of application being similar to white wash coat. The number of coats of colour wash shall be as specified, the next coat being given after the earlier coat dries. Due care shall be taken to stir the mix constantly before it is applied to avoid settling of the colour matter (at the bottom of the box).
- **Mode of measurement and payment :** The mode of measurement for this item shall be as specified in I.S. 1200 of 1965, in square metres necessary deductions etc. being made depending upon the size of openings; from one face or two faces as the case may be. The contractor shall be paid for the net area of the surface colour washed at the agreed rate per square metre basis.

15. Roof of Mangalore Tiled with Class A-A Tiles :

- **Materials Required :**
    - **Mangalore Tiles :** The Mangalore tiles (class A-A) to be used for roof shall be as specified in I.S. 654 of 1957. The tiles shall be got approved by the Engineer-in-charge before laying in position.
    - **Battens :** They shall be prepared from approved seasonal teak wood and sawn true to line, width and thickness as specified for the item on the drawings. The portion of the batten to be embedded in the wall shall be coal tarred and the other exposed portion shall be coated with (linseed) oil, to prevent its decay when laid in position.
    - **Iron Fastenings :** All iron work such as M.S. flats, nails, bolts, nuts and binding wire used shall be of standard quality and shall be brushed with coal tar for the embedded portion and the remaining iron work to be oiled with linseed oil.
    - **Preliminary Arrangement :** Before fixing of battens start, it shall be verified that the lines, levels and slopes of the trusses, ridges, purlines, common rafters, wall plates etc. are as shown on the drawings and defects noticed if any, shall be rectified accordingly.
    - **Laying of Roof :** The laying of roof is split into two parts :
    - **(a) Fixing Battens :** The battens of the required size shall be fixed on the upper surface of the rafters with the iron nails at centre to centre distance (i.e. spacing) of 31.75 cm. The thickness of the lowest battens is twice the normal thickness and is placed at 25 cm from that placed immediately above it.

    - **(b) Laying of Tiles :** Laying of tiles shall be carried from eaves towards ridge. Tiles shall be laid square and with breaking joints and shall fit properly as regards one to another so that 'catches' rest fully against battens. The hip and valley tiles shall be cut to the desired shape so that the ridge and hip tiles can be fixed appropriately. The tiles placed at the end of gables and eaves shall be tied by 1.22 mm wire underneath the battens. Also wind ties of steel flat (40 mm x 3 mm) shall be provided near the eaves with proper arrangement of fastening the same through the Mangalore tiles to the (common) rafters by suitable screws or hooks after every alternate rafter as shown on the drawings. The top surface of the roof so formed shall be of uniform plane from ridge to the eaves.

    - **Drip Moulding :** Stone or brick drip moulding shall be provided at the end of roof against a wall as specified on the drawings.

    - **Mode of Measurement and Payment :** The item shall be measured as specified in I.S. 1200 of 1965, the unit of measurement being in square meters. The contractor shall be paid for the completed work limited to that shown on the drawings at the agreed rate as per square meter basis.

16. **Reinforced Cement Concrete (1 : 2 : 4) for Slab Work Inclusive of Centering, Form Work (but Excluding Reinforcement) :**

- **Materials :**

  (a) **Cement :** As specified for item no. 3 (a) of P.C.C.

  (b) **Sand :** As mentioned in item no. 3 (b) for P.C.C.

  (c) **Coarse Aggregates :** As stated in item no. 3 (c) of P.C.C. The maximum size of aggregate shall be 20 mm.

  (d) **Water :** Only drinking water shall be used for the preparation of concrete.

  - **Proportion of the Mix :** The cement, sand and coarse aggregates shall be mixed either on volumetric or weight basis in the proportion of 1 : 2 : 4.

  - **Mixing :** The concrete shall be prepared in the mechanical mixer the drum being rotated atleast for 2 minutes. The water cement ratio shall be about 0.55 or as directed by the Engineer-in-charge. The slump test carried on site shall be about 100 mm.

  - **Form Work :** The form work shall conform to the pare 7.2 of the I.S. 456 of 1957.

  - **Placing of Concrete in Position :** Before placing concrete in position, the entire form work and the arrangement of steel reinforcement shall be checked thoroughly and got approved by the Engineer-in-charge. The item of reinforcing steel is not to be included in the slab portion but will form a separate item and shall be paid for accordingly.

    The concrete in the slab is then laid to the required thickness throughout as shown on the drawing. The entire concreting for the slab is to be completed in one continuous operation. The labour shall not be allowed to cross over the freshly laid green concrete portion.

    Any fixtures such as hooks, clamps etc. shall be placed in their correct position at the time of laying of slab.

  - **Compaction :** Compaction shall be carried out either manually by tamping bars, rods, etc. or by mechanical vibrators so as to get a homogeneous dense mass of concrete without any cavities.

  - **Finishing :** After the form work is removed after the specified period, the surface of the slab shall if necessary roughened and plastered with a cement mortar (1 : 3) to obtain uniform smooth surface and then cured as usual.

  - **Mode of Measurement and Payment :** The mode of measurement shall be as per I.S. 1200 of 1965 in cubic meters of the slab laid to correct thickness as shown on the drawings and the contractor shall be paid at the agreed rate on per cubic metre basis.

Note :

- Any portion of the slab resting over the column shall be excluded from the slab portion and shall be included in the column and paid accordingly.
- In case of slab and beam connections, the slab shall be considered as running continuously throughout and the beam shall be measured as that portion lying above or below the slab.

17. Specifications for Items of Construction other than Building works :

(1) **Road work : Cement Concrete (1 : 2 : 4) Rigid Pavement :** The item pertaining to road work provides for laying of cement concrete (1 : 2 : 4) pavement of required thickness inclusive of subgrade of lean mix of cement concrete (1 : 4 : 8), compacting, finishing curing etc. complete.

- **Materials Required :**

(a) **Cement :** It shall be ordinary Portland cement satisfying all I.S. requirements as specified in item 3 (a) of plain cement concrete.

(b) **Coarse Aggregate :** The grading of coarse aggregates shall be arranged to obtain dense concrete having maximum large size of aggregates size with minimum voids. The grading of aggregate shall preferably be as follows:

(a) Aggregate i.e. metal 40 mm   ... 60 to 65%
(b) Aggregate i.e. metal 20 mm   ... 40 to 35%
(c) Aggregate size i.e. metal 10 mm   ... 40 to 35%

Samples of metals shall be tested as per I.S. requirements by the contractor. Measurement of aggregates shall be carried out on volumetric basis by approved measuring boxes.

(c) **Fine Aggregates :** It may be natural river sand or crushed stone screened to required size, satisfying the I.S. 383 of 1952 requirements that will have maximum density and strength etc.

(d) **Water :** Only drinking water shall be used for mixing.

(e) **Reinforcement :** Steel reinforcement if required shall conform to the I.S. specifications.

- **Mix Proportion :** The cement, fine aggregates and coarse aggregates for this work are generally mixed in 1 : 2 : 4 proportion.

On the basis of one ordinary portland cement bag weighing 50 kg, the proportion corresponding to 1 : 2 : 4 mix will be as follows :

O.P. Cement 1 bag　　= 50 kg.
Fine aggregates i.e. sand　= 70 litres
Coarse aggregates　= 140 litres.

The desired water cement ratio shall be 0.55 and the results of slump test carried out on site shall not exceed 40 mm.

- **Measuring Boxes :** When volumetric batching is to be carried out, the boxes provided with handles for lifting shall be strong and sturdy. The size of the boxes shall be so arranged as to measure the necessary quantity of each type in complete boxes or multiples thereof.

- **Equipment :** All tools, equipment, mixers, machinery required for the subgrade preparation batching, mixing, transporting, laying, finishing and curing of the pavement of concrete, shall be of standard design approved by Engineer-in-charge.

  The batch type concrete mixers of approved standard shall have a capacity of at least 0.2 m³ of mixed concrete. Appropriate measuring device for the water to be added during mixing shall be arranged by the contractor. The mixer provided with time measuring device shall be rotated for specified time for each mix to obtain a homogenenous dense mass of cement concrete.

- **Sub-grade and Sub-base Preparation :** All weak, soft patches in the subgrade shall be removed and filled with coarse aggregate, watered and rammed. All low lying portion and hollows etc. shall then be filled by a lean mix of concrete (1 : 4 : 8) layer and compacted well.

- **Final Preparation of the Base :** Before concreting (1 : 2 : 4) the surface, the sub-grade and sub-base work shall be completed as required, so as to make the entire base smooth and even. The entire surface shall then be cleaned and carefully moistened.

- **Forms :** The side forms of either mild steel or wooden shall have the depths equal to the thickness of the pavement slab. Such forms are to be placed to the required grade and alignment 60 m in advance of the concrete deposition point. These forms are to be removed after 24 hours of laying of concrete, without disturbing the concrete and its edges. The forms can be reused after cleaning, oiling, etc.

- **Construction Joints :** The joints shall be transverse expansion, contraction or construction and longitudinal joints.

  The transverse expansion joints of premoulded type are to provided at 35 m interval and of 12 mm thickness.

  The transverse construction joints must be at 8 m interval and shall be of dummy grove type.

  Transverse construction joints are required when the concreting work is stopped for more than 30 minutes.

The longitudinal joints of plain butt type shall be formed by placing the concrete against the face of the slab already concreted. For concrete slabs thicker than 10 cm, tie bars shall be provided for longitudinal joints.

- **Laying or Placing of Concrete :** After the sub base is moistened the concrete shall be laid in position to the required width and depth of the pavement as shown on the drawings. After laying the concrete, it shall be rodded or vibrated to prevent honey combing . Crossing of freshly laid concrete shall be strictly prohibited.

- **Compacting and Finishing the Surface :** Concrete after it is laid shall be spread uniformly to the given longitudinal and transverse slope and thickness. The compaction can be carried out by a vibrating screed. The concrete shall then be smoothened and by using longitudinal float (1.2 m long × 0.1 m wide) the laitance is removed. The slab is then tested for the true surface by a straight edge and surface corrected if necessary. All the joints are then finished to have level surface across it. The entire pavement is then broom finished and the edges of the slab are neatly finished to have a radius of 10 mm.

- **Curing :** The curing consists of initial curing by covering the slab, to avoid rapid drying, by wet empty cement bags till the surface hardens sufficiently to be walked on without causing any damage. The wet cement bags are then removed and surface cured finally by ponding by creating earthen bunds (1 m × l m) and filling them with water for 21 days.

- **Cleaning :** After final curing is over the entire surface is wiped clean and allowed to dry. All the joints are then sealed properly and opened for traffic after about 28 days of placing of concrete.

- **Testing :** The strength of the pavement shall be tested according I.S. requirements.

- **Mode of Measurement and Payment :** The mode of measurement is per square meter of completed pavement of specified thickness and strength.

  The length shall be the actual length measured along the centre line of the pavement and width shall be taken at right angles to the centre line of the pavement. The quantity of pavement of specified thickness shall be measured in square meters to two places of decimals and contractor shall be paid at the agreed rate on per hundred square metre basis.

2. Road work : Laying Full Grout Bituminous Road Surface 50 mm thick :

Flexible Pavement :

The flexible pavement item in general includes the labour to be arranged for laying the full grout bituminous surface for the road of finished thickness of 50 mm and is inclusive of preparation of road surface, equipment, plant, fuel etc. but exclusive of metal (i.e. stone aggregates), bitumen and compaction.

- **Materials :** The bitumen and stone aggregates required for road surface shall confirm to the relevant I.S. specifications. The quantities of stone aggregates and bitumen required shall be as shown below.

Sr. No.	Name of Material	Rate of Application
1.	Dry chips of 10 mm size	1.2 m³ per 100 m²
2.	Dry chips of 12 mm size	1.5 m³ per 100 m²
3.	Dry stone aggregate 40 mm size	0.6 m³ per 100 m²
4.	Bitumen 30/40 penetration for grouting	490 to 500 kg
5.	Bitumen 50/100 penetration for seal coal	160 to 170 kg

- **Preparation of the Base :** The entire road surface shall be thoroughly cleaned of all dust, dirt, loose materials etc. and the entire blindage shall be brushed off completely so as to expose the stone metal completely. The surface so prepared shall be banned for the traffic. Edge lines shall clearly be marked for sufficiently long length for spreading the metal.

- **Spreading the Material and Compacting :** At first 40 mm size metal shall be evenly spread @ 6 m³ per 100 m² and the section checked for grade, alignment etc. and well compacted so as to make the entire surface even and uniform.

- **Application of Bitumen :** The bitumen of grade S - 35 of 30/40 penetration heated in a boiler to a temperature of about 185°C shall be applied through cans with rose or pressure sprayers at a uniform rate of 490 to 500 kg/100 square metre.

- **Blindage :** Stone chips of 12 mm size shall then be uniformly spread over the surface of the road @ 1.5 m³ per 100 m² immediately after applying the bitumen which is still hot.

- **Compaction :** The entire road surface shall be compacted as specified or directed by the Engineer-in-charge.

- **Seal Coat :** After the above surface is prepared the seal coat shall be applied within 30 days of laying of the full grout surface.

  Before the application of seal coat, the existing surface shall be cleaned off all dust, dirt, loose matter etc. by brooms or gunny bags. The Bitumen of I.S. Grade S - 90 with 80/100 penetration, heated in a boiler to temperature of 170°C shall be uniformly applied @ 170 kg per 100 square meter area with a rose can or sprayer.

- **Blindage :** After the application of seal coat of bitumen, the surface shall be uniformly blinded with stone chips of 10 mm size @ 1.2 m³ per 100 m².

- **Rolling :** After the blindage has been spread evenly, the surface shall be thoroughly rolled to obtain a uniform continuous road surface of desired quality.

- **Mode of Measurement and Payment :** The mode of measurement as per I.S. shall be per 100 square meter of completed work. The length shall be measured along the center line of the road surface and the width shall be limited to that specified on the drawings. The length and width dimensions shall be measured correct upto two decimal places of meter and the area covered by the road surface shall be calculated to one place of decimal of square meter. The contractor shall be paid at the agreed rate for 100 sq. m of the completed work.

3. **Water Supply to Building : Water Supply Pipe Line of Cast Iron (A or B Class) :**

The item is related to providing and laying C.I. pipe line of specified diameter etc. complete including excavating, laying of pipe and back filling.

- **Materials :** The C.I. pipe shall satisfy all I.S. 1537 - 1960 requirements and the specified pipe diameter shall be the inside diameter. All fitting etc. shall be according to I.S. 1538 - 1960. The sockets and spigot, flanges etc. shall be as shown on plan.

- **Excavation for Laying Pipe :** The trench to be excavated for laying pipe shall be true to lines, levels and grades as approved by the Engineer-in-charge. The trench shall be excavated to a depth such that there will be minimum cover of 0.75 m and the width of the trench shall be 0.30 m more than pipe socket to enable ramming the material refilled below and at the sides of the pipe. The bed of the trench shall be even and uniform and to the desired grade. Dewatering, if any shall be arranged by the contractor at his cost. All existing pipes, service lines, underground cables etc. if met with during excavation shall be properly supported and well protected, without causing any damage. In case of the road crossing the pipe shall be laid below the road crust.

- **Laying of Pipes :** To start with the pipes shall be placed along the side of the trench in its correct position. The pipes are then inspected for any defects, cracks etc. and are cleaned by a brush from inside to remove the material adhered to it. The pipes are then lowered into the trench and spigots placed into sockets. The whole length of pipe shall rest on the bed of the trench uniformly throughout. All lead joints are completed and are paid for separately. The open end of the pipe at the end of day's work shall be closed properly. Laying of pipe usually includes its cutting, waste etc.

- **Testing the Joints and back Filling :** After completing lead joints, the pipe line shall be tested to check for leakage etc. and then back filling is carried out in layers and suitably rammed. The back filling is carried out to original ground level before excavation. To allow for subsequent settlement by traffic etc. over it, the filling is usually raised by 8 cm per metre of depth of the trench.

- **Mode of Measurement and Payment :** The item is measured per metre length of the pipe laid inclusive of all necessary fitting, cutting, wastages etc. The length completed shall be measured correct to one centimetre and the payment to the contractor made at the agreed rate per metre length. For lead and flagged joints contractor shall be paid separately.

4. **Sanitary Arrangement for Building :**

Providing and fixing Water Closet Pan (Indian style) White Glazed Earthenware of specified size with trap (P or S type), foot rest etc.

The item in general relates to W.C. Pan (Indian style) of white glazed earthenware of specified size with C.I. flushing cistern 13.5 litres capacity, soil and vent pipes to be provided on the outside of wall.

- **Materials Required :**

  (a) **Water closet pan** (Indian style), trap and foot rest shall be in accordance with I.S. 771 of 1958 and best Indian make available in the market.

  (b) **C. I. Pipe and Fitting :** It shall be of good quality available in the market.

  (c) **C.I. High Level Flushing Cistern :** This shall conform to I.S. 774 of 1960 of 13.5 litres capacity.

  (d) Lead pipe 32 mm diameter shall be as per I.S. 404 - 1952.

  (e) G.I. pipe 20 mm diameter shall be as per I.S. 1239 - 1958.

  (f) G.I. iron chain and pull shall be as per I.S. 774 - 1960

  (g) Brick bat lime concrete (1: 2: 4) shall be as per relevant I.S.

  - **Fixing the W.C. Pan and Cistern :** The W.C. pan and flushing cistern shall be fixed in the appropriate places as shown on the detailed drawings. The trap shall be in position with trap joined in C.M. (1 : 1).

  - **The Vent and Soil Pipes :** The vent and soil pipes shall project through the cavity left in the wall and wall made good.

  - **Brick Bat Line Concrete** (1 : 2 : 4) shall be pressed properly around the pan surface to fill all hollow portions. The level of the pan shall be slightly at lower level than the surrounding floor level sloping towards the pan.

  - **The Flushing Cistern** shall rest on two C.I. cantilever brackets projecting from the walls at the appropriate height. The inlet pipe, lead flushing pipe etc. shall be connected correctly as shown on the drawings.

  - **Foot Rests :** After the flooring is ready, foot rests shall be placed in exact position in C.M. (1 : 1). The payment for the item of flooring shall be made separately.

- **The Chain and Pulling Arrangement** shall be fixed to the flushing cistern as shown on the drawings The cistern, bracket and pipes shall be oil painted.

- **Testing :** The entire installation shall be checked for leak proof joints if any; and should function satisfactorily.

- **Mode of Measurement and Payment :** The mode of measurement shall be per unit of water closet pan fixed with all necessary arrangement and payment shall be made to the contractor at the agreed rate per item of W.C. pan fixed, complete in all respects.

THEORETICAL QUESTIONS

1. What do you mean by specifications of an item of construction ?
2. What is the purpose of writing specifications ?
3. State the different types of specifications indicating the purpose of each.
4. What care should be taken while drafting specifications of an item of   construction ?
5. State the legal aspects of specifications.
6. Write detailed specifications for the following items of construction
   (i) Excavation of foundations in ordinary soil
   (ii) P.C.C. (1 : 4 : 8) in foundations
   (iii) U.C.R. masonry in foundations in C.M. (1 : 6)
   (iv) Brickwork in superstructure in C.M. (1 : 6)
   (v) R.C.C. (1 : 2 : 4) for slab
   (vi) Internal plastering 12 mm thick with neeru finish
   (vii) Shahabad stone flooring
   (viii) Mangalore tiled roofing
   (ix) Wood work for doors and windows
   (x) Cement concrete (1 : 2 : 4) Rigid Pavement.
7. Why specifications are necessary ? How the specifications are useful to
   (i) Contractor
   (ii) Supervisor
   (iii) Estimator
8. Write detailed specifications for the following :
   (i) Excavation for foundations
   (ii) P.C.C. (1 : 4 : 8) for foundations
   (iii) B.B. masonry, IInd sort in C.M. (1 : 4) for superstructure

9. Distinguish between particular and general specifications.

10. Write detailed specifications for the following :

    (i) 15 mm thick sand faced cement plaster (1 : 4) to brick masonry

    (ii) Excavation for foundations in ordinary soils

11. State the necessity of specifications and explain the term general specifications.

12. What are standard specifications ? Distinguish between 'technical specifications' and 'general specifications'.

13. Define specification. What is the necessity of specification ? State the principle of specification drafting.

14. Enumerate the types of specifications. Write the purpose of each type. What is the necessity of specifications ? Explain its legal importance.

15. What are specifications ? Enumerate the types of specifications and state the purpose of each type.

16. Write detailed specifications for the following items of construction:

    (i) II class B.B. masonry in cement mortar (1: 6) in super structure.

    (ii) C.C. (1 : 2 : 4) for R.C.C. roof slab.

17. Write detailed specifications for sand faced cement plaster to brick masonry work.

18. State how the specifications are useful for supervising the work.

19. Write detailed specifications for any one of the following items :

    (i) Uncoursed rubble masonry in C.M. (1 : 6) in foundations

    (ii) Doors and windows of timber for residential buildings.

20. Explain the terms used in brief specifications

    (i) Lead and lift for earthwork, (ii) Dewatering and back filling.

21. Write a note on the art and science of writing specifications covering the following aspects.

    (i) Necessity of specifications in addition to drawing.

    (ii) Style, composition, numbering of clauses and cross referring

    (iii) Procedure in drafting specifications, type of data and information to be collected before drafting.

    (iv) What you should write and what you should avoid while drafting specifications ?

22. Write detailed specifications for any one :

    (i) Centering and form work for cantilever canopies.

    (ii) First class B.B. masonry in C.M. (1 : 6) in superstructure.

Chapter 6
RATE ANALYSIS

6.1 INTRODUCTION

The process of determining the rate per unit of a particular item of construction after taking into consideration

- The cost of quantities of materials required.
- The cost of labour to be employed.
- The cost of hire charges of ordinary and special (if any) tools and plants required.
- Overhead charges.
- Establishment charges of Head office, of the contractor, and
- The contractor's reasonable profit, is known as 'Analysis of Rates' (or Prices) or 'Rate Analysis (or Prices).

6.2 PURPOSE (OR OBJECT) OF ANALYSIS OF RATES (OR PRICES)

Analysis of Rates :

The purpose of analysis of rates of various items of construction may be as stated below :

- It enables the contractor in quoting the appropriate rate for the various items of construction.
- It is useful for preparing detailed estimates of the proposed project.
- The analysis of rates also helps in the comparison of actual cost incurred with the estimated cost of the work.
- It also enables in comparing the expenditure of the other similar works.
- In Government Organizations, it helps in checking or comparing the rates quoted by the contractor in the tenders.
- It also helps in arriving at the reasonable rate for different items of construction not included under the District Schedule of Rates (DSR).

6.3 FACTORS AFFECTING THE RATE (OR PRICE) ANALYSIS

The various factors that affect the rate or price of an item are as follows :

(i) Material :

For the completion of an item, the exact quantities of various materials required can be calculated mathematically from the known specifications of the item. The rates or prices of various materials required, however, varies from time to time and from place to place. The term cost of material implies cost of material at the site and thus includes the cost of material at its origin (or source), cost of transport, railway freight, octroi taxes, etc. If the distance through which the material is to be transported is more than 8 kilometers, additional transport charges are to be included to the cost of material.

Obviously, as the cost of material varies from place to place and from time to time, the rate or price of an item will also vary accordingly.

(ii) Labour :

In order to complete an item of construction different categories of labour (i.e. skilled, semi-skilled and unskilled) are to be employed. The number of labours required for the completion of an item is determined either by past experience or by carrying out actual experiments on work site.

The cost of labour is generally inclusive of ordinary tools required by the respective labourer e.g. pick axes, crow bars, ghamelas for excavation, hammers, chisels etc. to be brought by mason etc.

The wages to be paid to labourer depend upon their availability, and category (i.e. skilled, semi-skilled or unskilled), cost of living in the area (i.e. rural or urban), amenities available to the labourer and nearness to the work site.

Thus knowing the number of labourers to be employed and the wages to be paid to them the cost of labour for the completion of an item can be worked out accurately.

(iii) Tools and Plants :

Separate provision is to be made for the cost of hiring ordinary tools and plants such as concrete mixers, vibrators (inclusive of cost of fuel, electric charges and operators required etc.). For multi-storeyed buildings, special concrete hoist, cranes etc. are to be used for concerting purposes.

They are usually taken as 1 % of the total cost of material and labour required for the completion of an item.

(iv) Overhead Charges :

These are unproductive and indirect expenses required for the completion of an item and include establishment of office at the work-site, supervision charges etc. They are generally taken as 5% of the total cost of material and labour required for completion of the item. Overheads are further sub-divided into :

　(a)　General overheads and (b) Job overheads.

(a) **General Overheads :** General overheads include the establishment charges of the office staff, telephone bill, stationery, printing, postage charges, travel expenses, rent and taxes etc.

(b) **Job Overheads :** The expenses included under job overheads are salaries of supervisor staff, material handling charges, repair charges, labour welfare amenities, workmens compensation expenses, insurance charges, losses on advances, interest on investment, paid holidays, provision for incentive, bonus for early completion of work etc.

Thus overhead charges are the expenses to be incurred by the contractor for a particular work site but which cannot be included under the basic cost of any item of construction e.g. say concreting work.

The overhead charges can also be classified as 'one time' (i.e. fixed) and 'time related' (i.e. variable overheads). Items such as establishment of an office at the worksite, hutments for labours, tea stall, approaches to the worksite, electric and telephone connection etc. come under 'one time' over heads, whereas salaries of supervisor, and clerical staff, watchman, office expenses, postage and telephone charges, repair and maintenance charges pertaining to the work etc. are included under the *'Time Related Overheads.'*

(v) Establishment Charges (of Head Office) :

The permanent head office of the contracting company is different from the temporary office at the worksite. The amount to be spent for running the head office such as salaries of quantity surveyors, accountants, cashiers, clerks, etc. are all included under establishment charges. It is usually assumed as 1 % of the cost of material and labour.

(vi) Contractor's Profit :

The contractor's profit is usually taken as 10 to 15 % of the total cost of construction of an item. It is equal to the total amount received by the contractor for the completion of an item minus the initial investment the contractor has made for its completion. Even though the net profit amounts to about 10 to 15 % the return on the rolling capital employed may be very much higher even upto 100 % per year as the contract provides for interim payment to be made to the contractor after fixed interval of time depending upon the volume of work completed by him. Longer the duration of the completion of the work lesser (say upto 10%) will the percentage of profit and vice-a-versa The cost of items (i), (ii) and (iii) as stated above is known as 'basic cost ' whereas the overhead charges are indirect costs. The summation of cost of the items (i), (ii), (iii), (iv), (v) as indicated above amounts to the 'cost of an item' i.e. the initial investment or the amount the contractor has to spend for the completion of an item. After contractors reasonable profit i.e. (vi) is added to the cost of the item it becomes its 'rate' or 'price'.

6.4 TASK WORK (OR OUT TURN)

Definition :

'Task Work' or 'Out Turn' is defined as the quantity, of a particular item of construction which an average labourer of a particular trade can complete in a working day of eight clock hours. The 'task work' varies from individual to individual, place to place and depends upon various factors such as physical fitness and skill of the labourer, type, nature and place of work, climatic conditions of the place, and amenities available to the labourer etc.

The usual procedure of determining the task work for any item of construction is by keeping a record of labour employed and the work carried out by him in a day of eight hours or it may be determined by past experience. However determination of exact task work of a labour for a particular type of work is a difficult job. It is observed that the out turn (i.e. task work) of a labour in case of item rate contracts is much higher than if the same work is executed by employing daily labour. Thus determination of exact number of labourer for the completion of a particular item work is a very difficult task.

The table given below indicates the 'Task work' (i.e. approximate quantity of work) for an average labourer (or artesian) in a day of eight hours.

6.5 TABLE SHOWING THE 'TASK WORK'

The task work stated below is to be used as a guidance only and should not be quoted as a rule.

Sr. No.	Item of construction	Quantity of work per day per mason/labour
1.	Excavation for foundations in ordinary soil including normal lead of 30 m and lift of 1.5 m.	2.5 cub. m
2.	Excavation for foundations in Hard Soil including normal lead of 30 m and lift of 1.5 m.	1.8 cub. m
3.	Excavation for foundations in ordinary rock including normal lead of 30 m and lift of 1.5 m.	0.80 cub. m
4.	Excavation for foundation in Hard Rock including normal lead of 30 m and lift of 1.5 m.	0.48 cub. m
5.	Time concrete in foundation.	8.5 cub. m
6.	U.C.R. (i.e. Random Rubble Stone Masonry) in lime or cement mortar stone.	0.85 to 1.00
7.	C.R. stone masonry in lime or cement mortar including dressing of stones.	0.75 to 0.8
8.	Ashlar masonry is lime or cement mortar or arch work in stone.	0.4 cub. m
9.	P.C.C. (1 : 2 : 4)	5.00 cub. m
10.	R.C.C. (1 : 2 : 4)	3.00 cub. m

... Contd.

11.	Brick work in lime or cement mortar in foundation and plinth	1.25 cub. m
12.	Brick work in lime or cement mortar in superstructure	1.00 cub. m
13.	Brick work in lime or cement mortar in arches	0.55 cub. m
14.	Half brick work in lime or cement mortar in partition	5 sq. m.
15.	13 mm thick plastering with lime or cement mortar	8.00 sq. m
16.	Pointing with lime or cement mortar	10.00 sq. m
17.	White washing or colour washing (one coat)	200 sq. m
18.	White washing or colour washing (three coats)	70 sq. m
19.	Painting or varnishing of doors or windows (one coat)	25.00 sq. m
20.	Distempering (one coat)	35 sq. m
21.	Flooring of cement concrete (25 mm thick)	7.50 sq. m
22.	6 mm thick terrazo mosaic floor over 20 min thick cement concrete (1 : 2 : 4)	5 sq. m
23.	Timber framing in Sal or Teak wood	0.07 m^3
24.	Timber framing in country cut wood	0.15 m^3
25.	Panelled or glazed shutters for doors or windows	0.15 sq. m
26.	Door or window shutters battened	0.80 sq. m
27.	Mangalore or Allahabad single tiling	6.00 sq. m
28.	Allahabad double tiling	4.00 sq. m
29.	Number of bricks that will be laid by a mason in a brickwork of height 10 m	600 Nos. per mason

6.6 TABLE SHOWING MATERIALS REQUIRED FOR DIFFERENT ITEMS OF CONSTRUCTION

The table below shows the quantities of materials required for different items of construction :

Sr. No.	Description of item	Unit	Quantity required
	Brick work	cub. m	
	(i) Bricks (without wastage) I.S. size 190 mm × 90 mm × 90 mm	cub. m	500 Nos.
	(ii) Mortar (dry) (assumed as 30%)	cub. m	0.3 cub. m
2.	Stone masonry		
	(i) Stone required for rubble masonry (including 25% wastage)	cub. m	1.25 cub. m
	(ii) Mortar (dry) (assumed as 42%)	cub. m	0.42 cub. m
3.	Cement concrete (1 : 2 : 4)		
	(i) Cement	cub. m	6.51 bags
	(ii) Fine aggregates i.e. sand	cub. m	0.435 cub. m
	(iii) Coarse aggregates i.e. ballast	cub. m	0.870 cub. m

... Contd.

4.	25 mm thick cement concrete (1 : 2 : 4) flooring		
	(i) Cement	sq. m	0.24 bags
	(ii) Fine aggregates i.e. sand	sq. m	0.012 cub. m
	(iii) Coarse aggregates i.e. ballast	sq. m	0.024 cub. m
5.	12 mm thick plastering		
	(i) Dry mortar required	sq. m	0.002 cub. m
6.	Pointing to brick work		
	(i) Dry mortar required	sq. m	0.006 cub. m
7.	White washing (one coat)		
	Lime required	sq. m	0.1 kg
8.	Dry distemper (initial or first coat)	sq. m.	0.065 kg
9.	Dry distemper (second coat)	sq. m	0.05 kg
10.	Snowcem water proofing 1st coat	sq. m	0.03 kg
11.	Snowcem water proofing 2nd coat	sq. m	0.02 kg
12.	Damp proof course (D.P.C.) 20 cm thick in cement mortar (1 : 2)		
	(i) Cement	sq. m	0.27 bags
	(ii) Sand	s.q. m	0.018 cub. m
	(iii) Impermo	sq. m	0.27 kg
13.	D.P.C., 25 mm thick in cement concrete (1 : 1.5 : 3)		
	(i) Cement	sq. m.	0.22 bags
	(ii) Sand	sq. m.	0.0125 cub. m
	(iii) Coarse aggregate	sq. m	0.0250 cub. m
	(iv) Impermo	sq. m	0.22 kg
14.	Sloping roof of galvanised corrugated iron sheets	100 sq. m.	128 sq. m (considering overlap)
15.	Sloping roof of asbestos cement corrugated sheets	100 sq. m	115 sq. m (considering overlaps)
16.	Ready made paint mix one coat	100 sq. m	10 litres
17.	Timber		
	(i) For panelled door shutter 40 mm thick	100 sq. m	4.5 cub. m
	(ii) For battened door shutter 40 mm thick	100 sq. m	4.00 cub. m
	(iii) For party glazed and party panelled shutters 40 mm thick	100 sq. m	3.00 cub. m
	(iv) For fully glazed shutter 40 mm thick	100 sq.m	2 cub. m

6.7 LABOUR REQUIREMENTS FOR DIFFERENT ITEMS OF WORKS

The report of productivity project of National Building Organisation (N.B.O.) New Delhi specifies the labour requirements of various categories for different items of works as follows :

Sr. No.	Description of item	Unit	Type of labour	Labour constant in days (i.e. of 8 hours) per unit			
				Soft Soil	Hard Soil	Soft rock	Hard rock
1.	**Excavation and earth work**						
(i)	Excavation over areas upto 1.5 m deep and removing out (the excavated materials)	1 cub. m	Mazdoor	0.35	0.60	1.4	2.4
(ii)	Excavation in trenches upto 1.5 m deep and removing out (the excavated material)	1 cub. m	Mazdoor	0.54	0.94	2.15	3.40
(iii)	For excavation exceeding 1.5 deep but not more than 3 m	1 cub. m	Additional mazdoor	0.10	0.10	0.10	0.10
(iv)	(a) Removing excavated material upto 50 m from the spoil heap including loading, unloading and depositing	1 cub. m	Mazdoor	0.25	0.25	0.35	0.35
	(b) For each addition at 50 m or part thereof, add to the above (a).	1 cub. m	Additional mazdoor	0.05	0.05	0.1	0.1
(v)	Return fill including ramming the excavated material around the foundation	1 cub. m	Mazdoor	0.20	0.20	0.25	0.25
(vi)	Levelling, ramming bottom of foundation	1 sq. m	Mazdoor	0.03	0.03	0.03	0.03
2.	**Concreting (mixing)**		Mason	Mazdoor	Bhisti		Bullock with driver
(i)	Lime concrete						
	(a) For mixing	cub. m			1.20	0.25	0.12
(ii)	(b) For laying in foundation	1 cub. m	0.15	1.50	0.05		–
	P.C.C.						
	(a) Hand mixing	1 cub. m	–	0.85	0.10		–
	(b) Mixing by machine	1 cub. m	–	0.3	0.10		–

... Contd.

3.	**Placing the concrete (P.C.C. or R.C.C.) in position**						
(i)	P.C.C. to be laid in foundation	1 cub. m	0.15	1.50	0.60		
(ii)	R.C.C. in foundations	1 cub. m	0.18	1.50	0.60		
(iii)	R.C.C. in slab	1 cub. m	0.25	2.50	0.80		
(iv)	R.C.C. in beam	1 cub. m	0.55	2.22	0.60		
(v)	R.C.C. in column	1 cub. m	1.15	2.1	0.60		
(vi)	Lintels	1 cub. m	1.20	2.1	0.60		
(vii)	R.C.C. in staircases	1 cub. m	1.20	2.75	0.60		
(viii)	R.C.C. in walls	1 cub. m	0.90	1.75	0.60		
4.	**Form work for concrete**		**Mazdoor and Carpenter**				
(i)	Slabs	sq. m		0.22			
(ii)	Walls	sq. m		0.20			
(iii)	Lintels	sq. m		0.30			
(iv)	Beams	sq. m		0.45			
(v)	Columns	sq. m		0.45			
(vi)	Staircases	sq. m		0.45			
5.	**Brick work** **(A) Mixing Mortar**						Bullock with driver
(i)	Mud mortar			0.70	0.30		
(ii)	Lime mortar (of any proportion)	1 cub. m		1.00	0.20		0.12 –
(iii)	Cement mortar (hand mix) of any proportion)	1 cub. m		0.90	0.12		
(iv)	Cement mortar (of any proportion machine mix)	1 cub. m		0.40	0.12	Mixer 0.08	Operator 0.08
	(B) Laying brick work (excluding required in mixing mortar)						
(i)	Brick work in mud mortar		Mason	Mazdoor	Bhisti		
	(a) In foundations and upto plinth	1 cub. m	0.65	1.65	0.2		
	(b) In superstructure (upto 3 m height above the plinth level)	1 cub. m	0.80	1.90	0.2		
(ii)	Brick work in lime mortar	1 cub. m					
	(a) In foundations and upto plinth	1 cub. m	0.80	1.7	0.20		
	(b) In superstructure upto 3 m above plinth	1 cub. m	0.95	1.90	0.20		

... Contd.

(iii)	Brick work in cement mortar						
	(a) In foundation and upto plinth	1 cub. m	0.82	1.70	0.20		
	(b) In superstructure upto 3 m above plinth	1 cub. m	0.95	1.90	0.20		
	Add extra for following brick work as follows :						
	(c) Brick work curved in plan, radius not exceeding 6.5 m	1 cub. m	0.25	0.50	–	–	
	(d) Hall brick work in walls	1 sq. m	0.20	0.20			
	(e) Arch work in brick	1 cub. m	0.40	0.30			
	(f) Raking joints and pointing (flush type) along with the brick work	1 sq. m	0.025	0.025			
	(g) Damp proof course (D.P.C.) 15 to 25 mm thick, in cement mortar exclusive of labour required in mortar mixing	1 sq. m	0.015	0.015	0.015		
	(h) Honey combed half brick work	1 sq. m	0.2	0.2	0.05		
	Additional labour for brick work above 3 m and upto 30 m						
			Multiplier				
	(i) 3 m to 12 m		1.00				
	(ii) 12 m to 18 m		1.20				
	(iii) 18 m to 24 m		1.30				
	(iv) 24 m to 30 m		1.40				
6.	**Stone masonry (excluding labour required for mortar mixing)**						
	(i) Random rubble masonry in foundations and plinth	1 cub. m	0.70	1.60			
	(ii) Random rubble masonry in superstructure	1 cub. m	0.80	2.00			
	(iii) Random rubble masonry brought upto courses	1 cub. m	1.00	1.70			
	(iv) Ashlar masonry	1 cub. m	3.00	0.90			

Note : The same multiplier used for brick work is to be adopted for additional heights of stone masonry.

Sr.	Description of item	Unit	Carpenter	Assistant
7N(A)	**Wood work**			
(i)	Scantlings (soft wood) clean sawn	1 cub. m	3.00	3.00
(ii)	Scantlings soft wood wrought	1 cub. m	6.0	6.0
(iii)	Scantlings (hard wood) clean sawn	1 cub. m	4.5	4.5
(iv)	Scantlings (hard wood) wrought	1 cub. m	9.00	9.00
(v)	Timber battens	per 10 m	0.4	0.20
7. (B)	**Wood work-joinery**			
	(i) Door and window frames (chowkat)	1 cub. m	12	6
	(ii) For panelled, glazed shutters etc.			
	(a) Soft wood	1 sq. m	1.4	0.25
	(b) Hard wood	1 sq. m	2.00	0.25

Sr.	Description of item	unit	Mason	Mazdoor	Polisher
No.	**Flooring**				
(i)	Shahabad stone flooring 30 mm thick	10 sq. m	0.8	1.30	–
(ii)	Cement tile or polished terrazo flooring	10 sq. m	1.90	1.90	4.5
(iii)	Tile flooring (white glazed)	10 sq. m	2.90	1.90	–
(iv)	P.C.C. flooring (10 mm thick)	10 sq. m	0.60	0.60	–
(v)	Lime concrete flooring	10 sq. m	0.4	0.4	–

Labour constants in days per 10 sq.m.

Sr.	Description	Unit	Mason	Mazdoor	Bhisti
No.	**Plastering and pointing**				
(i)	13 mm thick plaster for brick work and concrete surfaces	10 sq. m	0.45	1.20	0.4
(ii)	13 mm thick plaster for rubble masonry works	10 sq. m	0.75	1.20	0.4
(iii)	Rough cast cement plaster (on the previously rendered surface)	10 sq. m	0.7	0.5	0.3
(iv)	Plastering for ceiling (extra labour)	10 sq. m	0.2	0.1	
(v)	Pointing to brick work				
	(a) Struck	10 sq. m	1.1	0.50	
	(b) Flush	10 sq. m	0.70	0.50	
	(c) Keyed or ruled	10 sq. m	0.96	0.50	
(vi)	Pointing to uncoursed (random rubble) masonry				
	(a) Tuck	10 sq. m	0.90	0.50	
	(b) Struck	10 sq. m	0.70	0.50	
(vii)	Pointing to Ashlar work	10 sq. m	0.60	0.30	

... Contd.

10.	White washing, colour washing, distempering				
(a)	Brooming i.e. preparation of surface to be plastered	10 sq. m	–	0.025	
(b)	First coat white washing or colour washing	10 sq. m.	Lime water 0.065	0.035	
(c)	First coat white washing or colour washing for each subsequent coats	10 sq. m	0.05	0.025	
(d)	Distempering		Painter	Mazdoor	
	(i) First coat	10 sq. m	0.25	0.05	
	(ii) Subsequent coats	10 sq. m	0.13	0.03	
(e)	Dry distemper (washable) first coat subsequent coat	10 sq. m	0.25	0.06	
(f)	Oil bond distemper first coat,	10 sq. m	0.28	0.065	
	Subsequent coat		0.22	0.05	
(g)	Snowcem i.e. water proof cement paint first coat,	10 sq. m	0.35	0.15	0.15
	subsequent coat		0.25	0.12	0.15
(h)	Painting to steel or wood work	10 sq. m	Painter		
	Prime coat	10 sq. m	0.35		
	Subsequent coat	10 sq. m	0.40		
(i)	Varnishing	10 sq. m	0.60		
			Polisher		
(j)	French polishing	10 sq. m	0.55		

6.8 COMPUTATIONS OF QUANTITIES OF MATERIALS REQUIRED FOR VARIOUS ITEMS OF WORKS

6.8.1 Plain Cement Concrete (P.C.C.)

The materials required for preparation of cement concrete are cement, sand (i.e. fine aggregates) and ballast (i.e. coarse aggregates) which are to be mixed in the predetermined proportion. The voids in the coarse aggregates are filled by fine aggregates and that in the fine aggregates are filled by cement paste (i.e. cement and water). Thus the wet volume of the cement concrete (i.e. when water is added to the dry cement concrete mix) will always be less than its corresponding dry volume (i.e. sum total volume of each of ingredient added together). It has been observed that in order to prepare 1 cub. m of wet cement concrete, the corresponding dry volume required is about 1.52 cub. m. Knowing the mix of the cement concrete (i.e. 1 : 4 : 8 or 1 : 3 : 6 or 1 : 2 : 4 etc.) the ingredient materials required can be determined as follows :

To determine the materials required for 1 cub. m of (wet) concrete of 1 : 4 : 8 proportion, the dry volume of concrete required will be 1.52 cub. m (which shrinks to 1 cub. m after addition of water to it).

$$\therefore \quad \text{Quantity of cement required} = \frac{1.52}{1 + 4 + 8} = \frac{1.52}{13} = 0.117 \text{ cub. m.}$$

As 1 cub. m of cement is equivalent to 30 bags of cement (each bag weighing 50 kg).

The quantity of cement required = 0.117×30 = 3.51 bags ≈ 3.50 bags.

Similarly quantity of sand required = $\left(\dfrac{1.52}{1 + 4 + 8}\right) \times 4$ = 0.468 cub. m ≈ 0.47 cub. m.

and quantity of course aggregate required = $\dfrac{1.52}{1 + 4 + 8} \times 8$ = 0.936 cub. m ≈ 0.94 cub. m.

The following table gives the quantities of materials required for cement concrete of various proportion (i.e. mix) by volume.

Unit : 1 Cubic Metre

Sr. No.	Proportion of mix on volumetric basis	Cement	Fine aggregates or sand	Coarse aggregate or ballast
1.	1 : 1.5 : 3	8.4 bags	0.42 cub. m	0.84 cub. m
2.	1 : 2 : 4	6.6. bags	0.44 cub. m	0.88 cub. m
3.	1 : 3 : 6	4.5 bags	0.45 cub. m	0.90 cub. m
4.	1 : 4 : 8	3.5 bags	0.47 cub. m	0.94 cub. m
5.	1 : 5 : 10	2.85 bags	0.475 cub. m	0.95 cub. m

6.8.2 Reinforcement for Reinforced Cement Concrete

It is usual practice to express the steel required for reinforced cement concrete as percentage of volume of concrete e.g. 1 % steel in R.C.C. slab indicates that the quantity of steel required will be equal to the 1 % of the volume of concrete i.e. for every one square metre sectional area of the slab cut, there will be 0.01 sq.m of steel bar utilised.

As the steel weighs 7830 kg per cubic metre, the 1 % steel reinforcement means there will be 78 kg of steel per cubic metre of volume of concrete.

The values of usual percentage of steel assumed for various items will be as shown below.

Sr. No.	Item	Percentage of steel (By volume of concrete)
1.	Slab	0.9 to 1.5 %
2.	Foundations	0.5 to 1 %
3.	Walls	1 to 2 %
4.	Columns	1 to 3 %
5.	Lintels, beams	1.5 to 3 %

The quintal of binding wire for reinforced steel is usually assumed as 1 to 1.3 kg per quintal of steel reinforcement. Due allowance is to be made for wastage of steel which is 5 to 10 %.

6.8.3 Main Brick Work in Superstructure

In order to calculate the quantities of materials required for brick work in cement mortar, it is necessary to decide the size of the bricks to be used in the masonry.

The size of the conventional or traditional bricks vary from $8\frac{3}{4}" \times 3\frac{3}{16}" \times 2\frac{5}{8}"$

(i.e. 22.23 cm × 10.64 cm × 6.67 cm) to $9" \times 4\frac{1}{2}" \times 3"$ (i.e. 22.86 cm × 11.43 cm × 7.62 cm).

The new I.S. size brick i.e. modular brick is actual 19 cm × 9 cm × 9 cm with a frog of 10 cm × 4 cm × 1 cm size. Normally, the mortar joint is taken as 1 cm throughout, therefore, the nominal size of brick will be 20 cm × 10 cm × 10 cm.

∴   Volume of one I.S. size brick, with thickness of joint as 1 cm

$$= 0.20 \times 0.1 \times 0.1 = 0.002 \text{ cub. m}$$

∴   For 1 cubic metre of brick work, the total number of I.S. size (i.e. modular) bricks required

$$= \frac{1 \text{ cub. m}}{0.002} = 500 \text{ Nos.}$$

∴   Adding 5% towards wastage = 25

∴   Total number of I.S. bricks required = 525 nos.

Now,

$$\begin{pmatrix} \text{Quantity or volume of} \\ \text{wet mortar required} \end{pmatrix} = \begin{pmatrix} \text{Total volume of} \\ \text{brick work} \end{pmatrix} - \begin{pmatrix} \text{Volume occupied} \\ \text{by 500 bricks} \\ \text{of 19 cm} \times \text{9 cm} \times \text{9 cm size} \end{pmatrix}$$

$$= [1 - 500 \times 0.19 \times 0.09 \times 0.09] \text{ cub. m}$$

$$= 1 - 0.7695 = 0.2305 \text{ cub. m.}$$

In order to allow for mortar for filling the frog, bonding and wastage during its use, 10% is to be added.

∴   Volume of wet mortar required   = $0.2305 + 0.10 \times 0.2305$

                                                        = 0.253 cub. m

∴   Dry volume of mortar required   = 1.25×0.253

                                                        = $0.316 \approx 0.30$

i.e. Approximately for 1 cubic metre of brick work, 30 % of the dry mortar will be required.

Calculations of materials for 1 cub. m of brick work in C. M. (1 : 6) with traditional size bricks 9" × 4.375" × 2.75" (i.e. 22.86 cm × 11.11 cm × 6.985 cm.)

Assuming thickness of joint as 1 cm throughout, the nominal size of traditional bricks = 23.86 cm × 12.11 cm × 7.985 cm.

∴   Volume of one traditional size brick with 1 cm as thickness of joint

$$= (0.2386 \times 0.1211 \times 0.07985) \text{ cub. m} = 0.002307 \text{ cub. m}$$

Number of traditional bricks required for 1 cub. m of brick work	$= \dfrac{1}{0.002307}$	= 433 Nos.
Add 5% towards wastage	= 22	
∴ Total number of traditional bricks required	= 455 nos.	
Now, $\left(\begin{array}{c}\text{Value of wet}\\ \text{mortar required}\end{array}\right)$	$= 1 - 433 \times (0.2286 \times 0.1111 \times 0.06985)$	
	= 1 − 0.77	
	= 0.23 cub. m which is practically same as derived above	
∴ Adding 10 % extra for wastage	= 0.023 cub. m	
∴ Wet volume of mortar required	= 0.253 cub. m	
∴ Dry volume required	= 1.25 (wet volume)	
	$= 1.25 \times 0.253$	
	= 0.316 cub. m	
	≈ 0.30 cub. m	

i.e. approximately 30 % of dry volume of mortar is required for constructing 1 cub. m of brick work. Further, knowing the proportion of cement mortar the quantities of cement (in bags) and sand can be worked out as usual.

e.g. knowing the proportion of the cement mortar the quantities of cement and sand required can be determined as follows.

For cement mortar (1 : 6) proportion,

$$\begin{pmatrix} \text{Quantity of cement} \\ \text{required} \end{pmatrix} = \frac{\text{Dry volume of mortar}}{1 + 6} = \frac{0.316}{7}$$

$$= 0.045 \text{ cub. m} = 0.045 \times 30$$

$$= 1.35 \text{ bags of cement}$$

and $$\begin{pmatrix} \text{Quantity of sand} \\ \text{required} \end{pmatrix} = \frac{0.316}{7} \times 6 = 0.2708 \text{ cub. m}$$

$$\approx 0.27 \text{ cub. m}$$

Approximate method :

The above quantities can be determined by an approximate method as follows :

For 1 cubic metre of brick work divide 0.3 by the sum of the proportion of the material to obtain the quantity of cement in cubic metre

i.e. quantity of cement required $\frac{0.3}{1 + 6} = \frac{0.3}{7} = 0.043$ cubic m.

But as certain amount of cement will be required to fill the voids in the sand, add 0.002 cubic metre extra

∴　　　　Quantity of cement required $= 0.043 + 0.002$

$$= 0.045 \text{ cub. m which is same as above}$$

∴　　Number of cement bags required $= 0.045 \times 30 = 1.35$ bag

and Quantity of sand required $= 0.045 \times 6 = 0.27$ cub. metre

6.8.4 10 cm Thick Brick Work in Partition Walls in Cement Mortar (1 : 4)

In order to calculate the quantities of cement and sand required for 10 cm thick brick partition wall, with I.S. size (i.e. modular) bricks, the procedure would be as follows.

Considering 10 sq. m area of the brick work to be constructed with 10 cm thick wall.

The quantity of brick work in partition $= 10 \times \frac{10}{100} = 1$ cub. m.

∴　　Number of bricks required (considering the thickness of joints on 10 cm)

$$= \frac{1.00}{0.20 \times 0.1 \times 0.1}$$

$$= 500$$

Adding 5 % extra for wastage $= 25$

∴　　　　Total number of bricks $= 525$

∴　　Quantity of mortar required $= (10 \times 0.1) - 500 (0.19 \times 0.9 \times 0.9)$

$$= 1 - 0.77 = 0.23$$

Adding 10 % extra for frog, bonding, wastage etc.

$$= 0.023$$

∴ Wet volume of mortar required $= 0.253$ cub. m

∴   Dry volume required $= 1.25 \times 0.253 = 0.316$ cub. m

$$\approx 0.30 \text{ cub. m}$$

i.e. for 10 sq. m area of brick work of thickness 10 cm, the quantity of dry mortar required = 0.3 cub. m

Further, knowing the proportion of mix, the quantities of cement and sand can be found out by dividing the total quantity of dry volume of mortar by the sum of the numerical figures of the proportion or mix of the mortar and then multiplying it by the individual numerals.

6.8.5 Plastering

To determine the quantity of cement (or lime) and sand, required for plastering unit square metre of the area of various thickness is to work out the volume of mortar required per sq. m of plaster by multiplying the area to be plastered by its thickness. In order to allow extra mortar for raked out joints, cavities, uneven surfaces, etc. the above worked out quantity is to be increased approximately by 30 %. Further to convert the wet volume of mortar into its corresponding dry volume it should further be increased by about 30 %. Then the quantities of cement and sand required can be determined by dividing the total dry volume of mortar by the sum of the numerical figures of proportion or mix of the mortar and multiplying it by the individual numerical figures.

e.g. To determine the quantities of cement and sand for 12 mm thick plaster in cement mortar (1 : 4) the procedure would be as follows:

Considering the area to be plastered as 10 sq.m, with a thickness of 12 mm, the quantity of wet mortar required

$$= 10 \text{ (sq. m)} \times \frac{1.2}{100} \text{ (m)}$$

$$= 0.12 \text{ cub. m}$$

∴ Adding 30 % extra for filling joints, and uneven surface etc., quantity of wet mortar required = 0.12 + 0.3 (0.12).

$$= 0.156 \text{ cub. m}$$

∴ Quantity of dry mortar required $= 0.156 + 0.3 (0.156)$

$$= 0.156 + 0.0468$$

$$= 0.2028 \text{ cub. m}$$

Further, allowing for wastage etc.

The total quantity of dry mortar required = 0.203 cub. m.

$$\therefore \qquad \text{Quantity of cement required} \quad = \frac{0.203}{1+4} = 0.041 \text{ cub. m}$$

$$= 0.042 \times 30 = 1.23 \text{ bags}$$

$$\text{and} \qquad \text{Quantity of sand required} \quad = \frac{0.203}{1+4} \times 4 = 0.162 \text{ cub. m}$$

Approximate method

The approximate method of determining the volume of dry mortar required is to multiply the quantity of wet mortar required by a factor 1.8.

$$\text{i.e. volume of wet mortar required} = 0.12 \text{ cub. m}$$

$$\therefore \qquad \text{Volume of dry mortar required} = 0.12 \times 1.8$$

$$= 0.216 \text{ cub. m}$$

$$\therefore \qquad \text{Quantity of cement required} \quad = \frac{0.216}{1+4} = 0.043 \text{ cub. m}$$

$$= 0.043 \times 30 = 1.29$$

$$\approx 1.3 \text{ bags}$$

$$\text{and} \qquad \text{quantity of sand required} \quad = \frac{0.216}{1+4} \times 4 = 0.0.173 \text{ cub. m}$$

which is same as determined above.

Neeru finish coat of 1.5 mm thickness.

If the inside face is to be plastered further with a Neeru finish of 1.5 mm thickness then the quantity of Neeru required for 10 sq.m surface

$$= 10 \text{ (sq. m)} \times \frac{1.5}{1000} \text{ (m)}$$

$$= 0.015 \text{ cub. m}$$

i.e. $\qquad 0.015 \times 30 = 0.45 \text{ bags}$

i.e. $\qquad \approx 0.5 \text{ bags of Neeru}$

which is available as "Sagol' or 'Sunala' as brand name in the market.

6.8.6 Pointing

The volume of dry mortar required for pointing depends upon the type of surface i.e. either brick work or masonry work.

For pointing (which may be flush, struck or keyed) to the brick work, the dry volume of mortar, including wastage, required for 10 sq. m area is about 0.036 cub. m, and for random rubble masonry it is 0.076 cub. m. Thus knowing the proportion of the mix of the mortar say 1 : 3 the quantity of cement and sand can be found out as follows :

- For pointing to brick work

$$\text{Volume of cement required} \quad = \frac{0.036}{1 + 3} = 0.009 \text{ cub. m}$$

$$= 0.009 \times 30$$

$$= 0.270 \text{ bags}$$

and $$\text{volume of sand required} \quad = \frac{0.036}{1 + 3} \times 3 = 0.027 \text{ cub. m}$$

- For pointing to random or coursed rubble masonry, the volume of dry mortar required = 0.076 cub. m

∴   For pointing in cement mortar (1 : 3) proportion,

$$\text{the quantity of cement required} \quad = \frac{0.076}{1 + 3} = 0.019 \text{ cub. m}$$

$$= 0.019 \times 30 = 0.57 \text{ bags of cement}$$

$$\approx 0.60 \text{ bags}$$

$$\text{and quantity of mortar required} \quad = \frac{0.076}{1 + 3} \times 3 = 0.057 \text{ cub. m}$$

6.8.7 Floor Finishes

Item : Plain cement tiles 20 mm thick over cement mortar (1 : 6) screeding, including cement float etc.

The quantities of plain cement tiles, cement and sand required for flooring 10 sq. m area will be determined as follows :

- Plain cement tiles including 5% wastage = 10.5 sq. m
- Quantity of mortar for screeding, assuming 20 mm thickness

$$= 10 \text{ (sq. m)} \times \frac{2}{1000} \text{ (m)} = 0.2 \text{ cubic metre}$$

$$\left(\begin{array}{l} \text{Quantity of dry mortar required} \\ \text{to allow for shrinkage, wastage etc.} \end{array} \right) = 1.3 \times 0.2 = 0.26$$

∴   Quantity of cement required for (1 : 6) proportion

$$= \frac{0.26}{1 + 6} = 0.037 \text{ cub. metre}$$

or $$= 0.037 \times 30$$

$$= 1.11 \text{ bags of cement} \qquad \text{... (i)}$$

and quantity of cement required for float, assuming, 1.5 mm thickness

$$= 10 \times 0.0015$$

$$= 0.015 \text{ cub. m}$$

$$= 0.015 \times 30 = 0.45 \text{ bags of cement} \qquad \text{... (ii)}$$

∴   Total quantity of cement required

$$= (i) + (ii)$$

$$= 1.11 + 0.45 = 1.56 \text{ bags}$$

and quantity of sand required $= \dfrac{0.26}{1 + 6} \times 6 = 0.222 \text{ cub. m} \approx 0.25 \text{ cub. m}$

6.8.8 Mangalore Tiled Roof

To calculate the number of Mangalore tiles and battens required to cover an area of 10 sq.m.

$$\text{Size of Mangalore tiles} = 41 \text{ cm} \times 24 \text{ cm}$$

and it can cover an area of 32 cm × 21 cm.

∴ $\left(\begin{array}{c} \text{Area covered by one tile} \\ \text{with overlap} \end{array} \right) = 32 \text{ cm} \times 21 \text{ cm}$

$$= 0.32 \times 0.21 \text{ sq. m}$$

$$= 0.672 \text{ sq. m}$$

∴   Total number of tiles required $= \dfrac{\text{Area to be covered}}{\text{Area of one tile with overlap}}$

$$= \dfrac{10}{0.0672} = 148.81 \approx 149 \text{ Nos.}$$

$$\text{Length of the ridge tile} = 40 \text{ cm}$$

The size of teak wood battens is equal to 5 cm × 2.5 cm and are usually fixed at 30 cm centre to centre.

Therefore the length of the battens required = 36 m

6.9 INCREASE IN RATES OR PRICES FOR ADDITIONAL FLOORS

Note : For items of construction of superstructure of a building, the prices (i.e. rates) are to be increased for subsequent floor as more effort is required for transporting material to subsequent floors :

Sr. No.	Floor Level	Percentage price increase
1.	Ground and first floors	No increase
2.	Second floor	1 % increase
3.	Third floor	2 % increase
4.	Fourth floor	3 % increase
5.	For every additional floor	1 % increase

The above increase in price shall be over the ground floor rates only.

6.10 WATER CHARGES

The water charges @ 1 % is to be considered for the items of construction that need water for the completion of that time.

e.g. P.C.C. in foundations, brick work in superstructure in cement mortar etc.

6.11 REQUIREMENT OF CEMENT IN BAGS FOR VARIOUS COMMON ITEMS OF CONSTRUCTION

Sr. No.	Item of Work		Cement required in bags	Unit
I.	**Plain cement concrete (P.C.C.)**			
1.	P.C.C.	1 : 5 : 10	2.65 bags	cub. m
2.	P.C.C.	1 : 4 : 8	3.40 bags	cub. m
3.	P.C.C.	1 : 3 : 6	4.40 bags	cub. m
4.	P.C.C.	1 : 2 : 4	6.25 bags	cub. m
II.	**Reinforcement cement concrete (R.C.C.)**			
5.	R.C.C.	(1 : 2 : 4) (i.e. M-15)	6.25 bags	cub. m
6.	R.C.C.	(1 : 1.5 : 3) (i.e. M-20)	8.00 bags	cub. m
7.	R.C.C.	(i.e. M-25)	11.2 bags	cub. m
III.	**Stone masonry**			
8.	U.C.R stone masonry in cement mortar (1 : 6)		1.75 bags	cub. m
9.	C.R. stone masonry in cement mortar (1 : 6)		1.60 bags	cub. m
10.	C.R. stone masonry in cement mortar (1 : 5)		1.80 bags	cub. m
IV.	**Brick masonry or brick work**			
11.	Burnt brick masonry in cement mortar (1 : 8)		1.12 bags	cub. m
12.	Burnt brick masonry in cement mortar (1 : 6)		1.45 bags	cub. m
13.	Half brick work in cement mortar (1 : 3)		0.23 bags	sq. m
V.	**Damp proof course (D.P.C.)**			
14.	D.P. course 5 cm thick in cement mortar (1 : 2 : 4)		0.36 bags	sq. m
15.	Terrace slab 2 cm thick in cement mortar (1 : 3)		0.20 bags	sq. m
VI.	**Plastering the surface**			
16.	6 mm thick cement mortar (1 : 3) internal plaster (single coat)		0.07 bags	m^2
17.	6 mm thick cement mortar (1 : 4) internal plaster (single coat)		0.045 bags	m^2
18.	12 mm thick cement mortar (1 : 3) plaster (single coat)		0.15 bags	m^2
19.	12 mm thick cement mortar (1 : 4) plaster (single coat)		0.11 bags	m^2
20.	12 mm thick cement mortar (1 : 5) plaster (single coat)		0.095 bags	m^2
21.	Rough cast cement mortar (1 : 4) plaster in two coats, 25 mm thick		0.22 bags	m^2

VII.   Pointing work

22.	Flush groove type pointing in cement mortar (1 : 3) for brick work	0.03 bags	m²
23.	Flush groove type pointing in cement mortar (1 : 3) for stone masonry	0.026 bags	m²
24.	Veer pointing in cement mortar (1 : 3) for stone masonry	0.031 bags	m²
25.	Weathered pointing in cement mortar (1 : 3) for stone masonry.	0.041 bags	m²

VIII.   Flooring etc.

26.	25 mm thick rough/polishing Shahabad stone flooring on a cement mortar (1 : 6) bed and cement mortar pointing (1 : 3)	0.136 bags	m²
27.	Skirting and Dado of (polished) Shahabad stone 25 mm thick in cement mortar (1 : 4)	0.185 bags	m²
28.	Plain cement tiles 25 mm × 25 mm on a cement mortar (1 : 6) bed for flooring	0.15 bags	m²
29.	Skirting and Dado of plain cement tiles in cement mortar (1 : 4)	0.185 bags	m²
30.	Coloured tiles (25 mm × 25 mm)	0.15 bags	m²
31.	Skirting and Dado of coloured tiles	0.18 bags	m²
32.	Marble mosaic tiles 10 mm thick		
	(a) in white cement	0.135 bags	m²
	(b) in grey cement	0.21 bags	m²
33.	Polished Shahabad stone 25 mm thick tread and riser of stair-case	0.185 bags	m²

6.12 APPROXIMATE RATES OF MATERIALS OF CONSTRUCTION

The rates mentioned below have been taken from D.S.R. – P.W.D [Mumbai Region] for **year 2015-2016**. These rates have been used for analysis of rates of various items carried out in this chapter. For current DSR. Please visit www.matrapwd.com.

Sr. No.	Name of the material	Rate (₹)	Unit
1.	A.C. plain sheet 6 mm thick	162.00	m²
2.	A.C. sheet ridge	183.00	pair
3.	Aggregate 10 mm and below	780.00	m³
4.	Aggregate 20 mm to 6 mm	780.00	m³
5.	Aggregate 25 cm to 40 mm	765.00	m³
6.	Aluminium paint	460.00	litre
7.	Barbed wire	76.00	kg
8.	Binding wire	67.00	kg
9.	Bitumen-bulk (80/100 grade)	42012.00	M.T.
10.	Bitumen-bulk (60/70 grade)	43038.00	M.T.
11.	Black kadappa – 35 mm thick	443.00	m²
12.	Boiled linseed oil (double boiled)	105.00	litre
13.	Boundary stone 75 × 20 × 15 cm	389.00	No.
14.	Brick bats	239.00	m³
15.	Bricks (I class)	6.50	No.
16.	Bricks (II class)	6.00	No.
17.	Bricks aggregate (20 to 40 mm)	340.00	m³
18.	C.C. 1 : 4 : 8	3639.00	m³
19.	C.C. septic tank, 1.2 m dia (2.5 m) L	10500.00	No.
20.	C.I. manhole cover – 75 kg	2546.00	No.
21.	Cement	300.00	Bag [50 kg]
22.	Cement [White]	1060.00	Bag [50 kg]
23.	Chicken proof mesh	46.00	m²
24.	Coal tar	23.00	kg
25.	Colour wash basin 55 × 40 cm	1133.00	No.
26.	Decorative ply veneer – 4 mm thick	487.00	m²
27.	Epoxy water proof paint	410.00	litre
28.	Sand [Crushed]	1000.00	m³
29.	Sand [Natural]	1400.00	m³
30.	Glass – 5 mm thick	420.00	m²
31.	Granite (16-20 mm)	2839.00	m²
32.	Green marble	874.00	m²
33.	Kadappa stone both sides polished 25 mm thick	480.00	m²
34.	Kota stone (machine cut) 25 mm thick	483.00	m²
35.	Lime (unslaked)	15.00	kg
36.	M.S. angle 50 × 50 × 6 mm	43.00	kg

...Contd

37.	M.S. plate	43.00	kg
38.	Mangalore ridge/Hip tiles	25.00	No.
39.	Mangalore tiles class "AA"	25.00	No.
40.	Vitrified tiles [Matt finish 2 ft × 2 ft]	869.00	m^2
41.	Mild steel	38500.00	M.T.
42.	TMT FE - 500	40500.00	M.T.
43.	Nails	63.00	kg
44.	Nerru/Sanala	6.00	kg
45.	Water bound distemper	71.00	kg
46.	Oil paint [Ready Mixed]	225.00	litre
47.	Plywood 12 mm thick	487.00	m^2
48.	Plywood 9 mm thick	389.00	m^2
49.	Polished Shahabad 25-30 mm thick	242.00	m^2
50.	Primer for plaster surface	105.00	litre
51.	Rolling shutter	1820.00	m^2
52.	Rubble stone (blasted)	300.00	m^3
53.	Steel primer	116.00	litre
54.	T.W. batten 50 × 25 mm	63.00	R.M.
55.	Tor steel [HYSD]	39000.00	M.T.
56.	High Tensile Steel	169000.00	M.T.
57.	Varnish	113.00	litre
58.	W.C. pan 68 CM I[st] class (Orissa)	1329.00	No.
59.	Oil bound distemper	103.00	kg

6.13 APPROXIMATE RATES OF EQUIPMENT / MACHINERY REQUIRED FOR WORKS [2015-2016 : PUNE]

Sr. No.	Machinery rates	Rate (₹)	Unit
1.	Air compressor	752.00	Hour
2.	Bitumen pressure sprayer	211.00	M.T.
3.	Boring machine for core sample	6215.00	R.M.
4.	Boring machine without core	3110.00	R.M.
5.	Cart on hire with driver	1120.00	Day
6.	Chain and pulley	226.00	Day
7.	Concrete mixer [Reversible with SCADA]	545.00	Hour
8.	Drum mix plant [with SCADA]	4220.00	Hour
9.	Electrical drill machine	239.00	Day

...Contd.

10.	Excavator/300 ck H.P. 51	4536.00	Hour
11.	Guniting gun	310.00	Hour
12.	Hot mix mini plant	1216.00	Hour
13.	Rent of generator set 33 kVA	584.00	Hour
14.	Road roller [8 to 10 tonnes]	690.00	Hour
15.	Self propelled paver finishes	1460.00	Hour
16.	Tile polishing machine	680.00	Day
17.	Tractor with trolley	457.00	Hour
18.	Truck (7.5 M.T.)	57.20	km
19.	Vibrator [Electrical]	157.00	Hour
20.	Water pump – 15 H.P.	227.00	Hour
21.	Welding machine	336.00	Day
22.	Winch or Hoist	2640.00	Day

6.14 TRANSPORTATION OF MATERIAL AND ITS COST

6.14.1 Introduction

Various material required for the construction of the structure is to be carried to the work site. For short distances usually bullock carts are used whereas for long distances trucks are to be used. The capacity of bullock carts is about 1 tonne whereas trucks can carry a load of 3 to 8 tonnes depending upon the size of the truck used.

6.14.2 Transportation of Materials by Truck (or Vehicles)

The cost of transportation of material by truck (i.e. vehicle) depends upon the following :

- The maximum load the vehicle can safely carry.
- Distance to which the material is to be transported.
- Cost of hire charges of the vehicle.
- (Average) speed of the vehicle.
- Labour required for loading and unloading the material.
- Average number of trips in a day of 8 working hours.
- Cost of fuel (i.e. petrol or diesel) and oil required.
- Time required for checking, octroi post etc.

The speed of the vehicle usually varies directly with the distance to be travelled. A speed of about 10 km/hour is assumed for a lead of 10 km, with an increase of 0.5 km/hour for every additional lead of 1 km.

The total number of trips (denoted by N) in a working day of 8 hours is determined as follows :

$$\text{Number of trips } = N = \left\{ \frac{\text{Number of working hours per day}}{\frac{2L}{S} + \frac{T}{60}} \right\} = \left\{ \frac{8}{\frac{2L}{S} + \frac{T}{60}} \right\}$$

where,
- L = Distance to be travelled i.e. lead (one way) in km
- S = Average speed of the vehicle in km/hour
- T = Time measured in minutes for loading, unloading, checking and at octroi post etc. which is usually assumed as 60 minutes for the entire operation.

$$\therefore \quad N = \left\{ \frac{8}{\frac{2L}{S} + 1} \right\}$$

Thus after calculating the total number of trips, the total distance covered for to and fro (i.e. both ways) in km.

= 2 NL + parking i.e. travel from parking place to work and back, which is usually assumed as 6 km.

= (2NL + 6) kilometers.

The average speed of the vehicle may be assumed as 25 to 30 km/hour.

Thus knowing the total distance covered (i.e. 2 NL + 6), the cost of fuel and oil consumed can be worked out. Thus the total cost of the transporting and the total quantities of material transported can be found out. Generally, the cost of hiring a truck of 7.5 to 8 tonnes capacity is assumed as ₹ 400/per day (inclusive of all expenses including driver, cleaner, fuel, oil, etc. complete); or the contract may be on the rate per unit rate of material transported. Usually, 6 workers are allowed to travel in a truck by Government Regional Transport Authorities for loading and unloading of materials. Usually, the rates or prices of items worked out are inclusive of initial lead of 5 km for all completed items of building construction.

For the lead charges of major items. e.g. earth, murum, lime, sand, coarse aggregates, cement, timber, steel, cement or concrete blocks, bamboos, bullies, A.C. sheets, bricks, roof tiles, C.I. or R.C.C. pipes etc. the statement 'C' published by the Government of Maharashtra under the **'Schedule of Rates'** for appropriate Public Works Region is to be referred. In the statement 'C' the cost of carriage of materials over distance exceeding 0.5 upto 200 km including labour for loading and unloading are even in a tabular form and cost per trip is specified in the last column (No. 14). The number of trips that will be done by a truck per day of 8 hours is to be calculated by the formula given below.

$$\text{Number of trips } = N = \left\{ \frac{8}{\frac{2L}{S} + \frac{T}{60}} \right\}$$

where
$$L = \text{Distance (one way) measured in km}$$
$$S = \text{Truck speed in km/hour}$$
$$T = \text{Time consumed in loading, unloading and}$$
$$\text{at check posts, toll post, etc. in minutes}$$

Assuming this T about 60 minutes,

$$\frac{T}{60} = \frac{60}{60} = 1$$

$\therefore$ Number of trips $= \left\{ \dfrac{8}{\dfrac{2L}{S} + 1} \right\}$

For all other minor or petty items the usual lead charges are assumed @ 1/2% of the cost of such item required for the completion of the work e.g. white cement putty etc. irrespective of distance to which they are transported or at 10 paise for the unit items.

6.14.3 Transportation of Material by Bullock Carts

Usually, the bullock carts are capable of transporting 1 tonne of material, the average speed being assumed as 3 km/hour including time required for loading and unloading of materials. Thus the number of trips that can be completed in a day of 8 working hours can be calculated by making use of the formula stated above and then the total quantity of material that can be carried per day and the total number of days required for transporting the entire material is found out.

Usually, the hire charges of bullock cart including the driver is assumed as ₹ 80 to 100 per day or the entire work of transporting may be alloted on the contract basis per unit of material transported by the bullock cart.

On and average a bullock cart may carry 1 tonne load when travelling at 3.5 km/hour.

Weight carrying capacities of other modes of transport

1.	Basket or Ghamela	0.015 m^3 per trip
2.	Wheel barrows	0.06 m^3 per trip
3.	Donkey load	0.08 m^3 per trip

A load of one tonne is equivalent

1.	Sand	0.675 m^3
2.	Coarse aggregates	0.60 m^3
3.	Stone	0.50 m^3
4.	Mangalore tiles	370 Nos. (average size)
5.	Bricks	325 Nos. (conventional size)
6.	Water	1000 lires (i.e. 1 m^3)
7.	Timber	1.3 m^3
8.	Flag stones (50 mm thick)	8 m^2
9.	Cement mortar	0.50 m^3
10.	Scaffolding poles (of average size)	About 36 to 40 Nos.

6.15 RATES SPECIFIED FOR VARIOUS CATEGORIES OF LABOURS IN BUILDING INDUSTRY

The wages as specified in the "Schedule of Rates" 2015-2016 of Public Works. Department – Pune Region of Government of Maharastra for the various categories (skilled, semi-skilled and unskilled etc.) of adult labour employed for 8.0 hrs/day in the building industry are as follows :

Sr. No.	Description of labour	Category	Wages (Rs/day)
1.	Bar bender	skilled	367.00
2.	Beldar	skilled	367.00
3.	Compressor operator	skilled	407.00
4.	Electrician	skilled	407.00
5.	Excavator (heavy)	unskilled	367.00
6.	Fitter IInd class with tools	skilled	384.00
7.	Gunman for guiniting	skilled	384.00
8.	Helper	unskilled	367.00
9.	Labour for Excavator heavy rock (unblast)	unskilled	367.00
10.	Mixer operator	skilled	407.00
11.	Mason/carpenter (IInd class)	skilled	384.00
12.	Mason/carpenter (I^{st} class)	skilled	407.00
13.	Mazdoor	unskilled	367.00
14.	Painter – I^{st} class	skilled	384.00
15.	Painter – IInd class	skilled	384.00
16.	White washer	semi-skilled	367.00
17.	Plumber with tools	skilled	407.00
18.	Polishman	semi-skilled	384.00
19.	Skilled labour	skilled	384.00
20.	Vibrator operator	skilled	384.00
21.	Watchman	skilled	367.00
22.	Welder/driller	skilled	407.00

6.16 ANALYSIS OF RATES OF PRINCIPLE ITEMS OF WORK IN BUILDING CONSTRUCTION

The analysis of rates of some of the principle items of work in building construction are worked out as follows. The rates worked out should not be taken as authority but shall be used for guidance. The actual rates of the items of the work may be slightly more or less than those worked out due to fluctuations in the rates of materials required for the completion of the item and also due to variation in the wages to be paid to the labourers and their out-turns. (The rates are for the year 1994-95)

The items of work for which the analysis of rates is worked out and entered in the 'Rate Analysis Sheet' are as follows :

Rates are for Year 2010 - 11

ANALYSIS OF RATE

6.16.1 For : Excavation for foundations in earthen soil including removal of excavated material to normal lead of 50 m and lift of 1.5 m, shoring, strutting, preparing the bed for foundations, dewatering and backfilling etc. complete.

Unit 1 cub. m.

Material	Quantity	Rate	Per	Amount	Labour	No.	Rate	Per	Amount
		Rs.		Rs.			Rs.		Rs.
For 1.0 m^3					For 1.0 m^3				
					1. Mazdoor for excavation and getting out	0.35	367.00	day	128.45
					2. Mazdoor for lead	0.25	367.00	day	91.75
					3. Mazdoor for back filling	0.20	367.00	day	73.40
Nil				NIL			Cost of labour per m^3 =		293.60
		Cost of material per m^3 =					Cost of material per m^3 =		NIL
							Total =		293.60

Add 10% for contractor's profit and overhead charges and 1/2% for T and P.

So, Total cost = 1.105×293.60 = **324.43 Rs./m^3**.

ANALYSIS OF RATE

6.16.2 For : Providing and laying P.C.C. [1 : 4 : 8] in foundations including bailing out of water manually, formwork, compaction, curing etc. complete.

Unit : 1 cub.m

Material	Quantity	Rate	Per	Amount
For 1.0 m³		Rs.		Rs.
1. Cement	3.5 bags	300.00	bag	1050.00
2. Sand [Crushed]	0.46 m³	1000.00	cub.m	460.00
3. Coarse aggregate [Stone metal 25-40 mm]	0.92 m³	725.00	cub.m	667.00
	Cost of material per m³ =			2177.00

Labour	No.	Rate	Per	Amount
For 1.0 m³		Rs.		Rs.
1. Mason – IInd class	0.15	384.00	day	57.60
2. Mazdoor	1.50	367.00	day	550.50
3. Bhisti	0.60	367.00	day	220.20
4. Concrete mixer with operator	0.10	2353.00	day	235.30
		Cost of labour per m³ =		1063.60
		Cost of material per m³ =		2177.00
			Total =	3240.60

Add 10% for contractor's profit and overhead charges and $1\frac{1}{2}$ % for water charges and $\frac{1}{2}$ % for T and P.

So, Total cost = 1.12×3240.60 = **3629.47 Rs./m³**

ANALYSIS OF RATE

6.16.3 For : Providing and laying uncoursed (Random) rubble masonry in cement in mortar (1 : 6) including watering. scaffolding etc. complete.

Note : For 1.0 m^3 of U.C.R., 0.49 m^3 of dry mortar is required.

So, for [1 : 6] cement mortar,   Cement $= \dfrac{0.49 \times 1}{1 + 6} = 0.07 \text{ m}^3 = 0.07 \times 30 = 2.1$ bags and

Sand $= 0.49 \times \dfrac{6}{7} = 0.42 \text{ m}^3$ will be required.

Unit : **1 cub.m**

Material	Quantity	Rate	Per	Amount		Labour	No.	Rate	Per	Amount
		Rs.		Rs.				Rs.		Rs.
For 1.0 m^3						For 1.0 m^3				
1. Cement	2.10 bags	300.00	bag	630.00		1. Mason – IInd class	1.00	384.00	day	384.00
2. Sand [Crushed]	0.42 m^3	1000.00	cub.m	420.00		2. Mazdoor	2.00	367.00	day	734.00
3. Rubble stone [blasted]	1.25 m^3	300.00	cub.m	375.00		3. Bhisti	0.20	367.00	day	734.00
		Cost of material per m^3 =		**1425.00**				Cost of labour per m^3 =		1191.40
								Cost of material per m^3 =		1425.00
									Total =	**2616.40**

Add 10% for contractor's profit and overhead charges $1\frac{1}{2}$ % for water charges and $\frac{1}{2}$ % for T and P.

So, Total cost $= 1.12 \times 2616.40 =$ **2930.37 Rs./m^3**

Note : For constructing stone wall of 1.0 m^3 volume, heap of stone of volume 1.25 m^3 is required, since stones kept in scattered/unarranged way will consume more volume as compared to properly constructed stone wall.

ANALYSIS OF RATE

6.16.4 For : Providing and laying coursed rubble masonry in superstructure in cement mortar (1 : 6) including watering, scaffolding etc. complete.

Note : For 1.0 m³ of coursed stone masonry, approximately 0.42 m³ of dry mortar is required.

So, for cement mortar (1 : 6),   Cement = $0.42 \times \dfrac{1}{1+6}$ = 0.06 m³ = 0.06 × 30 = 1.80 bags and

Sand = $0.42 \times \dfrac{6}{7}$ = 0.36 m³ will be required.

Unit : 1 cub.m

Material	Quantity	Rate	Per	Amount	Labour	No.	Rate	Per	Amount
For 1.0 m³		Rs.		Rs.	For 1.0 m³		Rs.		Rs.
1. Cement	1.80 bags	300.00	bag	540.00	1. Mason – IInd class	1.25	384.00	day	480.00
2. Sand [Crushed]	0.36 m³	1000.00	cub.m	360.00	2. Mazdoor	2.00	367.00	day	734.00
3. Trap metal/quartzite [40-50 mm]	1.25 m³	344.00	cub.m	430.00	3. Bhisti	0.20	367.00	day	73.40
	Cost of material per m³ =			1330.00					
					Cost of labour per m³ =				1287.40
					Cost of material per m³ =				1330.00
								Total =	2617.40

Add 10% for contractor's profit and overhead charges, $1\frac{1}{2}$ % for water charges and $\frac{1}{2}$ % for T and P.

So, Total cost = 1.12 × 2617.40 = **2931.49 Rs./m³**

ANALYSIS OF RATE

6.16.5 For : Providing 1st class brickwork in superstructure in cement mortar (1 : 6) with I.S. size bricks 19 cm × 9 cm × 9 cm including raking of joints, watering, scaffolding etc. complete.

Unit : 1 cub.m

	Material	Quantity	Rate	Per	Amount		Labour	No.	Rate	Per	Amount
	For 1.0 m³		Rs.		Rs.		For 1.0 m³		Rs.		Rs.
1.	Bricks [1st class]	525.00 No.	6.50	No.	3412.00	1.	Mason – II nd class	1.00	384.00	day	384.00
2.	Cement	1.35 bags	300.00	bag	405.00	2.	Mazdoor	2.00	367.00	day	734.00
3.	Sand [Crushed]	0.27 m³	1000.00	cub.m	270.00	3.	Bhisti	0.20	367.00	day	73.40
		Cost of material per m³ =			**4087.50**			Cost of labour per m³ =			1191.40
								Cost of material per m³ =			4087.50
										Total =	**5278.90**

Add 10% for contractor's profit and overhead charges, $1\frac{1}{2}$ % for water charges and $\frac{1}{2}$ % for T and P.

So, Total cost = 1.12 × 5278.90 = **5912.37 Rs./m³**

ANALYSIS OF RATE

6.16.6 For : Providing cast in situ R.C.C. work in beams, slabs etc. using M 20 concrete [1 : 1.5 : 3] excluding steel but including centering, shuttering, bending and binding.

Unit : 1 cub.m

Material	Quantity	Rate	Per	Amount	Labour	No.	Rate	Per	Amount
For 10.0 m³		Rs.		Rs.	For 10.0 m³		Rs.		Rs.
1. Cement	84.00 bags	300.0	bag	25200.00	1. Mason – IInd class	2.50	384.00	day	960.50
2. Sand [Crushed]	4.20 m³	1000.00	m³	4200.00	2. Mazdoor	25.0	367.00	day	9125.00
3. Aggregate [6-20 mm]	8.40 m³	780.00	m³	6552.00	3. Bhisti	8.00	367.00	day	2936.00
4. Binding wire [Binding wire @ 1 kg/quintal]	7.85 kg	67.00	kg	525.00	4. Conc. mixer with operator	1.00	2353.00	day	2353.00
					Bending, cracking and Binding steel in position				
					1. Barbender	8.00	367.00	day	2936.00
					2. Mazdoor	8.00	367.00	day	2936.00
					Provision of centering and shuttering				
					1. Timber planks & ballies	–	2000.00	day	2000.00
					2. Carpenter [IInd class]	10.00	367.00	day	3670.00
					3. Mazdoor	10.00	367.00	day	3670.00
		Cost of material per 10 m³ =		**36477.50**		Total cost of labour per 10 m³ =			**30586.00**

Total cost of material and labour = 36477.00 + 30586.00 = 67063 Rs. Add 10 % for contractor's profit and overhead charges, $1\frac{1}{2}$ % for water charges and $\frac{1}{2}$ % for T and P. So, Total cost = 1.12 × 67063.00 = **75111.00 Rs./10 m³**.

OR Total cost = **7511.00 Rs./m³** [Excluding steel]

ANALYSIS OF RATE

6.16.7 For : Providing cast in situ R.C.C. work in beams, slabs etc. using M 20 concrete [1 : 1.5 : 3] including steel along with centering, shuttering, bending and binding.

Unit : 1 cub.m

Material	Quantity	Rate Rs.	Per	Amount Rs.
For 10.0 m³				
1. Cement	84.0 bags	300.00	bag	25200.00
2. Sand [Crushed]	4.20 m³	1000.00	m³	4200.00
3. Aggregate [6-20 mm]	8.40 m³	780.00	m³	6552.00
4. Binding wire [@ 1 kg/quintal]	7.85 kg	67.00	kg	525.00
5. Steel @ 1 % of R.C.C. [By volume] $= \frac{1}{100} \times 10^3 = 0.10\ m^3$ = 785.0 kg	7850 kg/m³ × 0.10 m³ = 785.0 kg	39.00 [TOR Steel]	kg	30615.00
Cost of material per 10 m³ =				67092.00

Labour	No.	Rate Rs.	Per	Amount Rs.
For 10.0 m³				
1. Mason – IInd class	2.50	384.00	day	960.00
2. Mazdoor	25.0	367.00	day	9125.00
3. Bhisti	8.00	367.00	day	2936.00
4. Conc. mixer with operator	1.00	2353.00	day	2353.00
Bending, cracking and Binding steel in position				
1. Barbender	8.00	367.00	day	2936.00
2. Mazdoor	8.00	367.00	day	2936.00
Provision of centering and shuttering				
1. Timber planks and ballies	–	2000.00	day	2000.00
2. Carpenter [IInd class]	10.00	367.00	day	3670.00
3. Mazdoor	10.00	367.00	day	3670.00
Total cost of labour per 10 m³ =				30586.00

Total cost of material and labour = 67092.00 + 30586.00 = 97678.00 Rs. Add 10 % for contractor's profit and overhead charges, $1\frac{1}{2}$ % for water charges and $\frac{1}{2}$ % for T and P. So, Total cost = 1.12 × 69125.00 = 109399.00 Rs./10 m³.

OR Total cost = **10940.00 Rs./m³** [Including steel]

ANALYSIS OF RATE

6.16.8 For : Providing and fixing in position TOR steel reinforcement [HYSD STEEL] including bending, binding, hooking, wastage, laps etc. complete.

Unit : 1 tonne

Material	Quantity	Rate	Per	Amount	Labour	No.	Rate	Per	Amount
		Rs.		Rs.			Rs.		Rs.
For 1.0 tonne					For 1.0 tonne				
1. TOR steel bars [HYSD]	1.05 tonne	39000.00	Ton	40950.00	1. Bars bender	12	367.00	day	4404.00
2. Binding wire 1.63 mm φ	2.00 kg	67.00	kg	703.50	2. Mazdoor	12	367.00	day	4404.00
Binding wise @ 10 kg/ton [or 1 kg/quintal]	Total cost of material per ton =			41653.50	Total cost of labour per ton =				8808.00
					Total cost of material per ton =				41653.00
								Total =	50461.00

Add 10% for contractor's profit and overhead charges, $\frac{1}{2}$ % for T and P.

So, Total cost = 1.105 × 50461 = **55759.40 Rs./tonne**

ANALYSIS OF RATE

6.16.9 For : Providing & laying 2.50 cm thick cement concrete flooring using M 15 (1:2:4) concrete for 10 m² area.

Solution : For 2.5 cm thick cement concrete floor, for 10 m² area, the quantity of cement concrete = $10 \times 0.025 = 0.25$ m³.

Adding 10% for unevenness of base, so wet volume of concrete required = $1.1 \times 0.25 = 0.275$ m³

For dry volume of concrete, adding 52% more. So dry volume of concrete = $1.52 \times 0.275 = 0.418$ m³

For M 15 concrete, cement = $0.418 \times \dfrac{1}{(1+6)} = 0.06$ m³ = $0.06 ? \ 30 = 1.80$ bags

Sand = $0.06 \times 2 = 0.12$ m³, 　aggregate = $0.06 \times 4 = 0.24$ m³.

For neat surface finish, additional 0.02 m³ (0.6 bags) of cement will be required.

So total cement required = 2.4 bags.

Material	Quantity	Rate	Per	Amount
For 10.0 m²		Rs.		Rs.
1. Cement	2.40 bags	300.00	bag	720.00
2. Sand [Crushed]	0.12 m³	1000.00	m³	120.00
3. Aggregate [6-20 mm]	0.24 m³	780.00	m³	187.20
		Cost of material per 10 m² =		1027.20

Unit : 1 sq.m

Labour	No.	Rate	Per	Amount
For 10.0 m²		Rs.		Rs.
1. Mason [Ist class]	0.80	407.00	day	325.60
2. Mazdoor	1.20	367.00	day	440.40
3. Bhisti	0.20	367.00	day	73.40
	Cost of labour per 10 m² =			839.40
	Cost of material per 10 m² =			1027.20
			Total =	1866.60

Add 10% for contractor's profit and overhead charges, $1\frac{1}{2}$ % for water charges, $\frac{1}{2}$ % for T and P.

So, Total cost = $1.12 \times 1866.60 = $ **2090.59 Rs./10 m²** or **209.06 Rs./m²**

ANALYSIS OF RATE

6.16.10 For : Providing and laying vitrified tiles, over 20 mm thick cement mortar (1 : 6) for 10 m² area.

Solution : Vitrified tiles required = 10.5 m² (5 % wastage considered)

Volume of wet mortar for screeding, for 20 mm thickness = 10 m² × 0.02 m = 0.2 m³.

Volume of dry mortar required = 1.25 × 0.20 = 0.25 m³ [Adding 25% extra for shrinkage etc.]

Quantity of cement = $0.25 \times \dfrac{1}{7}$ = 0.036 m³ = 1.07 bags and sand = 0.036 × 6 = 0.21 m³.

Additional quantity of cement required for float, assuming 1.5 mm.

Thickness = 10 × 0.0015 = 0.015 m³ = 0.45 bags.

So, total quantity of cement required = 1.07 + 0.45 = 1.52 bags.

Unit : 1 sq.m

Material	Quantity	Rate	Per	Amount	Labour	No.	Rate	Per	Amount
		Rs.		Rs.			Rs.		Rs.
For 10.0 m²					For 10.0 m²				
1. Cement	1.52 bags	300.00	bag	456.00	1. Mason [1st class]	2.00	407.00	day	814.00
2. Sand [Crushed]	0.21 m³	1000.00	m³	210.00	2. Mazdoor	2.00	367.00	day	734.00
3. Vitrified tiles [Matt finish] [2 ft. × 2 ft.]	10.50 m²	869.00	m²	9124.50	3. Bhisti	0.20	367.00	day	73.40
	Cost of material per 10 m² =			9790.50		Cost of labour per 10 m² =			1621.40
						Cost of material per 10 m² =			9790.50
								Total =	11411.90

Add 10% for contractor's profit and overhead charges, $1\frac{1}{2}$ % for water charges, $\frac{1}{2}$ % for T and P.

So, Total cost = 1.12 × 11411.90 = **12781.33 Rs./10 m²** or **1278.13 Rs./m²**

ANALYSIS OF RATE

6.16.11 For : Providing 12 mm thick internal plastering in cement mortar (1 : 4) without neeru finish to concrete or brick surfaces including scaffolding and curing etc. complete.

Unit : 1 sq.m

	Material	Quantity	Rate	Per	Amount	Labour	No.	Rate	Per	Amount
			Rs.		Rs.			Rs.		Rs.
	For 10.0 m^2					For 10.0 m^2				
1.	Cement	1.26 bags	300.00	bag	378.00	1. Mason [1st class]	0.45	407.00	day	183.15
2.	Sand [Crushed]	0.17 m^3	1000.00	m^3	170.00	2. Mazdoor	1.20	367.00	day	440.40
						3. Bhisti	0.40	367.00	day	146.80
		Cost of material per 10 m^2 =			548.00		Cost of labour per 10 m^2 =				770.35
							Cost of material per 10 m^2 =			548.0
									Total =	1318.35

Add 10% for contractor's profit and overhead charges, $1\frac{1}{2}$ % for water charges, $\frac{1}{2}$ % for T and P.

So, Total cost = 1.12 × 1318.35 = **1476.55 Rs./10 m^2 = 147.65 Rs./m^2**

ANALYSIS OF RATE

6.16.12 For : Providing 12 mm thick plastering in cement mortar (1 : 4) with neeru finish to internal surfaces including scaffolding, curing etc. complete.

Unit : 1 sq. m

Material	Quantity	Rate	Per	Amount	Labour	No.	Rate	Per	Amount
For 10.0 m²		Rs.		Rs.	For 10.0 m²		Rs.		Rs.
1. Cement	1.26 bags	300.00	bag	378.00	1. Mason [1st class]	0.55	407.00	day	223.85
2. Sand [Crushed]	0.17 m³	1000.00	m³	170.00	2. Mazdoor	1.50	367.00	day	550.50
3. Neeru	0.50 bags	300.00	bag	150.00	3. Bhisti	0.50	367.00	day	183.50
	Cost of material per 10 m² =			**698.00**	Cost of labour per 10 m² =				957.85
					Cost of material per 10 m² =				698.00
								Total =	**1655.85**

Add 10% for contractor's profit and overhead charges, $1\frac{1}{2}$ % for water charges, $\frac{1}{2}$ % for T and P.

So, Total cost $= 1.12 \times 1655.85 = $ **1854.55 Rs./10 m²** $= $ **185.45 Rs./m²**

ANALYSIS OF RATE

6.16.13 For : Providing flush grooved pointing with cement mortar (1 : 3) for brickwork including scaffolding and curing etc complete.

Unit : 1 sq. m^2

Material	Quantity	Rate	Per	Amount		Labour	No.	Rate	Per	Amount
For 10.0 m^2		Rs.		Rs.		For 10.0 m^2		Rs.		Rs.
1. Cement	0.35 bags	300.00	bag	105.00		1. Mason [IInd class]	0.80	384.00	day	307.20
2. Sand [Crushed]	0.035 m^3	1000.00	m^3	35.00		2. Mazdoor	1.20	367.00	day	440.40
						3. Bhisti	0.20	367.00	day	73.40
		Cost of material per 10 m^2 =		**140.00**			Cost of labour per 10 m^2 =			821.00
							Cost of material per 10 m^2 =			140.00
									Total =	**961.00**

Add 10% for contractor's profit and overhead charges, $\frac{1}{2}$ % for T and P.

So, Total cost = 1.12 × 961.00 = **1076.32 Rs./10 m^2** = 107.63 Rs./m^2

ANALYSIS OF RATE

6.16.14 For : Providing and fixing mangalore tiled roofing with class A-A tiles with horizontal teak wood battens, iron works and oiling the battens etc. complete.

Unit : 1 sq.m

Material	Quantity	Rate	Per	Amount	Labour	No.	Rate	Per	Amount
For 10.0 m²		Rs.		Rs.	For 10.0 m²		Rs.		Rs.
1. Mangalore tiles [41 cm × 24 cm]	150.00 No.	19.00	No.	2850.00	1. Carpenter [IIst class]	1.00	384.00	day	384.00
2. Teak wood battens [5 cm × 2.5 cm]	36.0 m	75.00	R.M.	2700.00	2. Tile layer	1.00	384.00	day	384.00
3. Ridge tiles	10.0 m	32.00	No.	320.00	3. Mazdoor	2.00	367.00	day	734.00
4. Nails	2.50 kg	85.00	kg	212.00	4. Sundries [Ladder etc.]	L.S.	40.00	day	40.00
5. Linseed oil	1/2 litre	105.00	litre	52.50					
	Cost of material per 10 m² =			**6135.00**		Cost of labour per 10 m² =			1542.00
						Cost of material per m² =			6135.00
								Total =	**7677.00**

Add 10% for contractor's profit and overhead charges, $\frac{1}{2}$ % for T and P.

So, Total cost = 1.105×7677.00 = 7677.00 Rs./10 m² = 767.70 Rs./m²

ANALYSIS OF RATE

6.16.15 For : Providing water bound distemper of approved brand and shade in two coats [inclusive of priming coat of white wash], scaffolding etc. complete.

Unit : 1 sq.m

Material	Quantity	Rate	Per	Amount
For 10.0 m²		Rs.		Rs.
1. Water bound distemper	1.25 kg	71.00	kg	88.75
2. Lime powder for white wash	1.25 kg	15.00	kg	18.75
Cost of material per 10 m² =				107.50

Labour	No.	Rate	Per	Amount
For 10.0 m²		Rs.		Rs.
1. Painter (IInd class)	0.50	384.00	day	192.00
2. Mazdoor	0.50	367.00	day	183.50
3. Sundries (Ladder etc.)	L.S.	40.00	day	40.00
Cost of labour per 10 m² =				415.50
Cost of material per 10 m² =			=	107.50
			Total =	523.00

Add 10% for contractor's profit and overhead charges, $1\frac{1}{2}$ % for water charges and $\frac{1}{2}$ % for T and P.

So, Total cost = 1.12×523.00 = **585.76 Rs./10 m²** = **58.58 Rs./m²**

ANALYSIS OF RATE

Unit : 1 sq.m

6.16.16 For : Painting two coat over a coat of priming for 10 m² area.

Material	Quantity	Rate	Per	Amount	Labour	No.	Rate	Per	Amount
		Rs.		Rs.			Rs.		Rs.
For 10.0 m²					For 10.0 m²				
1. Primer paint	0.6 litre	105.00	litre	63.00	1. Painter (IInd class)	0.70	384.00	day	268.80
2. Paint [Ready mixed]	1.0 litre	225.00	litre	225.00	2. Mazdoor	0.70	367.00	day	268.80
					3. Sundries, brushes, sandpaper etc.	–	80.00	L.S.	80.00
	Cost of material per 10 m² =			**288.00**		Cost of labour per 10 m² =			617.60
						Cost of material per 10 m² =			288.00
								Total =	**905.60**

Add 10% for contractor's profit and overhead charges, $\frac{1}{2}$ % for T and P.

So, Total cost = 1.105×905.60 = **1000.69 Rs./10 m²** = **100.07 Rs./m² [Including primer]**

6.17 ESCALATION OF PRICES

Now-a-days, in almost all the item rate contracts, *a price variation clause* is introduced under the conditions of contract.

According to the price variation clause if during the operative period of contract, there shall be variation in the Consumers Price Index and or in the Wholesale Price Index of all commodities prepared by the office of the Economic Advisor, Ministry of Industry, Government of India, as compared to the respective figures, thereof, on the date 30 days prior to the last date prescribed for accepting the tender and or in the prices of Diesel oil, Petrol, Lubricants etc. then adjustment of rates on account of labour, materials and diesel oil/petrol etc. will be computed by the following procedure:

(i) Price variation (P.V.) for labour component :

$$(P.V.)_L = 0.85 \left(\begin{array}{c} \text{P-cost of schedule A} \\ \text{of material used} \end{array} \right) \left(\frac{K_1}{100} \times \frac{CI - C_o}{C_o} \right)$$

where, $(P.V.)_L$ = Price variation (for labour) in rupees to be permitted.

P = Total cost of work executed during the period under consideration

K_1 = Percentage of labour component.

C_o = Basic consumer's price index on the date 30 days preceding the last date mentioned for receipt of tender.

CI = Average consumer price index during the period under consideration.

(ii) Price variation for materials (Component)

$$(P.V.)_M = 0.85 \left(\begin{array}{c} \text{P-cost of schedule A} \\ \text{of material used} \end{array} \right) \times \left(\frac{K_2}{100} \times \frac{WI - W_o}{W_o} \right)$$

where, $(P.V.)_M$ = Price variation for materials in rupees to be permitted.

P = Total cost of work executed during the period under consideration

K_2 = Percentage of material component.

W_o = Basic wholesale price index on the date 30 days prior to the last date mentioned for receipt of tender.

WI = Average wholesale price index during the period under consideration

(iii) Price variation in diesel oil, petrol, lubricants etc.

$$(P.V.)_0 = 0.85 \left(\begin{array}{c} \text{P-cost of schedule A} \\ \text{of material used} \end{array} \right) \left(\frac{K_3}{100} \times \frac{PI - P_o}{P_o} \right)$$

where, $(P.V.)_0$ = Price variation for (Diesel, Petrol, Lubricants) in rupees to be permitted.

P = Total cost of work executed during the period under consideration

K_3 = Percentage of Diesel, Petrol, Lubricants component

PI = Average price for H.S.D. (at origin i.e. Mumbai for Maharashtra State) during the period under consideration.

P_o = Average price of H.S.D. at origin i.e. Mumbai on the date 30 days prior to the last date prescribed.

The total percentages of all the three components i.e. *labour material* and *diesel, petrol lubricants* i.e. K_1, K_2 and K_3 should be equal to 100.

THEORETICAL QUESTIONS

1. What is meant by 'Analysis of Rates' ? What points are taken into consideration while preparing rate analysis ?

2. Explain the purpose of analysis of rates.

3. Explain the various factors on which the rate of an item depends.

4. What do you mean by overhead charges ? Distinguish between 'General overheads' and 'Job overheads'.

5. Define 'Task Work' and state the procedure of determining 'task work' for various items of construction.

6. Determine the quantities of various materials required for one cubic meter of wet P.C.C. (1 : 3 : 6) for foundations.

7. State the percentage of steel required for R.C.C. in case of the following:
   (i) R.C.C. slab
   (ii) R.C.C. beam
   (iii) R.C.C. columns
   (iv) R.C.C. lintels
   (v) R.C.C. foundation

8. Determine the quantities of various materials required for one cubic meter of brick work in superstructure, IInd sort in cement mortar (1 : 6).
   (i) For I.S. size bricks.
   (ii) Conventional types of bricks.

9. Determine the quantities of various materials required for 10 cm thick brick work for partition walls 10 sq. m area in cm (1 : 4). Assume I.S. size of the bricks for calculations.

10. Determine the quantities of various materials required for 12 cm thick cement plaster (1 : 4) of 10 sq. m area in case of the following :
    (i) With neeru finish 1.5 mm thick
    (ii) Without neeru finish.

11. Determine the quantities of various materials required for 10 sq. m. area of pointing in C.M. (1 : 3) in case of the following:

    (i)   For pointing to brick work

    (ii)   For pointing to R. R. stone masonry.

12. Determine the quantities of various materials required for plain cement tile flooring 20 mm thick over c.m. (1 : 6) for 10 sq. m area to be covered.

13. Calculate the number of Mangalore Tiles and battens (of standard size) required to cover a sloping roof of 10 sq. m. area.

14. Find out the materials required for

    (i)   P.C.C. (1 : 2 : 4) mix - for 100 m^3

    (ii)   U. C. R. masonry in C.M. - for 100 m^3

    (iii)   Brick masonry, IInd sort in C.M. (1 : 5) for 10 m^3

15. Work out cement quantity in bags, required for the following items of work.

    (i)   Cement concrete (1 : 2 : 4) mix - 10 m^3

    (ii)   U.C.R. masonry in C.M. (1 : 5) - 10 m^3

16. Explain the term task work and state task work for the following items.

    (i)   U.C.R. masonry in plinth

    (ii)   Cement plaster (1 : 5) in neeru finish

    (iii)   Cement pointing (1 : 3) for brick work

    (iv)   Distempering to new surfaces in two coats

17. Discuss the factors considered while analysing the rate for an item

18. Prepare rate analysis for any one of the following items

    (i)   Providing and laying C.C. (1 : 4 : 8) in foundations.

    (ii)   Providing and laying marble mosaic tiled floor 25 mm thick

19. Write a note on overhead charges.

20. Discuss briefly the factors which affect the unit price of an item of work.

21. What are direct and indirect overhead charges ?

22. State and explain the various factors affecting the rate of an item.

23. Define task work and state the task work for the following items

    (i)   II class B.B. masonry in superstructure

    (ii)   13 mm thick cement plaster to brick masonry in superstructure

24. Prepare rate analysis for the item of P.C.C. (1 : 4 : 8) in foundations

25. Work out the rate analysis for U.C.R. masonry in cement mortar (1 : 6) in foundation.

26. Write a short note on overhead charges.

27. 36 m³ of U.C.R. masonry in cement mortar (1 : 6) is to be constructed for the foundation of a school building. Calculate :

    (i)   Requirement of different materials.

    (ii) Number of masons and mazdoors required if the work is to be completed in 10 days.

28. (a) Work out rate analysis for the following items of work.

        (i)   U.C.R. masonry in C.M. (1 : 4) for foundations.

        (ii) 12 mm thick cement plaster in C.M. (1 : 4) with neeru finish.

    (b) Prepare analysis of rate for

        (i)   P.C.C. (1 : 4 : 8) bed

        (ii) C. R. masonry in C. M. (1 : 5) for plinth.

29. Work out the rate analysis for the following : (i) P. C. C. (1 : 4 : 8) in foundations, (ii) 12 mm thick cement plaster with neeru finish to internal surface of brick masonry in superstructure.

30. Give rate analysis for any one of the following (i) II class B.B. masonry in C.M. (1 : 6) in superstructure (ii) C.C. (1 : 2 : 4) for R.C.C. slab

31. Site conditions affect the rate of an item ? Comment in brief.

32. What is a task work ?

33. Work out the number of bricks and mortar required per cubic meter of brick wall one brick thick in English bond using $19 \times 9 \times 9$ cm size. Thickness of joint is 1 cm. Bricks are having a frog of $10 \times 4 \times 1$ cm size. No rounding off or any allowance for wastage is to be made. Mortar requirement is to be worked out correct to the fourth decimal place.

34. Cement concrete (1 : 2 : 4) is to be laid in foundation trenches. The total quantity of concrete is 7.5 cubic metres. Calculate the quantities of different materials required for the work.

35. Cement required in bags (approximately) per cubic metre of 1 : 2 : 4 concrete is

    (A) 2.2 (B) 4.4 (C) 6.6 (D) 8.8   **Answer (C)**

36. Volume of 1 bag of cement weighing 50 kg is (A) 3.400 cub. m, (B) 0.034 cub. m, (C) 1.050 cub. m, (D) 0.020 cub. m   **Answer (B)**

37. Number of bricks required for 100 cub. m of brick work in cement mortar for nominal brick size of 200 mm x 100 mm $\times$ 100 mm is about (A) 500 (B) 15,000 (C) 50,000 (D) 25,000.   **Answer (C)**

38. Weight of 1 cub. m of plain cement concrete (1 : 2 : 4) is about (A) 2400 kN (B) 24.00 kN (C) 240.00 kN, (D) 2.4 kN.   **Answer (D)**

39. Estimate the requirements of materials i.e. cement (nos. of bags), sand (cub. m) and coarse aggregates (i.e. stone chips-cub. m) for 10 cub. m of cement concrete (1: 2: 4) of nominal mix.

40. Per cubic metre of brick work (brick length 22.5) in cement mortar the requirements of bricks and wet mortar are: (A) 500 Nos. and 0.50 cub. m (B) 460 Nos. and 0.50 cub. m (C) 500 Nos. and 0.25 cub. m (D) 460 Nos. and 0.25 cub. m   **Answer (D)**

41. To prepare 10 cubic metres of concrete of nominal mix (1 : 2 : 4) the quantity of cement required in bags.

42. A room of internal dimensions 2.6m × 3.0 m has four windows each of size 1.0 m × 1.5 m and three doors each of size 1.2 m × 2.10 m and one built in almirah of size 1.1 m × 1.6 m. The ceiling is at a height of 3.1 m. For purpose of Jamb/reveals 25 % of window areas are allowed. What is the area of the colour washing on the walls ?

Chapter 7

TENDERS AND TENDER NOTICE

7.1 TENDERS

7.1.1 Introduction to Tenders

The very first step to be taken for the execution of works is to invite tenders. Tender is defined as an offer in writing for execution of certain specified work or for supply of specified materials subject to certain terms and conditions such as rates, time limits etc.

Depending upon the type of contract, the tender may be item-rate tender, lump-sum tender, cost-plus tender, labour tender or demolition tender.

Tender presupposes that the person submitting the tender is well equipped with required material and labour for the completion of the work.

Before inviting tenders, an Architect or Engineer has to see that the following particulars are ready :

- Complete plans, specifications and details of the work are ready in all respects, without any ambiguity.
- Bill of quantities of various items are fairly accurate.
- Necessary conditions regarding the manner in which the entire work is to be executed are checked and correct.

The contractor interested in submitting his tenders has to make a thorough study of plans, specifications of the work to be executed and also the terms and conditions etc. In addition, he has to inspect the proposed work site to ascertain the complexity of the work, probable time of completion, material, and personnel (technical and non-technical) required and the difficulties that will be encountered during the execution of the work. After considering all the factors stated above, he will be in a position to quote the rates for the various items of work to be executed, execution of certain specified work, for supply of specified material or transportation of materials etc.

7.1.2 Invitation of Tenders

The tenders for the execution of a work may be invited by any one of the following three methods :

- Open or Public tenders,
- Private or Limited or selected tenders, and
- Negotiated or Single tender

- **Open or Public Tenders**

  Tenders should invariably be invited in open and public manner by giving an advertisement in the local leading news papers or by a notice in a regional language and also in English to be displayed in public places. For a work costing more than Rs. 25,000 tender notice should be published in local leading news papers having large coverage.

  All public works are invariably to be advertised in the local newspaper by giving a public tender notice so that any eligible new contractor can submit his tender as all contractors are given equal opportunity. Thus there are chances of getting the work executed at the cheapest rate. However, there is possibility of entrusting the work to an unknown, inexperienced and less qualified contractor which may lead to dispute, sub-standard quality of work etc. The method is suitable for public works.

- **Private or Limited or Selected Tenders**

  In this case, tenders are invited from the limited number of reputed contractors for the execution of the work. This results into fair competition on the limited scale and eliminates a new inexperienced contractor. This method is advantageous for the works of specialised nature which an ordinary new contractor will not be able to complete it satisfactorily. Moreover it leads to speedy and successful completion of the work. This method is suitable for carrying out private works.

- **Negotiated or Single Tender**

  This is similar to limited tender but instead of inviting tenders from the limited contractors, it is invited from a single well-known reputed contractor. This method is adopted in case of execution of work of specialised nature or for the supply of articles of proprietary nature.   As there is no fair competition, this method may prove to be costly. However for the execution of work within the target time without sacrificing its quality, the method is found to be of great advantage. The method is also followed for the purchase of articles or materials (irrespective of its cost) included under the rate contract system.

7.1.3 Tender Notice

7.1.3.1 Procedure of Issuing Tender Notice

As already stated public tenders should invariably be invited by giving an advertisement in the regional and English language in the local newspapers having large coverage in the prescribed form of the department. The person filling the tender should have an open access to the contract document kept in the office of the person issuing tender notice.

The tender notice should include the following information :

- Name of the agency (i.e. department) inviting tenders
- Name of the work and its exact location.
- Estimated cost of the work and the type or category of contractors eligible to tender for the work.

- Time of completion of the work.
- The place and time where the contract documents can be seen and blank tender forms can be obtained.
- The cost of the blank tender form.
- Specifications of the work and conditions of contract.
- Place, date and time of accepting the tenders.
- Place, date and time of opening the tenders.
- Earnest money to be deposited along with the tender.
- Security deposit to be paid (applicable only to the successful tenderer) and its nature.
- Validity and right to reject any or all tenders and the name of authority accepting tenders.

7.1.3.2 Period of Notice (W-2010)

The following schedule for period of notices of first and second or subsequent calls may be followed :

Sr. No.	Cost of the work	Minimum Notice period for first call	Minimum Notice period for second or subsequent calls
1.	Cost of work upto ₹ 50,000	Two weeks	10 days
2.	Cost of work > ₹ 50,000		
	< ₹ 5,00,000	Four weeks	Two weeks
3.	Cost of work above ₹ 5,00,000	Six weeks	Four weeks

7.1.3.3 Interval of Time between Last Date of Accepting Tender forms and date of Opening of Tender (W-2010)

The time interval between last date for issuing tender forms and date of opening of tenders will be as follows :

Sr. No.	Type of Work	Time Interval
1.	Acceptance of tender within the powers of Superintending Engineer	4 days
2.	Acceptance of tender within the powers of Chief Engineer	One week

Note : Under no circumstances the blank tender forms should be issued during the above time.

7.1.3.4 Specimen form of a Tender Notice

Sealed tenders are invited in (type of) tender form from registered Contractors ...... class, for the work as mentioned below and will be received in sealed covers addressed to ...... (Name of agency inviting tender), duly superscribed with the name of the work, by the undersigned, in his office upto the date and time noted as below and will be opened on the same day, in the presence of intending contractors, if possible. A certified true copy of the registration will have to be tendered with the application, by the contractor, for the issue of tender form.

1. An amount as mentioned below should be paid on account of earnest money by cash, or demand draft drawn in the favour of .... Name of agency inviting tenders.

    (i)   Name of work ....

    (ii)   Estimated cost of the work ₹   ....

    (iii) Earnest money ....   ₹   ....

    (iv)   Security Deposit ....   ₹   .... in cash

                        and   ₹   ....   through

                                                            interim bills

    (v)   Time of completion ....

    (vi)   Cost of blank tender form ₹ ..... (Non-refundable) ₹ 50 extra if required by post.

    (vii) Blank tender forms will be available between 11 a.m. to 5 p.m. on week days except on Sunday and holidays.

    (viii) Last date of receiving tenders .... at .... p.m.

    (ix)   Date of opening the tenders .... at ....

    (x)   Class of registration of the contractors to whom the tender is open ....

2. Additional information if any regarding the contract can be obtained from the office of the undersigned during office hours only.

3. The offer shall remain valid for 90 days from the date of opening of tenders.

4. The rates to be quoted by the contractor will be in metric units only.

5. The right to reject any or all tenders without assigning any reason is reserved with the undersigned.

**Executive Engineer
or Name of the authority
inviting tender**

7.1.4 Submission of Tenders

The intending contractors have to submit their tenders in special envelops marked as 1, 2, 3 and 4 as follows :

• 'Envelope number 1' contains the earnest money to be deposited by the contractor in manner indicated in the notice inviting tenders.

• 'Envelope number 2' contains the information regarding solvency certificate from appropriate bank authorities, latest tax clearance certificate from the income tax office, a list of similar works carried out by the contractor in the past and works in progress at present, list of plants and machinery owned by the contractor, and technical personnel that can be employed by him and a letter covering the tender.

- Envelope number 3' shall contain tender form complete with all the rates quoted in figures and words duly signed by the contractor, and

- Envelope number 4', shall be a large size outer envelope containing the above envelopes 1, 2, and 3 properly sealed and superscribed as Tender for ……. (i.e. name of the work) and submitted in person or sent by 'registered post acknowledgement, due to the authorities inviting tenders so as to reach the place on or before the last date and time indicated in the tender notice.

7.1.5 Opening of Tenders

All the public tenders received on or before due date must be opened on the date and time mentioned in the tender notice in the following sequence. The outer envelope number 4, should be opened in office on date and time (as mentioned in the tender notice) in the presence of contractors present at that time. Subsequently, envelope number 1 which contains earnest money deposit shall be opened and if earnest money deposited is not as prescribed then the tender is to be returned unopened to the concerned contractor if present. After this, the envelope number 2 containing covering letter, solvency and income tax clearance certificate etc. is opened, thoroughly scrutinized and his financial status determined. Lastly, the envelope number 3 containing tender form (with duly quoted rates) is to be opened on the same or any other date that will be announced and intimated to the contractor. The tenders should preferably be opened in the alphabetical order (of names of contractors) and the authority opening the tender shall prepare a list of contractors (or tenderer) or their representatives who are present and their signatures are taken of their presence. However, in case of tenders invited by the private agencies, the contractors may not be required to remain present at the time of opening of tenders.

Tenders of the persons directly or indirectly related to the Government service should not be accepted.

7.1.6 Scrutiny of Tenders   (W-2010)

Before accepting any tender, it is required to thoroughly check all the tenders received so that there are no mistakes. Generally, the tenders which are far below the estimated cost of the work should not be accepted. Acceptance of such tenders leads to delay in completion of the work, poor quality of material, sub-standard work etc.

The following precautions should be taken at the time of scrutiny of all the tenders received.

- The person opening the tender shall initial against the name of tenderer entered in the register of tender forms issued.

- A complete list of tenders received with the details of deposit cheques (towards earnest money) should be prepared.

- It should be scrupulously seen that each tender is signed by the contractor and it contains his address.

- There should be no alterations and additions or deletions in the terms and conditions included in the tender form submitted by the contractor.

- It should be verified that the rates against each item are written in figures as well as words. The multiplication of the quantity of each item and its corresponding rate should be verified very carefully.

- Additions of amounts page wise (in the tender form) should be done very carefully to arrive at the final cost of work, in case of each tender.

- After scrutinising all the tenders received, a comparative statement should be prepared, indicating the lowest tender first and the highest tender at the last.

- All the over writings and corrections in the tender submitted by the contractor should be attested at all such places with dated initial of the person opening the tender, and also noted at the end of each page indicating the total number of over writings or corrections on that page. All such corrections or over writings should invariably be signed by the tenderer.

- If the rates are written only in figures, the person opening the tender has to write them in words also after pointing out this omission to the tenderer present at that time.

- If there is any omission in mentioning the rate against any item in tender, the person opening the tender shall put a dash against such blank spaces and attested by the dated initials.

- Whenever there is difference between rates quoted in figures and words, the rate taken by the tenderer for calculating the total amount of that item should be considered as correct. In other cases, the lower rate of the two (i.e. figures and words) should be assumed as correct.

- If any rate quoted by the contractor is not clear or doubtful, the tender may be considered as invalid.

- The person scrutinising the tenders shall read out the rates (quoted in the tender) to the tenderer or their agents who are present.

- After scrutinising the tenders received, a comparative statement of all the tenders should be prepared with the lowest tendered amount placed first and the highest tendered amount at the last as shown below :

Sr. No.	Name of tenderer or contractor	Total amount of tender	Remarks
1.	X	₹ 3,15,600	Lowest
2.	Y	₹ 3,32,500	
3.	Z	₹ 3,60,200	
4.	P	₹ 3,70,000	
5.	Q	₹ 3,74,400	Highest

• The tenders, if beyond the powers of acceptance of the person inviting tenders should be sent to the appropriate higher authorities for disposal.

The additional points to be considered before accepting any tender will be as follows :

• The previous experience of the contractor and his reputation in the society.

• Contractor's capability in organising the work.

• The financial status of the contractor as regards the total estimated cost of the work.

• The intelligence, sincerity, general behaviour and temperament of the contractor.

• The other works in progress, at present, by the contractor.

• The solvency certificate from the bank and the latest income tax clearance certificate received by the contractor.

• Details of plants and machinery (required for the work) available with the contractor.

• Details of Govt. registration of the contractor.

7.1.7 Acceptance of Tender

(i) **General Procedure :** It is usual practice to accept the tender quoting the lowest amount. However, if lowest amount quoted by the contractor is far below the estimated cost of the work, it is quite likely that the contractor will not be capable of executing the work resulting in poor quality of work, delay in completion of the work etc. Under such circumstances it is advisable to accept the second lowest tender which is very nearer to the estimated cost of the work. It is utmost important that the acceptance of the tender must be done within the specified or reasonable time limit. The tender should be accepted as an absolute and unqualified without bringing any conditional or counter-offer. The contractor has a right to withdraw his offer or tender before it is accepted, by forfeiting the earnest money deposited by him. The offer of the contractor becomes invalid if the acceptance of the tender is not done by him within the specified or reasonable time limit or in the event of death of either party.

After acceptance of a particular tender, all the tenders (including the rejected ones) accompanied by the comparative statement should be forwarded by the Sub-divisional officer to the Division office of Executive Engineer for completing contract documents and refund of earnest money of the unsuccessful contractors etc.

(ii) **Definition of Term 'Acceptance' :** The definition of the term 'acceptance' as mentioned in the section 2 (b) of Indian Contract Act of 1872 is as follows :

"When the person to whom the proposal is made signifies his assent thereto, the proposal is said to be accepted". It may be noted that the word 'proposal' as mentioned in Indian Contract Act of 1872, is synonymous to the word 'offer' in the English Law.

(iii) **Methods of Acceptance :** The various methods of acceptance of tender (i.e. offer) from view point of law are as follows :

(a) **Conduct as a proof of acceptance :** In certain cases the conduct of the person may be considered as a proof of acceptance of the offer. The communication of intention may be made in many ways other than spoken, written or signalled words. e.g. if an owner allows contractor to commence the work without completing the formalities of the acceptance, his conduct implies the acceptance of the offer (i.e. tender) of the contractor.

(b) **Acceptance by telegram :** Communication of acceptance of the offer by a telegram will be valid, provided it is proved beyond doubt that the telegram was sent by a competent person authorised to send it to the contractor.

(c) **Written acceptance :** When it is clearly mentioned in the tender to communicate acceptance in writing, the verbal acceptance is not sufficient, unless it is communicated in writing, within the reasonable time limit and in a prescribed manner.

(d) **Absolute and unqualified acceptance :** The Indian contract law states that the acceptance of the offer must be absolute and unqualified. An acceptance with variation is nothing but a counter offer which must be acceptable to the original promissor before a contract is made.

LETTER OF ACCEPTANCE

(On letterhead paper of the Employer)

.... (date)

To : .... (name and address of the Contractor).

Dear Sirs,

This is to notify you that your Bid dated .... for execution of the .... (name of the contract and identification number, as given in the instructions to Bidders) for the Contract Price of Rupees ....(amount in words and figures as corrected and modified in accordance with the instructions to Bidders is hereby accepted by our Agency.

We accept / do not accept that .... be appointed as the conciliator 2.

You are hereby requested to furnish Performance Security, in the form detailed in para 34.1 of ITB for an amount of ₹ .... within 21 days of the receipt of this letter of acceptance valid upto 28 days from the date of expiry of taking over certificate subject to removal of defects Period i.e. upto .... and sign the contract, failing which action as stated in para 34.3 of ITB will be taken.

Please acknowledge receipt.

Your faithfully,

Authorised Signature

Name and Title of Signatory

Name of Agency

....

1.   Delete "corrected and" or "and modified" if only one of these actions applies. Delete "as corrected and modified in accordance with the instructions to Bidders" if corrections or modifications have not been effected.

ISSUE OF NOTICE TO PROCEED WITH THE WORKS

(letterhead of the Employer)

.... dated

To

.... (name and address of the Contractors)

....

....

Dear Sirs,

Pursuant to your furnishing the requisite security as stipulated in ITB clause 34.1 and signing of the contract for the implementation/construction .... a Bid Price of ₹ .... you are hereby instructed to proceed with the execution of the said works in accordance with the contract documents.

Yours faithfully

(Signature, name and title of signatory authorised to sign on behalf of Employer)

7.1.7.1 Rejection of all Tenders

The last para of any tender notice invariably says that right to reject any or all tenders without assigning any reason is reserved with the undersigned.

All the tenders received are sometimes rejected under the following circumstances :

- If all the tenderers or contractors have formed an unholy alliance or syndicate, to defraud the owner or the Government;

- The amount quoted by the lowest tenderer or contractor is in excess of the funds earmarked or allotted for the execution of the work;

- The owner or Government decides to make drastic changes in the proposed work (e.g. an original load bearing structure is now proposed to be converted into a framed structure) in between the period of invitation of tenders and the opening of tenders; and

- There is poor response to the invitation of tender from the contractors.

7.1.7.2 Rejection of the Lowest Tender

When tenders are invited by the Government by giving an open advertisement in the news paper, it is usual practice to accept the tender of a contractor who has quoted the lowest rates. However, the lowest tender may also be rejected under the following circumstances.

- The lowest tender is not found as per the specifications and general requirement laid down in the tender documents;
- The tenderer instead of quoting his rates for the various items in the bill of quantities has offered to execute the entire work for an amount that will be less than the lowest offer received.
- The lowest tenderer is not financially sound to execute the entire proposed work or is a bankrupt;
- The credibility of the lowest tenderer is suspicious and his reputation is not good;
- The lowest tenderer is totally inexperienced or has no experience of carrying out similar works in the past.
- The lowest tender can also be rejected if the tenderer has made any additions and alterations or removed any pages in the tender form or has not signed all the corrections he has made in the rates quoted by him.

7.1.7.3 Readvertisement of the Tender

In case of rejection of all tenders it becomes necessary to readvertise the tender if the same work is to be executed. In such cases certain changes are effected in the original designed structure and fresh tenders are invited for this new proposed work independently. In case tenders are reinvited for the same work without any changes, the new offers from the same contractors will be influenced by the experience they have gained by the earlier proposal.

7.1.8 Revocation of Tender

An offer or tender becomes a contract (which is enforceable by law) if it is accepted by the offeree (or owner or promisee). As tender is only a offer, the owner can reject it without any liability. Similarly, the tenderer (or contractor) has a right to revoke his offer (or tender), as long as it is not accepted and converted into legal contract e.g. if after, submitting his tender, the tenderer (or contractor) realises his mistakes in tendering, or is not interested in carrying out the work, or wants to withdraw from the work, he can do so by revoking his offer (or tender). Sections 4 and 5 of Indian contract Act 1872 pertains to the revocation of offer (i.e. tender). 'Section 4' states communication of a proposal is complete when it comes to the knowledge of the person to whom it is made. 'Section 5' states that a proposal may be revoked at any time before communication of acceptance is complete as against the proposer, but not afterwards. An acceptance may be revoked at any time before the communication of acceptance is complete as against acceptor but not afterwards.

7.1.9 Powers of Accepting Tenders

The powers of accepting public tenders of Govt. works by the various Government officers are as follows :

Sr. No.	Name of the Government Officer	Extent to which the power is delegated
1.	Chief Engineer (C.E.)	Full powers
2.	Superintending Engineer (S.E.)	₹ 50,00,000
3.	Executive Engineer (E.E.)	₹ 10,00,000
4.	Assistant Engineer (Class I)	₹ 50,000
5.	Assistant Engineer (Class II)	₹ 40,000
6.	Deputy Engineer	
7.	Sub-divisional Engineer	₹ 30,000
8.	Sub-divisional Officer (S.D.O.)	₹ 20,000

Notes :

- The amount of tender should not exceed the sanctioned amount in the estimate.
- The tenders are to be received by the Deputy Engineer in case of sub-divisional office, by the divisional accountant for the divisional office and by the head clerk for the circle office.

7.1.10 Earnest Money

No tender for the execution of the works is to be accepted unless it is accompanied by a chalan indicating deposit of required cash in the treasury/State Bank etc. in name of the department inviting tenders as 'Earnest money' as stated in the tender notice. This money indicates as to how 'earnest' is the contractor in accepting the work. This amount is approximately 1% to 2% of the estimated cost as a guarantee of the tenderer, to accept the work, if allotted. This earnest money serves as a check so that the contractor will not refuse the work if his tender is accepted. If successful contractor refuses to accept the work, his earnest money is to be forfeited. The earnest money of the other unsuccessful contractors is to be refunded.

The amount of earnest money is related to the estimated cost of work as shown below :

Sr. No.	Estimated cost of the work	Earnest money as percentage of estimated cost
1.	Upto Rs. 1 crore	1%
2.	More than Rs. 1 crore but less than Rs. 2 crores	3/4% (minimum ₹ 1 lakh)
3.	More than Rs. 2 crores	1/2% (minimum ₹ 1.5 lakhs)

The earnest money to be accompanied with the tender must be sufficiently large to be security against inconvenience or loss to the department (or owner) in case the successful contractor whose tender is accepted, refuses or fails to complete contract documents and furnish the necessary 'security deposit' within the specified time. Name of such contractor should be debarred in allotting any work in future.

The right of acceptance or otherwise of the tenders received is left entirely to the discretion of the person inviting tenders and no reason or explanation thereof is to be demanded by the tenderers.

In case the lowest offer (i.e. tender) is to be rejected and any other than the lowest is to be accepted or negotiated, a committee of Executive Engineer and the Collector of that district or Superintending Engineer and the Divisional Commissioner or Chief Engineer and Secretary P.W.D., as the case may be is to be appointed to take the unanimous decision in the matter.

The main object of earnest money to be deposited by the contractor along with the tender is to have 'restriction on the unnecessary competition' of the contractors. Because of the imposition of earnest money, only genuine, interested contractors who are financially sound will submit their tenders. The contractor, if after the allotment of work refuses to commence the work then as a punishment, his earnest money is to be forfeited. In the absence of earnest money to be deposited with the tender, any contractor who is not earnest to accept the work will submit his tender quoting lowest rates and in the event of work allotted to him, he may refuse to enter into a contract, causing great hardship to the owner or Government Authority. Lastly, the forfeited earnest money of the lowest contractor, may be considered as 'compensation' to the owner or Government department for the delay etc. in the execution of the work.

7.1.11 Security Deposit

After the acceptance of tender of a particular contractor, he has to deposit a certain amount with the department or owner and is known as *'Security Deposit'* and it varies from 5 to 10 per cent of the total estimated cost of the work to be executed. Usually, the contractor has to deposit this amount prior to the commencement of the work. However, if the amount of security deposit is more as is in case of large works, the contractor may be asked to remitt part of the security deposit to start with, the remaining amount being deducted in installments from his running bills. Usually, the earnest money deposited by the successful contractor is considered as part of security deposit and the balance amount collected from him.

The main objects of security deposit are as given below :

   (i) **Deposit for Loans :** This deposit serves as security against plant, machinery or material such as steel, cement etc. issued by the owner or department to the contractor on loan.

(ii) As a Punishment : If the contractor is not following the terms and conditions as mentioned in the contract e.g. poor quality of material, inferior type of work, delay in completion of the work or leaving the work incomplete, then as a punishment his security deposit may be forfeited. Such a forfeited security deposit also serves as compensation for the damages caused to the department or owner by the contractor.

After the satisfactory completion of the work by a contractor, as per the drawings and specification, within the stipulated time, his security deposit is to be refunded after the maintenance period (which is usually six month) is over.

The Government norms for accepting the amount of security deposit from the contractor are as follows :

Sr. No.	Estimated amount of the work	% age of security deposit	Minimum amt. of security deposit
	(I) For Earth Work		
1.	Upto ₹ 10,000	4 to 6%	....
2.	Above ₹ 10,000 and upto ₹ 50,000	3 to 5%	₹ 500
3.	Above ₹ 50,000 and upto ₹ 1,00,000	2 to 4%	₹ 2,000
4.	Above ₹ 1,00,000	2%	₹ 3,000
	(II) For other works		
5.	Upto ₹ 20,000	5 to 7%	....
6.	Above ₹ 20,000 and upto ₹ 50,000	4 to 6%	₹ 1,200
7.	Above ₹ 50,000 and upto ₹ 1,00,000	3 to 5%	₹ 2,500
8.	Above ₹ 1,00,000	2 to 4%	₹ 4,000

Notes : • Contractor should not be permitted to start the work before the security deposit is paid.

• In case of any reduction in the above percentages the matter should be reported, to the next higher authorities, with full justification.

• The security deposit amount to be deducted from the running bills of the contractor should not be more than 50% of the amount of security deposit.

7.1.12 Retention Amount

After the work is assigned to a contractor, the contractor has to deposit 10% of the estimated amount as 'Security deposit' before he commences the work. However, it may not be possible for a contractor to deposit the entire amount of security deposit as this amount remains blocked till the completion of the work and his business depends upon the rolling of his capital. To overcome this difficulty, the contractor may be permitted to pay the amount of security deposit in installments from the running bills due to him for the work completed. Such an installment which is 'retained' by the department or owner from the payment to be made to the contractor is called as 'retention amount' or 'retention money'. The amount to be retained from contractor's running bill everytime is about 10% of the amount of the work executed by the contractor. Such 'retention' is continued till the entire amount of 'security deposit' is collected from the contractor's bills, thereafter the running bills of the contractor are paid in full without any deductions.

'Retention amount' is the money earned by the contractor but not payable to him under the conditions of contract. After the completion of the work 50% of the retention money is paid to the contractor and remaining 50% is to be paid after the 'maintenance or defect liability period' (which is generally six months or one rainy season) is over. No interest will be paid by the owner or Government on the 'retention amount' collected. The contractor can assign the 'retention amount' to his nominated person. The main object of retention money is to make good any defects noticed in the work executed by the contractor or to meet compensation for delay in execution of the work.

7.1.13 Draft Tender Papers

Before assigning any Government work to the contractor, the Executive Engineer has to prepare 'draft tender papers' which should contain the following details :

- A complete set of drawings (i.e. plan, elevation, section, details etc.) indicating the overall dimensions of the work to be executed.

- Tender notice to the press in the prescribed form (by the Government).

- Notice to the contractor in the prescribed form (by the Government).

- General description of the work and conditions of work.

- Additional conditions and instructions to the contractor if any.

- Brief general specifications about the work.

- Statement of the details of design.

- Detailed specifications for all items of work to be executed.

- Special specifications, if any, for P.C.C. and R.C.C. works etc.

- Prescribed agreement form to be signed by the contractor.

- Availability of Government machinery for the execution of work with hire changes etc. and

- A certificate by the competent authority regarding careful scrutiny of the plans and estimates on which the tenders are prepared.

7.1.14 Tender Form or Tender Documents

The tenders received from the various tenderers or contractors are to be compared and a comparative statement is to be prepared before allotting work to a particular contractor. In order to have a common base for the comparison of tenders each tenderer is supplied with a specified form known as a *'Tender form'*, which should include the following details :

- 'Notice inviting tenders' in the name of the owner or department.

- Letter of 'tender acceptance' from the contractor.

- 'Earnest money' to be deposited by the tenderer or contractor along with the tender.

- 'Security deposit' to be paid by the contractor whose tender will be accepted.

- General specifications of all the items of work.

- *Rates to be quoted by the contractor :* The tender form should include the various items of work (in case of item rate tender) with their estimated quantities, known as bill of quantities, against which the tenderer or contractor has to quote his rates or prices, both in figures and words. In case of lump-sum tender, specifications of the works and special conditions if any are to be mentioned in the tender form and the contractor has to write only one figure i.e. the price at which he intends to execute the entire work.

- *Time of completion :* The time in which the entire work is to executed by the contractor after intimation to start the work should be mentioned in the tender form.

- Articles of agreement and special conditions if any should be included in the tender form.

- *Validity period :* The validity period, after opening of tender, should also be included in the tender form. This period generally varies from 1 to 4 months after the tenders are opened.

- Other information regarding the contractor is aware of site conditions, details of plan, estimate and conditions of contract etc. and his willingness to execute the work.

7.1.15 Unbalanced Tender

In case of 'item rate tender', the contractor has to quote his rates against each item indicated in the tender form. If the rates quoted by the contractor are not varying much from those mentioned in the 'Schedule of rates', prepared by the 'Public Works Department' the tender is said to be 'balanced' one. However, if the rates quoted by the contractor for initial items are higher and for the subsequent items are lower and the sum total amount remains practically unaffected, the tender is said to be 'unbalanced'.

The contractor may submit the unbalanced tender for the following reasons :

- The idea in quoting higher rates for the initial items is to get an excess payment in the initial stages of the work, which can be reutilised as a working capital for the completion of subsequent items. This may be true in case of genuine contractors, but in case of unreliable contractors this may not be true as he may terminate the contract after completing the initial items of work of huge profit. Even with the security deposit paid by the contractor, it may not be possible to complete the remaining part of the work.

- The contractor may be well equipped with certain plant, machinery, technical personnel etc. for items of work for which he has quoted lower rates, whereas for other items his rates may be higher. Thus the owner may be tempted to accept such tender which is favourable to the contractor.

- An experienced contractor will immediately make out from the 'tender form' the items which are over-estimated and under-estimated and accordingly he will quote lower rates for over-estimated items and higher rates for the under-estimated items. The owner or department will be tempted to assign the work to such a contractor. Thus the contractor is not only assigned the work but also assured of huge profit.

To overcome the difficulty of unbalanced tenders, the tenders, instead of inviting on 'item rate basis' (also called as unit-price system) may be invited on lump-sum or cost plus percentage basis.

7.1.16 Types or Classification of Tenders (Forms)

The various types of tenders may be classified as follows :

1. Unit price tender which may be
   (a) Item rate tender (B$_2$ form)
   (b) Percentage (up and down) item rate tender (B$_1$ form)
2. (a) Lump-sum (L.S.) tender (C form)
   (b) Lump-sum plus percentage or target tender
3. Cost plus tender which may be
   (a) Cost plus percentage or cost plus fee tender
   (b) Cost plus fixed fee tender
   (c) Cost plus fixed percentage with bonus and punishment clause
4. Labour rate tender
5. Demolition work tender

1. Unit Price Tenders

(a) Item Rate Tender (B₂ form) :

As the name suggest, in this method the approximate quantities of all the items of work (i.e. bill of quantities) with their full description are mentioned and the contractor has to quote his rates (i.e. prices) for these items. The quantities of items mentioned are approximate and may be more or less than that mentioned. The contractor agrees to carry out the work at the quoted rates for the various items. Thus the 'rates of various items' and not the quantities of such items form a part of contract.

The item rate tender method is more balanced as compared to other methods and there is no risk involved on the part of the contractor as he will be paid on the quantity of the work carried out by him at the quoted rates. The quality of the work can be maintained. The method is commonly adopted in building industries, construction of roads etc.

(b) Percentage (Up and Down) Item Rate Tender (B₁ form) :

The only difference between 'item rate tender' and 'percentage item rate tender' is that in the former only the quantities of various items of work are mentioned in the bill of quantities whereas in the latter the quantities of various items of work are given with their prices (i.e. rates) and the contractor has to quote his prices (i.e. rates) as percentage above or below the prices already mentioned against quantities of each item of work, at which he is willing to execute the work. All other terms and conditions in this case will be similar to the 'item rate tender' as stated above.

The method is generally adopted for annual maintenance and repair works of buildings and also for construction of new buildings.

2. (a) Lump sum (L.S.) Tender (C form) :

In this method, the contractor is willing to execute the entire work as per the approved plans and specifications for a fixed amount i.e. lump sum amount or at a fixed price per square metre or per cubic metre of construction. The contractor has to arrange for all material and labour required for the execution of work. Interim payments for the completed items of work may be made or he may be paid after completion of the entire work depending upon the conditions laid down in the contract. If as per agreement, payment is to be made to the contractor after the completion of the work, and if the contractor leaves the work in between, no payment is to be made to him even for the completed items of work as the lump sum contract is not divisible and hence cannot be apportioned. The L.S. tender is convenient to the owner, as the total cost of the work is known to him in advance.

(b) Lump sum plus percentage or Target Tender :

It is modified form of a 'lump sum tender' with an incentive clause which assures the contractor a certain percentage over the total cost of the project as a bonus if he completes the entire work before the stipulated time i.e. target. All other terms and conditions are similar to the lump-sum tender.

3. Cost Plus Tenders :

(a) Cost plus percentage or cost plus fee tender :

In this type of tender the owner agrees to pay to the contractor the entire cost of the work plus a certain percentage (of the entire cost of the work) as his fees for hiring his expert services for the execution of the work. However, the total cost of the work and the time of its completion are not known to start with. The contractor may try to increase the cost as his profit is linked with the total cost of the work.

(b) Cost plus fixed fee tender :

It is similar to cost plus percentage tender but the contractor is not paid at certain percentage of total cost but he is given fixed fees irrespective of the total cost of the work. The owner arranges for the entire material and labour required for the execution of the work and the contractor is paid fixed fees for rendering his professional services and advices from time to time.

(c) Cost plus fixed percentage with bonus and punishment (or penalty) clause :

It is a modified form of cost plus fixed fee tender in which the contractor is paid the fixed fee if the total cost of the work remains same as the estimated cost. If there is saving in the cost of the work, the contractor is paid certain percentage (upto 50% of) of the amount saved. However, if the cost of the work is in excess of the estimated cost certain percentage of the excess cost shall be deducted from his agreed fees (i.e. to the extent of 66% of his fixed fees).

4. Labour Rate Tender :

In this system the owner has to supply all materials required for the work and the contractor agrees to arrange for all labour, including centering, scaffolding, tools and plants required for the execution of the work. The advantage of this method is that the owner can bring quality material for the work as only labour charges are to be paid to the contractor. The owner has to keep a strict watch over the misuse of the material brought by him.

The labour rates may be for completed items of work or on the square metre (or cubic metre) of the work executed by the contractor. There are very less chances of any dispute arising between the owner and contractor in this method.

5. Demolition Work Tender:

Such tenders are invited for the demolition of the existing structure upto ground or road level and disposing off the demolished material away from it. The contractor may dispose off the entire demolished material by paying certain amount to the owner or department. Contrary to the practice of accepting lowest tender in the usual cases, in *demolition work* the tenderer who gives highest offers is to be accepted. In this case the tenderer disposes off (i.e. sells) all the materials obtained from the dismantled building and in turn makes payment of specified amount to the owner. The tenderer should be asked to deposit the entire amount of tender before the demolition work starts.

THEORETICAL QUESTIONS

1. List out any size important instructions given to a tender.

2. Explain the basic point with respect to which any tender is scrutinized by the client.

3. Draft a brief tender notice to execute the construction work of a concrete road of estimated cost of 30 laks to be completed in one year under JUNURM scheme.

4. Explain the purpose of taking the security deposit in a tender.

5. Discuss merits, demerits of open tenders as against negotiated tender.

6. How cartel formation in a tender can be detected? What action is then subsequently taken.

7. Before working out a tender and before submitting it, what information and data needs to be collected and ascertained. Elaborate.

8. What is meant by a 'tender'? Explain the standard way of opening the tender and its scruting.

9. State the advantages and disadvantages of post-qualification of contractors.

10. Explain the terms earnest money and security deposits.

Chapter 8

METHOD OF EXECUTING WORK

8.1 METHODS OF EXECUTING WORKS

8.1.1 Introduction to Public Works Government Organisations

In order to construct original (public) works and to maintain them in good working condition after their construction, various engineering organisations have been formed by the Central and State Governments in our country as mentioned below :

(1) Central Government of India has its own Central Public Works Department (C.P.W.D.), which looks after the construction and maintenance of roads, buildings, airports etc.

(2) State Government (e.g. Maharashtra State) has its own works organisation comprising of various wings of several departments, namely :

    (i) Public Works Department

    (ii) Irrigation Works Department consisting of :

        (a) Irrigation wing and

        (b) Command Area Development Authority (C.A.D.A.)

    (iii) Environment engineering wing

    (iv) Ports wing and

    (v) Energy wing.

All the above wings except (iii), (iv) and (v) are headed by a secretary on the administrative side.

The 'Environment Engineering Wing' comes under the Secretary to Urban Development; 'Ports Wings' is looked after by Secretary to Home department and 'Energy wing' is taken care of by Secretary to Industries, Energy and Labour Department.

For technical side the above wings except C.A.D.A. and ports wings are headed by a technical person called as Chief Engineer.

On the administrative side, each wing is divided into :

    (i) *'Circles'* separately for

        (a) Roads and buildings

    (b)   Irrigation

    (c)   Hydro-Electrical

    (d)   Environmental engineering, etc. each headed by a Superintending Engineer.

(ii)   *'Directorate'* of Engineering and Irrigation Research, and Training college for in service engineers, looked by the Director of the Superintending Engineer's rank.

(iii) *'Command Area Development'* is looked by an Administrator.

(iv) *Offices* of the

    (a)   Chief Officer, Ports and

    (b)   Superintendent for parks and gardens.

For the efficient execution of the works each circle is further divided into Divisions, each division looked by an Executive Engineer. Each such division is further sub-divided into number of sub-divisions looked after either by an Assistant Engineer (Junior class I) or Sub-divisional Officer (Class II).

Roads and Buildings wing looks after the construction and maintenance of Roads and Buildings in the State.

Irrigation wing is responsible for the construction and maintenance of major and minor irrigation projects in their own state. Hydro-electrical wing has to look after the construction and maintenance of Hydro-Power projects, whereas Environmental Engineering wing takes care of construction and maintenance of water supply and sanitary engineering works in the state.

8.1.2 Organisational Set Up

As stated above, the administrative and technical head of each wing is a Chief Engineer (C.E.) who is overall incharge of the works in that wing and is directly responsible to the Government. His job is to prepare 'Budget Estimates' every year for the various works of that wing and allocate grants, considering the priority, to the various works. He has to keep constant watch over the progress of the work, the expenditure incurred and to maintain proper accounts of the works in consultation with the Accountant General of the State.

Chief Engineer may, if required, be assisted by the Additional Chief Engineers, Deputy Chief Engineers depending upon the volume of work involved in the wing.

The entire work under the control of Chief Engineer is further divided for administrative purposes, into various circles, having Superintending Engineer (S.E.) as its administrative and technical head. He is directly responsible to the Chief Engineer. He has to keep close watch over the quality and progress of the work of each division under his circle. In Military Engineering Services (M.E.S.) of Central Government, Superintending Engineer is known as *surveyor of the works*.

Each circle is further divided into various divisions for the efficient execution of works and the overall incharge of execution and efficient management of works of each division is called as Executive Engineer (E.E.) or Divisional Engineer (D.E.). He is directly responsible to the Superintending Engineer. He has to execute works and maintain proper accounts of the expenditure on various works in his division. He has to see that the expenditure incurred does not exceed the estimated amount of the works. In addition, he has to prepare the project reports including designs and also to prepare detailed estimates of the works in his charge.

Each 'Division' is further sub-divided into number of sub-divisions for the speedy execution of the works and is headed by an Assistant Engineer (A.E.), Sub-divisional Officer (S.D.O.) or Deputy Engineer (Dy. E.) as an overall incharge of the works in his Sub-division. He is directly responsible to the Executive Engineer for the execution and proper maintenance of accounts of the works under his Sub-division. He has to make payments for the works executed, either departmentally or through a contractor, under his jurisdiction and submit monthly accounts, for approval, to the Divisional officer.

Each such sub-division is further sub-divided into number of small sections, headed by 'Sectional Officers' (S.O.) who are stationed at the work site and are directly responsible for the day-to-day work, its quality and satisfactory progress. The works completed under his control, either departmentally or through a contractor, are to be properly measured and entered by him in the measurement book (M.B.). The bills of payment for the completed works are also to be prepared by him. He is responsible to maintain day-to-day accounts of departmental labour employed, Government material including tools and plants issued at the work site etc. Section officers, may, if required, be assisted by sub-overseers or junior supervisor, at the work site depending upon the volume of the work.

Executive Engineer's Divisional Office consists of the following three sections :

(i)   Accounts section

(ii)   Establishment or Correspondence section, and

(iii) Drawing and Designs section

(i) Accounts Section : A Divisional Accountant assisted by accounts clerk looks after the entire accounts i.e. expenditure incurred on works of the division. The Executive Engineer has to consult the Divisional Accountant in all matters relating to finance. Divisional Accountant is directly responsible to the Accountant General of the State.

(ii) Establishment Section : Head clerk assisted by senior and junior clerks looks after all correspondence of the division with Superintending Engineer's offices and sub-divisional offices under its division.

(iii)　Drawing and Designs Section : Head Draftsman assisted by draftsman, tracer etc. looks after the preparation of drawings, designs, estimates, tenders, contracts etc.

Office of the Account General has to inspect and audit every year the accounts of each division and point out the irregularities, if any, in the divisional accounts and send necessary report to the Government for appropriate action in the matter.

In the budget, certain amount is to be allocated every year for the works of various divisions to be undertaken by the Government. The allocated amount is to be spent for the specified work during that financial year only, otherwise, the unspent amount if any will lapse and fresh requisition will have to be made for the reallocation of the funds during the next year.

8.1.3 P.W.D. Procedure of Execution of Works

8.1.3.1 Definitions

- Work.

- Works expenditure and works outlay.

- Appropriation.

- **Work :** The work to be executed may be either a public or private work, the former being constructed by Government and the latter by an individual or private body. The expenditure on public works is met from public funds and is dealt with here in after.

  The term *work* taken in its comprehensive sense refers to all works pertaining to construction, repairs, supply of materials, repairs and carriages of tools and plants, and supply and or manufacture of other stores' operation of workshop, etc.

- **Works expenditure and works outlay :** The terms 'work expenditure' and 'work outlay' refer respectively to the *expenditure* and 'capital charges' (i.e. outlay) on the special services required for the construction, or repairs or maintenance of any work.

  The charges under these two classes may be *net* when any receipts obtained are taken in reduction of the charges. However, they exclude the cost of routine (general) services, tools and plants and establishment charges or any other charges not included into final head of account but included under any of the suspense accounts.

- **Appropriation :** It is the authorised amount of expenditure that can be incurred under major or minor head or sub-head by the disbursing officer. Technically the term 'appropriation' also refers to the provision made in respect of charged expenditure.

The entire control of operations of the various works organisation, whether the funds are made available through Government or Public contribution etc. vests with the State Government.

8.1.3.2 Requirements of 'Works' prior to its Execution

Before execution of any public works is undertaken, it is necessary to fulfil certain requirements as stated below.

- The 'work' to be executed should have 'Administrative Approval' from the department in whose interest the work is to be undertaken.

- The plans and detailed estimates prepared on the basis of 'administrative approval' should be accorded 'Technical sanction' from the State Government.

- Appropriation of funds to the expenditure to be incurred on the original works during the financial year, in which the work is to be undertaken, and

- Provision for the annual repairs and maintenance of the works in the budget of the financial year and execution of such works to the extent of amount specified thereof in the budget.

However certain deviations from the above norms may be permitted in the exceptional cases such as sudden damage to the roads due to excessive floods, breach in the earthen bund, collapse of a building etc. In such cases, the work can be started in anticipation of the sanction, after sending a detailed report, justifying the action taken, to the appropriate higher authorities. The appropriate authorities say Superintending Engineer, may accord post-facto sanction for such urgent 'works'.

8.1.3.3 Classification of Works

The classification of works will be as follows :

- The term *'Original Work'* implies entirely new works or of additions and alterations to the existing works. It also includes all repairs to newly acquired, purchased or previously abandoned properties which are to be brought into reuse again.

- The terms *'Repairs and Maintenance'* include all works undertaken to maintain the existing building in ordinary working condition.

Notes :

- When a certain portion of the existing structure other than road, road surface, road bridge etc. is to be remodelled or replaced, that will result in the increase in the value of that property, is also included under 'original work' and the entire cost of such work is to be credited to 'original work' and is to be debited to repairs. In all other cases except as stated above, the entire cost of the new work is to be charged to 'repairs works'.

- In case of replacement or remodelling of an existing portion of a road, road bridge, causeway etc., that results in increase in the value of the property, the entire cost of such works comes under 'new work' and is chargeable to 'original works'.

8.1.4 Administrative Approval

8.1.4.1 General

For any new original work, including special repairs works, but excluding ordinary repairs, initiated by or related to the requirements of a department, it is necessary to obtain formal 'acceptance' known as **'Administrative Approval'** from the competent authorities of the concerned department to execute such work at a specified amount to fulfil the administrative requirements of that department. Generally, administrative approval is accorded to such proposals if they are found technically sound and the preliminary (or block) estimates are fairly accurate. Other information such as the proposed site of the work, preliminary plans and justification thereof should accompany the proposal.

In case of the works costing upto Rs. 10,000/- detailed plans and estimates can be prepared and sent for administrative approval to competent authorities which will then be sent to the competent authorities of public works department for according technical sanction.

On the basis of priority of the work and the availability of funds, administrative approval is accorded, by the Government, to a particular new work.

8.1.4.2 Stages of Administrative Approval

In order to obtain administrative approval for a particular work, it has to pass through the following three stages :

- Initiation of the proposal by the concerned department.
- Preparation of 'block estimate' (also called preliminary estimate) by the Engineering department (i.e. Public Works Organisation), and
- Approval of the competent authority of the head of the concerned department.

Whenever a particular work is accorded 'Administrative Approval', a certain provision of funds is to be made in the budget during the plan period (e.g. five year plans) proposed by the Government.

A block estimate or preliminary estimate to be submitted to the concerned Head of Department should include the following information :

- Letter addressed to the Head of Department giving full justification for the proposal.
- Block estimate based upon the 'plinth-area' basis (i.e. prevalent market rate per square meter of the built up area in the locality) including 5% provision for contingencies (i.e. unforeseen expenditure) and 1% towards work-charged establishment and electrification charges on percentage basis (10 to 12% of the estimated cost) as per Government circular in force from time to time.
- General description of the proposed new work, its necessity in the public interest.

- Site plan and layout of the proposed work and
- Necessary certificate about the arithmetical check for the estimate.

8.1.4.3 Revised Administrative Approval

The procedure as stated above also applies for obtaining revised administrative approval in the following cases :

- When the estimated cost of the proposed work exceeds the amount administratively approval by more than 10% or rupees 1 crore (whichever is less).
- There is change in the original proposal, even though the cost of the same is likely to be covered by effecting savings on other items of works (i.e. even if original amount of approval is not exceeded), and
- There are modifications in the originally approved proposals resulting in the preparation of a revised estimate.

After obtaining the administrative approval, the Engineering Department (i.e. P.W.D.) prepares detailed drawings (including plan, elevation, sections, details etc.), and detailed estimate of the proposed work to be submitted to the competent authority of the Public Works Department for Technical Sanction.

8.1.4.4 Expenditure Sanction

It implies concurrence of the Finance Department (F.D.) of the Government for the expenditure proposed and allotment of funds to meet the expenditure thereof. Unless there is expenditure sanction, no amount can be spent on the proposed work.

8.1.4.5 Powers of Administrative Approval

The powers vested with the various authorities of the State Government to accord administrative approval to the State Works are as specified below :

Sr. No.	Nature and name of the work	Authority to whom the power is delegated	Extent of power
1.	Roads, buildings	Chief Engineer	Rs. 5 lakhs
		Superintending Engineer	Rs. 2 lakhs
		Executive Engineer	Rs. 50,000/-

8.1.5 Technical Sanction

8.1.5.1 Necessity

After obtaining administrative approval to a work, it is necessary to prepare detailed drawings and estimates of the proposed work, which are to be submitted to the appropriate authority of Public Works Department of the State Government for according sanction. Such a sanction by the competent authority is known as **'Technical Sanction'**. The technical sanction implies sanction for the detailed drawings including structural drawings, designs and quantities of different items of works shown in the detailed estimate and the proposed rates thereof for all items of work in the estimate.

If the estimated amount of the work exceeds 10% of the amount administratively approved, technical sanction can only be accorded after obtaining revised administrative approval for the work. Technical Sanction is not required for annual repair works not costing more than 5,000/- for which a lump-sum provision will be sanctioned by Superintending Engineer.

Technical sanction must be accorded to the work before it is commenced.

8.1.5.2 Powers of Technical Sanction (Roads and Buildings)

The powers to accord technical sanction to original and revised estimates are as follows :

Sr. No.	Nature and name of the work	Authority to whom the power is delegated	Extent of power
(i)	Original works	Chief Engineer	Full powers
		Superintending Engineer	₹ 25 lakhs
		Executive Engineer	₹ 10 lakhs
		Assistant Engineer (Class I)	Upto ₹ 50,000
		Assistant Engineer (Class II)	Upto ₹ 40,000
		Deputy Engineer	Upto ₹ 30,000
		Sub-divisional Engineer	Upto ₹ 20,000
		Sub-divisional Officer	Upto ₹ 20,000
(ii)	Ordinary Repairs	Superintending Engineer	Full powers within the budget allotment for the circle.
		Executive Engineer	Full powers within the budget allotment for the division.
		Assistant Engineer (Class I)	₹ 10,000 subject to allotment for sub-division
		Assistant Engineer (Class II) Deputy Engineer →	₹ 5,000
		Sub-divisional Engineer	₹ 2,500
		Sub-divisional Officer	₹ 1,000
(iii)	Special Repairs	Superintending Engineer	Full powers within the budget allotment.
		Executive Engineer	₹ 1,00,000 for each case with-in the budget allotment.

		Assistant Engineer (Class I)	₹ 10,000

...Conti.

		Assistant Engineer (Class II) Deputy Engineer →	₹ 5,000
		Sub-divisional Engineer	₹ 2,500
		Sub-divisional Officer	₹ 1,000
(iv)	Special Tools & Plants	Chief Engineer	Full powers
		Superintending Engineer	₹ 5,00,000
		Executive Engineer	₹ 1,00,000
(v)	Excess over Estimates	Chief Engineer	Full powers
		Superintending Engineer	Upto 5% of the sanctioned estimate
		Executive Engineer	Upto 5% of the sanctioned estimate

8.1.6 Comparison between Original Works and Repair Works

Original Works	Repair Works
(i) It may be entirely new work such as new buildings, roads, bridges etc.	(i) The works, which do not fall under the category of original works and are carried out to maintain the works. e.g. building etc. in ordinary use.
(ii) It may also be additions and alterations carried out to existing works such as building etc. that will enhance its value of the property i.e. conversion of a big hall into two or three usable rooms.	(ii) It may be annual maintenance work such as white washing, colour washing to buildings or surface coats to the roads and are called as annual maintenance works.
(iii) It may also be previously abandoned structure e.g. building, road etc. which is to be put to reuse.	(iii) It may also be minor additions and alterations that will not increase the value of property such as providing additional door or window to the existing building upto a maximum amount of ₹ 2,500/-

(iv) Special repairs such as renovation of a structure or repairs carried out to damaged structure to bring it to reuse are also classified under original works.	(iv) It is also be either annual repairs or emergency repairs to an existing building due to its normal wear and tear i.e. repairs to damaged plaster or emergency repairs to be carried out to existing works which are damaged during monsoon floods etc.

8.1.7 Classification of Original works on the basis of Expenditure

Another classification of original works on the basis of expenditure incurred on it is as follows :

    (i)   Major work

    (ii)   Minor work

    (iii) Petty work

(i) Major Work :

It is an original work, estimated cost of which excluding departmental charges, is more than Rs. 1 lakhs or any other ceiling fixed by the engineering department i.e. P.W.D.

(ii) Minor Work :

It is also an original work, the estimated cost of which excluding departmental charges is not more than Rs. 1 lakhs or any other ceiling fixed by the department i.e. P.W.D.

(iii) Petty Work :

It may be either original work or repair work, the estimated cost of which is upto ₹ 5,000/- or any other limit fixed by the Public Works Department of the Government.

8.1.8 Execution of Works

The works are to be executed either departmentally or through an outside agency called as a **'Contractor'**; the former being used for 'Minor works' and the latter for the 'Major works'.

8.1.8.1 Execution of Major works

For major works it is common practice to invite open tenders for the works by giving an advertisement in the leading local news papers called as 'Tender Notice'. The tenders from the contractors received upto the last date mentioned in the tender notice, are scrutinised by the competent authorities depending upon the estimated cost of the work and normally the lowest tender is accepted and the work is allotted to the lowest tenderer (i.e. contractor) and the execution of the work commences.

It is not binding on the competent authorities to always accept the lowest tender. The competency of the tenderer, his past experience of carrying out similar works, and financial status are some of the yard sticks that are applied while accepting tender of a particular contractor. After accepting a particular tender, of a contractor, he is invited and the work is allotted to him after completion of certain Government formalities. The topic is discussed in details in a subsequent chapter on 'Tender and Tender Notice'.

8.1.8.2 Execution of Minor Works

The various methods of executing or carrying out 'minor works' are as follows :

- (i)   Piece Work Agreement (P.W.A.)
- (ii)   Rate List
- (iii) Day work and
- (iv)   Daily Labour or Departmental work

(i) Piece Work Agreement (P.W.A.) :   **(W-2010)**

In Piece Work agreement only the rates are agreed upon by a piece worker without any reference to the total quantity of work to be done or the time of completion. Advertisement for such work costing ₹ 2,500/- is not given in any news paper. Notice inviting tenders (or quotations) is displayed on the notice board of the office of the Executive Engineer without mentioning the quantities of work to be done. Works upto ₹ 2 lakhs can be carried out through a contractor by piece work agreement (P.W.A.) system subject to the following conditions :

- (a)   For work costing over ₹ 50,000/- the Executive Engineer has to take the prior permission from the higher officer (i.e. Superintending Engineer).

- (b)   Item rate quotations either in A_1 or A_2 form shall be invited from the piece work contractor by the Executive Engineer for the items of work to be let out. The time limit for inviting quotations in A_1 or A_2 tender forms for works costing upto ₹ 50,000/- is 7 days, and for the works costing more than ₹ 50,000 and upto ₹ 1,00,000/ is 15 days. For the piece works costing more than ₹ 2,50,000 an advertisement should be given in the local news paper.

The piece worker has to arrange for all material and labour required for carrying out the work. In the Piece Work Agreement only the descriptions of various items of work to be carried out and the rate at which payment is to be made and the total amount of work is mentioned. It also includes detailed specifications of various items of work to be done but does not include the total quantity of work nor its time of completion.

'Piece work agreement' may be either in A_1 or A_2 tender form. In A_1 type of tenders, the rates of various items are mentioned in the schedule attached to the tender form and the piece worker has to quote his rates above or below the scheduled rate at which he is willing to carry out the works. Generally, the work is allotted to the lowest tenderer.

In case of A_2 type of tender, instead of schedule of rate as in A_1 type, schedule of all items of work is mentioned and the piece worker has to quote his rates for the various items included in the schedule of item.

As the 'time is the essence of contract', and since no time limit for the completion of piece work is mentioned, in the real sense the piece work agreement is not a contract. There is no earnest money nor security deposit to be paid by the piece-worker and there is no mention of penalty clause in the agreement. However the agreement can be terminated at any time by serving notice, mentioning the date of termination, to the piece worker.

The rates at which the work is to be allotted to the piece worker should be within sanctioned divisional schedule of rate or within the sanctioned estimated rates. For the rates in excess of sanctioned divisional schedule of rates of the year, Executive Engineer has to take prior permission of Superintending Engineer. The Superintending Engineer may sanction the rates provided the excess over the estimated amount is within his powers.

Piece work Agreement (P.W.A.) is generally adopted for small works of very urgent nature and where labour co-operative societies are not willing to accept such works. The piece worker is paid as per the measurement of the actual work carried out by him at the agreed rate. The specimen piece work agreement form is shown on the next page.

(ii) Rate List: **(W-2010)**

Petty works costing less than ₹ 5,000 can be carried out by a piece worker as per 'Schedule of Cost' which is called as **'Rate List'**. The method is generally adopted when small urgent repair works are to be carried out immediately. As there is no mention about the total quantity of work done nor the time of completion, it is similar to piece work agreement system.

The drawback of carrying out work either by 'Piece Work Agreement' or 'rate list' is that if the early part of the work is more.

PIECE WORK AGREEMENT FORM

District ....   Division ....

Name of work........   Name of Party tendering ....

I hereby agree to execute the undermentioned description of work by piecework and in accordance with the conditions noted below in consideration of payment being made by the Executive Engineer/Sub-divisional Officer .... Division for the quantity of work executed at the rates specified in the following Schedule :

Name of work	Number of item	Class & description of work to be executed	Unit of calculation	Rate of payment

N.B. : Piecework is that which involves the payment for the work done at the stipulated rate only without reference to the total quantity or time.

Dated ....   Signature of party making tender (contractor)

Witness ......   Residence ....

                                Accepted by me (Signature) ....

                                Executive Engineer/Sub-divisional Officer ..

                                Division

Profitable then the later part (of the work) the piece worker may complete the earlier easy and profitable part, accept the payment thereof, and abandon the work thereafter. To guard against this it is advisable to provide different rates for different parts of the work or to make provision for separate rates for extra lift and lead in excess of minimum.

Executive Engineer can execute work under rate list upto Rs. 25,000/-.

(iii) Day Work :

There are certain items of works which can neither be measured accurately nor valued correctly due to its complexity e.g. decorative plaster work or ornamental door etc. where it is not possible to carry out the work at fixed rate. In such cases **'Day work'** method is adopted for the valuation of above items on the basis of actual material used, the number and class of labour employed and the tools and plants required for its completion. The contractor has to maintain day to day account of material consumed, the hours for which each type of labour was employed in a 'day work sheet' which may be checked by the owner or Engineer-in-charge occasionally.

The contractor is paid on the basis of net cost of various material required and the wages paid to the labour plus 20 to 25% as his profit which includes overhead charges and rent for tools and plant utilised if any :

DAY WORK SHEET				
(i) Name of Work to be carried out				
(ii) Name of the Owner				
(iii) Name of the Engineer-in-charge				
(iv) Items for which day work is sanctioned				
(v) Sanction date				
(vi) Date of Commencement of Day Work				
Material Required		Labour Employed and Type of labour	Number	Out turn of the day work
Name of material	Quantity required			
Date				
Working hours Signature of owner or Engineer-in-charge		Signature of Contractor		

The following points should be noted while carrying out daywork method :

- Day work should only be commenced after obtaining necessary sanction from the Engineer-in-charge or owner.
- The contractor should intimate to the Engineer-in-charge or owner the date of the commencement of the work.
- The Engineer-in-charge has to certify the weekly day work statement prepared by the contractor.

The day work method needs strict supervision on the out turn of the work. Moreover, as the contractor's profit depends upon the cost of the work, he will try to increase the cost and as such this expensive method should as far as possible be avoided.

(iv) Daily Labour or Departmental Work :

(a) Necessity :

When no contractor is willing to accept the work due to small margin of profit or is not competent enough to carry out the work, then the work is to be executed departmentally by employing labour on daily wages. The material required for the work such as cement, steel, sand, coarse aggregate, bricks etc. and ordinary and special tools and plants required for the work can be issued from the (Govt.) stores on indent or directly brought from the market.

(b) Muster roll :

The attendance of the total number of labours employed is maintained in Muster Roll form No. 21, by the concerned engineer-in-charge. The Assistant Engineer or Deputy Engineer has to check the Muster roll during inspection and put his signature over it. The payment is made to the labour weekly, fortnightly or monthly as agreed upon. At the time of closing the muster roll for payment it is necessary to measure the work done during that period and enter it in the measurement book (M.B.). The amount to be paid to the each labour and the total amount to be paid and the total quantity of work done is also to be entered at the time of closing the muster roll. The muster roll is then submitted to the higher competent officer for issuing pay order. The amount in the form of imprest or advance is then handed over to the site engineer for making payment to the labour. The site engineer then disburses the amount to the labour and puts his signature against each such payment. After the payment is made the muster roll is sent to Assistant Engineer or Sub-divisional officer, the expenditure incurred is then included in the monthly statement account of the sub-division. The amount of undisbursed wages if any, is to be deposited in cash in the sub-division accounts. The amount can subsequently be withdrawn and payment made to the labour on the hand receipt (form no. 28).

The daily labour method is adopted for maintenance works such as repairs to roads, canals, etc. The material required is to be supplied through Government Central Stores. There is no time limit mentioned for the completion of the work. There is also no monetary ceiling for executing the work departmentally.

The muster roll is divided into two parts :

(a) The part I is called as 'Nominal Roll' in which daily attendance of the labour employed is to be marked with their name, father's name, designation, attendance dates, rates of wages, total amount to be paid to each labour, total amount of the muster roll, signature of the person marking the attendance and signature of the officer making the payment etc. are entered.

(b) In the part II details of quantities of work carried out by the labour and the progress of the work are recorded. Details of measurement that are taken are entered in the measurement book (M.B.) and then abstract of quantities is prepared and written in this part of the muster roll quoting the reference of M.B. page number. The entries once made in the muster roll should in no case be altered nor duplicate muster roll prepared.

The following rules must be followed while maintaining muster roll at the work site :

- For each work there may be one or more than one muster roll.
- Muster roll should never be prepared in duplicate.
- For each period of payment (which may be more than one) there shall be one muster roll.

- The attendance and absence of daily labour with fine if applicable must be marked in ink in the muster roll so that there will be little scope for tampering afterwards.

- After the muster roll is closed and passed for payment the amount should be disbursed immediately and each payment initialled with date by the officer making payment. Details of undisbursed amount should be entered in the register of unpaid labour wages.

- The attendance in the muster roll should tally with the daily labour report sent to the higher authorities.

The earlier muster rolls were in three parts Part I for Nominal Roll, Part II for Register of arrears of wages and Part III for details of measurement of work done.

8.1.9 Relationship between Owner, Engineer, Architect and Contractor

8.1.9.1 Introduction

Whenever any building is to be constructed on a vacant plot, the owner has to seek the guidance of other persons, who will undertake the assignment of 'planning', designing' and subsequently its construction and supervision of the work. The owner, who is a laymen does not understand the exact meaning of plan, elevation section etc. of the building and is also not aware of certain formalities to be completed before the actual construction of the building commences. Thus, the owner is a person who intends to construct a building and expresses his ideas about the proposed building to a person called as **'Architect'**. The 'architect' carefully considers all the requirements of the 'owner' and after visiting the site, tries to put the 'owners' ideas about the building in the form of drawings i.e. plan, elevation, etc. of the building and tries to convince the owner that his requirements are fulfilled. Once the 'owner' approves the architect's proposal i.e. plans, elevations etc., the architect then represents the owner in getting necessary sanction to his plan from the concerned municipal authorities and after obtaining the sanction he assigns the work in consultation with the owner to an outside agency called as the **'Contractor'**. The task of structural design and safety of the structure is assigned to another person known as structural engineer or consulting engineer. Thus, the four persons involved in the construction of a proposed new building are 'Owner', 'Architect', 'Engineer' and 'Contractor', who are supposed to work together in the execution of the proposed work. The 'architect' and 'engineer' are supposed to safeguard the interest of the owner at all stages of the work till its completion. They should possess required knowledge, imagination, skill etc. required for the efficient execution of the work and maintain harmonious relations with the owner and the contractor.

Once a particular contractor is fixed for the execution of the work, it is necessary to prepare 'contract documents' to be signed by the owner and contractor. Such documents develop a legal bond between the owner and contractor for the execution of the work and indicate in details the responsibilities of each to the contract. The duties of architect also emerge from the contract documents and thus his responsibilities towards the execution of the work are also decided.

The duties and liabilities of the above four agencies in the execution of the work may be explained as follows :

8.1.9.2 Owner

The owner should possess a free-hold or lease hold plot without any legal embrances and should have proposal for the construction of his building for which he should have sufficient finance. At any stage the work should not be held up for want of finance. The 'owner' has to express his ideas about the proposed work to an 'architect' and appoints him as his representative to look after the execution of the work. The owner who is prepared to spend the amount to the extent of estimated cost of the building is constantly worried about the actual cost of construction which may be very much higher than the estimated one.

8.1.9.3 Architect

Architect is a person appointed by the 'owner' to put his ideas in the form of drawing. He should be conversant with all municipal bye-laws and is responsible for the preparation of complete drawings of the work. He has to get the relevant drawings (i.e. plan etc.) sanctioned from the municipal corporation and safeguard the interest of the owner throughout the execution of the work till the award of completion certificate from the proper authorities. He has to handover all completed drawings to the contractor for the execution of work.

The architect has to prepare an estimate of the proposed work and has to assure the owner, that under no circumstances the actual cost of construction will be more than the estimated cost. He has to work as liason officer between the owner and the contractor. He has to satisfy and safeguard the interest of the owner and at the same time he has to see that no injustice is done to the contractor. He has to scrutinise the running and final bills prepared by the contractor and pass them for payment.

8.1.9.4 Structural Engineer (or Consulting Engineer)

Structural engineer is responsible for the overall safety of the structure. His R.C.C. and steel designs should be safe, bold and economical. He has to supervise the structural work during its construction stages and certify accordingly. He has also to take care of the type of foundations to be provided depending upon soil strata met with. Also he has to see that their is no unequal settlement of foundation that develops cracks in the superstructure.

8.1.9.5 Contractor

The contractor is a person who brings the ideas of owners expressed in the form of drawing (i.e. plans etc.) by the architect, into reality. The contractor is legally bound to the owner for the completion of the work in the stipulated time. He has to receive instructions from time to time from the architect who represents the owner in the execution of the work. He has to follow strictly all the specifications of various items of construction mentioned in the contract document and prepare running and final bills of the work executed and sent it to the architect for scrutiny and arranging payment for the work carried out by him.

He should get complete set of accurate drawings from the architect, for the speedy completion of the work. The architect has to immediately convey the decisions taken by him or the owner (as regards execution of the work) to the contractor.

The contractor should not be put to inconvenience or financial loss due to handing over of incorrect and insufficient drawings to him. Moreover, all his interim and final bill should be immediately scrutinised by the architect and passed for payment by the owner.

In short owner, architect, engineer and contractor have to work together sincerely, honestly and contribute their best towards the speedy completion of the work as per the drawings and specifications.

THEORETICAL QUESTIONS

1. Differentiate between piece-work agreement and rate list with an example.

2. Explain process of administrative approval and technical sanction in the PWD with an example.

3. Explain the PWD procedure of executing a minor work.

4. Explain the PWD method of execution of a work.

5. Explain the organisational set-up.

6. Differentiate between original works and repair works.

7. Give the classification of original work on the basis of Expenditure.

8. Discuss the relationship between owner, engineer, Architect and Contractor.

Chapter 9

CONTRACTS AND ARBITRATION

9.1 CONTRACTS

9.1.1 Introduction

Contracts play an important role in our every day life. Even without realising it, we enter into contract, for example: when one enters a vacant rickshaw and asks the driver of the rickshaw to take to his destination he has entered into an 'implied contract'. The rickshaw-driver agrees to take that person to his destination for the payment to be made to him as shown by the rickshaw meter. All such transactions in our every day life are based on agreements that create mutual rights and obligations.

The 'principles of contract' are as laid down in sections 1 to 75 of 'Indian Contract Act' 1872 which came into force from 1st September 1872.

9.1.2 Definition and Basic Concept of Law of Contracts

(1) Definition of Contract

"A contract is an agreement that arises out of the 'acceptance' of a 'proposal' or 'offer', and is enforceable by law".

(2) The Basic Concepts of Law of Contracts are as follows

  (i) **Proposal or offer :** The section 2 (a) of the Indian Contract Act 1872, defines the 'proposal' in the following manner.

  When a person signifies to another person his willingness to do or to abstain from doing anything, with a view to obtain the consent (i.e. assent) of that other he is said to make a 'proposal' or 'offer'.

  The 'offer' gives rise to a 'contract' when it creates legal relationship.

  (ii) **Acceptance :** Section 2.C of Indian Contract Act defines the acceptance as :

  "When the person to whom the proposal or offer is made signifies his assent (i.e. consent), the 'proposal' or 'offer' is said to be 'accepted'.

  The acceptance is said to be valid when it is 'absolute' and 'unqualified' and is expressed in 'usual and acceptable manner.' The acceptance may be communicated by 'words' or by 'conduct'. A 'conditioned' or 'qualified' acceptance is not an acceptance but is a 'counter proposal'.

(iii) Promise : When a 'proposal' or 'offer' is accepted without any condition and or reservation, it becomes a 'promise'. The person who initiates the proposal is said to be 'promissor' and the one who accepts is called as 'promisee'.

When the acceptance of any proposal or offer is given in words, the promise is termed as 'express'.

When the acceptance of any proposal or offer is made in any form other than in words, it is said to be 'implied'.

(iv) Consideration : Ordinarily, when a person makes a promise to another he will do so to derive certain benefit out of it, and is known as 'consideration' of the promise. The section 2 (d) of Indian Contract Act, defines 'consideration' as "When at the desire of promissor, the promisee or any other person has done or abstained from doing, or does or abstains from doing, or promises to do or to abstain from doing such act or abstinence or promise is called 'consideration' for the promise.

(v) Agreement : The Section 2 (e) of the Indian Contract Act, says that any promise or every set of promises, forming the consideration for each other (i.e. promissor and promisee), is known as an 'agreement'. The agreement is further classified as :

- 'Valid agreements' are those that are enforceable by law.
- 'Void agreements' are those that are not enforceable by law.
- 'Voidable agreements' are those which are valid as long as they are not avoided by the parties competent to do so. i.e. it is enforceable by law at the option of parties to such an agreement but not at the option of those who are not party to such agreement.
- Unenforceable agreements are those which cannot be enforced by law due to some technical flaws in the agreement.
- 'Illegal agreements' are those which are against the law and hence are void.

(vi) Contract : As per Section 2 (h) of Indian Contract Act, the 'contract' is an agreement enforceable by law. If an agreement enables a person to compel another to do something or not to do something, it is termed as 'contract' e.g. If B agrees to build a house for A in consideration for Rs. 1 lakh, the agreement is said to be a contract.

It may be noted that, all contracts are (necessarily) agreements but all agreements are not (necessarily) contracts, as they are not enforceable by law.

9.1.3 Voidable and Void Contracts   (W-2010)

The various conditions that an agreement should satisfy so as to become a 'contract', mentioned in section 10 of Indian Contract Act are discussed as follows :

(a) Voidable Contract:

As agreement that can be enforced by law at the option of one or more parties to the agreement but not at the option of others (not concerned with the agreement) is called as a 'voidable contract'.

(b) Void Contract:

A contract which cannot be enforced by law is said to be 'void contract'. Such a contract cannot be enforced by law due to presence of technical flaw into it of which any of the parties may take advantage of it. e.g. agreement forced by coercion, fraud etc. amounts to 'voidable contract'. If the objects or considerations of the contract are against law, the contract is said to be 'void'.

Under the following circumstances, an agreement (and hence contract) becomes voidable.

(i)   When consent to agreement is forced by coercion, or undue influence or fraud etc.

(ii)   When a party to contract, in which time is essence of contract, fails to complete in a stipulated time.

9.1.4 Speciality and Simple Contracts

(a) Speciality Contract: It is a contract in 'writing' and is signed, sealed and delivered by the concerned parties, without any 'consideration'. It is also known as deed.

(b) Simple Contracts: The contracts which are not under seal but with considerations are called simple contracts.

9.1.5 Essentials (i.e. Requirements) of a Valid Contract

As stated earlier a 'contract' is an agreement which is enforceable by law, as such there will be no contract which will be 'void'. An 'agreement' may be 'void' but the 'contracts' are all 'valid' (i.e. can be enforced by either party) or 'voidable' (i.e. enforceable by any one of the parties, at its option).

The following agreements are contracts, as per Section 10 of Indian Contract Act which reads as follows :

All agreements are contracts if they are made :

- by the free consent of the parties.
- who are competent to contract.
- for a lawful consideration and with a lawful object and
- are not expressly declared as void.

9.1.5.1 Free Consent

Section 13 of Indian Contract Act states that two or more persons are said to consent, when they agree upon the same thing in the same sense. In order that the contract should be valid, not only 'consent' but **'Free consent'** is necessary. Consent is said to be 'free' when it is free from coercion, undue influence, misrepresentation, fraud, mistake etc.

When the concerned parties agree upon the same thing in the same sense, they are said to be 'ad idem'.

In case of 'building contracts', the terms and conditions of contracts are clearly understood by both the parties and their signatures on such documents clearly indicate their free consent to the agreement. However, if it can be reasonably proved that the agreement was without free consent, the contract may become 'void'.

Thus there should be a sound proposal (i.e. offer) initiated by a party to be accepted by another party without any reservation or qualification to become an agreement i.e. there should be 'meeting of minds' of the two parties entering into contract regarding the subject matter of 'agreement'.

- **Coercion :** Coercion as per Section 15 of Indian Contract Act is any action forbidden by the Indian Penal Code (I.P.C.) i.e. Any contract that takes place under coercion is said to be void.

- **Undue influence :** Section 16 of Indian Contract Act states that any consent taken under 'undue influence' is said to be invalid under the following circumstances :

(a) that one of the parties was in a position to dominate the will of the other, and

(b) makes use of domination to gain an unfair benefit over the other.

    Thus undue influence results in the absence of 'free consent'.

- **Misrepresentation and fraud :** It may be either due to 'innocence' or wilful. If it is due to 'innocence' it is termed as 'misrepresentation' and if 'wilful' it is considered as 'fraud'.

    The person misguided by misrepresentation has a right to avoid the contract, whereas defrauded party can also avoid the contract and claim for the loss or damage caused to the party.

- **Mistake of law or of fact :** As per Section 21 of Indian Contract Act, the contract is not voidable, if it is caused by a mistake as to any law in force in that country. As ignorance of law is not an excuse, such mistakes of law are not grounds for relief from contract.

    For mistakes of fact, if both the contracting parties are under mistake to the matter of fact the agreement (or contract) becomes void.

9.1.5.2 Who are Competent to Contract

Section 11 of Indian Contract Act states that all agreements are contracts if the agreements are made by a competent party i.e. the one

- Who is not a minor (i.e. who has attended the age of majority).
- Who is of sound mind and
- Who is not disqualified from contracting by any law to which he is subject to :

(i) **Minor :** The person who has not attended the age of 18 is said to be minor, and any agreement during the age of minority is said to be void.

(ii) Sound mind : Section 12 of Indian Contract Act states that a person will be said to be of sound mind, if at the time of entering contract he is capable of understanding it and can form a rational judgement as to its effect upon his interests. A person who is normally of unsound mind but occasionally of sound mind, may enter into a contract when he is of sound mind. Thus a person having unsound mind or lunatic is incompetent to enter into a contract. Similarly, the contract entered by a 'drunkard' is also voids.

9.1.5.3 Lawful Consideration with a Lawful Object

All works carried out by contract are not done free of cost and thus for a contract to be legal there must be some lawful valid consideration. Section 2 (d) of I.C.A. defines consideration as follows : "When at the desire of the promisor, the promisee or any other person, has done or abstained from doing or does or abstains from doing or promises to do or to abstain from doing, then such act of abstinence or promise is called a consideration for the promise. In practice, all building contracts are based on lawful valid considerations in terms of certain amount of money. As per section 23 of I.C.A., the consideration is lawful unless it is not forbidden by law or is fraudulent or court regards it as immoral or opposite to public policy.

Thus an agreement having unlawful consideration or object is said to be void. Unusual promises or acts without any valid consideration will not be entertained by the Court of law. However, section 25 of Indian Contract Act quotes certain exceptions to valid consideration as stated below "An agreement without valid consideration is void unless :

The contract is in writing and registered according to the law and is made out of natural love or affection between the contracting parties or to compensate for the voluntary services rendered to the promisor or it is promise to pay time barred debts. i.e. under the above cases the agreement entered without valid consideration will be said to be valid".

9.1.5.4 Not Expressely Declared as Void

A contract which cannot be enforced by law is termed as 'void contract' and is due to the presence of technical flaw into it.

9.1.6 Guidelines While Entering into Contracts

- The terms and conditions laid down in contract should be very precise and definite and without any ambiguity. Under no circumstances alternatives should be provided in any form.
- Prescribed standard forms of 'Contracts' should invariably be used wherever applicable.
- Where such standard forms are not prescribed expert legal and financial advice should be sought from the competent authorities at the time of preparing contract documents.
- The terms and conditions of contract once entered should not be materially altered.
- The contract should not involve any uncertain or unusual condition detrimental to the department.
- The work should be allotted to the contractor only after written agreement is obtained.
- All government machinery, property etc. entrusted to the contractor must be well safe guarded.

- Provision as regards cancellation of contract, after giving due notice to the contractor should be made in the contract.
- In case the work is to be started in between the period of the 'acceptance of tender' and 'execution of contract', temporary agreement in A_2 form should be completed. Subsequently this should be followed by main agreement in the regular form of contract.

9.1.7 Classification of Contractors

Depending upon the technical capability and financial status, the contractors are classified, by the competent Maharashtra Government authorities with effect from 6th September 1982, as follows :

General Works Category

Earlier category of contractors before 6.9.1982	Limit for tendering	New category of contractors from 6.9.1982	Limit for tendering
A_1	No limits	I	No limits
		II	Rs. 3 crores
A	Rs. 1 crore	III	Rs. 1 crore
B_+	Rs. 60 lakhs		
B	Rs. 30 lakhs	IV	Rs. 50 lakhs
B_1	Rs. 15 lakhs	V	Rs. 15 lakhs
C	Rs. 5 lakhs	VI	Rs. 5 lakhs
D	Rs. 2 lakhs		
E	Rs. 50,000/-	VII	Rs. 2 lakhs

Note : Before registration of a contractor into the appropriate category, a full inquiry as to his financial stability, professional capacity and reliability must be made. The contractor has to furnish full information in the following proforma.

Sr. No.	Name of work	Amount of work put to tender	Date & Year of commencement of work	Amount spend during each of last 5 years	Amount of work that remains to be executed	Remarks

9.1.8 Registration of Contractors

The contractor interested in registering his name with the Government shall submit an application in the following form, to the authority competent to sanction it. The applicant has to furnish documents regarding his financial status supported by a certificate of solvency obtained from the District collector or S.D.O. of that district or Bankers' certificate and also certificate regarding his professional capacity and reliability from the officers known to the contractor.

In addition to the above, the contractor's application should be accompanied by the following documents :

- Latest income-tax clearance certificate.
- Technical staff with the qualification and experience, employed by the contractor.
- List of machinery possessed by the contractor including its location, condition etc.
- In case of partnership firms, an attested copy of the partnership deed.
- Copy of power of attorney, duly attested.
- The contractor has to pay half the registration fees (non-refundable) for the class in which he intends to register himself.

Prescribed Application form for registration as contractor

1. Name of applicant with full address   :
2. Details of firm i.e. Joint Stock Company,

   Hindu Undivided Family, Individual etc.   :
3. Name of person holding power of attorney   :
4. Name of sole proprietors/partners with

   particulars   :
5. Name of bankers with full address   :
6. Place of business   :
7. Class in which registration is sought   :
8. Whether contractor desires to deposit

   Lump-sum money for securing exemption

   from earnest deposit or will pay earnest money

   with each tender   :
9. List of works executed during last three years

   preceding the date of application :

   - Name of work

- Amount of work put to tender
- Date and year of commencement
- Amount spent during each of last three years
- Amount of work still to be completed

10. List of tools and plants possessed by the contractor   :

11. Technical qualifications and experience of
    the partner/proprietor and details of technical
    employees in the firm.   :

12. Tools and plants, machineries etc. owned
    by the contractor   :

13. Whether enlisted in any other Department/Orga-
    nisation or other State   :

14. Has the applicant or his partner black listed
    by the Govt., in the past and whether the
    applicant had applied for registration
    elsewhere and whether the application
    was rejected.   :

15. Up-to-date income-tax clearance certificate
    enclosed or not   :

16. Amount of solvency certificate which the
    applicant has held or produced   :

17. I/we certify that I/we have been not and will
    not get myself/ourselves registered as contractor
    in the department under more than
    one name   :
    Signature and Address.

9.1.9 Upgradation of Contractors

The contractors desirous of upgrading themselves to higher class have to submit fresh application in prescribed form accompanied by new solvency certificate and all other relevant documents through the Executive Engineer and have to pay fresh registration fees. The Executive Engineer has to forward such application with recommendations accompanied by confidential reports of contractors to the concerned competent authorities. The competent authority has to decide all such applications on merits taking into account the works in hand of contractor and his annual turnover.

9.1.10 Renewal of Registration

For the renewal of registration the contractors have to send their applications in prescribed form accompanied by fresh solvency certificate and other relevant documents and requisite fees to the Executive Engineer at least three months before the expiry of his earlier registration. The Executive Engineer with his recommendations will forward such applications to the concerned competent authorities for approval.

9.1.11 Pre-qualification of Contractors

In this process, the financial stability and competency of the contractors is determined before the tenders for the work are invited. After the contractors are pre-qualified, the tender forms are supplied to the only eligible contractors who possess requisite qualifications for the job.

The contractors are classified based on their financial status and technical capability as explained in the Art 7.3.7.

Before 6th September 1982, the contractors were classified as A_1, A, B_+, B, B_1, C, D and E but with effect from 6th September 1982, they are classified into new category as I, II, III, IV, V, VI and VII.

Contractor has to sent a standard application form giving all detailed information regarding his past experience of carrying out similar works, works on hand at present, financial status, qualifications, tools and plants and equipment available (with him) for executing the work. After going through all information supplied in application form, the appropriate authorities decide the category of the contractor and his name is entered in the schedule of that category.

Merits of Pre-qualification:

- As only competent qualified contractors can only submit their tender, the question of verifying the competency of contractor will not arise. Moreover under this process, the work can be allotted to the lowest tenderer who is capable to carry out the work.
- The selected contractors (usually lowest) are capable of executing the work as they are qualified to do the job.
- *Fair competition :* As only eligible and qualified contractors can submit their tenders, there will be fair competition amongst the qualified contractors.
- *Elimination of unqualified contractor :* The contractors unqualified for work cannot apply thus their time, energy etc. in filling the tender form is saved.

Demerits of Pre-qualifications:

- *No open competition :* As only qualified contractors have to apply (i.e. submit their tender) for the work, there is no open competition.
- *Mal practices in classification :* There is every possibility of malpractice at the time of pre-qualification of contractors.

- *Complicated application form :* Any ordinary contractor may not be able to fill the complicated application form correctly.

Weighted Point Score Method of Pre-qualification of Contractors :

- First of all the weightage of each criteria/parameters in ratio/decimal is determined by considering the total weightage of all parameters like profitability, annual turnover, networth etc.
- The score of the first contractors (in points) for the different parameters/criteria is determined.
- The weighted point score of the first contractor, for different parameters is determined by multiplying the weightage (in ratio/decimal) with the score (in points).
- The total weighted point score of the first contractor is determined by adding the weighted point score for the various parameters.
- Following this method, the total weighted point score of the other contractors is also determined.
- The maximum (possible) weighted point score for the different parameters is determined by multiplying the maximum point earmarked for the parameter with its corresponding weightage (in ratio/decimal).
- The maximum (possible) total weighted point score is determined by adding the maximum (possible) weighted point score for the various parameters.
- The cutoff weighted point score is determined by considering the guidelines given for pre-qualification [for example, if it is mentioned that the contractors, who will get more than 60% of the total points, will only pre-qualify. Then cutoff weighed point score will be 60% of maximum (possible) total weighted point score.]
- All those contractors whose total weighted point score is more than cutoff weighted point score will prequalify. (The method can be understood by persuing the following solved problem.)

Q. 1. **For the assessment of pre-qualification of the contractors as regards their "Financial capability" it is decided to evaluate the contractors on a 3 point scale for the following :**   **(Dec. 2003 – 8 Marks)**

I. **Liquidity – Weightage 10**

    (i)   Adequate liquidity of 1 crore – 3 points

    (ii)   Liquidity less than one crore – 0 point.

II. **Profitability – Weightage 10**

    [From balance sheet of last 3 years]

    (i)   If +ve in all the three years – 3 points

    (ii)   If +ve in any two years – 2 points.

    (iii) If +ve in any one year – 1 point.

III. Average net worth (over last 3 years) – Weightage 5

    (i)   If ≥ 2 crores – 3 points.

    (ii)   If ≥ 1.5 crores but < 2.0 crores – 2 points.

    (iii) If ≥ 1 crore but < 1.5 crores – 1 points.

IV. Annual turnover (of last 3 years) – Weightage 5

    (i)   If turnover is > 10 crores – 3 points.

    (ii)   If turnover is ≤ 10 crores but > 8 crores – 2 points.

    (iii) If turnover is ≤ 8 crores but > 5 crores – 1 point.

Solution : From the comparative statements of the contractors, who have submitted their pre-qualifying bids, the following data is obtained :

Sr. No.	Criteria	Data of		
		Contractor A	**Contractor B**	**Contractor C**
I.	Liquidity (in crores)	1.50	0.750	1.20
II.	Profitability in last 3 years (+ve in last 3 years)	2 years	3 years	3 years
III.	Average net worth in 3 years (in crores)	3 crores	1.8 crores	1.3 crores
IV.	Average annual turnover in 3 years in crores	9 crores	6 crores	8 crores

Q. 2. **Further it is decided that, the contractors who will get more than 60% of the total points, will only prequalify.**

    Assess the contractors by weighted point score average method, and decide which contractors will prequalify; with seasons.

Solution : Weightage of liquidity is 10, while the total weightage of all parameters will be 10 + 10 + 5 + 5 = 30, therefore weightage of liquidity in terms of ratio will be 10/30 = $\frac{1}{3}$.

Contractor A will get 3 points for liquidity parameter, since his liquidity is 1.5 crore, (which is more than 1 crore, as mentioned) therefore weighted point score of contractor A for liquidity will be $3 \times \frac{1}{3}$ = 1.0. Similarly, the W.P.S. of contractors B and C for liquidity will be $0 \times \frac{1}{3}$ = 0 and $3 \times \frac{1}{3}$ = 1.0 respectively. W.P.S. of the contractors have been determined in the following table :

Sr. No.	Criteria	Weighted point score		
		Contractor A	Contractor B	Contractor C
1.	Liquidity	$3 \times \frac{1}{3} = 1.0$	$0 \times \frac{1}{3} = 0.0$	$3 \times \frac{1}{3} = 1.0$
2.	Profitability	$2 \times \frac{1}{3} = \frac{2}{3}$	$3 \times \frac{1}{3} = 1.0$	$3 \times \frac{1}{3} = 1.0$
3.	Average net worth	$3 \times \frac{1}{6} = \frac{1}{2}$	$2 \times \frac{1}{6} = \frac{1}{3}$	$1 \times \frac{1}{6} = \frac{1}{6}$
4.	Average annual turnover	$2 \times \frac{1}{6} = \frac{1}{3}$	$1 \times \frac{1}{6} = \frac{1}{6}$	$1 \times \frac{1}{6} = \frac{1}{6}$
	Total weighted point score	**2.5**	**1.5**	**2.33**

Maximum (possible) total weighted point score :

$$= \left(3 \times \frac{1}{3}\right) + \left(3 + \frac{1}{3}\right) + \left(3 \times \frac{1}{6}\right) + \left(3 \times \frac{1}{6}\right) = 3.0$$

Cutoff weighted point score : 60% of M.T.W.P.S. $= 0.6 \times 3.0 = 1.8$.

Since total weighted point score of contractors A **(2.5)** and C **(2.33)** are more than cutoff weighted point score **(1.8)**, therefore, **contractors A and C will pre-qualify.**

9.1.12 Labour Co-operative Societies

As per Government directive, the works whose estimated cost is upto ₹ 1,00,000 should be let out to 'labour co-operative societies', without calling for tenders. The estimated rates should be as per the updated divisional schedule of rates (D.S.R.). The classification of labour co-operative societies depending upon their financial status, managerial and technical capacity and man power is as follows :

Sr. No.	Type of labour co-operative society	Authority competent to classify	Estimated cost of the work
1.	A class	Superintending Engineer	Upto ₹ 1 lakh
2.	B class	Executive Engineer	Upto ₹ 50,000
3.	C class	Executive Engineer	Upto ₹ 20,000

Usually, co-operative societies are formed from local landless backward class persons and other persons, the backward class persons being in majority.

As regards allotment of work between labour co-operative societies and piece-workers, preference should be given to the former. However, in the absence of labour co-operative societies coming forward to take up the work, it can be allotted to piece workers.

Such labour co-operative societies are exempted from producing solvency certificates but they have to produce a certificate from District Deputy Registrar regarding their financial status and capacity to execute the work. Not more than three works should be allotted to any society at one time. The total cost of the works so allotted should not exceed twice the limit prescribed for allotting a single work. The classification of labour co-operative societies should be reviewed every three years depending upon their financial status and managerial capacity. For the works costing upto ₹ 1,00,000 the work can be allotted to labour co-operative societies without calling for tenders, and as such there is no necessity of earnest money to be deposited by them. Similarly, the works which do not involve supply of Government materials i.e. cement, steel, etc. no security deposit is required to be collected. However, works in which Govt. material is to be supplied fifty percent of amount due towards deposits, is to be recovered.

9.1.13 Methods of Carrying Out Works

The various systems of carrying out works other than by the employment of daily labour are :

- Piece work
- Rate list and
- Contract work
- In 'piece work system' only the rate is agreed upon by a piece worker without any reference to the total quantity of work to be carried out or its time of completion. The entire work is completed either on A – 1 or A – 2 forms.
- In case of 'rate list' system, small, petty works are carried by number of piece-workers as per schedule of costs, called as 'rate list' without making any reference to the total quantity of work and the time of its completion.
- All other work (not included in the above) carried out or supplies of material made under agreement is called as 'contract work'. The agreement for carrying out such contract work is invariably in writing in which the total quantity of work to be carried out and the time within which it is to be completed is also mentioned besides other conditions such as penalty and liabilities etc.

As already stated a contract is an agreement which is enforceable by law. The contract comes into existence when there is 'free consent' between the contracting parties with valid consideration.

In the 'contract system', all the work is carried out through contractor who arranges all required materials, labour, tools and plants for the satisfactory completion of the work, as per specifications within the prescribed time limit. Contracts are generally arranged by invitation of sealed tenders, the work being allotted to the lowest tenderer.

9.1.14 Types of Contract   (W-2010)

As already stated a 'proposal' or 'offer' made and accepted by both the parties becomes a 'promise'. The acceptance must be absolute and unqualified. Every 'promise' with valid considerations is an 'agreement', and agreement that can be enforced by law is a 'contract'.

Types or Kinds or Forms of Contract :

Various types of contracts are as follows :

    (1)   Lump-sum contracts

    (2)   Schedule or unit price or Item rate contracts, and

    (3)   Lump-sum and schedule contracts

    (4)   Cost plus or percentage contracts.

(1) Lump-Sum Contracts:

The Public Works Manual defines lump-sum contract as one in which the contractor agrees to execute the entire work with all its contingencies in accordance with the drawings and specifications for a fixed sum, the following being its essential characteristics.

- In case of additions and alterations not covered by the contract and not involving any increase or decrease of quantities except when the design is changed, it should clearly be specified that the rates provided for such items will be as sanctioned in the schedule of rates of the division.

- Except as stated in clause (a) above, no allusion is made in the contract to the departmental estimate of work, schedule of rates or quantities of the work to be executed.

- Detailed measurements of the work executed are not required to be recorded except in case of additions and alterations.

In this type of contract, the quantities of items do not form part of contract. The prescribed form C is to be used for all such lump-sum contracts.

The method is suitable when it is possible to calculate the exact quantities of all items of work to be executed and when there are limited number of well defined items of work. e.g. construction of a compound wall or type designs for a housing scheme etc.

The method is also followed in case of miscellaneous items which cannot be executed by any other type of contract e.g. ornamental plaster work, providing an opening in the existing main wall etc.

Merits and Demerits of Lump-sum Contracts:

- **Economical :** Contractor tendering for lump-sum contract will quote his amount with certain margin of profit. Because of fair competition amongst the contractor, the margin of profit is likely to come down, resulting in the saving in the cost and hence economical.

- **Fixed Amount :** The contract being a 'lump-sum', owner knows the total cost of the work before hand and thus he is well prepared to arrange the fixed amount of the contract.

- **Speedy Execution of the Work :** The contractor's profit is related to the time of completion of the work. As the contractor is assured a fixed sum, he will try to complete the work as early as possible increasing percentage of profit. Moreover, he can utilise the machinery, tools and plants on this work after its completion to some other work.

- **No Measurement of Items of Work :** As it is a lump-sum contract, the measurement of works will be restricted only to the extra items, thus reducing the burden of measurements.

Demerits of Lump-sum Contract:

- **Unbalanced Contract :** The contract may result in excessive profit or loss to the contractor and is thus of speculative in nature.

- **More Dispute :** As the contractor's and owner's interest will be clashing all the while it may result in dispute between them.

- **Extra Items and Extra Cost :** As all the plans, specifications and details of the work are to be prepared completely before the commencement of work, it is very difficult to adjust any additions and alterations during the execution of the work, thus resulting in 'extra items of works', and extra cost, which is contrary to the essence of lump-sum contract.

- **Delay in Commencement of the Work :** Unless all plans, specifications and other formalities are completed, the work cannot be commenced.

- **Quality of Material :** Good workmanship is not guaranteed, as contractor will try to bring substandard material and complete the work as early as possible to have higher margin of profit.

- **Loss of Material :** For any loss or pilferage of material from the site, the contractor will be held responsible, and hence it is disadvantageous to the contractor.

(2) Schedule or Unit Price or Item Rate Contracts:

Schedule contracts are those in which the tenderer or contractor agrees to undertake the execution of work at the fixed rate, the amount to be paid to him being dependent on the quantities and kind of work executed or material supplied. Thus, in this type of contract, the quantities of items form part of the contract and the contractor has to execute the entire work as shown in drawing and as per the description given in the bill of quantities, the rates of various items of work being agreed upon. The rates quoted by the contractor are inclusive of material, labour, tools and plants, overhead charges and contractor's profit. The actual quantities of items of work may be more or less than the estimated quantities but the rate of the item remains fixed.

In the B_2 tender form, the approximate quantities of all items of work Ex. Excavation for foundations, filling foundations with plain cement concrete (1 : 3 : 6), U.C.R. masonry in foundations etc., are mentioned and the contractor has to quote his rates against all such items and arrive at the total cost of the work. Though the exact quantities of the various items of work are not known, the quality of construction is well defined by detailed specifications for such items. The item-wise work executed by the contractor is accurately measured and priced as per the rates quoted in the bill of quantities. For any extra work, the rate quoted by the contractor in the bill of quantities is binding on him. The method is generally followed for most of the public works executed by the Government.

Merits of Schedule Contracts:

- **Balanced Contract :** As the contractor is paid as per the rates agreed upon item wise, there are no chances of excessive profit or loss to the contractor and hence it is a balanced type of contact.

- **Flexibility :** This type of contract is 'flexible' one as reasonable variations can be made in the quantities of the items as shown in the tender, during the progress of the work.

- **Early Commencement of the Work :** The work can be let out immediately to the contractor after the acceptance of his tender, other formalities i.e. final plan and specifications etc. being completed afterwards.

- **Economical :** As the contractor is to be paid on the basis of actual quantity of work that will carried out, the method may prove to be economical.

- **Possibility of Variations :** Variations in the plans are possible as the items of works executed are to be actually measured and paid for at the agreed rates.

- **No Element of Uncertainty :** Any uncertainties in the plans etc. will not have any adverse effect on the contractor's interest, as the contractor will be paid for the completed item at the agreed price or rate.

- **Extra Work :** As the contractor is to be paid at the agreed rates of the various items, the extra works are minimised.

- **Early Completion of the Work :** In this type of contract, the contractor tries to complete the work as early as possible so that he can utilise the tools and plants etc. on some other work.

Demerits of Schedule Contracts

- **Total Cost of the Work Unknown :** As the quantities of various items of work are likely to be more or less than the estimated, the exact cost of the work to be executed is not known to start with.

- **More Measurements :** As all the items for which the payment is to made are to be actually measured, the work load of architect/or engineer is considerably increased.

- **Clashing of Interests :** The contractor will try to do more quantity of work of such items for which he has quoted more rates, whereas the owner will try to extract more work of items for which the contractor has quoted less rates thus resulting in the confliction of interests.

- **Variations in the Plan :** As the work commences well before the final plan and detailed specifications are prepared, it is quite likely that demolition of certain works may be necessary, resulting in the extra cost of the work.

- **Loss of Material :** The contractor will have to suffer for any loss or pilferage of material.

The schedule contract may be either 'item rate' (i.e. unit priced) or 'percentage item rate' contract.

- In case of an item rate contract, the contractor quotes his rates separately against each item in figures as well as in words.

- In case of percentage item rate contract, the estimated rates are also mentioned against each item in the tender and the contractor has to quote his rates against such items in percentage by which the estimated rates are to be decreased or increased, in case the work is allotted to him. This second method is to be adopted for the works where the actual quantities are likely to vary considerably from those shown in the tender form (i.e. estimated quantities). There is very little possibility of such tenders being unbalanced one.

(3) Lump-Sum and Schedule Contracts:

This type of contract is similar in nature to the lump-sum contract. i.e. the contractor will be paid fixed sum for the execution of the entire work as specified in the stipulated time and in addition schedule of rates for various items of work is also provided to regulate the rates at which the contractor will be paid for any additions or alterations that will be effected during the progress of the work.

At the time of making payment, it is not necessary to measure the items of original work but only the measurement of extra items of work will be required and paid for as per the schedule of rate agreed upon.

This type of contract is not in common use but is followed in the organisations which are permitted to do so.

The merits and demerits of this system are same as that mentioned in the lump-sum contract mentioned in (i) above, with only change that schedule of rate is also included in the contract for the payment to be made to the contractor for any additions or alterations made during the execution of the work.

(4) Cost Plus or Percentage Contracts:

In this type of contract, the contractor agrees to execute the work for a certain percentage over the actual cost of construction as fees for his expert services. This type of contract is suitable where both quantity and quality of the work are unknown to start with and there are frequent fluctuations in the market rates of labour and material and no contractor is willing to come forward to execute the work either on lump-sum or item-rate basis. The method is not suitable for public works but can be adopted for private works.

In this method the owner maintains the complete record of expenditure incurred on construction work and the contractor is paid at the certain percentage over it as his fees. According to the manner in which such fees are paid to the contractor, this method is further classified as follows :

- Cost plus fixed percentage
- Cost plus fixed sum

- Cost plus fixed sum with profit sharing
- Cost plus fixed sum with bonus
- Cost plus fixed sum with penalty
- Cost plus variable percentage.

(i) Cost Plus Fixed Percentage: In this method, the owner agrees to pays to the contractor a certain fixed percentage of the total expenditure incurred on the work, towards his fees for the overall supervision and other services. This percentage usually varies from 10 to 15 percent of the total cost of the work.

(ii) Cost Plus Fixed Sum: In this method instead of making payment to the contractor on the fixed percentage basis, a fixed sum is paid to him for his services. Thus it is a predetermined amount that is to be paid to the contractor.

(iii) Cost Plus Fixed Sum with Profit Sharing: In order to bring the cost of work lower than the estimated cost, this method is adopted. If the contractor completes the work and brings down the cost (lower than the estimated one), he is paid certain share from the amount thus saved in addition to the fixed sum to be paid to him. The usual percentage to be paid to the contractor from such saving is upto a maximum 50 percent. This is a sort of incentive to the contractor to finish the work early and that well below the estimated cost.

(iv) Cost-Plus Fixed Sum with Bonus: This type of contract is preferred when the work is to be completed urgently and before time.

A certain date (known as target date) is fixed for the completion of entire work and if the contractor completes the work before the target date, he is paid a certain amount as bonus per day of early completion in addition to the fixed sum agreed upon earlier.

(v) Cost Plus Fixed Sum with Penalty: This method is similar to the above method with little modification. A target date is fixed for the completion of the work. If the contractor completes the work by the target date, he is paid the fixed sum as agreed upon earlier. However, if there is delay in the completion of the work, he is penalised a certain fixed amount per day of delay in completion. This method, thus compels the contractor to complete the work by target date, else he will be penalised every day of delay.

(vi) Cost Plus Varying Percentage: In this method payment to the contract is made on varying percentage basis. The contractor's percentage is linked with the cost of the construction. It increases or decreases with the decrease or increase in cost of construction from the estimated amount. Thus he gets more profit if he can bring down the cost of construction, and (he gets) less profit if the actual cost of construction exceeds the estimated amount.

Merits of Cost-Plus Contracts

- **Interest Not Clashing :** In this method, the contractor is assured a certain fixed amount towards his profit and thus he will not run in loss. The owner can spend as much amount as he likes towards the work. Thus interest of both owner and contractor will not be clashing with each other.

- **No Speculation :** As the contractor's profit is linked with the total cost of construction there is no scope for speculation.
- **Early Commencement of the Work :** Immediately after the acceptance of tender, the work can be started without waiting for all formalities to complete.
- **No Necessity of Preparing all Details :** It is not necessary to prepare all detailed drawings etc. prior to the commencement of the work.
- **Good Quality of Material and Workmanship :** Good quality of material and workmanship can be achieved.
- **Elimination of Extra Work :** As the contractor will be paid a certain percentage of total cost, there will be no botheration of extra work and determination of its rate.
- **Speedy Completion of Work :** As the contractor is assured fixed sum or percentage over the total cost of work, he will try to complete the work as early as possible.

Demerits of Cost-Plus Contracts:
- **Unbalanced contract :** As the contractor's profit depends upon the total cost of the work, he will try to increase the cost of construction.
- **Cost of construction unknown :** As the total cost of construction is not known to start with, the owner is likely to face financial difficulties.
- **Unsuitable for public works :** This type of contract is unsuitable and illegal for public works.
- **No economy :** As the contractor's profit is linked with the total cost of the work, he will try to produce fictitious bills, thus increasing the cost of the work.
- **Carelessness of the contractor :** The contractor will be careless throughout the execution of work, thus increasing the total cost.
- **Loss of material :** Owner has to suffer for any loss or pilferage of material from the work site.

9.1.15 Contract Documents

Before a work is given out on contract, the Executive Engineer or owner prepares 'contract documents' to be signed by both the parties and it should include the following documents :
- Title page - indicating the name of the work.
- Index page - showing the contents of the agreement with page numbers.
- Brief tender notice giving description of the work estimated cost, earnest money and security amount to be deposited, time of completion of the work etc.
- Tender form showing rates quoted by the contractor, total cost of the work, time of completion, progress of work, security money, penalty etc. This is also called as schedule 'B'.
- Schedule of quantities or bill of quantities showing description of each item, rates and price of each item, total cost of the work.
- General specifications of the work mentioning the class and type of work.

- Detailed specifications of all items of works and of materials to be used unless reference can be made to some standard specifications.
- Schedule A of materials to be issued or supplied by the department or owner to the contractor, with their rates and the place of issue etc.
- A complete set of drawings indicating the general dimensions of the proposed work with necessary details of the various parts.
- Complete statement of machinery available with the department indicating terms and conditions and hire charges etc.
- 'Conditions of contract' indicating detailed terms and conditions of contract to be complied with by the contractor, which should include the following :
- All rates inclusive of materials, tools and plants, transport, labour and all the other arrangement required for the completion of the work.
- Security deposit to be paid.
- Progress of work to be maintained.
- Time of completion of the entire work.
- Penalty to be imposed on the contractors for slow and or unsatisfactory progress of the work, bad quality of work and delay in completion of the work.
- Mode of payment to the contractor, running account payment, final payment and refund of security deposit.
- Rules for employment of debitable agency.
- Extension of time limit.
- Termination of contract, sub-letting.
- Wages to the labour as per Minimum Wages Act and compensation to labour.
- Additions and alterations, Extra items of works, Escalation of rates and contractor's claim.
- Defect liability period of works after its completion.
- Breach of contract.
- 'Special conditions' which depend on the nature of work, special tools and plants, taxes, royalities which are included in the rates, amenities to be provided to labour and the compensation to be paid to labour in case of accidents at work site.

9.1.16 Conditions of Contract

(i) Introduction:

These are the general terms and conditions of contract to be complied with by the contractor and are mainly related to the work to be executed. The main object of specifying these terms and conditions is to see that no dispute arises between the department (or owner) and the contractor and both the parties are kept out of the court of law. Advice of the competent legal advisers must be taken while preparing such terms and conditions of contract.

(ii) Duties, Reponsibilities and Liabilities of Contractor:

The contract spells out the duties, responsibilities and liabilities of the contractor right from the commencement of the work till its completion and defect liability period is over. They may be classified into :

- Administrative and organisational responsibilities and
- Responsibilities regarding execution of the work

9.1.16.1 Administrative and Organisational Responsibilities

- **Inspection of Site by Contractor :** Before submitting the tender, a contractor should inspect the work site and find out the facilities available such as access to work site and difficulties that are likely to crop up during the execution of the work. Under no circumstances the contractor is entitled for any 'extra payment' or 'extension of time limit' for such difficulties.

- **Performance Bond (in the Form of Security Deposits) :** The contractor has to submit a 'performance bond' in the form of security deposit (which may be 5 to 10 percent of the total estimated cost) which may be by way of Government securities or bonds and is to be returned to the contractor only after the defect liability period of work is over. It is a security from the contractor towards non-performance of the work or loss from the defects that will be noticed within six months after the completion of the work. If the amount of security deposit to be paid is large, the same may be recovered in installments from his interim payments to be made.

- **Organisational Set up at Work Site :** The contractor has to bring all equipment, machinery etc. required for the execution of the work and has to set up a small office at the work site.

- **Legal Obligations, Licences etc. :** The amount agreed upon in the contract includes, all taxes, royalties, fees etc. to be paid by the contractors to the appropriate authorities. He has to procure all the relevant licences, permits etc. required for transporting materials to the work site.

- **Anticipated Progress of the Work :** After a contract is awarded to the contractor, he has to prepare progress chart reports of the work and submit it to the department, or owner or architect.

- **Water Supply and Power Connections :** The contractor has to make all arrangement at his own cost to get the water supply and power connections from the appropriate authorities.

- **Miscellaneous Items :** (a) To make arrangement to protect the work site and any existing structure on it from damages, (b) To keep the work site clean and clear of all obstructions, (c) Not to employ any child labour below the age of 14 years, (d) To hand over the work after its completion in a good condition to the department or owner.

9.1.16.2 Responsibilities Regarding Execution of the Work

General and Particular Conditions of Work : The terms and conditions of the contract should be such that there is no ambiguity in their interpretations and no dispute should arise between the contracting parties. The contract provides that in case of dispute, the decision of an architect or engineeer (appointed by the owner) should be final and conclusive. The various conditions of contract depend upon the type of work to be executed may be as follows :

(1) Drawings and Specifications : As regards interpretation of the drawings and specifications related to the work, the decision of the architect or engineer (appointed by owner or Government) shall be final and conclusive.

(2) Quality of Materials and Workmanship : The material required for the construction and its workmanship should be as per specifications laid down by the Bureau of Indian standard (former I.S.I.). If any special type of material is specified, the contractor has to use the same type or its equivalent subject to approval by the architect or engineer.

All material brought on the site and the workmanship is subject to inspection, examination and test by the engineer or architect. Defective or doubtful material and workmanship is to removed and replaced by the approved standard one as specified in the contract. If the contractor refuses to do so, the same will be replaced by the owner or his representative at the cost of the contractor and the contractor shall not be permitted to proceed further with the work.

(3) Tolerances : The entire execution of the work should be in line, level and plumb and as per the dimensions shown on the drawings. Any variation will be rectified by the contractor at his own cost.

(4) Setting Out of the Work : The entire work is to be set out by the contractor as per the dimensions indicated on the plan and it should be in true line, level and plumb (i.e. vertical).

(5) Detail Drawings of the Work : For the construction of certain items such as lifts, steel windows etc. the contractor has to get the relevant drawings, samples approved by the engineer or architect of the owner. Generally, such works are carried through sub-contractor by the main contractor.

(6) Contractor's Engineer-In-Charge of the Work : The contractor has to appoint a full time engineer as in-charge of the work who will be responsible for proper planning and efficient execution of the work and maintain upto date record of the work. He has to follow the instructions given by the architect or engineer appointed by the owner.

(7) Miscellaneous Items Such as Commencement of Work, Accesses to the Work Site: The contractor should be allowed to commence the work on the date as shown in the contract documents. The architect and engineer (also called as clerk of the work) should have free and easy access for inspection of the work site.

(8) Standing Earnest Money (S.E.M.) : A Standing Earnest Money (S.E.M.) of the amount shown below can be accepted from a tenderer or contractor to cover tendering against any number of works costing upto the amount shown below :

Sr. No.	Works costing upto	Standing Earnest Money
1.	Works upto ₹ 1 lakh	₹ 5,000
2.	Above ₹ 1 lakh and upto ₹ 5 lakhs	₹ 10,000
3.	Above ₹ 5 lakhs	₹ 25,000

However, this amount shall not be adjusted towards the security deposit of the individual contracts obtained by the contractor.

Form in which the Earnest Money is acceptable : The earnest money should be in cash or pay orders, deposit receipts, demand drafts or guarantee bonds executed by State Bank of India or Nationalized or Schedule bank. The Government securities are not to be accepted as earnest money deposit.

Note : The amount of earnest money to be deposited by the tenderer should be large enough to be security against loss, in case the contractor whose tender is accepted, refuses to undertake the work or fails to furnish the necessary security deposit within the specified time (after his tender is accepted). The amount of earnest money may be $2\frac{1}{2}$ % for works costing upto ₹ 5 lakhs and 2% for works costing more than 5 lakhs, subject to a maximum of ₹ 20,000.

(9) Security Deposit : Security deposit is to be paid by a contractor, whose tender has been accepted, in token for the due fulfillment of contract. The normal amount of security deposit for contracts upto ₹ 1 lakh is 10% of the price of contract and for the contracts costing ₹ 2 lakhs, it will be 10% of the first ₹ 1 lakh, plus 7.5% of the balance, and for the contracts costing more than ₹ 2 lakhs, it will be 10% for the first 1 lakh, and 7.5% for the next 1 lakh and 5% for remaining amount subject to a maximum of ₹ 1.5 lakhs.

Under special circumstances where reduction in security deposit may enable the department to obtain more favourable contract, the percentage of security deposit may be reduced.

If the amount of security deposit to be paid in lump-sum within the specified period is not paid by the contractors, the tender already accepted shall be considered as cancelled.

The initial security deposit to be collected should be moderate (i.e. 50% of the total amount of security deposit) and remaining amount of deposit shall be deducted from the running bills of the contractor. The contractor should never be allowed to start the work before he pays the security desposit. The security deposit shall be refunded to the contractor after the expiry of period of guarantee or after the defect liability period is over.

The security deposit may be in the following form :

- Cash deposit

- Government securities, State loan bonds.
- A deposit in the post office savings bank
- A deposit in the National Saving Certificate
- 12 years National Defence Certificate
- Unit Trust of India certificates
- Demand drafts, pay orders, deposit receipts.
- Deposit receipts from all Scheduled banks

(10) Time of Completion : A Civil Engineering project is made up of number of activities, each activity requiring certain specified time for its completion. As the cost of execution of the work is dependant on its time of completion, it is necessary to determine the optimum time of its construction. The optimum time of completion is one that results in the minimum cost of the project. Before inviting tenders from the contractors, for a particular project, it is essential to decide the reasonable and realistic time for its completion. Generally, the time of completion is specified in the contract by stipulating its *'date of completion'* or by mentioning the number of calender months in which it is to be completed or within specified number of working days. Section 55 of the Indian Contract Act reads as : "If a party to contract promises to complete a certain thing on or before a specified time and fails to do so on or before the specified times the contract (or so much of it has been already performed) becomes voidable at the promisee's option, if the intention of parties was that time must be the essence of contract." "However, if it was not intention of the parties that time must be of the essence of the contract, the contract does not become voidable, in the event of failure to perform such thing on or before the specified time, but the promisee in that case is entitled to compensation from the promissor (i.e. contractor) for any loss occured to him by such failure".

Thus it can be said that the law does not always consider stipulation of time as a rigid or strict condition in the contract and may not allow owner or department to rescind a contract simply because the contractor has failed to complete the work within the specified time, but considers as to whether the time was essence of contract or not. In short, whether time is a essence of the contract or not depends upon the intention of parties. Usually, for the public works to be carried out by contractor, the time allowed for the completion of the work is mentioned in the tender form and is to be scrupulously followed by the contractor, and shall be reckoned from the date on which the order to commence the work is issued to the contractor by the deparment. The work shall throughout the stipulated period of the contract be proceeded with, with all due deligence time being deemed to be of essence of contract on the part of the contractor.

Thus the contractor has not only to complete the work within the stipulated time but has to maintain sufficient progress of the work every month. If he fails to maintain satisfactory progress as per the schedule or fails to complete the work in a stipulated time, the contractor shall pay as compensation or penalty as per terms and conditions of contract an amount equal to 1% of or such smaller amount as Superintending Engineer, whose decision shall be final, may decide, for everyday that the work remains uncommenced or unfinished after the due date of its completion. The maximum limit of compensation or penalty to be paid will be restricted to 10% of the total amount of contract.

'Time is the essence of contract' will be true for mercantile transactions e.g. in case of shipping contracts, failure by the promiser to fulfil his promise within the stipulated time will make the contract voidable at the option of the promisee.

(11) Progress of the Work : Civil Engineering contracts also provide four stages to review the progress of the work executed by the contractor as follows :

Sr. No.	Percentage of work to be executed	Percentage of time (within which the work is to be completed)
1.	25% of the work	n_1 % of time stipulated
2.	50% of the work	n_2 % of time stipulated
3.	75% of the work	n_3 % of time stipulated
4.	100% i.e. Entire work	Stipulated time mentioned in the contract

Where values of n_1, n_2 and n_3 will be decided by the competent authorities accepting the tender. In case the contractor fails to maintain satisfactory progress as stated above, he is liable to pay compensation or penalty an amount equal to 1% or such smaller amount (as decided by the Superintending Engineer) of the estimated cost of the work shown in the 'contract' per day that the due quantity of work remains to be completed, subject to a total amount of such compensation or penalty does not exceed 10% of estimated amount of the work as shown in the contract documents.

(12) Extension of Time for Delay in Completion : When the contractor is unable to execute the work within the prescribed time limit on account of certain valid reasons, he has to apply for the extension of time before the due date of its completion as provided in the terms and conditions of contract. Such extension of time may be granted on any one or more of the following grounds :

- By force majeure.
- Act of God.
- Exceptionally bad weather conditions
- Serious loss or damage due to fire, storm etc.
- Due to civil commotion, local combination of workman, lockout or strikes resulting in non-availability of construction material.
- Acute shortage of essential labour.

- Land required for construction of the work not made available in time.

- Non-availability of plans and instructions from the architect or engineer in time.

- Non-availability of stores and tools and plants to be supplied by the department.

- Due to delay on the part of other sub-contractor or nominated suppliers appointed by the department, but not included in the contract.

- Any other valid reasons, which are beyond the control of the contractor.

The Executive Engineer is the competent authority who can grant necessary extension of time to the contractor on the valid grounds as stated above.

(13)   Extension of Time due to Additions and Alterations : The time limit for the execution of the work shall be extended in the proportion to the increase in its cost due to additions and or alterations bears to the original cost of the contract work and a certificate of the Engineer-in-charge of the work as to such proportion shall be conclusive and final.

(14) Rates of the Works not Included in the Estimate : If the additional and or altered work includes any type of work for which no rates are specified in the contract, then such class of work shall be carried out at the rates given in the schedule of rates of the division or at the rates mutually agreed upon by the Engineer-in-charge and the contractor, whichever is lower. However, if for the additional and or altered works, for which no rates are given in the schedule of rates of the division, is to be carried out before the rates are decided, the contractor shall within one week of the date of receipt of the order to execute such works, intimate the Engineer-in-charge of rates he proposes to charge for such work, and if the Engineer-in-charge does not agree to his rates, he may cancel his order to execute this work and may arrange to execute it in such a manner as he may consider advisable. In case of dispute, the decision of Superintending Engineer of the circle shall be conclusive and final.

(15) Extra Items : The items of work which are not included in the accepted tender, are to be sanctioned by and paid for (at the agreed rate) by the Executive Engineer, subject to the following limitations :

- The amount of each such extra item should not be more than ₹ 10,000/-

- The total cost of all such extra items should be within the amount upto which the Executive Engineer is empowered to accept the tender.

- The rate for the extra item, which is fairly comparable with any similar item already included in the accepted tender should be decided by the Executive Engineer after convincing the contractor. However, such rate should not exceed the rate quoted for the same item in the schedule of rates of the division.

- When extra item is not comparable with any item in the accepted tender, it should be paid at the rate to be mutually agreed upon by the Engineer-in-charge of the work and the contractor provided such rate does not exceed the rate for the same item included in the schedule of rate.

- The work of extra item should be carried out by the contractor after receiving formal written orders from the Engineer-in-charge of the work.

- The rates of extra items are subject to the careful scrutiny by the Divisional Account of the division, before they are sanctioned and paid by the competent authorities.

(16) Ex-gratia Payment to Contractor : While making ex-gratia payment to the contractor, the following criteria should be applied :

- The contractor has to submit documentary evidence, of the actual loss suffered by him, duly certified by Chief Auditor of Local Fund Accounts.

- The loss should be such for which the contractor cannot be held responsible for it.

- While determining the extent of the loss to be compensated, it is also necessary to consider the profit made by the contractor in any other government work executed at about the same time.

- Ex-gratia payment can be paid to the contractor provided he has worked sincerely and efficiently throughout the execution of the work avoiding wasteful methods of work and with utmost economy.

- The compensation to be paid in the form of ex-gratia payment should never exceed the actual loss by the contractor.

- The ex-gratia payment should never be paid due to subsequent increase in the prices of material required for the execution of work.

- The contractor is eligible to apply for ex-gratia payment provided he has utilised his capacity to the fullest extent, avoiding wastage.

(17) Debitable Agency : Under any clauses of conditions of contract the contractor is liable to pay compensation amounting to the whole of his security deposit (either paid in lump-sum or deducted by installments) or in case of abandonment of work due to illness or death of the contractor, the Executive Engineer shall have the power to adopt any of following courses as he may think appropriate :

- To rescind the contract and in that case the security deposit of the contractor stands forfeited.

- To carry out the work or any part of it departmentally, debiting the contractor with the cost of the work. The certificate of the Executive Engineer to the cost and such other expenses incurred on the work carried out departmentally will be final.

- To order that the work of the contractor carried out so far be measured and the unexecuted part of the work be handed over to another contractor to complete. The work carried out by the new contract agency will be debited to the contractor and the amount of work done through the new contractor be credited to the contractor in all respects and in the same way and at the same price or rates as if it had been carried out by the contractor as per terms and conditions of contract. The certificate of the

Executive Engineer as regards the cost, the work and other expenses incurred in getting the unexecuted work done by the new contractor etc. shall be final. The new agency which is employed to complete the remaining work at the cost of original contractor who failed to execute the work or was unable to show satisfactory progress of the work is known as "Debitable Agency". It may be in the form of a new contractor or daily labour and may be employed by serving proper notice to the original contractor.

(18) Terminal of Contract : Termination of contract may be in any one of the following ways :

• **By mutual agreement :** The contract may be terminated at any stage by mutual agreement between the owner and contractor. In such cases contractor will be paid for the work executed upto the time of termination and the owner will be free to appoint another contractor to continue further work.

• **After completion of the work :** After the contractor completes the entire work, as per terms and conditions, it stands automatically terminated. The performance of the contractor under such cases is known as **'specific performance'**.

• **Due to impossibility of performance :** Sometimes due to certain peculiar circumstances, the execution of the work by the contractor becomes impossible e.g. due to excessive floods, everything on the work site has been washed away, then it is practically impossible for the contractor to continue the work further and thus the contract can be terminated.

• **By the provision of the law :** If any one of the party becomes bankrupt or due to the death of one party (i.e. contractor or owner), the law provides for the termination of contract.

• **Breach of contract :** It is failure to perform an obligation arising out of contract i.e. If any contracting party fails to perform the promise, then other party, need not perform his part of agreement and is eligible for compensation or damages caused due to breach of the contract by the former. In case of breach of contract, the injured party is entitled to damages, even though they may be nominal, as a compensation only and not as punishment. The damages to be recovered will be to the extent of the actual loss caused to him (i.e. the aggrieved party).

The breach of agreement is said to be 'total' or 'partial' depending upon whether there is failure to perform the 'whole' or 'partial' obligation, without any sufficient valid justification, and the other party is then entitled for compensation. Breach of contract may constitute means of termination of contract.

Section 39 of the Indian Contract Act reads as follows : "When a party to a contract has refused to perform or has disabled himself from performing his promise, in its entirely, the promisee (i.e. owner or department) may put an end to the contract unless he (i.e. contractor) has signified by words or conduct, his acquiescene in its continuance.

(19) Measure of Damages : Section 73 of Indian Contract Act regarding measure of damages reads as follows :

When a contract is broken, the party who suffers by such breach is entitled to receive, from the party, who has broken the contract, compensation for any loss or damage caused to him thereby.

- (a) Which naturally arose in the usual course of things from such breach or
- (b) Which the parties knew, when they made the contract, to be likely to result from the breach of contract.

- Such compensation is not allowed for any remote and indirect loss or damage sustained by reason of the breach.

- While estimating the loss or damage due to breach of contract, the means which existed of remedying the inconvenience caused by not performing the contract must be taken into account.

Compensation of Breach of Contract : The amount of compensation to be paid should be commensurate with loss or damage caused to the other party. Thus in case of breach of contract, the 'Court of law' would assess the extent of damages with a view to restore to the aggrieved party, such benefits as he might have derived from the contract, had there been no such breach.

Any Civil Engineering contract includes certain provision for the payment of certain amount of money to be paid by the contractor, if he fails to complete the work as laid down in the terms and conditions of contract. Such a sum as agreed upon by the parties to be paid as compensation for damages is known as 'Liquidated Damages'. Sometimes this sum is also called as **'Penalty'**, which is an amount stipulated as in terrorem of the offending party.

Thus 'penalty' is a fine for not complying with the terms and conditions of contract agreement. Such a penalty is to be imposed for not maintaining satisfactory progress of the work, bad workmanship, delay in the completion of the work, work not being carried out as per the specification laid out in the contract etc. The main purpose of penalty is to secure performance of the agreement, the amount being according to true intention of parties only a maximum of damage. Liquidated damages, on the other hand are real or genuine convenanted pre-estimates of damages. In this case parties do not make any attempt to estimate the real loss that might occur to them due to breach of contract. In short the liquidated damages are an assessment of the amount which will compensate the wrong party for the breach of contract.

The 'damages' due to breach of contract are classified as follows :

- Liquidated damages
- Unliquidated damages and
- Penalty

Liquidated Damages	Unliquidated Damages	Penalty
(1) It is a genuine convenanted pre-estimate of damage.	They are ordinary damages with fixed relation with the actual damage.	It is a sort of fine as in terrorem of offending party.
(2) It has no relationship with the actual damage done.	It increases with the increase in damage and decreases with decrease of damage.	It may be exhorbitant as compared to real damages. Any amount but not exceeding the sum mentioned, can be recovered, however this may not be the whole amount.
(3) The whole sum can be recovered, even if the actual loss may be greater or smaller than pre-estimated or anticipated by contracting parties. It may be fixed percentage varying from ₹ 50 to ₹ 100 per day of the delay.	Such damages are for not maintaining sufficient progress of the work and or for not completing the work in the stipulated time.	The maximum penalty will be 10% of the total estimated cost of the work to be executed.

The breach of contract may be on the part of the contractor or owner and the general procedure of ascertaining the 'damages' will be as follows :

Breach of contract by the contractor	Breach of contract by the owner
The damage will be to the extent of present market price of executing the contractor's performance or it may be the difference between the price of the defective construction and that of the construction which should have been completed as per terms and conditions of contract.	The damage will be to the extent of the entire amount of contract minus the cost of the work already completed or the expenditure incurred by the contractor to the date of breach plus reasonable profit, that he would have obtained in case of completion of the work or value of entire work he has executed to the date of contract plus reaso-nable percentage of profit.

(20) Sub-contractor : In addition to the main contractor required for the execution of the building works other specialised agencies are required for certain works such as provision of lifts, air conditioning etc. Thus it is necessary to employ sub-contractors who will work under the main contractor who co-ordinates all such activities in fulfillment of the building work.

The main contractor has to submit the list of such sub-contractors who will be carrying out specialised job and are deemed to be employed by him. The sub-contractors have to execute their job satisfactorily and receive payment for the work carried out by them through the main contractor. If their is delay in the execution of their job, they have to pay liquidated damages to main contractor. The final payment to the sub-contractor is to be made after their payment bills are certified by the architect or engineer appointed by the owner.

(21) Bonus Clause : In order to give incentive to the contractor to complete work well before its stipulated time, and also within the estimated cost in the tender, sometime a bonus clause is also incorporated in the contract agreement. The bonus clause says that if the contractor executes the entire work well before the time and that within the estimated price in the tender, he will be eligible for the extra amount in the form of bonus at the rate agreed upon by both the parties. If after agreeing upon the bonus clause, the owner refuses to pay the agreed sum, the contractor can recover the amount of the bonus from the owner. If for some reason, the time of completion of the work is extended by the architect or engineer appointed by the owner, due to additions and alterations in the work, it automatically means the extension of the date of bonus of completion.

(22) Execution of Work According to Drawings and Specifications : It is the duty of the contractor to execute all work and every part of the work both as regards materials and workmanship strictly in according to the drawings and specifications. All work should conform exactly, fully and faithfully to the drawings and designs and according to the written instructions given to the contractor. The contractor will be supplied complete set of contract drawings and working drawings and certified copy of the accepted tender along with the work order.

Additions and Alterations in Specifications and Designs : The Executive Engineer has full powers to make any alterations and or additions in the original specifications, designs and drawings and such other changes that appear him to be necessary during the progress of the work and the contractor is bound to follow all such changes and instructions issued to him in writing duly signed by the Executive Engineer and such additions, alterations etc. in no case shall make the contract invalid.

(23) Payment on Intermediate or Interim Certificates : Usually, no payment shall be made for any work estimated to cost less than ₹ 1000. In case of work estimated to cost more than ₹ 1000 the contractor shall submit monthly bill thereof and be entitled to receive payment proportionate to the part of the work approved, passed and certified by the Engineer-in-charge and his decision will be final. All such intermediate payments will be considered as payments by way of advances against the final payments and are not to be considered as payments for work actually carried out and shall not preclude the Engineer-in-charge form ordering removal of any bad, imperfect or unsound work noticed at latter stage. The final bill shall be submitted by the contractor within a month of the date of completion of the work, otherwise Executive Engineer's certificate regarding measurements and total amount to be paid for the work shall be final.

Final Certificate : After the completion of the work the contractor has to remove from the site all scaffolding, scattered surplus materials and rubbish and dirt, dust etc. from all doors, windows, floors, walls and other parts of the work executed and then the contractor shall be furnished with a certificate by the Executive Engineer of such completion.

If the contractor fails to remove the scaffolding, surplus materials etc., after the work is completed, the Executive Engineer will order the removal of such scaffolding, surplus material etc. and the contractor will have to bear the entire cost of all such expenses and shall loose his claim of scaffolding, surplus materials etc., except for the any amount realised by the sale thereof.

(24) Sub-letting of Contract : In no case the contractor shall assign or sublets the work without the written approval of the Executive Engineer. If he assigns or sublets his contract or attempts to do so, or become insolvent, the Executive Engineer may there upon by issuing a notice in writing to the contractor rescind the contract and his security deposit shall stand forfeited and will be absolutely at the disposal of Government and in addition the contractor shall not be entitled to recover or be paid for any work he has actually executed under the contract.

(25) Escalation or Price Variation Clause : The contract does not allow the contractors to claim any extra amount for variations of prices during the progress of the work. Thus the contract price (i.e. estimated cost) shall not be subject to any increase or decrease in prices. In the present day inflationary market this clause has an adverse effect on the contractor, and results in the contractor abonding the work or adopting go slow tactic. In order to overcome this difficulty and to do fair justice to the contractor in case of escalation of prices it is advisable to introduce **'Escalation or Price variation clause'** in the conditions of contract, by incorporating in the contract the basic rates of the important materials of construction such as steel, cement, sand, teak wood etc. which are likely to fluctuate in their prices.

The following guidelines may be followed in ascertaining variations of prices (i.e. escalation) of materials.

Guidelines for Escalation Clause :

- Escalation clause will not be applicable if the price variation is upto 5 percent.
- Escalation clause shall be applied only for the works whose time of completion is more than one year and whose contract price is above ₹ 10 lakhs.
- For the lump-sum contracts whose value is equal to or more than 15% of the contract price no escalation clause will be applicable.
- The escalation or price variation shall be based on the average price index of the last 3 months.

(26) Delay in Supply of Material by the Department : In no case, the contractor shall be entitled to claim any compensation from the department for the loss suffered by him on account of delay in the supply of material entered in the Schedule A, when such delay is caused by reasons which are beyond the control of the department e.g. non-availability of railway wagons, act of God, force majeure etc. However, the department may grant reasonable extension of time for delay in the supply of such materials. The decision of the Executive Engineer, in this matter will be conclusive and final.

(27) Works Open for Inspection : All works being executed by the contractor shall at all times be open for inspection of the Engineer-in-charge and his subordinates and either contractor or his duly appointed responsible agent must be present at the time of such inspections.

(28) Defect Liability Period Clause : The clause regarding 'defects and its liability' is incorporated in a contract so as to safeguard the interest of the owner. It is the responsibility of the contractor to remove the defective work executed due to bad workmanship or use of substandard material. Generally, such works may pass unnoticed at the time of inspection of the work by an architect or Engineer appointed by the owner. If the work is carried out hurriedly and in improper manner the defects are developed after the completion of the work. The defect and maintenance clause provides for the rectification of defects, that are noticed either during or after the execution of the work, by the contractor at his own cost. Such a clause specifies a period of six months to one year after completion during which the defects are noticed. The period actually starts from date of certified completion of the work, by an architect or engineer. If the contractor refuses or fails to rectify the defects noticed during the 'defect-liability period' (which is generally 6 to 12 months after the completion of works) the department or owner may rectify such defects and deduct the amount of rectification of defects from the payments due to the contractor from the 'security deposits' in the custody of the department. The contractor is not liable for any normal wear and tear that occurs during the maintenance or defect liability period. However, if it can be conclusively proved that wear and tear are the direct results of defects, the contractor is bound to rectify them. If such defects are noticed due to natural calamities such as cyclones, storms etc., the contractor is not responsible for such defects. The security deposit of the contractor is to be refunded only after the defect liability period is over.

(29) Advances to Contractors : As a general rule no advance payments is to be made to the contractor except for the work actually executed by him.

However, exceptions are to be made in the interest of the speedy completion of the work under the following circumstances,

(i) Secured Advance : Sometimes, a contractor, who is to receive payment after the completion of the work, needs an 'advance payment' on the security of the construction material brought by him on the work site. In such case, the concerned Divisional Officer, be kind enough, to sanction an advance upto a maximum of 75% of the present value of such material (which is imperishable) brought on site.

The following points are to be noted in this regard :

- The material must have been actually brought on site by the contractor.

- No previous advance has been received by the contractor for the above material.

- The materials are really required for the items of construction (included under the contract) for which the rate has been already agreed upon.

- The recoveries of advances shall be made from the contractor's bill for the work done as and when the materials are consumed.

- The items of construction material on which secured advance may be given include asphalt, bitumen, sand etc., required for the work.

- No secured advance is permissible in case of piece workers.

- Secured advance is not to be paid for material brought for centering, laying of water line etc.

- In case of advances (other than secured advances) to be made to the contractor against security of (materials) machinery brought by him the said machinery should invariably be hypothecated to the Government on the standard prescribed form 50 A after the machinery has been duly insured by the contractor with some insurance company.

Standard Contract Conditions Published by Ministry of Statistics and Programme Implementation (MOS and PI)

TWELVE STANDARD CONTRACT CLAUSES   **(W-2010)**

The 12 Standard Contract Clauses are the basic clauses which provide the structure for a contract between two parties for carrying out specific activities in a desired manner.

Whereas the Standard General Conditions for domestic contracts as given in Part II of the document provide a complete framework for preparation of the contract documents.

Clause 1 : Eligibility and Pre-qualification (PQ) :

A. Eligibility Criteria :

(a) Experience on similar works executed during the last five years; and details like monetary value, clients, proof of satisfactory completion;

(b) Registration, if any, with specified departments/organisations, class/type of registration;

(c) Documentary evidence of adequate financial standing.

B. Pre-qualification Information to be called for :

- Constitution and legal status. Joint-venturing or other tie-ups for technology, equipment, financial backing and/or project management;

- Registration (class and type) with specified agencies and previous pre-qualification(s) for similar projects.

- Experience on similar work(s) during last 5 years with details including year wise monetary value, clients, and proof of satisfactory completion of works.

- Financial standing as certified by Bankers, Audited Profit and Loss Account and Balance Sheet, Annual turnover in last 5 years, access to adequate working capital.

- Construction Equipment proposed to be deployed for the project and proof of its availability; equipment proposed to be purchased or leased.

- Key personnel available and proposed to be engaged for management and supervision of the project, their qualifications and experience.

- Project planning and quality control procedures to be adopted.

- Information regarding projects in hand, current litigation, orders regarding exclusion/expulsion or black listing, if any.

- The capacity of a construction agency to take up a new project under consideration in addition to his present commitments must be carefully assessed on the basis of the above information. The method of this assessment may be left to the owner or his Consultants.

- It may be mentioned, as an example, that some organisations, like, the World Bank, adopt the following formula:

- The cut of grade obtained by Construction Company under the Grading Scheme of CIDC should be

$$\text{Bid capacity} = A \times N \times 2 - B, \text{ where}$$

$$'N' = \text{Number of years prescribed for completion of the subject contract}$$

$$'A' = \text{Maximum value of works executed in any one year during last five years (at current price level)}$$

$$'B' = \text{Value, at current price level, of existing commitments and on going works to be completed in the next 'N' years.}$$

Clause 2 : Earnest Money (EM)

A. For projects estimated to cost ₹ 25 crores and above, earnest money should be 1% of the estimated cost; and maximum amount of earnest money should be ₹ 50 lakh.

B. For projects estimated to cost less than ₹ 25 crores also, the earnest money should be 1% of the estimated cost . Maximum amount of earnest money may be stipulated at the discretion of the owner .

C. Earnest money may be submitted in the form of irrecoverable Bank Guarantee with Banks to be specified by the Owners. Certified cheques and Demand Drafts should also be acceptable; Bank Guarantees submitted as Earnest Money shall be valid for 28 days beyond the validity of the bid.

D. Earnest money of unsuccessful bidders should be refunded as promptly as possible, but not later than 28 days after the expiry of the bid validity.

Clause 3 - Security Deposit (SD)

A. Security Deposit shall consist of two parts; (a) Performance Guarantee to be submitted at award of work, and (b) Retention money to be recovered from Running Bills.

B. Performance Guarantee should be 5% of Contract amount and should be submitted as Bank Guarantee, Government Securities, FDR or any other form of deposit stipulated by the Owner, within 28 days of receipt of letter of acceptance.

C. Retention Money should be deducted at 5% from Running Bills. Total of Performance Guarantee and Retention Money should not exceed 10% of Contract amount or lesser sum indicated in the bid document.

D. 5% Performance Guarantee should be refunded within 14 days of the issue of the defect liability Certificate (taking over Certificate with a list of defects). Retention money should be refunded after issue of No. Defects Certificate. This balance amount can be substituted by "**On demand**" Bank Guarantee.

Clause 4 - Variations, Extra / Substituted Items

A. Variation permitted should be ± 25% in quantity of each individual item, and ± 10% of the total contract price. Within 14 days of the date of instruction for executing varied work, extra work or substitution, and before the commencement of such work, notice shall be given either (a) by the contractor to the owner of his intention to claim extra payment or a varied rate or price, or (b) by the owner to the contractor of his intention to vary a rate or price

B. For items not existing in the Bill of Quantities or substitutions to items in the Bill of Quantities, rate payable should be determined by methods given below and in the order given below :

   • Rates and prices in contract, if applicable;
   • Rates and prices in the Schedule of Rates applicable to the contract ± tendered percentage, where appropriate;
   • Market rates of materials and labor, plus 10% for overheads and Profits of contractor
   • Escalation to be paid as admissible.

C. If there is delay in the owner and the contractor coming to an agreement on the rate of an extra item, provisional rates as proposed by the owner should be payable till such time as the rates are finally determined.

D. For items existing in the Bill of Quantities but where quantities have increased beyond the variation limits, the rate payable for quantity in excess of the quantity in the Bill of Quantity plus the permissible variation should be :

1. Rates and prices in contract, if reasonable, failing which
2. Market rates of material and labour, plus 20% for overheads and profits of contractor.

Clause 5 - Payment of Running Bills :

A. Bills should be prepared and submitted by the Contractor. Joint measurements should be taken continuously and need not be connected with billing stage. System of four copies of measurements, one each for Contractor, Client and Engineer, and signed by both Contractor and Client can be tried.

B. 75% of bill amount should be paid within 14 days of submission of the bill. Balance amount of the verified bill should be paid within 28 days of the submission of the bill.

C. For delay in payment beyond these periods specified in (B) above, interest at a pre-specified rate (suggested rate 12% p. a.) should be paid.

Clause 6 - Payment of Final Bills :

A. Contractor should submit final bill within 60 days of issue of defects liability certificate. Client's engineer should check the bill within 60 days after its receipt and return the bill to contractor for corrections, if any are needed. 50% of undisputed amount should be paid to the contractor at the stage of returning the bill.

B. The contractor should re-submit the bill, with corrections within 30 days of its return by the Engineer. The re-submitted bill should be checked and paid within 60 days of its receipt.

C. Interest at a pre-specified rate (say 12%) should be paid if the bill is not paid within the time limit specified above.

Clause 7 – Advance Payment :

A. Mobilisation Advance and Construction Equipment Advance should be given at 12% interest or free of interest at the discretion of the owner and against Bank Guarantee for Mobilisation Advance and against hypothecation of Construction Equipment to the Owner for Construction Equipment Advance.

B. Mobilisation Advance should be given upto 10% of Contract price, payable in two equal installments. The first installment should be paid after mobilisation has started and next installments should be paid after satisfactory utilisation of earlier advance(s).

C. Construction Equipment Advance should be paid upto 5% of Contract price, limited to 90% of assessed cost of machinery. For special cases, a higher advance for construction equipment upto 10% of contract price may be considered.

D. Construction Equipment advances should be paid in two or more installments. First installment should be paid after Construction Equipment has arrived at the site and next installments should be paid after satisfactory utilisation of earlier advance(s).

E. Recovery of Mobilisation and Construction Equipment advance should start when 15% of the work is executed and recovery of total advance should be complete by the time 80% of the original contract price is executed.

Clause 8 - Secured Advance: (W-2010)

A. 75% of cost of materials brought to site for incorporation into works only should be paid as Secured Advance. Materials which are of perishable nature should be adequately insured. In case, advance is not payable against any particular items, they should be listed in the Contract Document.

Clause 9 - Liquidated Damages and Incentives:

Liquidated Damages:

9A. In case of delay in completion of the contract, liquidated damages (LD) may be levied at the rate of half percent (1/2%) of the contract price per week of delay, subject to a maximum of 10 percent of the contract price.

9A (i)   The owner, if satisfied, that the works can be completed by the contractor within a reasonable time after the specified time for completion, may allow further extension of time at its discretion with or without the levy of L.D. In the event of extension granted being with L.D, the owner will be entitled without prejudice to any other right or remedy available in that behalf, to recover from the contractor as agreed damages equivalent to half percent (1/2%) of the contract value of the works for each week or part of the week subject to the ceiling defined in sub-clause 9 A.

9A (ii)   The owner, if not satisfied that the works can be completed by the contractor, and in the event of failure on the part of the contractor to complete work within further extension of time allowed as aforesaid, shall be entitled, without prejudice to any other right, or remedy available in that behalf, to rescind the contract.

9A (iii) The owner, if not satisfied with the progress of the contract and in the event of failure of the contractor to recoup the delays in the mutually agreed time frame, shall be entitled to terminate the contract.

9A (iv)   In the event of such termination of the contract as described in clauses 9A (ii) or 9A (iii) or both the owner shall be entitled to recover L.D. upto ten percent (10%) of the contract value and forfeit the security deposit made by the contractor besides getting the work completed by other means at the risk and cost of the contractor.

9A (v)   The ceiling of LD shall be 10% of the project cost in turnkey contracts. Lower limits for LDs should be clearly justified while formulating the contract. Each public sector undertaking/Ministry will take a considered view for adopting any deviations on LDs with necessary legal advice.

9A (vi)   Ministries/Departments/Project Enterprises may adopt a suitable percent of the contract price as liquidated damages and allowable time-limit depending upon the nature of turnkey contract.

Incentives or Bonus (Optional Clause):

9B   For early completion of the contract before the stipulated date of completion of an incentive amount at the rate of half percent (1/2 %) of the contract price per week of early completion, subject to a maximum of five percent (5%) of the contract price may be paid to the contractor.

9B (i)   The incentive or bonus (optional clause) would be applicable in time-critical projects.

9B (ii)   The owner (Project Enterprise/Ministry/Department) may determine accurately the quantum of incentive and the period of early completion as the eligibility criteria before the award of contract.

9B (iii) Each Public Sector Undertaking/Ministry will consider and take a considered view whether the clause regarding incentives are to be included in the contract along with justifications based on legal advice.

Clause 10 - Escalation :

A (i)   All short duration contracts upto 24 months should be awarded on fixed price basis and are not subject to any escalation what soever. However, only statutory variation limited to duties and taxes are considered for adjustment in contract price.

A (ii)   For calculating escalation, base prices should be taken as on the date of opening of the Bids.

B.   The Contract document should specify the suitable percentage of input for labour, materials like cement, steel, bitumen, POL and other materials and equipment usage for the purposes of calculating escalation.

C.   Escalation should be calculated based on

- Notified fair wages and in the absence of which consumer price index for labour would be applicable,
- Market rate for cement and steel,
- Average official retail price of bitumen and POL,
- Whole sale price index for other materials,
- Published Government Documents should be used for calculation of escalation amount.

D.   Escalation Reimbursement should be calculated for to the extent of 85% of the escalation so calculated.

Clause 11 - Disputed Items and Arbitration:

A. Conciliation:

(a)   Disputes between the Employer and the Contractor shall first be submitted to Conciliation. The procedure outlined in the Arbitration and Conciliation Act, 1996 shall be followed.

(b) The party initiating conciliation shall send to the other party a written invitation to conciliate. Conciliation proceedings shall commence when the other party accepts in writing the invitation to conciliate. If the other party rejects the invitation, or does not reply within thirty days from the date of invitation, there will be no Conciliation Proceedings.

(c) There shall be one Conciliator, unless the parties agree that there shall be two or three Conciliators; where there is more than one Conciliator, they ought, as a general rule, to act jointly.

(d) When it appears to the Conciliator that there exists elements of a settlement which may be acceptable to the parties, he shall submit them to parties for their observation. He may reformulate the terms of a possible settlement in the light of their observations.

(e) If the parties reach agreement of the dispute, they may draw up and sign a written settlement agreement. They may request the Conciliator to draw up or assist them in drawing up the settlement agreement.

(f) If settlement agreement shall have the same status and effect as if it is an arbitral award on agreed terms on the substance of the dispute rendered by an arbitral tribunal under section 30 of the Act.

(g) If a settlement does not appear possible, the Conciliator, after consultation with the parties, will give a written declaration that further efforts at Conciliation are no longer justified and the Conciliation Proceedings are terminated.

B. When Conciliation Proceedings have become infructious or have been terminated, the party, which initiated the Conciliation, shall refer the disputes for Arbitration. The reference to Arbitration should be made preferably within 28 days of the termination of Conciliation Proceedings.

C. The Arbitration shall be conducted in accordance with the Indian Arbitration and Conciliation Act, 1996. For Contracts costing upto ₹ 10 Crores, a Sole Arbitrator should be appointed. For Contracts costing over ₹ 10 Crores, a Committee of Arbitrators should be appointed composed of one Arbitrator to be nominated by the Contractor, one to be nominated by the Owner and the third Arbitrator, who will act as a Chairman but not as umpire, to be chosen jointly by the two nominees. The decision of majority of Arbitrators shall be final and binding on both parties.

Clause 11A-Dispute Resolution Board:

If a dispute of any kind whatsoever arises between the Employer and the Contractor in connection with, or arising out of the Contract or the execution of the Works, whether during the execution of the Works or after their completion and whether before or after the repudiation or other termination of the Contract, including any disagreement by either party with any action, inaction, opinion. instruction, determination, certificate or valuation of the

Engineer, the matter in dispute shall, in the first place, be referred to the Dispute Review Board.

The Board shall be established by signature of the Dispute Review Board Agreement ("the Board Agreement") which shall occur at the same time as the signature of the Contract Agreement.

Membership of the Board in all contracts of value upto ₹ 3.00 crores will consist of one Member, experienced in the type of construction involved in the Works and in the interpretation of document, to be appointed by the President, Institution of Engineers (India) at the request of the employer. In all other cases, membership of the Board shall comprise three Members similarly experienced. One Member shall be selected by each of the Employer and the Contractor and approved by the other. If either of these Members is not so selected and approved within 14 days of the date of the Contract Agreement, then upon the request of either or both parties such Member shall be selected within 14 days of such request by the President, Institution of Engineers (India).

The third Member shall be selected by the other two and approved by the parties. If the two Members selected by or on behalf the parties fail to select the third Member within 14 days after the later of their selections, then upon the request of either or both parties such third Member shall be selected within 14 days by the same international / national appointment authority as above who shall seek the approval of the proposed third Member by the parties before selection, but failing such approval nevertheless shall select the third Member. The third Member shall serve as Chairman of the Board.

In the event of death, disability, or resignation of any Member, such Member shall be replaced in the same manner as the Member being replaced was selected. If for whatever other reason a Member shall fail or be unable to serve, the Chairman (or failing the action of the Chairman then either of other Members) shall inform the parties and such non-serving Member shall be replaced in the same manner as the Member being replaced was selected. Any replacement made by the parties shall be completed within 30 days, failing which the replacement shall be made by the same international/national appointing authority as above in the same manner as described above. Replacement shall be considered complete when the new Member signs the Board Agreement. Throughout any replacement process the Members not being replaced shall continue to serve and the Board shall continue to function and its activities shall have the same force and effects as if the vacancy had not occurred.

Either the Employer or the Contractor may refer a dispute to the Board and the Board's recommendations shall be binding on the Employer and the Contractor in respect of disputes involving individual claims upto one percent of the contract value subject to a ceiling of ₹ 1 (one) million for contracts valued upto three hundred million or and (ii) ceiling of ₹ 10 (Ten) million for contracts valued above ₹ 300 (Three hundred) million. In all other cases, upon receipt of Board's Recommendation (s), these shall be deemed accepted. Accepted and deemed accepted Recommendations shall be final and binding on the parties.

Any dispute on which the Board has not issued a Recommendation within 42 days of its final hearing on the dispute, or regarding which the Recommendation (s) are not accepted, may be referred in writing by either party to arbitration in accordance with this Clause, by written notice to the other party with copies to the Engineer and the Board. Such notice shall state that it is being made pursuant to this Clause and shall establish the entitlement of the party giving it to commence arbitration provided that no such arbitration may be commenced until such notice is given. Such reference shall be made within 14 days of receipt of the Board's recommendation(s), or within 14 days of the day on which said period of 42 days expired, as the case may be, failing which reference any recommendation(s) previously rejected or not accepted shall be deemed accepted despite such previous rejection or non-acceptance and shall be final and binding upon the parties.

All Recommendations, which have become final and binding, shall be implemented by the parties forthwith; such implementation shall include any relevant action of the Engineer.

Whether or not accepted or deemed accepted, all of the Recommendations shall be admissible in any subsequent dispute resolution procedure, including any arbitration or any litigation having any relation to the dispute or disputes to which the Recommendation(s) relate.

Unless the Contract has already been repudiated or terminated, the Contractor shall, in every case, continue to proceed with the Works with all due diligence and the Contractor and the Employer shall give effect forthwith to every decision of the Engineer unless and until the same shall be revised, as hereinafter provided, in an arbitral award.

Clause 12 - Owner's Risk and Compensation Events:

A. Owners Risks : The owner is responsible for the excepted risks, which are :

(a) War, hostilities, invasion, act of foreign enemies, rebellion, revolution, insurrection of military or usurped power, or civil war;

(b) Riot, commotion, disorder, unless solely restricted to employees of the Contractor or his sub-contractors and arising from the conduct of the works;

(c) Contamination by radioactivity from any nuclear fuel, or from any nuclear waste radioactive toxic explosive;

(d) A cause due solely to the design of the Works, other than the Contractor's design;

(e) Pressure waves caused by aircraft or other aerial devices travelling at sonic or supersonic speeds;

(f) Flood, tornadoes, earthquakes and landslides;

(g) Loss or damage due to the use or occupation by the Employer of any Section or part of the Permanent Works except as may be provided for in the Contract;

(h) Any operation of the forces of nature (in so far as it occurs on the site) which an experienced contractors could :

- not have reasonably foreseen or could

- reasonably have foreseen, but against which he could not reasonably have taken at least one of the following measures :

    (i) prevent loss or damage to physical property from occurring by taking appropriate measures; and

    (ii) insure against.

B. Compensation Events: The compensation events mutually agreed should be provided in the contract document.

C. In the event of any such loss or damage happening from any of the owners risks defined in (A) above, as in combination with other risks, the contractor shall, if so required by the owner, rectify the loss or damage. An addition to the contract price shall be determined treating the work done as variation / extra / substituted item, as given in the relevant clauses.

D. Whenever any compensation event occurs, the contractor will notify the owner, within 14 days and provide a forecast cost of the compensation event. As soon as information demonstrating the effect of such event is available, the owner shall assess the compensation to be paid. In case contractors' forecast is deemed unreasonable, the owner shall adjust the contract price and/or extend the completion date based on his assessment.

9.1.17 Arbitration

(1) Introduction :

The main object of incorporating this clause in the conditions of contracts is to avoid lengthy and tedious procedure of litigation and to avoid inordinate delays and expenses when the dispute between the contractor and the owner or department is referred to the court of law. 'Arbitration' is a procedure in which dispute between the contractor and the owner or department is referred to a third impartial party known as an **'Arbitrator'**. The arbitrator(s), after hearing both the parties in a judicial manner gives their decision and is known as 'Award', which is executed on the stamp paper in accordance with the 'Stamp Duty Act'. The award (i.e. decision of the arbitrators) is binding on both the parties.

As per Arbitration Act 1940, the term 'arbitration agreement' means a written agreement to refer present or future differences to arbitration, irrespective of whether an arbitrator is named therein or not.

Arbitration is thus an alternative to regular 'Civil suits' of settling disputes between the contracting parties and is a quasijudicial process of adjudication by a third person or persons acceptable to both the disputing parties. All disputed matters except those of criminal nature can be referred to arbitration.

An arbitrator is a judge appointed by the disputing parties to resolve their dispute. He must be fair, frank and honest throughout the arbitration proceedings and must have complete idea about the contractual obligations and should have sufficient knowledge of the law and legal proceedings. If both parties agree to appoint only one person as an arbitrator, he is known as a **'Sole arbitrator'**. However if each party appoints their own arbitrator then they are known as joint arbitrators. In case of even number of joint arbitrators, the appointed arbitrators will refer the matter to another person known as **'Umpire'** whose decision i.e. award will be final.

(2) Causes of Disputes :

The common causes of dispute between the contracting parties may be any one or all of the following :

- Variation or escalation of rates.
- Delays on the part of the owner or department to supply necessary drawings, or decisions to the contractor.
- Delays in payment to be made to the contractor.
- Extra-claims by the contractor.
- Termination of contract
- Hire charges to be paid for the tools and plant supplied by the department.
- Extension of time.

The arbitration proceedings are similar to the regular law court's proceedings. The arbitrator will consider all the evidence and record the statements of both the parties and witnesses appearing before him and considering all pros and cons of the dispute will declare his award (which is similar to judgement in the court of law) which will be binding on both the parties.

(3) Merits of Arbitration Procedure :

- The entire procedure of arbitration is very simple as compared to the Court of law proceedings,
- It takes less time to declare the award,
- It is cheap as compared to filing civil suits,
- The dispute between the contracting parties is not made public as it is decided privately,
- The time and place for arbitration proceedings can be fixed to suit the convenience of both the parties.

The arbitrator after finalising the award, informs both the parties accordingly and asks them to pay necessary fees and expenses. The award is then filed in the court of law and then the decree is issued by the court and the award is implemented. Usual time prescribed for declaring award is four calender months from the date of appointing arbitrator.

Thus it can be concluded that the method of arbitration is effective, expedious and economical as compared to regular court proceedings. The award of the arbitrators can be challenged in the higher court of laws and can be set aside for some valid reasons and in exceptional cases.

Sanction of the court of law is necessary to convert the decision of the arbitrator into a valid award.

(4) Qualifications of an Arbitrator :

The following are some of the desired qualifications required for an arbitrator.

- Arbitrator should be fair, impartial, honest and disinterested person.
- He should be knowledgeable and expert in the field of dispute and having good reputation.
- He should have sufficient knowledge of the law.
- He should be conversant with the arbitration proceedings.
- He should be capable of handling the entire procedure of arbitration.
- For the disputes in building industries, he may be an eminent engineer or an architect, acceptable to both the parties.
- He should not be a person of suspicious character.

(5) Powers of an Arbitrator :

As per the Arbitration Act, 1940, an arbitrator is bestowed with the following powers :

- He can administer oath to both the disputed contracting parties and also witnesses appearing before him for collecting the evidence.
- In certain special disputes, he is at liberty to refer it to court of law for its opinion in the matter.
- The arbitrator has full powers to ask any questions related to the disputed matter to both the parties and witnesses.
- He is empowered to declare his judgement, called as 'award' in the disputed matter, which will be binding on both the parties.

(6) Duties of an Arbitrator :

- Throughout the arbitration proceeding he has to be impartial and fair to both the disputed parties.
- He should not yield to undue influence or pressurization from either parties.
- During the process of arbitration he has to assume a role of third party and disinterested judge.

- While collecting evidence he must give equal opportunities to both the disputing parties to plead their case and should always talk to one party only in the presence of other party to prove his impartiality.

- The arbitrator should be conscious and always abide by the norms of natural justice and equality while carrying out arbitration proceedings.

THEORETICAL QUESTIONS

1. Explain in brief the nature of any four types of contracts.

2. Explain the importance of contract conditions and differentiate between general conditions and particular conditions.

3. Explain (a) Secured advance (b) Mobilization advance.

4. Explain valid, voidable and void contracts with an example of each. Discuss essential requirements as per ICA (1872) for forming a valid contract.

5. State the advantages and disadvantages of post-qualification of contractors.

6. Enlist the essential requirements of a valid contract.

7. What is meant by arbitration ? State its necessity in civil engineering contracts.

 ❖ ❖ ❖

Sample Question Paper for
In-Semester Examination (30 Marks)

Time: 1 Hour   **Marks: 30**

Q. 1.   **(a)** What is an approximate estimate? State the purposes of preparing approximate estimate.   **[2 + 4 = 6]**

         (b) Differentiate between supplementary and revised estimate.   **[4]**

OR

Q. 2.   **(a)** Prepare an approximate estimate for a two storried R.C.C. building using the following data.   **[6]**

            (i)   Floor area on each floor = 200 sq.m.

            (ii)   Built up area = 1.2 time the floor area.

            (iii)   Plinth area rate = ₹ 1800/- per sq.m.

            (iv)   Work charge establishment and contingencies = 8% of construction cost.

            (v)   Cost of water supply, drainage and electrification = 16% of the sum total.

         (b) Explain the rule for measurement of plastering work as per IS 1200.   **[4]**

Q. 3.   **(a)** Fig. 1 shows the plan and section of an office building. Determine the quantities of the following items and prepare the measurement sheet with appropriate description of each item.

            (i)   Earth work in excavation in hard murrum for foundation.   **[5]**

            (ii)   UCR masonry in C.M. (1 : 6) in plinth and foundation.   **[5]**

OR

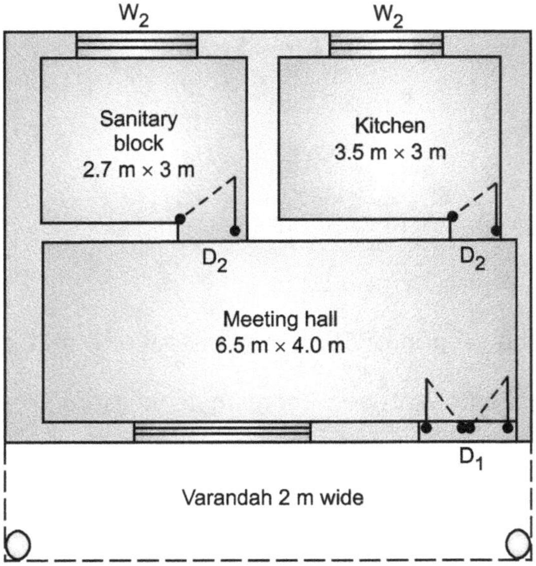

Fig. 1(a) : Plan

Q. 4.   **(a)** A R.C.C. beam 4 m long, 0.23 × 0.45 m in cross-section is provided with reinforcement as given below. Reinforcement at bottom = 2 No./ 12 mm diameter straight and 2 No. / 12 mm diameter bent up bars.

Reinforcement at top = 2 No. / 8 mm diameter anchor bars stirrups = 6 mm diameter at 150 mm C/C.

Prepare bar bending schedule and determine the quantity of 6 mm, 8 mm and 12 mm diameter steel reinforcement.   **[5]**

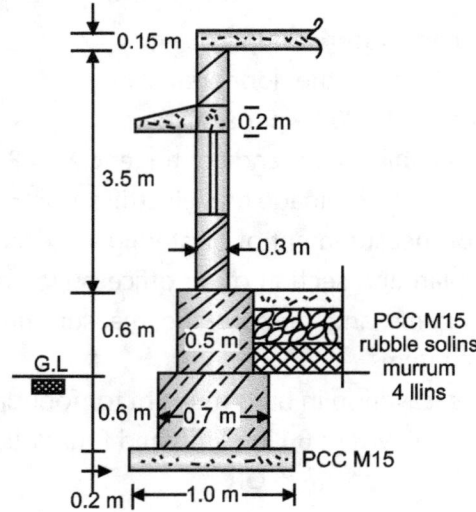

Fig. 1 (b) : Section

D_1 = 1.5 m × 2.1 m

D_2 = 1.0 m × 2.1 m

W_1 = 1.5 m × 1.2 m

W_2 = 1.2 m × 1.2 m

(b) Fig. 2 shows the section of 10 m long masonry wier. Determine the quantities of the following items, entering them in a measurement sheet with appropriate description of each item.

(i) Earthwork in excavation.   **[3]**

(ii) P.C.C. M 15 in foundation.   **[2]**

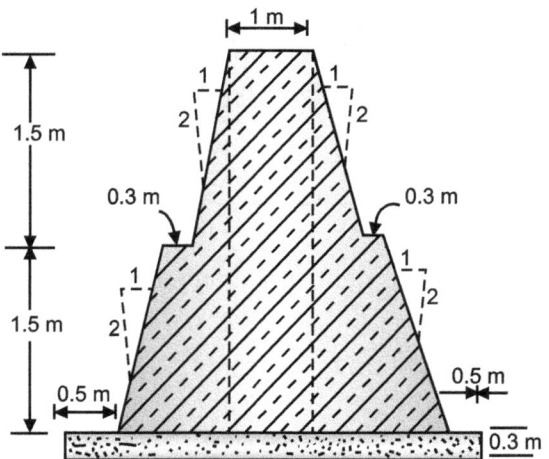

Fig. 2 : Section

Q. 5.   Refer Q. 3 (a) and Fig. 1 and find out the following :

(i)   Brick masonry in C.M. (1 : 6) in superstructure.   **[5]**

(ii) RCC M20 in slab and lintels assuming 15 cm projection on either side of openings.   **[5]**

OR

Q. 6.   **(a)** Explain the purpose of valuation.   **[5]**

(b) Differentiate between the terms Cost, Price and Value of an item with the help of suitable example.   **[5]**

◈ ◈ ◈

Sample Question Paper for
End-Semester Examination (70 Marks)

Time: 2:30 Hours   **Marks: 70**

Q. 1.   **(a)** Fig. 1 shows plant of a residential building. Determine quantities of the following items :

       (i)   Excavation of foundation for tooting.   **[3]**

       (ii) R.C.C. in footing.   **[3]**

       (iii) R.C.C. in columns.   **[3]**

       (iv) R.C.C. in slab.   **[3]**

       (v) R.C.C. in beam.   **[3]**

       (vi) Steel reinforcement, if percentage of steel for various element is   **[3]**
            Column : 2%, Beam an lintel : 1.2%, Slab : 1%, Footing : 0.8%.

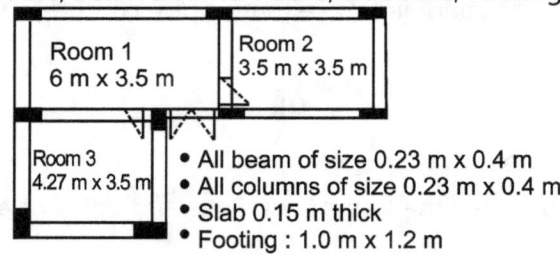

Fig. 1 (a)

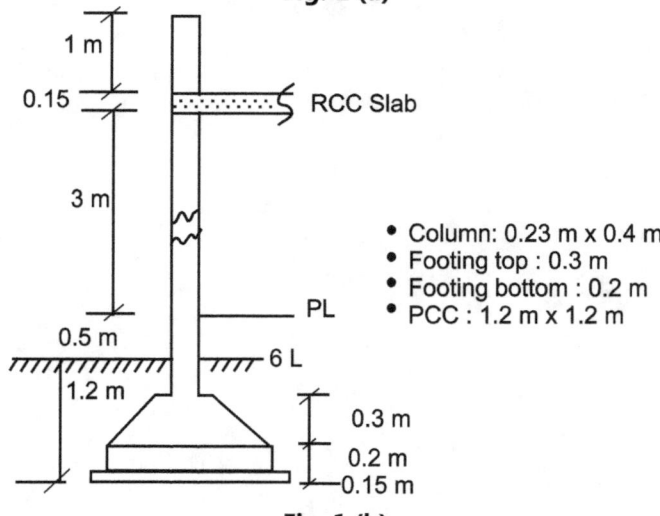

Fig. 1 (b)

   (b) Explain the terms "Taking Out" and "Squaring".   **[2]**

OR

Q. 2. **(a)** A (G + 2) building has a carpet area of 800 m^2 in each floor. The area occupied by corridor verandah, staircase, etc is 25% and area occupied by wall, column is 10%, water supply 7.5% Electrification 8.5%, contingency 4%. Prepare a preliminary estimate considering cost of ground floor ₹ 1500/- sq-m, ₹ 1700/- for I floor, ₹ 1850/- for I floor. **[10]**

(b) Determine book value of a property consisting of a land (plot of area 1000 m^2) and building (built-up area of 600 m^2) in the year 2013 assuming scrap value 10% of the original cost. The original land cost is 1973 was ₹ 100/- per m^2 and the cost of built-up area in the same year was ₹ 900/- per m^2. Assume that the construction specifications are first class and the land cost has remained unchanged. **[8]**

(c) Explain the terms "Scrap Value" and "Salvage Value". **[2]**

Q. 3. **(a)** Explain the importance of specification in preparing estimate and what are the objectives of Specifications. What are standard specification and specification for performance? Explain how control over quality of material and workmanship is achieved by specification. **[8]**

(b) Draft a detailed specification for earthwork embankment (without OMC). **[8]**

OR

Q. 4. **(a)** Explain importance of Rate Analysis and what are the factors affecting rate analysis. Explain in detail the procedure for rate analysis. **[4]**

(b) Explain task work and how does it vary. Work out the labour requirement for

(i) Reinforcement for R.C.C. work and

(ii) I class brick masonry in CM 1 : 6 in superstructure. **[4]**

(c) Prepare rate analysis for R.C.C. work in column with proportion 1 : 1. 5 : 3, with cement course sand, 2.5 cm ballast with all material, T and P complete. **[8]**

Q. 5. **(a)** Enlist various methods of execution of minor works in PWD. Explain any one method giving its merits and demerits. **[6]**

(b) A 6 + 1 residential bunglow of estimated cost ₹ 60 lakhs is to be constructed in a plot lying on Mumbai-Pune expressway near to Monawala. Draft a tender notice for inviting tenders under '2-bid' system for execution of the work. **[6]**

(c) Briefly discuss different forms of BOT tenders. **[6]**

Q. 6. **(a)** What is administrative approval ? Explain its significance in PWD method of execution of works. **[6]**

(b) Write notes on: [6]

  (i) Pre-bid conference.

  (ii) Method of inviting tenders.

(c) Explain the term 'Scruting of Tenders'. [4]

Q. 7. **(a)** Discuss in brief essential requirements of a valid contract. [6]

  (b) State merits and demerits of pre-qualification of contractors. [6]

  (c) Write a note on cost plus or percentage contracts. [4]

OR

Q. 8 Write notes on any four of the following : [16]

  (a) Lump-sum contracts.

  (b) Arbitration and arbitrator.

  (c) Responsibilities of contractor regarding execution of work.

  (d) Registration of contractors.

  (e) Contents of F.I.D.I.C. document.

University Question Papers

Time : 4 Hours   Max. Marks : 100

Section – I

1. (a) Distinguish between an estimate and estimation. Explain approximate estimate, detailed estimate, supplementary estimate and revised estimate with an example of each. **(10)**

   (b) Explain all the rules associated with deductions, additions for the plaster item as per IS 1200. **(8)**

OR

2. (a) Explain the logic behind deciding the units of measurement, with suitable examples,

   (i) m^3, (ii) m^2, (iii) m, (iv) Rg, (v) No.

   (b) Explain all the rules as per IS 1200 associated with measurement of RCC items without steel reinforcement for **(8)**

   (i) Columns

   (ii) Beams

   (iii) Slabs, with suitable examples.

3. A dog-legged stair consists of 10 steps in each flight of width 300 mm. Length of step is 1.5 m and rise is 150 mm. Width of landing is 2.0 m. Waist slab thickness is 200 mm. The steel reinforcement consists of :

   – Longitudinal steel – 12 mm ϕ ToR at 200 mm C-C and

   – Transverse steel – 10 mm ϕ ToR 250 mm C-C.

   Determine :

   (a) Quantities for RCC $(1 : 1\frac{1}{2} : 3)$ items as per IS 1200 and DSR requirements. **(3)**

   (b) % of steel in staircase. **(5)**

   (c) Bill of materials required to execute the above work. (3% wastage, 5% safety stock may be considered). **(5)**

   (d) Draw bar-bending schedule. **(3)**

OR

4. A masonry wall of 300 mm thickness is to be constructed with IS bricks in C.M., 1:6. Sieved sand is to be used for masonry joints. The dimensions of the wall are 5 m $\times$ 4 m. The wall was the following openings :

   Window – W_1 – 1.5 m $\times$ 1.2 m

   Door – D_1 – 1.2 m $\times$ 2.1 m.

   Assume suitable sizes for lintels, chajjas. Determine :

(a) Item quantity for BB masonry in C.M., 1:6 as per IS 1200. **(3)**

(b) Item quantity for R.C.C. lintel. **(2)**

(c) Item quantity for R.C.C. chajja. **(2)**

(d) Bill of materials required to execute the entire above work. (3% wastage, 5% safety stock may be considered). **(9)**

Assume mix for RCC as M (25).

5. (a) Draft a detailed specification for providing and laying RCC of M (25) grade including formwork and including steel reinforcement for a slab, with all other standard requirements which are normally specified in the BOQ. **(12)**

(b) Discuss the various factors affecting the rate of any item. **(4)**

OR

6. (a) Explain various types of specifications such as brief, detailed, standard, open, closed with examples. Elaborate the do's and dont's w.r.t. specification writing. Discuss the importance of specifications from the legal as well as the construction point of view.

(12)

(b) What is taskwork ? Why does it vary ? Explain its importance with an example. **(4)**

Section – II

7. (a) Explain any five factors affecting value of a property in brief, with suitable examples.

(10)

(b) Determine value of property based on following information :

(i) Plot area 2000 m^2.

(ii) Land rate when purchased in year 2000 – ₹ 1000 per m^2.

(iii) Appreciation of land rate – 4% per annum at a compounded worth.

(iv) Year of valuation – 2011.

(v) FSI consumed – 0.5.

(vi) Construction cost in the year 2005 when building was constructed is – ₹ 8000/- per sq.m.

(vii) Interest rate on sinking fund – 5%.

(viii) Expected life of buildings – 50 years. Use present land value method.

OR

8. (a) Explain with examples, any five types of value. **(5)**

(b) Explain any two methods of working out depreciation, in brief. **(6)**

(c) Explain "method of yield", with an example. **(5)**

(d) Explain concept of land reversion and reversionary value. **(2)**

9. (a) Draft a brief tender notice, so as to construct a multistoreyed mall building of 50 crores to be completed in 18 calendar months, involving pre-qualifications of tenderers. **(7)**

(b) Explain process of administrative approval and technical sanction in the PWD with an example. **(5)**

(c) Explain the purpose of taking the security deposit in a tender. **(4)**

OR

10. (a) Discuss merits, demerits of open tenders as against negotiated tender. **(6)**

(b) How cartel formation in a tender can be detected ? What action is then subsequently taken ? **(4)**

(c) Before working out a tender and before submitting it, what information and data needs to be collected and ascertained. Elaborate. **(6)**

11. (a) Explain valid, voidable and void contracts with an example of each. Discuss essential requirements as per ICA (1872) for forming a valid contract. **(8)**

(b) In the recent Japanase earthquake scenario, a major on-going construction work got devasted. You were the contractor of that work. Which conditions in the contract will enable you to recover the losses incurred ? Explain the reasoning. **(8)**

OR

12. (a) On a construction work, the following defects are noticed :

(i)   Door shutters are not fitting in the door frames because of faulty line, level and dimensioning.

(ii) Toilet slabs are leaking after water proofing is done.

(iii) Non-uniformity in the paint colour shades is observed.

(iv) Shrinkage cracks in plaster item are observed, before paining.

As an Engineer in charge of the works, what action you will take against the contractor, in accordance with the contract conditions ? Explain for each defect, separately. **(12)**

(b) Explain B.O.T. contract with an example. **(4)**

◈ ◈ ◈

May 2012

Time : 4 Hours　　　　　　　　　　　　　　　　　　　　　　**Max. Marks : 100**

Section – I

1. (a) State the purposes of preparing detailed estimate. Hence differentiate between supplementary and revised estimate. **(8)**

(b) What is an approximate estimate? Prepare the approximate estimate for a three storied R.C.C. building with following details : **(8)**

　(i)　Carpet area on each floor = 600 sq.m.

　　　Total number of floors = 3.

　(ii)　Area occupied by walls = 15% of carpet area.

　(iii)　Area occupied by passage, sanitary block and staircase = 30% of carpet area.

　(iv)　Rate of construction = ₹ 20,000/- sq. m. of built-up area.

　(v)　Work charged establishment and contingencies = 3% and 5% of construction cost respectively.

　vi)　Water supply, drainage and electrification = 15% of sum total.

OR

2. (a) Enlist various methods used for preparing approximate estimate of civil engineering projects. State the purposes of preparing approximate estimate and explain plinth area method. **(8)**

(b) Explain the following terms in brief : **(8)**

　(i)　Provisional sum item

　(ii)　Prime cost items

　(iii)　Work charge establishment

　(iv)　Contingencies.

3. Fig. 1 shows plan and section of a load bearing office building. Determine the quantities of following items and enter in a measurement sheet.

　(i)　Earthwork in excavation for foundation. **(3)**

　(ii)　UCR masonry in C.M. (1 : 6) in plinth and foundation. **(3)**

　(iii)　Brick masonry (1:4) in superstructure. **(3)**

　(iv)　R.C.C. (M20) in slab and lintels. **(4)**

(v) Steel reinforcement, if steel reinforcement is 1% of R.C.C. work. Schedule for openings is given below:

Door D1 : 1.5 × 2.1, D2 = 1.2 × 2.1

Windows W1 : 1.5 × 1.2

W2 : 1.0 × 1.2

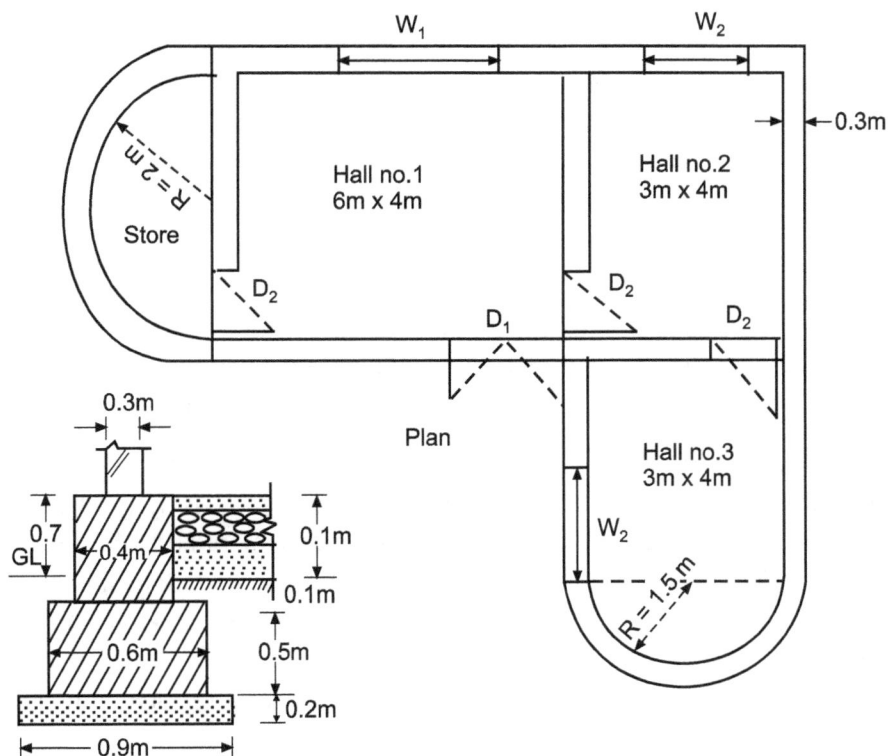

Floor to floor height = 3.2 m

Slab thickness = 0.15 m

Fig. 1

(b) Explain with neat sketch the method for taking out quantity for R.C.C. work in footing.

(3)

OR

4. (a) Fig. 2 shows a section of 10 m long R.C.C. retaining wall. Determine

   (i)   R.C.C. M20 in retaining wall.   **(3)**

   (ii) Steel reinforcement, 8 mm, 10 mm and total. Also prepare bar bending schedule.

   (6)

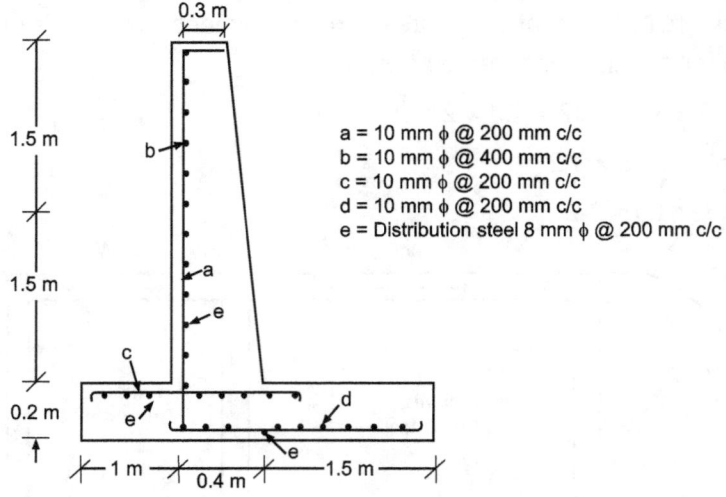

Fig. 2

(b) Determine the quantity of earthwork for the portion of a road between chainage 00 to 300 m. The ground levels at various chainages are given below: **(9)**

Ch. (m)	0	30	60	90	120	150	180	210	240	270	300
G.L. in m	150	150.45	150.85	151.2	152.00	152.5	151.8	151.2	150.5	150	149.50

The formation level at Ch. 00 is 149.50 and the road is in rising gradient of 1 in 150. The formation width is 12 m, side slope 2:1 in embankment and 1.5:1 in cutting.

5. (a) Draft a detailed specification for execution of R.C.C. M20 work in superstructure with reference to materials, proportions, method of execution, workmanship, tests, mode of measurement and payment.   **(8)**

   (b) A brick masonry wall in C.M. (1:6) is to be provided for a residential building. Details are as below: **(4)**

   Total length = 50 m, height above plinth = 3 m, thickness of wall = 0.2 m.

   Determine

   (i) Materials like bricks, cement and sand required for masonry work.   **(6)**

   (ii) If 3 masons and 8 mazdoors are employed for the construction, find the time in days required for the construction of masonry work.   **(2)**

OR

6. (a) Determine the rate/cu.m. for providing and laying R.C.C. (1:1.5:3) for slab excluding form work and steel reinforcement.

   If the total R.C.C. work in slab is 75 m^3, find the basic materials like cement, sand and coarse aggregate required for the work.   **(9)**

   (b) Draft a detailed specification for providing and laying brick masonry in C.M. (1 : 6) in super structure.   **(7)**

SECTION - II

7. (a) Differentiate between the following (write 2 differences each) : **(8)**
　　(i)　Distress value – scrap value
　　(ii)　Value cost
　　(iii)　Freehold property – Leasehold property.
　　(iv)　Depreciation – obsolescence.
　(b) Explain five purposes of valuation in brief. **(5)**
　(c) Briefly explain the belting method used for land valuation. **(5)**

OR

8. (a) State various methods used for valuation of land with buildings. Explain any one method in detail. **(5)**
　(b) What is meant by 'land reversion'? Explain briefly 'reversionary value'. **(5)**
　(c) Determine fair market value of the property using the following data : **(8)**
　　(i)　Built-up area of building = 250 m^2.
　　(ii)　Plot area = 500 m^2.
　　(iii)　Year of construction = 1980.
　　(iv)　Present land cost = ₹ 10000/- per m^2.
　　(v)　Present construction rate = 20000/- per m^2.
　　(vi)　Rate of interest on Government securities = 6%.
　　(vii)　Scrap value = 10%.
　　Building was constructed with all 'First Class' specifications. Assume expected life of building = 60 years.

9. (a) What is meant by a 'tender'? Explain the standard (usual) way of opening the tender and its scrutiny. **(4)**
　(b) State the advantages and disadvantages of 'post-qualification' of contractors. **(4)**
　(c) Explain the terms 'earnest money' and 'security deposit'. **(4)**
　(d) Explain the PWD method (procedure) of execution of a work. **(4)**

OR

10. (a) Draft out a typical tender notice to be advertised in an English Newspaper for construction of tenements of a residential co-operative housing society with an approximate construction cost of 1 crore of rupees. **(6)**
　(b) Enlist the essential elements of a typical tender form. Briefly (in 1 or 2 sentences) explain their necessity. **(5)**
　(c) Explain the PWD procedure of executing a minor work. **(5)**

11. (a) Enlist the essential requirements of a valid contract. **(4)**
　(b) What is meant by 'arbitration'? State its necessity/advantages in civil engineering contracts. **(4)**

(c) Justify the 'bankruptcy of contractor' clause in the conditions of a civil engineering contract. **(4)**

(d) State the advantages of an 'item-rate contract'. **(4)**

OR

12. (a) Write a note on 'termination of a contract'. **(4)**

(b) You are owner of a proposed building under construction. During your visit you have come across the following situations at the site: **(4)**

(i) Your found that inferior quality sand and bricks are being used for construction.

(ii) The labour is asking for more money (compensation) from you, telling that the contractor is paying wages less than the minimum wages prescribed by the government.

Briefly explain the action you will take as owner to salvage the situation in each case. Mention clearly the relevant (appropriate) typical clause of the contract to support your action. **(4)**

(c) State whether following statements are 'True' or 'False'. Give reason for each of them. (No marks will be given if reason not given) **(4)**

(i) The method of measurement of completed works (items) should be a part of the contract document.

(ii) The patent rights and royalties clause should be included in the contract conditions (document).

(d) State the advantages of a 'lump-sum contract'. **(4)**

◈ ◈ ◈

Dec. 2012

Time : 4 Hr.   **Max. Marks : 100**

Section – I

1. (a) What is an approximate estimate? State the purposes of preparing approximate estimate. **[6]**

(b) Differentiate between supplementary and revised estimate. **[4]**

(c) What factors are considered while deciding the plinth area rate for preparing approximate estimate? **[6]**

OR

2. (a) Enlist the different types of estimate used in civil engineering projects. Hence, explain the method of preparing detailed estimate of a building. **[6]**

(b) Prepare an approximate estimate for a two storried R.C.C. building using the following data. **[6]**

(i) Floor area on each floor = 200 sq.m.

    (ii) Built up area = 1.2 time the floor area.

    (iii) Plinth area rate = ₹ 1800/- per sq.m.

    (iv) Work charge establishment and contingencies = 8% of construction cost.

    (v) Cost of water supply, drainage and electrification = 16% of the sum total.

  (c) Explain the rule for measurement of plastering work as per IS 1200.   **[4]**

3. (a) Fig. 1 shows the plan and section of an office building. Determine the quantities of the following items and prepare the measurement sheet with appropriate description of each item.

    (i) Earth work in excavation in hard murrum for foundation.   **[3]**

    (ii) UCR masonry in C.M. (1: 6) in plinth and foundation.   **[3]**

    (iii) Brick masonry in C.M. (1 : 6) in superstructure.   **[3]**

    (iv) RCC M20 in slab and lintels assuming 15 cm projection on either side on openings.   **[4]**

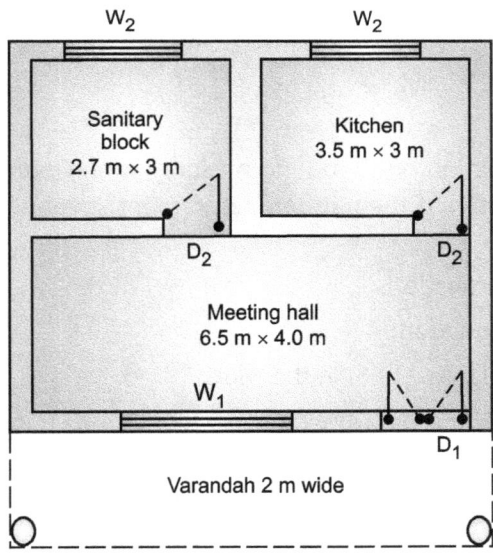

Fig. 1(a) : Plan

  (b) A R.C.C. beam 4 m long, 0.23 × 0.45 m in cross-section is provided with reinforcement as given below. Reinforcement at bottom = 2 No./ 12 mm diameter straight and 2 No. / 12 mm diameter bent up bars.

  Reinforcement at top = 2 No. / 8 mm diameter anchor bars stirrups = 6 mm diameter at 150 mm C/C.

  Prepare bar bending schedule and determine the quantity of 6 mm, 8 mm and 12 mm diameter steel reinforcement.   **[5]**

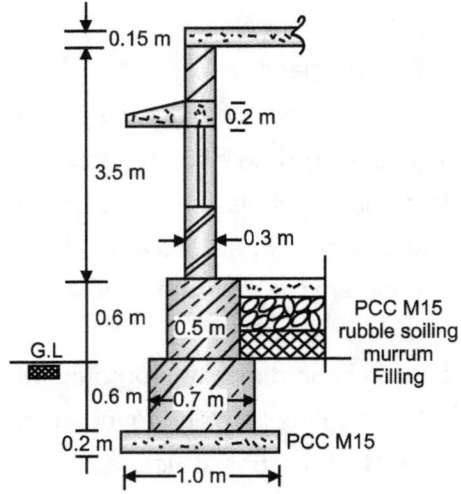

Fig. 1 (b) : Section

D_1 = 1.5 m × 2.1 m

D_2 = 1.0 m × 2.1 m

W_1 = 1.5 m × 1.2 m

W_2 = 1.2 m × 1.2 m   **OR**

4. (a) Fig. 2 shows the section of 10 m long masonry wier. Determine the quantities of the following items, entering them in a measurement sheet with appropriate description of each item.

  (i)   Earthwork in excavation.   **[2]**

  (ii) P.C.C. M 15 in foundation.   **[2]**

  (iii) C.R. Masonry in C.M. (1 : 6) in the wier.   **[4]**

  (iv) Pointing in C.M. (1 : 4) for the masonry work.   **[4]**

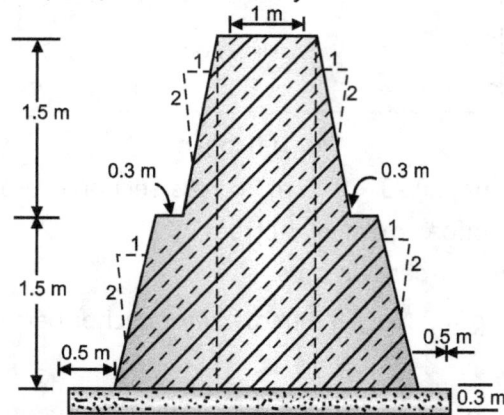

Fig. 2 : Section

    (b) State the methods used for calculation of earthwork in roads and hence explain any one method. **[6]**

5. (a) Draft a detailed specification for item of brick masonry work in superstructure with reference to **[8]**

      (i) The materials and proportion,

      (ii) Method of execution, workmanship and

      (iii) Mode of measurement and payment.

    (b) A compound wall 40 m long, 0.3 m wide and 1.5 m in height is constructed in UCR masonry in C.M. (1 : 6). Determine, **[8]**

      (i) The quantity of basic materials like rubble, cement and sand required for the work.

      (ii) If two masons and eight mazdoors are employed for the work, find the time in days required to complete the work. **[8]**

OR

6. (a) Determine the rate per unit for construction BM (1 : 4) in superstructure. **[8]**

    (b) Draft a detailed specification for construction of C.R. masonry in superstructure with reference to **[8]**

      (i) The materials and proportions

      (ii) Method of execution, workmanship and

      (iii) Mode of measurement and payment.

Section – II

7. (a) An old bungalow is purchased today for ₹ 80000/-. Determine the amount of sinking fund and annual installment of sinking fund for a future life of 20 years for this bungalow. Given: The scrap value is 10% of the cost of purchase and rate of interest is 5%. **[5]**

    (b) Discuss five types of values of a property in brief. **[5]**

    (c) Briefly explain 'land and building basis' of valuation. **[4]**

    (d) Explain briefly the essential characteristics of 'Value' of a property. **[4]**

OR

8. (a) Owner of a building earns a net annual income of ₹ 50000/-. Calculate years Purchase and value of the building for an expected life of 50 years if :

      (i) The property is perpetual and simple rate of interest is 6%.

      (ii) The property is receivable with a dual rate of interest 6% and sinking fund is 3%. **[5]**

    (b) What is meant by 'Value' of a property? Briefly discuss the factors on which the value or valuation of property depends. **[5]**

    (c) Clearly explain four objectives of valuation. **[4]**

    (d) State various methods used for valuation of buildings. Explain in short any one method. **[4]**

9. (a) Discuss the amounts of Earnest Money and Security Deposit and their necessity (purpose). **[5]**

   (b) What is meant by a 'tender notice'? State eight essential factors which must be a part of tender notice. **[5]**

   (c) Write a note on 'registration as a contractor' with respect to the following points:
       (i) Different classes of contractors and corresponding limits for amount of works
       (ii) Application form (information to be filled)
       (iii) Documents to be submitted along with the form. **[6]**

OR

10. (a) Discuss the 'balanced' and 'unbalanced' types of tenders with examples. **[5]**

    (b) Explain essential elements of a typical tender form. **[5]**

    (c) Write a detailed note on various categories (classes) of works executed by PWD. **[6]**

11. (a) What is meant by a 'contract' in civil engineering? Elaborate on three essential requirements (characteristics) of a valid (lawful) contract. **[4]**

    (b) What is meant by 'arbitration'? Explain its necessity with examples. State four matters which can not be lawfully referred to an arbitrator. **[4]**

    (c) Explain 'general' and 'special' conditions of contract with examples. **[4]**

    (d) List out the advantages and disadvantages of a 'labour contract'. **[4]**

OR

12. (a) Write a note on 'breach of contract'. **[4]**

    (b) Discuss the meaning and necessity of :
        (i) Interim payment
        (ii) Liquidated damages **[4]**

    (c) Clearly explain 'legally competent parties' for a lawful (valid) contract. **[4]**

    (d) Enlist various types of civil engineering contracts. Explain any one type of contract in detail. **[4]**

◈ ◈ ◈

May 2013

Time : 4 Hours   **Max. Marks : 100**

Section – I

1. (A) What is an estimate ? State the purposes of preparing a detailed estimate ? **(4)**

   (B) State the unit of measurement and rule for deductions to be made for openings in cases of following items : **(6)**

       (i) Plastering to the wall surface (internal and external).
       (ii) Brick masonry in superstructure for main walls and partition walls.

   (C) Prepare an approximate estimate for a school building. Use following data : **(6)**

(i)   Number of students in the school = 400.

(ii)   Floor area for class rooms = 1 m²/student.

(iii) Area for administration building = 20% of classroom area class including staffroom, office head.

(iv)   Area for sanitary block for girls = 20% of class room area boys, ladies an gents staff.

(v)   Area occupied by walls, passage etc. = 25% total floor area.

(vi)   Plinth area rate of construction = ₹ 1000/m².

(vii) Contingencies and work charge establishment = 5% of construction.

(viii) Water supply, drainage and electrification = 16% of total cost.

OR

2. (A) State different types of estimate and hence differentiate between revised estimate and supplimentary estimate. **(6)**

(B) What is a construction item ? Write brief description as required in the measurement and billing of any item. **(4)**

(C) State different methods of preparing approximate estimate. Explain any one method and elaborate various factors to be considered during preparation of approximate estimate. **(6)**

3. (A) Figure 1 shows plant of a residential building. Determine quantities of following items :

(i)   Excavation of foundation for tooting. **(3)**

(ii)   R.C.C. in tooting. **(3)**

(iii) R.C.C. in columns. **(3)**

(iv)   R.C.C. in slab. **(3)**

(v)   R.C.C. in beam. **(3)**

(vi)   Steel reinforcement, if percentage of steel for various element is **(3)**

Column : 2%, Beam an lintel : 1.2%, Slab : 1%, Footing : 0.8%.

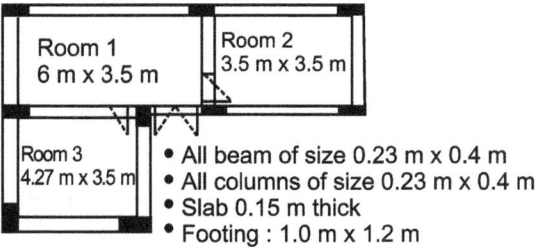

Fig. 1 (a)

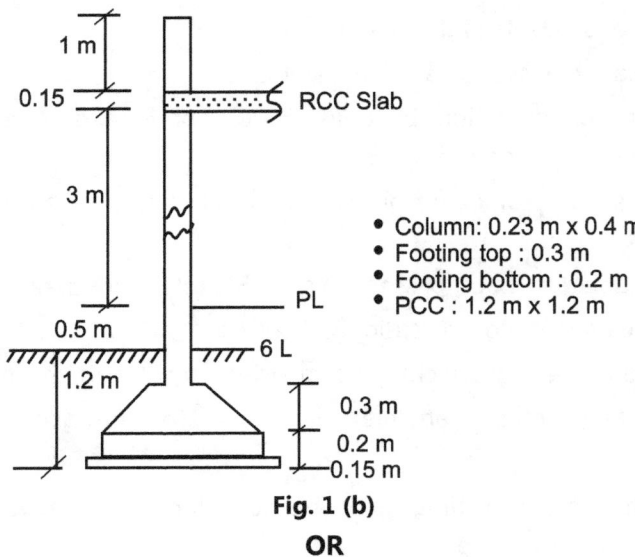

- Column: 0.23 m x 0.4 m
- Footing top : 0.3 m
- Footing bottom : 0.2 m
- PCC : 1.2 m x 1.2 m

Fig. 1 (b)

OR

4. **(A)** Figure 2 shows section of a circular R.C.C. storage reservoir. Determine the quantities of following items :

    (i)   Excavation for foundation in hard murram. **(2)**

    (ii) P.C.C. M15 in plinth and foundation. **(3)**

    (iii) U.C.R. masonry in C.M. (1 : 6) in plinth and foundation. **(3)**

    (iv) R.C.C. M20 in base slab and roof slab. **(3)**

    (v)   R.C.C. M20 in container wall of the tank. **(3)**

    (vi) Steel reinforcement in kg if the percentage of steel in all R.C.C. member is 1.5%

    (4)

5. **(A)** Determine the rate per unit for the item of U.C.R. masonry in C.M.C. (1 : 6) in superstructure. Use following rates for materials and labour, also assume any other data if necessary stating it clearly.

    Rubble : ₹ 500/m³, Sand : ₹ 1500/m³, Cement : ₹ 270/bat, Mazdoor : ₹ 300/day,

    Mason : ₹ 600/day and head mason : ₹ 800/day. **(6)**

    (B) A residential building is constructed in brick masonry in C.M. (1 : 6). The details of the masonry are as below. **(6)**

    Main wall cone brick thick : L = 62 m, h = 3 m, b = 0.2 m for our brick thick wall.

    (i)   Determine the basic materials like bricks, sand and cement to required complete the work.

    (ii) If 5 masons and 12 mazdoors are employed for the work, determine the time in days required to complete the work.

    (C) Draft a detailed specification for providing and laying **(4)**

P.C.C. (1 : 2 : 4) in plinth and foundation bed with reference to following points :

(i)   Materials quality proportions etc.

(ii) Method of execution and work mans chip.

(iii) Method of measurement and payment.

OR

6. (A) Determine the rate per Cu.m for providing and laying Brick Masonry in C.M. (1 : 6). Assume following rates for materials and labour and assume other details if required. **(6)**

Materials : Bricks : ₹ 4000/1000 Nos., Cement : ₹ 280/bag, Sand : ₹ 1200/m³.

Labour Head mason : ₹ 800/day, Mason : ₹ 600/day and Mazdoor : ₹ 300/day.

(B) U.C.R. masonry in C.M. (1 : 6) for a retaining wall is 412 m³. Determine the basic materials required for the construction of retaining wall. Also if 6 masons and 12 mazdoors are employed for this work, find the time in days required to complete the work. **(6)**

(C) Draft a detailed specification for providing internal plaster in C.M. (1 : 3) with reference to following points :

(i)   Materials, quality etc.

(ii) Method of execution, work manship and

(iii) Method of measurement and payment. **(4)**

Section – II

7. (A) A construction equipment is purchased for ₹ 160,000/-. Knowing that the salvage value of ₹ 20,000/- at the end of 5 years calculate book value of the equipment at the end of each year using constant percentages method of depreciation. **(8)**

(B) Explain in brief the following terms : **(6)**

(i)   Sinking fund.

(ii) Depreciation and

(iii) Leasehold property.

(C) Discuss any four purposes of valuation of a property. **(4)**

OR

8. (A) A plot of land has the shape as shown in Fig. 2. **(10)**

Determine the value of the plot using belting method. The depth of the front belt is 24 m its rate is ₹ 400 per square meter. Assume number of belts, sizes of belts and their rates as per usual standard practice. **(10)**

(B) What do you understand by the term outgoing ? Discuss the specification of outgoings in valuation. **(4)**

(C) What is meant by value of a property ? Briefly explain any three types of values of a property. **(4)**

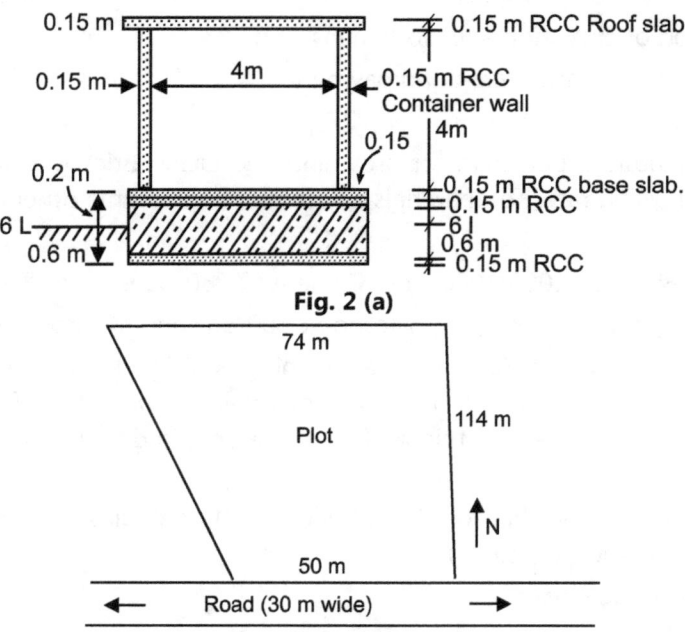

Fig. 2 (a)

Fig. 2. (b)

9. (A) Enlist various methods of execution of minor works in PWD. Explain any one method giving its merits and demerits. **(6)**

(B) A 6 + 1 residential bunglow of estimated cost ₹ 60 lakhs is to be constructed in a plot lying on Mumbai-Pune expressway near to Monawala. Draft a tender notice for inviting tenders under '2-bid' system for execution of the work. **(6)**

(C) Briefly discuss different forms of BOT tenders. **(4)**

OR

10. (A) What is administrative approval ? Explain its significance in PWD method of execution of works. **(6)**

(B) Write notes on **(6)**

    (i)   Pre-bid conference.

    (ii) Method of inviting tenders.

(C) Explain the term 'Scruting of Tenders'. **(4)**

11. (A) Define 'arbitration' and hence explain various matters which can be referred to an arbitrator. **(4)**

(B) State different types of contract and explain any one in detail. **(6)**

(C) Discuss the responsibilities of an owner and a contractor with reference to the contract signed between them while execution of the work. **(6)**

OR

12. (A) State with reasons whether following sentences indicate the instances of legal valid contract or not. **(6)**

  (i)   A contractor agrees orally to construct an additional floor on an existing ground floor of a bunglow. During discussion the owner and contractor agree to proceed with the work urgently.

  (ii) A contract signed by an owner undergoing treatment for severe headache.

  (iii) Contract signed for sharing of smuggled goods.

  (B) State four advantages of arbitration. Discuss the matters which cannot be referred to an 'arbitrator' as per Arbitration Act 1940. **(6)**

  (C) Write a note on conditions of valid contract. **(4)**

◈ ◈ ◈

Dec. 2013

Time : 4 Hours   **Max. Marks : 100**

Section – I

1. (a) Enlist different types of estimates and explain any one in detail. **(4)**

  (b) Describe various factors to be considered while preparing estimate for a project. **(4)**

  (c) Determine approximate estimated cost of a residential building, using following data : **(8)**

  (i)   Built-up area of the proposed building = 250 sq.m.

  (ii) Cost of building of built-up area 300 sq.m and with same specification as proposed building constructed 2 years before = ₹ 1500000/-

  (iii) Assume 10% rise in construction cost over the rates 2 years before.

  (iv) Assume a provision of 15% of construction cost for water supply, drainage and electrification.

OR

2. (a) Differentiate between prime cost items and provisional items. **(4)**

  (b) Explain the data required for preparation of estimate. **(4)**

  (c) Determine approximate estimated cost of a residential building, using following data : **(8)**

  (i)   Built-up area of the proposed building = 350 sq.m.

  (ii) Cost of buiulding of built-up area 300 sq.m and with same specification as proposed building constructed 3 years before = ₹ 1600000/-.

  (iii) Assume 15% rise in construction cost over rates before three years.

  (iv) Assume a provision of 15% of construction cost for water supply, drainage and electriciation.

3.   Fig. 1 shows plane and section of a residential building. The schedule for opening is as below :

Doors, D1 = 1.2 m × 2.1 m, windows, W1 = 1.5 m × 1.2 m. R.C.C. Lintel of size 0.23 m × 0.23 m with 15 cm projection on either side is provided over the opening. Determine quantities of following items and enter them in a measurement sheet with appropriate description.

(a) Excavation in hard murum for foundation. **(3)**

(b) UCR masonry in plinth and foundation. **(3)**

(c) Brick masonry in C.M. (1 : 6) in superstructure. **(3)**

(d) RCC M20 for slab and lintel. **(3)**

(e) Steel reinforcement if percentage of steel reinforcement is 2%. **(3)**

(f) 12 mm thick internal plaster in C.M. (1 : 4). **(3)**

OR

4. Fig. 2 shows plan and section of a residential building. The schedule for opening is as below :

Doors, D1 = 1.2 m × 2.1 m; Windows, W1 = 1.5 × 1.2 m. R.C.C. Lintel of size 0.23 m × 0.23 m with 15 cm projection on either side is provided over the openings. Determine quantities of following items and enter them in a measurement sheet with appropriate description.

(a) Excavation in hard murum for foundation. **(3)**

(b) UCR masonry in plinth and foundation. **(3)**

(c) Brick masonry in C.M. (1 : 6) in superstructure. **(3)**

(d) RCC M20 for slab and lintel. **(3)**

(e) Steel reinforcement if percentage of steel reinforcement is 1.8%. **(3)**

(f) 12 mm thick internal plaster in C.M. (1 : 4). **(3)**

5. (a) Explain the factors to be considered while determining rate per unit of an item. **(4)**

(b) The quantity of stonemasonry in C.M. (1 : 6) for plinth and fundation is 150 Cu.M. Determine the quantities of basic materials required to complete the work. **(6)**

(c) Draft detailed specification for the item of providing and laying brick masonry (1 : 6) in superstructure with reference to

(i) Different materials, quality and testing.

(ii) Method of execution and workmanship and

(iii) Mode of measurement and payment. **(6)**

OR

6. (a) What is task work ? Explain how the task work is useful in rate analysis of an item. **(4)**

(b) The quantity of R.C.C. (1 : 1.5 : 3) work for a residential building is 28 Cu.M. Determine the quantities of basic materials required for execute the R.C.C. work. **(6)**

(c) Draft a detailed specification for the item of providing and laying U.C.R. masonry (1 : 6) in plinth and foundation with reference to **(6)**

(i) Different materials, quality and testing.

(ii) Method of execution and workmanship.

(iii) Mode of measurement and payment.

Section – II

7. (a) Define 'outgoings' and explain how the outgoings are important in valuation of a property. **(4)**

   (b) Define' depreciation' and explain how it is useful in determining value of a property. **(4)**

   (c) Determine standard monthly rent for a property. Use following data : **(8)**

      (i) Area of plot = 500 sq.m.

      (ii) Total (G + 1) built-up area = 500 sq.m.

      (iii) Present land cost = ₹ 1200 sq.m.

      (iv) Present construction rate = ₹ 12000 sq.m.

      (v) Expected return on land and building cost = 5% respectively.

      (vi) Rate of interest for redemption of capita and sinking fund = 6% respectively.

      (vii) Total outgoings = 30% of gross rent.

      (viii) Expected future life of the building = 80 years.

OR

8. (a) Differentiate between scrap value and salvage value. **(4)**

   (b) State the different methods for calculating depreciation of built-up properties and explain any one. **(4)**

   (c) The details of certain built-up property are given below. Determine the present market value of the property. **(8)**

      (i) Built-up area = 400 sq.m., plot area = 400 sq.m.

      (ii) Past age of the building = 30 years.

      (iii) Expected future life of the building = 60 years.

      (iv) Present construction rate = ₹ 14000 sq.m.

      (vi) Present land cost = ₹ 8000 sq.m.

      (vi) Rate of interest for sinking fund = 6%.

9. (a) Explain the P.W.D. procedure for execution of minor works. **(4)**

   (b) Explain the purpose of administrative approval and technical sanction during execution of civil engineering works. **(6)**

   (c) Explain various forms of B.O.T. tenders. **(6)**

OR

10. (a) Explain the unbalanced tender with suitable example. **(6)**

    (b) Write short note on : **(10)**

       (i) Security deposit.

       (ii) Earnest money deposit.

       (iii) Pre-bid conference.

(iv) Liquidated damages.

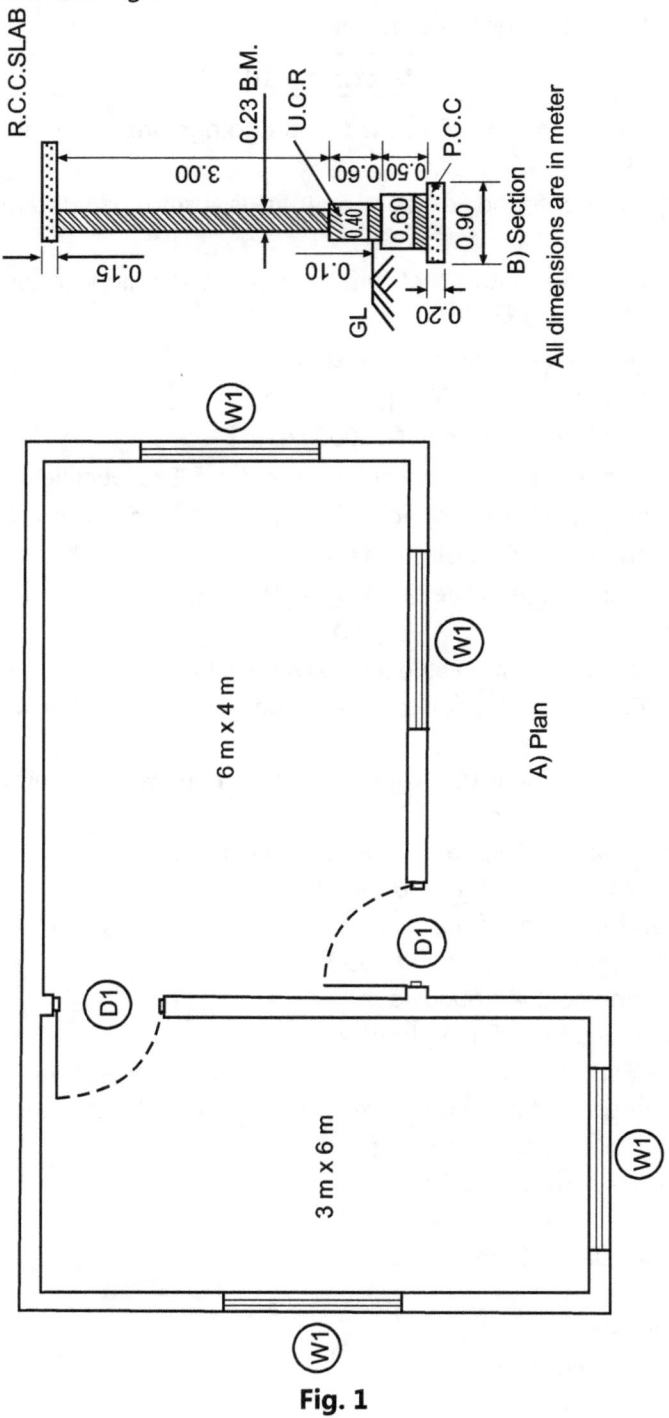

Fig. 1

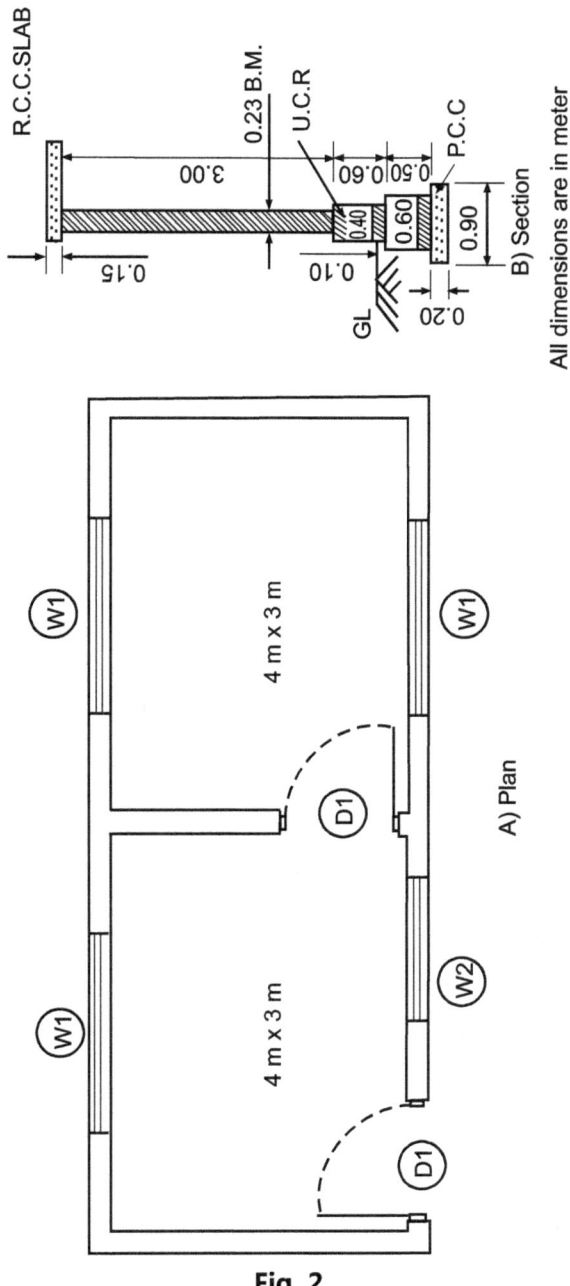

Fig. 2

10. (a) Compare Lump Sum Contracts and Item Rate Contracts with reference to

    (i)   nature of agreement,

    (ii)   contract documents and

    (iii) advantages. **(6)**

(b) Explain the following with suitable examples :   **(12)**

    (a) Valid contract.

    (b) Null or void contract.

    (c) Arbitration.

    (d) Termination of contract.

OR

12. (a) State the different types of civil engineering contract and hence explain any one. **(6)**

    (b) List out advantages and disadvantages of labour contract. **(4)**

    (c) Explain the B.O.T. type of contracts and state its advantages to the client. **(8)**

◈ ◈ ◈

Nov. 2014

Time : 4 Hours   **Max. Marks : 100**

Section – I

1. (a) Enlist the different types of estimate used in civil engineering and hence explain the supplementary estimate in brief. **[6]**

    (b) Explain the importance of brief description of an item required in the measurement sheet. **[4]**

    (c) Explain how the knowledge of quantity surveying is essential to civil engineer during execution of a project. **[6]**

OR

2. (a) List out various methods of preparing approximate estimate and the necessity of preparation of approximate estimate. **[6]**

    (b) Explain the provisional sum and the provisional sum items in construction project. **[4]**

    (c) State the range of provisions to be made for following items during preparation of detailed estimate : **[6]**

      (i)   Contingencies

      (ii) Workcharge establishment

      (iii) Water supply and drainage

      (iv) Electrification

3. (a) Fig. 1 shows the plans of an office building. Prepare a measurement sheet and determine the quantities of following ites, writing brief description of each item in the measurement sheet.

      (i)   Excavation in earthwork for foundation. **[2]**

      (ii) R.C.C. in slab. **[2]**

    (iii) UCR masonry in plinth and foundation. **[3]**

    (iv) Brick masonry (1 : 6) in superstructure. **[3]**

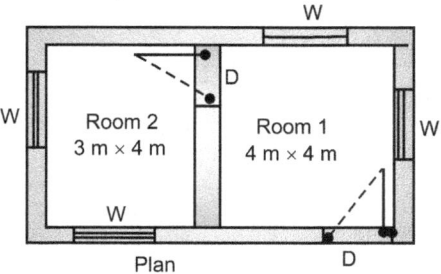

Fig. 1 (a) : Plan

$$D = 1.2^{m} \times 2.1 \text{ m}$$

$$W = 1.5 \text{ m} \times 1.2 \text{ m}$$

All walls 0.2 m thick.

  (b) Explain the method of taking out quantities for RCC in footing, column, beam with necessary formula if any. **[6]**

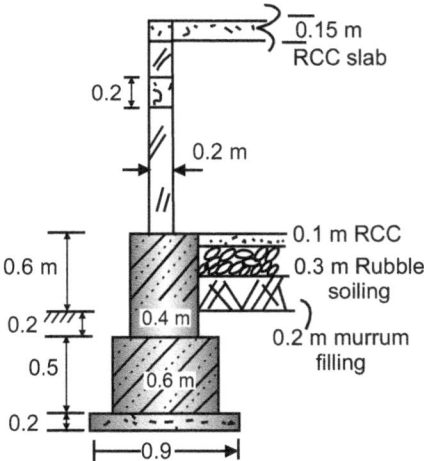

Fig. 1 (b) : Section

  (c) Explain the prime cost items. **[2]**

OR

4. (a) Fig. 2 shows the plan for an ottah provided infront of a building. Determine the quantities of following items.

    (i)   Earthwork in excavation. **[3]**

    (ii) Brick masonry in C.M. (1 6) **[3]**

    (iii) Tile flooring **[3]**

    (iv) Plastering to the surfaces **[3]**

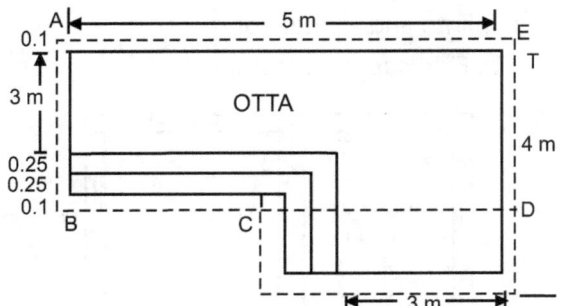

Fig. 2 (a) : Plan

(b) Write short note on: [6]

(i)   Method of measurement and rule for deduction for item of plastering.

(ii) Method of measurement of timber work for doors and windows.

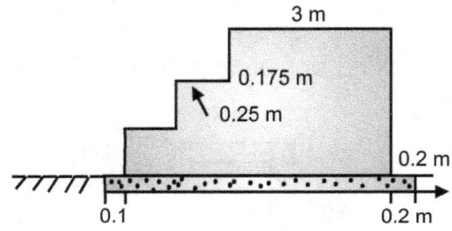

Fig. 2 (b) : Section

5. (a) Explain the purposes of preparing rate analysis for various items.   [4]

    (b) Explain the factors which affect the rate of an item.   [4]

    (c) Determine the rate per unit of measurement for brick masonry in C.M. (1 : 6) in superstructure.   [8]

OR

6. (a) Determine the basic materials required for construction of 135 Cu.m. of brick masonry (1 : 6).   [6]

    (b) Explain the overhed charges.   [4]

    (c) Draft a detailed specification for execution of U.C.R. masonry in plinth and foundation with reference to :   [6]

    (i)   Materials, quality of material, proportions.

    (ii) Method of execution and work man ship.

    (iii) Method of measurement and payment.

Section – II

7. (a) What is meant by 'value' of a commodity? State four parameters or characteristics a commodity should have to possess value. Also state six factors which affect valuation.

    [6]

(b) Explain two types of ownership or tenure of property. **[6]**

(c) State various methods of calculating 'depreciation' explain any one method in detail stating the formula used, merits / demerits of the method, etc. **[6]**

OR

8. (a) Explain in brief six factors considered for valuation of a building. **[6]**

(b) Write notes on : **[6]**

    (i)   Sinking fund

    (ii) Years purchase

(c) Write three differences between the following : **[6]**

    (i)   Scrap value - Salvage value

    (ii) Building Lease - occupational Lease

9. (a) Explain PWD procedure of administrative approval and technical sanction. **[6]**

(b) Briefly explain the essential information of a tender notice. **[6]**

(c) Justify earnest money and security deposit for a construction work. **[4]**

OR

10. (a) Give types (Classification) of tenders (forms) and briefly explain them. **[6]**

(b) Write notes on : **[6]**

    (i)   Opening of sealed tenders

    (ii) Scrutiny of tenders

(c) State and briefly explain any one method of execution of minor works in PWD. **[4]**

11. (a) Discuss in brief essential requirements of a valid contract. **[6]**

(b) State merits and demerits of pre-qualification of contractors. **[6]**

(c) Write a note on cost plus or percentage contracts. **[4]**

OR

12. Write notes on any four of the following : **[16]**

(a) Lump-sum contracts.

(b) Arbitration and arbitrator.

(c) Responsibilities of contractor regarding execution of work.

(d) Registration of contractors.

(e) Contents of F.I.D.I.C. document.

May 2015

Time : 4 Hours   **Max. Marks : 100**

1. (a) A person wish to construct a building as per the following plan Fig. 1 Explain the utility of plan, sectional elevation in working out the detailed estimate.   **[5]**

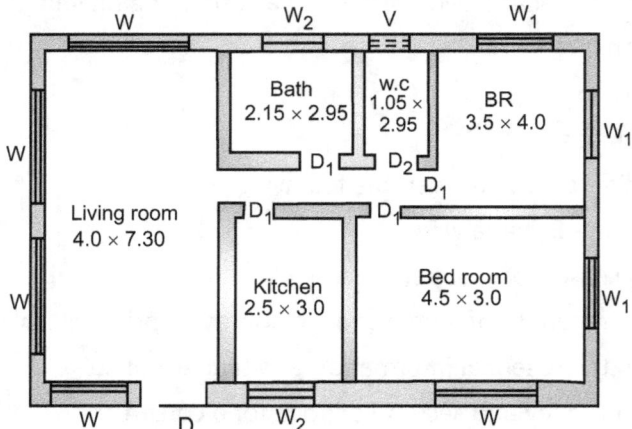

Fig. 1 : Plan

   (b) Work out the cost of construction of the following items by (1) long and short method   **[13]**

   (i)   PCC in foundation

   (ii) DPC

   (iii) RCC lintel and beam assuming steel at 1 % of RCC

   (iv) BM 1.6 for superstructure

OR

2. (a) What are the different methods of detail estimate? Explain centre line method of estimation and carryout the detailed estimate and obtain the quantity for following Fig 2.   **[14]**

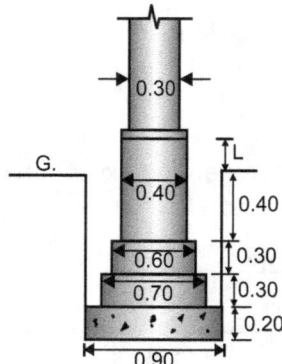

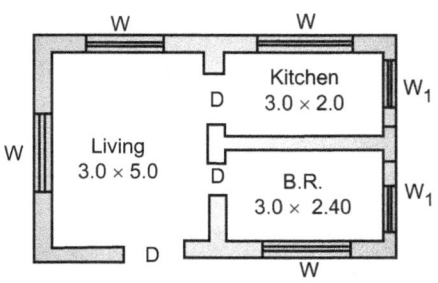

Fig. 2 : Plan

Fig. 1 : Door,	D	= 0.90 × 2.10
	D_1	= 0.75 × 2.10
	D_2	= 0.60 × 1.80
Window,	W	= 1.50 × 1.20
	W_1	= 1.20 × 0.90
	W_2	= 0.90 × 1.05
Vertialates	V	= 0.45 × 0.60
Fig. 2 : Door,	D	= 0.90 × 2.10
Window	W	= 1.20 ×1 .50
	W_1	= 0.90 × 1.20

Note : Foundation detail common to both Q. 1 (a) and 2 (a) as per Fig. 2 (a) Door, window, etc. common for both. All dimension in metre.

Q. 1 (a) and (2) (a).

(i)   Earth Work Excavation for foundation

(ii) Brick Masonry in CM 1:6

(iii) Damp Proof Course

(b) What is the unit of measurement of   **[4]**

(i)   Pointing.

(ii) Plastering

(iii) RCC lintel

(iv) Wood works for doors

3. (a) What is approximate or preliminary estimate and what is the purpose of approximate estimate. Explain the annual maintenance estimate and revised estimate.   **[6]**

(b) A (G+2) building has a carpet area of 800 M^2 in each floor. The area occupied by corridor verandah, staircase, etc is 25% and area occupied by wall, column is 10%, water supply 7.5% Electrification 8.5%, contingency 4%. Prepare a preliminary estimate considering cost of ground floor ₹ 1500/- sq-m, ₹ 1700/-for I floor, ₹ 1850/- for I floor.   **[10]**

OR

4. (a) Fig 3, shows section along the shorter span of a room of size 7 x 12 m internal dimension. The thickness of slab is 15 cm. Assume 5cm end cover and 2.5 cm cover at top and bottom.   **[10]**

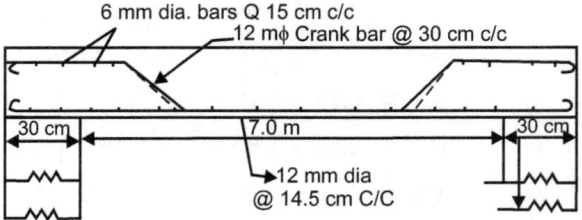

Fig. 3

(b) What are the different methods of calculating sectional area of road in banking. Explain the Mid section method of calculating earthwork with typical table for calculation.   **[6]**

5. (a) Explain the importance of specification in preparing estimate and what are the objectives of Specifications. What are standard specification and specification for performance? Explain How control over quality of material and workmanship is achieved by specification.   **[8]**

(b) Draft a detailed specification for earthwork embankment (without OMC).   **[8]**

OR

6. (a) Explain importance of Rate Analysis and what are the factors affecting rate analysis. Explain in detail the procedure for rate analysis.   **[4]**

(b) Explain task work and how does it vary. Work out the labour requirement for
   (i)   Reinforcement for R.C.C. work and
   (ii) I class brick masonry in CM 1:6 in super structure.   **[4]**

(c) Prepare rate analysis for RCC work in column with proportion 1:1.5:3, with cement course sand, 2.5 cm ballast with all material, T and P complete.   **[8]**

Section – II

7. (a) A construction equipment was purchased for ₹ 5,00,000/-with annual rate of interest of 6%. Determine life of the equipment ('n' years) if annual sinking fund is ₹ 3,000/- and salvage value is ₹ 60,000/-.   **[8]**

(b) What is meant by 'Depreciation' State its significance in valuation with example. Discuss merits and demerits of 2 methods of finding depreciation.   **[6]**

(c) Enlist the factors that may affect the value of a building. Discuss any one factor in detail with example.   **[4]**

OR

8. (a) Determine book value of a property consisting of a land (plot of area 1 000 m^2) and building (built-up area of 600 m^2) in the year 2013 assuming scrap value 10% of the original cost. The original land cost is 1973 was Rs. 100/- per m^2 and the cost of built-up area in the same year was Rs. 900/- per m^2. Assume that the construction specifications are first class and the land cost has remained unchanged.   **[8]**

(b) A rectangular plot has 35 m width along the road and 95 m depth at right angles to the road. Calculate the value of the land using method of belting. Assume that cost of the first belt of 20 m depth is ₹ 200/- per ml.   **[6]**

(c) State two differences each between: **[4]**

(i)   Sentimental Value-Distress Value

(ii) Salvage Value - Scrap Value

9. (a) Give the classification of 'works' as per the P.V.D.   **[6]**

Explain the essential pre-requisites as per the P.W.D. procedure before starting the execution of a 'work'.

(b) What is meant by a tender? Discuss importance of types of tenders and tendering procedure with respect to any one specific construction work.   **[5]**

(c) State various methods of tendering systems with respect to civil engineering works.**[5]**

A billionaire lady wants to construct a bungalow with all possible modern security provisions and facilities in it. Suggest a suitable tendering method she should adopt for inviting tenders for construction of the bungalow. Justify your suggestion.

OR

10 (a) State two differences each between: **[6]**

(i)   Sentimental Value-Distress Value

(ii) Salvage Value - Scrap Value

(b) Discuss the terms: Retention Money, Acceptance of a Tender.   **[5]**

(c) Discuss the following terms as per the P.W.D.   **[5]**

(i)   Original Works

(ii) Revised administrative approval

11. (a) State whether True or False, giving proper justification : (Zero marks will be given if justification is not written) **[6]**

    (i)   A wife approaches an arbitrator for her divorce case.

    (ii)   A contractor may sign a contract with the divorced wife of an industrialist.

    (iii) Only a judge retired from High Court or higher court can be an arbitrator for dispute with respect to a dispute in the execution of a Civil Engineering contract.

  (b) Briefly explain the contents of a typical contract. **[5]**

  (c) What is the meaning of 'arbitration'? Discuss various types of arbitration. **[5]**

OR

12. (a) Differentiate clearly between: Item Rate Contract and Lump-sum Contract. **[6]**

  (b) State four issues that may be referred to an arbitrator. Discuss the powers of an arbitrator. **[5]**

  (c) What is meant by 'General' and 'Special' conditions of contract? Clearly explain with appropriate examples. **[5]**

Time : 1 Hour   **Max. Marks : 30**

Instruction to the candidates:

(1) Answer Q.1 or Q.2, Q.3 or Q.4, Q.5 or Q.6.

(2) Figures to the right indicate full marks.

(3) Use of logarithmic tables, slide rule, Mollier charts, electronic pocket calculator and steam table allowed.

(4) Assume suitable data, if necessary.

---

1. **(a)** "Estimation gives exact cost of any construction", Comment. Explain the purpose and necessity of estimation and valuation of any work. What are the different types of data required for estimating any work. **[6]**

(b) What are the different types of estimate? Explain difference between. **[4]**

(i) Supplementary and revised estimate (ii) Site plan & layout plan   **OR**

2. **(a)** Under what conditions approximate estimate is made and explain the various purpose of approximate estimate. **[3]**

(b) Explain the approximate method for estimating the water supply and Sewage project. **[3]**

(c) A multi Storied office building has carpet area of 2500 sq-m. 30% of building area is covered by corridor, verandah, toilet, staircase. 10% of building area by walls. Assume a plinth area-rate of 6450 per sq-m. Add 25% of total cost for water supply. sanitary. electrical fittings, and contingences. Prepare a preliminary estimate for the building. **[4]**

3. **(a)** What do you understand by taking out quantities. Explain detailed and abstract estimate with necessary estimate form. **[4]**

(b) What is the necessity for accuracy in measurement? Give the limits of measurement and degree of accuracy for, Dimensions, Area. Volume of work. Weight. Rates **[6]OR**

4. **(a)** Work out the quantity of work for the following item of works for the plan shown in **Fig. 1 (a) and (b) by centre line method.**

(i) Earthwork excavation for foundation. **[3]**

(ii) Damp proof course (1:2:4) 2.5 cm thick. **[3]**

(iii) Brick work in cement mortar 1:6 in foundation and plinth as per section in Fig. (1.b).

5. **(a)** Work out the quantity of work for the following item of works for the plan and section shown in **Fig. 1 (a) and (b) by long and short wall method.**

(i) Brick work in cement mortar 1:6 for superstructure including parapet. **[4]**

(ii) RCC work in Roof slab, lintel. Also find the quantity of steel requirement for the work. **[4]**

(iii) Woodwork for door DI. The frame size may be taken as 100 mm × 300 mm. **[2]**

OR

6. **(a)** Define valuation of property. What are the important factors influencing the value of building. **[3]**

(b) What are the various methods of valuation? Explain value, cost , Gross income and Net Income of a property? **[3]**

(c) What are the various factors contributing to depreciation of a structure and what are the various methods to work out the depreciation. A person wish to purchase a building at an estimated cost of Rs. 10.00 lakhs. The age of building is 40 years and well maintained. The life of structure may be considered as 80 years. At cost should the person purchase the building? **[4]**

Q. 4 (a) and Q. 5 (a)

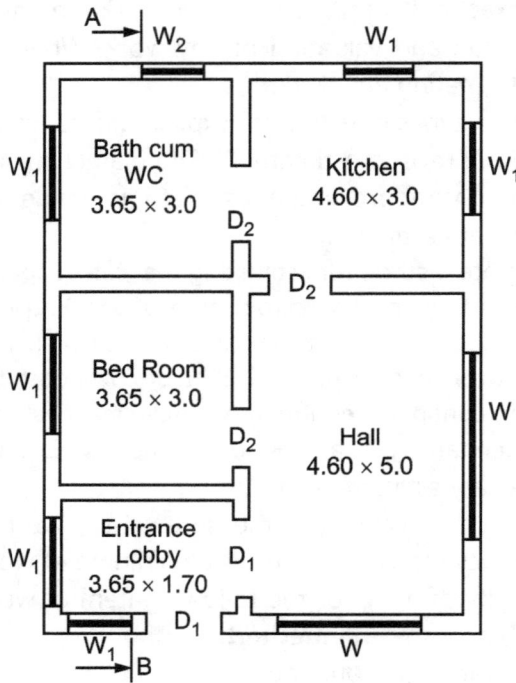

Fig. 1(a) Plan of building

Schedule of opening

Door

$D_1 = 1.80 \times 2.10$

$D_2 = 1.50 \times 2.10$

Window

$W = 3.0 \times 1.80$

$W_1 = 1.80 \times 1.50$

$W_2 = 1.50 \times 1.20$

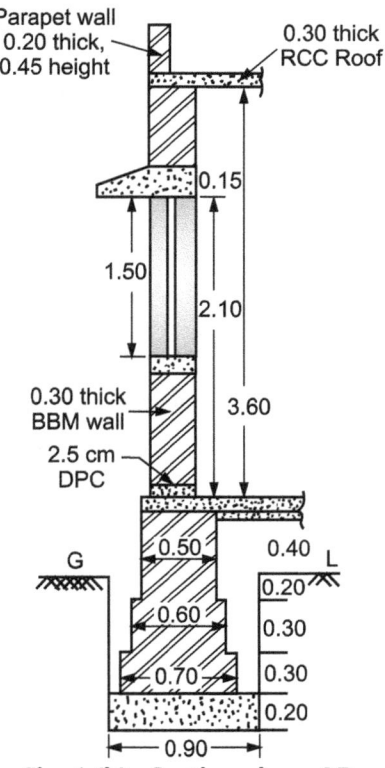

Parapet wall
0.20 thick,
0.45 height

0.30 thick
RCC Roof

0.15

1.50

2.10

0.30 thick
BBM wall

3.60

2.5 cm
DPC

G

0.50   0.40   L

0.20

0.60   0.30

0.70   0.30

0.20

0.90

Fig. 1 (b) : Section along AB

All Door and window frame – 100 mm × 300 mm (All dimension in meter)

END SEM. EXAM. MAY 2016

Time : $2\frac{1}{2}$ Hours   **Max. Marks : 70**

Instructions to the candidates :

(1) Answer Q. 1 or Q. 2, Q. 3 or Q. 4, Q. 5 or Q. 6, Q. 7 or Q. 8, Q. 9 or Q. 10, Q. 11 or Q. 12.

(2) Neat diagrams should be drawn whenever necessary.

(3) Figures to the right side indicate full marks.

(4) use of electronic pocket calculator is allowed.

(5) Assume suitable data, if necessary.

1. **(a)** What is an estimate? Hence state the different types and state under which conditions the particular estimate is prepared.   **[3]**

    (b) What do you mean by contingencies? How much provision is made for contingencies while preparing estimate?   **[3] OR**

2. **(a)** Explain the following with suitable example;   **[3]**

    (i)   The provisional sum item   (ii) Prime cost items

    (b) Explain the method of measurement and rule for making deductions for openings for following items;   **[3]**

    (i)   Plastering to the wall surface, and (ii) Brick masonry in superstructure.

3. Figure 1(a) and 1(b) shows plans and section of residential building. Determine the quantities of following items.   **[8]**
 (i)   Excavation in foundation (ii) UCR masonry in CM (1:6) in foundation
 (iii) Damp proof course.   **OR**
4. Refer Figure 1(A) and 1(B), determine the quantities of following items.   **[8]**
 (i)   12 mm thick internal plaster.
 (ii) Steel reinforcement in slab for both rooms is 8mm Dia. Bars provided at 120 mm c/c along short and long span with alternate bars bent up at support. Determine the quantity of reinforcement.
5. (a) A person wish to sell his building at Rs 15.00 lakhs. The life of building may be considered as 80 years and scrap value as 10%. Find the depreciated value on the building if the current age of building is 20 year also at what price the building should be purchased.
 (b) State true or false and comment on the following.   **[2]**
 (i)   The amount of sinking fund to be accumulated is nothing but the total depreciation of the property.
 (ii) Value of a building may be higher than it's estimated cost.   **OR**
6. What is reversionary value of land? Hence determine the present value of a building including land using following data.   **[6]**
 (i)   Income available from the property : Rs 96000/- per annum.
 (ii) Life of the property : 80 years.
 (iii) The rate for redemption of is 60% and rate of interest on Government securities is 5%.
 (iv) All outgoing : 35% of gross income.
 (v)   Present cost of land : Rs 30 lacs.
7. (a) Explain the purpose of Rate analysis. What factors should be considered while working out rate per unit for an item and explain how specification of an item of work affect the rate of an item?   **[4]**
 (b) Determine the material requirement for construction of 126 Cu.m of brick masonry in C.M. (1:6). Also determine the quantity of water required if W/C ratio for the mortar is 0.55.   **[8]**
 (c) Prepare the rate analysis for Brick masonry in CM 1:6 for super structure. The following rates for material and labour may be considered for rate analysis.   **[6]**
 (i)   Cement = Rs 300/bag   (ii) Sand = Rs 1400/m^3
 (iii) Aggregate = Rs 1400/m^3 (iv) Bricks = Rs 4500/1000No
 (v)   Steel = Rs 38,500/ MT
 Labour rate/day
 (i)   Head mason = Rs 600/-   (ii) Mason = 450/-
 (iii) Mazdoor = Rs 350/-   (iv) Bhisti/Helper = Rs 300/-   **OR**
8. (a) Draft a detailed specification with respect to materials, labour, workmanship, mode of measurement etc for the UCR masonry foundations and plinth.   **[6]**
 (b) What are the different factors to be considered while drafting specification of an item and explain the step by step method of drafting a specification?   **[6]**

(c) Explain : (i) Advantages and Disadvantages of open specification   **[6]**
  (ii) Restricted Specification
  (iii) General specification for second class building

9. (a) Explain the unbalanced tender with suitable example.   **[4]**
  (b) Write short note on (any three) :   **[6]**
  (i)   Security deposit (ii) Pre-bid conference (iii) Liquidated damages
  (c) Prepare a tender notice to be advertised in news paper for extension of a college building. The estimated amount is Rs 1.75 crores and work is to be completed in 15 months. Give also the pre qualification criteria's.   **[6] OR**

10. (a) Explain the purpose of administrative approval and technical sanction during execution of civil engineering works.   **[6]**
  (b) Explain the organizational set up of P.W.D giving the hierarchy of the officers in the P.W.D. Explain the duties and responsibilities of each.   **[6]**
  (c) What is the necessity of engaging daily labour by P.W.D. Explain Muster Roll (MR). Draft a page of Register of Muster Roll form.   **[4]**

11. (a) Compare Lump Sum Contracts and Item Rate Contracts with reference to   **[6]**
  (i)   Nature of agreement (ii) Contract documents and (iii) Advantages
  (b) Explain the followings (any two) with suitable examples.   **[6]**
  (i)   Valid contract (ii) Null of void contract (iii) Termination of contract
  (c) What is a contract document and explain the contents of a contact document.   **[4]**

12. (a) Define Arbitration and need for arbitration. What are the powers and duties of arbitrators?   **[6]**
  (b) What are the different types of arbitration and explain any one.   **[4]**
  (c) Explain the necessary precaution the Engineer-in Charge should take to avoid arbitration.   **[6]**

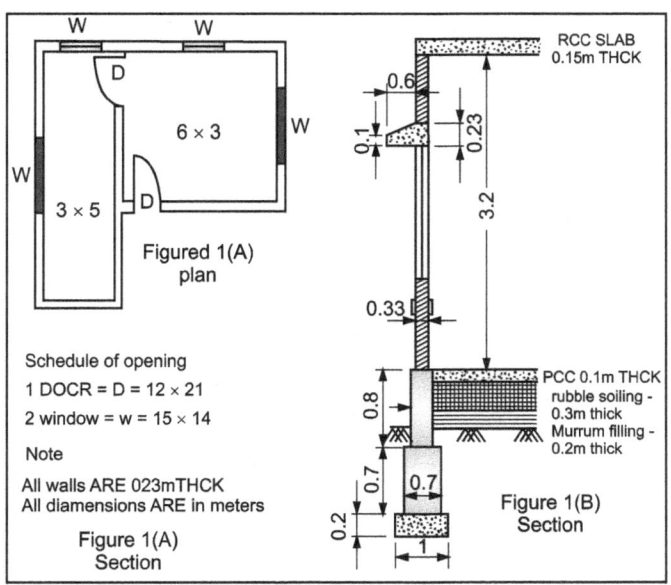

Fig. 2

END SEM. EXAM. NOVEMBER 2016

Time : 2$\frac{1}{2}$ Hours   **Max. Marks : 70**

Instructions to the candidates :

   (1) Solve Q. 1 or Q. 2, Q. 3 or Q. 4, Q. 5 or Q. 6, Q. 7 or Q. 8, Q. 9 or Q. 10, Q. 11 or Q. 12.
   (2) Figures to the right indicate full marks.
   (3) Use of electronic pocket calculator is allowed.
   (4) Assume Suitable data f necessary.
   (5) Neat diagrams must be drawn wherever necessary.

1. **(a)** Define Estimate. State various purposes of estimates.   **[3]**
   (b) Explain following :   **[3]**
       (i)   Contingencies   (ii) Work Charge Establishment   **OR**
2. **(a)** Enlist any 6 of the items of work for estimation of building project and give their unit of measurement.   **[3]**
   (b) State various methods of approximate estimate and explain any one.   **[3]**
3. Figure 1(a) and 1(b) shows plan and elevation of residential building. Determine the quantities of following items.   **[8]**

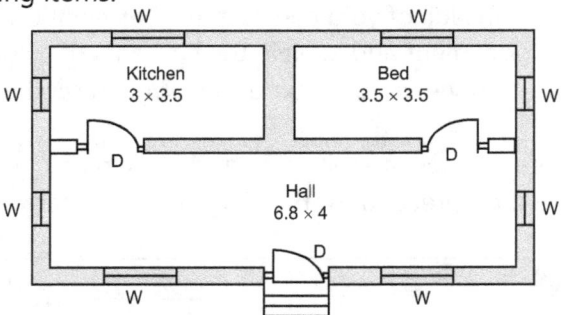

Fig. 1(a) : PLAN

D = 1.2 × 2.0 m   W = 1 × 1.8 m All dimensions are in mm.

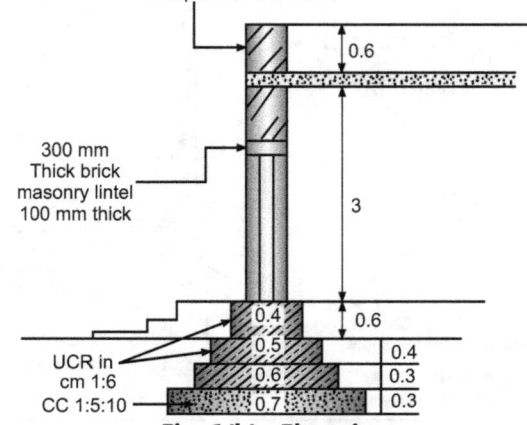

Fig. 1(b) : Elevation

(i) Excavation in foundation

(ii) Cement Concrete (1:5:10) in foundation

(iii) UCR masonry in CM (1:6) in foundation   **OR**

4. Prepare bar bending schedule for Fig. 1(a) and 1(b) shows the L-section and cross section of RCC beam. Also determine the % steel in the beam (Assume Density of Steel is 7860 kg/m³)   **[8]**

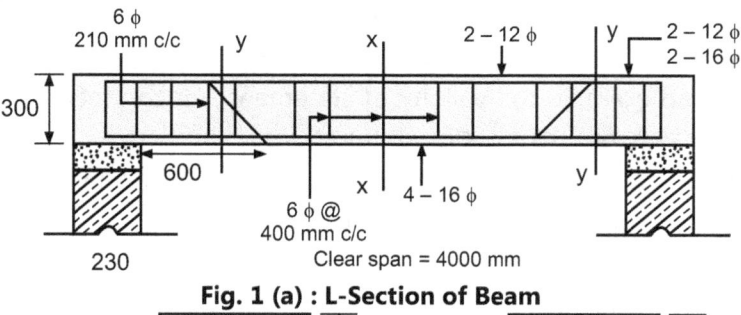

Fig. 1 (a) : L-Section of Beam

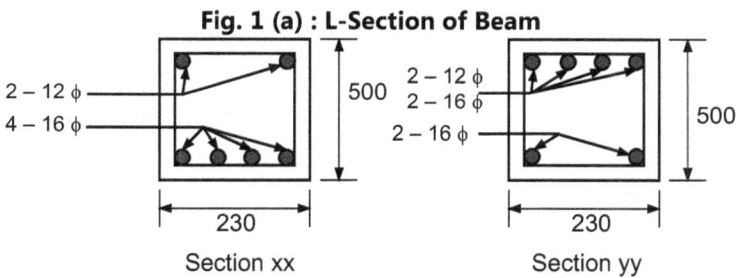

Section xx   Section yy

Fig. 1 (b) : C/S of Beam

5. **(a)** Define following :   **[3]**

    (i)   Market Value   (ii) Book Value   (iii) Distressed Value

    (b) Explain meaning of Price, Cost and Value and also discuss the purpose of valuation.   **[3] OR**

6. Define Depreciation and state the methods for its determination.

    The estimated cost of a building is RS. 200000. It is 20 years old and well maintained. The life of the structure is assumed to be 80 years. Determine the depreciated value of the building. The fixed percentage of depreciation is unity.   **[6]**

7. **(a)** Draft a detailed specification for providing and laying RCC of M25 grade including form work and including steel reinforcement for a slab with all other standard requirements which are normally specified in BOQ.   **[6]**

    (b) Explain how the various direct cost and indirect cost are considered in analysis of rate of building item.   **[6]**

    (c) What is task work? Why does it vary? Explain its importance with an example. **[6] OR**

8. **(a)** Prepare rate analysis for providing and laying RCC of M25 grade for plinth and Foundation using basic rates as per the current DSR.   **[6]**

    (b) Explain purpose of specifications and state its different types.   **[6]**

    (c) Explain the terms overheads and sundries.   **[6]**

9. (a) Draft a specimen tender notice for the construction of a bridge assuming suitable details. **[6]**

   (b) Discuss merits, demerits of Open Tenders as against Negotiated Tender. **[6]**

   (c) Explain the purpose of taking Security Deposit in tender. **[4] OR**

10. (a) Explain the PWD procedure for execution of minor works. **[6]**

   (b) State true or false with justification: A lowest tender can be rejected. **[6]**

   (c) State and explain the prequalifications for tenders. **[4]**

11. (a) Explain with an example the validity of statement "All contracts are agreements but all agreements are not necessarily contracts". **[6]**

   (b) Explain "3 Bid system" of submitting tenders. What is its advantage? **[6]**

   (c) Explain "Pre-Bid conference" stating its advantages. **[4] OR**

12. (a) Explain the following with examples : **[6]**

   (i)   Detection of unbalanced bid

   (ii) Time is the essence of contract

   (b) Explain B.O.T. type of tender and quote any one field example wherein it is actually being utilized. **[6]**

   (c) Explain Arbitration. **[4]**